The Collected Stories of R

John Mortin   923–2009) was a barrister, playwright and novelist. His fictional trilogy about the inexorable rise of an ambitious Tory MP in the Thatcher years (*Paradise Postponed*, *Titmuss Regained* and *The Sound of Trumpets*) has recently been republished in Penguin Modern Classics, together with his autobiography, *Clinging to the Wreckage*, and his play, *A Voyage Round My Father*. His most famous creation was the barrister Horace Rumpole, who featured in four novels and around eighty short stories. Sir John, who was knighted in 1998 for his services to the arts, died in January 2009.

Sam Leith is the former literary editor of the *Daily Telegraph*, and the author of the novel *The Coincidence Engine* and three non-fiction books, of which the most recent was *You Talkin' To Me? – Rhetoric From Aristotle to Obama*. He writes regularly for the *Evening Standard*, *Guardian*, *Prospect* and the *Spectator*.

JOHN MORTIMER

The Collected Stories
of Rumpole

Edited by CHLOE CAMPBELL
with an introduction by SAM LEITH

PENGUIN BOOKS

PENGUIN CLASSICS

Published by the Penguin Group
Penguin Books Ltd, 80 Strand, London WC2R ORL, England
Penguin Group (USA) Inc., 375 Hudson Street, New York, New York 10014, USA
Penguin Group (Canada), 90 Eglinton Avenue East, Suite 700, Toronto, Ontario,
Canada M4P 2Y3 (a division of Pearson Penguin Canada Inc.)
Penguin Ireland, 25 St Stephen's Green, Dublin 2, Ireland (a division of Penguin Books Ltd)
Penguin Group (Australia), 707 Collins Street, Melbourne, Victoria 3008, Australia
(a division of Pearson Australia Group Pty Ltd)
Penguin Books India Pvt Ltd, 11 Community Centre, Panchsheel Park,
New Delhi – 110 017, India
Penguin Group (NZ), 67 Apollo Drive, Rosedale, Auckland 0632, New Zealand
(a division of Pearson New Zealand Ltd)
Penguin Books (South Africa) (Pty) Ltd, Block D, Rosebank Office Park,
181 Jan Smuts Avenue, Parktown North, Gauteng 2193, South Africa

Penguin Books Ltd, Registered Offices: 80 Strand, London WC2R ORL, England

www.penguin.com

This edition first published in Penguin Classics 2012
001

Copyright © John Mortimer, 1978, 1979, 1981, 1983, 1987, 1988, 1990, 1992, 1995, 2001, 2002
Editorial material copyright © Chloe Campbell, 2012
Introduction copyright © Sam Leith, 2012
All rights reserved

The moral right of the author, editor and introducer has been asserted

The acknowledgements on page xiii constitutes an extension of this page.

Set in 10/12.5pt Dante MT Std
Typeset by Jouve (UK), Milton Keynes
Printed in England by Clays Ltd, St Ives plc

ISBN: 978-0-141-19829-3

www.greenpenguin.co.uk

Penguin Books is committed to a sustainable
future for our business, our readers and our planet.
This book is made from Forest Stewardship
Council™ certified paper.

ALWAYS LEARNING   **PEARSON**

Contents

Introduction

'Being Horace Rumpole in his sixties, still slogging round the Old Bailey with sore feet, a modest daily hangover and an aching back was certainly no great shakes, but who else could I be?' (p. 167).

Such is the situation of John Mortimer's greatest creation. Who else could Rumpole be, but a hungover Old Bailey Hack in his sixties? His own account tells us he was born some time around 1910, but he actually drew his first breath, already in his sixties and, as it were, pre-crumpled, in December 1975, when 'Rumpole of the Bailey' went out on the BBC's long-running TV series *Play For Today*.

Rumpole, then, had his first incarnation on the small screen. In fittingly Rumpolian fashion, he got the second choice of name and third choice of actor. Originally, he was to have been called 'Rumbold' (a decision hastily modified after the discovery that there already existed, in Guildford, a barrister called Horace Rumbold). And though he was brought brilliantly to life by Leo McKern, his creator had originally eyed Michael Hordern (too busy) and Alastair Sim (too dead) for the part.

The many prose stories that Mortimer went on to write, of which you hold in your hands a selection of the best, are more than just TV spin-offs, however. They have an independent, and enduring, life. McKern's stentorian Rumpole on the small screen may have defined the character in the public mind, but what we find in the stories is a subtly different creature: camper, more feline, more Mortimeresque.

Rumpole, on the page, is quite a cocktail: there's a very generous slosh of P. G. Wodehouse, a dash of Falstaff at his more benign, a tincture of Tony Hancock and a faint but discernible backnote of G. K. Chesterton's Father Brown. His readiness with a quotation from the *Oxford Book of English Verse* (the Quiller-Couch original, be it noted: not

Dame Helen Gardner's 1972 reboot) and fondness for *The Times* cross-word even seem to anticipate Inspector Morse.

Rumpole takes his place among these figures without apology. He is an enduring comic character with the potential to live in any number of stories: a creation, as John Mortimer put it, 'to keep me in my old age'.[1] He is the one character Mortimer created who outlived him.

One of the great joys of these stories – like Wodehouse's, setting a time and place in aspic – is the deep consolatory joy of familiarity. You settle into Rumpole's world with the same easeful sigh you imagine Rumpole emitting as he settles into his place at Pommeroy's. Each story is different, but each story is also, deep down, the same. Each twists in an eminently satisfactory way.

The geography of the world in which these stories are set is bounded by the mansion flat in Froxbury Court, from which Rumpole leaves each morning on the 8.45 tube; his Chambers at Equity Court, where every morning he searches his corner of the mantelpiece for a brief, and steps politely over one of 'Uncle Tom's' putts across the rug; the Old Bailey, where the struggle against the irascible Judge Bullingham continues; and Pommeroy's Wine Bar, where our hero repairs to refuel, reflect and cash cheques. He seldom ventures outside this ambit, though necessity, from time to time, forces him into a branch of the 'Caring Bank' – resented custodians of the Rumpole overdraft. Crime, as Rumpole is fond of reminding us, does not pay.

Familiar, too, is the cast of characters, known – as if Rumpole's world really were the minor public school it resembles – by their affectionately deflating nicknames: the loathsome 'Hearthrug' and the pious 'Bollard', the amiably superannuated 'Uncle Tom', the foxy 'Portia', the formidable 'Mad Bull', the silkily capable private investigator F. I. G. – 'Fig' – Newton, and the innumerable scions of that irredeemably villainous family, the Timsons – locked like Montagues and Capulets in their immemorial rivalry with the Molloys.

Also, of course – known by an epithet that has left Mortimer's stories and passed into the wider culture (see p. 66) – there is She Who Must Be Obeyed: Rumpole's wife Hilda, the daughter of his old pupil master, C. H. Wystan. John Mortimer's biographer, Valerie Grove, describes Hilda Rumpole as 'dreadful'[2], but there's no great evidence of nastiness. If anything, Hilda is long suffering and occasionally ill used, forced as she is to pester Rumpole (she always calls her husband by his second name) for the wherewithal to buy Vim – her enthusiasm for which baffles her husband to the extent that he at one point asks: 'Do we *eat* Vim?'

Rumpole makes a great performance of being in terror of her, but he always does exactly what he wants. Theirs is recognizably the companionable, undersexed, affectionate and somewhat separate partnership of a married couple in it for the long haul. Exasperation rather than hostility marks the temper of their relationship – and Hilda's triumph over the wretched Perivale Blythe in 'Rumpole and the Last Resort' (pp. 266–7) is token of a closer and shrewder co-operation than appearances suggest.

Like all the immortals, Rumpole comes with his identifying paraphernalia. St Sebastian has his arrows and his palm frond; Sherlock Holmes his pipe and his violin. Rumpole has his egg-stains, his waistcoat marked too with the ash from a 'small cigar', his shabby wig, acquired 'from an ex-Attorney General of Tonga in 1932', and his glass of Pommeroy's Very Ordinary Claret – aka 'Château Fleet Street' or 'Château Thames Embankment'.

These, then, in their form and in their style, are deeply conservative stories. The encroachment of modernity is registered – Space Invaders machines appear in pubs; flashy computerized systems do their owners precious little good; smarmy modernizers infiltrate the Chambers and have to be seen off – and it is resisted. Rumpole himself is always looking backwards. The conceit is that our hero is writing his memoirs, and their guiding star is a past glory: successfully defending in the case of the Penge Bungalow Murders as a junior barrister 'alone and without a leader'.

To the despair of Hilda, Rumpole positively resists forward movement. He finds ways of avoiding being promoted – having no ambition to take silk, mustering only a half-hearted enthusiasm at the prospect of becoming Head of Chambers, and treating the idea of being a 'Deputy Circus Judge' with bemused contempt.

So the stories are conservative. But there is more to them than that. At the core of Rumpole's conservatism is his regard for the law: a time-hallowed institution through which the presumption of innocence, as he often reminds us, runs like a golden thread. But Rumpole – defender of the underdog, upsetter of judicial applecarts – is resolutely anti-authoritarian.

He is proud to identify himself as 'an Old Bailey Hack', and evinces positive affection for the criminals who provide his living. He shows no interest in the more 'respectable' areas of law. Crime, he explains in 'Rumpole and the Man of God', 'not only pays moderately well, but [. . .] is also by far the greatest fun. Give me a murder on a spring morning with a decent run and a tolerably sympathetic jury, and Rumpole's happiness is complete' (p. 70).

One account of his origin – and a telling one as to Rumpole's moral make-up – is that he was modelled on the real-life QC James Burge, a bon vivant and self-declared anarchist, whom Mortimer once heard refer to 'my old darling Prince Peter Kropotkin'. 'Burge referred to everyone as an "old darling",' Mortimer recalled, 'except his wife, [. . .] and there I had Rumpole.'[3]

Rumpole is a classic Establishment rebel. As he puts it in 'Rumpole and the Blind Tasting' (responding to his pupil Mizz Probert's earnest sociological account of criminality): 'I was brought up in appalling conditions, in an ice-cold vicarage with no mod cons or central heating. My old father, being a priest of the Church of England, had only the sketchiest notion of morality, and my mother was too occupied with jam-making and the Women's Institute to notice my existence. Is it any real wonder that I have taken to crime?' (p. 290).

Disambitious and determinedly suburban, Rumpole operates from a very particular place in the English class system, and the stories are coloured with sharp and funny little nuggets of social stereotyping. Hunter's Hill, for instance, home of the defendant in 'Rumpole and the Expert Witness', is a 'delightful little dormitory town in Surrey, where nothing is heard but the whirr of the kitchen mixers running up Provençal specialities from the Sunday supplements and the purr of the hi-fis playing baroque music to go with the Buck's Fizz' (p. 135). The criminal patriarch Fred Timson, meanwhile, is 'a grey-haired man, his face bronzed by the suns of Marbella, wearing a discreet sports jacket, cavalry-twill trousers and an MCC tie [. . .] flanked by two substantial ladies who had clearly both been for a recent tint and set at the hairdressers [. . .] brightly dressed as though for a wedding or some celebration other than their husbands' day in Court' (p. 348). Part of the joke is how little difference there is between the two worlds.

Rumpole is a paladin disguised as a rogue: a trickster hero. He is part barrister, part stage actor; delighting in the courtroom *coup de théâtre*. His raffishness is a form of generosity, a marker of his wide and perpetually amused tolerance of human folly. Adulterers, pornographers and honest villains don't disturb him half so much as do prigs, punishment junkies and whited sepulchres, like the odious Hearthrug.

Rumpole makes it a point of principle always to defend. When it's suggested that he might take up prosecuting, he retorts in the negative, 'with the determined air of a man who has to draw the line somewhere': 'I'm not going to use my skills, such as they are, to force some poor devil into a condemned Victorian slum where he can be banged up with a couple of psychopaths and his own chamber pot' (p. 197).

This, in essence, is the golden thread of seriousness that runs through these stories intended to delight: a recognition of mortal folly, and an effort to spare the fools – as far as possible – the harshest consequences of it. This applies outside the Old Bailey as well as in it. When he spies Phillida Erskine-Brown gearing up for a fling with an unsuitable lover, Rumpole gently sabotages the affair; not from moral censoriousness, but to be kind to her.

It's a mark of Mortimer's deftness that, even in the essentially comic and consolatory universe of Rumpole – one in which no real harm ever comes to anybody, and Uncle Tom will forever have a place in the office to play golf – the odd note of melancholy occasionally, like the faint chill in a summer evening, intrudes.

Just look at the lovely temper of the payoff to 'Rumpole and the Heavy Brigade':

I suppose it was a waltz. As I steered Hilda out on to the great open spaces it seemed quite easy to go round and round, vaguely in time to the music. I heard a strange sound, as if from a long way off.

'*I'll have the last waltz with you, / Two sleepy people together . . .*' Or words to that effect. I was in fact singing. Singing and dancing to celebrate a great victory in a case I was never meant to win. (p. 69).

That, ladies and gentlemen, is life itself. Let us raise a glass of Château Thames Embankment to it.

Sam Leith, 2012

Notes

1. John Mortimer, *The Best of Rumpole* (London: Viking, 1993), author's introduction.
2. Valerie Grove, *A Voyage Round John Mortimer: The Authorized Biography* (London: Viking, 2007), p. 283.
3. Grove, *A Voyage Round John Mortimer*, pp. 284–5.

Acknowledgements

'Rumpole and the Younger Generation' and 'Rumpole and the Heavy Brigade' first appeared in *Rumpole of the Bailey*, 1978. 'Rumpole and the Man of God' and 'Rumpole and the Showfolk' first appeared in *The Trials of Rumpole*, 1979. 'Rumpole and the Expert Witness', 'Rumpole and the Spirit of Christmas' and 'Rumpole and the Boat People' first appeared in *Regina v. Rumpole*, 1981, and then under the title *Rumpole for the Defence*, 1982. 'Rumpole and the Genuine Article' and 'Rumpole and the Last Resort' first appeared in *Rumpole and the Golden Thread*, 1983. 'Rumpole and the Blind Tasting', 'Rumpole and the Judge's Elbow' and 'Rumpole's Last Case' first appeared in *Rumpole's Last Case*, 1987. 'Rumpole and the Tap End', 'Rumpole and the Bubble Reputation' and 'Rumpole and Portia' first appeared in *Rumpole and the Age of Miracles*, 1988. 'Rumpole à la Carte' first appeared in *Rumpole à la Carte*, 1990. 'Rumpole on Trial' first appeared in *Rumpole on Trial*, 1992. 'Rumpole and the Model Prisoner' first appeared in *Rumpole and the Angel of Death*, 1995. 'Rumpole and the Old Familiar Faces' first appeared in *Rumpole Rests His Case*, 2001. 'Rumpole and the Primrose Path' first appeared in *Rumpole and the Primrose Path*, 2002. All the books were first published by Penguin, Viking Penguin or Allen Lane; and all the stories are copyright © Advanpress Ltd.

A version of the case in which Rumpole 'gained an acquittal alone and without a leader' is published in *Rumpole and the Penge Bungalow Murders* (Penguin, 2004).

'Fig' Newton boasts two sets of middle names in these stories, and Uncle Tom's sister has varying marital status.

The Collected Stories of Rumpole

Rumpole and the Younger Generation

I, Horace Rumpole, barrister-at-law, 68 next birthday, Old Bailey Hack, husband to Mrs Hilda Rumpole (known to me only as She Who Must Be Obeyed) and father to Nicholas Rumpole (lecturer in social studies at the University of Baltimore, I have always been extremely proud of Nick); I, who have a mind full of old murders, legal anecdotes and memorable fragments of the *Oxford Book of English Verse* (Sir Arthur Quiller-Couch's edition) together with a dependable knowledge of bloodstains, blood groups, fingerprints and forgery by typewriter; I, who am now the oldest member of my Chambers, take up my pen at this advanced age during a lull in business (there's not much crime about, all the best villains seem to be off on holiday in the Costa Brava), in order to write my reconstructions of some of my recent triumphs (including a number of recent disasters) in the Courts of Law, hoping thereby to turn a bob or two which won't be immediately grabbed by the taxman, or my clerk Henry, or by She Who Must Be Obeyed, and perhaps give some sort of entertainment to those who, like myself, have found in British justice a life-long subject of harmless fun.

When I first considered putting pen to paper in this matter of my life, I thought I must begin with the great cases of my comparative youth, the 'Penge Bungalow Murders', where I gained an acquittal alone and without a leader, or the 'Great Brighton Benefit Club Forgery', which I contrived to win by reason of my exhaustive study of typewriters. In these cases I was, for a brief moment, in the Public Eye, or at least my name seemed almost a permanent feature of the *News of the World*, but when I come to look back on that period of my life at the Bar it all seems to have happened to another Rumpole, an eager young barrister whom I can scarcely recognize and whom I am not at all sure I would like, at least not enough to spend a whole book with him.

3

I am not a public figure now, so much has to be admitted; but some of the cases I shall describe, the wretched business of the Honourable Member, for instance, or the charge of murder brought against the youngest, and barmiest, of the appalling Delgardo brothers, did put me back on the front page of the *News of the World* (and even got me a few inches in *The Times*). But I suppose I have become pretty well known, if not something of a legend, round the Old Bailey, in Pommeroy's Wine Bar in Fleet Street, in the robing room at London Sessions and in the cells at Brixton Prison. They know me there for never pleading guilty, for chain-smoking small cigars and for quoting Wordsworth when they least expect it. Such notoriety will not long survive my not-to-be-delayed trip to Golders Green Crematorium. Barristers' speeches vanish quicker than Chinese dinners, and even the greatest victory in Court rarely survives longer than the next Sunday's papers.

To understand the full effect on my family life, however, of that case which I have called 'Rumpole and the Younger Generation', it is necessary to know a little of my past and the long years that led up to my successful defence of Jim Timson, the sixteen-year-old sprig, the young hopeful, and apple of the eye of the Timsons, a huge and industrious family of South London villains. As this case was, by and large, a family matter, it is important that you should understand my family.

My father, the Reverend Wilfred Rumpole, was a Church of England clergyman who, in early middle age, came reluctantly to the conclusion that he no longer believed any one of the 39 Articles. As he was not fitted by character or training for any other profession, however, he had to soldier on in his living in Croydon and by a good deal of scraping and saving he was able to send me as a boarder to a minor public school on the Norfolk coast. I later went to Keble College, Oxford, where I achieved a dubious third in law – you will discover during the course of these memoirs that, although I only feel truly alive and happy in Law Courts, I have a singular distaste for the law. My father's example, and the number of theological students I met at Keble, gave me an early mistrust of clergymen whom I have always found to be most unsatisfactory witnesses. If you call a clergyman in mitigation, the old darling can be guaranteed to add at least a year to the sentence.

When I first went to the Bar, I entered the Chambers of C. H. Wystan. Wystan had a moderate practice, acquired rather by industry than talent, and a strong disinclination to look at the photographs in murder cases, being particularly squeamish on the fascinating subject of blood. He also had a daughter, Hilda Wystan as was, now Mrs Hilda Rumpole and She Who Must Be Obeyed. I was ambitious in those days. I did my best to cultivate Wystan's clerk Albert, and I started to get a good deal of criminal work. I did what was expected of me and spent happy hours round the Bailey and Sessions and my fame grew in criminal circles; at the end of the day I would take Albert for a drink in Pommeroy's Wine Bar. We got on extremely well and he would always recommend 'his Mr Rumpole' if a solicitor rang up with a particularly tricky indecent assault or a nasty case of receiving stolen property.

There is no point in writing your memoirs unless you are prepared to be completely candid, and I must confess that, in the course of a long life, I have been in love on several occasions. I am sure that I loved Miss Porter, the shy and nervous, but at times liberated daughter of Septimus Porter, my Oxford tutor in Roman Law. In fact we were engaged to be married, but the engagement had to be broken off because of Miss Porter's early death. I often think about her, and of the different course my home life might have taken, for Miss Porter was in no way a girl born to command, or expect, implicit obedience. During my service with the ground staff of the RAF. I undoubtedly became helplessly smitten with the charms of an extremely warmhearted and gallant officer in the WAAFs by the name of Miss Bobby O'Keefe, but I was no match for the wings of a Pilot Officer, as appeared on the chest of a certain Sam 'Three-Fingers' Dogherty. During my conduct of a case, which I shall describe in a later chapter which I have called 'Rumpole and the Alternative Society', I once again felt a hopeless and almost feverish stirring of passion for a young woman who was determined to talk her way into Holloway Prison. My relationship with Hilda Wystan was rather different.

To begin with, she seemed part of life in Chambers. She was always interested in the law and ambitious, first for her widowed father, and then, when he proved himself unlikely Lord Chancellor material, for me. She often dropped in for tea on her way home from shopping, and Wystan used to invite me in for a cup. One year I was detailed off to be her partner at an Inns of Court ball. There it became clear to me that I was expected to marry Hilda; it seemed a step in my career like getting a brief in the Court of Appeal, or doing a murder. When she proposed to me, as she did over a glass of claret cup after an energetic waltz, Hilda made it clear that, when old Wystan finally retired, she expected to see me Head of Chambers. I, who have never felt at a loss for a word in Court, found absolutely nothing to say. In that silence the matter was concluded.

So now you must picture Hilda and me twenty-five years later, with a son at that same east coast public school which I just managed to afford from the fruits of crime, in our matrimonial home at 25B Froxbury Court, Gloucester Road. (A mansion flat is a misleading description of that cavernous and underheated area which Hilda devotes so much of her energy to keeping shipshape, not to say Bristol fashion.) We were having breakfast, and, between bites of toast, I was reading my brief for that day, an Old Bailey trial of the sixteen-year-old Jim Timson charged with robbery with violence, he having allegedly taken part in a wage snatch on a couple of elderly butchers: an escapade planned in the playground of the local comprehensive. As so often happens, the poet Wordsworth, that old sheep of the Lake District, sprang immediately to mind, and I gave tongue to his lines, well knowing that they must only serve to irritate She Who Must Be Obeyed.

'*Trailing clouds of glory do we come / From God, who is our home; / Heaven lies about us in our infancy!*'

I looked at Hilda. She was impassively demolishing a boiled egg. I also noticed that she was wearing a hat, as if prepared to set out upon some expedition. I decided to give her a little more Wordsworth, prompted by my reading the story of the boy Timson.

'*Shades of the prison house begin to close / Upon the growing boy.*'

Hilda spoke at last.

'Rumpole, you're not talking about your son, I hope. You're never referring to Nick . . .'

'*Shades of the prison house begin to close*? Not round our son, of course. Not round Nick. Shades of the public school have grown round him, the thousand-quid-a-year remand home.'

Hilda always thought it indelicate to refer to the subject of school fees, as if being at Mulstead were a kind of unsolicited honour for Nick. She became increasingly businesslike.

'He's breaking up this morning.'

'Shades of the prison house begin to open up for the holidays.'

'Nick has to be met at 11.15 at Liverpool Street and given lunch. When he went back to school you promised him a show. You haven't forgotten?'

Hilda was clearing away the plates rapidly. To tell the truth I had forgotten the date of Nick's holidays; but I let her assume I had a long planned treat laid on for him.

'Of course I haven't forgotten. The only show I can offer him is a robbery with violence in Number 2 Court at the Old Bailey. I wish I could lay on a murder. Nick's always so enjoyed my murders.'

It was true. On one distant half term Nick had sat in on the 'Peckham Billiard Hall Stabbing', and enjoyed it a great deal more than *Treasure Island*.

'I must fly! Daddy gets so crotchety if anyone's late. And he does love his visits.'

Hilda removed my half-empty coffee cup.

'Our father which art in Horsham. Give my respects to the old sweetheart.'

It had also slipped my mind that old C. H. Wystan was laid up with a dicky ticker in Horsham General Hospital. The hat was, no doubt, a clue I should have followed. Hilda usually goes shopping in a headscarf. By now she was at the door, and looking disapproving.

' "Old sweetheart" is hardly how you used to talk of the Head of your Chambers.'

'Somehow I can never remember to call the Head of my Chambers "Daddy".'

The door was open. Hilda was making a slow and effective exit.

'Tell Nick I'll be back in good time to get his supper.'

'Your wish is my command!' I muttered in my best imitation of a slave out of *Chu Chin Chow*. She chose to ignore it.

'And try not to leave the kitchen looking as though it's been hit by a bomb.'

'I hear, oh Master of the Blue Horizons.' I said this with a little more confidence, as she had by now started off on her errand of mercy, and I added, for good measure, 'She Who Must Be Obeyed'.

I had finished my breakfast, and was already thinking how much easier life with the Old Bailey judge was than marriage.

Soon after I finished my breakfast with Hilda, and made plans to meet my son at the start of his holidays from school, Fred Timson, star of a dozen Court appearances, was seeing *his* son in the cells under the Old Bailey as the result of a specially arranged visit. I know he brought the boy his best jacket, which his mother had taken specially to the cleaners, and insisted on his putting on a tie. I imagine he told him that they had the best 'brief' in the business to defend him, Mr Rumpole having always done wonders for the Timson family. I know that Fred told young Jim to stand up straight in the witness-box and remember to call the Judge 'my Lord' and not show his ignorance by coming out with any gaffe such as 'your Honour', or 'Sir'. The world, that day, was full of fathers showing appropriate and paternal concern.

The robbery with which Jim Timson was charged was an exceedingly simple one. At about 7 p.m. one Friday evening, the date being 16 September, the two elderly Brixton butchers, Mr Cadwallader and Mr Lewis Stein, closed their shop in Bombay Road and walked with their week's takings round the corner to a narrow alley-way known as Green's Passage, where their grey Austin van was parked. When they got to the van they found that the front tyres had been deflated. They stooped to inspect the wheels and, as they did so, they were attacked by a number of boys, some armed with knives and one flourishing a cricket stump. Luckily, neither of the butchers was hurt, but the attaché case containing their money was snatched.

Chief Inspector 'Persil' White, the old darling in whose territory this outrage had been committed, arrested Jim Timson. All the other boys got clean away, but no doubt because he came from a family well known, indeed almost embarrassingly familiar, to the Chief Inspector, and because of certain rumours in the school playground, he was charged and put on an identity parade. The butchers totally failed to identify him; but, when he was in the Remand Centre, young Jim, according to the evidence, had boasted to another boy of having 'done the butchers'.

As I thought about this case on my way to the Temple that morning, it occured to me that Jim Timson was a year younger than my son, but that he had got a step further than Nick in following his father's profession. I had always hoped Nick would go into the law, and, as I say, he seemed to thoroughly enjoy my murders.

In the clerk's room in Chambers Albert was handing out the work for the day: rather as a trainer sends his string of horses out on the gallops. I looked round the familiar faces, my friend George Frobisher, who is an old sweetheart but an absolutely hopeless advocate (he can't ask for costs without writing down what he's going to say), was being fobbed off with a nuisance at Kingston County Court. Young Erskine-Brown, who wears striped shirts and what I believe are known as 'Chelsea Boots', was turning up his well-bred nose at an indecent assault at Lambeth (a job I'd have bought Albert a double claret in Pommeroy's for at his age) and saying he would prefer a little civil work, adding that he was sick to death of crime.

I have very little patience with Erskine-Brown.

'A person who is tired of crime,' I told him quite candidly, 'is tired of life.'

'Your Dangerous and Careless at Clerkenwell is on the mantelpiece, Mr Hoskins,' Albert said.

Hoskins is a gloomy fellow with four daughters; he's always lurking about our clerk's room looking for cheques. As I've told him often enough crime doesn't pay, or at any rate not for a very long time.

When a young man called MacLay had asked in vain for a brief I invited him to take a note for me down at the Old Bailey. At least he'd get a wig on and not spend a miserable day unemployed in Chambers. Our oldest member, Uncle Tom (very few of us remember that his name is T. C. Rowley) also asked Albert if there were any briefs for him, not in the least expecting to find one. To my certain knowledge, Uncle Tom hasn't appeared in Court for fifteen years, when he managed to lose an undefended divorce case, but, as he lives with a widowed sister, a lady of such reputed ferocity that she makes She Who Must Be Obeyed sound like Mrs Tiggywinkle, he spends most of his time in Chambers. He looks remarkably well for 78.

'You aren't actually *expecting* a brief, Uncle Tom, are you?' Erskine-Brown asked. I can't like Erskine-Brown.

'Time was,' Uncle Tom started one of his reminiscences of life in our Chambers. 'Time was when I had more briefs in my corner of the mantelpiece, Erskine-Brown, than you've seen in the whole of your short career at the Bar. Now,' he was opening a brown envelope, 'I only get invitations to insure my life. It's a little late for that.'

Albert told me that the robbery was not before 11.30 before Mr Justice Everglade in Number 1 Court. He also told me who was prosecuting, none other than the tall, elegant figure with the silk handkerchief and gold wristwatch, leaning against the mantelpiece and negligently reading a large cheque from the Director of Public Prosecutions, Guthrie Featherstone, MP. He removed the silk handkerchief, dabbed the end of his nose and his small moustache and asked in that voice which comes over so charmingly, saying nothing much about any important topic of the day in 'World at One'.

'Agin me, Rumpole? Are you agin me?' He covered a slight yawn with the handkerchief before returning it to his breast pocket. 'Just come from an all-night sitting down at the House. I don't suppose your robbery'll be much of a worry.'

'Only, possibly, to young Jim Timson,' I told him, and then gave Albert his orders for the day. 'Mrs Rumpole's gone down to see her father in Horsham.'

'How is Wystan? No better, is he?' Uncle Tom sounded as gently pleased as all old men do when they hear news of illness in others.

'Much the same, Uncle Tom, thank you. And Young Nick. My son . . .'

'Master Nick?' Albert had always been fond of Nick, and looked forward to putting him through his paces when the time came for him to join our stable in Chambers.

'He's breaking up today. So he'll need meeting at Liverpool Street. Then he can watch a bit of the robbery.'

'We're going to have your son in the audience? I'd better be brilliant.' Guthrie Featherstone now moved from the fireplace.

'You needn't bother, old darling. It's his Dad he comes to see.'

'Oh, *touché*, Rumpole! *Distinctement touché!*'

Featherstone talks like that. Then he invited me to walk down to the Bailey with him. Apparently he was still capable of movement and didn't need a stretcher, even after a sleepless night with the Gas Mains Enabling Bill, or whatever it was.

We walked together down Fleet Street and into Ludgate Circus,

Featherstone wearing his overcoat with the velvet collar and little round bowler hat, I puffing a small cigar and with my old mac flapping in the wind; I discovered that the gentleman beside me was quietly quizzing me about my career at the Bar.

'You've been at this game a long while, Rumpole,' Featherstone announced. I didn't disagree with him, and then he went on.

'You never thought of taking silk?'

'Rumpole, QC?' I almost burst out laughing. 'Not on your Nelly. Rumpole "Queer Customer". That's what they'd be bound to call me.'

'I'm sure you could, with your seniority.' I had no idea then, of exactly what this Featherstone was after. I gave him my view of QCs in general.

'Perhaps, if I played golf with the right judges, or put up for Parliament, they might make me an artificial silk, or, at any rate, a nylon.' It was at that point I realized I had put up a bit of a black. 'Sorry. I forgot. You *did* put up for Parliament.'

'Yes. You never thought of Rumpole, QC?' Featherstone had apparently taken no offence.

'Never,' I told him. 'I have the honour to be an Old Bailey Hack! That's quite enough for me.'

At which point we turned up into Newgate Street and there it was in all its glory, touched by a hint of early spring sunshine, the Old Bailey, a stately Law Court, decreed by the City Fathers, an Edwardian palace, with an extensive modern extension to deal with the increase in human fallibility. There was the Dome and the Blindfold Lady. Well, it's much better she doesn't see *all* that's going on. That, in fact, was our English version of the Palais de Justice, complete with murals, marble statues and underground accommodation for some of the choicest villains in London.

Terrible things go on down the Bailey – horrifying things. Why is it I never go in the revolving door without a thrill of pleasure, a slight tremble of excitement? Why does it seem a much *jollier* place than my flat in Gloucester Road under the strict rule of She Who Must Be Obeyed? These are questions which may only be partly answered in the course of these memoirs.

At the time when I was waving a cheerful umbrella at Harry, the policeman in the revolving door of the Old Bailey extension, my wife Hilda was at her Daddy's bedside at the Horsham General arranging her dozen early daffs and gently probing, so she told me that evening, on the subject of his future, and mine.

'I'll have to give up, you know. I can't go on forever. Crocked up, I'm afraid,' said Wystan.

'Nonsense, Daddy. You'll go on for years.'

I imagine Hilda did her best to sound bracing, whilst putting the daffs firmly in their place.

'No, Hilda. No. They'll have to start looking for another Head of Chambers.'

This gave Hilda her opportunity. 'Rumpole's the senior man. Apart from Uncle Tom and he doesn't really practise nowadays.'

'Your husband the senior man.' Wystan looked back on a singularly uneventful life. 'How time flies! I recall when he was the junior man. My pupil.'

'You said he was the best youngster on bloodstains you'd ever known.' Hilda was doing her best for me.

'Rumpole! Yes, your husband was pretty good on bloodstains. Shaky, though, on the law of landlord and tenant. What sort of practice has Rumpole now?'

'I believe . . . Today it's the Old Bailey.' Hilda was plumping pillows, doing her best to sound casual. And her father showed no particular enthusiasm for my place of work.

'It's always the Old Bailey, isn't it?'

'Most of the time. Yes. I suppose so.'

'Not a frightfully good *address*, the Old Bailey. Not exactly the SW1 of the legal profession.'

Sensing that Daddy would have thought better of me if I'd been in the Court of Appeal or the Chancery Division, Hilda told me she thought of a masterstroke.

'Oh, Rumpole only went down to the Bailey because it's a family he knows. It seems they've got a young boy in trouble.'

This appealed to Daddy, he gave one of his bleak smiles which amount to no more than a brief withdrawal of lips from the dentures.

'Son gone wrong?' he said. 'Very sad that. Especially if he comes of a really good family.'

★

That really good family, the Timsons, was out in force and waiting outside Number 1 Court by the time I had got on the fancy dress, yellowing horsehair wig, gown become more than a trifle tattered over the years and bands round the neck that Albert ought to have sent to the laundry after last week's death by dangerous driving. As I looked at the Timson clan assembled, I thought the best thing about them was the amount of work of a criminal nature they had brought into Chambers. They were all dressed for the occasion, the men in dark blazers, suede shoes and grey flannels; the ladies in tight-fitting suits, high heels and elaborately piled hairdos. I had never seen so many ex-clients together at one time.

'Mr Rumpole.'

'Ah, Bernard! You're instructing me.'

Mr Bernard, the solicitor, was a thirtyish, perpetually smiling man in a pinstriped suit. He regarded criminals with something of the naive fervour with which young girls think of popular entertainers. Had I known the expression at the time, I would have called him a grafters' 'groupie'.

'I'm always your instructing solicitor in a Timson case, Mr Rumpole.' Mr Bernard beamed and Fred Timson, a kindly man and most innocent robber, stepped out of the ranks to do the honours.

'Nothing but the best for the Timsons, best solicitor and best barrister going. You know my wife Vi?'

Young Jim's mother seemed full of confidence. As I took her hand, I remembered I had got Vi off on a handling charge after the Croydon bank raid. Well, there was really no evidence.

'Uncle Cyril.' Fred introduced the plumpish uncle with the small moustache whom I was sure I remembered. What was *his* last outing exactly? Carrying housebreaking instruments by night?

'Uncle Dennis. You remember Den, surely, Mr Rumpole?'

I did. Den's last little matter was an alleged conspiracy to forge logbooks.

'And Den's Doris.'

Aunty Doris came at me in a blur of hennaed hair and darkish perfume. What was Doris's last indiscretion? Could it have been receiving a vast quantity of stolen scampi? Acquitted by a majority, at least I was sure of that.

'And yours truly. Frederick Timson. The boy's father.'

Regrettable, but we had a slip-up with Fred's last spot of bother. I was away with flu, George Frobisher took it over and he got three years. He must've only just got out.

'So, Mr Rumpole. You know the whole family.'

A family to breed from, the Timsons. Must almost keep the Old Bailey going single-handed.

'You're going to do your best for our young Jim, I'm sure, Mr Rumpole.'

I didn't find the simple faith of the Timsons that I could secure acquittals in the most unlikely circumstances especially encouraging. But then Jim's mother said something which I was to long remember.

'He's a good boy. He was ever so good to me while Dad was away.'

So that was Jimbo's life. Head of the family at fourteen, when Dad was off on one of his regular visits to Her Majesty.

'It's young Jim's first appearance, like. At the Old Bailey.' Fred couldn't conceal a note of pride. It was Jim boy's Bar Mitzvah, his first Communion.

So we chatted a little about how all the other boys got clean away, which I told them was a bit of luck as none of them would go into the witness-box and implicate Jim, and Bernard pointed out that the identification by the butchers was pretty hopeless. Well, what did he expect? Would you have a photographic impression of the young hopeful who struck you a smart blow on the back of the head with a cricket stump? We talked with that curious suppressed excitement there always is before a trial, however disastrous the outcome may be, and I told them the only thing we had to worry about, as if that were not enough, was Jim's confession to the boy in the Remand Centre, a youth who rejoiced in the name of Peanuts Molloy.

'Peanuts Molloy! Little grass.' Fred Timson spoke with a deep contempt.

'Old "Persil" White fitted him up with that one, didn't he?' Uncle Cyril said it as if it were the most natural thing in the world, and only to be expected.

'Chief Detective Inspector White,' Bernard explained.

'Why should the Chief Inspector want to fit up your Jimbo?' It was a question to which I should have known what their answer would be.

'Because he's a Timson, that's why!' said Fred.

'Because he's the apple of our eye, like,' Uncle Den told me, and the boy's mother added:

'Being as he's the baby of the family.'

'Old Persil'd fit up his mother if it'd get him a smile from his Super.' As Fred said this the Chief Inspector himself, grey-haired and avuncular, walked by in plain clothes, with a plain-clothes sergeant.

'Morning, Chief Inspector,' Fred carried on without drawing breath.

'Morning, Fred. Morning, Mrs Timson.' The Chief Inspector greeted the family with casual politeness, after all they were part of his daily work, and Vi sniffed back a 'Good morning, Chief Inspector.'

'Mr Timson. We'll shift our ground. Remove, good friends.'

Like Hamlet, after seeing the ghost, I thought it was better to continue our conference in private. So we went and sat round a table in the canteen, and, when we had sorted out who took how many lumps, and which of them could do with a choc roll or a cheese sandwich, the family gave me the lowdown on the chief prosecution witness.

'The Chief Inspector put that little grass Peanuts Molloy into Jim's painting class at the Remand Centre.' Fred had no doubt about it.

'Jim apparently poured out his soul to Peanuts.' The evidence sounded, to my old ears, completely convincing, and Bernard read us a snatch from his file.

'We planned to do the old blokes from the butcher's and grab the wages . . .'

'That,' I reminded the assembled company, 'is what Peanuts will say Jim told him.'

'You think I'd bring Jim up to talk in the nick like that? The Timsons ain't stupid!' Fred was outraged, and Vi, pursing her lips in a sour gesture of wounded respectability, added, 'His Dad's always told him. Never say a word to anyone you're banged up with – bound to be a grass.'

One by one, Aunty Doris, Uncle Den and Uncle Cyril added their support.

'That's right. Fred's always brought the boy up proper. Like the way he should be. He'd never speak about the crime, not to anyone he was banged up with.'

'Specially not to one of the Molloys!'

'The Molloys!' Vi spoke for the Timsons, and with deep hatred. 'Noted grasses. That family always has been.'

'The Molloys is beyond the pale. Well known for it.' Aunty Doris nodded her hennaed topknot wisely.

'Peanuts's Grandad shopped my old father in the "Streatham Co-op Robbery". Pre-war, that was.'

I had a vague memory then of what Fred Timson was talking about. The Streatham Co-op case, one of my better briefs – a long case with not much honour shown among thieves, as far as I could remember.

'Then you can understand, Mr Rumpole. No Timson would ever speak to a Molloy.'

'So you're sure Jimbo never said anything to Peanuts?' I was wondering exactly how I could explain the deep, but not particularly creditable, origins of this family hostility to the jury.

'I give you my word, Mr Rumpole. Ain't that enough for you? No Timson would ever speak to a Molloy. Not under any circumstances.'

There were not many matters on which I would take Fred Timson's word, but the history of the Streatham Co-op case came back to me, and this was one of them.

It's part of the life of an Old Bailey Hack to spend a good deal of his time down in the cells, in the basement area, where they keep the old door of Newgate, kicked and scarred, through which generations of villains were sent to the treadmill, the gallows or the whip. You pass this venerable door and ring a bell, you're let in and your name's taken by one of the warders who bring the prisoners from Brixton. There's a perpetual smell of cooking and the warders are snatching odd snacks of six inches of cheese butties and a gallon of tea. Lunch is being got ready, and the cells under the Bailey have a high reputation as one of the best caffs in London. By the door the screws have their pin-ups and comic cartoons of judges. You are taken to a waiting-room, three steel chairs and a table, and you meet the client. Perhaps he is a novice, making his first appearance, like Jim Timson. Perhaps he's an old hand asking anxiously which judge he's got, knowing their form as accurately as a betting-shop proprietor. Whoever he is, the client will be nervously excited, keyed up for his great day, full of absurd hope.

The worst part of a barrister's life at the Old Bailey is going back to the cells after a guilty verdict to say 'goodbye'. There's no purpose in it, but, as a point of honour, it has to be done. Even then the barrister probably gets the best reaction, and almost never any blame. The client is stunned, knocked out by his sentence. Only in a couple of weeks' time, when the reality of being banged up with the sour smell of stone walls and his own chamber pot for company becomes apparent, does the convict start to weep. He is then drugged with sedatives, and Agatha Christies from the prison library.

When I saw the youngest Timson before his trial that morning, I couldn't help noticing how much smaller, and how much more experienced, he looked than my Nick. In his clean sports jacket and carefully knotted tie he was well dressed for the dock, and he showed all the carefully suppressed excitement of a young lad about to step into the limelight of Number 1 with an old judge, twelve jurors and a mixed bag of lawyers waiting to give him their undivided attention.

'Me speak to Peanuts? No Timson don't ever speak to a Molloy. It's a point of honour, like,' Jim added his voice to the family chorus.

'Since the raid on the Streatham Co-op. Your grandfather?'

'Dad told you about that, did he?'

'Yes. Dad told me.'

'Well, Dad wouldn't let me speak to no Molloy. He wouldn't put up with it, like.'

I stood up, grinding out the stub end of my small cigar in the old Oxo tin thoughtfully provided by HM's government. It was, I thought, about time I called the meeting to order.

'So Jim,' I asked him, 'what's the defence?'

Little Jim knitted his brows and came out with his contribution. 'Well. I didn't do it.'

'That's an interesting defence. Somewhat novel – so far as the Timsons are concerned.'

'I've got my alibi, ain't I?'

Jim looked at me accusingly, as at an insensitive visitor to a garden who has failed to notice the remarkable display of gladioli.

'Oh, yes. Your alibi.' I'm afraid I didn't sound overwhelmed with enthusiasm.

'Dad reckoned it was pretty good.'

Mr Bernard had his invaluable file open and was reading from that less-than-inspiring document, our Notice of Alibi.

'Straight from school on that Friday September 2nd, I went up to tea at my Aunty Doris's and arrived there at exactly 5.30. At 6 p.m. my Uncle Den came home from work accompanied by my Uncle Cyril. At 7 p.m. when this alleged crime was taking place I was sat round the television with my Aunty and two Uncles. I well remember we was watching "The Newcomers".'

All very neat and workmanlike. Well, that was it. The family gave young Jim an alibi, clubbed together for it, like a new bicycle. However, I had to disappoint Mr Bernard about the bright shining alibi as we went through the swing doors on our way into Court.

'We can't use that alibi.'

'We can't?' Mr Bernard look wounded, as if I'd just insulted his favourite child.

'Think about it, Bernard. Don't be blinded by the glamour of the criminal classes. Call the Uncles and the Aunties? Let them all be cross-examined about their records? The jury'll realize our Jimbo comes from a family of villains who keep a cupboard full of alibis for all occasions.'

Mr Bernard was forced to agree, but I went into my old place in Court (nearest to the jury, furthest from the witness-box) thinking that the devilish thing about that impossible alibi was that it might even be true.

So there I was, sitting in my favourite seat in Court, down in the firing line, and there was Jim boy, undersized for a prisoner, just peeping over the edge of the dock, guarded in case he ran amok and started attacking the Judge, by a huge Dock Officer. There was the jury, solid and grey, listening impassionately as Guthrie Featherstone spread out his glittering mass of incriminating facts before them. I don't know why it is that juries all look the same; take twelve good men and women off the street and they all look middle-aged, anonymous, slightly stunned, an average jury, of average people trying an average case. Perhaps being a jury has become a special profession for specially average people. 'What do you want to do when you grow up my boy?' 'Be a juryman, Daddy.' 'Well done, my boy. You can work a five-hour day for reasonable expenses and occasionally send people to chokey.'

So, as the carefully chosen words of Guthrie Featherstone passed over our heads like expensive hair oil, and as the enthusiastic young MacLay noted it all down, and the Rumpole Supporters Club, the

Timsons, sat and pursed their lips and now and then whispered, 'Lies. All lies' to each other, I sat watching the Judge rather as a noted torea- dor watches the bull from the barrier during the preliminary stages of the corrida, and remembered what I knew of Mr Justice Everglade, known to his few friends as 'Florrie'. Everglade's father was Lord Chancellor about the time when Jim's grandfather was doing over the Streatham Co-op. Educated at Winchester and Balliol, he always cracked *The Times* crossword in the opening of an egg. He was most happy with International Trust companies suing each other on nice points of law, and was only there for a fortnight's slumming down the Old Bailey. I wondered exactly what he was going to make of Peanuts Molloy.

'Members of the jury, it's right that you should know that it is alleged that Timson took part in this attack with a number of other youths, none of whom have been arrested,' Featherstone was purring to a halt.

'*The boy stood on the burning deck/whence all but he had fled,*' I muttered, but the Judge was busy congratulating learned Counsel for Her Majesty the Queen who was engaged that morning in prosecuting the pride of the Timsons.

'It is quite right you should tell the jury that, Mr Featherstone. Per- fectly right and proper.'

'If your Lordship pleases.' Featherstone was now bowing slightly, and my hackles began to rise. What was this? The old chums' league? Fellow members of the Athenaeum?

'I am most grateful to your Lordship for that indication.' Feather- stone did his well-known butler passing the sherry act again. I wondered why the old darling didn't crawl up on the bench with Mr Justice Ever- glade and black his boots for him.

'So I imagine this young man's defence is – he wasn't *ejusdem generis* with the other lads?' The Judge was now holding a private conversation, a mutual admiration society with my learned friend. I decided to break it up, and levered myself to my feet.

'I'm sorry. Your Lordship was asking about the defence?'

The Judge turned an unfriendly eye on me and fumbled for my name. I told you he was a stranger to the Old Bailey, where the name of Rumpole is, I think, tolerably well known.

'Yes, Mr . . . er . . .' The clerk of the Court handed him up a note on which the defender's name was inscribed. 'Rumpole.'

'I am reluctant to intrude on your Lordship's confidential conversation with my learned friend. But your Lordship was asking about the defence.'

'You are appearing for the young man . . . Timson?'

'I have that honour.'

At which point the doors of the Court swung open and Albert came in with Nick, a boy in a blazer and a school-tie who passed the boy in the dock with only a glance of curiosity. I always thank God, when I consider the remote politeness with which I was treated by the Reverend Wilfred Rumpole, that I get on extremely well with Nick. We understand each other, my boy and I, and have, when he's at home, formed a strong but silent alliance against the almost invincible rule of She Who Must Be Obeyed. He is as fond as I am of the Sherlock Holmes tales, and when we walked together in Hyde Park and Kensington Gardens, young Nick often played the part of Holmes whilst I trudged beside him as Watson, trying to deduce the secret lives of those we passed by the way they shined their shoes, or kept their handkerchiefs in their sleeves. So I gave a particularly welcoming smile to Nick before I gave my attention back to Florrie.

'And, as Jim Timson's Counsel,' I told his Lordship, 'I might know a little more about his case than Counsel for the prosecution.'

To which Mr Justice Everglade trotted out his favourite bit of Latin. 'I imagine,' he said loftily, 'your client says he was not *ejusdem generis* with the other lads.'

'*Ejusdem generis*? Oh yes, my Lord. He's always saying that. *Ejusdem generis* is a phrase in constant use in his particular part of Brixton.'

I had hit a minor jackpot, and was rewarded with a tinkle of laughter from the Timsons, and a smile of genuine congratulation from Nick.

Mr Justice Everglade was inexperienced down the Bailey, he gave us a bare hour for lunch and Nick and I had it in the canteen. There is one thing you can say against crime, the catering facilities aren't up to much. Nick told me about school, and freely confessed, as I'm sure he wouldn't have done to his mother, that he'd been in some sort of trouble that term. There was an old deserted vicarage opposite Schoolhouse (my old House and Nick's) and he and his friends had apparently broken in the scullery window and assembled there for poker parties and the consumption of cherry brandy. I was horrified as I drew up the indictment which seemed to me to contain charges of burglary at common law, housebreaking under the Forcible Entries Act, contravening the Betting, Gaming, Lotteries Act and Serving Alcohol on Unlicensed Premises.

'Crabtree actually invited a couple of girls from the village,' Nick continued his confession. 'But Bagnold never got to hear of that.'

Bagnold was Nick's headmaster, the school equivalent of 'Persil' White. I cheered up a little at the last piece of information.

'Then there's no evidence of girls. As far as your case goes there's no reason to suppose the girls ever existed. As for the other charges, which are serious . . .'

'Yes, yes, I suppose they are rather.'

'I imagine you were walking past the house on Sunday evening and, attracted by the noise . . . You went to investigate?'

'Dad. Bagnold came in and found us – playing poker.'

Nick wasn't exactly being helpful. I tried another line.

'I know, "My Lord. My client was only playing poker in order not to look too pious whilst he lectured his fellow sixth-formers on the evils of gambling and cherry brandy."'

'Dad. Be serious.'

'I am serious. Don't you want me to defend you?'

'No. Bagnold's not going to tell the police or anything like that.'

I was amazed. 'He isn't? What's he going to do?'

'Well . . . I'll miss next term's exeat. Do extra work. I thought I should tell you before you got a letter.'

'Thank you, Nick. Thank you. I'm glad you told me. So there's no question of . . . the police?'

'The police?' Nick was laughing. 'Of course not. Bagnold doesn't want any trouble. After all, we're still at school.'

I watched Nick as he finished his fish and chips, and then turned my thoughts to Jim Timson, who had also been at school; but with no kindly Bagnold to protect him.

Back in Court I was cross-examining that notable grass, Peanuts Molloy, a skinnier, more furtive edition of Jim Timson. The cross-examination was being greatly enjoyed by the Timsons and Nick, but not much by Featherstone or Chief Detective Inspector 'Persil' White who sat at the table in front of me. I also thought that Mr Justice 'Florrie' Everglade was thinking that he would have been happier snoozing in the Athenaeum, or working on his gros-point in Egerton Terrace, than listening to me bowling fast in-swingers at the juvenile chief witness for the prosecution.

'You don't speak. The Molloys and the Timsons are like the Montagues and the Capulets,' I put it to Peanuts.

'What did you say they were?' The Judge had, of course, given me my opportunity. I smacked him through the slips for a crafty single. 'Not *ejusdem generis*, my Lord,' I said.

Nick joined in the laughter and even the ranks of Featherstone had to stifle a smile. The usher called 'Silence'. We were back to the business in hand.

'Tell me, Peanuts . . . How would you describe yourself?'

'Is that a proper question?' Featherstone uncoiled himself gracefully. I ignored the interruption.

'I mean artistically. Are you a latter-day Impressionist? Do all your oils in little dots, do you? Abstract painter? White squares on a white background? Do you indulge in watches melting in the desert like dear old Salvador Dali?'

'I don't know what you're talking about.' Peanuts played a blocking shot and Featherstone tried a weary smile to the Judge.

'My Lord, neither, I must confess, do I.'

'Sit quietly, Featherstone,' I muttered to him. 'All will be revealed to you.' I turned my attention back to Peanuts. 'Are you a dedicated artist? The Rembrandt of the Remand Centre?'

'I hadn't done no art before.' Peanuts confirmed my suspicions.

'So we are to understand that this occasion, when Jim poured out his heart to you, was the first painting lesson you'd ever been to?'

Peanuts admitted it.

'You'd been at the Remand Centre how long?'

'Couple of months. I was done for a bit of an affray.'

'I didn't ask you that. And I'm sure the reason you were on remand was entirely creditable. What I want to know is, what inspired you with this sudden fascination for the arts?'

'Well, the chief screw. He suggested it.'

Now we were beginning to get to the truth of the matter. Like his old grandfather in the Streatham Co-op days, Jim had been banged up with a notable grass.

'You were suddenly told to join the painting class, weren't you . . . and put yourself next to Jim?'

'Something like that, yeah.'

'What did he say?' Florrie frowned. It was all very strange to him and yet he was starting to get the hint of something that wasn't quite cricket.

'Something like that, my Lord,' I repeated slowly, giving the judge a chance to make a note. 'And you were sent there, not in the pursuit of art, Peanuts, but in the pursuit of evidence! You knew that and you supplied your masters with just what they wanted to hear – even though Jim Timson didn't say a word to you!'

Everyone in Court, including Nick, looked impressed. DI White bit hard on a polo mint and Featherstone oozed to his feet in a rescue bid.

'That's great, Dad!'

'Thanks, Nick. Sorry it's not a murder.'

'I don't know quite what my learned friend is saying. Is he suggesting that the police . . .'

'Oh, it's an old trick,' I said, staring hard at the Chief Inspector. 'Bang the suspect up with a notable grass when you're really pushed for evidence. They do it with grown-ups often enough. Now they're trying it with children!'

'Mr Rumpole,' the Judge sighed, 'you are speaking a language which is totally foreign to me.'

'Let me try and make myself clear, my Lord. I was suggesting that Peanuts was put there as a deliberate trap.'

By now, even the Judge had the point. 'You are suggesting that Mr Molloy was not a genuine "amateur painter"?'

'No, my Lord. Merely an amateur witness.'

'Yes.' I actually got a faint smile. 'I see. Please go on, Mr Rumpole.'

Another day or so of this, I felt, and I'd get invited to tea at the Athenaeum.

'What did you say first to Jim? As you drew your easel alongside?'

'Don't remember.'

'Don't you?'

'I think we was speaking about the Stones.'

'What "stones" are these?' The Judge's ignorance of the life around him seemed to be causing him some sort of wild panic. Remember this was 1965, and I was in a similar state of confusion until Nick, whispering from behind me, gave me the clue.

'The Rolling Stones, my Lord.' The information meant nothing to him.

'I'm afraid a great deal of this case seems to be taking place in a foreign tongue, Mr Rumpole.'

'Jazz musicians, as I understand it, my Lord, of some notoriety.' By courtesy of Nick, I filled his Lordship in on 'the scene'.

'Well, the notoriety hasn't reached me!' said the Judge, providing the obedient Featherstone with the laugh of the year, if not the century. When the learned prosecuting Counsel had recovered his solemnity, Peanuts went rambling on.

'We was talking about the Stones concert at the Hammersmith Odeon. We'd both been to it, like. And, well . . . we talked about that. And then he said . . . Jim said . . . Well, he said as how he and the other blokes had done the butchers.'

The conversation had now taken a nasty turn. I saw that the Judge was writing industriously. 'Jim said . . . that he and the other blokes . . . had done the butchers.' Florrie was plying his pencil. Then he looked up at me, 'Well, Mr Rumpole, is that a convenient moment to adjourn?'

It was a very convenient moment for the prosecution, as the evidence against us would be the last thing the jury heard before sloping off to their homes and loved ones. It was also a convenient moment for Peanuts. He would have his second wind by the morning. So there was nothing for it but to take Nick for a cup of tea and a pile of crumpets in the ABC, and so home to She Who Must Be Obeyed.

So picture us three that evening, finishing dinner and a bottle of claret, celebrating the return of the Young Master at Hack Hall, Counsel's Castle, Rumpole Manor, or 25B Froxbury Court, Gloucester Road. Hilda had told Nick that his grandpa had sent his love and expected a letter, and also dropped me the encouraging news that old C. H. Wystan was retiring and quite appreciated that I was the senior man. Nick asked me if I was really going to be Head of Chambers, seeming to look at me with a new respect, and we drank a glass of claret to the future, whatever it might be. Then Nick asked me if I really thought Peanuts Molloy was lying.

'If he's not, he's giving a damn good imitation.' Then I told Hilda as she started to clear away, 'Nick enjoyed the case. Even though it was only a robbery. Oh, Nick . . . I wish you'd been there to hear me cross-examine about the bloodstains in the "Penge Bungalow Murders".'

'Nick wasn't born, when you did the "Penge Bungalow Murders".'

My wife is always something of a wet blanket. I commiserated with my son. 'Bad luck, old boy.'

'You were great with that Judge!'

I think Nick had really enjoyed himself.

'There was this extraordinary Judge who was always talking Latin and Dad was teasing him.'

'You want to be careful,' Hilda was imposing her will on the pudding plates. 'How you tease judges. If you're to be Head of Chambers.' On which line she departed, leaving Nick and I to our claret and conversation. I began to discuss with Nick the horrifying adventure of *The Speckled Band*.

'You're still reading those tales, are you?' I asked Nick.

'Well . . . not lately.'

'But you remember. I used to read them to you, didn't I? After She had ordered you to bed.'

'When you weren't too busy. Noting up your murders.'

'And remember we were Holmes and Watson? When we went for walks in Hyde Park.'

'I remember *one* walk.'

That was odd, as I recall it had been our custom ever at a weekend, before Nick went away to boarding school. I lit a small cigar and looked at the Great Detective through the smoke.

'Tell me, Holmes. What did you think was the most remarkable piece of evidence given by the witness Peanuts Molloy?'

'When he said they talked about the Rolling Stones.'

'Holmes, you astonish me.'

'You see, Watson. We were led to believe they were such enemies I mean, the families were. They'd never spoken.'

'I see what you're driving at. Have another glass of claret – stimulates the detective ability.' I opened another bottle, a clatter from the kitchen telling me that the lady was not about to join us.

'And there they were chatting about a pop concert. Didn't that strike you as strange, my dear Watson?'

'It struck me as bloody rum, if you want to know the truth, Holmes.' I was delighted to see Nick taking over the case.

'They'd both been to the concert . . . Well, that doesn't mean anything. Not necessarily . . . I mean, *I* was at that concert.'

'Were you indeed?'

'It was at the end of the summer holidays.'

'I don't remember you mentioning it.'

'I said I was going to the Festival Hall.'

I found this confidence pleasing, knowing that it wasn't to be shared with Hilda.

'Very wise. Your mother no doubt feels that at the Hammersmith Odeon they re-enact some of the worst excesses of the Roman Empire. You didn't catch sight of Peanuts and young Jimbo, did you?'

'There were about two thousand fans – all screaming.'

'I don't know if it helps . . .'

'No.'

'If they were old mates, I mean. Jim might really have confided in him. All the same, Peanuts is lying. And *you* noticed it! You've got the instinct, Nick. You've got a nose for the evidence! Your career at the Bar is bound to be brilliant.' I raised my glass to Nick. 'When are you taking silk?'

Shortly after this She entered with news that Nick had a dentist's appointment the next day, which would prevent his reappearance down the Bailey. All the same, he had given me a great deal of help and before I went to bed I telephoned Bernard the solicitor, tore him away from his fireside and instructed him to undertake some pretty immediate research.

Next morning, Albert told me that he'd had a letter from old C. H. Wystan, Hilda's Daddy, mentioning his decision to retire.

'I think we'll manage pretty well, with you, Mr Rumpole, as Head of Chambers,' Albert told me. 'There's not much you and I won't be able to sort out, sir, over a glass or two in Pommeroy's Wine Bar . . . And soon we'll be welcoming Master Nick in Chambers?'

'Nick? Well, yes.' I had to admit it. 'He is showing a certain legal aptitude.'

'It'll be a real family affair, Mr Rumpole . . . Like father, like son, if you want my opinion.'

I remembered Albert's words when I saw Fred Timson waiting for me outside the Court. But before I had time to brood on family tradition, Bernard came up with the rolled-up poster for a pop concert. I grabbed it from him and carried it as unobtrusively as possible into Court.

'When Jim told you he'd done up the butchers . . . He didn't tell you the date that that had happened?' Peanuts was back, facing the bowling, and Featherstone was up to his usual tricks, rising to interrupt.

'My Lord, the date is set out quite clearly in the indictment.'

The time had come, quite obviously, for a burst of righteous indignation.

'My Lord, I am cross-examining on behalf of a sixteen-year-old boy on an extremely serious charge. I'd be grateful if my learned friend didn't supply information which all of us in Court know – except for the witness.'

'Very well. Do carry on, Mr Rumpole.' I was almost beginning to like Mr Justice Everglade.

'No. He never told me when, like. I thought it was sometime in the summer.' Peanuts tried to sound co-operative.

'Sometime in the summer? Are you a fan of the Rolling Stones, Peanuts?'

'Yes.'

'Remind me . . . they were . . .' Still vaguely puzzled the Judge was hunting back through his notes.

Sleek as a butler with a dish of peas, Featherstone supplied the information. 'The musicians, my Lord.'

'And so was Jim a fan?' I ploughed on, ignoring the gentleman's gentleman.

'He was. Yes.'

'You had discussed music, before you met in the Remand Centre?'

'Before the nick. Oh yes.' Peanuts was following me obediently down the garden path.

'You used to talk about it at school?'

'Yes.'

'In quite a friendly way?' I was conscious of a startled Fred Timson looking at his son, and of Jim in the dock looking, for the first time, ashamed.

'We was all right. Yes.'

'Did you ever go to a concert with Jimbo? Please think carefully.'

'We went to one or two concerts together,' Peanuts conceded.

'In the evening?'

'Yes.'

'What would you do? . . . Call at his home and collect him?'

'You're joking!'

'Oh no, Peanuts. In this case I'm not joking at all!' No harm, I thought, at that stage, in underlining the seriousness of the occasion.

'Course I wouldn't call at his home!'

'Your families don't speak. You wouldn't be welcomed in each other's houses?'

'The Montagues and the Capulets, Mr Rumpole?' The old sweetheart on the bench had finally got the message. I gave him a bow, to show my true love and affection.

'If your Lordship pleases . . . Your Lordship puts it extremely aptly.' I turned back to Peanuts. 'So what would you do, if you were going to a concert?'

'We'd leave school together, like – and then hang around the caffs.'

'Hang around the caffs?'

'Cafays, Mr Rumpole?' Mr Justice Everglade was enjoying himself, translating the answer.

'Yes, of course, the cafays. Until it was time to go up West? If my Lord would allow me, up to the "West End of London" together?'

'Yes.'

'So you wouldn't be separated on these evenings you went to concerts together?' It was one of those questions after which you hold your breath. There can be so many wrong answers.

'No. We hung around together.'

Rumpole breathed a little more easily, but he still had the final question, the great gamble, with all Jim Timson's chips firmly piled on the red. *Fait vos jeux, m'sieurs et mesdames* of the Old Bailey jury. I spun the wheel.

'And did that happen . . . When you went to the Rolling Stones at the Hammersmith Odeon?'

A nasty silence. Then the ball rattled into the hole.

Peanuts said, 'Yes.'

'That was this summer, wasn't it?' We were into the straight now, cantering home.

'In the summer, yeah.'

'You left school together?'

'And hung around the caffs, like. Then we went up the Odeon.'

'Together . . . All the time?'

'I told you – didn't I?' Peanuts looked bored, and then amazed as I unrolled the poster Bernard had brought, rushed by taxi from Hammersmith, with the date clearly printed across the bottom.

'My Lord. My learned friend might be interested to know the date of the only Rolling Stones concert at the Hammersmith Odeon this year.' I gave Featherstone an unwelcome eyeful of the poster.

'He might like to compare it with the date so conveniently set out in the indictment.'

When the subsequent formalities were over, I went down to the cells. This was not a visit of commiseration, no time for a 'sorry old sweetheart, but . . .' and a deep consciousness of having asked one too many questions. All the same, I was in no gentle mood, in fact, it would be fair to say that I was bloody angry with Jimbo.

'You had an alibi! You had a proper, reasonable, truthful alibi, and, joy of joys, it came from the prosecution! Why the hell didn't you tell me?'

Jim, who seemed to have little notion of the peril he had passed, answered me quite calmly, 'Dad wouldn't've liked it.'

'Dad! What's Dad got to do with it?' I was astonished.

'He wouldn't've liked it, Mr Rumpole. Not me going out with Peanuts.'

'So you were quite ready to be found guilty, to be convicted of robbery, just because your Dad wouldn't like you going out with Peanuts Molloy?'

'Dad got the family to alibi me.' Jim clearly felt that the Timsons had done their best for him.

'Keep it in the family!' Though it was heavily laid on, the irony was lost on Jim. He smiled politely and stood up, eager to join the clan upstairs.

'Well, anyway. Thanks a lot, Mr Rumpole. Dad said I could rely on you. To win the day, like. I'd better collect me things.'

If Jim thought I was going to let him get away as easily as that, he was mistaken. Rumpole rose in his crumpled gown, doing his best to represent the majesty of the law. 'No! Wait a minute. I didn't win the day. It was luck. The purest fluke. It won't happen again!'

'You're joking, Mr Rumpole.' Jim thought I was being modest. 'Dad told me about you . . . He says you never let the Timsons down.'

I had a sudden vision of my role in life, from young Jim's point of view and I gave him the voice of outrage which I use frequently in Court. I had a message of importance for Jim Timson.

'Do you think that's what I'm here for? To help you along in a career like your Dad's?' Jim was still smiling, maddeningly. 'My God! I shouldn't have asked those questions! I shouldn't have found out the date of the concert! Then you'd really be happy, wouldn't you? You could follow in Dad's footsteps all your life! Sharp spell of Borstal training to teach you the mysteries of housebreaking, and then a steady life in the nick. You might really do well! You might end up in Parkhurst, Maximum Security Wing, doing a glamorous twenty years and a hero to the screws.'

At which the door opened and a happy screw entered, for the purpose of springing young Jim – until the inevitable next time.

'We've got his things at the gate, Mr Rumpole. Come on, Jim. You can't stay here all night.'

'I've got to go,' Jim agreed. 'I don't know how to face Dad, really. Me being so friendly with Peanuts.'

'Jim,' I tried a last appeal. 'If you're at all grateful for what I did . . .'

'Oh I am, Mr Rumpole, I'm quite satisfied.' Generous of him.

'Then you can perhaps repay me.'

'Why – aren't you on legal aid?'

'It's not that! Leave him! Leave your Dad.'

Jim frowned, for a moment he seemed to think it over. Then he said, 'I don't know as how I can.'

'You don't know?'

'Mum depends on me, you see. Like when Dad goes away. She depends on me then, as head of the family.'

So he left me, and went up to temporary freedom and his new responsibilities.

My mouth was dry and I felt about ninety years old, so I took the lift up to that luxurious eatery, the Old Bailey canteen, for a cup of tea and a Penguin biscuit. And, pushing his tray along past the urns, I met a philosophic Chief Inspector 'Persil' White. He noticed my somewhat lugubrious expression and tried a cheering, 'Don't look so miserable, Mr Rumpole. You won didn't you?'

'Nobody won, the truth emerges sometimes, Inspector, even down the Old Bailey.' I must have sounded less than gracious. The wiley old copper smiled tolerantly.

'He's a Timson. It runs in the family. We'll get him sooner or later!'

'Yes. Yes. I suppose you will.'

At a table in a corner, I found certain members of my Chambers, George Frobisher, Percy Hoskins and young Tony MacLay, now resting from their labours, their wigs lying among cups of Old Bailey tea, buns and choccy bics. I joined them. Wordsworth entered my head, and I gave him an airing . . . *'Trailing clouds of glory do we come.'*

'Marvellous win, that. I was telling them.' Young MacLay thought I was announcing my triumph.

'Yes, Rumpole. I hear you've had a splendid win.' Old George, ever generous, smiled, genuinely pleased.

'It'll be *years* before you get the cheque,' Hoskins grumbled.

'Not in entire forgetfulness and not in utter nakedness,/But trailing clouds of glory do we come/From God who is our home . . .' I was thinking of Jim, trying to sort out his situation with the help of Wordsworth.

'You don't get paid for years at the Old Bailey. I try to tell my grocer that. If you had to wait as long to be paid for a pound of sugar, I tell him, as we do for an armed robbery . . .' Hoskins was warming to a well-loved theme, but George, dear old George was smiling at me.

'Albert tells me he's had a letter from Wystan. I just wanted to say,

I'm sure we'd all like to say, you'll make a splendid Head of Chambers, Rumpole.'

'Heaven lies about us in our infancy, / Shades of the prison house begin to close / Upon the growing boy . . . / But he beholds the light, and whence it flows, / He sees it in his joy.' I gave them another brief glimpse of immortality. George looked quite proud of me and told MacLay, 'Rumpole quotes poetry. He does it quite often.'

'But does the growing boy behold the light?' I wondered. 'Or was the old sheep of the Lake District being unduly optimistic?'

'It'll be refreshing for us all, to have a Head of Chambers who quotes poetry,' George went on, at which point Percy Hoskins produced a newspaper which turned out to contain an item of news for us all.

'Have you seen *The Times*, Rumpole?'

'No, I haven't had time for the crossword.'

'Guthrie Featherstone. He's taken silk.'

It was the apotheosis, the great day for the Labour-Conservative Member for wherever it was, one time unsuccessful prosecutor of Jim Timson and now one of Her Majesty's Counsel, called within the Bar, and he went down to the House of Lords tailored out in his new silk gown, a lace jabot, knee breeches with diamanté buckles, patent shoes, black silk stockings, lace cuffs and a full-bottomed wig that made him look like a pedigree, but not over-bright, spaniel. However, Guthrie Featherstone was a tall man, with a good calf in a silk stocking, and he took with him Marigold, his lady wife, who was young enough, and I suppose pretty enough, for Henry, our junior clerk, to eye wistfully, although she had the sort of voice that puts me instantly in mind of headscarves and gymkhanas, that high-pitched nasal whining which a girl learns from too much contact with the saddle when young, and too little with the Timsons of this world in later life. The couple were escorted by Albert, who'd raided Moss Bros for a top hat and morning coat for the occasion, and when the Lord Chancellor had welcomed Guthrie to that special club of Queen's Counsel (on whose advice the Queen, luckily for her, never has to rely for a moment) they came back to Chambers where champagne (the N.V. cooking variety, bulk bought from Pommeroy's Wine Bar) was served by Henry and old Miss Patterson, our typist, in Wystan's big room looking out over Temple

Gardens. C. H. Wystan, our retiring Head, was not among those present as the party began, and I took an early opportunity to get stuck into
the beaded bubbles.

After the fourth glass I felt able to relax a bit and wandered to where
Featherstone, in all his finery, was holding forth to Erskine-Brown about
the problems of appearing *en travestie*. I arrived just as he was saying,
'It's the stockings that're the problem.'

'Oh yes. They would be.' I did my best to sound interested.

'Keeping them up.'

'I do understand.'

'Well, Marigold. My wife Marigold . . .' I looked across to where
Mrs QC was tinkling with laughter at some old legal anecdote of
Uncle Tom's. It was a laugh that seemed in some slight danger of break-
ing the wine glasses.

'*That* Marigold?'

'Her sister's a nurse, you know . . . and she put me in touch with
this shop which supplies suspender belts to nurses . . . among other
things.'

'Really?' This conversation seemed to arouse some dormant sexual
interest in Erskine-Brown.

'Yards of elastic, for the larger ward sister. But it works miracu-
lously.'

'You're wearing a suspender belt?' Erskine-Brown was frankly fascinated. 'You sexy devil!'

'I hadn't realized the full implications,' I told the QC, 'of rising to
the heights of the legal profession.'

I wandered off to where Uncle Tom was giving Marigold a brief history of life in our Chambers over the last half-century. Percy Hoskins
was in attendance, and George.

'It's some time since we had champagne in Chambers.' Uncle Tom
accepted a refill from Albert.

'It's some time since we had a silk in Chambers,' Hoskins smiled at
Marigold who flashed a row of well-groomed teeth back at him.

'I recall we had a man in Chambers once called Drinkwater –
oh, before you were born, Hoskins. And some fellow came and paid
Drinkwater a hundred guineas – for six months' pupillage. And you
know what this Drinkwater fellow did? Bought us all champagne – and

the next day he ran off to Calais with his junior clerk. We never saw hide nor hair of either of them again.' He paused. Marigold looked puzzled, not quite sure if this was the punchline.

'Of course, you could get a lot further in those days – on a hundred guineas,' Uncle Tom ended on a sad note, and Marigold laughed heartily.

'Your husband's star has risen so quickly, Mrs Featherstone. Only ten years call and he's an MP *and* leading counsel.' Hoskins was clearly so excited by the whole business he had stopped worrying about his cheques for half an hour.

'Oh, it's the PR you know. Guthrie's frightfully good at the PR'

I felt like Everglade. Marigold was speaking a strange and incomprehensible language.

'Guthrie always says the most important thing at the Bar is to be polite to your instructing solicitor. Don't you find that, Mr Rumpole?'

'Polite to solicitors? It's never occurred to me.'

'Guthrie admires you so, Mr Rumpole. He admires your style of advocacy.'

I had just sunk another glass of the beaded bubbles as passed by Albert, and I felt a joyous release from my usual strong sense of tact and discretion.

'I suppose it makes a change from bowing three times and offering to black the judge's boots for him.'

Marigold's smile didn't waver. 'He says you're most amusing out of Court, too. Don't you quote poetry?'

'Only in moments of great sadness, Madam. Or extreme elation.'

'Guthrie's so looking forward to leading you. In his next big case.'

This was an eventuality which I should have taken into account as soon as I saw Guthrie in silk stockings; as a matter of fact it had never occurred to me.

'Leading *me*? Did you say, *leading* me?'

'Well, he has to have a junior now . . . doesn't he? Naturally he wants the best junior available.'

'Now he's a leader?'

'Now he's left the Junior Bar.'

I raised my glass and gave Marigold a version of Browning. 'Just for a pair of knee breeches he left us . . . Just for an elastic suspender belt, as supplied to the Nursing profession . . .' At which the QC himself bore down on us in a rustle of silk and drew me into a corner.

'I just wanted to say, I don't see why recent events should make the slightest difference to the situation in Chambers. You *are* the senior man in practice, Rumpole.'

Henry was passing with the fizzing bottle. I held out my glass and the tide ran foaming in it.

'*You wrong me, Brutus,*' I told Featherstone. '*You said an older soldier, not a better.*'

'A quotation! *Touché*, very apt.'

'Is it?'

'I mean, all this will make absolutely no difference. I'll still support you, Rumpole, as the right candidate for Head of Chambers.'

I didn't know about being a candidate, having thought of the matter as settled and not being much of a political animal. But before I had time to reflect on whatever the Honourable Member was up to, the door opened letting in a formidable draught and the Head of Chambers. C. H. Wystan, She's Daddy, wearing a tweed suit, extremely pale, supported by Albert on one side and a stick on the other, made the sort of formidable entrance that the ghost of Banquo stages at dinner with the Macbeths. Wystan was installed in an armchair, from which he gave us all the sort of wintry smile which seemed designed to indicate that all flesh is as the grass, or something to that effect.

'Albert wrote to me about this little celebration. I was determined to be with you. And the doctor has given permission, for no more than one glass of champagne.' Wystan held out a transparent hand into which Albert inserted a glass of non-vintage. Wystan lifted this with some apparent effort, and gave us a toast.

'To the great change in Chambers! Now we have a silk. Guthrie Featherstone, QC, MP!'

I had a large refill to that. Wystan absorbed a few bubbles, wiped his mouth on a clean, folded handkerchief and proceeded to the oration. Wystan was never a great speech maker, but I claimed another refill and gave him my ears.

'You, Featherstone, have brought a great distinction to Chambers.'

'Isn't that nice, Guthrie?' Marigold proprietorially squeezed her master's fingers.

'You know, when I was a young man. You remember when we were young men, Uncle Tom? We used to hang around in Chambers for weeks on end.' Wystan had gone on about these distant hard times at every Chambers meeting. 'I well recall we used to occupy ourselves with an old golf ball and mashie niblick, trying to get chip shots into the waste-paper baskets. Albert was a boy then.'

'A mere child, Mr Wystan,' Albert looked suitably demure.

'And we used to pray for work. *Any* sort of work, didn't we, Uncle Tom?'

'We were tempted to crime. Only way we could get into Court,' Uncle Tom took the feed line like a professional. Moderate laughter, except for Rumpole who was busy drinking. And then I heard Wystan rambling on.

'But as you grow older at the Bar you discover it's not having any work that matters. It's the *quality* that counts!'

'Here, here! I'm always saying we ought to do more civil.' This was the dutiful Erskine-Brown, inserting his oar.

'Now Guthrie Featherstone, QC, MP, will, of course, command briefs in all divisions – planning, contract,' Wystan's voice sank to a note of awe, 'even Chancery! I was so afraid, after I've gone, that this Chambers might become known as merely a criminal set.' Wystan's voice now sank in a sort of horror. 'And, of course, there's no doubt about it, too much criminal work does rather lower the standing of a Chambers.'

'Couldn't you install pithead baths?' I hadn't actually meant to say it aloud, but it came out very loud indeed.

'Ah, Horace.' Wystan turned his pale eyes on me for the first time.

'So we could have a good scrub down after we get back from the Old Bailey?'

'Now, Horace Rumpole. And I mean no disrespect whatever to my son-in-law.' Wystan returned to the oration. From far away I heard myself say, 'Daddy!' as I raised the hard-working glass. 'Horace does practise almost exclusively in the Criminal Courts!'

'One doesn't get the really fascinating points of *law*. Not in criminal work,' Erskine-Brown was adding unwanted support to the motion. 'I've often thought we should try and attract some really lucrative tax cases into Chambers.'

That, I'm afraid, did it. Just as if I were in Court I moved slightly to the centre and began my speech.

'Tax cases?' I saw them all smiling encouragement at me. 'Marvellous! Tax cases make the world go round. Compared to the wonderful world of tax, crime is totally trivial. What does it matter? If some boy loses a year, a couple of years, of his life? It's totally unimportant! Anyway, he'll grow up to be banged up for a good five, shut up with his own chamber pot in some convenient hole we all prefer not to think about.' There was a deafening silence, which came loudest from Marigold Featherstone. Then Wystan tried to reach a settlement.

'Now then, Horace. Your practice no doubt requires a good deal of skill.'

'Skill? Who said "skill"?' I glared round at the learned friends. 'Any fool could do it! It's only a matter of life and death. That's all it is. Crime? It's a sort of a game. How can you compare it to the real world of Off Shore Securities. And Deductible Expenses?'

'All you young men in Chambers can learn an enormous amount from Horace Rumpole, when it comes to crime.' Wystan now seemed to be the only one who was still smiling. I turned on him.

'You make me sound just like Fred Timson!'

'Really? Whoever's Fred Timson?' I told you Wystan never had much of a practice at the Bar, consequently he had never met the Timsons. Erskine-Brown supplied the information.

'The Timsons are Rumpole's favourite family.'

'An industrious clan of South London criminals, aren't they, Rumpole,' Hoskins added.

Wystan looked particularly pained. 'South London criminals?'

'I mean, do we want people like the Timsons forever hanging about in our waiting-room? I merely ask the question.' He was not bad, this Erskine-Brown, with a big future in the nastier sort of Breach of Trust cases.

'Do you? Do you merely ask it?' I heard the pained bellow of a distant Rumpole.

'The Timsons . . . and their like, are no doubt grist to Rumpole's mill,' Wystan was starting on the summing up. 'But it's the balance that *counts*. Now, you'll be looking for a new Head of Chambers.'

'Are we still looking?' My friend George Frobisher had the decency to ask. And Wystan told him, 'I'd like you all to think it over carefully. And put your views to me in writing. We should all try and remember. It's the good of the Chambers that matters. Not the feelings, however deep they may be, of any particular person.'

He then called on Albert's assistance to raise him to his feet, lifted his glass with an effort of pure will and offered us a toast to the good of Chambers. I joined in, and drank deep, it having been a good thirty seconds since I had had a glass to my lips. As the bubbles exploded against the tongue I noticed that the Featherstones were holding hands, and the brand-new artificial silk was looking particularly delighted. Something, and perhaps not only his suspender belt, seemed to be giving him special pleasure.

Some weeks later, when I gave Hilda the news, she was deeply shocked.

'*Guthrie Featherstone*! Head of Chambers!' We were at breakfast. In fact Nick was due back at school that day. He was neglecting his cornflakes and reading a book.

'By general acclaim.'

'I'm sorry.' Hilda looked at me, as if she'd just discovered that I'd contracted an incurable disease.

'He can have the headaches – working out Albert's extraordinary book-keeping system.' I thought for a moment, yes, I'd like to have been Head of Chambers, and then put the thought from me.

'If only you could have become a QC.' She was now pouring me an unsolicited cup of coffee.

'QC? C.T. That's enough to keep me busy.'

'C.T.? Whatever's C.T.?'

'Counsel for the Timsons!' I tried to say it as proudly as I could. Then I reminded Nick that I'd promised to see him off at Liverpool Street, finished my cooling coffee, stood up and took a glance at the book that was absorbing him, expecting it to be, perhaps, that spine-chilling adventure relating to the Footprints of an Enormous Hound. To my amazement the shocker in question was entitled simply *Studies in Sociology*.

'It's interesting,' Nick sounded apologetic.

'You astonish me.'

'Old Bagnold was talking about what I should read if I get into Oxford.'

'Of course you're going to read law, Nick. We're going to keep it in the family.' Hilda the barrister's daughter was clearing away deafeningly.

'I thought perhaps PPE and then go on to Sociology.' Nick sounded curiously confident. Before Hilda could get in another word I made my position clear.

'PPE, that's very good, Nick! That's very good indeed! For God's sake. Let's stop keeping things in the family!'

Later, as we walked across the barren stretches of Liverpool Street Station, with my son in his school uniform and me in my old striped trousers and black jacket, I tried to explain what I meant.

'That's what's wrong, Nick. That's the devil of it! They're being born around us all the time. Little Mr Justice Everglades . . . Little Timsons . . . Little Guthrie Featherstones. All being set off . . . to follow in father's footsteps.' We were at the barrier, shaking hands awkwardly. 'Let's have no more of that! No more following in father's footsteps. No more.'

Nick smiled, although I have no idea if he understood what I was trying to say. I'm not totally sure that I understood it either. Then the train removed him from me. I waved for a little, but he didn't wave back. That sort of thing is embarrassing for a boy. I lit a small cigar and went by tube to the Bailey. I was doing a long firm fraud then; a particularly nasty business, out of which I got a certain amount of harmless fun.

Rumpole and the Heavy Brigade

The story of my most recent murder, and my defence of Petey Delgardo, the youngest, and perhaps the most appalling of the disagreeable Delgardo brothers, raises several matters which are painful, not to say embarrassing for me to recall. The tale begins with Rumpole's reputation at its lowest, and although it has now risen somewhat, it has done so for rather curious and not entirely creditable reasons, as you shall hear.

After the case of the 'Dartford Post Office Robbery', which I have recounted in the previous chapter, I noticed a distinct slump in the Rumpole practice. I had emerged, as I thought, triumphant from that encounter with the disciplinary authority; but I suppose I was marked, for a while, as a barrister who had been reported for professional misconduct. The quality of briefs which landed on the Rumpole corner of the mantelpiece in our clerk's room was deteriorating and I spent a great deal more time pottering round Magistrates' Courts or down at Sessions than I did in full flood round the marble halls of the Old Bailey.

So last winter picture Rumpole in the November of his days, walking in the mists, under the black branches of bare trees to Chambers, and remembering Thomas Hood.

'No warmth, no cheerfulness, no healthful ease, / No comfortable feel in any member, / No shade, no shine, no butterflies, no bees, / No fruits, no flowers, no leaves, no birds, – November!'

As I walked, I hoped there might be some sort of trivial little brief waiting for me in Chambers. In November an old man's fancy lightly turned to thoughts of indecent assault, which might bring briefs at London Sessions and before the Uxbridge Justices. (Oh God! Oh, Uxbridge Justices!) I had started forty years ago, defending a charge of unsolicited grope on the Northern Line. And that's what I was back to. In my end is my beginning.

I pushed open the door of my Chambers and went into the clerk's room. There was a buzz of activity, very little of it, I was afraid, centring round the works of Rumpole, but Henry was actually smiling as he sat in his shirtsleeves at his desk and called out, 'Mr Rumpole.'

'Stern daughter of the Voice of God! Oh, duty! Oh my learned clerk, what are the orders for today, Henry? Mine not to reason why. Mine but to do or die, before some Court of Summary Jurisdiction.'

'There's a con. Waiting for you, sir. In a new matter, from Maurice Nooks and Parsley.'

Henry had mentioned one of the busiest firms of criminal solicitors, who had a reputation of being not too distant from some of their heavily villainous clients. In fact the most active partner was privately known to me as 'Shady' Nooks.

'New matter?'

' "The Stepney Road Stabbing". Mr Nooks says you'll have read about it in the papers.'

In fact I had read about it in that great source of legal knowledge, the *News of the World*. The Delgardo brothers, Leslie and Basil, were a legend in the East End; they gave copiously to charity, they had friends in 'show business' and went on holiday with a certain Police Superintendent and a well-known Member of Parliament. They hadn't been convicted of any offence, although their young brother, Peter Delgardo, had occasionally been in trouble. They ran a club known as the Paradise Rooms, a number of protection rackets and a seaside home for orphans. They were a devoted family and Leslie and Basil were said to be particularly concerned when their brother Peter was seen by several witnesses kneeling in the street outside a pub called the Old Justice beside the bloodstained body of an East End character known as Tosher MacBride. Later a knife, liberally smeared with blood of MacBride's group, was found beside the driver's seat of Peter Delgardo's elderly Daimler. He was arrested in the Paradise Rooms to which he had apparently fled for protection after the death of Tosher. The case seemed hopeless but the name 'Delgardo' made sure it would hit the headlines. I greeted the news that it was coming Rumpole's way with a low whistle of delight. I took the brief from Henry.

'*My heart leaps up when I behold . . . a rainbow in the sky*. Or a murder in the offing. I have to admit it.'

I suddenly thought of the fly in the ointment.

'I suppose they're giving me a leader – in a murder?'

'They haven't mentioned a leader,' Henry seemed puzzled.

'I suppose it'll be Featherstone. Well, at least it'll get me back to the Bailey. My proper stamping ground.'

I moved towards the door, and it was then my clerk Henry mentioned a topic which, as you will see, has a vital part to play in this particular narrative, my hat. Now I am not particularly self-conscious as far as headgear is concerned and the old black Anthony Eden has seen, it must be admitted, a good many years' service. It has travelled to many far-flung courts in fair weather and foul, it once had a small glowing cigar-end dropped in it as it lay under Rumpole's seat in Pommeroy's, it once blew off on a windy day in Newington Causeway and was run over by a bicycle. The hat is therefore, it must be admitted, like its owner, scarred and battered by life, no longer in its first youth and in a some-what collapsed condition. All the same it fits me comfortably and keeps the rain out most of the time. I have grown used to my hat and, in view of our long association, I have a certain affection for it. I was therefore astonished when Henry followed me to the door and, in a lowered tone as if he were warning me that the coppers had called to arrest me, he said,

'The other clerks were discussing your hat, sir. Over coffee.'

'My God! They must be hard up for conversation, to fill in a couple of hours round the ABC.'

'And they were passing the comment, it's a subject of a good many jokes, in the Temple.'

'Well, it's seen some service.' I took off the offending article and looked at it. 'And it shows it.'

'Quite frankly, Mr Rumpole, I can't send you down the Bailey, not on a top-class murder, in a hat like it.'

'You mean the jury might get a peep at the titfer, and convict with-out leaving the box?' I couldn't believe my ears.

'Mr Featherstone wears a nice bowler, Mr Rumpole.'

'I am not leading Counsel, Henry,' I told him firmly. 'I am not the Conservative-Labour MP for somewhere or other, and I don't like nice bowlers. Our old clerk Albert managed to live with this hat for a good many years.'

'There's been some changes made since Albert's time, Mr Rumpole.'

Henry had laid himself open, and I'm afraid I made the unworthy comment.

'Oh, yes! I got some decent briefs in Albert's time. The "Penge Bungalow Murders", the Brighton forgery. I wasn't put out to grass in the Uxbridge Magistrates' Court.'

The chairs in my room in Chambers have become a little wobbly over the years and my first thought was that the two large men sitting on them might be in some danger of collapse. They both wore blue suits made of some lightweight material, and both had gold wristwatches and identity bracelets dangling at their wrists. They had diamond rings, pink faces and brushed-back black hair. Leslie Delgardo was the eldest and the most affable, his brother Basil had an almost permanent look of discontent and his voice easily became querulous. In attendance, balanced on my insecure furniture, were 'Shady' Nooks, a silver-haired and suntanned person who also sported a large gold wristwatch, and his articled clerk, Miss Stebbings, a nice-looking girl fresh from law school, who had clearly no idea what area of the law she had got into.

I lit a small cigar, looked round the assembled company and said, 'Our client is not with us, of course.'

'Hardly, Mr Rumpole,' said Nooks. 'Mr Peter Delgardo has been moved to the prison hospital.'

'He's never been a well boy, our Petey.' Leslie Delgardo sounded sorrowful.

'Our client's health has always been an anxiety to his brothers,' Nooks explained.

'I see.' I hastily consulted the brief. 'The victim of the murder was a gentleman called Tosher MacBride. Know anything about him?'

'I believe he was a rent collector.' Nooks sounded vague.

'Not a bad start. The jury'll be against murder but if someone has to go it may as well be the rent collector.' I flipped through the depositions until I got to the place where I felt most at home, the forensic report on the blood.

'Bloodstains on your brother's sleeve.'

'Group consistent with ten per cent of the population,' said Nooks.

'Including Tosher MacBride? And Exhibit 1, a sheath knife. Mr MacBride's blood on that, or, of course, ten per cent of the population.

Knife found in your brother's ancient Daimler. Fallen down by the driver's seat. Bloodstains on his coat sleeve? Bloodstained sheath knife in his car?'

'I know it looks black for young Peter.' Leslie shook his head sadly.

I looked up at him sharply. 'Let's say it's evidence, Mr Delgardo, on which the prosecution might expect to get a conviction, unless the Judge has just joined the Fulham Road Anarchists – or the jury's drunk.'

'You'll pull it off for Petey.' It was the first time Basil Delgardo had spoken and his words showed, I thought, a touching faith in Rumpole.

'Pull it off? I shall sit behind my learned leader. I presume you're going to Guthrie Featherstone, QC, in these Chambers?'

Then Nooks uttered words which were, I must confess, music to my ears.

'Well, actually, Mr Rumpole. On this one. No.'

'Mr Rumpole. My brothers and I, we've heard of your wonderful reputation,' said Basil.

'I did the "Penge Bungalow Murder" without a leader,' I admitted. 'But that was thirty years ago. They let me loose on that.'

'We've heard golden opinions of you, Mr Rumpole. Golden opinions!' Leslie Delgardo made an expansive gesture, rattling his identity bracelet. I got up and looked out of the window.

'No one mentioned the hat?'

'Pardon me?' Leslie sounded puzzled, and Nooks added his voice to the vote of confidence.

'Mr Delgardo's brothers are perfectly satisfied, Mr Rumpole, to leave this one entirely to you.'

'Now is the Winter of my Discontent, Made Glorious Summer by a first-class murder.' I turned back to the group, apologetic. 'I'm sorry, gentlemen. Insensitive, I'm afraid. All these months round the Uxbridge Magistrates' Court have blunted my sensitivity. To your brother it can hardly seem such a sign of summer.'

'We're perfectly confident, Mr Rumpole, you can handle it.' Basil lit a cigarette with a gold lighter and I went back to the desk.

'Handle it? Of course I can handle it. As I always say, murder is nothing more than common assault, with unfortunate consequences.'

'We'll arrange it for you to see the doctor.' Nooks was businesslike.

'I'm perfectly well, thank you.'

'Doctor Lewis Bleen,' said Leslie, and Nooks explained patiently, 'The well-known psychiatrist. On the subject of Mr Peter Delgardo's mental capacity.'

'Poor Petey. He's never been right, Mr Rumpole. We've always had to look after him,' Leslie explained his responsibilities, as head of the family.

'You could call him Peter Pan,' Basil made an unexpected literary reference. 'The little boy that never grew up.'

I doubted the accuracy of this analogy. 'I don't know whether Peter Pan was actually responsible for many stabbings down Stepney High Street.'

'But that's it, Mr Rumpole!' Leslie shook his head sadly. 'Peter's not responsible, you see. Not poor old Petey. No more responsible than a child.'

Doctor Lewis Bleen, Diploma of Psychological Medicine from the University of Edinburgh, Head-Shrinker Extraordinaire, Resident Guru of 'What's Bugging You' answers to listeners' problems, had one of those accents which remind you of the tinkle of cups and the thud of dropped scones in Edinburgh tea-rooms. He sat and sucked his pipe in the interview room at Brixton and looked in a motherly fashion at the youngest of the Delgardos who was slumped in front of us, staring moodily at nothing in particular.

'Remember me, do you?'

'Doctor B . . . Bleen.' Petey had his brothers' features, but the sharpness of their eyes was blurred in his, his big hands were folded in his lap and he wore a perpetual puzzled frown. He also spoke with a stammer. His answer hadn't pleased the good doctor, who tried again.

'Do you know the time, Petey?'

'N . . . N . . . No.'

'Disorientated . . . as to time!' Better pleased, the doctor made a note.

'That might just be because he's not wearing a watch,' I was unkind enough to suggest.

The doctor ignored me. 'Where are you, Peter?'

'In the n . . . n . . .'

'Nick?' I suggested.

'Hospital wing.' Peter confirmed my suggestion.

'Orientated as to place!' was my diagnosis. Doctor Bleen gave me a sour look, as though I'd just spat out the shortcake.

'Possibly.' He turned back to our patient. 'When we last met, Peter, you told me you couldn't remember how MacBride got stabbed.'

'N . . . No.'

'There appears to be a complete blotting out of all the facts,' the doctor announced with quiet satisfaction.

'Mightn't it be worth asking him whether he was *there* when Tosher got stabbed?' I was bold enough to ask, at which Nooks chipped in.

'Mr Rumpole. As a solictor of some little experience, may I interject here?'

'If you have to.' I sighed and fished for a small cigar.

'Doctor Bleen will correct me if I'm wrong but, as I understand, he's prepared to give evidence that at the relevant moment . . .'

'So far I have no idea when the relevant moment was.' I lit the cigar, Nooks carried on regardless.

'Mr Delgardo's mind was so affected that he didn't know the nature and quality of his act, nor did he know that what he was doing was wrong.'

'You mean he thought he was giving Tosher a warm handshake, and welcome to the Rent Collectors' Union?'

'That's not exactly how I suggest we put it to the learned Judge.' Nooks smiled at me as though at a wayward child.

'Then how do you suggest we tell it to the old sweetheart?'

'Guilty but insane, Mr Rumpole. We rather anticipated your advice would be that, guilty but insane in law.'

'And have you anticipated what the prosecution might say?'

'Peter has been examined by a Doctor Stotter from the Home Office. I don't think you'll find him unhelpful,' said Doctor Bleen. 'Charles Stotter and I play golf together. We've had a word about this case.'

'Rum things you get up to playing golf. It always struck me as a good game to avoid.' I turned and drew Peter Delgardo into the conversation. 'Well, Peter. You'll want to be getting back to the telly.'

Peter stood up. I was surprised by his height and his apparent strength, a big pale man in an old dressing-gown and pyjamas.

'Just one question before you go. Did you stab Tosher MacBride?'

The doctor smiled at me tolerantly. 'Oh I don't think the answer to *that* will be particularly reliable.'

'Even the question may strike you as unreliable, Doctor. All the same, I'm asking it.' I moved closer to Peter. 'Because if you did, Peter, we can call the good shrink here, and Doctor Stotter fresh from the golf course, and they'll let you off lightly! You'll go to Broadmoor at Her Majesty's Pleasure, and of course Her Majesty will be thinking of you constantly. You'll get a lot more telly, and some exciting basket-weaving, and a handful of pills every night to keep you quiet, Petey, and if you're very good they might let you weed the doctors' garden or play cricket against the second eleven of male warders . . . but I can't offer you these delights until I know. Did you stab Tosher?'

'I think my patient's tired.'

I turned on the trick cyclist at last, and said, 'He's not your patient at the moment. He's my client.'

'Doctor Bleen has joined us at great personal inconvenience.' Nooks was distressed.

'Then I wouldn't dream of detaining him a moment longer.' At which point Doctor Lewis Bleen DPM (Edinburgh) left in what might mildly be described as a huff. When he'd been seen off the premises by a helpful trusty, I repeated my question.

'Did you do it, Peter?'

'I c . . . c . . . c . . .' The answer, whatever it was, was a long time in coming.

Nooks supplied a word. 'Killed him?' but Peter shook his head.

'Couldn't of. He was already c . . . cut. When I saw him, like.'

'You see, I can't let you get sent to hospital unless you did it,' I explained as though to a child. 'If you didn't, well . . . just have to fight the case.'

'I wants you to f . . . f . . . fight it. I'm not going into any nuthouse.' Peter Delgardo's instructions were perfectly clear.

'And if we fight we might very well lose. You understand that?'

'My b . . . b . . . brothers have told me . . . You're hot stuff, they told me . . . Tip-top l . . . awyer.'

Once again I was puzzled by the height of my reputation with the Delgardos. But I wasn't going to argue. 'Tip-top? Really? Well, let's say

I've got to know a trick or two, over the years . . . a few wrinkles . . .
Sit down, Peter.'

Peter sat down slowly, and I sat opposite him, ignoring the restive
Nooks and his articled clerk.

'Now, hadn't you better tell me exactly what happened, the night
Tosher MacBride got stabbed?'

I was working overtime a few days later when my door opened and in
walked no less a person than Guthrie Featherstone, QC, MP, our
Head of Chambers. My relations with Featherstone, ever since he
pipped me at the post for the position of Head, have always been somewhat uneasy, and were not exactly improved when I seized command of
the ship when he was leading me in the matter of the 'Dartford Post
Office Robbery'. We have little enough in common. Featherstone, as
Henry pointed out, wears a nice bowler and a black velvet collar on his
overcoat; his nails are well manicured, his voice is carefully controlled,
as are his politics. He gets on very well with judges and solicitors and
not so well with the criminal clientele. He has never been less than
polite to me, even at my most mutinous moments, and now he smiled
with considerable bonhomie.

'Rumpole! You're a late bird!'

'Just trying to feather my nest. With a rather juicy little murder.'

Featherstone dropped into my tattered leather armchair, reserved
for clients, and carefully examined his well-polished black brogues.

'Maurice Nooks told me, he's not taking in a leader.'

'That's right.'

'I know the last time I led you wasn't *succès fou*.'

'I'm a bit of a back-seat driver, I'm afraid.'

'Of course, you're an old hand at crime,' Featherstone conceded.

'An old lag you might say.'

'But it's a question of tactics in this case. Maurice said, if I appeared,
it might look as if they'd rather over-egged the pudding.'

'You think the jury might prefer – a bit of good plain cooking?'
I looked at him and he smiled delightfully.

'You put things rather well, sometimes.'

There was a pause, and then the learned leader got down to what
was, I suppose, the nub and the purpose of his visit.

'Horace. I'm anxious to put an end to any sort of rift between the two senior men in Chambers. It doesn't make for a happy ship.'

'Aye aye, sir.' I gave him a brief nautical salute from my position at the desk.

'I'm glad you agree. *Sérieusement*, Horace, we don't see enough of each other socially.' He paused again, but I could find nothing to say. 'I've got a couple of tickets for the Scales of Justice ball at the Savoy. Would you join me and Marigold?'

To say I was taken aback would be an understatement. I was astonished. 'Let's get this quite clear, Featherstone.'

'Oh "Guthrie", please.'

'Very well, Guthrie. You're asking me to trip the light fantastic toe . . . . with your wife?'

'And if you'd like to bring *your* good lady.'

I looked at Featherstone in total amazement. 'My . . .'

'Your missus.'

'Are you referring, at all, to my wife? She Who Must Be Obeyed? Do I take it you actually want to spend an evening out with She!'

'It'll be great fun.'

'Do you really think so?' He had lost me now. I went to the door and unhooked the mac and the old hat, preparatory to calling it a day. However, Featherstone had some urgent matter to communicate, apparently of an embarrassing nature.

'Oh, and Horace . . . this is rather embarrassing. It's just that . . . It's well . . . your name came up on the Bench at our Inn only last week. I was lunching with Mr Justice Prestcold.'

'That must have been a jolly occasion,' I told him. 'Like dinner with the Macbeths.' I knew Mr Justice Prestcold of old, and he and I had never hit it off, or seen eye to eye. In fact you might say there was always a cold wind blowing in Court between Counsel and the Bench whenever Rumpole rose to his feet before Prestcold, J. He could be guaranteed to ruin my cross-examination, interrupt my speech, fail to sum up the defence and send any Rumpole client down for a hefty six if he could find the slightest excuse for it. Prestcold was an extraordinarily clean man, his cuffs and bands were whiter than white, he was forever polishing his rimless glasses on a succession of snowy handkerchiefs. They say, and God knows what truth there is in it, that Prestcold travels on circuit with a portable loo seat wrapped in plastic. His clerk has the unenviable job of seeing that it is screwed in at the lodgings, so his Lordship may not sit where less fastidious judges have sat before.

'He was asking who we had in Chambers and I was able to tell him Horace Rumpole, *inter alia*.'

'I can't imagine Frank Prestcold eating. I suppose he might just be brought to sniff the bouquet of a grated carrot.'

'And he said, "You mean the fellow with the disgraceful hat?"'

'Mr Justice Prestcold was talking about my *hat*?' I couldn't believe my ears.

'He seemed to think, forgive me for raising this, that your hat set the worst possible example to younger men at the Bar.'

With enormous self-control I kept my temper. 'Well, you can tell Mr Justice Prestcold – the next time you're sharing the Benchers' Vegetarian Platter . . . That when I was last before him I took strong exception to his cufflinks. They looked to me just as cheap and glassy as his eyes!'

'Don't take offence, Horace. It's just not worth it, you know, taking offence at Her Majesty's judges. We'll look forward to the Savoy. Best to your good lady.'

I crammed on the hat, gave him a farewell wave and left him. I felt, that evening, that I was falling out of love with the law. I really couldn't believe that Mr Justice Prestcold had been discussing my hat. I mean, wasn't the crime rate rising? Wasn't the State encroaching on our liberties? Wasn't Magna Carta tottering? Whither Habeus Corpus? What was to be done about the number of twelve-year-old girls who are making advances to old men in cinemas? What I thought was, hadn't judges of England got enough on their plates without worrying about my hat! I gave the matter mature consideration on my way home on the Inner Circle, and decided that they probably hadn't.

A few mornings later I picked up the collection of demands, final demands and positively final demands which constitutes our post and among the hostile brown envelopes I found a gilded and embossed invitation card. I took the whole lot into the kitchen to file away in the tidy bin when She Who Must Be Obeyed entered and caught me at it.

'Horace,' She said severely. 'Whatever are you doing with the post?'

'Just throwing it away. Always throw bills away the first time they come in. Otherwise you only encourage them.'

'If you had a few decent cases, Rumpole, if you weren't always slumming round the Magistrates' Courts, you might not be throwing away bills all the time.' At which she pedalled open the tidy bin and spotted the fatal invitation.

'What's that?'

'I think it's the gas.' It was too late, She had picked the card out from among the potato peelings.

'I never saw a gas bill with a gold embossed crest before. It's an invitation! To the Savoy Hotel!' She started to read the thing. 'Horace Rumpole and Lady.'

'You wouldn't enjoy it,' I hastened to assure her.

'Why wouldn't I enjoy it?' She wiped the odd fragment of potato off the card, carried it into the living room in state, and gave it pride of place on the mantelpiece. I followed her, protesting.

'You know what it is. Boiled shirts. Prawn cocktail. Watching a lot of judges pushing their wives round the parquet to selections from *Oklahoma*.'

'It'll do you good, Rumpole. That's the sort of place you ought to be seen in: the Scales of Justice ball.'

'It's quite impossible.' The situation was becoming desperate.

'I don't see why.'

I had an inspiration, and assumed an expression of disgust. 'We're invited by Marigold Featherstone.'

'The wife of your Head of Chambers?'

'An old boot! A domestic tyrant. You know what the wretched Guthrie calls her? She Who Must Be Obeyed. No. The ball is out, Hilda. You and Marigold wouldn't hit it off at all.'

Well, I thought, She and sweet Marigold would never meet, so I was risking nothing. I seized the hat and prepared to retreat. 'Got to leave you now. Murder calls.'

'Why didn't you tell me we were back to murder? This *is* good news.' Hilda was remarkably cheerful that morning.

'Murder,' I told her, 'is certainly better than dancing.' And I was gone about my business. Little did I know that the moment my back was turned Hilda looked up the Featherstones' number in the telephone book.

'You can't do it to Peter! I tell you, you can't do it! Fight the case? How can he fight the case?' Leslie Delgardo had quite lost the cool and knowing air of a successful East End businessman. His face was flushed and he thumped his fist on my table, jangling his identity bracelet and disturbing the notice of additional evidence I was reading, that of Bernard Whelpton, known as 'Four Eyes'.

'Whelpton's evidence doesn't help. I'm sure you'll agree, Mr Rumpole,' Nooks said gloomily.

'You read that! You read what "Four Eyes" has to say.' Leslie collapsed breathless into my client's chair. I read the document which ran roughly as follows. 'Tosher MacBride used to take the mick out of Peter on account he stammered and didn't have no girlfriends. One night I saw Peter try to speak to a girl in the Paradise Rooms. He was asking the girl to have a drink but his stutter was so terrible. Tosher said to her, "Come on, darling . . . It'll be breakfast time before the silly git finishes asking for a light ale." After I heard Peter Delgardo say as he'd get Tosher. He said he'd like to cut him one night.'

'He's not a well boy.' Leslie was wiping his forehead with a mauve silk handkerchief.

'When I came out of the Old Justice pub that night I see Tosher on the pavement and Petey Delgardo was kneeling beside him. There was blood all over.' I looked up at Nooks. 'You know it's odd. No one actually *saw* the stabbing.'

'But Petey was there wasn't he?' Leslie was returning the handkerchief to his breast pocket. 'And what's the answer about the knife?'

'In my humble opinion,' Nooks's opinions were often humble, 'the knife in the car is completely damning.'

'Oh completely.' I got up, lit a small cigar and told Leslie my own far from humble opinion. 'You know, I'd have had no doubts about this case if you hadn't just proved your brother innocent.'

'I did?' The big man in the chair looked at me in a wild surmise.

'When you sent Doctor Lewis Bleen, the world-famous trick cyclist, the head-shrinker extraordinaire, down to see Petey in Brixton. If you'd done a stabbing, and you were offered a nice quiet trip to hospital, wouldn't you take it? If the evidence was dead against you?'

'You mean *Peter* turned it down?' Leslie Delgardo clearly couldn't believe his ears.

'Of course he did!' I told him cheerfully. 'Petey may not be all that bright, poor old darling, but he knows he didn't kill Tosher MacBride.'

The committal was at Stepney Magistrates' Court and Henry told me that there was a good deal of interest and that the vultures of the press might be there.

'I thought I should warn you, sir. Just in case you wanted to buy . . .'

'I know, I know,' I interrupted him. 'Perhaps, Henry, there's a certain amount of force in your argument. "Vanity of vanities, all is vanity," said the preacher.' Here was I a barrister of a certain standing, doing a notable murder alone and without a leader, the type of person whose picture might appear in the *Evening Standard*, and I came to the reluctant conclusion that my present headgear was regrettably unphotogenic. I took a taxi to St James's Street and invested in a bowler, which clamped itself to the head like a vice but which caused Henry, when he saw it, to give me a smile of genuine gratitude.

That evening I had forgotten the whole subject of hats and was concerned with a matter that interests me far more deeply: blood. I had soaked the rubber sponge that helps with the washing-up and, standing at the kitchen sink, stabbed violently down into it with a table knife. It produced, as I had suspected, a spray of water, leaving small spots all over my shirt and waistcoat.

'Horace! Horace, you look quite different.' Hilda was looking at the evening paper in which there was a picture of Pete Delgardo's heroic defender arriving at Court. 'I know what it is, Horace! You went out. And bought a new hat. Without me.'

I stabbed again, having resoaked the sponge.

'A bowler. Daddy used to wear a bowler. It's an improvement.' Hilda was positively purring at my dapper appearance in the paper.

'Little splashes. All over the place,' I observed, committing further mayhem on the sponge.

'Horace. Whatever are you doing to the washing-up?'

'All over. In little drops. Not one great stain. Little drops. Like a fine rain. And plenty on the cuff.'

'Your cuff's soaking. Oh, why couldn't you roll up your sleeve?'

I felt the crook of my arm, and was delighted to discover that it was completely dry.

'Now I know why you didn't want to take me to the Scales of Justice annual ball.' Hilda looked at the *Evening Standard* with less pleasure. 'You're too grand now, aren't you, Rumpole? New hat! Picture in the paper! Big case! "Horace Rumpole. Defender of the Stepney Road Stabber". Big noise at the Bar. I suppose you didn't think I'd do you credit.'

'That's nonsense, Hilda.' I mopped up some of the mess round the sink, and dried my hands.

'Then why?'

I went and sat beside her, and tried to comfort her with Keats. 'Look. We're in the Autumn of our years. *Season of mists and mellow fruitfulness,/ Close bosom-friend of the maturing sun . . .* '

'I really can't understand *why*!'

'*Where are the songs of Spring? Ay, where are they?/Think not on them, thou hast thy music too.* But not jigging about like a couple of Punk Rockers. At a dance!'

'I very much doubt if they have Punk Rockers at the Savoy. Doesn't it occur to you, Rumpole? We never go out!'

'I'm perfectly happy. I'm not longing to go to the ball, like bloody Cinderella.'

'Well, I am!'

I thought Hilda was being most unreasonable, and I decided to point out the fatal flaw in the entire scheme concerning the Scales of Justice ball.

'Hilda. I can't dance.'

'You can't what?'

'Dance. I can't do it.'

'You're lying, Rumpole!'

The accusation was so unexpected that I looked at her in a wild surmise. And then she said,

'Would you mind casting your mind back to the 14th of August 1938?'

'What happened then?'

'You proposed to me, Rumpole. As a matter of fact, it was when you proposed. I shouldn't expect you to remember.'

'1938. Of course! The year I did the "Euston Bank Robbery". Led by your father.'

'Led by Daddy. You were young, Rumpole. Comparatively young. And where did you propose, exactly? Can't you try and remember that?'

As I have said, I have no actual memory of proposing to Hilda at all. It seemed to me that I slid into the lifetime contract unconsciously, as a weary man drifts off into sleep. Any words, I felt sure, were spoken by her. I also had temporarily forgotten where the incident took place and hazarded a guess.

'At a bus stop?'

'Of course it wasn't at a bus stop.'

'It's just that your father always seemed to be detaining me at bus stops. I thought you might have been with him at the time.'

'You proposed to me in a tent.' Hilda came to my aid at last. 'There was a band. And champagne. And some sort of cold collation. Daddy had taken me to the Inns of Court ball to meet some of the bright young men in Chambers. He told me then, you'd been very helpful to him on blood groups.'

'It was the year before I did the "Penge Bungalow Murders",' I remembered vaguely. 'Hopeless on blood, your father, he could never bring himself to look at the photographs.'

'And we danced together. We actually waltzed together.'

'That's simple! That's just a matter of circling round and round. None of your bloody jigging about concerned with it!'

It was then that Hilda stood up and took my breath away. 'Well, we can waltz again, Rumpole. You'd better get into training for it. I rang up Marigold Featherstone and I told her we'd be delighted to accept the invitation.' She gave me a little smile of victory. 'And I tell you what. She didn't sound like an old boot at all.'

I was speechless, filled with mute resentment. I'd been double-crossed.

My toilette for the Delgardo murder case went no further than the acquisition of a new hat. As I sat in Court listening to the evidence for the prosecution of Bernard 'Four Eyes' Whelpton, I was vaguely conscious of the collapsed state of the wig (bought second-hand from an ex-Chief Justice of Tonga in the early thirties), the traces of small cigar and breakfast egg on the waistcoat, and the fact that the bands had lost their pristine crispness and were forever sagging to reveal the glitter of the brass collar-stud.

I looked up and saw the Judge staring at me with bleak disapproval and felt desperately to ensure that the fly buttons were safely fastened. Fate span her bloody wheel, and I had drawn Mr Justice Prestcold; Frank Prestcold, who took such grave exception to my hat, and who now looked without any apparent enthusiasm at the rest of my appearance. Well, I couldn't help him, I couldn't even hold up the bowler to prove I'd tried. I did my best to ignore the Judge and concentrate on the evidence. Mr Hilary Painswick, QC, the perfectly decent old darling who led for the prosecution, was just concreting in 'Four Eyes's story.

'Mr Whelpton. I take it you haven't given this evidence in any spirit of enmity against the man in the dock?'

The man in the dock looked, as usual, as if he'd just been struck between the eyes with a heavy weight. Bernie Whelpton smiled charmingly, and said indiscreetly, 'No. I'm Petey's friend. We was at university together.'

At which Rumpole rose up like thunder and, to Prestcold, J's intense displeasure, asked for the jury to be removed so that he could lodge an objection. When the jury had gone out the Judge forced himself to look at me.

'What is the basis of your objection, Mr Rumpole? On the face of it the evidence that this gentleman was at university with your client seems fairly harmless.'

'This may come as a surprise to your Lordship.'

'May it, Mr Rumpole?'

'My client is not an old King's man. He didn't meet Mr "Four Eyes" Whelpton at a May Ball during Eights Week. The university referred to is, in fact, Parkhurst Prison.'

The judge applied his razor-sharp mind and saw a way of overruling my objection.

'Mr Rumpole! I very much doubt whether the average juryman has your intimate knowledge of the argot of the underworld.'

'Your Lordship is too complimentary.' I gave him a bow and a brassy flash of the collar-stud.

'I think no harm has been done. I appreciate your anxiety to keep your client's past record out of the case. Shall we have the jury back?'

Before the jury came back I got a note from Leslie Delgardo telling me, as I knew very well, that Whelpton had a conviction for perjury. I ignored this information, and did my best to make a friend of the little Cockney who gazed at me through spectacles thick as ginger-beer bottles.

'Mr Whelpton, when you saw my client, Peter Delgardo, kneeling beside Tosher MacBride, did he have his arm round Mr MacBride's neck?'

'Yes, sir.'

'Supporting his head from behind?'

'I suppose so.'

'Rather in the attitude of a nurse or a doctor who was trying to bring help to the wounded man?'

'I didn't know your client had any medical qualifications!' Mr Justice Prestcold was trying one of his glacial jokes. I pretended I hadn't heard it, and concentrated on Bernie Whelpton.

'Were you able to see Peter Delgardo's hands when he was holding Tosher?'

'Yes.'

'Anything in them, was there?'

'Not as I saw.'

'He wasn't holding this knife, for instance?' I had the murder weapon on the desk in front of me and held it up for the jury to see.

'I tell you. I didn't see no knife.'

'I don't know whether my learned friend remembers.' Hilary Painswick uncoiled himself beside me. 'The knife was found in the car.'

'Exactly!' I smiled gratefully at Painswick. 'So my client stabbed Tosher. Ran to his car. Dropped the murder weapon in by the driver's seat and then came back across the pavement to hold Tosher in his arms and comfort his dying moments.' I turned back to the witness. 'Is *that* what you're saying?'

'He might have slipped the knife in his pocket.'

'Mr Rumpole!' Prestcold, J, had something to communicate.

'Yes, my Lord?'

'This is not the time for arguing your case. This is the time for asking questions. If you think this point has any substance you will no doubt remind the jury of it when you come to make up your final address; at some time in the no doubt distant future.'

'I'm grateful. And no doubt your Lordship will also remind the jury of it in your summing-up, should it slip my memory. It really is *such* an unanswerable point for the defence.'

I saw the Prestcold mouth open for another piece of snappy repartee, and forestalled him by rapidly restarting the cross-examination.

'Mr Whelpton. You didn't see Tosher stabbed?'

'I was in the Old Justice wasn't I?'

'You tell us. And when you came out, Tosher . . .'

'Might it not be more respectful to call that good man, the deceased, "Mr MacBride"?' the Judge interrupted wearily.

'If you like. "That good man Mr MacBride" was bleeding in my client's arms?'

'That was the first I saw of him. Yes.'

'And when he saw you Mr Delgardo let go of Tosher, of that good man Mr MacBride, ran to his car and got into it?'

'And then he drove away.'

'Exactly. You saw him get into his car. How did he do it?'

'Just turned the handle and pulled the door open.'

'So the car was unlocked?'

'I suppose it was. I didn't really think.'

'You suppose the door was unlocked.' I looked at the Judge who appeared to have gone into some sort of a trance. 'Don't go too fast, Mr Whelpton. My Lord wants an opportunity to make a note.' At which the Judge returned to earth and was forced to take up his pencil. As he wrote, Leslie Delgardo leaned forward from the seat behind me and said,

'Here, Mr Rumpole. What do you think you're doing?'

'Having a bit of fun. You don't grudge it to me, do you?'

The next item on the agenda was the Officer-in-Charge of the case, a perfectly reasonable fellow with a grey suit, who looked like the better type of bank manager.

'Detective Inspector. You photographed Mr Delgardo's antique Daimler when you got it back to the station?'

'Yes.' The officer leafed through a bundle of photographs.

'Was it then exactly as you found it outside the Old Justice?'

'Exactly.'

'Unlocked? With the driver's window open?'

'Yes. We found the car unlocked.'

'Then it would have been easy for anyone to have thrown something in through the driver's window, or even put something in through the door?'

'I don't follow you, sir. Something?'

I found my prop and held it up. Exhibit 1, a flick knife. 'Something like this knife could have been dropped into Peter Delgardo's car, in a matter of moments?'

I saw the Judge actually writing.

'I suppose it could, sir.'

'By the true murderer, whoever it was, when he was running away?'

The usher was beside me, handing me the fruit of Mr Justice Prestcold's labours; a note to Counsel which read, 'Dear Rumpole. Your bands are falling down and showing your collar-stud. No doubt you would wish to adjust accordingly.' What was this, a murder trial, or a bloody fashion parade? I crumpled the note, gave the bands a quick shove in a northerly direction and went back to work.

'Detective Inspector. We've heard Tosher MacBride described as a rent collector.'

'Is there to be an attack on the dead man's character, Mr Rumpole?'

'I don't know, my Lord. I suppose there are charming rent collectors, just as there are absolute darlings from the Income Tax.'

Laughter in Court, from which the Judge remained aloof.

'Where did he collect rents?'

'Business premises.' The officer was non-committal.

'What sort of business premises?'

'Cafés, my Lord. Pubs. Minicab offices.'

'And if the rent wasn't paid, do you know what remedies were taken?'

'I assume proceedings were taken in the County Court.' The Judge sounded totally bored by this line of cross-examination.

'Alas, my Lord, some people have no legal training. If the rents weren't paid, sometimes those minicab offices caught on fire, didn't they, Detective Inspector?'

'Sometimes they did.' I told you, he was a very fair officer.

'To put it bluntly, that "good man" Tosher MacBride was a collector for a protection racket.'

'Well, Officer, was he?' said Prestcold, more in sorrow than in anger.

'Yes, my Lord. I think he was.'

For the first time I felt I was forcing the Judge to look in a different direction, and see the case from a new angle. I rubbed in the point. 'And if he'd been sticking to the money he'd collected, that might have provided a strong motive for murder by someone other than my client? Stronger than a few unkind words about an impediment in his speech?'

'Mr Rumpole, isn't that a question for the jury?' I looked at the jury then, they were all alive and even listening, and I congratulated the old darling on the Bench.

'You're right! It is, my Lord. *And for no one else in this Court!*'

I thought it was effective, perhaps too effective for Leslie Delgardo, who stood up and left Court with a clatter. The swing doors banged to after him.

By precipitously leaving Court, Leslie Delgardo had missed the best turn on the bill, my double act with Mr Entwhistle, the forensic expert, an old friend and a foeman worthy of my steel.

'Mr Entwhistle, as a scientific officer I think you've lived with bloodstains as long as I have?'

'Almost.'

The jury smiled, they were warming to Rumpole.

'And you have all the clothes my client was wearing that night. Have you examined the pockets?'

'I have, my Lord.' Entwhistle bowed to the Judge over a heap of Petey's clothing.

'And there are no bloodstains in any of the pockets?'

'There are none.'

'So there can be no question of a bloodstained knife having been hidden in a pocket whilst my client cradled the deceased in his arms?'

'Of course not.' Entwhistle smiled discreetly.

'You find that a funny suggestion?'

'Yes, I do. The idea's ridiculous.'

'You may be interested to know that it's on that ridiculous idea the prosecution are basing their case.'

Painswick was on his feet with a well-justified moan. 'My Lord . . .'

'Yes. That was a quite improper observation, Mr Rumpole.'

'Then I pass from it rapidly, my Lord.' No point in wasting time with him, my business was with Entwhistle. 'Had Mr Delgardo stabbed the deceased, you would expect a spray of blood over a wide area of clothing?'

'You might have found that.'

'With small drops spattered from a forceful blow?'

'I should have expected so.'

'But you found nothing like it?'

'No.'

'And you might have expected blood near the area of the cuff of the coat or the shirt?'

'Most probably.'

'In fact, all we have is a smear or soaked patch in the crook of the arm.'

Mr Entwhistle picked up the overcoat, looked and, of course, admitted it.

'Yes.'

'Totally consistent with my client having merely put an arm round the deceased when he lay bleeding on the pavement.'

'Not inconsistent.'

'A double negative! The last refuge of an expert witness who doesn't want to commit himself. Does "not inconsistent" translated into plain English mean consistent, Mr Entwhistle?'

I could have kissed old Entwhistle on the rimless specs when he turned to the jury and said, 'Yes, it does.'

So when I got outside and saw Leslie Delgardo sitting on a bench chewing the end of a cigar, I thought he would wish to congratulate me. I didn't think of a gold watch, or a crinkly fiver, but at least a few warm words of encouragement. So I was surprised when he said, in a tone of deep hostility, 'What're you playing at, Mr Rumpole? Why didn't you use Bernie's conviction?'

'You really want to know?' Other members of the family were thronging about us, Basil and a matronly person in a mink coat, dabbing her eye make-up with a minute lace hanky.

'We all want to know,' said Basil, 'all the family.'

'I know I'm only the boy's mother,' sobbed the lady in mink.

'Don't underestimate yourself, madam,' I reassured her. 'You've bred three sons who have given employment to the legal profession.' Then I started to explain. 'Point one. I spent all this trial trying to keep your brother's record out. If I put in the convictions of a prosecution witness the jury'll get to know about Peter's stretch for unlawful wounding, back in 1970. You want that?'

'We thought it was helpful,' Basil grumbled.

'Did you?' I looked at him. 'I'm sure you did. Well, point two, the perjury was forging a passport application. I've already checked it. And point three.'

'Point three, Mr Rumpole. You're sacked.' Leslie's voice was high with anger. I felt grateful we weren't in a turning off Stepney High Street on a dark night.

'May I ask why?'

'You got that Judge's back up proper. He'll do for Petey. Good afternoon, Mr Rumpole. I'm taking you off the case.'

'I don't think you can do that.' He'd started to walk away, but now turned back with a look of extreme hostility.

'Oh, don't you?'

'The only person who can take me off this case is my client, Mr Peter Delgardo. Come along, Nooks, we'd better go down to the cells.'

'Your brother wants to sack me.'

Petey looked at me with his usual lack of understanding. Nooks acted as a smooth interpreter.

'The position is, Mr Leslie Delgardo is a little perturbed at the course this case is taking.'

'Mr Leslie Delgardo isn't my client,' I reminded Peter.

'He thinks we've got on the wrong side of the Judge.'

I was growing impatient. 'Would he like to point out to me, strictly for my information, the *right* side of Mr Justice Prestcold? What *does* that Judge imagine he is? Court correspondent for *The Tailor and Cutter*?'

I stamped out my small cigar. 'Look, Peter, dear old sweetheart. I've abandoned the Judge. He'll sum up dead against you. That's obvious. So let the jury think he's nothing but a personal anti-pollution programme who shoves Air Wick up his nostrils every time he so much as smells a human being and we might have *got* somewhere.'

'Mr Leslie Delgardo is definitely dissatisfied. This puts me in a very embarrassing position.' Nooks looked suitably embarrassed.

'Cheer up, Nooks!' I smiled at him. 'Your position's nothing like so embarrassing as Peter's.' Then I concentrated on my client. 'Well. What's it going to be? Do I go or stay?'

Peter began to stammer an answer. It took a long time to come but, when it did, it meant that just one week later, on the day of the Scales of Justice ball, I was making a final speech to the jury in the case of the Queen against Delgardo. I may say that I never saw Leslie, or Basil, or their dear old Mum again.

'Members of the jury, may I call your attention to a man we haven't seen. He isn't in the dock. He has never gone into that witness-box. I don't know where he is now. Perhaps he's tasting the delights of the Costa Brava. Perhaps he's very near this Court waiting for news. I'll call him Mr X. Did Mr X employ that "good man" Tosher MacBride to collect money in one of his protection rackets? Had Tosher MacBride betrayed his trust and was he to die for it? So that rainy night, outside the Old Justice pub in Stepney, Mr X waited for Tosher, waited with this knife and, when he saw his unfaithful servant come out of the shadows, he stabbed. Not once. Not twice. But you have heard the evidence. Three times in the neck.'

The jury was listening enrapt to my final speech; I was stabbing violently downwards with my prop when Prestcold cleared his throat and pointed to his own collar meaningfully. No doubt my stud was winking at him malevolently, so he said, 'Hm! . . . Mr Rumpole.'

I ignored this, no judge alive was going to spoil the climax of my speech, and I could tell that the jury were flattered, not to say delighted, to hear me tell them,

'Of course you are the *only* judges of fact in this case. But if you find Peter Delgardo guilty, then Mr X will smile, and order up champagne. Because, wherever he is, he will know . . . he's safe at last!'

Frank Prestcold summed up, as I knew he would, dead against Petey. He called the prosecution evidence 'overwhelming' and the jury listened politely. They went out just after lunch, and were still out at 6.30 when I telephoned Hilda and told her that I'd change in Chambers, and meet her at the Savoy, and I wanted it clearly understood that I wasn't dancing. I was just saying this when the usher came out and told me that the jury were back with a verdict.

After it was all over, I looked round in vain for Nooks. He had apparently gone to join the rest of the Delgardos in the great unknown. So I went down to say 'goodbye' to Peter in the cells. He was sitting inert, and staring into the middle distance.

'Cheer up, Peter.' I sat down beside him. 'Don't look so bloody miserable. My God. I don't know how you'd take it if you'd lost.'

Peter shook his head, and then said something I didn't wholly understand. 'I was . . . meant to l . . . l . . . lose.'

'Who meant you to? The prosecution? Of course. Mr Justice Prestcold? Undoubtedly, Fate. Destiny. The Spirit of the Universe? Not as it turned out. It was written in the stars. "Not Guilty of Murder. And is that the verdict of you all?"'

'That's why they ch . . . chose you. I was meant to lose.'

What the man said puzzled me. I admit I found it enigmatic. I said, 'I don't follow.'

'Bloke in the cell while I was w . . . w . . . waiting. Used to be a mate of Bernie "Four Eyes". He told me why me brothers chose you to defend me.'

Well, I thought I knew why I had been chosen for this important case. I stood up and paced the room.

'No doubt I have a certain reputation around the Temple, although my crown may be a little tarnished; done rather too much indecent assault lately.'

'He heard them round the P . . . P . . . Paradise Rooms. Talking about this old feller Rumpole.' Peter seemed to be pursuing another line of thought.

'The "Penge Bungalow Murders" is in *Notable British Trials*. I may have become a bit of a household name, at least in criminal circles.'

'They was l . . . looking for a barrister who'd be sure to lose.'

'After this, I suppose, I may get back to better quality crime.' The full force of what Peter had said struck me. I looked at him and checked carefully. '*What* did you say?'

'They wanted me defended by someone they could c . . . count on for a guilty verdict. That's why they p . . . p . . . picked you for it.'

It was, appallingly, what I thought he'd said.

'They wanted to fit me up with doing Tosher,' Peter Delgardo went on remorselessly.

'Let me get this clear. Your brothers selected *me* to nobble your defence?'

'That's it! You w . . . was to be the jockey, like.' That pulled me back.

'How did they light on me exactly? Me . . . Rumpole of the Bailey?'

My entire life, Sherlock Holmes stories, law degree, knock-about apprenticeship at Bow Street and Hackney, days of triumph in murder and forgery, down to that day's swayed jury and notable victory, seemed to be blown away like autumn leaves by what he said. Then, the words came quickly now, tumbling out of him, 'They heard of an old bloke. Got p . . . past it. Down to little bits of cases . . . round the M . . . M . . . Magistrates' Courts. Bit of a muddler, they heard. With a funny old broken-down hat on him.'

'The hat! Again.' At least I had bought a bowler.

'So they r . . . reckoned. You was just the bloke to lose this murder, like.'

'And dear old Nooks. "Shady" Nooks. Did he help them to choose me?' I suspected it.

'I d . . . don't know. I'm n . . . n . . . not saying he didn't.'

'So that's my reputation!' I tried to take stock of the situation, and failed abysmally.

'I shouldn't've told you.' He sounded genuinely apologetic.

'Get Rumpole for the defence – and be sure of a conviction.'

'Perhaps it's all lies.' Was he trying to cheer me up? He went on. 'You hear lots of s . . . s . . . stories. In the cells under the Bailey.'

'And in the Bar Mess too. They rubbish your reputation. Small cigar?' I found a packet and offered him one.

'All right.'

We lit up. After all, one had to think of the future.

'So where does this leave you, Peter?' I asked him.

'I'd say, Mr Rumpole, none too s . . . safe. What about you?'

I blew out smoke, wondering exactly what I had left.

'Perhaps not all that safe either.'

I had brought my old dinner jacket up to Chambers and I changed into it there. I had a bottle of rum in the cupboard, and I gave myself a strong drink out of a dusty glass. As I shut the cupboard door, I noticed my old hat; it was on a shelf, gathering dust and seemed to have about it a look of mild reproach. I put it on, and noticed how comfortably it fitted. I dropped the new, hard bowler into the waste-paper basket and went on to the Savoy.

'You look charming, my dear.' Hilda, resplendent in a long dress, her shoulders dusted with powder, smiled delightedly at Mrs Marigold Featherstone, who was nibbling delicately at an after-dinner mint.

'Really, Rumpole.' Hilda looked at me, gently rebuking.

'She!'

'She?' Marigold was mystified, but anxious to join in any joke that might be going.

'Oh "She",' I said casually. 'A woman of fabulous beauty. Written up by H. Rider Haggard.' A waiter passed and I created a diversion by calling his attention to the fact that the tide had gone out in my glass. Around us prominent members of the legal profession pushed their bulky wives about the parquet like a number of fresh-faced gardeners executing elaborate manoeuvres with wheelbarrows. There were some young persons among them, and I noticed Erskine-Brown, jigging about in solitary rapture somewhere in the vicinity of Miss Phillida Trant. She saw me and gave a quick smile and then she was off circling Erskine-Brown like an obedient planet, which I didn't consider a fitting occupation for any girl of Miss Trant's undoubted abilities.

'Your husband's had a good win.' Guthrie Featherstone was chatting to Hilda.

'He hasn't had a "good win", Guthrie.' She put the man right. 'He's had a triumph!'

'Entirely thanks . . . to my old hat.' I raised my glass. 'Here's to it!'

'What?' Little of what Rumpole said made much sense to Marigold.

'My triumph, indeed, my great opportunity, is to be attributed solely to my hat!' I explained to her, but She couldn't agree.

'Nonsense!'

'What?'

'You're talking nonsense,' She explained to our hosts. 'He does, you know, from time to time. Rumpole won because he knows so much about blood.'

'Really?' Featherstone looked at the dancers, no doubt wondering how soon he could steer his beautiful wife off into the throng. But Hilda fixed him with her glittering eye, and went on, much like the ancient mariner.

'You remember Daddy, of course. He used to be *your* Head of Chambers. Daddy told me. "Rumpole", Daddy told me. In fact, he told me that on the occasion of the Inns of Court summer ball, which is practically the last dance we went to.'

'Hilda!' I tried, unsuccessfully, to stem the flow.

'No. I'm going to say this, Horace. Don't interrupt! "Horace Rumpole," Daddy told me, "knows more about bloodstains than anyone we've got in Chambers."'

I noticed that Marigold had gone a little pale.

'Do stop it, Hilda. You're putting Marigold off.'

'Don't you find it,' Marigold turned to me, 'well, sordid sometimes?'

'What?'

'Crime. Don't you find it terribly sordid?'

There was a silence. The music had stopped, and the legal fraternity on the floor clapped sporadically. I saw Erskine-Brown take Miss Trant's hand.

'Oh, do be careful, Marigold!' I said. 'Don't knock it.'

'I think it must be sordid.' Marigold patted her lips with her table napkin, removing the last possible trace of after-dinner mint.

'Abolish crime,' I warned her, 'and you abolish the very basis of our existence!'

'Oh, come now, Horace!' Featherstone was smiling at me tolerantly.

'He's right,' Hilda told him. 'Rumpole knows about bloodstains.'

'Abolish crime and we should all vanish.' I felt a rush of words to the head. 'All the barristers and solicitors and dock officers and the dear old matron down the Old Bailey who gives aspirins away with sentences of life imprisonment. There'd be no judges, no Lord Chancellor. The Commissioner of the Metropolitan Police would have to go out selling encyclopedias.' I leant back, grabbed the wine from the bucket and started to refill all our glasses. 'Why are we here? Why've we got prawn cocktail and *duck à l'orange* and selections from dear old *Oklahoma*? All because a few villains down the East End are kind enough to keep us in a regular supply of crime.'

A slightly hurt waiter took the bottle from me and continued my work.

'Don't *you* help them?' Marigold looked at me, doubtfully.

'Don't I *what*?'

'Help them. Doing all these crimes. After all. You get them off.'

'Today,' I said, not without a certain pride. 'Today, let me tell you, Marigold, I was no help to them at all. I showed them . . . no gratitude!'

'You got him off!'

'What?'

'You got Peter Delgardo off.'

'Just for one reason.'

'What was that?'

'He happened to be innocent.'

'Come on, Horace. How can you be sure of that?' Featherstone was smiling tolerantly but I leant forward and gave him the truth of the matter.

'You know, it's a terrifying thing, my learned friend. We go through all that mumbo-jumbo. We put on our wigs and gowns and mutter the ritual prayers. "My Lord, I humbly submit." "Ladies and gentlemen of the jury, you have listened with admirable patience . . ." Abracadabra. Fee Fo Fi Bloody Fum. And just when everyone thinks you're going to produce the most ludicrously faked bit of cheese-cloth ectoplasm, or a phoney rap on the table, it comes. Clear as a bell. Quite unexpected. The voice of truth!'

I was vaguely aware of a worried figure in a dinner jacket coming towards us across the floor.

'Have you ever found that, Featherstone? Bloody scaring sometimes. All the trouble we take to cloud the issues and divert the attention.

Suddenly we've done it. There it is! Naked and embarrassing. The truth!'

I looked up as the figure joined us. It was my late instructing solicitor.

'Nooks. "Shady" Nooks!' I greeted him, but he seemed in no mood to notice me. He pulled up a chair and sat down beside Featherstone.

'Apparently it was on the nine o'clock news. They've just arrested Leslie Delgardo. Charged him with the murder of Tosher MacBride. I'll want a con with you in the morning.'

I was left out of this conversation, but I didn't mind. Music started again, playing a tune which I found vaguely familiar. Nooks was muttering on; it seemed that the police now knew Tosher worked for Leslie, and that some member of the rival Watson family may have spotted him at the scene of the crime. An extraordinary sensation overcame me, something I hadn't felt for a long time, which could only be described as happiness.

'I don't know whether you'll want to brief me for Leslie, Nooks,' I raised a glass to old 'Shady'. 'Or would that be rather over-egging the pudding?'

And then an even more extraordinary sensation, a totally irrational impulse for which I can find no logical explanation, overcame me. I put out a hand and touched She Who Must Be Obeyed on the powdered shoulder.

'Hilda.'

'Oh yes, Rumpole?' It seemed I was interrupting some confidential chat with Marigold. 'What do you want now?'

'I honestly think,' I could find no coherent explanation, 'I think I want to dance with you.'

I suppose it was a waltz. As I steered Hilda out on to the great open spaces it seemed quite easy to go round and round, vaguely in time to the music. I heard a strange sound, as if from a long way off.

'*I'll have the last waltz with you, / Two sleepy people together . . .*' Or words to that effect. I was in fact singing. Singing and dancing to celebrate a great victory in a case I was never meant to win.

Rumpole and the Man of God

As I take up my pen during a brief and unfortunate lull in crime (taking their cue from the car-workers, the villains of this city appear to have downed tools causing a regrettable series of lay-offs, redundancies and slow-time workings down the Old Bailey), I wonder which of my most recent Trials to chronicle. Sitting in Chambers on a quiet Sunday morning (I never write these memories at home for fear that She Who Must Be Obeyed, my wife Hilda, should glance over my shoulder and take exception to the manner in which I have felt it right, in the strict interests of truth and accuracy, to describe domestic life *à coté de* Chez Rumpole); seated, as I say, in my Chambers I thought of going to the archives and consulting the mementoes of some of my more notorious victories. However when I opened the cupboard it was bare, and I remembered that it was during my defence of a South London clergyman on a shoplifting rap that I had felt bound to expunge all traces of my past, and destroy my souvenirs. It is the curse, as well as the fascination of the law, that lawyers get to know more than is good for them about their fellow human beings, and this truth was driven home to me during the time that I was engaged in the affair that I have called 'Rumpole and the Man of God'.

When I was called to the Bar, too long ago now for me to remember with any degree of comfort, I may have had high-flown ideas of a general practice of a more or less lush variety, divorcing duchesses, defending stars of stage and screen from imputations of unchastity, getting shipping companies out of scrapes. But I soon found that it's crime which not only pays moderately well, but which is also by far the greatest fun. Give me a murder on a spring morning with a decent run and a tolerably sympathetic jury, and Rumpole's happiness is complete. Like most decent advocates, I have no great taste for the law; but I flatter myself I can cross-examine a copper on his notebook, or charm the Uxbridge Magistrates off their Bench, or have the old darling sitting number four in the jury-box sighing with pity for an embezzler with two wives and six starving children. I am also, and I say it with absolutely no desire to boast, about the best man in the Temple on the subject of bloodstains. There is really nothing you can tell Rumpole about blood, particularly when it's out of the body and on to the clothing in the forensic laboratory.

The old Head of my Chambers, C. H. Wystan, now deceased (also known reluctantly to me as 'Daddy', being the father of Hilda Wystan, whom I married after an absent-minded proposal at an Inns of Court ball. Hilda now rules the Rumpole household and rejoices in the dread title of 'She Who Must Be Obeyed'), old C. H. Wystan simply couldn't stand bloodstains. He even felt queasy looking at the photographs, so I started by helping him out with his criminal work and soon won my spurs round the London Sessions, Bow Street and the Old Bailey.

By the time I was called on to defend this particular cleric, I was so well known in the Ludgate Circus Palais de Justice that many people, to my certain knowledge, called Horace Rumpole an Old Bailey Hack. I am now famous for chain-smoking small cigars, and for the resulting avalanche of ash which falls down the waistcoat and smothers the watch-chain, for my habit of frequently quoting from the *Oxford Book of English Verse*, and for my fearlessness in front of the more savage type of Circuit Judge (I fix the old darlings with my glittering eye and whisper 'Down Fido' when they grow overexcited).

Picture me then in my late sixties, well nourished on a diet consisting largely of pub lunches, steak-and-kidney pud and the cooking claret from Pommeroy's Wine Bar in Fleet Street, which keeps me astonishingly regular. My reputation stands very high in the remand wing of Brixton Nick, where many of my regular clients, fraudsmen, safe-blowers, breakers-in and carriers of offensive weapons, smile with everlasting hope when their solicitors breathe the magic words, 'We're taking in Horace Rumpole.'

I remember walking through the Temple Gardens to my Chambers one late September morning, with the pale sun on the roses and the first golden leaves floating down on the young solicitors' clerks and their girlfriends, and I was in a moderately expansive mood. Morning was at seven, or rather around 9.45, the hillside was undoubtedly dew-pearled, God was in his heaven, and with a little luck there was a small crime or two going on somewhere in the world. As soon as I got into the clerk's department of my Chambers at Number 3 Equity Court Erskine-Brown said, 'Rumpole. I saw a priest going into your room.'

Our clerk's room was as busy as Paddington Station with our young and energetic clerk Henry sending barristers rushing off to distant destinations. Erskine-Brown, in striped shirt, double-breasted waistcoat and what I believe are known as 'Chelsea Boots', was propped up against the mantelpiece reading the particulars of some building claim Henry had just given him.

'That's your con, Mr Rumpole,' said Henry, explaining the curious manifestation of a Holy Man.

'Your *conversion*? Have you seen the light, Rumpole? Is Number 3 Equity Court your Road to Damascus?'

I cannot care for Erskine-Brown, especially when he makes jokes. I chose to ignore this and go to the mantelpiece to collect my brief, where I found old Uncle Tom (T. C. Rowley), the oldest member of our Chambers, who looks in because almost anything is preferable to life with his married sister in Croydon.

'Oh dear,' said Uncle Tom. 'A vicar in trouble. I suppose it's the choirboys again. I always think the Church runs a terrible risk having choirboys. They'd be far safer with a lot of middle-aged lady sopranos.'

I had slid the pink tape off the brief and was getting the gist of the clerical slip-up when Miss Trant, the bright young Portia of Equity Court (if Portias now have rimmed specs and speak with a Roedean accent) said that she didn't think vicars were exactly my line of country.

'Of course they're my line of country,' I told her with delight. 'Anyone accused of nicking half a dozen shirts is my line of country.' I had gone through the brief instructions by this time. It seems that the cleric in question was called by the somewhat Arthurian name of the Reverend Mordred Skinner. He had gone to the summer sales in Oxford Street (a scene of carnage and rapine in which no amount of gold would have persuaded Rumpole to participate), been let off the leash in the gents' haberdashery, and later apprehended in the Hall of Food with a pile of moderately garish shirtings for which he hadn't paid.

Having spent a tough ten minutes digesting the facts of this far from complex matter (well, it showed no signs of becoming a State trial or House of Lords material), I set off in the general direction of my room, but on the way I was met by my old friend George Frobisher exuding an almost audible smell of 'bay rum' or some similar unguent.

I am not myself against a little *Eau de Cologne* on the handkerchief, but the idea of any sort of cosmetic on my friend George was like finding a Bishop *'en travestie'*, or saucy seaside postcards on sale in the vestry. George is an old friend and a dear good fellow, a gentle soul who stands up in Court with all the confidence of a sacrificial virgin waiting for the sunrise over Stonehenge, but a dab hand at *The Times* crossword and a companionable fellow for a drink after Court in Pommeroy's Wine Bar off Fleet Street. I was surprised to see he appeared to have a new suit on, a silvery tie, and a silk bandana peeping from his top pocket.

'You haven't forgotten about tonight, have you?' George asked anxiously.

'We're going off for a bottle of Château Fleet Street in Pommeroy's?'

'No . . . I'm bringing a friend to dinner. With you and Hilda.'

I had to confess that this social engagement had slipped my mind. In any event it seemed unlikely that anyone would wish to spend an evening with She Who Must Be Obeyed unless they were tied to her by bonds of matrimony, but it seemed that George had invited himself some weeks before and that he was keenly looking forward to the occasion.

'No Pommeroy's then?' I felt cheated of the conviviality.

'No, but . . . We might bring a bottle with us! I have a little news. And I'd like you and Hilda to be the first to know.' He stopped then, enigmatically, and I gave a pointed sniff at the perfume-laden haze about him.

'George . . . You haven't taken to brilliantine by any chance?'

'We'll be there for 7.30.' George smiled in a sheepish sort of fashion and went off whistling something that someone might have mistaken for the 'Tennessee Waltz' if he happened to be tone deaf. I passed on to keep my rendezvous with the Reverend Mordred Skinner.

The Man of God came with a sister, Miss Evelyn Skinner, a brisk woman in sensible shoes who had foolishly let him out of her sight in the haberdashery, and Mr Morse, a grey-haired solicitor who did a lot of work for the Church Commissioners and whose idea of a thrilling trial was a gentle dispute about how many candles you can put over the High Altar on the third Sunday in Lent. My client himself was a pale, timid individual who looked, with watery eyes and a pinkish tingle to his nostrils, as if he had caught a severe cold during his childhood and had never quite got over it. He also seemed puzzled by the mysteries of the Universe, the greatest of which was the arrival of six shirts in the shopping-bag he was carrying through the Hall of Food. I suggested that the whole thing might be explained by absent-mindedness.

'Those sales,' I said, 'would induce panic in the hardiest housewife.'

'Would they?' Mordred stared at me. His eyes behind steel-rimmed glasses seemed strangely amused. 'I must say I found the scene lively and quite entertaining.'

'No doubt you took the shirts to the cash desk, meaning to pay for them.'

'There were two assistants behind the counter. Two young ladies, to take money from customers,' he said discouragingly. 'I mean there was no need for me to take the shirts to any cash desk at all, Mr Rumpole.'

I looked at the Reverend Mordred Skinner and relit the dying cheroot with some irritation. I am used to grateful clients, co-operative clients, clients who are willing to pull their weight and put their backs to the wheel in the great cause of Victory for Rumpole. The many murderers I have known, for instance, have all been touchingly eager to help, and although one draws the line at simulated madness or futile and misleading alibis, at least such efforts show that the customer has a will to win. The cleric in my armchair seemed, by contrast, determined to put every possible obstacle in my way.

'I don't suppose you realized that,' I told him firmly. 'You're hardly an *habitué* of the sales, are you? I expect you wandered off looking for a cash desk, and then your mind became filled with next week's sermon, or whose turn it was to do the flowers in the chancel, and the whole mundane business of shopping simply slipped your memory.'

'It is true,' the Reverend Mordred admitted, 'that I was thinking a great deal, at the time, of the Problem of Evil.'

'Oh really?'

With the best will in the world I didn't see how the Problem of Evil was going to help the defence.

'What puzzles the ordinary fellow is,' he frowned in bewilderment, 'if God is all-wise and perfectly good – why on earth did he put evil in the world?'

'May I suggest an answer?' I wanted to gain the poor cleric's confidence by showing that I had no objection to a spot of theology. 'So that an ordinary fellow like me can get plenty of briefs round the Old Bailey and London Sessions.'

Mordred considered the matter carefully and then expressed his doubts.

'No . . . No, I can't think *that*'s what He had in mind.'

'It may seem a very trivial little case to you, Mr Rumpole . . .' Evelyn Skinner dragged us back from pure thought. 'But it's life and death to Mordred.' At which I stood and gave them all a bit of the Rumpole mind.

'A man's reputation is never trivial,' I told them. 'I must beg you both to take it extremely seriously. Mr Skinner, may I ask you to address your mind to one vital question? Given the fact that there were six shirts in the shopping-basket you were carrying, how the hell did they get there?'

Mordred looked hopeless and said, 'I can't tell you. I've prayed about it.'

'You think they might have leapt off the counter, by the power of prayer? I mean, something like the loaves and the fishes?'

'Mr Rumpole.' Mordred smiled at me. 'Yours would seem to be an extremely literal faith.'

I thought that was a little rich coming from a man of such painful simplicity, so I lit another small cigar, and found myself gazing into the hostile and somewhat fishy eyes of the sister.

'Are you suggesting, Mr Rumpole, that my brother is guilty?'

'Of course not,' I assured her. 'Your brother's innocent. And he'll be so until twelve commonsensical old darlings picked at random off Newington Causeway find him otherwise.'

'I rather thought – a quick hearing before the Magistrates. With the least possible publicity.' Mr Morse showed his sad lack of experience in crime.

'A quick hearing before the Magistrates is as good as pleading guilty.'

'You think you might win this case, with a jury?' I thought there was a faint flicker of interest in Mordred's pink-rimmed eyes.

'Juries are like Almighty God, Mr Skinner. Totally unpredictable.'

So the conference wound to an end without divulging any particular answer to the charge, and I asked Mordred to apply through the usual channels for some sort of defence when he was next at prayer. He rewarded this suggestion with a wintry smile and my visitors left me just as She Who Must Be Obeyed came through on the blower to remind me that George was coming to dinner and bringing a friend, and would I buy two pounds of cooking apples at the tube station, and would I also remember not to loiter in Pommeroy's Wine Bar taking any sort of pleasure.

As I put the phone down I noticed that Miss Evelyn Skinner had filtered back into my room, apparently desiring a word with Rumpole alone. She started in a tone of pity.

'I don't think you quite understand my brother . . .'

'Oh, Miss Skinner. Yes, well . . . I never felt totally at home with vicars.' I felt some sort of apology was in order.

'He's like a child in many ways.'

'The Peter Pan of the Pulpit?'

'In a way. I'm two years older than Mordred. I've always had to look after him. He wouldn't have got anywhere without me, Mr Rumpole, simply nowhere, if I hadn't been there to deal with the Parish Council, and say the right things to the Bishop. Mordred just never thinks about himself, or what he's doing half the time.'

'You should have kept a better eye on him, in the sales.'

'Of course I should! I should have been watching him like a hawk, every minute. I blame myself entirely.'

She stood there, busily blaming herself, and then her brother could be heard calling her plaintively from the passage.

'Coming, dear. I'm coming at once,' Evelyn said briskly, and was gone. I stood looking after her, smoking a small cigar and remembering Hilaire Belloc's sound advice to helpless children:

> *Always keep tight hold of nurse,*
> *For fear of finding something worse.*

*

George Frobisher brought a friend to dinner, and, as I had rather suspected when I got a whiff of George's perfume in the passage, the friend
was a lady, or, as I think Hilda would have preferred to call her, a woman.
Now I must make it absolutely clear that this type of conduct was totally out of character in my friend George. He had an absolutely clean
record so far as women were concerned. Oh, I imagine he had a mother,
and I have heard him occasionally mutter about sisters; but George had
been a bachelor as long as I had known him, returning from our convivial claret in Pommeroy's to the Royal Borough Hotel, Kensington,
where he had a small room, reasonable *en pension* terms and coloured
television after dinner in the residents' lounge, seated in front of which
device George would read his briefs, occasionally taking a furtive glance
at some long-running serial of Hospital Life.

Judge of my surprise, therefore, when George turned up to dinner at
Casa Rumpole with a very feminine, albeit middle-aged, lady indeed.
Mrs Ida Tempest, as George introduced her, came with some species of
furry animal wreathed about her neck, whose eyes regarded me with a
glassy stare, as I prepared to help Mrs Tempest partially disrobe.

The lady's own eyes were far from glassy, being twinkling, and roguish in their expression. Mrs Tempest had reddish hair (rather the colour
of falsely glowing artificial coals on an electric fire) piled on her head,
what I believe is known as a 'Cupid's Bow' mouth in the trade, and the
sort of complexion which makes you think that if you caught its owner
a brisk slap you would choke in the resulting cloud of white powder.
Her skirt seemed too tight, and her heels too high, for total comfort;
but it could not be denied that Mrs Ida Tempest was a cheerful and even
a pleasant-looking person. George gazed at her throughout the evening
with mingled admiration and pride.

It soon became apparent that in addition to his lady friend, George
had brought a plastic bag from some off-licence containing a bottle of
non-vintage Moët. Such things are more often than not the harbinger
of alarming news, and sure enough as soon as the pud was on the table
George handed me the bottle, to cope with an announcement that he
and Mrs Ida Tempest were engaged to be married, clearly taking the
view that this news should be a matter for congratulation.

'We wanted you to be the first to know,' George said proudly.

Hilda smiled in a way that can only be described as 'brave' and further comment was postponed by the explosion of the warm Moët. I filled everyone's glasses and Mrs Tempest reached with enthusiasm for the booze.

'Oh, I do love bubbly,' she said. 'I love the way it goes all tickly up the nose, don't you, Hilda?'

'We hardly get it often enough to notice.' She Who Must Be Obeyed was in no celebratory mood that evening. I had noticed, during the feast, that she clearly was not hitting it off with Mrs Tempest. I therefore felt it incumbent on me to address the Court.

'Well then. If we're all filled up, I suppose it falls to me. Accustomed as I am to public speaking . . .' I began the speech.

'Usually on behalf of the criminal classes!' Hilda grumbled.

'Yes. Well . . . I think I know what is expected on these occasions.'

'You mean you're like the film star's fifth husband? You know what's expected of you, but you don't know how to make it new.' It appeared from her giggles and George's proud smile that Mrs Tempest had made a joke. Hilda was not amused.

'Well then!' I came to the peroration. 'Here's to the happy couple.'

'Here's to us, George!' George and Mrs Tempest clinked glasses and twinkled at each other. We all took a mouthful of warmish gas. After which Hilda courteously pushed the food in George's fiancée's direction.

'Would you care for a little more Charlotte Russe, Mrs Tempest?'

'Oh, Ida. Please call me Ida. Well, just a teeny-weeny scraping. I don't want to lose my sylph-like figure, do I, Georgie? Otherwise you might not fancy me any more.'

'There's no danger of that.' The appalling thing was that George was looking roguish also.

'Of you not fancying me? Oh, I know . . .' La Tempest simpered.

'Of losing your figure, my dear. She's slim as a bluebell. Isn't she slim as a bluebell, Rumpole?' George turned to me for corroboration. I answered cautiously.

'I suppose that depends rather on the size of the bluebell.'

'Oh, Horace! You are terrible! Why've you been keeping this terrible man from me, George?' Mrs Tempest seemed delighted with my enigmatic reply.

'I hope we're all going to see a lot of each other after we're married.'

George smiled round the table, and got a small tightening of the lips from Hilda.

'Oh yes, George. I'm sure that'll be very nice.'

The tide had gone down in Mrs Tempest's glass, and after I had topped it up she held it to the light and said admiringly. 'Lovely glasses. So tasteful. Just look at that, George. Isn't that a lovely tasteful glass?'

'They're rejects actually,' Hilda told her. 'From the Army and Navy Stores.'

'What whim of providence was it that led you across the path of my old friend George Frobisher?' I felt I had to keep the conversation going.

'Mrs Tempest, that is Ida, came as a guest to the Royal Borough Hotel.' George started to talk shyly of romance.

'You noticed me, didn't you, dear?' Mrs Tempest was clearly cast in the position of prompter.

'I must admit I did.'

'And I noticed him noticing me. You know how it is with men, don't you, Hilda?'

'Sometimes I wonder if Rumpole notices me at all.' Hilda struck, I thought, an unnecessarily gloomy note.

'Of course I notice you,' I assured her. 'I come home in the evenings – and there you are. I notice you all the time.'

'As a matter of fact we first spoke in the Manageress's Office,' George continued with the narration, 'where we had both gone to register a complaint, on the question of the bathwater.'

'There's not enough hot to fill the valleys, I told her, let alone cover the hills!' Mrs Tempest explained gleefully to Hilda, who felt, apparently, that no such explanation was necessary.

'George agreed with me. Didn't you, George?'

'Shall I say, we formed an alliance?'

'Oh, we hit it off at once. We've so many interests in common.'

'Really.' I looked at Mrs Tempest in some amazement. Apart from the basic business of keeping alive I couldn't imagine what interests she had in common with my old friend George Frobisher. She gave me a surprising answer.

'Ballroom dancing.'

'Mrs Tempest,' said George proudly, 'that is Ida, has cups for it.'

'George! You're a secret ballroom dancer?' I wanted Further and Better Particulars of this Offence.

'We're going for lessons together, at Miss McKay's *École de Dance* in Rutland Gate.'

I confess I found the prospect shocking, and I said as much to George. 'Is your life going to be devoted entirely to pleasure?'

'Does *Horace* tango at all, Hilda?' Mrs Tempest asked a foolish question.

'He's never been known to.' Hilda sniffed slightly and I tried to make the reply lightly ironic.

'I'm afraid crime is cutting seriously down on my time for the tango.'

'Such a pity, dear.' Mrs Tempest was looking at me with genuine concern. 'You don't know what you're missing.'

At which point Hilda rose firmly and asked George's intended if she wanted to powder her nose, which innocent question provoked a burst of giggles.

'You mean, do I want to spend a penny?'

'It is customary,' said Hilda with some *hauteur*, 'at this stage, to leave the gentlemen.'

'Oh, you mean you want a hand with the washing-up,' Mrs Tempest followed Hilda out, delivering her parting line to me.

'Not too many naughty stories now, Horace. I don't want you leading my Georgie astray.' At which I swear she winked.

When we were left alone with a bottle of the Old Tawney George was still gazing foolishly after the vanishing Ida. 'Charming,' he said, 'isn't she charming?'

Now at this point I became distinctly uneasy. I had been looking at La Belle Tempest with a feeling of *déjà vu*. I felt sure that I had met her before, and not in some previous existence. And, of course, I was painfully aware of the fact that the vast majority of my social contacts are made in cells, courtrooms and other places of not too good repute. I therefore answered cautiously. 'Your Mrs Tempest . . . seems to have a certain amount of vivacity.'

'She's a very able businesswoman, too.'

'Is she now?'

'She used to run an hotel with her first husband. Highly successful business apparently. Somewhere in Kent . . .'

I frowned. The word 'hotel' rang a distant, but distinctly audible, bell.

'So I thought, when we're married, of course, she might take up a small hotel again, in the West Country perhaps.'

'And what about you, George? Would you give up your work at the Bar and devote all your time to the veleta?' I rather wanted to point out to him the difficulties of the situation.

'Well. I don't want to boast, but I thought I might go for a Circuit Judgeship.' George said this shyly, as though disclosing another astonishing sexual conquest. 'In fact I *have* applied. In some rural area . . .'

'*You* a judge, George? A *judge*? Well, come to think of it, it might suit you. You were never much good in Court, were you, old darling?' George looked slightly puzzled at this, but I blundered on. 'It wasn't in Ramsgate, by any chance? Where your *inamorata* kept a small hotel?'

'Why do you ask?' George was lapping up the port in a sort of golden reverie.

'Don't do it, George!' I said, loudly enough, I hoped, to blast him out of his complacency.

'Don't be a judge?'

'Don't get married! Look, George. Your Honour. If your Lordship pleases. Have a little consideration, my dear boy.' I tried to appeal to his better nature. 'I mean – where would you be leaving me?'

'Very much as you are now, I should imagine.'

'Those peaceful moments of the day. Those hours we spend with a bottle of Château Fleet Street from 5.30 on in Pommeroy's Wine Bar. That wonderful oasis of peace that lies between the battle of the Bailey and the horrors of Home Life. You mean they'll be denied me from now on? You mean you'll be bolting like a rabbit down the Temple Underground back to Mrs Tempest and leaving me without a companion?'

George looked at me, thoughtfully, and then gave judgement with, I thought, a certain lack of feeling.

'I am, of course, extremely fond of you, Rumpole. But you're not exactly . . . Well, not someone who one can share *all* one's interests with.'

'I'm not a dab hand at the two-step?' I'm afraid I sounded bitter.

'I didn't *say* that, Rumpole.'

'Don't do it, George! Marriage is like pleading guilty, for an indefinite sentence. Without parole.' I poured more port.

'You're exaggerating!'

'I'm not, George. I swear by Almighty God. I'm not.' I gave him the facts. 'Do you know what happens on Saturday mornings? When free men are lying in bed, or wandering contentedly towards a glass of breakfast Chablis and a slow read of the Obituaries? You'll both set out with a list, and your lady wife will spend your hard-earned money on things you have no desire to own, like Vim, and saucepan scourers, and J-cloths . . . and Mansion polish! And on your way home, you'll be asked to carry the shopping-basket . . . I beg of you, don't do it!'

This plea to the jury might have had some effect, but the door then opened to admit La Belle Tempest, George's eyes glazed over and he clearly became deaf to reason. And then Hilda entered and gave me a brisk order to bring in the coffee tray.

'She Who Must Be Obeyed!' I whispered to George on my way out. 'You see what I mean?' I might as well have saved my breath. He wasn't listening.

Saturday morning saw self and She at the check-out point in the local Tesco, with the substantial fee for the Portsmouth Rape Trial being frittered away on such frivolous luxuries as sliced bread, Vim, cleaning materials and so on, and as the cash register clicked merrily up Hilda passed judgement on George's fiancée.

'Of course she won't do for George.'

I had an uneasy suspicion that she might be correct, but I asked for further and better particulars.

'You think not? Why exactly?'

'Noticing our glasses! It's such bad form noticing people's things. I thought she was going to ask how much they cost.'

Which, so far as She was concerned seemed to adequately sum up the case of Mrs Ida Tempest. At which point, having loaded up and checked that the saucepan scourers were all present and correct, Hilda handed me the shopping-basket, which seemed to be filled with lead weights, and strode off unimpeded to the bus stop with Rumpole groaning in her wake.

'What we do with all that Vim I can never understand.' I questioned our whole way of life. 'Do we *eat* Vim?'

'You'd miss it, Rumpole, if it wasn't there.'

On the following Monday I went down to Dockside Magistrates' Court to defend young Jim Timson on a charge of taking and driving away a Ford Cortina. I have acted for various members of the clan Timson, a noted breed of South London villain, for many years. They know the law, and their courtroom behaviour, I mean the way they stand to attention and call the magistrate 'Sir', is impeccable. I went into battle fiercely that afternoon, and it was a famous victory. We got the summons dismissed with costs against the police. I hoped I'd achieve the same happy result in the notable trial of the Reverend Mordred Skinner, but I very much doubted it.

As soon as I was back in Chambers I opened a cupboard, sneezed in the resulting cloud of dust and burrowed in the archives. I resisted the temptation to linger among my memories and pushed aside the Penge Bungalow photographs, the revolver that was used in the killing at the East Grimble Rep and old Charles Monti's will written on a blown ostrich egg. I only glanced at the drawing an elderly RA did, to while away his trial for soliciting in the Super Loo at Euston Station, of the Recorder of London. I lingered briefly on my book of old press cuttings from the *News of the World* (that fine Legal Textbook in the Criminal Jurisdiction), and merely glanced at the analysis of bloodstains from the old Brick Lane Billiard Hall Murder when I was locked in single-handed combat with a former Lord Chief Justice of England and secured an acquittal, and came at last, on what I was seeking.

The blue folder of photographs was nestling under an old wig tin and an outdated work on forensic medicine. As I dug out my treasure and carried it to the light on my desk, I muttered a few lines of old William Wordsworth's, the Sheep of the Lake District,

> '*Perhaps the plaintive numbers flow*
> *For old, unhappy, far-off things,*
> *And battles long ago.*'

On the cover of the photographs I had stuck a yellowing cutting from the *Ramsgate Times*. 'Couple Charged in Local Arson Case' I read again. 'The Unexplained Destruction of the Saracen's Head Hotel!' I opened the folder. There was a picture of a building on the seafront, and a number of people standing round. I took the strong glass off my desk to examine the figures in the photograph and saw the younger, but still roguishly smiling, face of Mrs Ida Tempest, my friend George's intended.

Having tucked the photographs back in the archive, I went straight to Pommeroy's Wine Bar, nothing unusual about that, I rarely go any-where else at six o'clock, after the day's work is done; but George wasn't in Chambers and I hoped he might drop in there for a strengthener before a night of dalliance with his *inamorata* in the Royal Borough Hotel. However when I got to Pommeroy's the only recognizable fig-ure, apart from a few mournful-looking journalists and the opera critic in residence, was our Portia, Miss Phillida Trant, drinking a lonely Cinzano Bianco with ice and lemon. She told me that she hadn't seen George and said, rather enigmatically, that she was waiting for a person called Claude, who, on further inquiry, turned out to be none other than our elegant expert on the civil side, my learned antagonist Erskine-Brown.

'Good God, is he Claude? Makes me feel quite fond of him. Why ever are you waiting for him? Do you want to pick his brains on the law of mortgages?'

'We *are* by way of being engaged,' Miss Trant said somewhat sharply.

The infection seemed to be spreading in our Chambers, like gippy tummy. I looked at Miss Trant and asked, simply for information, 'You're sure you know enough about him?'

'I'm afraid I do.' She sounded resigned.

'I mean, you'd naturally want to *know* everything, wouldn't you – about anyone you're going to commit matrimony with?' I wanted her confirmation.

'Go on, surprise me!' Miss Trant, I had the feeling, was not being entirely serious. 'He married a middle-aged Persian contortionist when he was up at Keble? I'd love to know that – and it'd make him *far* more exciting.'

At which point the beloved Claude actually made his appearance in a bowler and overcoat with a velvet collar, and announced he had some treat in store for Miss Trant, such as Verdi's *Requiem* in the Festival Hall, whilst she looked at him as though disappointed at the un-murkiness of the Erskine-Brown past. Then I saw George at the counter making a small purchase from Jack Pommeroy and I bore down on him. I had no doubt, at that stage, that my simple duty to my old friend was immediate disclosure. However when I reached George I found that he was investing in a bottle far removed from our usual Château Fleet Street.

'1967. Pichon-Longueville? Celebrating, George?'

'In a way. We have a glass or two in the room now. Can't get anything decent in the restaurant.' George was storing the nectar away in his briefcase with the air of a practised *boulevardier*.

'George. Look. My dear fellow. Look . . . will you have a drink?'

'It's really much more comfortable, up in the room,' George babbled on regardless. 'And we listen to the BBC Overseas Service, old Victor Sylvester records requested from Nigeria. They only seem to *care* for ballroom dancing in the Third World nowadays.' My old friend was moving away from me, although I did all I could to stop him.

'Please, George. It'll only take a minute. Something . . . you really ought to know.'

'Sorry to desert you, Rumpole. It would never do to keep Ida waiting.'

He was gone, as Jack Pommeroy with his purple face and the rosebud in his buttonhole asked what was my pleasure.

'Red plonk,' I told him. 'Château Fleet Street. A large glass. I've got nothing to celebrate.'

After that I found it increasingly difficult to break the news to George, although I knew I had to do so.

The Reverend Mordred Skinner was duly sent for trial at the Inner London Sessions, Newington Causeway in the South-east corner of London. Wherever civilization ends it is, I have always felt, somewhere just north of the Inner London Sessions. It is a strange thing but I always look forward with a certain eagerness to an appearance at the Old Bailey. I walk down Newgate Street, as often as not, with a spring in my stride and there it is, in all its glory, a stately Law Court, decreed by the

City Fathers, an Edwardian palace with a modern extension to deal with the increase in human fallibility. Terrible things go on down the Bailey, horrifying things. Why is it I never go through its revolving door without a thrill of pleasure, a slight tremble of excitement? Why does it seem a much jollier place than my flat in Gloucester Road under the strict rule of She Who Must Be Obeyed?

Such pleasurable sensations, I must confess, are never connected with my visits to the Inner London Sessions. While a hint of spring sunshine often touches the figure of Justice on the Dome of the Bailey, it always seems to be a wet Monday in November at Inner London. The Sessions House is stuck in a sort of urban desert down the Old Kent Road, with nowhere to go for a decent bit of steak-and-kidney pud during the lunch hour. It is a sad sort of Court, with all the cheeky Cockney sparrows turned into silent figures waiting for the burglary to come on in Court 2, and the juries there look as if they relied on the work to eke out their social security.

I met the Reverend gentleman after I had donned the formal dress (yellowing wig bought second-hand from an ex-Attorney General of Tonga in 1932, somewhat frayed gown, collar like a blunt extension). He seemed unconcerned and was even smiling a little, although his sister Evelyn looked like one about to attend a burning at the stake; Mr Morse looked thoroughly uncomfortable and as if he'd like to get back to a nice discussion of the Almshouse charity in Chipping Sodbury.

I tried to instil a suitable sense of the solemnity of the occasion in my clerical customer by telling him that God, with that wonderful talent for practical joking which has shown itself throughout recorded history, had dealt us his Honour Judge Bullingham.

'Is he very dreadful?' Mr Skinner asked almost hopefully.

'Why he was ever made a Judge is one of the unsolved mysteries of the universe.' I was determined not to sound reassuring. 'I can only suppose that his unreasoning prejudice against all black persons, defence lawyers and probation officers, comes from some deep psychological cause. Perhaps his mother, if such a person can be imagined, was once assaulted by a black probation officer who was on his way to give evidence for the defence.'

'I wonder how he feels about parsons.' My client seemed not at all put out.

'God knows. I rather doubt if he's ever met one. The Bull's leisure taste runs to strong drink and all-in wrestling. Come along, we might as well enter the corrida.'

A couple of hours later, his Honour Judge Bullingham, with his thick neck and complexion of a beetroot past its first youth, was calmly exploring his inner ear with his little finger and tolerantly allowing me to cross-examine a large gentleman named Pratt, resident flatfoot at the Oxford Street Bazaar.

'Mr Pratt? How long have you been a detective in this particular store?'

'Ten years, sir.'

'And before that?'

'I was with the Metropolitan Police.'

'Why did you leave?'

'Pay and conditions, sir, were hardly satisfactory.'

'Oh, really? You found it more profitable to keep your beady eye on the ladies' lingerie counter than do battle in the streets with serious crime?'

'Are you suggesting that this isn't a serious crime, Mr Rumpole?' The learned Judge, who pots villains with all the subtlety of his namesake animal charging a gate, growled this question at me with his face going a darker purple than ever, and his jowls trembling.

'For many people, my Lord,' I turned to the jury and gave them the message, 'six shirts might be a mere triviality. For the Reverend Mordred Skinner, they represent the possibility of total ruin, disgrace and disaster. In this case my client's whole life hangs in the balance.' I turned a flattering gaze on the twelve honest citizens who had been chosen to pronounce on the sanctity or otherwise of the Reverend Mordred. 'That is why we must cling to our most cherished institution, trial by jury. It is not the value of the property stolen, it is the priceless matter of a man's good reputation.'

'Mister Rumpole,' the Bull lifted his head as if for the charge. 'You should know your business by now. This is not the time for making speeches, you will have an opportunity at the end of the case.'

'And as your Honour will have an opportunity *after* me to make a speech, I thought it as well to make clear who the judges of *fact* in this matter are.' I continued to look at the jury with an expression of flattering devotion.

'Yes. Very well. Let's get on with it.' The Bull retreated momentarily. I rubbed in the victory.

'Certainly. That is what I was attempting to do.' I turned to the witness. 'Mr Pratt. When you were in the gents' haberdashery . . .'

'Yes, sir?'

'You didn't see my client remove the shirts from the counter and make off with them?'

'No, sir.'

'If he had, no doubt he would have told us about it,' Bullingham could not resist growling. I gave him a little bow.

'Your Honour is always so quick to notice points in favour of the defence.' I went back to work on the store detective. 'So why did you follow my client?'

'The Supervisor noticed a pile of shirts missing. She said there was a Reverend been turning them over, your Honour.'

This titbit delighted the Bull, he snatched at it greedily. 'He might not have told us that, if you hadn't asked the wrong question, Mr Rumpole.'

'No question is wrong, if it reveals the truth,' I informed the jury, and then turned back to Pratt. I had an idea, an uncomfortable feeling that I might just have guessed the truth of this peculiar case. 'So you don't know if he was carrying the basket when he left the shirt department?'

'No.'

'Was he carrying it when you first spotted him, on the moving staircase?'

'I only saw his head and shoulders . . .'

The pieces were fitting together. I would have to face my client with my growing notion of a defence as soon as possible. 'So you first saw him with the basket in the Hall of Food?'

'That's right, sir.'

At which point Bullingham stirred dangerously and raised the curtain of his top lip on some large yellowing teeth. He was about to make a joke. 'Are you suggesting, Mr Rumpole, that a basket full of shirts mysteriously materialized in your client's hand in the Tinned Meat Department?'

At which the jury laughed obsequiously. Rumpole silenced them in a voice of enormous gravity.

'Might I remind your Honour of what he said. This is a serious case.'

'As you cross-examined, Mr Rumpole, I was beginning to wonder.' Bullingham was still grinning.

'The art of cross-examination, your Honour, is a little like walking a tightrope.'

'Oh is it?'

'One gets on so much better if one isn't continually interrupted.'

At which Bullingham relapsed into a sullen silence and I got on with the work in hand.

'It would have been quite impossible for Mr Skinner to have paid at the shirt counter, wouldn't it?'

'No, sir. There were two assistants behind the counter.'

'Young ladies?'

'Yes, sir.'

'When you saw them, what were they doing?'

'I . . . I can't exactly recall.'

'Well then, let me jog your memory.' Here I made an informed guess at what any two young lady assistants would be doing at the height of business during the summer sales. 'Were they not huddled together in an act of total recall of last night in the disco or Palais de Hop? Were they not blind and deaf to the cries of shirt-buying clerics? Were they not utterly oblivious to the life around them?'

The jury was looking at me and smiling, and some of the ladies nodded understandingly. I could feel that the old darlings knew all about young lady non-assistants in Oxford Street.

'Well, Mr Pratt. Isn't that exactly what they were doing?'

'It may have been, your Honour.'

'So is it surprising that my client took his purchase and went off in search of some more attentive assistance?'

'But I followed him downstairs, to the Hall of Food.'

'Have you any reason to suppose he wouldn't have paid for his shirts there, given the slightest opportunity?'

'I saw no sign of his attempting to do so.'

'Just as you saw no sign of the salesladies attempting to take his money?'

'No but . . .'

'It's a risky business entering your store, isn't it, Pratt?' I put it to him. 'You can't get served and no one speaks to you except to tell you that you're under arrest.'

I sat down to some smiles from the jury and a glance from the Bull. An eager young man named Ken Rydal was prosecuting. I had run up against this Rydal, a ginger-haired, spectacled wonder who might once have been a Senior Scout, and won the Duke of Edinburgh award for being left out on the mountainside for a week. 'Ken' felt a strong sense of team spirit and loyalty to the Metropolitan Police, and he was keen as mustard to add the Reverend Mordred Skinner to the notches on his woggle.

'Did you see Mr Skinner make any attempt to pay for his shirts in the Hall of Food?' Ken asked Pratt.

I read a note from my client that had finally arrived by way of the usher.

'No. No, I didn't,' said Pratt.

Ken was smiling, about to make a little Scout-like funny. 'He didn't ask for them to be wrapped up with a pound of ham, for instance?'

'No, sir.' Pratt laughed and looked round the Court, to see that no one was laughing. And the Bull was glaring at Ken.

'This is not a music hall, Mr Rydal. As Mr Rumpole has reminded us, this is an extremely serious case. The whole of the Reverend gentleman's future is at stake.' The Judge glanced at the clock, as if daring it not to be time for lunch. The clock co-operated, and the Bull rose, muttering 'Ten past two, members of the jury.'

I crumpled my client's note with some disgust and threw it on the floor as I stood to bow to the Bull. The Reverend Mordred had just told me he wasn't prepared to give evidence in his own defence. I would have to get him on his own and twist his arm a little.

'I simply couldn't take the oath.'

'What's the matter with you? Have you no religion?'

The cleric smiled politely and said, less as a question than a statement of fact, 'You don't like me very much, do you?'

We were sitting in one of the brighter hostelries in Newington Cause-way. The bleak and sour-smelling saloon bar was sparsely populated by two ailing cleaning-ladies drinking stout, another senior citizen who was smoking the dog-ends he kept in an old Oxo tin and exercising his talents as a Cougher for England, and a large drunk in a woolly bobble-hat who kept banging in and out the Gents with an expression of increasing euphoria. I had entrusted to Mr Morse the solicitor the tricky task of taking Miss Evelyn Skinner to lunch in the public canteen at the Sessions House. I imagined he'd get the full blast of her anxiety over the grey, unidentifiable meat and two veg. Meanwhile I had whisked the Reverend out to the pub where he sat with the intolerably matey expression vicars always assume in licensed premises.

'I felt you might tell me the truth. You of all people. Having your collar on back to front must mean something.'

'Truth is often dangerous. It must be approached cautiously, don't you think?' My client bit nervously into a singularly unattractive saus-age. I tried to approach the matter cautiously.

'I've noticed with women,' I told him, 'with my wife, for instance, when we go out on our dreaded Saturday morning shopping expeditions, that She Who Must Be Obeyed is in charge of the shopping-basket. She makes the big decisions. How much Vim goes in it and so forth. When the shopping's bought, I get the job of carrying the damn thing home.'

'Simple faith is far more important than the constant scramble after unimportant facts.' Mordred was back on the old theology. 'I believe that's what the lives of the Saints tell us.'

Enough of this Cathedral gossip. We were due back in Court in half an hour and I let him have it between the eyes. 'Well, my simple faith tells me that your sister had the basket in the shirt department.'

'Does it?' He blinked most of the time, but not then.

'When Pratt saw you in the Hall of Food you were carrying the shopping-basket, which she'd handed you on the escalator.'

'Perhaps.'

'Because she'd taken the shirts and put them in the bag when you were too busy composing your sermon on the Problem of Evil to notice.' I lit a small cigar at that point, and Mordred took a sip of sour bitter. He was still smiling as he started to talk, almost shyly at first, then with increasing confidence.

'She was a pretty child. It's difficult to believe it now. She was attracted to bright things, boiled sweets, red apples, jewellery in Woolworth's. As she grew older it became worse. She would take things she couldn't possibly need ... Spectacles, bead handbags, cigarette cases although she never smoked. She was like a magpie. I thought she'd improved. I try to watch her as much as I can, although you're right, on that day I was involved with my sermon. As a matter of fact, I had no need of such shirts. I may be old-fashioned but I always wear a dog collar. Always.'

'Even on rambles with the Lads' Brigade?'

'All the same,' my client said firmly, 'I believe she did it out of love.'

Well, now we had a defence: although he didn't seem to be totally aware of it.

'Those are the facts?'

'They seem to be of no interest to anyone – except my immediate family. But that's what I'm bound to say, if I take my oath on the Bible.'

'But you were prepared to lie to me,' I reminded him. He smiled again, that small, maddening smile.

'Mr Rumpole. I have the greatest respect for your skill as an advocate, but I have never been in danger of mistaking you for Almighty God.'

'Tell the truth *now*. She'll only get a fine. Nothing!'

He seemed to consider the possibility, then he shook his head.

'To her it would be everything. She couldn't bear it.'

'What about you? You'd give up your whole life?'

'It seems the least I can do for her.' He was smiling again, hanging that patient little grin out like an advertisement for his humility and his deep sense of spiritual superiority to a worldly Old Bailey Hack.

I ground out my small cigar in the overflowing ashtray and almost shouted. 'Good God! I don't know how I keep my temper.'

'I do sympathize. He found His ideas irritated people dreadfully. Particularly lawyers.' He was almost laughing now. 'But you do understand? I am quite unable to give evidence on oath to the jury.'

As every criminal lawyer knows it's very difficult to get a client off unless he's prepared to take the trouble of going into the witness-box, to face up to the prosecution and to demonstrate his innocence or at least his credentials as a fairly likeable character who might buy you a pint after work and whom you would not really want to see festering in the nick. After all fair's fair, the jury have just seen the prosecution witnesses put through it, so why should the prisoner at the Bar sit in solemn silence in the dock? I knew that if the Reverend told his story, with suitable modesty and regret, I could get him off and Evelyn would merely get a well-earned talking to. When he refused to give evidence I could almost hear the rustle of unfrocking in the distance.

Short of having my client dragged to the Bible by a sturdy usher, when he would no doubt stand mute of malice, there was nothing I could do other than address the jury in the unlikely hope of persuading them that there was no reliable evidence on which they could possibly convict the silent vicar. I was warming to my work as Bullingham sat inert, breathing hoarsely, apparently about to erupt.

'Members of the jury,' I told them. 'There is a Golden Thread that runs throughout British justice. The prosecution must prove its case. The defence has to prove nothing.'

'*Mr* Rumpole . . .' A sound came from the Judge like the first rumble they once heard from Mount Vesuvius.

I soldiered on. 'The Reverend Mordred Skinner need not trouble to move four yards from that dock to the witness-box unless the prosecution has produced evidence that he *intended* to steal – and not to pay in another department.'

'Mr *Rumpole*.' The earth tremor grew louder. I raised my voice a semitone.

'Never let it be said that a man is forced to prove his innocence! Our fathers have defied kings for that principle, members of the jury. They forced King John to sign Magna Carta and sent King Charles to the scaffold and it has been handed down even to the Inner London Sessions, Newington Causeway.'

'If you'd let me get a word in edgeways . . .'

'And now it is in your trust!'

I'm not, as this narrative may have made clear, a religious man; but what happened next made me realize how the Israelites felt when the waters divided, and understand the incredulous reaction of the disciples when an uninteresting glass of water flushed darkly and smelt of the grape. I can recall the exact words of the indubitable miracle. Bullingham said, 'Mr Rumpole. I entirely agree with everything you say. And,' he added glowering threateningly at the Scout for the prosecution, 'I shall direct the jury accordingly.'

The natural malice of the Bull had been quelled by his instinctive respect for the law. He found there was no case to answer.

I met my liberated client in the Gents, a place where his sister was unable to follow him. As we stood side by side at the porcelain I congratulated him.

'I was quite reconciled to losing. I don't think my sister would have stood by me somehow. The disgrace you see. I think,' he looked almost wistful, 'I think I should have been alone.'

'You'd have been unfrocked.'

'It might have been extremely restful. Not to have to pretend to any sort of sanctity. Not to pretend to be different. To be exactly the same as everybody else.'

I looked at him standing there in the London Sessions loo, his mac over his arm, his thin neck half-strangled by a dog collar. He longed for the relaxed life of an ordinary sinner, but he had no right to it.

'Don't long for a life of crime, old darling,' I told him. 'You've obviously got no talent for it.'

Upstairs we met Evelyn and Mr Morse. The sister gave me a flicker of something which might have been a smile of gratitude.

'It was a miracle,' I told her.

'Really? I thought the Judge was exceedingly fair. Come along, Mordred. He's somewhere else you know, Mr Rumpole. He can't even realize it's all over.' She attacked her brother again. 'Better put your mac on, dear. It's raining outside.'

'Yes, Evelyn. Yes. I'll put it on.' He did so, obediently.

'You must come to tea in the Rectory, Mr Rumpole.' I had a final chilly smile from Evelyn.

'Alas, dear lady. The pressure of work. These days I have so little time for pleasure.'

'Say goodbye to Mr Rumpole, Mordred.'

The cleric shook my hand, and gave me a confidential aside. 'Goodbye, Mr Rumpole. You see it was entirely a family matter. There was no need for anyone to know anything about it.'

And so he went, in his sister's charge, back to the isolation of the Rectory.

> *Will no one tell me what she sings?*
> *Perhaps the plaintive numbers flow*
> *For old, unhappy, far-off things,*
> *And murders long ago.*

Had I, against all the odds, learned something from the Reverend? Was I now more conscious of the value of secrecy, of not dropping bombs of information which might cause ruin and havoc on the family front? It seems unlikely, but I do not know why else I was busily destroying the archive, pushing the photographs into the unused fireplace in my Chambers and applying a match, and dropping the durable articles, including the ostrich egg, into the waste-paper basket. As the flames licked across the paper and set Mrs Tempest the arsonist curling into ashy oblivion, the door opened to admit Miss Trant.

'Rumpole! What on earth are you doing?'

I turned from the smoking relics.

'You keep things, Miss Trant? Mementoes? Locks of hair? Old letters, tied up in ribbon? "Memories",' I started to sing tunelessly, '"were made of this."'

'Not really.'

'Good.'

'I've got my first brief. From when I prosecuted you in Dock Street.' This was the occasion when I tricked Miss Trant into boring the wretched Beak with a huge pile of law, and so defeated her.* It was not an incident of which I am particularly proud.

'Destroy it. Forget the past, eh? Miss Trant. Look to the future!'

'All right. Aren't you coming up to Guthrie Featherstone's room? We're laying on a few drinks for George.'

'George? Yes, of course. He'll have a lot to celebrate.'

Guthrie Featherstone, QC, MP, the suave and elegant Conservative-Labour MP for somewhere or another who, when he is not passing the 'Gas Mains Enabling Bill' or losing politely at golf to various of Her

---

* See 'Rumpole and the Married Lady' (*The First Rumpole Omnibus*).

Majesty's judges, condescends to exercise his duties as Head of Chambers (a post to which I was due to succeed by order of seniority of barristers in practice, when I was pipped at the post by young Guthrie taking silk. Well, I didn't want it anyway); Guthrie Featherstone occupied the best room in Chambers (first floor, high windows, overlooking Temple Gardens) and he was engaged in making a speech to our assembled members. In a corner of the room I saw our clerk Henry and Dianne the typist in charge of a table decorated by several bottles of Jack Pommeroy's cooking champagne. I made straight for the booze, and at first Featherstone's speech seemed but a background noise, like Radio Four.

'It's well known among lawyers that the finest advocates never make the best judges. The glory of the advocate is to be opinionated, brash, fearless, partisan, hectoring, rude, cunning and unfair.'

'Well done, Rumpole!' This, of course, was Erskine-Brown.

'Thank you very much, Claude.' I raised my glass to him.

'The ideal judge, however,' Featherstone babbled on, 'is detached, courteous, patient, painstaking and, above all, quiet. These qualities are to be found personified in the latest addition to our Bench of Circuit Judges.'

' "Circus" Judges, Rumpole calls them,' Uncle Tom said loudly, to no one in particular.

'Ladies and gentlemen,' the QC, MP concluded, 'please raise your glasses to his Honour Judge George Frobisher.'

Everyone was smiling and drinking. So the news had broken. George was a Circuit Judge. No doubt the crowds were dancing in Fleet Street. I moved to my old friend to add my word of congratulation.

'Your health, George. Coupled with the name of Mrs Ida Tempest?'

'No, Rumpole. No.' George shook his head, I thought sadly.

'What do you mean, "No"? Mrs Tempest should be here. To share in your triumph. Celebrating back at the Royal Borough Hotel, is she? She'll have the Moët on ice by the time you get back.'

'Mrs Tempest left the Royal Borough last week, Rumpole. I have no means of knowing where to find her.'

At which point we were rudely interrupted by Guthrie Featherstone calling on George to make a speech. Other members joined in and Henry filled up George's glass in preparation for the great oration.

'I'm totally unprepared to *say* anything on this occasion,' George said, taking a bit of paper from his pocket to general laughter. Poor old George could never do anything off the cuff.

'Ladies and gentlemen,' George started. 'I have long felt the need to retire from the hurly-burly of practice at the Bar.'

'Comes as news to me that George Frobisher had a practice at the Bar,' Uncle Tom said to no one much in a deafening whisper.

'To escape from the benevolent despotism of Henry, now our senior clerk.' George twinkled.

'Can you do a Careless Driving at Croydon tomorrow, your Honour?' Henry called out in the cheeky manner he had adopted since he was an office boy.

Laughter.

'No, Henry, I can't. So I have long considered applying for a Circuit Judgeship in a Rural Area . . .'

'Where are you going to, George? Glorious Devon?' Featherstone interrupted.

'I think they're starting me off in Luton. And I hope, very soon, I'll have the pleasure of you all appearing before me!'

'Where did George say they were sending him?' Uncle Tom asked.

'I think he said Luton, Uncle Tom,' I told him.

'Luton, glorious Luton!' Henry sometimes goes too far, for a clerk. I was glad to see that Dianne ssshed him firmly.

'Naturally as a Judge, as one, however humble, of Her Majesty's Judges, certain standards will be expected of me,' George went on, I thought in a tone of some regret.

'No more carousing in Pommeroy's with Horace Rumpole!' Uncle Tom was still barracking.

'And I mean to try, to do my best, to live up to those standards. That's really all I have to say. Thank you. Thank you all very much.'

There was tumultuous applause, increased in volume by the cooking champagne, and George joined me in a corner of the room. Uncle Tom was induced to make his speech, traditional and always the same on all Chambers' occasions, and George and I talked quietly together.

'George. I'm sorry. About Mrs Tempest . . .'

'It was your fault, Rumpole.' George looked at me with an air of severe rebuke.

'My fault!' I stood amazed. 'But I said nothing. Not a word. You know me, George. Discretion is Rumpole's middle name. I was silent. As the tomb.'

'When I brought her to dinner with you and Hilda. She recognized you at once.'

'She didn't show it!'

'She's a remarkable woman.'

'I was junior Counsel, for her former husband. I'm sure he led her on. She made an excellent impression. In the witness-box.' I tried to sound comforting.

'She made an excellent impression on me, Rumpole. She thought you'd be bound to tell me.'

'She thought that?'

'So she decided to tell me first.'

I stood looking at George, feeling unreasonably guilty. Somewhere in the distance Uncle Tom was going through the usual form of words.

'As the oldest member of Chambers, I can remember this set before C. H. Wystan, Rumpole's revered father-in-law, took over. It was in old Barnaby Hawks's time and the young men were myself, Everett Long-barrow and old Willoughby Grime, who became Lord Chief Justice of Basutoland . . . He went on Circuit, I understand, wearing a battered opera hat and dispensed rough justice . . .'

The other barristers joined in the well-known chorus 'Under a Bong Tree'.

'As I remember, Ida Tempest got three years.'

'Yes,' said George.

'Her former husband got seven.' I was trying to cheer him up. 'I don't believe Ida actually applied the match.'

'All the same, it was a risk I didn't feel able to take.'

'You didn't notice the smell of burning, George? Any night in the Royal Borough Hotel . . . ?'

'Of course not! But the Lord Chancellor's secretary had just told me of my appointment. It doesn't do for a Judge's wife to have done three years, even with full remission.'

I looked at George. Was the sacrifice, I wondered, really necessary? 'Did you *have* to be a Judge, George?'

'I thought of that, of course. But I had the appointment. You know, at my age, Rumpole, it's difficult to learn any new sort of trade.'

'We had no work in those days,' Uncle Tom continued his trip down memory lane. 'We had no briefs of any kind. We spent our days practising chip shots, trying to get an old golf ball into the waste-paper basket with . . .'

'A mashie niblick!' the other barristers sang.

'Well, that was as good a training as any for life at the Bar,' Uncle Tom told them.

I filled George's glass. 'Drink up, George. There may be other ladies . . . turning up at the Royal Borough Hotel.'

'I very much doubt it. Every night when I sit at the table for one, I shall think – if only I'd never taken her to dinner at Rumpole's! Then I might never have known, don't you see? We could have been perfectly happy together.'

'Of course, C. H. Wystan never ever took silk. But now we have a QC, MP and dear old George Frobisher, a Circus, beg his pardon, a Circuit Judge!' Uncle Tom was raising his glass to George, his hand was trembling and he was spilling a good deal on his cuff.

'Sometimes I feel it will be difficult to forgive you, Rumpole,' George said, very quietly.

'But I do recall when dear old Willoughby Grime was appointed to Basutoland, we celebrated the matter in song.'

'George, what did I do?' I protested. 'I didn't say anything.' But it wasn't true. My mere existence had been enough to deny George his happiness.

At which point the other barristers raised their glasses to George and started to sing 'For He's a Jolly Good Fellow'. I left them, and went out into the silence of the Temple, where I could still hear them singing.

Next Saturday morning I was acting the part of the native bearer with the Vim basket, following She Who Must Be Obeyed on our ritual shopping expedition.

'They've never made George Frobisher a Judge!' My wife seemed to feel it an occasion for ridicule and contempt.

'In my view an excellent appointment. I shall expect to have a good record of acquittals. In the Luton Crown Court.'

'When are they going to make you a judge, Rumpole?'

'Don't ask silly questions . . . I'd start every Sentence with "There but for the Grace of God goes Horace Rumpole."'

'I can imagine what *she's* feeling like.' Hilda sniffed.

'She . . . ?'

'The cat-that-swallowed-the-cream! Her Honour Mrs Judge. Mrs Ida Tempest'll think she's quite the thing, I'll be bound.'

'No. She's gone.'

'Gone, Rumpole? What did George say about that?'

> *'Cried, and the world cried too, "Our's the Treasure".*
> *Suddenly, as rare things will, she vanished.'*

We climbed on a bus, heavily laden, back to Casa Rumpole.

'George is well out of it, if he wants my opinion.'

'I don't think he does.'

'What?'

'Want your Opinion.'

Later, in our kitchen, as she stored the Vim away under the sink and I prepared our Saturday morning G and T, a thought occurred to me. 'Do you know? I'm not sure I should've taken up as a lawyer.'

'Whatever do you mean?'

'Perhaps I should have taken up as a vicar.'

'Rumpole. Have you been getting at the gin already?'

'Faith not facts, is what we need, do you think?'

Hilda was busy unpacking the saucepan scourers. Perhaps she didn't quite get my drift.

'George Frobisher has always been a bad influence, keeping you out drinking,' she said. 'Let's hope I'll be seeing more of you, now he's been made a Judge.'

'I'd never have got to know all these *facts* about people if I hadn't set up as a lawyer.'

'Of course you should have been a lawyer, Rumpole!'

'Why exactly?'

'If you hadn't set up as a lawyer, if you hadn't gone into Daddy's Chambers, you'd never have met me, Rumpole!'

I looked at her, suddenly seeing great vistas of what my life might have been.

'That's true,' I said. 'Dammit, that's very true.'

'Put the Gumption away for me, will you, Rumpole?'

She Who Must Be Obeyed. Of course I did.

Rumpole and the Showfolk

I have written elsewhere of my old clerk Albert Handyside who served me very well for a long term of years, being adept at flattering solicitors' clerks, buying them glasses of Guinness and inquiring tenderly after their tomato plants, with the result that the old darlings were inclined to come across with the odd Dangerous and Careless, Indecent Assault, or Take and Drive Away which Albert was inclined to slip in Rumpole's direction. All this led to higher things such as Robbery, Unlawful Wounding and even Murder; and in general for that body of assorted crimes on which my reputation is founded. I first knew Albert when he was a nervous office boy in the Chambers of C. H. Wystan, my learned father-in-law; and when he grew to be a head clerk of magisterial dimensions we remained firm friends and often had a jar together in Pommeroy's Wine Bar in the evenings, on which relaxed occasions I would tell Albert my celebrated anecdotes of Bench and Bar and, unlike She Who Must Be Obeyed, he was always kind enough to laugh no matter how often he had heard them before.

Dear old Albert had one slight failing, a weakness which occurs among the healthiest of constitutions. He was apt to get into a terrible flurry over the petty cash. I never inquired into his book-keeping system; but I believe it might have been improved by the invention of the Abacus, or a monthly check-up by a Primary School child well versed in simple addition. It is also indubitably true that you can't pour drink down the throats of solicitors' managing clerks without some form of subsidy, and I'm sure Albert dipped liberally into the petty cash for this purpose as well as to keep himself in the large Bells and sodas, two or three of which sufficed for his simple lunch. Personally I never begrudged Albert any of this grant-in-aid, but ugly words such as embezzlement were uttered by Erskine-Brown and others, and, spurred on by our second clerk Harry who clearly thirsted for promotion, my learned friends were induced to part with Albert Handyside. I missed him very much. Our new clerk Henry goes to Pommeroy's with our typist Dianne, and tells her about his exploits when on holiday with the *Club Mediterannée* in Corfu. I do not think either of them would laugh at my legal anecdotes.

After he left us Albert shook the dust of London from his shoes and went up North, to some God-lost place called Grimble, and there joined a firm of solicitors as managing clerk. No doubt Northerly barristers' clerks bought him Guinness and either he had no control of the petty cash or the matter was not subjected to too close an inspection. From time to time he sent me a Christmas card on which was inscribed among the bells and holly, 'Compliments of the Season, Mr Rumpole, sir. And I'm going to bring you up here for a nice little murder just as soon as I get the opportunity. Yours respectfully, A. Handyside.' At long last a brief did arrive. Mr Rumpole was asked to appear at the Grimble Assizes, to be held before Mr Justice Skelton in the Law Courts, Grimble: the title of the piece being the *Queen* (she does keep enormously busy prosecuting people) versus *Margaret Hartley*. The only item on the programme was 'Wilful Murder'.

Now you may have noticed that certain theatrical phrases have crept into the foregoing paragraph. This is not as inappropriate as it may sound, for the brief I was going up to Grimble for on the Inter-City train (a journey about as costly as a trip across the Atlantic) concerned a murder which took place in the Theatre Royal, East Grimble, a place of entertainment leased by the 'Frere-Hartley Players': the victim was one G. P. Frere, the leading actor, and my client was his wife known as 'Maggie Hartley', co-star and joint director of the company. And as I read on into *R.* v. *Hartley* it became clear that the case was like too many of Rumpole's, a born loser: that is to say that unless we drew a drunken prosecutor or a jury of anarchists there seemed no reasonable way in which it might be won.

One night after the performance, Albert's instructions told me, the stage-door keeper, a Mr Croft, heard the sound of raised voices and quarrelling from the dressing-room shared by G. P. Frere and his wife Maggie Hartley. Mr Croft was having a late cup of tea in his cubbyhole with a Miss Christine Hope, a young actress in the company, and they heard two shots fired in quick succession. Mr Croft went along the passage to investigate and opened the dressing-room door. The scene that met his eyes was, to say the least, dramatic.

It appeared from Mr Croft's evidence that the dressing-room was in a state of considerable confusion. Clothes were scattered round the room, and chairs overturned. The long mirror which ran down the length of the wall was shattered at the end furthest from the door. Near the door Mr G. P. Frere, wearing a silk dressing-gown, was sitting slumped in a chair, bleeding profusely and already dead. My client was standing halfway down the room still wearing the long white evening-dress she had worn on the stage that night. Her make-up was smudged and in her right hand she held a well-oiled service revolver. A bullet had left this weapon and entered Mr Frere's body between the third and fourth metacarpal. In order to make quite sure that her learned Counsel didn't have things too easy, Maggie Hartley had then opened her mouth and spoken, so said Croft, the following unforgettable words, here transcribed without punctuation.

'I killed him what could I do with him help me.'

In all subsequent interviews the actress said that she remembered nothing about the quarrel in the dressing-room, the dreadful climax had been blotted from her mind. She was no doubt, and still remained, in a state of shock.

I was brooding on this hopeless defence when an elderly guard acting the part of an air hostess whispered excitedly into the intercom, 'We are now arriving at Grimble Central. Grimble Central. Please collect your hand baggage.' I merged into a place which seemed to be nestling somewhere within the Arctic Circle, the air bit sharply, it was bloody cold and a blue-nosed Albert was there to meet me.

'After I left your Chambers in disgrace, Mr Rumpole . . .'

'After a misunderstanding, shall we say.'

'My then wife told me she was disgusted with me. She packed her bags and went to live with her married sister in Enfield.'

Albert was smiling contentedly, and that was something I could understand. I had just had, *à coté de* Chez Albert Handyside, a meal which his handsome, still youngish second wife referred to as tea, but which had all the appurtenances of an excellent cold luncheon with the addition of hot scones, Dundee cake and strawberry jam.

'Bit of luck then really, you getting the petty cash so "confused".'

'All the same. I do miss the old days clerking for you in the Temple, sir. How are things down South, Mr Rumpole?'

'Down South? Much as usual. Barristers lounging about in the sun. Munching grapes to the lazy sounds of plucked guitars.'

Mrs Handyside the Second returned to the room with another huge pot of dark-brown Indian tea. She replenished the Rumpole cup and Albert and I fell to discussing the tea-table subject of murder and sudden death.

'Of course it's not the Penge Bungalow Job.' Albert was referring to my most notable murder and greatest triumph, a case I did at Lewes Assizes alone and without the so-called aid of leading Counsel. 'But it's quite a decent little case, sir, in its way. A murder among the showfolk, as they terms them.'

'The showfolk, yes. Definitely worth the detour. There is, of course, one little fly in the otherwise interesting ointment.'

Albert, knowing me as he did, knew quite well what manner of insect I was referring to. I have never taken silk. I remain, at my advanced age, a 'junior' barrister. The brief in *R. v. Hartley* had only one drawback, it announced that I was to be 'led' by a local silk, Mr Jarvis Allen, QC. I hated the prospect of this obscure North Country Queen's Counsel getting all the fun.

'I told my senior partner, sir. I told him straight. Mr Rumpole's quite capable of doing this one on his own.' Albert was suitably apologetic.

'Reminded him, did you? I did the Penge Bungalow Murders alone and without a leader.'

'The senior partner did seem to feel . . .'

'I know. I'm not on the Lord Chancellor's guest list. I never get invited to breakfast in knee breeches. It's not Rumpole, QC. Just Rumpole, Queer Customer . . .'

'Oo, I'm sure you're not,' Mrs Handyside the Second poured me another comforting cup of concentrated tannin.

'It's a murder, sir. That's attracted quite a lot of local attention.'

'And silks go with murder like steak goes with kidney! This Jarvis Allen, QC . . . Pretty competent sort of man, is he?'

'I've only seen him on the Bench . . .'

'On the what?'

The Bench seemed no sort of a place to see dedicated defenders.

'Sits as Recorder here. Gave a young tearaway in our office three years for a punch-up at the Grimble United Ground.'

'There's no particular *art* involved in getting people into prison, Albert,' I said severely. 'How is he at keeping them out?'

After tea we had a conference fixed up with my leader and client in prison. There was no women's prison at Grimble, so our client was lodged in a room converted from an unused dispensary in the Hospital Wing of the masculine nick. She seemed older than I had expected as she sat looking composed, almost detached, surrounded by her legal advisers. It was, at that first conference, as though the case concerned someone else, and had not yet engaged her full attention.

'Mrs Frere.' Jarvis Allen, the learned QC started off. He was a thin, methodical man with rimless glasses and a general rimless appearance. He had made a voluminous note in red, green and blue Biro: it didn't seem to have given him much cause for hope.

'Our client is known as Maggie Hartley, sir,' Albert reminded him. 'In the profession.'

'I think she'd better be known as Mrs Frere. In Court,' Allen said firmly. 'Now, Mrs Frere. Tommy Pierce is prosecuting and of course I know him well . . . and if we went to see the Judge, Skelton's a perfectly reasonable fellow. I think there's a sporting chance . . . I'm making no promises, mind you, there's a sporting chance they might let us plead to manslaughter!'

He brought the last sentence out triumphantly, like a Christmas present. Jarvis Allen was exercising his remarkable talent for getting people locked up. I lit a small cigar, and said nothing.

'Of course, we'd have to accept manslaughter. I'm sure Mr Rumpole agrees. You agree, don't you, Rumpole?' My leader turned to me for support. I gave him little comfort.

'Much more agreeable doing ten years for manslaughter than ten years for murder,' I said. 'Is that the choice you're offering?'

'I don't know if you've read the evidence . . . Our client was found with the gun in her hand.' Allen was beginning to get tetchy.

I thought this over and said, 'Stupid place to have it. If she'd actually *planned* a murder.'

'All the same. It leaves us without a defence.'

'Really? Do you think so? I was looking at the statement of Alan Copeland. He is . . .' I ferreted among the depositions.

'What they call the "juvenile", I believe, Mr Rumpole,' Albert reminded me.

'The "juvenile", yes.' I read from Mr Copeland's statement. 'I've worked with G. P. Frere for three seasons . . . G. P. drank a good deal. Always interested in some girl in the cast. A new one every year . . .'

'Jealousy might be a powerful motive, for our client. That's a two-edged sword, Rumpole.' Allen was determined to look on the dreary side.

'Two-edged, yes. Most swords are.' I went on reading. 'He quarrelled violently with his wife Maggie Hartley. On one occasion, after the dress rehearsal of *The Master Builder*, he threw a glass of milk stout in her face in front of the entire company . . .'

'She had a good deal of provocation, we can put that to the Judge. That merely reduces it to manslaughter.' I was getting bored with my leader's chatter of manslaughter.

I gave my bundle of depositions to Albert and stood up, looking at our client to see if she would fit the part I had in mind.

'What you need in a murder is an unlikeable corpse . . . Then if you can find a likeable defendant . . . you're off to the races! Who knows? We might even reduce the crime to innocence.'

'Rumpole.' Allen had clearly had enough of my hopeless optimism. 'As I've had to tell Mrs Frere very frankly. There is a clear admission of guilt – which is not disputed.'

'What she said to the stage-door man, Mr . . .'

'Croft.' Albert supplied the name.

'I killed him, what could I do with him? Help me.' Allen repeated the most damning evidence with great satisfaction. 'You've read that, at least?'

'Yes, I've read it. That's the trouble.'

'What *do* you mean?'

'I mean, the trouble is, I read it. I didn't *hear* it. None of us did. And

I don't suppose Mr Croft had it spelled out to him, with all the punctuation.'

'Really, Rumpole. I suppose they make jokes about murder cases in London.'

I ignored this bit of impertinence and went on to give the QC some unmerited assistance. 'Suppose she said . . . Suppose our client said, "I killed him" and then,' I paused for breath, '"What could I do with him? Help me!"?'

I saw our client look at me, for the first time. When she spoke her voice, like Desdemona's, was ever soft, gentle and low, an excellent thing in woman.

'That's the reading,' she said. I must admit I was puzzled, and asked for an explanation.

'What?'

'The reading of the line. You can tell them. That's exactly how I said it.'

At last, it seemed, we had found *something* she remembered. I thought it an encouraging sign; but it wasn't really my business.

'I'm afraid, dear lady,' I gave her a small bow, 'I shan't be able to tell them anything. Who am I, after all, but the ageing juvenile? The reading of the line, as you call it, will have to come from your QC, Mr Jarvis Allen, who is playing the lead at the moment.'

After the conference I gave Albert strict instructions as to how our client was to dress for her starring appearance in the Grimble Assize Court (plain black suit, white blouse, no make-up, hair neat, voice gentle but audible to any OAP with a National Health deaf-aid sitting in the back row of the jury, absolutely no reaction during the prosecution case except for a well-controlled sigh of grief at the mention of her deceased husband) and then I suggested we met later for a visit to the scene of the crime. Her Majesty's Counsel for the defence had to rush home to write an urgent, and no doubt profitable, opinion on the planning of the new Grimble Gas Works and so was unfortunately unable to join us.

'You go if you like, Rumpole,' he said as he vanished into a funereal Austin Princess. 'I can't see how it's going to be of the slightest assistance.'

THE THEATRE ROYAL, EAST GRIMBLE

The Frere-Hartley Players
present
G. P. Frere and Maggie Hartley

in

'PRIVATE LIVES'

by

NOËL COWARD

with

Alan Copeland
Christine Hope

Directed by Daniel Derwent

Stalls £1.50 and £1. Circle £1 and 75p.
Matinées and Senior Citizens 50p.

The Theatre Royal, an ornate but crumbling Edwardian Music Hall, which might once have housed George Formby and Rob Wilton, was bolted and barred. Albert and I stood in the rain and read a torn poster.

A cat was rubbing itself against the poster. We heard the North Country voice of an elderly man calling 'Puss . . . Puss . . . Bedtime, pussy.'

The cat went and we followed, round to the corner where the stage-door man, Mr Croft, no doubt, was opening his door and offering a saucer of milk. We made ourselves known as a couple of lawyers and asked for a look at the scene.

'Mr Derwent's round the front of the house. First door on the right.'

I moved up the corridor to a door and, opening it, had the unnerving experience of standing on a dimly lit stage. Behind me flapped a canvas balcony, and a view of the Mediterranean. As I wandered forward a voice called me out of the gloom.

'Who is it? Down here, I'm in the Stalls Bar.'

There was a light somewhere, a long way off. I went down some steps that led to the stalls and felt my way towards the light with Albert blundering after me. At last we reached the open glass door of a small bar, its dark-red walls hung with photographs of the company, and we were in the presence of a little gnome-like man, wearing a bow tie and a double-breasted suit, and that cheerily smiling but really quite expressionless apple-cheeked sort of face you see on some ventriloquist's dolls. His boot-black hair looked as if it had been dyed. He admitted to Albert that he was Daniel Derwent and at the moment in charge of the Frere-Hartley Players.

'Or what's left of them. Decimated, that's what we've been! If you've come with a two-hander for a couple of rather untalented juveniles, I'd be delighted to put it on. I suppose you *are* in the business.'

'The business?' I wondered what business he meant. But I didn't wonder long.

'Show business. The profession.'

'No . . . Another . . . profession altogether.'

I saw he had been working at a table in the empty bar, which was smothered with papers, bills and receipts.

'Our old manager left us in a state of total confusion,' Derwent said. 'And my ear's out to *here* answering the telephone.'

'The vultures can't hear of an actor shot in East Grimble but half the Character Men in *Spotlight* are after me for the job. Well, I've told everyone. Nothing's going to be decided till after Maggie's trial. We're not reopening till then. It wouldn't seem right, somehow. *What* other profession?'

'We're lawyers, Mr Derwent,' Albert told him. 'Defending.'

'Maggie's case?' Derwent didn't stop smiling.

'My name's Handyside of Instructing Solicitors. This is Mr Rumpole from London, junior Counsel for the defence.'

'A London barrister. In the Sticks!' The little Thespian seemed to find it amusing. 'Well, Grimble's hardly a number-one touring date. All the same, I suppose murder's a draw. Anywhere . . . Care for a tiny rum?'

'That's very kind.' It was bitter cold, the unused theatre seemed to be saving on central heating and I was somewhat sick at heart at the prospect of our defence. A rum would do me no harm at all.

'Drop of orange in it? Or as she comes?'

'As she comes, thank you.'

'I always take a tiny rum, for the chords. Well, we depend on the chords, don't we, in our professions.'

Apart from a taste for rum I didn't see then what I had in common, professionally or otherwise, with Mr Derwent. I wandered off with my drink in my hand to look at the photographs of the Frere-Hartley Players. As I did so I could hear the theatre manager chattering to Albert.

'We could have done a bomb tonight. The money we've turned away. You couldn't buy publicity like it,' Derwent was saying.

'No . . . No, I don't suppose you could.'

'Week after week all we get in the *Grimble Argus* is a little para. "Maggie Hartley took her part well." And now we're all over the front page. And we can't play. It breaks your heart. It does really.' I heard him freshen his rum with another slug from the bottle. 'Poor old G. P. could have drawn more money dead than he ever could when he was alive. Well, at least he's sober tonight, wherever he is.'

'The late Mr G. P. Frere was fond of a drink occasionally?' Albert made use of the probing understatement.

'Not that his performance suffered. He didn't act any worse when he was drunk.'

I was looking at a glossy photograph of the late Mr G. P. Frere, taken about ten years ago I should imagine: it showed a man with grey sideburns and an open-necked shirt with a silk scarf round his neck and eyes that were self-consciously quizzical. A man who, despite the passage of the years, was still determined to go on saying 'Who's for tennis?'

'What I admired about old G. P.,' I heard Derwent say, 'was his selfless concern for others! Never left you with the sole responsibility of entertaining the audience. He'd try to help by upstaging you. Or moving on your laugh line. He once tore up a newspaper all through my long speech in *Waiting for Godot* . . . Now you wouldn't do that, would you, Mr Rumpole? Not in anyone's long speech. Well, of course not.'

He had moved, for his last remarks, to a point rather below, but still too close to, my left ear. I was looking at the photographs of a moderately pretty young girl, wearing a seafaring sweater, whose lips were parted as if to suck in a quick draft of ozone when out for a day with the local dinghy club.

'Miss Christine Hope?' I asked.

'Miss Christine Hopeless I called her.' This Derwent didn't seem to have a particularly high opinion of his troupe. 'God knows what G. P. saw in her. She did that audition speech from St Joan. All breathless and excited . . . as if she'd just run up four flights of stairs because the angel voices were calling her about a little part in *Crossroads*. "We could *do* something with her," G. P. said. "I know what," I told him. "Burn her at the stake."'

I had come to a wall on which there were big photographs of various characters, a comic charlady, a beautiful woman in a white evening-dress, a duchess in a tiara, a neat secretary in glasses and a tattered siren who might have been Sadie Thompson in *Rain* if my theatrical memory served me right. All the faces were different, and they were all the faces of Maggie Hartley.

'Your client. My leading lady. I suppose *both* our shows depend on her.' Derwent was looking at the photographs with a rapt smile of appreciation. 'No doubt about it. She's good. Maggie's good.'

I turned to look at him, found him much too close and retreated a step. 'What do you mean,' I asked him, 'by good exactly?'

'There is a quality. Of perfect truthfulness. Absolute reality.'

'Truthfulness?' This was about the first encouraging thing we'd heard about Maggie Hartley.

'It's very rare.'

'Excuse me, sir. Would you be prepared to say that in Court?' Albert seemed to be about to take a statement. I moved tactfully away.

'Is that what you came here for?' Derwent asked me nervously.

I thought it over, and decided there was no point in turning a friendly source of information into a hostile witness.

'No. We wanted to see . . . the scene of the crime.'

At which Mr Derwent, apparently reassured, smiled again. 'The Last Act,' he said and led us to the dressing-room, typical of a provincial rep. 'I'll unlock it for you.'

The dressing-room had been tidied up, the cupboards and drawers were empty. Otherwise it looked like the sort of room that would have been condemned as unfit for human habitation by any decent local authority. I stood in the doorway, and made sure that the mirror, which went all along one side of the room, was shattered in the corner furthest away from me.

'Any help to you, is it?'

'It might be. It's what we lawyers call the *locus in quo*.'

Mr Derwent was positively giggling then.

'Do you? How frightfully camp of you. It's what we actors call a dressing-room.'

So I went back to the Majestic Hotel, a building which seemed rather less welcoming than Her Majesty's Prison, Grimble. And when I was breaking my fast on their mixed grill consisting of cold greasy bacon, a stunted tomato and a sausage that would have looked ungenerous on a cocktail stick, Albert rang me with the unexpected news that at one bound put the Theatre Royal Killing up beside the Penge Bungalow Murders in the Pantheon of Rumpole's forensic triumphs. I was laughing when I came back from the telephone, and I was still laughing when I returned to spread, on a slice of blackened toast, that pat of margarine which the management of the Majestic were apparently unable to tell from butter.

★

Two hours later we were in the Judges' room at the Law Courts discussing, in the hushed tones of relatives after a funeral, the unfortunate event which had occurred. Those present were Tommy Pierce, QC, Counsel for the prosecution, and his junior Roach, the learned Judge, my learned leader and my learned self.

'Of course these people don't really live in the real world at all,' Jarvis Allen, QC, was saying. 'It's all make-believe for them. Dressing up in fancy costumes . . .'

He himself was wearing a wig, a tailed coat with braided cuffs and a silk gown. His opponent, also bewigged, had a huge stomach from which a gold watch-chain and seal dangled. He also took snuff and blew his nose in a red spotted handkerchief. That kind and, on the whole, gentle figure Skelton, J, was fishing in the folds of his scarlet gown for a bitten pipe and an old leather pouch. I didn't think we were exactly the ones to talk about dressing up.

'You don't think she appreciates the seriousness,' the Judge was clearly worried.

'I'm afraid not, Judge. Still, if she wants to sack me . . . Of course it puts Rumpole in an embarrassing position.'

'Are you embarrassed, Rumpole?' His Lordship asked me.

As a matter of fact I was filled with a deeper inner joy, for Albert's call at breakfast had been to the effect that our client had chosen to dismiss her leading Counsel and put her future entirely in the hands of Horace Rumpole, BA, that timeless member of the Junior Bar.

'Oh yes. Dreadfully embarrassed, Judge.' I did my best to look suitably modest. 'But it seems that the lady's mind is quite made up.'

'Very embarrassing for you. For you both.' The Judge was understanding. 'Does she give any reason for dispensing with her leading Counsel, Jarvis?'

'She said . . .' I turned a grin into a cough. I too remembered what Albert had told us. 'She said she thought Rumpole was "better casting".'

' "Better casting"? Whatever can she mean by that?'

'Better in the part, Judge,' I translated.

'Oh dear.' The Judge looked distressed. 'Is she very actressy?'

'She's an actress,' I admitted, but would go no further.

'Yes. Yes, I suppose she is.' The Judge lit his pipe. 'Do you have any views about this, Tommy?'

'No, Judge. When Jarvis was instructed we were going to ask your views on a plea to manslaughter.'

The portly Pierce twinkled a lot and talked in a rich North Country accent. I could see we were in for a prosecution of homely fun, like one of the comic plays of J. B. Priestley.

'Manslaughter, eh? Do you want to discuss manslaughter, Rumpole?' I appeared to give the matter some courteous consideration.

'No, Judge, I don't believe I do.'

'If you'd like an adjournment you shall certainly have it. Your client may want to think about manslaughter . . . Or consider another leader. She should have leading Counsel. In a case of this . . .' the Judge puffed out smoke . . . 'seriousness.'

'Oh, I don't think there's much point in considering another leader.'

'You don't?'

'You see,' I was doing my best not to look at Allen, 'I don't honestly think anyone else would get the part.'

When we got out of the Judges' room, and were crossing the imposing Victorian Gothic hallway that led to the Court, my learned ex-leader, who had preserved an expression of amused detachment up to that point, turned on me with considerable hurt.

'I must say I take an extremely dim view of that.'

'Really?'

'An extremely dim view. On this Circuit we have a tradition of loyalty to our leaders.'

'It's a local custom?'

'Certainly it is.' Allen stood still and pronounced solemnly, 'I can't imagine anyone on this Circuit carrying on with a case after his leader has been sacked. It's not in the best traditions of the Bar.'

'Loyalty to one's leader. Yes, of course, that is extremely important . . .' I thought about it. 'But we must consider the other great legal maxim, mustn't we?'

'Legal maxim? What legal maxim?'

' "The show must go on." Excuse me. I see Albert. Nice chatting to you but . . . Things to do, old darling. Quite a number of things to do . . .' So I hurried away from the fired legal eagle to where my old clerk was standing, looking distinctly anxious, at the entrance of the

Court. He asked me hopefully if the Judge had seen fit to grant an adjournment, so that he could persuade our client to try another silk, a course on which Albert's senior partner was particularly keen.

'Oh dear,' I had to disappoint him. 'I begged the Judge, Albert. I almost went down on my knees to him. But would he grant me an adjournment? I'm afraid not. No, Rumpole, he told me, the show must go on.' I put a comforting hand on Albert's shoulder. 'Cheer up, old darling. There's only one thing you need say to your senior partner.'

'What's that, sir?'

'The Penge Bungalow Murders.'

I sounded supremely confident of course; but as I went into Court I suddenly remembered that without a leader I would have absolutely no one to blame but myself when things went wrong.

'I don't know if any of you ladies and gentlemen have actually attended *performances* at the Theatre Royal . . .' Tommy Pierce, QC, opening the case for the prosecution, chuckled as though to say, 'Most of us got better things to do haven't we, members of the jury?' 'But we all have passed it going up the Makins Road in a trolley-bus on the way to Grimble Football Ground. You'll know where it is, members of the jury. Past the Snellsham Roundabout, on the corner opposite the Old Britannia Hotel, where we've all celebrated many a win by Grimble United . . .'

I didn't know why he didn't just tell them: 'The prisoner's represented by Rumpole of the Bailey, a smart-alecky lawyer from London, who's never ever heard of Grimble United, let alone the Old Britannia Hotel.' I shut my eyes and looked uninterested as Tommy rumbled on, switching, now, to portentous seriousness.

'In this case, members of the jury, we enter an alien world. The world of the showfolk! They live a strange life, you may think. A life of make-believe. On the surface everyone loves each other. "You were wonderful, darling!" said to men and women alike . . .'

I seriously considered heaving myself to my hind legs to protest against this rubbish, but decided to sit still and continue the look of bored indifference.

'But underneath all the good companionship,' Pierce was now trying to make the flesh creep, 'run deep tides of jealousy and passion which welled up, in this particular case, members of the jury, into brutal and, say the Crown, quite cold-blooded murder . . .'

As he went on I thought that Derwent, the little gnome from the theatre, whom I could now see in the back of the Pit, somewhere near the dock, was perfectly right. Murder *is* a draw. All the local nobs were in Court including the Judge's wife Lady Skelton, in the front row of the Stalls, wearing her special matinée hat. I also saw the Sheriff of the County, in his fancy dress, wearing lace ruffles and a sword which stuck rather inconveniently between his legs, and Mrs Sheriff of the County, searching in her handbag for something which might well have been her opera glasses. And then, behind me, the star of the show, my client, looking as I told her to look. Ordinary.

'This is not a case which depends on complicated evidence, members of the jury, or points of law. Let me tell you the facts.'

The facts were not such that I wanted the jury to hear them too clearly, at least not in my learned friend's version. I slowly, and quite noisily, took a page out of my notebook. I was grateful to see that some of the members of the jury glanced in my direction.

'It simply amounts to this. The murder weapon, a Smith and Wesson revolver, was found in the defendant's hand as she stood over her husband's dead body. A bullet from the very weapon had entered between the third and fourth metacarpal!'

I didn't like Pierce's note of triumph as he said this. Accordingly I began to tear my piece of paper into very small strips. More members of the jury looked in my direction.

'Ladies and gentlemen. The defendant, as you will see on your abstract of indictment, was charged as "Maggie Hartley". It seems she prefers to be known by her maiden name, and that may give you some idea of the woman's attitude to her husband of some twenty years, the deceased in this case, the late Gerald Patrick Frere . . .'

At which point, gazing round the Court, I saw Daniel Derwent. He actually winked, and I realized that he thought he recognized my paper-tearing as an old ham actor's trick. I stopped doing it immediately.

'It were a mess. A right mess. Glass broken, blood. He was sprawled in the chair. I thought he were drunk for a moment, but he weren't. And she had this pistol, like, in her hand.' Mr Croft, the stage-door man was standing in the witness-box in his best blue suit. The jury clearly liked him, just as they disliked the picture he was painting.

'Can you remember what she said?' The learned prosecutor prompted him gently.

'Not too fast . . .' Mr Justice Skelton was, worse luck, preparing himself to write it all down.

'Just follow his Lordship's pencil . . .' said Pierce, and the judicial pencil prepared to follow Mr Croft.

'She said, "I killed him, what could I do with him?"'

'What did you understand that to mean?'

I did hoist myself to my hind legs then, and registered a determined objection. 'It isn't what this witness understood it to mean. It's what the jury understands it to mean . . .'

'My learned friend's quite wrong. The witness was there. He could form his own conclusion . . .'

'Please, gentlemen. Let's try and have no disagreements, at least not before luncheon,' said the Judge sweetly, and added, less charmingly, 'I think Mr Croft may answer the question.'

'I understood her to say she was so fed up with him, she didn't know what else to do . . .'

'But to kill him . . . ?' Only the Judge could have supplied that and he did it with another charming smile.

'Yes, my Lord.'

'Did she say anything else? That you remember?'

'I think she said, "Help me."'

'Yes. Just wait there, will you? In case Mr Rumpole has some questions.'

'Just a few . . .' I rose to my feet. Here was an extremely dangerous witness whom the jury liked. It was no good making a head-on attack. The only way was to lure Mr Croft politely into my parlour. I gave the matter some thought and then tried a line on which I thought we might reach agreement.

'When you saw the deceased, Frere, slumped in the chair, your first thought was that he was drunk?'

'Yes.'

'Had you seen him slumped in a chair drunk in his dressing-room on many occasions?'

'A few.' Mr Croft answered with a knowing smile, and I felt encouraged.

'On most nights?'

'Some nights.'

'Were there some nights when he *wasn't* the worse for drink? Did he ever celebrate, with an evening of sobriety?'

I got my first smile from the jury, and the Joker for the prosecution arose in full solemnity.

'My Lord . . .'

Before Tommy Pierce could interrupt the proceedings with a speech I bowled the next question.

'Mr Croft. When you came into the dressing-room, the deceased Frere was nearest the door . . .'

'Yes. Only a couple of feet from me . . . I saw . . .'

'You saw my client was standing halfway down the room?' I asked, putting a stop to further painful details. 'Holding the gun.'

Pierce gave the jury a meaningful stare, emphasizing the evidence.

'The dressing-room mirror stretches all the way along the wall. And it was broken at the far end, away from the door?'

'Yes.'

'So to have fired the bullet that broke that end of the glass, my client would have had to turn away from the deceased and shoot behind her back . . .' I swung round, by way of demonstration, and made a gesture, firing behind me. Of course I couldn't do that without bringing the full might of the prosecution to its feet.

'Surely that's a question for the jury to decide.'

'The witness was there. He can form his own conclusions,' I quoted the wisdom of my learned friend. 'What's the answer?'

'I suppose she would,' Croft said thoughtfully and the jury looked interested.

The Judge cleared his throat and leaned forward, smiling politely, and being as it turned out, surprisingly unhelpful.

'Wouldn't that depend, Mr Rumpole, on where the deceased was at the time that particular shot was fired . . . ?'

Pierce glowed in triumph and muttered 'Exactly!' I did a polite bow and went quickly on to the next question.

'Perhaps we could turn now to the little matter of what she said when you went into the room.'

'I can remember that perfectly.'

'The words, yes. It's the reading that matters.'

'The *what*, Mr Rumpole?' said the Judge, betraying theatrical ignorance.

'The stress, my Lord. The intonation . . . It's an expression used in show business.'

'Perhaps we should confine ourselves to expressions used in Law Courts, Mr Rumpole.'

'Certainly, my Lord.' I readdressed the witness. 'She said she'd killed him. And then, after a pause, "What could I do with him. Help me."'

Mr Croft frowned. 'I . . . That is, yes.'

'Meaning. What could I do with his dead body, and asking for your help . . . ?'

'My Lord. That's surely . . .' Tommy Pierce was on his hind legs, and I gave him another quotation from himself.

'He was there!' I leant forward and smiled at Croft trying to make him feel that I was a friend he could trust.

'She never meant that she had killed him because she didn't know what to do with him?'

There was a long silence. Counsel for the prosecution let out a deep breath and subsided like a balloon slowly settling. The Judge nudged the witness gently. 'Well. What's the answer, Mr Croft? Did she . . . ?'

'I . . . I can't be sure how she said it, my Lord.'

And there, on a happy note of reasonable doubt, I left it. As I came out of Court and crossed the entrance hall on my way to the cells I was accosted by the beaming Mr Daniel Derwent, who was, it seemed, anxious to congratulate me.

'What a performance, Mr Rumpole. Knock-out! You were wonderful! What I admired so was the timing. The pause, before you started the cross-examination.'

'Pause?'

'You took a beat of nine seconds. I counted.'

'Did I really?'

'Built-up tension, of course. I could see what you were after.' He put a hand on my sleeve, a red hand with big rings and polished fingernails. 'You really must let me know. If ever you want a job in Rep.'

I dislodged my fan club and went down the narrow staircase to the cells. The time had clearly come for my client to start remembering.

Maggie Hartley smiled at me over her untouched tray of vegetable pie. She even asked me how I was; but I had no time for small talk. It was zero hour, the last moment I had to get some reasonable instructions.

'Listen to me. Whatever you do or don't remember . . . it's just impossible for you to have stood there and fired the first shot.'

'The first shot?' She frowned, as if at some distant memory.

'The one that *didn't* kill him. The one that went behind you. He must have fired that. He *must* . . .'

'Yes.' She nodded her head. That was encouraging. So far as it went.

'Why the hell . . . why in the name of sanity didn't you tell us that before?'

'I waited. Until there was someone I could trust.'

'Me?'

'Yes. You, Mr Rumpole.'

There's nothing more flattering than to be trusted, even by a confirmed and hopeless villain (which is why I find it hard to dislike a client), and I was convinced Maggie Hartley wasn't that. I sat down beside her in the cell and, with Albert taking notes, she started to talk. What she said was disjointed, sometimes incoherent, and God knows how it was going to sound in the witness-box, but given a few more breaks in the prosecution case, and a following wind I was beginning to get the sniff of a defence.

One, two, three, four . . .

Mr Alan Copeland, the juvenile lead, had just given his evidence-in-chief for the prosecution. He seemed a pleasant enough young man, wearing a tie and a dark suit (good witness-box clothing) and his evidence hadn't done us any particular harm. All the same I was trying what the director Derwent had admired as the devastating pause.

Seven . . . eight . . . nine . . .

'Have you any questions, Mr Rumpole?' The Judge sounded as if he was getting a little impatient with 'the timing'. I launched the cross-examination.

'Mr Alan . . . Copeland. You know the deceased man owned a Smith and Wesson revolver? Do you know where he got it?'

'He was in a spy film and it was one of the props. He bought it.'

'But it was more than a bit of scenery. It was a real revolver.'

'Unfortunately, yes.'

'And he had a licence for it . . . ?'

'Oh yes. He joined the Grimble Rifle and Pistol Club and used to shoot at targets. I think he fancied himself as James Bond or something.'

'As James who . . . ?' I knew that Mr Justice Skelton wouldn't be able to resist playing the part of a mystified judge, so I explained carefully.

'A character in fiction, my Lord. A person licensed to kill. He also spends a great deal of his time sleeping with air hostesses.' To Tommy Pierce's irritation I got a little giggle out of the ladies and gentlemen of the jury.

'Mr Rumpole. We have quite enough to do in this case dealing with questions of *fact*. I suggest we leave the world of fiction . . . outside the Court, with our overcoats.'

The jury subsided into serious attention, and I addressed myself to the work in hand. 'Where did Mr Frere keep his revolver?'

'Usually in a locker. At the Rifle Club.'

'Usually?'

'A few weeks ago he asked me to bring it back to the theatre for him.'

'He asked *you*?'

'I'm a member of the Club myself.'

'Really, Mr Copeland.' The Judge was interested. 'And what's your weapon?'

'A shotgun, my Lord. I do some clay pigeon shooting.'

'Did Frere say *why* he wanted his gun brought back to the theatre?' I gave the jury a puzzled look.

'There'd been some burglaries. I imagine he wanted to scare any intruder . . .'

I had established that it was Frere's gun, and certainly not brought to the scene of the crime by Maggie. I broached another topic. 'Now you have spoken of some quarrels between Frere and his wife.'

'Yes, sir. He once threw a drink in her face.'

'During their quarrels, did you see my client retaliate in any way?'

'No. No, I never did. May I say something, my Lord . . .'

'Certainly, Mr Copeland.'

I held my breath. I didn't like free-ranging witnesses, but at his answer I sat down gratefully.

'Miss Hartley, as we knew her, was an exceptionally gentle person.'

I saw the jury look at the dock, at the quiet almost motionless woman sitting there.

'Mr Copeland. You've told us you shot clay pigeons at the Rifle Club.' The prosecution was up and beaming.

'Yes, sir.'

'Nothing much to eat on a clay pigeon, I suppose.'

The jury greeted this alleged quip with total silence. The local comic had died the death in Grimble. Pierce went on and didn't improve his case.

'And Frere asked for this pistol to be brought back to the theatre. Did his wife know that, do you think . . . ?'

'I certainly didn't tell her.'

'May I ask why not?'

'I think it would have made her very nervous. I certainly was.'

'Nervous of what, exactly?'

Tommy Pierce had broken the first rule of advocacy. Never ask your witness a question unless you're quite sure of the answer.

'Well . . . I was always afraid G. P.'d get drunk and loose it off at someone . . .'

The beauty of that answer was that it came from a witness for the prosecution, a detached observer who'd only been called to identify the gun as belonging to the late-lamented G. P. Frere. None too soon for the health of his case Tommy Pierce let Mr Copeland leave the box. I saw him cross the Court and sit next to Daniel Derwent, who gave him a little smile, as if of congratulation.

In the course of my legal career I have had occasion to make some study of firearms; not so intensive, of course, as my researches into the subject of blood, but I certainly know more about revolvers than I do about the law of landlord and tenant. I held the fatal weapon in a fairly expert hand as I cross-examined the Inspector who had recovered it from the scene of the crime.

'It's clear, is it not, Inspector, that two chambers had been fired?'

'Yes.'

'One bullet was found in the corner of the mirror, and another in the body of the deceased, Frere?'

'That is so.'

'Now. If the person who fired the shot into the mirror pulled back this hammer,' I pulled it back, 'to fire a second shot . . . the gun is now in a condition to go off with a far lighter pressure on the trigger?'

'That is so. Yes.'

'Thank you.'

I put down the gun and as I did so allowed my thumb to accidentally press the trigger. I looked at it, surprised, as it clicked. It was a moderately effective move, and I thought the score was fifteen-love to Rumpole. Tommy Pierce rose to serve.

'Inspector. Whether the hammer was pulled back or not, a woman would have no difficulty in firing this pistol?'

'Certainly not, my Lord.'

'Yes. Thank *you*, Inspector.' The prosecution sat down smiling. Fifteen-all.

The last witness of the day was Miss Christine Hope who turned her large *ingénue* eyes on the jury and whispered her evidence at a sound level which must have made her unintelligible to the audiences at the Theatre Royal. I had decided to cross-examine her more in sorrow than in anger.

'Miss Hope. Why were you waiting at the stage door?'

'Somehow I can never bear to leave. After the show's over . . . I can never bear to go.' She gave the jury a 'silly me' look of girlish enthusiasm. 'I suppose I'm just in love with The Theatre.'

'And I suppose you were also "just in love with G. P. Frere"?'

At which Miss Hope looked helplessly at the rail of the witness-box, and fiddled with the Holy Bible.

'You waited for him every night, didn't you? He left his wife at the stage door and took you home.'

'Sometimes . . .'

'You're dropping your voice, Miss Hope.' The Judge was leaning forward, straining to hear.

'Sometimes, my Lord,' she repeated a decibel louder.

'Every night?'

'Most nights. Yes.'

'Thank you, Miss Hope.'

Pierce, wisely, didn't re-examine and La Belle Christine left the box to looks of disapproval from certain ladies on the jury.

I didn't sleep well that night. Whether it was the Majestic mattress, which appeared to be stuffed with firewood, or the sounds, as of a giant suffering from indigestion, which reverberated from the central heating, or mere anxiety about the case, I don't know. At any rate Albert and I were down in the cells as soon as they opened, taking a critical look at the client I was about to expose to the perils of the witness-box. As I had instructed her she was wearing no make-up, and a simple dark dress which struck exactly the right note.

'I'm glad you like it,' Maggie said. 'I wore it in *Time and the Conways*.'

'Listen to the questions, answer them as shortly as you can.' I gave her her final orders. 'Every word to the North Country comedian is giving him a present. Just stick to the facts. Not a word of criticism of the dear departed.'

'You want *them* to like me?'

'They shouldn't find it too difficult.' I looked at her, and lit a small cigar.

'Do I have to swear on . . . the Bible?'

'It's customary.'

'I'd rather affirm.'

'You don't believe in God?' I didn't want an obscure point of theology adding unnecessary difficulties to our case.

'I suppose He's a possibility. He just doesn't seem to be a very frequent visitor to the East Grimble Rep.'

'I know a Grimble jury,' Albert clearly shared my fears. 'If you *could* swear on the Bible?'

'The audience might like it?' Maggie smiled gently.

'The jury,' I corrected her firmly.

'They're not too keen on agnostic actresses. Is that your opinion?'

'I suppose that puts it in a nutshell.'

'All right for the West End, is that it? No good in Grimble.'

'Of course I want you to be *yourself* . . .' I really hoped she wasn't going to be difficult about the oath.

'No, you don't. You don't want me to be myself at all. You want me to be an ordinary North Country housewife. Spending just another ordinary day on trial for murder.' For a moment her voice had hardened. I looked at her and tried to sound as calm as possible as I pulled out my watch. It was nearly time for the curtain to go up on the evidence for the defence.

'Naturally you're nervous. Time to go.'

'Bloody sick to the stomach. Every time I go on.' Her voice was gentle again, and she was smiling ruefully.

'Good luck.'

'We never say "good luck". It's bad luck to say "good luck". We say "break a leg" . . .'

'Break a leg!' I smiled back at her and went upstairs to make my entrance.

Calling your client, I always think, is the worst part of any case. When you're cross-examining, or making a final speech, you're in control. Put your client in the witness-box and there the old darling is, exposed to the world, out of your protection, and all you can do is ask the questions and hope to God the answers don't blow up in your face.

With Maggie everything was going well. We were like a couple of ballroom dancers, expertly gyrating to Victor Sylvester and certain to walk away with the cup. She seemed to sense my next question, and had her answer ready, but not too fast. She looked at the jury, made herself audible to the Judge and gave an impression, a small, dark figure in the witness-box, of courage in the face of adversity. The Court was so quiet and attentive that, as she started to describe that final quarrel, I felt we were alone, two old friends, talking intimately of some dreadful event that took place a long time ago.

'He told me . . . he was very much in love with Christine.'

'With Miss Hope?'

'Yes. With Christine Hope. That he wanted her to play Amanda.'

'That is . . . the leading lady? And what was to happen to you?'

'He wanted me to leave the company. To go to London. He never wanted to see me again.'

'What did you say to that?'

'I said I was terribly unhappy about Christine, naturally.'

'Just tell the ladies and gentlemen of the jury what happened next.'

'He said it didn't matter what I said. He was going to get rid of me. He opened the drawer of the dressing-table.'

'Was he standing then?'

'I would say, staggering.'

'Yes, and then . . . ?'

'He took out the . . . the revolver.'

'This one . . . ?'

I handed the gun to the usher, who took it to Maggie. She glanced at it and shuddered.

'I . . . I think so.'

'What effect did it have on you when you first saw it?'

'I was terrified.'

'Did you know it was there?'

'No. I had no idea.'

'And then . . . ?'

'Then. He seemed to be getting ready to fire the gun.'

'You mean he pulled back the hammer . . . ?'

'My Lord . . .' Pierce stirred his vast bulk and the Judge was inclined to agree. He said:

'Yes. Please don't lead, Mr Rumpole.'

'I think that's what he did,' Maggie continued without assistance. 'I didn't look carefully. Naturally I was terrified. He was waving the gun. He didn't seem to be able to hold it straight. Then there was a terrible explosion. I remember glass, and dust, everywhere.'

'Who fired that shot, Mrs Frere?'

'My husband. I think . . .'

'Yes?'

'I think he was trying to kill me.' She said it very quietly, but the jury heard, and remembered. She gave it a marked pause and then went on. 'After that first shot. I saw him getting ready to fire again.'

'Was he pulling . . . ?'

'Please don't lead, Mr Rumpole.' The trouble with the great comedian was that he couldn't sit still in anyone else's act.

'He was pulling back . . . That thing.' Maggie went on without any help.

Then I asked the Judge if we could have a demonstration and the usher went up into the witness-box to play the scene with Maggie. At my suggestion he took the revolver.

'We are all quite sure that thing isn't loaded?' The Judge sounded nervous.

'Quite sure, my Lord. Of course, we don't want *another* fatal *accident!*'

'Really, my Lord. That was quite improper!' Pierce rose furiously. 'My learned friend called it an accident.'

I apologized profusely, the point having been made. Then Maggie quietly positioned the usher. He raised the gun as she asked him. It was pointed murderously at her. And then Maggie grabbed at the gun in his hand, and forced it back, struggling desperately, against the usher's chest.

'I was trying to stop him. I got hold of his hand to push the gun away . . . I pushed it back . . . I think . . . I think I must have forced back his finger on the trigger.' We heard the hammer click, and now Maggie was struggling to hold back her tears. 'There was another terrible noise . . . I never meant . . .'

'Yes. Thank you, Usher.'

The usher went back to the well of the Court. Maggie was calm again when I asked her:

'When Mr Croft came you said you had killed your husband?'

'Yes . . . I had . . . By accident.'

'What else did you say?'

'I think I said . . . What could I do with him? I meant, how could I help him, of course.'

'And you asked Mr Croft to help you?'

'Yes.'

It was time for the curtain line.

'Mrs Frere. Did you ever at any time have any intention of killing your husband?'

'Never . . .! Never . . .! Never . . .!' Now my questions were finished she was crying, her face and shoulders shaking. The Judge leaned forward kindly.

'Don't distress yourself. Usher, a glass of water?'

Her cheeks hot with genuine tears, Maggie looked up bravely.

'Thank you, my Lord.'

'Bloody play-acting!' I heard the cynical Tommy Pierce mutter ungraciously to his junior, Roach.

If she was good in chief Maggie was superb in cross-examination. She answered the questions courteously, shortly, but as if she were genuinely trying to help Tommy clear up any doubt about her innocence that may have lingered in his mind. At the end he lost his nerve and almost shouted at her:

'So according to you, you did nothing wrong?'

'Oh yes,' she said. 'I did something terribly wrong.'

'Tell us. What?'

'I loved him too much. Otherwise I should have left him. Before he tried to kill me.'

During Tommy's final speech there was some coughing from the jury. He tried a joke or two about actors, lost heart and sat down upon reminding the jury that they must not let sympathy for my client affect their judgement.

'I agree entirely with my learned friend,' I started my speech. 'Put all sympathy out of your mind. The mere fact that my client clung faithfully to a drunken, adulterous husband, hoping vainly for the love he denied her; the terrible circumstance that she escaped death at his hands only to face the terrible ordeal of a trial for murder; none of these things should influence you in the least . . .' and I ended with my well-tried peroration. 'In an hour or two this case will be over. You will go home and put the kettle on and forget all about this little theatre, and the angry, drunken actor and his wretched infidelities. This case has only been a few days out of your lives. But for the lady I have the honour to represent . . .' I pointed to the dock, '*all* her life hangs in the balance. Is that life to be broken and is she to go down in darkness and disgrace, or can she go back into the glowing light of her world, to bring us all joy and entertainment and laughter once again? Ask yourselves that question, members of the jury. And when you ask it, you know there can only be one answer.'

I sank back into my seat exhausted, pushing back my wig and

mopping my brow with a large silk handkerchief. Looking round the Court I saw Derwent. He seemed about to applaud, until he was restrained by Mr Alan Copeland.

There is nothing I hate more than waiting for a jury to come back. You smoke too much and drink too many cups of coffee, your hands sweat and you can't do or think of anything else. All you can do is to pay a courtesy visit to the cells to prepare for the worst. Albert Handyside had to go off and do a touch of Dangerous Driving in the Court next door, so I was alone when I went to call on the waiting Maggie.

She was standing in her cell, totally calm.

'This is the bad part, isn't it? Like waiting for the notices.'

I sat down at the table with my notebook, unscrewed my fountain pen.

'I had better think of what to say if they find you guilty of manslaughter. I think I've got the facts for mitigation, but I'd just like to get the history clear. You'd started this theatrical company together?'

'It was my money. Every bloody penny of it.' I looked up in some surprise. The hard, tough note was there in her voice; her face was set in a look which was something like hatred.

'I don't think we need go into the financial side.' I tried to stop her but she went on:

'Do you know what that idiotic manager we had then did? He gave G. P. a contract worth fifty per cent of the profits: for an investment of nothing and a talent which stopped short of being able to pour out a drink and say a line at the same time. Anyway I never paid his percentage.' She smiled then, it was quite humourless. 'Won't need to say that, will we?'

'No.' I said firmly.

'Fifty per cent of ten years' work! He reckoned he was owed around twenty thousand pounds. He was going to sue us and bankrupt the company . . .'

'I don't think you need to tell me any more.' I screwed the top back on my fountain pen. Perhaps she had told me too much already.

'So don't feel too badly, will you? If we're not a hit.'

I stood up and pulled out my watch. Suddenly I felt an urgent need to get out of the cell.

'They should be back soon now.'

'It's all a game to you, isn't it?' She sounded unaccountably bitter. 'All a wonderful game of "let's pretend". The costume. The bows. The little jokes. The onion at the end.'

'The onion?'

'An old music-hall expression. For what makes the audience cry. Oh, I was quite prepared to go along with it. To wear the make-up.'

'You didn't wear any make-up.'

'I know, that was brilliant of you. You're a marvellous performer, Mr Rumpole. Don't let anyone tell you different.'

'It's not a question of performance.' I couldn't have that.

'Isn't it?'

'Of course it isn't! The jury are now weighing the facts. Doing their best to discover where the truth lies.' I looked at her. Her face gave nothing away.

'Or at least deciding if the prosecution has proved its case.'

Suddenly, quite unexpectedly, she yawned, she moved away from me, as though I bored her.

'Oh, I'm tired. Worn out. With so much *acting*. I tell you, in the theatre we haven't got time for all that. We've got our livings to get.'

The woman prison officer came in.

'I think they want you upstairs now. Ready, dear?'

When Maggie spoke again her voice was low, gentle and wonderfully polite.

'Yes thanks, Elsie. I'm quite ready now.'

'Will your foreman please stand? Mr Foreman. Have you reached a verdict on which you are all agreed?'

'Not guilty, my Lord.'

Four words that usually set the Rumpole ears tingling with delight and the chest to swell with pleasure. Why was it, that at the end of what was no doubt a remarkable win, a famous victory even, I felt such doubt and depression? I told myself that I was not the judge of fact, that the jury had clearly not been satisfied and that the prosecution had not proved its case. I did the well-known shift of responsibility which is the advocate's perpetual comfort, but I went out of Court unelated. In the entrance hall I saw Maggie leaving, she didn't turn back to speak to me and I saw that she was holding the hand of Mr Alan Copeland. Such congratulations as I received came from the diminutive Derwent.

'Triumph. My dear, a total triumph.'

'You told me she was truthful . . .' I looked at him.

'I meant her acting. That's quite truthful. Not to be faulted. That's all I meant.'

At which he made his exit and my Learned Friend for the Prosecution came sailing up, beaming with the joy of reconciliation.

'Well. Congratulations, Rumpole. That was a bloody good win!'

'Was it? I hope so.'

'Coming to the Circuit dinner tonight?'

'Tonight?'

'You'll enjoy it! We've got some pretty decent claret in the mess.'

If my judgement hadn't been weakened by exhaustion I would never have agreed to the Circuit dinner which took place, as I feared, in a private room at the Majestic Hotel. All the gang were there, Skelton, J, Pierce, Roach and my one-time leader Jarvis Allen, QC. The food was indifferent, the claret was bad, and when the port was passed an elderly silk whom they called 'Mr Senior' in deference to his position as Leader of the Circuit, banged the table with the handle of his knife and addressed young Roach at the other end of the table.

'Mr Junior, in the matter of Rumpole.'

'Mr Senior,' Roach produced a scribble on a menu. 'I will read the indictment.'

I realized then that I had been tricked, ambushed, made to give myself up to the tender mercies of this savage Northerly Circuit. Rumpole was on trial, there was nothing to do but drink all the available port and put up with it.

'Count One,' Roach read it out. 'Deserting his learned leader in his hour of need. That is to say on the occasion of his leader having been given the sack. Particulars of Offence . . .'

'Mr Senior. Have five minutes elapsed?' Allen asked.

'Five minutes having elapsed since the loyal toast, you may now smoke.'

Tommy Pierce lit a large cigar. I lit a small one. Mr Junior Roach continued to intone.

'The said Rumpole did add considerably to the seriousness of the offence by proceeding to win in the absence of his learned leader.'

'Mr Junior. Has Rumpole anything to say by way of mitigation?'

'Rumpole.' Roach took out his watch, clearly there was a time limit in speeches. I rose to express my deepest thoughts, loosened by the gentle action of the port.

'The show had to go on!'

'What? What did Rumpole say?' Mr Justice Skelton seemed to have some difficulty in hearing.

'Sometimes. I must admit, sometimes . . . I wonder why.' I went on, 'What sort of show is it exactly? Have you considered what we are *doing* to our clients?'

'Has that port got stuck to the table?' Allen sounded plaintive and the port moved towards him.

'What are we *doing* to them?' I warmed to my work. 'Seeing they wear ties, and hats, keep their hands out of their pockets, keep their voices up, call the judge "my Lord". Generally behave like grocers at a funeral. Whoever they may be.'

'One minute,' said Roach, the timekeeper.

'What do we tell them? Look respectable! Look suitably serious! Swear on the Bible! Say nothing which might upset a jury of lay-preachers, look enormously grateful for the trouble everyone's taking before they bang you up in the nick! What do we find out about our clients in all these trials, do we ever get a fleeting glimpse of the truth? Do we . . . ? Or do we put a hat on the truth. And a tie. And a serious expression. To please the jury and my Lord the Judge?' I looked round the table. 'Do you ever worry about that at all? Do you *ever*?'

'Time's up!' said Roach, and I sat down heavily.

'All right. Quite all right. The performance is over.'

Mr Senior swigged down port and proceeded to judgement.

'Rumpole's mitigation has, of course, merely added to the gravity of the offence. Rumpole, at your age and with your experience at the Bar you should have been proud to get the sack, and your further conduct in winning shows a total disregard for the feelings of an extremely sensitive silk. The least sentence I can pass is a fine of twelve bottles of claret. Have you a chequebook on you?'

So I had no choice but to pull out a chequebook and start to write. The penalty, apparently, was worth thirty-six quid.

'Members of the Mess will now entertain the company in song,' Roach announced to a rattle of applause.

'Tommy!' Allen shouted.

'No. Really . . .' The learned prosecutor was modest but was prevailed upon by cries of 'Come along, Tommy! Let's have it. "The Road to Mandalay" . . . etc. etc.'

'I'm looking forward to this,' said Mr Justice Skelton, who was apparently easily entertained. As I gave my cheque to young Roach, the stout leading Counsel for the Crown rose and started in a light baritone.

> *'On the Road to Mandalay . . .*
> *Where the old Flotilla lay . . .*
> *And the dawn came up like thunder*
> *Out of China 'cross the Bay!'*

Or words to the like effect. I was not really listening. I'd had quite enough of show business.

Rumpole and the Expert Witness

Canst thou not minister to a mind diseased,
Pluck from the memory a rooted sorrow,
Raze out the written troubles of the brain,
And with some sweet oblivious antidote
Cleanse the stuffed bosom of that perilous stuff
Which weighs upon the heart . . .

Certainly not young Dr Ned Dacre, the popular GP of Hunter's Hill, that delightful little dormitory town in Surrey, where nothing is heard but the whirr of the kitchen mixers running up Provençal specialities from the Sunday supplements and the purr of the hi-fis playing baroque music to go with the Buck's Fizz.

Ned Dacre lived in a world removed from my usual clients, the Old Bailey villains whose most common disease is a criminal conviction. He had a beautiful wife, two cars, two fair-haired children called Simon and Sara at rather nice schools, an au pair girl, an Old English sheepdog, a swimming pool, a carport and a machine for recording television programmes so that he didn't have to keep watching television. His father, Dr Henry Dacre, had settled in Hunter's Hill just after the war and had built up an excellent practice. When his son grew up and qualified he was taken into the partnership, and father and son were the two most popular doctors for many miles around, the inhabitants being almost equally divided as to whether, in times of sickness, they preferred the attentions of 'Dr Harry' or 'Dr Ned'. With all these advantages it seemed that Ned Dacre had all that the heart of man could desire, except that he had an unhappy wife. One night, after they had enjoyed a quiet supper together at home, Dr Ned's wife Sally became extremely ill. As she appeared to lose consciousness, he heard her say,

'I loved you, Ned . . . I really did.'

These were her last words, for although her husband rang the casualty department of the local hospital, and an ambulance was quickly dispatched, the beautiful Mrs Sally Dacre never spoke again, and died before she was taken out of the house.

I learned, as did the world, about the death of Sally Dacre and its unfortunate consequences from *The Times*. I was seated at breakfast in the matrimonial home at Froxbury Court in the Gloucester Road, looking forward without a great deal of excitement to a fairly ordinary day practising the law, ingesting Darjeeling tea, toast and Oxford marmalade, when the news item caught my eye and I gave a discreet whistle of surprise. My wife, Hilda, who was reading her correspondence (one letter on mauve paper from an old school friend) wanted her share of the news.

'What's the news in *The Times*, Rumpole? Has war started?'

'A Dr Dacre has been arrested in Hunter's Hill, Surrey. He's charged with murdering his wife.'

Hilda didn't seem to find the intelligence immediately gripping. In fact she waved her correspondence at me.

'There's a letter from Dodo. You know, my friend Dodo, Rumpole?'

'The one who keeps the tea-shop in Devon?' I had a vague recollection of an unfriendly female in tweed who seemed to imagine that I tyrannized somewhat over She Who Must Be Obeyed.

'She's always asking me to pop down and stay.'

'Why don't you?' I muttered hopefully, and then returned to the Home News. ' "Dr Dacre . . . ? Dacre!" The name's distinctly familiar.'

'Dodo never cared for you, Rumpole,' Hilda said firmly.

'The feeling's mutual. Isn't she the one who wears amber beads and smells of scones?' I repeated the name, hoping to stir some hidden memory, 'Harry Dacre.'

'Dodo's been suffering from depression,' Hilda rambled on. 'Of course, she never married.'

'Then I can't think what she's got to be depressed about!' I couldn't resist saying it, perhaps not quite audibly from behind the cover of *The Times*. 'Dr Harry Dacre!' I suddenly remembered. 'He gave evidence in my greatest triumph, the Penge Bungalow Murders! He'd seen my client's bruises. Don't you remember?'

'Dodo writes that she's taking a new sort of pill for her depression. They're helping her, but she mustn't eat cheese.'

'Poor old Dodo,' I said, 'deprived of cheese.' I read the story in the paper again. 'It couldn't be him. This is Dr "Ned" Dacre. Oh well, it's just another nice little murder that's never going to come my way. "Cause of death, cerebral haemorrhage", that's the evidence in the Magistrates' Court, "sustained in an alleged attack..."'

As I read, Hilda was casting a critical eye over my appearance.

'You're never going to Chambers like that, are you, Rumpole?'

'Like what, Hilda?' I was wondering what sort of a savage attack by a local doctor could explain his wife's cerebral haemorrhage.

'Well, your stud's showing and you've got marmalade on your waist-coat, and do you *have* to have that old silk handkerchief half falling out of your top pocket?'

'That was the silk handkerchief I used to blow my nose on three times, tearfully, in my final speech in the double murder in the Deptford Old People's Home. It has a certain sentimental value. Will you leave me alone, Hilda?' She was dabbing at my waistcoat with a corner of a table napkin she had soaked in the hot-water jug.

'I just want you to look your best, Rumpole.'

'You mean, in case I get run over?'

'And I'll put that old hanky in the wash.' She snatched the venerable bandana out of my breast pocket. 'You'd be much better off with a few nice, clean tissues.'

'You know what that fellow Dacre's been accused of, Hilda?' I thought I might as well remind her. 'Murdering his wife.'

As I had no pressing engagement until 2.30, when I was due for a rather dull touch of defrauding the Customs and Excise at the Uxbridge Magistrates' Court, I loitered on my way to the tube station, walked up through the Temple Gardens smoking a small cigar and went into the clerk's room to complain to Henry of the run-of-the-mill nature of my legal diet.

'No nice murders on the menu, are there?' When I asked him this, Henry smiled in a secretive sort of way and said,

'I'm not sure, sir.'

'You're not *sure*?'

'There's a Dr Henry Dacre phoned to come and see you urgently, sir. It seems his son's in a bit of trouble. He's come with Mr Cossett, solicitor of Hunter's Hill. I've put them in your room, Mr Rumpole.'

Old Dr Dacre in my room! I began to sniff the memory of ancient battles and a never-to-be-forgotten victory. When I opened my door, I was greeted by a healthy-looking country solicitor, and a greying version of a witness whose evidence marked a turning point in the Penge Bungalow affair. Dr Harry Dacre held out his hand and said,

'Mr Rumpole. It's been a long time, sir.'

How long was it, perhaps a legal lifetime, since I did *R. v. Samuel Poulteny*, better known as the Penge Bungalow Murders, which altered the course of legal history by proving that Horace Rumpole could win a capital case, alone and without a leader? Young Dr Harry Dacre, then a GP at Penge, gave valuable evidence for the defence, and young Rumpole made the most of it. I motioned the good doctor to my client's chair and invited Mr Cossett, the instructing solicitor, to take a seat.

'Well now, Doctor,' I said, 'what can I do for you?'

'You may have read about my son's little trouble?' The old doctor spoke of the charge of wife murder as though it were a touch of the flu which might be cured by a couple of aspirin and a day in bed.

'Yes. Was it a stormy sort of marriage?' I asked him.

The doctor shook his head.

'Sally was an extraordinarily pretty girl. Terribly spoilt, of course. Ned gave her everything she wanted.'

I wondered if that included a cerebral haemorrhage, and then told myself to keep my mouth shut and listen quietly.

'She had her problems, of course,' Dr Dacre went on. 'Nervous trouble. Well. Half the women in Hunter's Hill have got a touch of the nervy. All these labour-saving devices in the kitchen, gives them too much time to think.'

Not a pioneer of women's lib, I thought, old Dr Harry. And I asked him, 'Was she taking anything for her nerves?'

'Sally was scared of pills,' the doctor shook his head. 'Afraid she might get hooked, although she didn't mind taking the odd drink too many.'

'Do you think she needed medical treatment?'

'Ned and I discussed it. He thought of a course of treatment but

Sally wouldn't co-operate. So he, well, I suppose he just put up with her.' Dr Harry seemed to think that no one would have found his daughter-in-law particularly easy to live with.

'And on, as the prosecutors say, the night in question?' I decided it was time to get down to the facts.

'Mr Rumpole! That's why we need you,' Dr Harry said flatteringly enough. 'I know from past experience. You're the man who can destroy the pathologist's evidence! I'll never forget the Penge Bungalow case, and the way you pulverized that expert witness for the Crown.'

I wouldn't have minded a lengthy reminiscence of that memorable cross-examination, but I felt we should get on with the work in hand.

'Just remind me of the medical evidence. We don't disagree with the Crown about the cause of death?'

'Cerebral haemorrhage? No doubt about that. But it's the other findings that are the difficulty.'

'Which are?'

'Multiple bruising on the body, particularly the legs, back and buttocks, and the wound on the head where the deceased girl fell and knocked the edge of the coffee table.'

'Which caused the haemorrhage to the brain?' I frowned. The evidence of bruising was hardly encouraging.

'No doubt about it,' Dr Harry assured me. 'The trouble is the pathologist says the bruising was inflicted *before* death; the implication being that my son beat his wife up.'

'Is that likely?' It sounded rather unlike the home life of a young professional couple in Hunter's Hill.

'I told you Sally was a spoilt and highly strung girl, Mr Rumpole.' Dr Harry shrugged. 'Her father was old Peter Gaveston of Gaveston Electronics. She always had everything she wanted. Of course she and Ned quarrelled. Don't all married couples?'

Not all married couples, of course, include She Who Must Be Obeyed, but I had reason to believe that the good doctor was right in his diagnosis.

'But Ned would never beat his wife up like that,' Ned's father assured me. 'Not beat her up to kill her.'

It sounded as if I would have to do battle with another pathologist, and I was anxious to find out who my opponent would be.

'Tell me, who's the Miracle of the Morgues, the Prosecution Prince of the Post-Mortems? Who's the great brain on the other side?'

'It's a local pathologist. Does all the work in this part of the country.'

'Would I have heard of him?' I asked casually.

'It's not a "him". It's a Dr Pamela Gorle. And the irony is, Ned knows her extremely well. They were at Barts together, before he met Sally, of course. He brought her home for the weekend once or twice, and I almost thought they might make a go of it.'

'You mean, get married?'

'Yes.' Dr Harry seemed to think that the lady with the formaldehyde might have been a better bet than Sally.

By this time I was beginning to feel some sympathy for Dr Ned. It's enough to be put on trial for murder without having your ex-girlfriend examine your deceased wife's body, and provide what turns out to be the only real evidence for the prosecution.

'I just don't understand! I simply don't understand it.'

Friendly young Dr Ned sat in the unfriendly surroundings of the prison interview room. He looked concerned but curiously detached, as though he had just hit on a mysterious tropical disease which had no known cure.

'Doctor,' I said, 'did you and your wife Sally get on moderately well together?'

'We had our quarrels, of course. Like all married couples.'

It was the second time I had heard that. But, I thought, all married couples don't end up with one dead and the other one in the nick awaiting trial on a charge of wilful murder.

I looked at Dr Ned. He was better-looking than his father had been at his age; but Dr Harry, as I remembered his appearance in the Penge Bungalow Murders trial, had seemed the stronger character and more determined. As I looked at the charming, but rather weak younger doctor (after all, he hadn't had to struggle to build up a practice, but had picked up his father's well-warmed stethoscope and married an extremely wealthy young woman) I found it hard to imagine him brutally beating his wife and so killing her. Of course I might have been mistaken; the most savage murder I was ever mixed up in was the axing of a huge Regimental Sergeant-Major by a five-foot-nothing Sunday school teacher from East Finchley.

'Your father told me that Mrs Sally Dacre was depressed from time to time. Was she depressed about anything in particular?'

'No. In fact I always thought Sally had everything she wanted.'

'But did she suffer from depression?'

'I think so. Yes.'

'And took nothing for it?'

'She didn't approve of pills. She'd heard too many stories about people getting hooked. Doctors and their wives.'

'So she took nothing?' I wanted to get the facts established.

'My father was her doctor. I thought that was more professional. I'm not sure if he prescribed her anything, but I don't think he did. There was nothing found in the stomach.'

He said it casually and seemed only politely concerned. I don't know why I felt a sudden chill at discussing the contents of his dead wife's stomach with the doctor.

'No pills,' I agreed with him. 'The medical evidence tells us that.'

'Dr Pamela Gorle's report,' Dr Ned went on, still quite dispassionately. I fished out the document in question.

'Yes. It talks of the remains of a meal, and a good deal of alcohol in the blood.'

'We had a bottle of Chianti. And a soufflé. We were alone that night. We ate our supper in front of the television.'

'Your wife cooked?' I asked, not that there was any question of the food being anything but harmless.

'Oh no.' Dr Ned smiled at me. 'I may not be an absolutely brilliant doctor, but my soufflés are nothing short of miraculous.'

'Did you quarrel that evening?' I asked him. 'I mean, like all married couples?'

'Not at all. We had a discussion about where we'd go for our holiday, and settled on Crete. Sally had never been there, and I had only once. Before we met, actually.'

Had that been, I wondered, a romantic packaged fortnight with the pathologist for the Crown? Mine not to reason who with, so I kept him at the job of telling me the story of that last night with his wife.

'And then?'

'Then Sally complained of a headache. I thought it was perhaps due to watching the television for too long, so I switched it off. She was standing up to get herself a brandy.'

'And?'

'She stumbled and fell forwards.'

'Face *forwards*? Are you sure of that?'

'Yes, I'm certain. It was then that her forehead hit the corner of the coffee table.'

'And caused the cerebral haemorrhage?'

Dr Ned paused, frowning slightly. He seemed to be giving the matter his detached and entirely professional opinion. At last, he said cautiously,

'I can only think so.'

'Doctor, your friend, the pathologist . . .'

'Hardly my *friend* any longer.' Dr Ned smiled again, ruefully this time, as though he appreciated the irony of having an old colleague and fiancée giving evidence against him on a charge of wilful murder.

'No,' I agreed with him. 'She isn't your friend, is she? She says she found extensive bruising on your wife's back, her buttocks and the back of her legs.'

'That's what I can't understand.' My client looked genuinely puzzled.

'You're quite sure she didn't fall backwards?' I asked after a careful silence. Dr Ned and his wife were quite alone. Who would quarrel with the description of her falling backwards and bruising herself? I had given him his chance. A professional villain, any member of the Timson family for instance, would have taken that hint and agreed with me. But not Dr Ned.

'No, I told you. She fell forwards.' He was either being totally honest or wilfully obtuse.

'And you can't account for the alleged bruises on her back?'

'No.' That was all he had to say about it. But then he frowned, in some embarrassment, and said,

'There is one thing perhaps I ought to tell you.'

'About your wife?'

'No. About Dr Pamela Gorle.' Again, he hesitated. 'We were at Barts together, you know.'

'And went to Crete together once, on a packaged holiday.'

'How did you know that?' He looked at me, puzzled. It was an inspired guess, so I didn't answer his question. As I am a perpetual optimist, I asked, 'Do you think the Crown's expert witness might be a little helpful to us in the witness-box?'

'Not at all. In fact, I'm afraid she'll do everything she can to get me convicted.'

As I have said, I am an incorrigible optimist, and for the first time in my conference with Dr Ned I began to sniff the faint, far-away odour of a defence.

'Pamela was an extraordinarily possessive girl,' the doctor told me. 'She was always unreasonably and abnormally jealous.'

'When you married Sally?'

'When I met Sally. I suppose, well, after that holiday in Crete Pam thought we might get married. Then I didn't ring her and I began to get the most awful letters and phone calls from her. She was threatening . . .'

'Threatening what?'

'It was all very vague. To tell my father, or my patients, or the GMC, that she was pregnant.'

'Would any of those august bodies have cared?'

'Not in the least. It wasn't true anyway. Then she seemed to calm down for a while, but I still got letters – on my wedding anniversary and on some date which Pamela seemed to think was important.'

'Perhaps the day your affair started, or ended?'

'Probably. I really can't remember. She'd got her job with the Home Office, retained as a pathologist for this part of the county. I hoped she might settle down and get married, and forget.'

'She never did? Get married, I mean?'

'Or forget. I had a dreadful letter from her about a month ago. She said I'd ruined her life by marrying a hopeless drunk, and that she'd tell Sally we were still meeting unless . . .'

'Yes?' I prompted him, he seemed reluctant to go on.

'Well. Unless we still met. And continued our affair.'

'Did your wife see the letter?'

'No. I always get up early and opened the post.'

'You've kept the letter, of course?'

'No. I tore it up at once.'

If only people had the sense to realize that they might be facing a murder trial at any moment, they might keep important documents.

'And what did the letter say?'

'That she'd find some way of ruining my life, however long it took her.'

Hell, I supposed, hath no fury like a lady pathologist scorned. But Dr Pamela Gorle's personal interest in the Dacre murder seemed to provide the only faint hope of a cure for Dr Ned's somewhat desperate situation. I didn't know if a murder case had ever been won by attacking the medical evidence on the grounds of a romantic bias, but I supposed there had to be a first time for everything.

Everything about the Dacre murder trial was thoroughly pleasant. The old, red brick, local Georgian courtroom, an object of beauty among the supermarkets and boutiques and the wine bar and television and radio stores of the little Surrey town, was so damned pleasant that you expected nice girls with Roedean accents to pass round the Court serving coffee and rock cakes whenever there was a lull in the proceedings. The jury looked as though they had dropped in for a rather gentle session of 'Gardeners' Question Time', and Owen Munroe, QC, was a pleasant prosecutor who seemed thoroughly distressed at having to press such a nasty charge as wilful murder against the nice young doctor who sat in the dock wearing his well-pressed suit and old Barts tie.

Worst of all, Nick McManus was a tremendously pleasant Judge. He was out to be thoroughly fair and show every courtesy to the defence, ploys which frequently lead to a conviction. It is amazing how many villains owe their freedom to the fact that some old sweetheart on the Bench seemed to be determined to get the jury to pot them.

We went quickly, and without argument, through the formal evidence of photographs, fingerprints and the finding of the body, and then my learned friend announced that he intended to call the pathologist.

'Will that be convenient to you, Mr Rumpole?' The Judge, as I have said, was a perfect gent.

'Certainly, my Lord. That will be quite convenient.' I made myself perfectly pleasant in return.

'I wish to make quite sure, Mr Rumpole, that you have every opportunity to prepare yourself to cross-examine the expert witness.'

You see what I mean? Old McManus was making sure I would have no alibi if I didn't succeed in cracking Dr Pamela. I'd've been far better off with someone like the mad Judge Bullingham, charging head-on at the defence. In this very pleasant trial, Rumpole would have no excuses. However, there was no help for it, so I bowed and said,

'I'm quite prepared, my Lord. Thank you.'

'Very well. Mr Munroe, as you are about to call the pathologist . . .'

'Yes, my Lord.' My opponent was on his feet.

'I suppose the jury will *have* to look at the photographs of the dead lady?'

'Yes, my Lord. It is Bundle No. 4.'

Pictures of a good-looking young woman, naked, bruised, battered and laid on a mortuary slab, are always harrowing and never helpful to the defence. McManus, J, introduced them to the jury quietly, but effectively.

'Members of the jury,' said the Judge. 'I'm afraid you will find these photographs extremely distressing. It is necessary for you to see them so you may understand the medical evidence fully, but I'm sure Counsel will take the matter as shortly as possible. These things are never pleasant.'

Death isn't pleasant, nor is murder. In the nicest possible way, the Judge was pointing out the horrific nature of the crime of which Dr Ned was charged. It was something you just didn't do in that part of Surrey.

'I swear by Almighty God that the evidence I shall give shall be the truth, the whole truth and nothing but the truth.'

I was aroused from my thoughts by the sound of the pathologist taking her Bible oath. Owen Munroe hitched up his gown, sorted out his papers and started his examination-in-chief.

'Dr Pamela Gorle?' he asked.

'Yes.'

'Did you examine the body of the late Sally Dacre, the deceased in this case?'

'I did. Yes.'

'Just tell us what you found.'

'I found a well-nourished, healthy woman of thirty-five years of age who had died from a cerebral haemorrhage. There was evidence of a recent meal.' The demure pathologist had a voice ever gentle and low, an excellent thing in a woman, but a bit of a drawback in the witness-box. I had to strain my ears to follow her drift. And unlike the well-nourished and healthy deceased, Dr Pamela was pale and even uninteresting to look at. Her hair was thin and mousy, she wore a black suit and National Health spectacles behind which her eyes glowed with some obsession. I couldn't be sure whether it was love of her gloomy work or hatred of Dr Ned.

'You say that you found widespread bruising on the deceased's back and buttocks. What was that consistent with?'

'I thought it was consistent with a violent attack from behind. I thought Mrs Dacre had probably been struck and kicked by . . . well, it appeared that she was alone that evening with her husband.'

'I object!' I had risen to protest, but the perfect gent on the Bench was ahead of me.

'Yes, Mr Rumpole. And you are perfectly right to do so. Dr Gorle, it is not for you to say *who* beat this lady and kicked her. That is entirely a matter for the jury. That is why Mr Rumpole has quite rightly objected.'

I wished his Lordship would stop being so lethally pleasant. 'But I understand,' the Judge continued, 'that your evidence is that she was kicked and beaten – by *someone*.' McManus, J, made it clear that Sally Dacre had been attacked brutally, and the jury could have the undoubted pleasure of saying who did it.

'Yes, my Lord.'

'Kicked and beaten!' His Lordship repeated the words for good measure, and after he'd written them down and underlined them with his red pencil, Munroe wound up his examination-in-chief.

'The immediate cause of death was?'

'A cerebral haemorrhage, as I said!'

'Could you form any opinion as to how that came about?' Munroe asked.

'Just a moment.' McManus, J, gave me one of his charming smiles from the Bench. 'Have you any objection to her opinion, Mr Rumpole?'

'My Lord, I wouldn't seek to prevent this witness saying anything she wishes in her effort to implicate my client in his wife's tragic death.'

McManus, J, looked slightly puzzled at that, and seemed to wonder if it was an entirely gentlemanly remark. However, he only said, 'Very well. Do please answer the question, Dr Gorle.'

'My opinion, my Lord, is that the deceased had received a blow to the head in the course of the attack.'

'The attack you have already described?'

'That is so, my Lord.'

'Thank you, Dr Gorle,' said Owen Munroe, and sat down with a quietly satisfied air and left the witness to me.

I stood up, horribly conscious that the next quarter of an hour would decide the future of my client. Would Dr Ned Dacre go back to his pleasant house and practice, or was he fated to vanish into some distant prison only to emerge, pale and unemployable, after ten or more long years? If I couldn't break down the medical evidence our case was hopeless. I stood in the silent Court, shuffling the photographs and the doctor's notes, wondering whether to lead up to my charge of bias gently laying what traps I could on the way, or go in with all my guns blazing. I seemed to stand for a long time undecided, with moist hands and a curious feeling of dread at the responsibility I had undertaken in the pit of my stomach, and then I made a decision. I would start with my best point.

'Dr Gorle. Just help me. You knew Dr Ned Dacre well, didn't you?'

The first question had been asked. We'd very soon find out if it were the right one.

'We were at Barts together.' Dr Gorle showed no sign of having been hit amidships.

'And went out together, as the saying is?' I said sweetly.

'Occasionally, yes.'

'"Going out" as so often nowadays meaning "staying in" together?' I used a slightly louder voice, and was gratified to see that the witness looked distinctly narked.

'What do you mean?'

'Yes. I think you should make that a little clearer, Mr Rumpole,' the Judge intervened, in the pleasantest possible way.

'You and Dr Ned Dacre went on holiday to Crete together, didn't you? Before he was married.'

There was a distinct pause, and the doctor looked down at the rail of the witness-box as she admitted it.

'Yes. We did.'

The dear old 'Gardeners' Question Time' fans on the jury looked suddenly interested, as if I had revealed a new and deadly form of potato blight. I pressed on.

'Did you become, what expression would you like me to use, his girlfriend, paramour, mistress?'

'We shared a bed together, yes.' Now the pathologist looked up at me, defiant.

'Presumably not for the purpose of revising your anatomy notes together?' I got a small chuckle from the jury which increased the witness's irritation.

'He was my lover. If that's how you want to put it.'

'Thank you, Dr Gorle. I'm sure the members of the jury understand. And I would also like the jury to understand that you became extremely angry when Dr Ned Dacre got married.' There was another long pause, but the answer she came up with was moderately helpful.

'I was disappointed, yes.'

'Angry and jealous of the lady whose dead body you examined?' I suggested.

'I suppose I was naturally upset that Ned Dacre had married someone else.'

'So upset that you wrote him a letter, only a week or so before this tragedy, in which you told him you wanted to hurt him as much as you possibly could?' Now the jury were entirely hooked. I saw Munroe staring at me, no doubt wondering if I could produce the letter. The witness may have decided that I could, anyway she didn't risk an outright denial.

'I may have done.'

'You may have done!' I tried the effect of a passage of fortissimo incredulity. 'But by then Dr Ned Dacre had been married for eight years and his wife had borne him two children. And yet you were still harbouring this terrible grudge?'

She answered quickly this time, and with a great intensity.

'There are some things you don't forget, Mr Rumpole.'

'And some things you don't forgive, Dr Gorle? Has your feeling of jealousy and hatred for my client in any way coloured your evidence against him?'

Of course I expected her to deny this. During the course of cross-examination you may angle for useful admissions, hints and half-truths which can come with the cunning cast of a seemingly innocent question. But the time always comes when you must confront the witness with a clear suggestion, a final formality of assertion and denial, when the subtleties are over. I was surprised, therefore, when the lady from the morgues found it difficult to answer the question in its simplest form. There was a prolonged silence.

'Has it, Dr Gorle?' I pressed her gently for an answer.

Only Dr Gorle knew if she was biased. If she'd denied the suggestion hotly no one could have contradicted her. Instead of doing so, she finally came out with,

'I don't *think* so.' And she said it so unconvincingly that I saw the jury's disapproval. It was the first game to Rumpole, and the witness seemed to have lost her confidence when I moved on to deal with the medical evidence. Fortunately a long career as an Old Bailey Hack has given me a working knowledge of the habits of dead bodies.

'Dr Gorle. After death a body becomes subject to a condition called "hypostasis"?'

'That is so. Yes.'

'The blood drains to the lowest area when circulation ceases?'

'Yes.'

'So that if the body has been lying on its back, the blood would naturally drain to the buttocks and the backs of the legs?'

'That's perfectly right,' she answered, now without hesitation.

'Did you say, Mr Rumpole's right about that?' The Judge was making a note of the cross-examination.

'Yes, my Lord.'

'Yes. Thank you, Doctor.' I paused to frame the next question carefully. 'And the draining of the blood causes discolouration of the skin of a dead body which can *look like bruising*?' I began to get an eerie feeling that it was all going too well, when the pale lady doctor admitted, again most helpfully,

'It can look exactly like bruising, yes.'

'Therefore it is difficult to tell simply by the colour of the skin if a patch is caused by "hypostasis" or bruising? It can be very misleading?'

'Yes. It can be.'

'So you must insert a knife under the skin to see what has caused the discolouration, must you not?'

'That is the standard test, yes.'

'If some blood flows, it is "hypostasis", but if the blood under the skin has coagulated and does *not* flow, it is probably a bruise?'

'What do you have to say about that, Dr Gorle?' the Judge asked the witness, and she came back with a glowing tribute to the amateur pathologist in the wig.

'I would say, my Lord, that Mr Rumpole would be well equipped to lecture on forensic medicine.'

'That test was carried out in a case called the Penge Bungalow Murders, Dr Gorle.' I disclosed the source of almost all my information, and added a flattering, 'No doubt before you were born.' I had never got on so well with a hostile witness.

'I'm afraid it was.'

'So what happened when you inserted a knife into the coloured portions?' I had asked the question in a manner which was almost sickeningly polite, but Dr Pamela looked greatly shaken. Finally, in a voice of contrition she admitted,

'I didn't.'

'What?'

'I didn't carry out that particular test.'

'You didn't?' I tried to sound encouragingly neutral to hide my incredulity.

'No.'

'Can you tell us *why* not?' The Judge now sounded more like an advocate than the calm, detached Mr Justice Rumpole.

'I'm afraid that I must have jumped to the conclusion that they were bruises and I didn't trouble to carry out any further test, my Lord.'

'You *jumped* to the conclusion?' There was no doubt about it. The courteous McManus was deeply shocked.

'Yes.' Dr Pamela looked paler, and her voice was trembling on the edge of inaudibility.

'You know, Dr Gorle, the jury aren't going to be asked to convict

Dr Dacre by "jumping to conclusions".' I blessed the old darling on the Bench when he said that, and began to see a distinct hope of returning my client to piles and prescriptions in the not-too-distant future.

'My Lord is, of course, perfectly right,' I told the witness. 'The case against Dr Ned Dacre has to be proved beyond reasonable doubt, so that the jury are *sure*. Can I take it that you're not sure there were any bruises at all?'

There was a pause and then out came the most beautiful answer.

'Not as you put it now. No. I'm not sure.'

Again I had the strange feeling that it was too easy. I felt like a torea-dor poised for a life-and-death struggle, seeing instead the ring doors open to admit a rather gentle and obedient cow.

'I'm not *sure* there were any bruises,' his Lordship repeated to him-self as he wrote it down in his note.

'And so you're not sure Mrs Dacre was attacked by anyone?' It was a question I would normally have avoided. With this witness, it seemed, I could dare anything.

'I can't be sure. No.'

And again, the Judge wrote it down.

'So she may simply have stumbled, hit her head against the coffee table and died of a cerebral haemorrhage?'

'It might have happened in that way. Yes.' Dr Gorle was giving it to me with jam on it.

'Stumbled because she had had too much to drink?'

The co-operative witness turned to the Judge.

'Her blood alcohol level was considerably above the breathalyser limit, yes, my Lord.'

'And you knew this family?'

'I knew about them. Yes.'

'And was it not one of your complaints that, in marrying Sally, Dr Ned had married a drunk?'

'I did say that in my letter.'

'The sort of girl who might drink too much wine, stumble against a chromium coffee table, hit her head and receive a cerebral haemor-rhage, *by accident*?' It was the full frontal question, but I felt no embarrassment now in asking it. The Judge was also keen on getting an answer and he said,

'Well, Dr Gorle?'

'I must admit it might've happened that way. Yes.'

It was all over then, bar the odd bit of shouting. I said, 'Thank you very much, Dr Pamela Gorle.' And meant it. It was game, set and match to Rumpole. We had a bit of legal argument between Counsel and then I was intoxicated by the delightful sensation of winning. The pleasant Judge told the jury that, in view of the concessions made by the expert witness, there really was no evidence on which they could possible convict the good doctor, and directed them to stop the case and pronounce those two words which are always music to Rumpole's ears, 'Not guilty'. We all went out into the corridor and loyal patients came to shake Ned's hand and congratulate him as politely as if he'd just won first prize for growing the longest leek.

'Mr Rumpole. I knew you'd come up trumps, sir. I shall never forget this, never!' Old Dr Harry was pumping my hand, slapping my shoulder, and I thought I saw tears in his eyes. But then I looked across the crowd, at a door through which the expert witness, the Crown's pathologist, Dr Pamela Gorle had just appeared. She was smiling at Dr Ned and, unless I was very much mistaken, he was smiling back. Was it only a smile, or did I detect the tremble of a wink? I left his father and went up to the young doctor. He smiled his undying gratitude.

'Mr Rumpole. Dad was right. You're the best!' Dr Ned was kind enough to say.

'Nonsense. It was easy.' I looked at him and said, 'Too easy.'

'Why do you say that?' Dr Ned looked genuinely puzzled.

I didn't answer him. Instead, I asked a question.

'I was meaning to ask you this before, Doctor. I don't suppose it matters now, but I'd like to know the answer, for my own satisfaction. What sort of soufflé was it you cooked for your wife that evening?' He might have lied, but I don't suppose he thought there was any point in it. Instead he answered as if he enjoyed telling the truth.

'Cheese.'

I was at breakfast with She Who Must Be Obeyed a few days later, after I had managed to spring the charming young doctor, and my wife was brandishing another mauve letter from her friend Dorothy or 'Dodo', the nervous tea-shop owner from the West Country.

'Another letter from Dodo! She's really feeling much better. So much more calm!'

'She's been taking these new pills, didn't you say?'

'Yes, I think that's what it must be.'

I remembered about a drug Dr Ned was discussing with his father for possible use on his nervous wife. Was it the same drug that was keeping Dodo off cheese?

'Then Dodo will be feeling better. So long as she doesn't eat cheese. If she eats cheese when she's on some sort of tranquillizer she's likely to go the way of the doctor's beautiful wife, and end up with a haemorrhage of the brain.'

I had a letter too. An invitation to a cocktail party in Hunter's Hill. Dr Ned Dacre, it seemed, felt that he had something to celebrate.

'Mr Rumpole! I'm so glad you could come.' Dr Ned greeted me enthusiastically.

I looked round the pleasant room, at the pleasant faces of grateful patients and the two thoroughly nice children handing round canapés. I noticed the Queen of the Morgues, Dr Pamela Gorle, dressed up to the nines, and then I looked at the nice young doctor who was now pouring me out a generous Buck's Fizz made, regardless of the expense, with the best Krug. I spoke to him quietly.

'You got off, of course. They can't try you again for the same murder. That was the arrangement, wasn't it?'

'What "arrangement"?' The young doctor was still smiling in a welcoming sort of way.

'Oh, the arrangement between you and the Crown pathologist, of course. The plan that she'd make some rather silly suggestions about bruises and admit she was wrong. Of course, she lied about the contents of the stomach. You're a very careful young man, Dr Ned. Now they can never try you for what you really did.'

'You're joking!' But I saw that he had stopped smiling.

'I was never more serious in my life.'

'What did I really do?' We seemed to be alone. A little whispering oasis of doubt and suspicion in the middle of the happy, chattering cocktail party. I told him what he'd done.

'You opened a few of those new tranquillizer capsules and poured them into your wife's Chianti. The cheese in the soufflé reacted in just the way you'd planned. All you had to do was make sure she hit her head on the table.'

We stood in silence. The children came up and we refused canapés. Then Dr Ned opened an alabaster box and lit a cigarette with a gold lighter.

'What're you going to do about it?' I could see that he was smiling again.

'Nothing I can do now. You know that,' I told him. 'Except to tell you that I know. I'm not quite the idiot you and Dr Pamela took me for. At least you know that, Dr Ned.'

He was a murderer. Divorce would have given him freedom but not his rich wife's money; so he became a simple, old-fashioned murderer. And what was almost worse, he had used me as part of his crime. Worst of all, he had done his best to spoil the golden memory of the Penge Bungalow Murders for me.

'Quiet everyone! I think Ned's got something to say!' Old Dr Harry Dacre was banging on a table with his glass. In due course quiet settled on the party and young Dr Ned made his announcement.

'I just wanted to say. Now all our friends are here. Under one roof. That of course no one can ever replace Sally. For me and the children. But with Simon and Sara's approval . . .' He smiled at his charming children. 'There's going to be another doctor in the Dacre family. Pamela's agreed to become my wife.'

In the ensuing clapping, kisses, congratulations and mixing of more Buck's Fizz, Rumpole left the party.

I hear it was a thoroughly nice wedding. I looked hard at the photograph in the paper and tried to detect, in that open and smiling young doctor's face, a sign of guilt.

> '. . . that perilous stuff.
> Which weighs upon the heart.'

I saw none.

Rumpole and the Spirit of Christmas

I realized that Christmas was upon us when I saw a sprig of holly over the list of prisoners hung on the wall of the cells under the Old Bailey.

I pulled out a new box of small cigars and found its opening obstructed by a tinselled band on which a scarlet-faced Santa was seen hurrying a sleigh full of carcinoma-packed goodies to the Rejoicing World. I lit one as the lethargic screw, with a complexion the colour of faded Bronco, regretfully left his doorstep sandwich and mug of sweet tea to unlock the gate.

'Good morning, Mr Rumpole. Come to visit a customer?'

'Happy Christmas, officer,' I said as cheerfully as possible. 'Is Mr Timson at home?'

'Well, I don't believe he's slipped down to his little place in the country.'

Such were the pleasantries that were exchanged between us legal hacks and discontented screws; jokes that no doubt have changed little since the turnkeys locked the door at Newgate to let in a pessimistic advocate, or the cells under the Coliseum were opened to admit the unwelcome news of the Imperial thumbs-down.

'My Mum wants me home for Christmas.'

'Which Christmas?' It would have been an unreasonable remark and I refrained from it. Instead, I said, 'All things are possible.'

As I sat in the interviewing room, an Old Bailey Hack of some considerable experience, looking through my brief and inadvertently using my waistcoat as an ashtray, I hoped I wasn't on another loser. I had had a run of bad luck during that autumn season, and young Edward Timson was part of that huge South London family whose criminal activities provided such welcome grist to the Rumpole mill. The charge in the seventeen-year-old Eddie's case was nothing less than wilful murder.

'We're in with a chance though, Mr Rumpole, ain't we?'

Like all his family, young Timson was a confirmed optimist. And yet, of course, the merest outsider in the Grand National, the hundred-to-one shot, is in with a chance, and nothing is more like going round the course at Aintree than living through a murder trial. In this particular case, a fanatical prosecutor named Wrigglesworth, known to me as the Mad Monk, was to represent Beechers and Mr Justice Vosper, a bright but wintry-hearted Judge who always felt it his duty to lead for the prosecution, was to play the part of a particularly menacing fence at the Canal Turn.

'A chance. Well, yes, of course you've got a chance, if they can't establish common purpose, and no one knows which of you bright lads had the weapon.'

No doubt the time had come for a brief glance at the prosecution case, not an entirely cheering prospect. Eddie, also known as 'Turpin' Timson, lived in a kind of decaying barracks, a sort of high-rise Lubianka, known as Keir Hardie Court, somewhere in South London, together with his parents, his various brothers and his thirteen-year-old sister, Noreen. This particular branch of the Timson family lived on the thirteenth floor. Below them, on the twelfth, lived the large clan of the O'Dowds. The war between the Timsons and the O'Dowds began, it seems, with the casting of the Nativity play at the local comprehensive school.

Christmas comes earlier each year and the school show was planned about September. When Bridget O'Dowd was chosen to play the lead in the face of strong competition from Noreen Timson, an incident occurred comparable in historical importance to the assassination of an obscure Austrian archduke at Sarajevo. Noreen Timson announced, in the playground, that Bridget O'Dowd was a spotty little tart quite unsuited to play any role of which the most notable characteristic was virginity.

Hearing this, Bridget O'Dowd kicked Noreen Timson behind the anthracite bunkers. Within a few days war was declared between the Timson and O'Dowd children, and a present of lit fireworks was posted through the O'Dowd front door. On what is known as the 'night in question', reinforcements of O'Dowds and Timsons arrived in old bangers from a number of South London addresses and battle was joined on the stone staircase, a bleak terrain of peeling walls scrawled with graffiti, blowing empty Coca-Cola tins and torn newspapers. The weapons seemed to have been articles in general domestic use such as bread knives, carving knives, broom handles and a heavy screwdriver.

At the end of the day it appeared that the upstairs flat had repelled the invaders, and Kevin O'Dowd lay on the stairs. Having been stabbed with a slender and pointed blade he was in a condition to become known as the 'deceased' in the case of the Queen against Edward Timson. I made an application for bail for my client which was refused, but a speedy trial was ordered.

So even as Bridget O'Dowd was giving her Virgin Mary at the comprehensive, the rest of the family was waiting to give evidence against Eddie Timson in that home of British drama, Number 1 Court at the Old Bailey.

'I never had no cutter, Mr Rumpole. Straight up, I never had one,' the defendant told me in the cells. He was an appealing-looking lad with soft brown eyes, who had already won the heart of the highly susceptible lady who wrote his social inquiry report. ('Although the charge is a serious one this is a young man who might respond well to a period of probation.' I could imagine the steely contempt in Mr Justice Vosper's eye when he read that.)

'Well, tell me, Edward. Who had?'

'I never seen no cutters on no one, honest I didn't. We wasn't none of us tooled up, Mr Rumpole.'

'Come on, Eddie. Someone must have been. They say even young Noreen was brandishing a potato peeler.'

'Not me, honest.'

'What about your sword?'

There was one part of the prosecution evidence that I found particularly distasteful. It was agreed that on the previous Sunday morning, Eddie 'Turpin' Timson had appeared on the stairs of Keir Hardie Court and flourished what appeared to be an antique cavalry sabre at the assembled O'Dowds, who were just popping out to Mass.

'Me sword I bought up the Portobello? I didn't have that there, honest.'

'The prosecution can't introduce evidence about the sword. It was an entirely different occasion.' Mr Bernard, my instructing solicitor who fancied himself as an infallible lawyer, spoke with a confidence which I couldn't feel. He, after all, wouldn't have to stand up on his hind legs and argue the legal toss with Mr Justice Vosper.

'It rather depends on who's prosecuting us. I mean, if it's some fairly reasonable fellow . . .'

'I think,' Mr Bernard reminded me, shattering my faint optimism and ensuring that we were all in for a very rough Christmas indeed, 'I think it's Mr Wrigglesworth. Will he try to introduce the sword?'

I looked at 'Turpin' Timson with a kind of pity. 'If it is the Mad Monk, he undoubtedly will.'

When I went into Court, Basil Wrigglesworth was standing with his shoulders hunched up round his large, red ears, his gown dropped to his elbows, his bony wrists protruding from the sleeves of his frayed jacket, his wig pushed back and his huge hands joined on his lectern in what seemed to be an attitude of devoted prayer. A lump of cottonwool clung to his chin where he had cut himself shaving. Although well into his sixties he preserved a look of boyish clumsiness. He appeared, as he always did when about to prosecute on a charge carrying a major punishment, radiantly happy.

'Ah, Rumpole,' he said, lifting his eyes from the police verbals as though they were his breviary. 'Are you defending *as usual?*'

'Yes, Wrigglesworth. And you're prosecuting *as usual?*' It wasn't much of a riposte but it was all I could think of at the time.

'Of course, I don't defend. One doesn't like to call witnesses who may not be telling the truth.'

'You must have a few unhappy moments then, calling certain members of the Constabulary.'

'I can honestly tell you, Rumpole,' his curiously innocent blue eyes looked at me with a sort of pain, as though I had questioned the doctrine of the immaculate conception, 'I have never called a dishonest policeman.'

'Yours must be a singularly simple faith, Wrigglesworth.'

'As for the Detective Inspector in this case,' Counsel for the prosecution went on, 'I've known Wainwright for years. In fact, this is his last

trial before he retires. He could no more invent a verbal against a defendant than fly.'

Any more on that tack, I thought, and we should soon be debating
how many angels could dance on the point of a pin.

'Look here, Wrigglesworth. That evidence about my client having a
sword: it's quite irrelevant. I'm sure you'd agree.'

'Why is it irrelevant?' Wrigglesworth frowned.

'Because the murder clearly wasn't done with an antique cavalry
sabre. It was done with a small, thin blade.'

'If he's a man who carries weapons, why isn't that relevant?'

'A man? Why do you call him a man? He's a child. A boy of seven-
teen!'

'Man enough to commit a serious crime.'

'*If* he did.'

'If he didn't, he'd hardly be in the dock.'

'That's the difference between us, Wrigglesworth,' I told him. 'I
believe in the presumption of innocence. You believe in original sin.
Look here, old darling.' I tried to give the Mad Monk a smile of friendship and became conscious of the fact that it looked, no doubt, like an
ingratiating sneer. 'Give us a chance. You won't introduce the evidence
of the sword, will you?'

'Why ever not?'

'Well,' I told him, 'the Timsons are an industrious family of criminals. They work hard, they never go on strike. If it weren't for people
like the Timsons, you and I would be out of a job.'

'They sound in great need of prosecution and punishment. Why
shouldn't I tell the jury about your client's sword? Can you give me one
good reason?'

'Yes,' I said, as convincingly as possible.

'What is it?' He peered at me, I thought, unfairly.

'Well, after all,' I said, doing my best, 'it is Christmas.'

It would be idle to pretend that the first day in Court went well, although
Wrigglesworth restrained himself from mentioning the sword in his
opening speech, and told me that he was considering whether or not to
call evidence about it the next day. I cross-examined a few members of
the clan O'Dowd on the presence of lethal articles in the hands of the

attacking force. The evidence about this varied and weapons came and went in the hands of the inhabitants of number twelve as the witnesses were blown hither and thither in the winds of Rumpole's cross-examination. An interested observer from one of the other flats spoke of having seen a machete.

'Could that terrible weapon have been in the hands of Mr Kevin O'Dowd, the deceased in this case?'

'I don't think so.'

'But can you rule out the possibility?'

'No, I can't rule it out,' the witness admitted, to my temporary delight.

'You can never rule out the possibility of anything in this world, Mr Rumpole. But he doesn't think so. You have your answer.'

Mr Justice Vosper, in a voice like a splintering iceberg, gave me this unwelcome Christmas present. The case wasn't going well but at least, by the end of the first day, the Mad Monk had kept out all mention of the sword. The next day he was to call young Bridget O'Dowd, fresh from her triumph in the Nativity play.

'I say, Rumpole. I'd be *so* grateful for a little help.'

I was in Pommeroy's Wine Bar, drowning the sorrows of the day in my usual bottle of the cheapest Château Fleet Street (made from grapes which, judging from the bouquet, might have been not so much trodden as kicked to death by sturdy peasants in gumboots) when I looked up to see Wrigglesworth, dressed in an old mackintosh, doing business with Jack Pommeroy at the sales counter. When I crossed to him, he was not buying the jumbo-sized bottle of ginger beer which I imagined might be his celebratory Christmas tipple, but a tempting and respectably aged bottle of Château Pichon-Longueville.

'What can I do for you, Wrigglesworth?'

'Well, as you know, Rumpole, I live in Croydon.'

'Happiness is given to few of us on this earth,' I said piously.

'And the Anglican Sisters of St Agnes, Croydon, are anxious to buy a present for their Bishop,' Wrigglesworth explained. 'A dozen bottles for Christmas. They've asked my advice, Rumpole. I know so little of wine. You wouldn't care to try this for me? I mean, if you're not especially busy.'

'I should be hurrying home to dinner.' My wife Hilda (She Who Must Be Obeyed), was laying on rissoles and frozen peas, washed down by my last bottle of Pommeroy's extremely ordinary. 'However, as it's Christmas, I don't mind helping you out, Wrigglesworth.'

The Mad Monk was clearly quite unused to wine. As we sampled the claret together, I saw the chance of getting him to commit himself on the vital question of the evidence of the sword, as well as absorbing an unusually decent bottle. After the Pichon-Longueville I was kind enough to help him by sampling a Boyd-Cantenac and then I said, 'Excellent, this. But of course the Bishop might be a Burgundy man. The nuns might care to invest in a decent Mâcon.'

'Shall we try a bottle?' Wrigglesworth suggested. 'I'd be grateful for your advice.'

'I'll do my best to help you, my old darling. And while we're on the subject, that ridiculous bit of evidence about young Timson and the sword . . .'

'I remember you saying I shouldn't bring that out because it's Christmas.'

'Exactly.' Jack Pommeroy had uncorked the Mâcon and it was mingling with the claret to produce a feeling of peace and goodwill towards men. Wrigglesworth frowned, as though trying to absorb an obscure point of theology.

'I don't quite see the relevance of Christmas to the question of your man Timson threatening his neighbours with a sword . . .'

'Surely, Wrigglesworth,' I knew my prosecutor well, 'you're of a religious disposition?' The Mad Monk was the product of some bleak Northern Catholic boarding school. He lived alone, and no doubt wore a hair shirt under his black waistcoat and was vowed to celibacy. The fact that he had his nose deep into a glass of Burgundy at the moment was due to the benign influence of Rumpole.

'I'm a Christian, yes.'

'Then practise a little Christian tolerance.'

'Tolerance towards evil?'

'Evil?' I asked. 'What do you mean, evil?'

'Couldn't that be your trouble, Rumpole? That you really don't recognize evil when you see it.'

'I suppose,' I said, 'evil might be locking up a seventeen-year-old during Her Majesty's pleasure, when Her Majesty may very probably forget all about him, banging him up with a couple of hard and violent cases and their own chamber pots for twenty-two hours a day, so he won't come out till he's a real, genuine, middle-aged murderer . . .'

'I did hear the Reverend Mother say,' Wrigglesworth was gazing vacantly at the empty Mâcon bottle, 'that the Bishop likes his glass of port.'

'Then in the spirit of Christmas tolerance I'll help you to sample some of Pommeroy's Light and Tawny.'

A little later, Wrigglesworth held up his port glass in a reverent sort of fashion.

'You're suggesting, are you, that I should make some special concession in this case because it's Christmas time?'

'Look here, old darling.' I absorbed half my glass, relishing the gentle fruitiness and the slight tang of wood. 'If you spent your whole life in that high-rise hellhole called Keir Hardie Court, if you had no fat prosecutions to occupy your attention and no prospect of any job at all, if you had no sort of occupation except war with the O'Dowds . . .'

'My own flat isn't particularly comfortable. I don't know a great deal about *your* home life, Rumpole, but you don't seem to be in a tearing hurry to experience it.'

'*Touché*, Wrigglesworth, my old darling.' I ordered us a couple of refills of Pommeroy's port to further postpone the encounter with She Who Must Be Obeyed and her rissoles.

'But we don't have to fight to the death on the staircase,' Wrigglesworth pointed out.

'We don't have to fight at all, Wrigglesworth.'

'As your client did.'

'As my client *may* have done. Remember the presumption of innocence.'

'This is rather funny, this is.' The prosecutor pulled back his lips to reveal strong, yellowish teeth and laughed appreciatively. 'You know why your man Timson is called "Turpin"?'

'No.' I drank port uneasily, fearing an unwelcome revelation.

'Because he's always fighting with that sword of his. He's called after Dick Turpin, you see, who's always duelling on the television. Do you watch the television, Rumpole?'

'Hardly at all.'

'I watch a great deal of the television, as I'm alone rather a lot.' Wrigglesworth referred to the box as though it were a sort of penance, like fasting or flagellation. 'Detective Inspector Wainwright told me about your client. Rather amusing, I thought it was. He's retiring this Christmas.'

'My client?'

'No. DI Wainwright. Do you think we should settle on this port for the Bishop? Or would you like to try a glass of something else?'

'Christmas,' I told Wrigglesworth severely as we sampled the Cock-burn, 'is not just a material, pagan celebration. It's not just an occasion for absorbing superior vintages, old darling. It must be a time when you try to do good, spiritual good to our enemies.'

'To your client, you mean?'

'And to me.'

'To you, Rumpole?'

'For God's sake, Wrigglesworth!' I was conscious of the fact that my appeal was growing desperate. 'I've had six losers in a row down the Old Bailey. Can't I be included in any Christmas spirit that's going around?'

'You mean, at Christmas especially it is more blessed to give than to receive?'

'I mean exactly that.' I was glad that he seemed, at last, to be following my drift.

'And you think I might give this case to someone, like a Christmas present?'

'If you care to put it that way, yes.'

'I do not care to put it in *exactly* that way.' He turned his pale blue eyes on me with what I thought was genuine sympathy. 'But I shall try and do the case of *R. v. Timson* in the way most appropriate to the greatest feast of the Christian year. It is a time, I quite agree, for the giving of presents.'

When they finally threw us out of Pommeroy's, and after we had considered the possibility of buying the Bishop brandy in the Cock Tavern, and even beer in the Devereux, I let my instinct, like an aged horse, carry me on to the Underground and home to Gloucester Road, and there discovered the rissoles, like some traces of a vanished civilization, fossilized in the oven. She Who Must Be Obeyed was already in bed, feigning sleep. When I climbed in beside her she opened a hostile eye.

'You're drunk, Rumpole!' she said. 'What on earth have you been doing?'

'I've been having a legal discussion,' I told her, 'on the subject of the admissibility of certain evidence. Vital, from my client's point of view. And, just for a change, Hilda, I think I've won.'

'Well, you'd better try and get some sleep.' And she added with a sort of satisfaction, 'I'm sure you'll be feeling quite terrible in the morning.'

As with all the grimmer predictions of She Who Must Be Obeyed this one turned out to be true. I sat in Court the next day with the wig feeling like a lead weight on the brain, and the stiff collar sawing the neck like a blunt execution. My mouth tasted of matured birdcage and from a long way off I heard Wrigglesworth say to Bridget O'Dowd, who stood looking particularly saintly and virginal in the witness-box, 'About a week before this did you see the defendant, Edward Timson, on your staircase flourishing any sort of weapon?'

It is no exaggeration to say that I felt deeply shocked and considerably betrayed. After his promise to me, Wrigglesworth had turned his back on the spirit of the great Christmas festival. He came not to bring peace but a sword.

I clambered with some difficulty to my feet. After my forensic efforts of the evening before, I was scarcely in the mood for a legal argument. Mr Justice Vosper looked up in surprise and greeted me in his usual chilly fashion.

'Yes, Mr Rumpole. Do you object to this evidence?'

Of course I object, I wanted to say. It's inhuman, unnecessary, unmerciful and likely to lead to my losing another case. Also, it's clearly contrary to a solemn and binding contract entered into after a number of glasses of the Bishop's putative port. All I seemed to manage was a strangled, 'Yes.'

'I suppose Mr Wrigglesworth would say,' Vosper, J, was, as ever, anxious to supply any argument that might not yet have occurred to the prosecution, 'that it is evidence of "system".'

'System?' I heard my voice faintly and from a long way off. 'It may be, I suppose. But the Court has a discretion to omit evidence which may be irrelevant and purely prejudicial.'

'I feel sure Mr Wrigglesworth has considered the matter most carefully and that he would not lead this evidence unless he considered it entirely relevant.'

I looked at the Mad Monk on the seat beside me. He was smiling at me with a mixture of hearty cheerfulness and supreme pity, as though I were sinking rapidly and he had come to administer supreme unction. I made a few ill-chosen remarks to the Court, but I was in no condition, that morning, to enter into a complicated legal argument on the admissibility of evidence.

It wasn't long before Bridget O'Dowd had told a deeply disapproving jury all about Eddie 'Turpin' Timson's sword. 'A man,' the Judge said later in his summing up about young Edward, 'clearly prepared to attack with cold steel whenever it suited him.'

When the trial was over, I called in for refreshment at my favourite watering hole and there, to my surprise, was my opponent Wrigglesworth, sharing an expensive-looking bottle with Detective Inspector Wainwright, the Officer-in-Charge of the case. I stood at the bar, absorbing a consoling glass of Pommeroy's ordinary, when the DI came up to the bar for cigarettes. He gave me a friendly and maddeningly sympathetic smile.

'Sorry about that, sir. Still, win a few, lose a few. Isn't that it?'

'In my case lately, it's been win a few, lose a lot!'

'You couldn't have this one, sir. You see, Mr Wrigglesworth had promised it to me.'

'He had *what*?'

'Well, I'm retiring, as you know. And Mr Wrigglesworth promised me faithfully that my last case would be a win. He promised me that, in a manner of speaking, as a Christmas present. Great man is our Mr Wrigglesworth, sir, for the spirit of Christmas.'

I looked across at the Mad Monk and a terrible suspicion entered my head. What was all that about a present for the Bishop? I searched my memory and I could find no trace of our having, in fact, bought wine for any sort of cleric. And was Wrigglesworth as inexperienced as he would have had me believe in the art of selecting claret?

As I watched him pour and sniff a glass from his superior bottle, and hold it critically to the light, a horrible suspicion crossed my mind. Had the whole evening's events been nothing but a deception, a sinister attempt to nobble Rumpole, to present him with such a stupendous hangover that he would stumble in his legal argument? Was it all in aid of DI Wainwright's Christmas present?

I looked at Wrigglesworth, and it would be no exaggeration to say the mind boggled. He was, of course, perfectly right about me. I just didn't recognize evil when I saw it.

Rumpole and the Boat People

'You'll have to do it, Rumpole. You'll be a different man.'

I considered the possibilities. I was far from satisfied, naturally, with the man I was, but I had grown, over the years, used to his ways. I knew his taste in claret, his rate of consumption of small cigars, and I had grown to have some respect for his mastery of the art of cross-examination. Difficult, almost impossible, as he was to live with on occasions, I thought we could manage to rub along together for our few remaining years.

'A different man, did you say?'

Dr MacClintock, the slow-speaking, Edinburgh-bred quack to whom my wife Hilda turns in times of sickness, took a generous gulp of the sherry she always pours him when he visits our mansion flat. (It's lucky that all his NHS patients aren't so generous or the sick of Gloucester Road would be tended by a reeling medico, yellow about the gills and sloshed on amontillado.) Then he said,

'If you follow my simple instructions, Rumpole, you'll become a different man entirely.'

Being Horace Rumpole in his sixties, still slogging round the Old Bailey with sore feet, a modest daily hangover and an aching back was certainly no great shakes, but who else could I be? I considered the possibilities of becoming Guthrie Featherstone, QC, MP, our learned Head of Chambers, or Claude Erskine-Brown, or Uncle Tom, or even Dr MacClintock, and retreated rapidly into the familiar flesh.

'All you have to do, old man, is lose two or three stone,' the doctor told me.

' "Old man"?' I looked closely at the sherry-swilling sawbones and saw no chicken.

'Just two or three stone, Rumpole. That's all you have to lose.'

Hilda was warming to her latest theme, that there was too much Rumpole.

'It's a very simple diet, perfectly simple. I've got it printed here.' Dr MacClintock produced a card with the deftness of a conjurer. The trick was known as the vanishing Rumpole, and the rapid materialization of a thinner and more eager barrister.

'No fat, of course.' The doctor repeated the oath on the card. 'Because it makes *you* fat. No meat, too rich in protein. No bread or potatoes, too many calories. No pastries, puddings, sweetmeats or sugar. No biscuits. No salt on the food. Steer clear of cheese. I don't recommend fruit to my patients because of its acid qualities. Eggs are perfectly all right if hard-boiled. Not too many though, or you won't do your business.'

'My business in the Courts?' I didn't follow.

'No. Your business in the lavatory.'

'Didn't you say,' Hilda put in encouragingly, 'that Rumpole could eat spinach?'

'Oh yes. As much spinach as he likes. And brown rice for roughage. Now you could manage a diet like that, couldn't you, Rumpole? Otherwise I can't be responsible for your heart.'

'I suppose I might manage it for a while.' The Rumpole ticker, I knew, had come to resent the pressure put on it during a number of hard-fought battles in front of the mad Judge Bullingham down the Bailey. 'Of course, it'd have to be washed down by a good deal of claret. Château-bottled. I could afford that with all this saving on pastries and puddings.'

'Oh, good heavens!' The quack held his sherry glass out for a refill. 'No alcohol!'

'You're asking me to give up claret?'

'No alcohol of any sort!'

'Certainly not, Rumpole.' Hilda was determined.

'But you might as well ask me to give up breathing.'

'It'll come quite easily to you, after a couple of days.'

'I suppose when you've been dead a couple of days you find it quite easy to give up breathing.'

'It's you that mentioned death, Rumpole.' The doctor smiled at me tolerantly. 'I haven't said a word about it. Now why not get your wife to take you away for a holiday? You could spare a couple of weeks at the seaside, surely? It's always easier to give things up when you're on holiday.'

Brown rice, spinach and a holiday were not an appetizing combination, but Hilda seemed delighted at the prospect.

'We could go down to Shenstone, Doctor. I've always wanted to go to Shenstone-on-Sea. My old friend Jackie Bateman, you know I've told you, Rumpole, Jackie Hopkins as was, we were at school together, runs a little business at Shenstone with her husband. Jackie's always writing begging me to come down to Shenstone. Apparently it's a dear little place and extremely quiet.'

'My partner, Dr Entwhistle, keeps his boat at Shenstone.' Dr Mac-Clintock seemed to think this fact might lend some glamour to the hole. 'It's quite a place for the boating community.'

'I don't boat,' I said gloomily.

'Better not, Rumpole,' the doctor was actually laughing. 'Better not take out a small dinghy. You might sink it! Shenstone sounds just the place for you to get a bit of rest. Pick a small hotel. A *temperance* hotel. That's all you'll be needing.'

That night, Hilda booked us in to the Fairview Private Hotel in Shenstone-on-Sea, and wrote off to Mrs Bateman, the former Miss Jackie Hopkins, announcing the glad tidings. I viewed the approaching visit with some dismay, tempered by the knowledge that it did seem to be becoming a minor Everest expedition for me to mount the shortest staircase. My bones ached, my head seemed stuffed with cottonwool and buttons were flying off me like bullets at the smallest unexpected move. Perhaps desperate measures were called for and a holiday *would* do me good. We set out for Shenstone armed with umbrellas, mackintoshes, heavy pullovers and, in my case, the *Complete Sherlock Holmes Stories*, Marjoribanks's *Life of Sir Edward Marshall Hall* and *The Oxford Book of English Verse* (I make it a rule not to read anything I haven't read before, except for *The Times* and briefs). We launched ourselves into the unknown as, up to the time of our departure, Mrs Jackie Bateman hadn't been heard from.

Shenstone-on-Sea, in the county of Norfolk, was to be seen, like most English pleasure resorts, through a fine haze of perpetual rain.

However, the main feature of Shenstone-on-Sea was undoubtedly the wind. It blew straight at you from the Ural mountains, crossing some very icy steppes, parky portions of Poland, draughty country round Dortmund and the flats of Holland, on the way. In this cruel climate the inhabitants gathered, stowing spinnakers and splicing ropes with bluish fingers, the wind blowing out their oilskins tight as a trumpeter's cheeks and almost doffing their bobble hats. For Shenstone-on-Sea was, as my Scottish medical man had said, quite the place for the boat community.

Apart from watching the daily armada of small boats set out, there was little or nothing to do at Shenstone. Hilda and I sat in the residents' lounge at the Fairview Hotel, and I read or did the crossword while she knitted or wrote postcards to other old school friends and we listened to the rain driven across the windows by the prevailing wind. On our arrival we telephoned Jackie Bateman and got no reply. Then we called on her at the address Hilda had, which turned out to be a shop on the harbour called Father Neptune's Boutique, a place for the sale of bobble hats, seamen's sweaters, yellow gumboots, tea mugs with the words 'Galley Slave' written on them and such-like nautical equipment. The Batemans, according to Hilda, owned this business and had a flat above the shop. We called, as I have said, but found the place silent and locked up, and got no answer when we rattled the door handle.

Hilda wrote a note for her elusive school friend, and put it through the door. We were standing looking helplessly at the silent shop, when someone spoke to us.

'She's moved. Gone away.'

A tallish, thin person clad in a balaclava helmet and a belted mackintosh, and sporting a large pair of field glasses, came by pushing a gaunt bicycle.

'Mrs Bateman's not here?' Hilda seemed slow to absorb the information.

'I tell you. She moved away. After it happened. Well. They reckoned she couldn't abide the place after that.'

'After what?' Hilda hadn't heard from Jackie Bateman since, she now remembered, the previous Christmas, and seemed not have been kept *au courant* with the major developments in her friend's life.

'Why, after the accident. When her husband got drowned. Hadn't you heard?'

'No, we hadn't. Oh dear.' Hilda looked surprised and shocked. 'What a terrible thing.'

The tall man pushed his bicycle away from us and we were left staring through the rain at the harbour where the frail boats were again putting out full of those, it now seemed, in considerable peril on the sea.

That night I was pecking away at a minute quantity of fish, almost entirely surrounded by spinach, in our private hotel, and moodily sipping water (an excellent fluid no doubt, most useful for filling radiators and washing socks, but of absolutely no value as a drink) when Hilda said,

'She was devoted to him, you know.'

'Devoted to whom?'

'To Barney. To her husband Barney Bateman. Jackie was. She always said he was such a wonderful man, and a terrific sailor with a really good sense of humour. Of course, he had your problem, Rumpole.'

'What's that? Judge Bullingham?'

'Don't be silly! Of course, I never met Barney, but Jackie told me he was a big man.'

'You mean fat?'

'That's what I think she meant. Jackie was always afraid he was going to get too heavy for dinghy racing. And he simply refused to go on a diet!'

'Sensible fellow.'

'How can you say he was sensible, Rumpole? Don't you remember, poor Jackie's husband's dead.'

Did Mr Bateman's weight become so gross that he simply sank with all hands? As I gave the lining of my stomach the unusual shock of a cascade of cold water, I decided not to ask the question, but to try at the earliest opportunity to get a little free time from She Who Must Be Obeyed.

My chance came the next day when Hilda said that she had a cold coming on, and I would have to take the morning walk alone. I sympathized with Hilda (although I supposed that the natural state of an inhabitant of Shenstone must be a streaming nose and a raised temperature) and left carefully in the direction of the cliffs, as a direct route towards licensed premises would have raised a questioning cry from the window of the residents' lounge.

I struggled up a path in a mist of rain and came, a little way out of town, upon the thin man with the balaclava helmet. He was staring through his powerful field glasses out to sea. I gave him a moderately depressed 'good morning', but he was too engrossed in watching something far out on the grey water to return my greeting. Then I took the next turn, down to the harbour and the Crab and Lobster, a large, old-fashioned pub with a welcoming appearance.

It was clearly the warmest place in Shenstone and the place was crowded. In very little time the landlord had supplied me with a life-restoring bottle of St Émilion and a couple of ham rolls, and I sat among the boat people in a cheerful fug, away from the knife-edged wind and the whining children in life jackets, among the polished brass and dangling lobster pots, looking at the signed photographs of regatta winners, all dedicated to 'Sam', whom I took to be the landlord. In pride of place among these pictures was one of a windswept but resolutely smiling couple in oilskins, proudly clutching a silver trophy with 'love from Jackie and Barney, to Sam and all the crowd at the Lobster' scrawled across it. The man seemed considerably and cheerfully overweight, and the colour print showed his flaming red hair and bushy beard. Jackie, Hilda's school friend, also looked extremely cheerful. She had clear blue eyes, short hair which must have been fair but was now going grey, and the sort of skin which showed its long exposure to force-nine gales. Such, I thought, were the women who flew round the world in primitive planes, crossed deserts or rode over No Man's Land on a bicycle. I bought Sam, the landlord, a large whisky and water, and in no time at all we were talking about the Batemans, a conversation in which a number of the regulars at the Crab and Lobster, also supplied with their favourite tipples, seemed anxious to join.

'One thing I could never understand about Jackie,' Sam said. 'I mean, she lost a wonderful personality like Barney Bateman, and they thought the world of each other. Never a cross word between the two of them!'

'And Barney was a man who always had a drink and a story for everyone. Never fumbled or rang the wife when it came to his round.'

A red-faced man in an anorak whom the others called Buster told me. 'As I say, I can't understand why after being married to Barney, the winner of the Shenstone regatta five years running, she ended up with a four-letter man like Freddy Jason! Hope he's not a friend of yours, is he?'

'Jason.' The name was entirely new to me.

'Jackie married him just six months after Barney died. We couldn't believe it.' A voluminous blonde bulging out of a pair of jeans and a fisherman's jersey shouted, 'Of course, I've never actually met Mr Jason. He's moved her up to Cricklewood.'

'Dreadful house,' said Buster. 'Absolutely miles from the sea.'

'Well, it is Cricklewood.' The blonde lady seemed prepared to excuse the house.

'Like I told you, Dora. I went there once when I was up in London. On business.'

'What business, Buster? Dirty weekend?' the seafaring woman addressed as Dora screamed, and after laughter from the boat people, Buster continued.

'Never you mind, Dora! Anyway, I looked up Freddy Jason in the book and rang Cricklewood. Finally Jackie came on the phone. Well, you remember what Jackie *used* to be like? "Come on over, Buster; stew's in the oven. We'll have a couple of bottles of rum and a sing-up round the piano." Not a bit of it. "Ever so sorry, dear. Freddy's not been all that well. We're not seeing visitors." '

'Can you imagine that coming from Jackie Bateman? "We're not seeing visitors!" ' Dora bawled at me, as though I would be bound to know. She was clearly used to conversation far out to sea, during gale-force winds.

'What you're saying is, there was a bit of a contrast between the two husbands?' I was beginning to get the sense of the meeting. 'At least she didn't repeat the same mistake; that's what most people do.'

'Barney wasn't a mistake,' Dora hailed me. 'Barney was a terrific yachtsman. And a perfect gent.'

I didn't repeat all this information to She Who Must Be Obeyed. To do so would only have invited a searching and awkward cross-examination about where I had heard it. But when we were back in London and recovering from our seaside holiday, Hilda told me she had had an unexpected telephone call from Jackie Bateman, Hopkins as was, Jason, as she had now discovered she had become. Apparently the boat woman had got our note by some means, and she wanted to bring her new husband to tea on Sunday to get 'a few legal tips' from Rumpole of the Bailey.

Hilda spent a great deal of Saturday with her baking tins in celebration of this unusual visit, and produced a good many rock cakes, jam tarts and a large chocolate sponge.

'Not for you, Rumpole,' she said in a threatening fashion. 'Remember, *you're* on a diet.'

In due course, Jackie turned up looking exactly like her photograph, bringing with her a thin and rather dowdy middle-aged man introduced as Freddy, who could not have been a greater contrast to the previous yachtsman and gent. Jason was dark, mouse-coloured and not red-haired; his one contribution to the conversation was to tell us that going out in any sort of boat made him seasick, and we discovered that he was a retired chartered accountant, whose hobby was doing chess problems. When Hilda pressed rock cakes and chocolate sponge on him, he waved her confections aside.

'What's the matter?' I asked him gloomily. 'Not on a diet too, are you?'

'Freddy never has to go on a diet,' his wife said with some sort of mysterious pride. 'He's one of nature's thin people.'

'That's right,' Freddy Jason told us. 'I simply never never put on weight.' All the same, I noticed that he didn't do any sort of justice to Hilda's baking, and he took his tea neat, without milk or sugar.

After some general chat we came on to the legal motive for the party.

'It's awfully boring, but naturally Barney was insured, and the insurance company paid out. That's how we were able to get married and buy the house. But now it seems that Chad Bateman, that's Barney's brother in New Zealand, has raised some sort of question about the estate. Look, can I leave you the letters? You see, we really don't know any lawyers we can trust.'

I had to say that I had only done one will case (in which I had been instructed from beyond the grave by a deceased military man) and that my speciality was violent death and classification of blood. However,

I was prepared to get the opinion of Claude Erskine-Brown, the civil lawyer in our Chambers (civil lawyers are concerned with money, criminal practitioners with questions of life and death) and I would give Mrs Jason, whose clear-eyed and sensible look of perfect trust I found appealing, the benefit of his deliberations in due course.

Before I had time to keep my promise, however, something happened of a dramatic nature. Hilda's old school-friend Jackie was arrested, as we heard the next week on the television news, on a charge of the wilful murder of her late husband, Barney Bateman.

We heard no more of Jackie Jason, Bateman, Hopkins and her troubles for a considerable period. And then, one morning, as I was walking into my Chambers in a state of some depression brought about by having mislaid about a stone of Rumpole in the course of my prolonged fast, my clerk Henry uttered words which were music to my ears.

'There's a new case for you, Mr Rumpole. A murder, from a new firm of solicitors.'

It was good news indeed. A new firm of solicitors meant a new source of work, claret and small cigars, and of all the dishes that figure on the Criminal Menu, murder is still the main course, or *pièce de résistance*.

'It's an interesting case, Mr Tonkin was telling me.' Henry handed me the bulky set of papers.

'Tonkin?'

'Of Teleman, Tonkin and Bird. That's the new firm from Norfolk. He says the odd thing about this murder is, they never found the body.'

'No corpse?' Without a corpse the thing should not, I thought, present much difficulty, although like all cases it would probably be easier without a client also. I looked down at the brief in my hands and saw the title on it '*R. v. Jason*'.

In due course, I read the papers and issued out into Fleet Street to find a taxi prepared to take me to Holloway Prison for an interview with Jackie Jason and Mr Tonkin. Waiting on the kerb, I was accosted by a tall figure wearing a bowler hat and an overcoat with a velvet collar, none other than our learned Head of Chambers, Guthrie Featherstone QC, MP.

'Hullo there, Horace!'

'Sorry, Guthrie. I'm just off to Holloway. Got a rather jolly murder.'

'I know.'

'Henry told you, did he? Strange thing, when I married She Who Must Be Obeyed, I never thought she'd be much help in providing me with work. But she's turned up trumps! She had the good luck to go to an excellent school where one of her form mates grew up to be charged with an extremely interesting . . .'

'I know.' Guthrie repeated himself. 'Jackie Jason.'

'*How* do you know?' Was Featherstone, I wondered, a spare-time boat person? His reply quite wiped off my grin of triumph and added, I thought, new difficulties to our defence.

'Because I'm leading you, of course. It'll be a pleasure to have you sitting behind me again, Horace. Ah, there's a cab. Holloway Prison, please.'

Because I never took silk and was not rewarded by the Lord Chancellor with a long wig and a pair of ceremonial knee breeches I am compelled, in certain cases, to sit behind some Queen's Counsel and, although I am old enough to be Featherstone's father, I must be his 'junior', and sit behind the QC, MP and listen, with what patience I can muster, to him asking the wrong questions. In the Shenstone-on-Sea murder, it would hardly be a pleasure. No doubt with his talent for agreeing with the Judge, Guthrie Featherstone could manage to lose even a corpseless case, in the nicest possible way.

'The evidence against us is pretty strong,' Featherstone said, as we sat together in the taxi bound for the ladies' nick. 'Two heads are better than one in a matter like this, Horace.'

'I didn't find that,' I told him, 'when I won the Penge Bungalow Murders, entirely on my own.'

'Penge Bungalow? Oh, I think you told me. That was one of your old cases, wasn't it? Well, people couldn't afford leading Counsel in those days. It was before legal aid.'

So, QCs have become one of the advantages of our new affluence, I was about to say, like fish fingers and piped music in Pommeroy's Wine Bar. However, I thought better of it and we reached the castellated turreted entrance to Holloway Prison in silence.

I may be, indeed I am, extremely old-fashioned. No doubt an army of feminists are prepared to march for women to have equal rights to long-term imprisonment, but I dislike the sight of ladies in the cooler. For a start, Holloway is a far less jovial place than Brixton. The lady screws look more masculine and malignant than gentleman screws, and female hands never seem made for slopping out.

When we got to the Holloway interview room, my new solicitor Tonkin rose to greet us. He was an upright, military-looking man with a ginger moustache and an MCC tie.

'Mr Featherstone. Mr Rumpole. Good of you to come, gentlemen. This is the client.'

Jackie Jason was looking as tanned and healthy as if she'd just stepped off a boat on a sunny day into the Crab and Lobster. She smiled at me from a corner of the room and said, 'I'm so glad I could find you a legal problem more in your line, Horace.'

I looked at her with gratitude. No doubt it was Jackie who had had the wisdom to choose Rumpole for the defence, and her solicitor Tonkin who had been weak-minded enough to choose Featherstone as a leader.

'I think it would help if you were just to tell us your story in your own way,' Featherstone kicked off the conference. I was sure that it would help him; no doubt he'd been far too busy with his parliamentary duties to read the brief.

'Well, Barney and I,' Jackie started.

'That was the late Mr Barney Bateman?' Featherstone asked laboriously.

'Yes. We used to live at Shenstone-on-Sea. Well, we were boat people.'

'Mrs Jason doesn't mean Far Eastern refugees,' I explained to my leader. 'She means those who take to the water in yellow oilskins and sailing dinghies, with toddlers in inflated life jackets, and usually call out the lifeboat to answer their cries of distress.'

'Barney and I never had toddlers,' Jackie said firmly.

'Horace, if I could put the questions?' Featherstone tried to assert his leadership.

'And we were pretty experienced sailors.'

'Yes,' I said thoughtfully, 'of course you were. And yet your husband died in a yachting accident.'

'Just remind me . . .' Featherstone continued to grope for the facts.

'We went out very early that day. We wanted to sail the regatta course without anyone watching.'

'You and your late . . . husband?' Featherstone was examining the witness.

'Barney and I.'

'You were on good terms?'

'Always. He was a marvellous man, Barney. Anyone'd tell you, anyone in the crowd in the Crab and Lobster at Shenstone. We were the best of pals.'

Dear old pals, jolly old pals. Everyone in the Crab and Lobster agreed with that. And yet one pal fell out of the boat and his body was never recovered.

'You say there was a sudden gust of wind?' Featherstone was making a nodding acquaintance with his brief.

'Yes,' Jackie told him. 'It came out of nowhere. Well, it will in that bit of sea. Barney was on his feet and the boom must have hit his head. It was all so unexpected. The boat went over and there I was in the drink.'

'And your husband?'

'Stunned, I suppose. By the boom, you see. I looked for him for ten minutes, swimming, and then, well, I clung to the boat. I couldn't get her righted, not on my own I couldn't. I waited almost half an hour like that and then the harbour motorboat came out. They'd got a phone call. Someone must have seen us. I was lucky, really. There aren't many people around in Shenstone at six o'clock in the morning.'

'But if you and your husband were on perfectly good terms . . .' Featherstone was frowning, puzzled, when Mr Tonkin gave him some unhelpful clarification.

'That's not really the point, is it, Mr Featherstone? It's the policy with the Colossus Mercantile that made them bring this prosecution.' He was referring to the subject of the correspondence that Jackie Jason had given me when she was still at liberty, so I knew a little about the Colossus policy. Featherstone looked blank. If he hadn't been a politician he would have said, 'All-night sitting last night. I never got round to reading the brief.' As it was, he said,

'Do just remind me . . .'

'Mrs Jason insured her first husband's life with the Colossus Mercantile just two weeks before the accident,' Tonkin explained. 'Before these inquiries got going she had remarried and collected the money.'

'How much was it? Just remind me,' Featherstone asked.

Mr Tonkin gave us the motive which had undoubtedly led to the prosecution of the yachtswoman.

'Just about two hundred thousand pounds.'

'You know I'm going to Norfolk today,' I reminded Hilda at breakfast some weeks later. 'It's Jackie's trial.'

'You will get her off, won't you, Rumpole? She's relying on you, you know.' Hilda said it as if the case presented no particular problem.

'I might get her off. I don't know about my friend.'

'You didn't tell me you were taking a friend with you.' Hilda looked at me with sudden suspicion.

'Didn't I? I'm taking Guthrie Featherstone. It's a secret romance. We've been passionately in love for years, Guthrie and I.'

'Rumpole, I don't know why you deliberately say things you know will annoy me. Also, it's not in the least degree funny!'

'I thought it was a *little* funny.'

'This is a letter from Lucy Loman.' This time Hilda showed me a pale green envelope.

'Is it really? I thought it was your pools.'

'Do stop being silly, Rumpole! I was at school with "Lanky" Loman!' As I wondered if there were anyone that Hilda *hadn't* been at school with, she went on, 'She tells me her daughter Tessa has just divorced a bankrupt garage proprietor with a foul temper and a taste for whisky.'

'Sounds a reasonable thing to do.'

'The problem is that Tessa has remarried.'

'Has she indeed?'

'Yes. A bankrupt ex-launderette owner with a much worse temper and a taste for gin.'

'So there's been no real change?'

'No. People don't change, do they?'

I was beginning to find She Who Must Be Obeyed unusually depressing that morning, when she went on thoughtfully,

'When they change partners, they always go for the same again, only slightly worse.'

Was there some similar, but even more ferocious version of She waiting to entrap me the second time around? The thought was too terrible to contemplate. I prepared to take self and brief off to Liverpool Street. On my way out, I said,

'Well, if you're going to change husbands while I'm gone . . .'

'Please don't be silly, Rumpole. I've had to tell you that once already. I'm quite prepared to make do with you, provided you're a good deal thinner.'

Make do for the rest of our natural lives, I thought. Matrimony and murder both carry a mandatory life sentence.

In the train from Liverpool Street Featherstone looked at me in a docile and trusting manner, as though he were depending on his learned junior to get him and his client out of trouble.

'I suppose you've read the birdwatcher's evidence?' he started gloomily.

'Mr "Nosey Parker" Spong? Saw the whole thing through a pair of strong opera glasses? Yes, I've read it.'

'Odd he never went to the police straight away.'

'The whole timetable's odd. The police and the insurance company accept her story of an accident. Colossus Mercantile pays out, she collects her two hundred thousand, calls herself a widow, marries Mr Jason, a retired accountant, buys a small house in Cricklewood and then . . .'

'The long-lost brother turns up from New Zealand.'

'Mr Chad Bateman. Hungry for his brother's estate which our client won't get if she's a murderess. So he disputes the insurance payment and starts inquiries. Advertises for the long-lost birdwatcher and puts together a case.'

'Puts together far too good a case for my liking.'

A silence fell between us, and somewhere in East Anglia I said,

'Featherstone?'

'Yes, Horace?'

'I get the feeling sometimes that you don't like me very much.'

'Now, whatever could have given you that idea?' My learned leader looked pained.

'We don't see eye to eye always on the running of Chambers. I find your cross-examination feeble and your politics anaemic and I don't mind saying so. I do ask you, however, to win this case. If you don't I may be in for a very rough time indeed from She Who Must Be Obeyed. She doesn't like having her old school chums convicted of murder.'

'You've got to help me, Horace.' The man looked positively desperate, so I gave my learned leader the benefit of a full account of my conversation with the habitués of the Crab and Lobster on the day I broke into my diet. When I had finished, Featherstone didn't look any more cheerful.

'Does that tell us anything?'

'Oh yes. Three things to be precise.'

'What on earth?'

'That the Batemans never had a cross word. That Jackie's second husband doesn't like visitors and that Barney Bateman won the regatta five times.'

'I don't see how that helps.'

'You're right. It doesn't help at all.'

'Now who's being depressing, Horace?'

'I know,' I told him perfectly frankly. 'I find the whole business very depressing indeed.'

In due course, I found myself sitting in the ancient, panelled Norfolk courtroom, in a place of importance behind my undecided leader, with a jury of solid East Anglian citizens and old Piers Craxton, a reasonably polite Judge, sent to try us. Our opponent was a jovial local silk named Gerald Gaunt who, being for the prosecution and with a strongish case, looked a great deal less gloomy than the nervous artificial silk in front of me. The witness-box was occupied by a figure familiar to me from my visit to Shenstone, the birdwatcher whom I had last seen surveying the North Sea with a pair of strong field glasses. Without his balaclava helmet, he looked older and slightly less dotty than when I had first seen him.

'Your name is Henry Arthur Spong?' Gaunt asked the ornithologist in the witness-box.

'Yes it is.'

'Do you remember being out very early one morning in July two years ago?'

'Tell him not to bloody well lead!' I whispered in a vain attempt to keep my learned leader on his toes.

'Ssh, Rumpole. I don't like to interrupt. It creates a bad impression.' Featherstone sounded deeply embarrassed.

'Creates a damn sight worse impression to let him lead the witness.'

'I remember it clearly. It was quite light at 6 a.m. and the date was July the 6th,' Mr Spong intruded on our private dialogue.

'How can he remember that?' I whispered to Guthrie Featherstone, and Mr Spong supplied the answer.

'I wrote a note in my diary. I saw a number of kittiwake and gannets and I thought I saw a Mediterranean shearwater. I have all that noted down in my birdwatcher's diary. I was looking out to sea through a pair of powerful field glasses.'

'Did you happen to spot a boat?' Gaunt asked and I prodded Featherstone again.

'Don't let him lead!'

'Please, Rumpole! Leave it to me.'

'Mr Spong. Out of deference to my learned friend's learned junior, I will frame the question in a non-leading form.' Gerald Gaunt raised a titter in Court. 'Did you see anything unusual?'

'Yes.' Spong clearly knew what he was being asked about. 'I saw a boat.'

'Surprise, surprise!' I whispered to Featherstone, who tried not to hear me.

'I noticed it because . . .'

'Yes. Tell us why you noticed it.' Gaunt encouraged the birdwatcher.

'There were two people standing up in it. One, I thought, was a man. He had a red beard. The other was a woman.'

'What did they appear to be doing?'

'I would say, struggling together. I couldn't see all that clearly.'

'And then?'

'Then the man seemed to fall from the side of the boat.' Gaunt, as any good barrister would, allowed a substantial pause for that to sink in, and then he asked,

'Tell me, Mr Spong. Was there any wind at the time?'

'No wind at all. No. It had been gusty a little earlier, but at the time the man fell from the boat it was perfectly calm.' It wasn't a helpful answer, being clean contrary to our client's instructions.

'And after he fell?'

'The woman waited for about five minutes.'

'She didn't dive in after him?'

'No.'

I saw the Judge make a note and the jury looked at the woman in the dock with no particular sympathy.

'What did she do then?'

'She deliberately upset the boat.'

During Gaunt's next and even longer pause, not only the Judge but the reporters were writing hard and the jury looked even less friendly.

'What do you mean by that, exactly?'

'She stood on the side and then swung herself out, pulling on the side ropes. She seemed to me to capsize the boat deliberately.'

'And after it had capsized?'

'She went into the water, of course. Then I saw her clinging to the boat.'

'What did you do?'

'Well, I thought she might be in some danger, so I bicycled off to telephone the police.'

'To the harbour?'

'Yes. The harbour office was locked up. It was so early you see. It took me some time to wake anyone in the cottages.'

'Thank you, Mr Spong.'

Gaunt sat down, clearly delighted with his witness and Guthrie Featherstone rose to cross-examine. Tall and distinguished, at least he managed to *look* like a barrister.

'Mr Spong,' he started, in his smoothest voice. 'You knocked up a Mr Newbold in one of the cottages?'

'Yes, I did. I banged on the door, and he put his head out of the window.'

'What did you tell him?'

'I asked him to phone the police and tell them that there was a woman in trouble with a boat.'

'You didn't tell him anything else you'd seen?'

'No, I didn't.'

'And having told Mr Newbold that a woman was in trouble with a boat, you got on your bicycle and rode away?'

'Yes. That is correct.'

Not a bad exchange, for Featherstone. I whispered my instructions to him.

'Leave it there.'

'What?' Guthrie whispered back, turning his head away from the witness.

'Don't give him a chance to explain! Comment on it later, to the jury.'

The trouble with leaders is that they won't take their learned junior's advice. Featherstone couldn't resist trying to gild the lily.

'Why didn't you tell Mr Newbold or the police the whole story? About the struggle in the boat and so on?'

'Well, sir. I thought I saw a Mediterranean shearwater, which would be extremely interesting so far out of its territory. I got on my bike to follow its flight, but when I spotted it later from the cliffs, it was a great shearwater, which is interesting enough.'

I sighed with resignation. From a dedicated birdwatcher, the answer was totally convincing.

'Mr Spong. Did you think sighting shearwaters was more important than a possible murder?' Featherstone asked with carefully simulated anger and incredulity.

'Yes, of course I did.'

Of course he did. The jury could recognize a man dedicated to his single interest in life.

'In fact, you only came forward when Mr Chad Bateman arrived from New Zealand and advertised for you?'

'That is correct.'

'How much did he get paid?' I whispered the question ferociously to my leader's back.

'Did you get paid for your information?' At least Featherstone obeyed orders, sometimes.

'I was given no money.'

'Thank you, Mr Spong.' My leader folded his silk gown about him and prepared to subside, but I stimulated him into a final question.

'Don't sit down! Ask him what he got apart from money,' I whispered, and my leader uncoiled himself. After a pause which made it look as though he'd thought of the question himself he said,

'Just one thing. Did you get rewarded in any other way?'

'I was offered a holiday in New Zealand,' Spong admitted.

'By the deceased's brother?'

'Yes.'

'Do you intend to take it?'

'Oh yes.' And Spong turned to the jury with a look of radiant honesty. 'There are some extremely interesting birds in New Zealand. But I must make this clear. It hasn't made the slightest difference to my telling the truth in this Court.'

I looked at the jury. I knew one thing beyond reasonable doubt. They believed the birdwatcher.

'Yes, thank you, Mr Spong.' Featherstone was finally able to sit down and turn to me for some whispered reassurance.

'It was a disaster, old darling,' I told him, but admitted, 'not entirely your fault.'

Later, Featherstone had another opportunity to practise the art of cross-examination on the police officer-in-charge of the case.

'Inspector Salter. The body of Barney Bateman was never recovered?' he asked. Well, at least it was a safe question, the answer to which was not in dispute.

'No, sir.' The Inspector, who looked as though he enjoyed fishing from his own small boat, had no trouble in agreeing.

'Is that not an unusual factor, in this somewhat unusual case?' Featherstone soldiered on, more or less harmlessly.

'Not really, sir.'

'Why do you say that?'

'There are particularly strong currents off Shenstone, sir. We have warnings put up to swimmers. Unfortunately, there have been many drowning accidents where bodies have never been recovered.'

'Did you say "accidents", Inspector?'

'Oh Featherstone, my old sweetheart. Don't try to be too brilliant,' I whispered, I hoped inaudibly. 'Just plod, Featherstone. It suits your style far better.'

'We have had bodies lost in accidents, yes, sir,' Inspector Salter answered carefully. 'I'm by no means suggesting that *this* was an accident. In fact, the view of the police is that it was deliberate.'

The Judge interrupted mercifully to spare Featherstone embarrassment.

'Yes. Thank you, Inspector Salter. I'm sure we all understand what the police are suggesting here.'

'If your Lordship pleases.' There was another rustle of silk as Featherstone sat. I had warned him. He should plod, just plod, and never attempt brilliance.

During the luncheon break we went to see our client in the cells.

'Mrs Jason. I'm sure it's a nerve-racking business, giving evidence on a charge of murder.' Featherstone was doing his best to prepare our client for the ordeal to come. But Jackie gave him a far too cheerful smile.

'I've been in cross-Channel races with Barney. And round Land's End in a force-nine gale which took away our mast in the pitch dark. I don't see that Mr Gaunt's questions are going to frighten me.'

'There's just one thing.' I thought I ought to insert a word of warning. 'I think the jury are going to believe the birdwatcher. It would be nice if we didn't have to quarrel with too much of his evidence.'

'What do you mean, it would be nice?' Jackie looked at me impatiently. 'That man Spong was talking absolute nonsense.'

'Well, for instance, he said that you were standing up in the boat together? Now, what could you have been doing – other than fighting, of course?'

'I don't know.' Jackie frowned. 'What could we have been doing?'

'Well, perhaps,' I made a suggestion, 'kissing each other goodbye?'

'That's ridiculous! Why on earth did you say that? Anyway,' she looked at Featherstone, 'who'll be asking me the questions in Court?'

'I shall, Mrs Jason,' he reassured her, 'as your leading Counsel. Mr Rumpole won't be asking you any questions at all.'

Our client looked as if the news came to her as a considerable relief. Featherstone's questions would be like a gentle following breeze, and Rumpole's awkward voice would not be heard. However, I had to warn her, and said,

'Gerald Gaunt's going to ask you some questions for the prosecution as well. You should be prepared for that, otherwise they're going to strike you like a force-nine gale amidships.'

'Don't worry, Mrs Jason.' Featherstone poured his well-oiled voice on the choppy waters of our conference. 'I'm sure you'll be more than a match for the prosecuting Counsel. Now, let's go through your proof again, shall we?'

In the course of time, Featherstone steered Jackie through her examination-in-chief, more or less smoothly. At least he managed to avoid the hidden rocks and shallows, but more by ignoring their existence and hoping for the best than by expert navigation. Finally, he had to sit down and leave her unprotected and without an anchor, to the mercy of such winds as might be drummed up by the cross-examination of our learned friend, Mr Gerald Gaunt, QC, who rose, and started off with a gentle courtesy which was deceptive.

'Mrs Jason. Your husband was a swimmer?'

'Barney could swim, yes. The point was,' Jackie answered confidently, 'we were too far out to swim ashore.'

'Oh, I quite agree,' Gaunt smiled at her. 'And he always said, didn't he, that it was far safer to cling to the wreckage and wait to be picked up than attempt a long and exhausting swim against the current?'

'Any experienced sailor would tell you that.' Jackie spoke to him as to a novice yachtsman.

'And that's exactly what *you* did?'

'Yes,' Jackie admitted.

'Why didn't your husband?'

'As I told you. He must have been stunned by the boom as we went about.'

Gaunt nodded and then produced a document from his pile of papers.

'I have here the account which you gave to the insurance company at the time. You said "the accident took place between the eighth and ninth marker buoys of the regatta course".'

'Yes.'

'Halfway between?'

'About that.'

'With the wind from the quarter it was on that morning, you could have sailed between those two points without going about at all, could you not?'

The healthy-looking woman in the witness-box seemed somewhat taken aback by his expertise. After a small hesitation she said,

'Perhaps we could.'

'Then why didn't you?' Gaunt was no longer smiling.

'Perhaps we're not all as clever as you, Mr Gaunt. Perhaps Barney made a mistake.'

'Made a mistake?' Gaunt looked extravagantly puzzled. 'On a course where he'd raced and won five times?'

Jackie Jason was proving to be the worst kind of witness. She was over emphatic, touchy and had treated the question as an insult. I could see the jury starting to lose faith in her defence.

'Anyway, you've never been out from Shenstone on the regatta course.' She raised her voice, making matters a good deal worse. 'I don't know what you know about it, Mr Gaunt!'

'Mrs Jason!' the Judge warned her. 'Just confine yourself to answering the questions. Mr Gaunt is merely doing his duty with his usual ability.'

'Mrs Jason.' Gaunt was quiet and courteous again. 'Did you tell your husband you'd taken out this large life insurance?'

The jury were looking hard at my client, as she did her best to avoid the question.

'I didn't tell him the exact amount. I ran our business affairs.'

'Which were in a terrible mess, weren't they?'

'Not terrible, no.' She answered cautiously, and our opponent fished out another devastating document.

'I have here the certified accounts for the shop, Father Neptune's Boutique, which you ran in Shenstone. Had a petition in bankruptcy been filed by one of your suppliers?'

'You seem to know all about it.' Again, the answer sounded angry and defensive.

'Oh yes, I do.' Gaunt assured her, cheerfully. 'And were the mortgage repayments considerably overdue on your cottage at Shenstone-on-Sea?'

'We only needed a bit of luck to pay off our debts.'

'And the "bit of luck" was your husband's death, wasn't it?'

It was a cruel question, but I knew her answer chilled the hearts of the jury. It came coldly, and after a long pause.

'I suppose it came at the right moment, from the business point of view.'

'I thought that she stood up to that reasonably well.'

Featherstone and I were removing the fancy dress in the local robing room and he turned to me, once again, for a reassurance that I failed to give.

'It was a disaster,' I said. 'Can't wait to chat. I'm off to London.'

'London?' Featherstone looked perplexed. 'We could have had dinner together and discussed my final speech.'

'Before your final speech, we ought to discuss whom we're going to call as a witness.'

'Witness? Have we got a witness?'

But I was on my way to the door.

'See you here in the morning. We'll talk about our witness.'

I left my puzzled leader and caught an Inter-City train. I sat munching an illicit teacake as a railway guard, pretending to be an air hostess, came over the intercom, and announced that we were due on the ground at Liverpool Street approximately twenty minutes late, and apologized for the delay. (I waited to be told to fasten my seat belt because of a spot of turbulence around Bishop's Stortford.) What I was doing was strictly unprofessional. We legal hacks are not supposed to chatter to witnesses in criminal matters, and Featherstone would have been deeply pained if he had known where I was going. And yet I was on a quest for the truth and justice for Jackie, although she, also, would not have thought my journey really necessary. We arrived at Liverpool Street Station after half an hour's delay (Please collect all your hand baggage and thank you for flying British Rail), and I persuaded a taxi to take me to Cricklewood.

When we stopped at the anonymous surburban house, I was glad to see a light on in a downstairs room. Freddy Jason came to the door when I rang the electric chime. He was wearing an old sweater and a pair of bedroom slippers. He led me into a room where a television set was booming, and I noticed a tray decorated with the remains of a pork pie, French bread and cheese, and a couple of bottles of Guinness.

'Aren't you afraid,' I asked him, 'of putting on weight?'

'I told you. I don't.' He clicked the television set into silence.

'How long can you keep it up, I wonder?'

'Keep what up?'

'Being a thin person.'

He looked at me, the skinny, mousy ex-accountant and said, with real anxiety,

'How's the trial going? Jackie won't let me near the place. Is it going well?' He had a dry, impersonal voice like the click of a computer adding up an overdraft.

'It's going down the drain.'

He sat down then. He seemed exhausted.

'I warned her,' he said. 'I was afraid of that. What can I do?'

'Do? Come and give evidence for her!'

'I don't know.' Jason looked at me helplessly. 'What can I say? I didn't get to know Jackie until after Barney's accident. I don't think I'd be much help in the witness-box, do you?'

'It depends,' I said, 'on what you mean by help.'

'Well. Does Jackie want me to come?'

'Jackie doesn't know I'm asking you.'

'Well, then. I can't help.'

'Listen,' I said. 'Do you want your wife to do a life sentence in Holloway? *For a murder she didn't commit?*'

He looked deeply unhappy. A thin man who had become, however unwillingly, involved in a fat man's death.

'No,' he said. 'I don't want that.'

'Then you'd better come back on the Inter-City to Norfolk. You might as well finish off your supper. I mean, you don't have to worry, do you? About your weight.'

When I got to the Court the next morning I found Featherstone and Mr Tonkin anxiously pacing the hall. I gave them what comfort I could.

'Cheer up, old darlings. Things may not be as bad as you think. Her husband's here. He'll have to give evidence.'

'Freddy Jason?' Tonkin frowned.

'What on earth can *he* do for us?' Featherstone asked.

'Well, he certainly can't make things any worse. He can say he didn't get to know Jackie until after the accident. At least we can scotch the idea that she pushed Barney out to marry another man.'

'I suppose he could say that.' Mr Tonkin sounded doubtful. 'You think we need this evidence, Mr Rumpole?'

'Oh yes. I'm sure we need it.' I turned to my leader. 'Featherstone, I have a certain experience in this profession. I did win the Penge Bungalow Murders alone and without a leader.'

'So you're fond of telling me.'

'In any case, the junior is accorded the privilege of calling at least one witness in a serious case, with the permission of his learned leader, of course.'

'*You* want to call Jason?' In fact, Featherstone sounded extremely grateful. If the witness turned out a disaster, at least I should get the blame.

'Would you leave him to me?' I asked politely.

'All right, Rumpole. You call him. If you think it'll do the slightest good. At least you won't be whispering instructions to me the whole time.'

When the Court had reassembled, and the Judge had been settled down on his seat, found his place in his notebook, been given a sharp, new pencil and put on his glasses, he looked at my leader encouragingly and said,

'Yes, Mr Featherstone.'

'My Lord,' Featherstone said with a good deal of detachment, 'my learned junior, Mr Rumpole, will call the next witness.'

'Yes, Mr Rumpole?' His Lordship switched his attention to my humble self.

For the first and last time in the Shenstone-on-Sea murder trial, I staggered to my feet. The calm woman in the dock gave me a little smile of welcome.

'Yes, my Lord,' I said. 'I will call the next witness. Call Frederick Jason.'

'No!' Jackie was no longer smiling. As the usher went out to fetch her husband I whispered to Tonkin to keep our client quiet and tell her that the evidence I was about to call was vital to her case. In fact, it was one of those rare defences which depended on nothing less than the truth.

Tonkin was busy whispering to the lady in the dock when her pale and nervous second husband was brought into the Court and climbed into the witness-box. He took the oath very quietly.

'I swear to God that the evidence I shall give shall be the truth, the whole truth and nothing but the truth.'

It was then that I asked the question which I had been waiting to put throughout the trial.

'Is your name Barney Bateman?'

The reactions were varied. The Judge looked shocked. Showing some tolerance towards an ageing junior who was undoubtedly past it, he said,

'Haven't you made a mistake, Mr Rumpole?'

Featherstone felt it was his turn to whisper disapproving instructions and said,

'*Jason*, Rumpole. His name's Jason.'

My client remained silent. I asked the question again.

'I repeat. Is your name Barney Bateman?' Then the witness looked, for the first time, at the prisoner with a sort of apology. She seemed, suddenly, much older and too tired to protest. I reflected that there is a strange thing about taking the oath, it sometimes makes people tell the truth. Anyway, we had at least found the corpse in the Shenstone murder. It was now speaking, with increasing liveliness, to the learned Judge.

'My Lord,' the witness said, 'you can't go on trying Jackie for murder. I'm still alive, you see.' He smiled then, and I got a hint of the old Barney Bateman. 'Still alive and living in Cricklewood.'

It took another couple of days, of course, for the whole story to be told and for the good citizens of East Anglia to find Jackie Bateman (as she always was) not guilty of the murder with which she had been charged. Featherstone and I were eventually released and sat opposite each other in the British Rail tea car. My leader looked at me with a contented smile.

'Well, Horace,' he said. 'I think that can be notched up among my successes.'

'Oh yes, Guthrie,' I agreed. 'Many congratulations.'

'Thanks. Of course one depends a good deal on one's learned junior. Two heads are better than one, Horace. That's what I always say.'

'Three heads. Don't forget Hilda's.'

'Your wife's, Horace?'

'You can't fool She Who Must Be Obeyed,' I said. 'She told me that people don't change, they keep on marrying the same husband. Jackie Bateman did exactly that.'

It was quite a touching story, really. I was right about what they were doing when the birdwatcher spotted them. Not fighting, of course, but kissing each other goodbye. It was only to be a temporary parting. Barney was to swim ashore, to some quiet little bit of beach. Then he shaved off his beard, went on a diet, dyed his hair and waited for his loving wife to collect the boodle. The murder trial was a nasty gust of wind, but she thought she'd sail through it. He knew she wasn't going to. So he *had* to tell the truth.

'They'll charge her with the insurance swindle,' my leader reminded me.

'Oh, I'm afraid they will,' I said, biting into another teacake. 'I think I'll do that case, Featherstone, if you don't mind – alone and without a leader.'

That night, still grateful to Hilda, I took her out for a celebration dinner at my favourite restaurant in the Strand. She looked at me, somewhat aghast as I placed my order.

'Potted shrimps, I think. With plenty of hot toast. Oh, and steak-and-kidney pud, potatoes, swedes and Brussels sprouts. After that, we might consider the sweet trolley and I'll have the wine list, please.'

'Rumpole! You *mustn't* eat all that,' said She Who Must Be Obeyed.

'Oh yes I must. You're married to Rumpole, you know. Not some skinny ex-chartered accountant. You're stuck with him and so am I. We can't alter him, can we? Jackie's case proved that. You can't just change people entirely to suit your own convenience.'

Rumpole and the Genuine Article

I would like to dedicate this small volume of reminiscences to a much-abused and under-appreciated body of men. They practise many of the virtues most in fashion today. They rely strictly on free enterprise and individual effort. They adhere to strong monetarist principles. They do not join trade unions. Far from being in favour of closed shops, they do their best to see that most shops remain open, particularly during the hours of darkness. They are against state interference of any kind, being rugged individualists to a man. No. I'm not referring to lawyers. Will you please charge your glasses, ladies and gentlemen, and drink to absent friends, to the criminals of England. Without these invaluable citizens there would be no lawyers, no judges, no policemen, no writers of detective stories and absolutely nothing to put in the *News of the World*.

It is better, I suppose, that I raise a solitary glass. I once proposed such a toast at a Chambers party, and my speech was greeted by a studied silence. Claude Erskine-Brown examined his fingernails, our clerk Henry, buried his nose in his Cinzano Bianco. Uncle Tom, our oldest inhabitant, looked as though he was about to enter a terminal condition. Dianne, who does what passes for typing in our little establishment at Equity Court in the Temple, giggled, it is true, but then Dianne will giggle at almost anything and only becomes serious, I have noticed, whenever I make a joke. A devout barrister known to me as Sam Bollard (of whom more, unfortunately, in the following pages) took me aside afterwards and told me that he considered my remarks to be in excessively bad taste, calculated to cause a breach of the peace and bring our Chambers into disrepute.

Well, where would he be, I asked him, should the carrying of house-breaking implements by night vanish from the face of the earth? He told me that he could manage very well with his civil practice and happily didn't have to rely on the sordid grubbing for a living round the Old Bailey which I appeared to enjoy. I left him, having regretted the fact that men with civil practices are often so remarkably un-civil when addressing their elders.

So, as the night wears on, and as my wife Hilda (whom I must be careful not to refer to as 'She Who Must Be Obeyed' – not, at any rate, when she is in earshot) sleeps in her hairnet, dreaming of those far-off happy days when she cantered down the playing fields of Cheltenham Ladies College cradling her lacrosse net and aiming a sneaky pass at her old friend Dodo Perkins; as I sit at the kitchen table filling a barrister's notebook with reminiscences (I see the bare bones of a nasty little man-slaughter on the opposite page), I pour a glass of Château Thames Embankment (on special offer this week at Pommeroy's Wine Bar – how else would Jack Pommeroy get anyone to buy it?) and drink, alone and in silence, to those industrious lawbreakers who seem to be partici-pating in the one growth industry in our present period of recession. I can safely write that here. Whoever may eventually read these pages, you can bet your life that it won't be Sam Bollard.

I have been back in harness a good three years since my abortive retirement. I had, as you may remember, upped sticks to join my son Nick and his wife Erica in Florida, the Sunshine State.*

She Who Must Be Obeyed apparently enjoyed life in that curious part of the world and was starting, somewhat painfully at first, to learn the language. I, as others have done before me, found that Miami had very little to offer unless you happened to be a piece of citrus fruit, and I began to feel an unendurable nostalgia for rain, secretaries rubbing their noses pink with crumpled paper handkerchiefs on the platform at Temple Station and the congealed steak-and-mushroom pie for lunch-eon in the pub opposite the Old Bailey. I got bored with cross-examining the nut-brown octogenarians we met on the beach, and longed for a good up-and-downer with the Detective Inspector in charge of the case, or even a dramatic dust-up with his Honour Judge Bullingham (other-wise known as the Mad Bull). I was a matador with nothing left to do but tease the cat. I needed a foeman worthy of my steel.

It was a nice problem of bloodstains which brought me home to real

* See *Rumpole's Return* (*The First Rumpole Omnibus*).

life at the Old Bailey, and a good deal of diplomatic skill and dogged endurance which eased me back into the peeling leather chair behind the desk in my old room in Equity Court. When I returned, our Head of Chambers, Guthrie Featherstone, QC, MP (SDP), didn't actually unroll the red carpet for me. In fact, and in the nicest possible way, of course, he informed me that there was no room at the Inn, and would have left me to carry on what was left of my practice from a barrow in Shepherd's Bush Market, if I hadn't seen a way back into my old tenancy.

Well, that's all water under the bridge by now, and the last three years have gone much as the last what is it, almost half a century? That is to say they have passed with a few triumphant moments when the jury came back and said in clear and ringing tones, 'Not Guilty', and a few nasty ones when you have to bid goodbye to a client in the cells (what do you say: 'Win a few, lose a few', or 'See you again in about eight years'?). I have spent some enjoyable evenings in Pommeroy's Wine Bar, and my health has been no worse than usual, my only medical problem being a feeling of pronounced somnolence when listening to my learned friends making speeches, and a distinct nausea when hearing his Honour Judge Bullingham sum up.

So life was going on much as usual, and I was pursuing the even tenor of my way in Equity Court, when I was faced with a somewhat unusual case which caused a good deal of a stir in artistic circles at the time, it being concerned, as so many artistic and, indeed, legal problems are, with the question so easily put yet answered with such confusion, 'What is real and what is the most diabolical fake?'

I first had the unnerving feeling that I was drifting away from reality, and that many of my assumptions were being challenged, when Guthrie Featherstone, QC, MP, knocked briefly on my door and almost immediately inserted his face, which wore an expression of profound, not to say haunted anxiety, into my room.

'Rumpole!' he said, gliding in and closing the door softly behind him, no doubt to block out eavesdroppers. 'I say, Horace, are you working?'

'Oh no, Featherstone,' I said, 'I'm standing on my head playing the bagpipes.' The sarcasm was intentional. In fact I was wrestling with a nasty set of accounts, carefully doctored by a delinquent bank clerk. As, like the great apes, my mathematical abilities stop somewhere short at 'one, two, three, many', I have a rooted aversion to fraud cases. Studying accounts leads me to a good deal of blood, tears and the consumption of box loads of small cigars.

Quite undeterred by the sharpness of my reply, the recently committed Social Democrat moved soundlessly towards my desk and ran a critical eye over my blurred and inaccurate calculations.

'Well,' said Featherstone, 'fraud's a nice clean crime really. Not like most of your practice. No blood. No sex.'

'Do you think so, Featherstone?' I asked casually, the QC, MP having failed to grip my full attention. 'A bank cashier seems to have lost about half a million pounds. Probably his adding up was no better than mine.'

'Still, it's almost a respectable crime. Your practice has become quite decent lately. We may even see you prosecuting.'

'No thank you,' I said with the determined air of a man who has to draw the line somewhere.

'Why ever not?'

'I'm not going to use my skills, such as they are, to force some poor devil into a condemned Victorian slum where he can be banged up with a couple of psychopaths and his own chamber pot.' I gave my learned Head of Chambers Article One of the Rumpole Creed.

'All the same, you being comparatively quiet of late, Horace, has led the Lord Chancellor's office, I know, to look on these Chambers with a certain amount of, shall we say, "goodwill"?'

I looked at Featherstone. He was wearing an expression which I can only describe as 'coy'. 'Shall we? Then I'd better get up to something noisy.' I was joking, of course, but Featherstone became distinctly agitated.

'Please, Horace. No. I beg you. Please. You heard about the awful thing that happened to old Moreton Colefax?'

'Featherstone! I'm trying to add up.' I tried to be firm with the fellow, but he sat himself down in my client's chair and started to unburden himself as though he were revealing a dire plot he'd recently stumbled on involving the assassination of the Archbishop of Canterbury and the theft of the Crown Jewels.

'The Lord Chancellor told Moreton that he was going to make him a judge. But the rule is, you mustn't tell anyone till the appointment's official. Well, Moreton told Sam Arbuckle, and Arbuckle told Grantley Simpson and Grantley told Ian and Jasper Rugeley over in

Paper Buildings, and Ian and Jasper told Walter Gains whom he happened to meet in Pommeroy's Wine Bar, and . . .'

'What is this, Featherstone? Some sort of round game?' My attention was not exactly held by this complicated account.

'Not for Moreton Colefax, it wasn't,' Guthrie Featherstone chuckled, and then went serious again. 'The thing became the talk of the Temple and the upshot was, poor old Moreton never got appointed. So if the Lord Chancellor sends for a fellow to make him a judge, Horace, that fellow's lips are sealed. He just mustn't tell a soul!'

'Why are you telling me then?' I only asked for information, I wasn't following the fellow's drift. But the effect was extraordinary. Guthrie sprang to his feet, paling beneath his non-existent tan. 'I'm not telling you anything, Horace. Good heavens, my dear man! What ever gave you the idea I was telling you anything?'

'I'm sorry,' I said, returning to the calculations. 'I should have realized you were just babbling away meaninglessly. What are you, Featherstone, a sort of background noise, like Muzak?'

'Horace, it is vital that you should understand that I have said nothing to you whatsoever.' Featherstone's voice sank to a horrified whisper. 'Just as it is essential to preserve the quiet, *respectable* image of our Chambers. There was that difficult period we went through when the Erskine-Browns were *expecting*, rather too early on in their married lives.'*

'They weren't married.' I recalled the happy event.

'Well, exactly! And of course that all passed over quite satisfactorily. We had a marquee in the Temple Gardens, if you remember, for the wedding. I believe I said a few words.'

'A *few* words, Guthrie? That's hardly like you.'

The above somewhat enigmatic conversation was interrupted by the telephone on my desk ringing and, after a few deft passes by Dianne on the intercom in our clerk's room, my wife Hilda's voice came over the line, loud, clear and unusually displeased.

'There's a young girl here, Rumpole,' She Who Must Be Obeyed was reading out the indictment over the phone. 'She is sitting in the kitchen, asking for you. Well, she's making her own cigarettes, and they smell of burnt carpets.'

* See 'Rumpole and the Course of True Love' (*The First Rumpole Omnibus*).

'But any sort of breath of scandal now. At this historic moment in the life of our Chambers.' Looking, if possible, more ashen than ever, Guthrie was still burbling in the background. And he didn't look particularly cheered up when he heard me address the instrument in my hand along the following lines:

'Something sort of arty-tarty, is she, do you say, Hilda? A young girl who says she's in trouble. What kind of trouble? Well, perhaps I haven't got your vivid imagination, but I quite honestly can't . . . Well, of course I'm coming home. Don't I always come home in the end?' I put down the telephone. Featherstone was looking at me, appalled, and started to say, in a voice of deep concern, 'I couldn't help overhearing.'

'Couldn't you?' Well I thought he might, if he were a man of tact, have filtered out of the room.

'Horace, is your home life completely satisfactory?' he asked.

'Of course it isn't.' I don't know what the man was thinking about. 'It's exactly as usual. Some girl seems to have aroused the wrath of She Who Must Be Obeyed.'

'Did you say . . . some *girl*?'

'Friend of yours, Guthrie?'

'What?'

'I thought it might be someone you had your eye on, from the typing pool, perhaps. I mean, I remember when . . .' But before I could call the Featherstone mind to remembrance of things past, he went on firmly, 'This is not a time for looking backwards, Horace. Let us look forward! To the fine reputation of this set of Chambers.'

He went to the door and opened it, but before he left the Rumpole presence he said, as though it were a full explanation, 'And do please remember, I haven't told you anything!'

I suppose that was true, in a manner of speaking.

As, from the sound of She Who Must Be Obeyed's voice, there appeared to be a bit of a cold wind blowing in Casa Rumpole (our so-called 'mansion' flat in the Gloucester Road, which bears about as much relation to a mansion as Pommeroy's plonk does to Château Pichon-Longueville), I delayed my return home and wandered into my usual retreat, where I saw our clerk Henry there before me. He was leaning nonchalantly against the bar, toying with his usual Cinzano Bianco, taken with ice and a twist of lemon. I began to press him for information which might throw some faint light on the great Featherstone mystery.

'As a barrister's clerk, Henry,' I said, 'you might be said to be at the very heart of the legal profession. You have your finger on the Lord Chancellor's pulse, to coin a phrase. Tell me honestly, has the old fellow lost his marbles?'

'Which old fellow, sir?' Henry seemed mystified. It was an evening for mystification.

'The Lord Chancellor, Henry! Has he gone off his rocker?'

'That's not for me to say, is it?' Our clerk Henry was ever the diplomat, but I pressed on. 'Is his Lordship seriously thinking of making Guthrie Featherstone, QC, MP, a Red Judge? I mean, I know our learned Head of Chambers has given up politics . . .'

'He's joined the SDP.'

'That's exactly what I mean. But a *judge!*'

'Speaking entirely for myself, Mr Rumpole, and I have no inside information . . .' Henry had decided to play it cautiously.

'Oh, come on. Don't be so pompous and legal, Henry.'

'I would say that Mr Featherstone would cut a fine figure on the Bench.' Our clerk had the sort of voice which could express nothing whatsoever, a genuinely neutral tone.

'Oh, he'd *look* all right,' I agreed. 'He'd fit the costume. But *is* he, Henry? That's what I want to know. *Is* he?'

'Is he *what*, Mr Rumpole?'

'He may *look* like a judge, but is he really the *genuine article*?'

So I left Henry, having hit, almost by chance I suppose, on one of the questions which troubled old Plato, led Bishop Berkeley to some of his more eccentric opinions and brought a few laughs to Bertrand Russell and a whole trainload of ideas to A. J. Ayer. It was that little matter of the difference between appearance and reality which lay at the heart of the strange case which was about to engage my attention.

As I say, I didn't expect much of a welcome from She Who Must Be Obeyed when I put into port at 25B Froxbury Court, and I wasn't disappointed. I had brought a peace offering in the shape of the last bunch of tulips I had found gasping for air in the shop at the Temple tube station.

'Where did you find those, Rumpole?' my wife Hilda asked tersely. 'Been raiding the cemetery?'

'Is she still here?' I hoped to see the cause of Hilda's discontent, and entered the kitchen. The place was empty. The bird, whoever she might have been, had flown.

'By *she* I suppose you mean your girl?' Hilda followed me into the kitchen and tried to bring back life to the tulips with the help of a cut-glass vase.

'She's not "my girl".'

'She came to see you. Then she burst into tears suddenly and left.'

'People who come to see me often burst into tears. It's in the nature of the legal profession.' I tried to sound reassuring. But I was distracted by a strange sound, a metallic clatter, as though someone were throwing beer cans up at our kitchen window.

'Hilda,' I put the question directly. 'What on earth's that?' She took a look out and reported – as it turned out, quite accurately – what she saw. 'There's a small man in a loud suit throwing beer cans up at our window, Rumpole. Probably another of your friends!' At which my wife made off in the direction of our living room with the vase of tulips, and I proceeded to the window to verify the information. What I saw was a small, cunning-looking old cove in a loud check suit, with a yellow stock round his neck. Beside him was a girl in ethnic attire, carrying a large, worn holdall, no doubt of Indian manufacture. The distant view I had of her only told me that she had red hair and looked a great deal too beautiful to have any business with the elderly lunatic who was shying beer cans up at our window. As I stuck my head out to protest, I was greeted by the old party with a loud hail of 'Horace Rumpole! There you are at last!'

'Who are you?' I had no idea why this ancient person, who had the appearance of a superannuated racing tipster, should know my name.

'Don't you remember Blanco Basnet? Fellow you got off at Cambridge Assizes? Marvellous, you were. Just bloody marvellous! Hang on a jiff. Coming up!' At which our visitors made off for the entrance of the building.

The name 'Blanco Basnet' rang only the faintest of bells. I had a vague recollection of some hanger-on round Newmarket, but what had he been charged with? Embezzlement? Common assault? Overfamiliarity with a horse? My reverie was interrupted by a prolonged peal on the front doorbell, and I opened up.

'Are you Basnet?' I asked the fellow as Hilda joined us, looking distinctly displeased.

'Course not. I'm Brittling.' He introduced himself. 'Harold Brittling. I was a close chum of old Blanco's though. And when you got him off without a stain on his bloody character, we drank the night away, if you will recall the occasion, at the Old Plough at Stratford Parva. Time never called while the landlord had a customer. We swapped addresses, don't you remember? I say, is this your girl?' This last remark clearly and inappropriately referred to She Who Must Be Obeyed.

'This is my wife Hilda,' I said with as much dignity as I could muster.

'This is my girl Pauline.' Brittling introduced the beauty dressed in a rug at his side.

'I've met her,' Hilda said coldly. 'Is she your daughter?'

'No, she's my girl.' Brittling enlarged on the subject. 'Don't talk much, but strips down like an early Augustus John. Thighs that simply call out for an HB pencil. I say, Rumpole, your girl Hilda looks distinctly familiar to me. Met before, haven't we?'

'I think it's hardly likely.' Hilda did her best to freeze the little man with a glance. It was ineffective.

'Round the Old Monmouth pub in Greek Street?' Brittling suggested. 'Didn't you hang a bit round the Old Monmouth? Didn't I have the pleasure of escorting you home once, Hilda, when the Guinness stout had been flowing rather too freely?'

At which Brittling, with the girl in tow, moved off towards the sitting room, and I was left with the thought that either the little gnome was completely off his chump or there were hidden depths to She Who Must Be Obeyed.

When we followed him into our room, Brittling furnished some further information.

'You two girls have chummed up already,' he said. 'I sent Pauline to find you, Horace, as I was temporarily detained in the cooler.'

It was with some relief that I began to realize that Brittling had not paid a merely social call. He brought business. He was a customer, a member of the criminal fraternity, and probably quite a respectable little dud-cheque merchant. However, legal etiquette demanded that I spoke to him sharply. 'Look, Brittling,' I said, 'if you've come here for legal advice, you'll have to approach me in the proper manner.'

'I shall approach you in the proper manner, bearing bubbly! Perhaps your girl will go and fetch a few beakers from the kitchen. Then we can start to celebrate!'

At which he started to yank bottles of champagne out of Pauline's holdall, with all the éclat of a conjurer producing rabbits from a hat.

'Celebrate what?' I was puzzled. Nothing good seemed to have happened.

'The case in which I'm going to twist the tail of the con-o-sewers,' Brittling almost shouted. 'And you, my dear Horace, are going to twist the tail of the legal profession. Game for a bit of fun, aren't you?'

At this moment he released the wine, which began to bubble out over the elderly Persian-type floor covering. This, of course, didn't add a lot to Hilda's approval of the proceedings. 'Do be careful,' she said tartly, 'that stuff is going all over the carpet.'

'Then get the glasses, Hilda.' Brittling was giving the orders. 'It's not like you, is it, to hold up a party?'

'Rumpole!' Hilda appealed to me with a look of desperation, but for the moment I couldn't see the point of allowing all the champagne to be drunk up by the carpet. 'No harm in taking a glass of champagne, Hilda,' I said reasonably.

'Or two.' Brittling winked at her. To my amazement, she then went off to fetch the beakers. When Hilda was gone I pressed on with the interrogation of Brittling.

'Who are you, exactly?' I asked, as a starter. The question seemed to provoke considerable hilarity in the old buffer.

'He asks who I am, Pauline!' He turned to his companion incredulously. 'Slade Gold Medal. Exhibited in the Salon in Paris. Hung in the Royal Academy. Executed in the Bond Street Galleries. And once, when I was *very* hungry, decorated the pavement outside the National Portrait Gallery. And the secret is – I can *do* it, Horace. So can you. We're pros. Give me a box of Conté crayons and I can run you up a Degas ballet dancer that old Degas would have given his eye teeth to have drawn.'

'His name's Harold Brittling.' The girl, Pauline, spoke at last, and as though that settled the matter. Brittling set off on a survey of the room as Hilda came back with four glasses.

'Who is he?' she asked anxiously as she handed me a glass.

'An artist. Apparently. Hung in the Royal Academy.' That was about all I was able to tell her.

'Not over-pictured, are you? What's this *objet d'art*?' Brittling had fetched up in front of a particularly watery watercolour presented to Hilda by her bosom chum Dodo, an artwork which I wouldn't give house room to were the choice mine, which of course it wasn't.

'Oh, that's a study of Lamorna Cove, done by my old school friend, Dorothy Mackintosh. Dodo Perkins, as was. She lives in the West Country now.'

' "Dodo" keeps a tea shop in St Ives.' I filled in the gaps in Hilda's narrative.

'She has sent in to the Royal Academy. On several occasions. Do you like it, Mr . . . ?' She actually seemed to be waiting anxiously for the Brittling verdict.

'Harold,' he corrected her. And, looking at her with particularly clear blue eyes, he added, in a way I can only describe as gallant, 'Do *you* like it, Hilda?'

'Oh, I think it's rather fine.' It was She, the connoisseur, speaking. 'Beautiful in fact. The way Dodo's caught the shadow on the rocks, you know.'

Brittling was sloshing the champagne around, smiling at Hilda and actually winking at Pauline as he said, 'Then if you think it's fine and beautiful, Hilda, that's what it is to you. To you it's worth a fortune. The mere fact that to me it looks like a rather colourless blob of budgerigar's vomit is totally irrelevant. You pay for what you think is beautiful. That's what our case is all about, isn't it, Horace? What's the difference between a Dodo and a Degas? Nothing but bloody talent which I can supply!'

'Look here, Brittling . . .' Although grateful for the glass full of nourishing bubbles, I thought the chap was putting the case against Dodo's masterpiece a little strongly.

'Harold,' he suggested.

'Brittling.' I was sticking to the full formality. 'My wife and I are grateful for this glass of . . .'

'The Widow Clicquot. Non-vintage, I'm afraid. But paid for with ready money.'

'But I certainly can't do any case unless you go and consult a solicitor and he cares to instruct me.'

'Oh I see.' Brittling was recharging all our glasses. 'Play it by the rules, eh?'

'Exactly.' I intended to get this prospective client under control.

'Then it's much more fun breaking them when the time comes,' said the irresponsible Brittling.

'I must make it quite clear that I don't intend to break any rules for you, Brittling,' I said. 'Come and see me in Chambers with a solicitor.'

' "Oh, I walk along the Bois du Boulogne . . . With an independent air . . ." ' Brittling began to sing in a way which apparently had nothing whatever to do with matters in question.

'Oh come along, Harold.' The girl, Pauline, took the old boy's arm and seemed to be urging him towards the door. 'He's not going to take your case on.'

'Why ever not?' Brittling seemed puzzled.

'*She* doesn't like you. And I don't think *he* likes you much either.'

' "You can hear them all *declare*, I must be a *millionaire*",' Brittling sang and then looked at me intently. 'Horace Rumpole may not like me,' he said at last, 'but he envies me.'

'Why should he do that?'

'Because of what he has to live with.' Brittling's magnificent gestures seemed to embrace the entire room. 'Pissy watercolours!'

And then they left us, as unexpectedly as they had come, abandoning the rest of the Veuve Clicquot, which we had with our poached eggs for supper. It wasn't until much later, when we were lying at a discreet distance in the matrimonial bed, that I happened to say to Hilda, by way of encouragement, 'I don't suppose we'll see either of them again.'

'Oh yes, you will,' she announced, as I thought, tartly. 'You'll do the case. You won't be able to resist it!'

'I can resist Mr Harold Brittling extremely easily,' I assured her.

'But *her*. Can you resist *her*, Rumpole?' And she went on in some disgust, 'Those thighs that simply seem to be *asking* for an HB pencil. I don't know when I've heard anything quite so revolting!'

'All the same, old Brittling seems to enjoy life.' I said it quietly, under my breath, but She almost heard me.

'*What* did you say?'

'I said I don't suppose he's got a wife.'

'That's what I thought you said.' And Hilda, somewhat mortified, snapped off the light, having decided it was high time we lost consciousness together.

To understand the extraordinary case of the Queen against Harold Brittling, it is necessary to ask if you have a nodding acquaintance with the work of the late Septimus Cragg, RA. Before he turned up his toes, which I imagine must have been shortly before the last war, Septimus Cragg appeared to the public gaze as just what they expected of the most considerable British painter of his time. His beard, once a flaming red, later a nicotine-stained white, his long procession of English and European mistresses, his farmhouse in Sussex, his huge collection of good-looking children who suffered greatly from never being able to paint as well as their father, his public denunciations of most other living artists, and his frequently pronounced belief that Brighton Pavilion was a far finer manifestation of the human spirit than Chartres Cathedral – all these things brought him constantly to the attention of the gossip columnists, and perhaps made his work undervalued in his final years.

Now, of course, as I discovered when I started to do a little preparation for the defence of Harold Brittling, there has been a considerable boom in Craggs. The generally held view is that he was by far the finest of the British post-Impressionists, and had he had the luck to be born in Dieppe, a port where a good deal of his life and a great many of his love affairs were celebrated, he might be mentioned in the same breath as such noted Frog artists as Degas and Bonnard. By now the art world will pay a great deal of hard cash for a Cragg in mint condition, particularly if it's a good nude. There's nothing that has the art world reaching for its chequebook, so it seems, as quickly as a good nude.

The rise in expert esteem of the paintings of Septimus Cragg was shown dramatically in the prices fetched in a recent sale at which Harold Brittling was seen to be behaving in a somewhat curious manner. The particular Cragg to come under the hammer was entitled *Nancy at the Hôtel du Vieux Port, Dieppe,* and it appeared to have an impeccable pedigree, having been put up for auction by a Miss Price, an elderly spinster lady who lived in Worthing and was none other than Septimus

Cragg's niece. As the bidding rose steadily from fifty to fifty-six thousand pounds, and as the picture was finally knocked down to a Mrs DeMoyne of New Haven, Connecticut, for a cool sixty thousand, Harold Brittling, sitting beside a silent and undemonstrative Pauline in the audience, could be seen giggling helplessly. On his way out of the auction, the beaming Brittling was fingered by two officers of the Fine Art and Antiques Department at Scotland Yard and taken into custody. Pauline was sent to enlist the immediate help of Horace Rumpole, and so earned the suspicious disapproval of She Who Must Be Obeyed.

Nancy, whoever she may have been, was clearly a generously built, cheerful young lady, who brought out the best in Septimus Cragg. He had painted her naked, with a mane of copper-coloured hair, standing against the light of a hotel bedroom window, through which the masts and funnels of the old port were hazily visible. In the foreground there was a strip of purplish carpet, a china basin and jug on a washstand, and the end of a brass bed, over which a man's trousers, fitted with a pair of braces, were dangling negligently. I was looking at a reproduction of the work in question in my Chambers. I hadn't yet seen the glowing original; but even in a flat, coloured photograph, the picture gave off the feeling of a moment of happiness, caught for ever. I felt, looking at it, I must confess, a bit of a pang. There hadn't, I had to face it, been many such mornings in hotel bedrooms in Dieppe in the long life and career of Horace Rumpole, barrister-at-law.

'It's only a reproduction,' Brittling said. 'Doesn't do it a bit of justice.'

And Mr Myers, old Myersy, the solicitor's managing clerk, who has seen me through more tough spots down the Bailey than I've had hot dinners, who sat there with his overcoat pockets bulging with writs and summonses, puffed at his nauseating, bubbling old pipe and said, as though we were looking at a bit of bloodstained sweatshirt or a mortuary photograph, 'That's it, Mr Rumpole. Exhibit J. L. T. (1). That's the evidence.'

Brittling, it seemed, had at least partially come to his senses. He had decided to consult a solicitor and approach me in a more formal manner than the mere lobbing of beer cans at my kitchen window. He looked at the exhibit in question and smiled appreciatively.

'It's a corker, though, as a composition, isn't it?'

'How is it as a forgery? That's what you're charged with, you know,' I reminded him, to bring the conversation down from the high aesthetic plane.

'A smashing composition,' Brittling went on as though he hadn't heard. 'And if you saw the texture of paint, and the way the curtains are moving in the wind from the harbour! There's only one man who could ever paint the air behind a curtain like that.'

'So it's the genuine article!' Myers assured me. 'That's what we're saying, Mr Rumpole.'

'Of course it's genuine!' Brittling called on the support of Keats: '*A thing of beauty . . . is a joy for ever.*'

I helped him with the quotation,

> *'Its loveliness increases; it will never*
> *Pass into nothingness; but still will keep*
> *A bower quiet for us, and a sleep*
> *Full of sweet dreams, and health, and quiet breathing . . .*

'Quiet breathing in the nick,' I reminded him somewhat brutally, 'if we don't keep our wits about us. Did you ever know Cragg?'

'Septimus . . . ?'

'Did you know him?' I asked, and Brittling embarked on a fragment of autobiography.

'I was the rising star of the Slade School,' he said. 'Cragg was the old lion, the king of the pack. He was always kind to me. Had me down to the farmhouse at Rottingdean. Full of his children by various mothers, and society beauties, waiting to have their portraits painted. There was such a lot of laughter in that house, and so many young people . . .'

'*Nancy at Dieppe.*' I picked up the reproduction. The features were blurred against the light, but didn't there seem to be something vaguely familiar about the girl in the hotel bedroom? 'Do you recognize the model at all?'

'Cragg had so many.' Brittling shrugged.

'Models or girlfriends?'

'It was usually the same thing.'

'Was it really? And *this* one?'

'Seems vaguely familiar.' Brittling echoed my thoughts. I gave him my searching look, reserved for difficult clients. 'The sort of thighs,' I asked him, 'which simply call out for an HB pencil, would you say?'

Brittling didn't seem to resent my suggestion. In fact he turned to me and gave a small but deliberate wink. I didn't like that. Clients who wink at you when you as good as tell them that you think they're guilty can be most unsettling.

I was still unsettled as I undressed in the matrimonial bedroom in Froxbury Court. Hilda, in hairnet and bedjacket, was propped up on the pillows doing the *Daily Telegraph* crossword puzzle. As I hung up the striped trousers I thought that it was a scene which would never have been painted by Septimus Cragg. I was reflecting on the difference between my life and that of the rip-roaring old RA and I said, thoughtfully, 'It all depends, I suppose, on where your talents lie.'

'What does?' Hilda asked in a disinterested sort of way.

'I mean, if my talents hadn't been for bloodstains, and cross-examining coppers on their notebooks, and addressing juries on the burden of proof . . . If I'd had an unusual aptitude for jotting down a pair of thighs in a hotel bedroom . . .'

'You've seen *her* again, haven't you?' Hilda was no longer sounding disinterested.

'I might have been living in a farmhouse in Sussex with eight pool-eyed children with eight different mothers, all devoted to me, and duchesses knocking on my door to have their portraits painted. My work might have meant trips to Venice and Aix-en-Provence instead of London Sessions and the Uxbridge Magistrates' Court! No, I didn't see her. She didn't come to the conference.'

'You want to concentrate on what you *can* do, Rumpole. Fine chance *I* ever have of getting invited to the Palace.'

'No need for the black jacket and pinstripes. Throw away the collar like a blunt execution. All you need is an old tweed suit and a young woman who's kind enough to wear nothing but a soulful expression. What's all that about the Palace?'

'They're making Guthrie Featherstone a judge, you know,' Hilda said, as though it were all, in some obscure way, my fault.

'Whoever told you that?'

I felt suddenly sorry for the old QC, MP, and worried that the chump's chances might be blown by a lot of careless talk. For Hilda told me that she had met Marigold Featherstone somewhere near Harrods, and that whilst she had been looking for bargains, the future Lady Marigold had told her that she had acquired a suitable outfit with the 'Princess Di' look for a visit to the Palace on the occasion of our not very learned Head of Chambers being awarded a handle to his name. When Hilda, not a little mystified, had asked her what sort of handle they had in mind, Marigold had rushed off in the direction of Sloane Street, urging Hilda to forget every word she had said, forgetting, of course, that She Who Must Be Obeyed never forgets.

'You didn't tell anyone else this, did you?' I asked.

'Well, no one except Phillida Erskine-Brown. I happened to run into her going into Sainsbury's.'

'You did *what*?'

'And Phillida explained it all to me. If you get made a judge you're knighted as a matter of course, and have to go to Buck House and all that sort of thing. So that was why Marigold was buying a new outfit.'

I was appalled, quite frankly. Phillida Erskine-Brown is a formidable lady advocate, the Portia of our Chambers. As for her husband, as I explained to Hilda, 'Claude Erskine-Brown gossips about the judiciary in the way teenagers gossip about film actors. Star-struck is our Claude. Practically goes down on his knees to anything in ermine! And he pops into Pommeroy's whenever he gets a legal aid cheque. Let's just hope he doesn't get paid until poor old Featherstone's got his bottom safely on the Bench.'

'One thing is quite certain, Rumpole,' said Hilda, filling in a clue. 'There's no earthly chance of your ever getting a handle.'

A few weeks later I had slipped into Pommeroy's Wine Bar for a glass of luncheon when Guthrie Featherstone came up to me and, having looked nervously over his shoulder like a man who expects to be joined at any moment by the Hound of Heaven, said, 'Horace! I came in here to buy a small sherry . . .'

'No harm in that, Guthrie.' I tried to sound reassuring.

'And Jack Pommeroy, you know what Jack Pommeroy called me?' His voice sank to a horrified whisper. 'He called me *"Judge"*!'

'Well, you'll have to get used to it.' I couldn't be bothered to whisper.

Featherstone looked round, appalled. 'Horace, for God's sake! Don't you see what this means? It means someone's been talking.'

And then his glance fell on a table where Claude Erskine-Brown was knocking back the Beaujolais Villages with assorted barristers. Featherstone's cup of unhappiness was full when Erskine-Brown raised his glass, as though in congratulation.

'Look! Claude Erskine-Brown, raising his glass at me!' Featherstone pointed it out, rather unnecessarily, I thought.

'Just a friendly gesture,' I assured him.

'You remember poor old Moreton Colefax, not made a judge because he couldn't keep his mouth shut.' The QC, MP, looked near to tears. 'It's all round the Temple.'

'Of course it's not. Don't worry.'

'Then why is Erskine-Brown drinking to me?'

'He thinks you *look* like a judge. Beauty, after all, Guthrie my old darling, is entirely in the eye of the beholder.' Curiously enough, when I said that, Guthrie Featherstone didn't look particularly cheered up.

In the course of time, however, Guthrie Featherstone, QC, MP, did cheer up, considerably. He fulfilled his destiny, and took on that role which led him to be appointed head boy of his prep school and a prefect at Marlborough, because, quite simply, he never got up anyone's nose and there were no other likely candidates available.

At long last Guthrie's cheerfulness round the Sheridan Club and his dedication to losing golf matches against senior judges earned him his just reward. A man who had spent most of his life in an agony of indecision, who spent months debating such questions as whether we should have a coffee machine in the clerk's room, or did the downstairs loo need redecorating; a fellow who found it so hard to choose between left and right that he became a Social Democrat; a barrister who agonized for hours about whether it would be acceptable to wear a light-grey tie in Chambers in April, or whether such jollifications should be confined to the summer months, was appointed one of Her Majesty's Judges, and charged to decide great issues of life and liberty.

Arise, Sir Guthrie! From now on barristers, men far older than you, will bow before you. Men and women will be taken off to prison at your decree. You will have made a Lady out of Marigold, and your old mother is no doubt extremely proud of you. There is only one reason, one very good reason, for that smile of amiable bewilderment to fade from the Featherstone features. You may make the most awful pig's breakfast of the case you're trying, and they'll pour scorn on you from a great height in the Court of Appeal.

So Guthrie Featherstone, in the full panoply of a Red Judge at the Old Bailey, was sitting paying polite and somewhat anxious attention to a piece of high comedy entitled *R. v. Brittling*, starring Claude Erskine-Brown for the prosecution, and Horace Rumpole for the defence. As the curtain rose on the second day of the hearing the limelight fell on a Mr Edward Gandolphini, an extremely expensive-looking art expert and connoisseur, with a suit from Savile Row, iron-grey hair and a tan fresh from a short break in the Bahamas. In the audience Pauline was sitting with her embroidered holdall, listening with fierce concentration, and in the dock, the prisoner at the Bar was unconcernedly drawing a devastating portrait of the learned Judge.

'Mr Gandolphini.' Erskine-Brown was examining the witness with all the humble care of a gynaecologist approaching a duchess who had graciously consented to lie down on his couch. 'You are the author of *Cragg and the British Impressionists* and the leading expert on this particular painter?'

'It has been said, my Lord.' The witness flashed his teeth at the learned Judge, who flashed his back.

'I'm sure it has, Mr Gandolphini,' said Featherstone, J.

'And are you also,' Erskine-Brown asked most respectfully, 'the author of many works on twentieth-century painting and adviser to private collectors and galleries throughout the world?'

'I am.' Gandolphini admitted it.

'And have you examined this alleged "Septimus Cragg"?' Erskine-Brown gestured towards the picture which, propped on a chair in front of the jury, revealed a world of secret delight miles away from the Central Criminal Court.

'I have, my Lord.' Mr Gandolphini again addressed himself to the learned Judge. 'I may say it isn't included in any existing catalogue of the artist's works. Of course, at one time, I believe, it was thought it came from a genuine source, the artist's niece in Worthing.'

'Now we know that to be untrue,' said Erskine-Brown with a meaningful look at the jury, and thereby caused me to stagger, filled with extremely righteous indignation, to my feet.

'My Lord!' I trumpeted. 'We know nothing of the sort – until that has been found as a fact by the twelve sensible people who sit in that jury-box and *no one else!*'

'Very well,' said his Lordship, trying to placate everybody. 'Very well, Mr Rumpole. Perhaps he suspected it to be untrue. Is that the situation, Mr Gandolphini?'

Guthrie turned to the witness, smiling, but I wasn't letting him off quite so easily. 'My Lord, how can what this witness suspected possibly be evidence?'

'Mr Rumpole. I know you don't want to be difficult.' As usual Featherstone exhibited his limited understanding of the case. I considered it my duty to be as difficult as possible.

'May I assist, my Lord?' said Erskine-Brown.

'I would be grateful if you would, Mr Erskine-Brown. Mr Rumpole, perhaps we can allow Mr Erskine-Brown to assist us?'

I subsided. I had no desire to take part in this vicarage tea-party, with everyone assisting each other to cucumber sandwiches. I thought that after one day on the Bench Guthrie had learnt the habit of getting cosy with the prosecution.

'Mr Gandolphini,' Erskine-Brown positively purred at the witness, 'if you *had* known that this picture did not in fact come from Miss Price's collection, would you have had some doubts about its authenticity?'

'That question is entirely speculative.' I was on my feet again.

'Mr Rumpole.' Featherstone was being extremely patient. 'Do you want me to rule on the propriety of Mr Erskine-Brown's question?'

'I think the time may have come to make up the judicial mind, yes.'

'Then I rule that Mr Erskine-Brown may ask his question.' Guthrie then smiled at me in the nicest possible way and said, 'Sorry, Mr Rumpole.' The old darling looked broken-hearted.

'Well, Mr Gandolphini?' Erskine-Brown was still waiting for his answer.

'I had a certain doubt about the picture from the start,' Gandolphini said carefully.

'From the start . . . you had a doubt . . .' Featherstone didn't seem to be able to stop talking while he wrote a note.

'Take it slowly now. Just follow his Lordship's pencil,' Erskine-Brown advised the witness and, in the ensuing pause, I happened to whisper to Myersy, 'And you may be sure his pencil's not drawing thighs in Dieppe.'

'Did you say something, Mr Rumpole?' his Lordship asked, worried.

'Nothing, my Lord, of the slightest consequence,' I rose to explain.

'I say that because I have extremely acute hearing.' Featherstone smiled at the jury, and I could think of nothing better to say than, 'Congratulations.'

'I thought the painting very fine.' Gandolphini returned to the matter in hand. 'And certainly in the manner of Septimus Cragg. It is a beautiful piece of work, but I don't think I ever saw a Cragg where the shadows had so much colour in them.'

'Colour? In the shadows? Could I have a look?' The Judge tapped his pencil on the Bench and called, 'Usher.' Obediently the usher carried the artwork up to his Lordship on the Bench, and his Lordship got out his magnifying glass and submitted Nancy's warm flesh tints and flowing curves to a careful, legal examination.

'There's a good deal of green, and even purple in the shadows on the naked body, my Lord,' Gandolphini explained.

'Yes, I do see that,' said the Judge. 'Have you seen that, Mr Rumpole? Most interesting! Usher, let Mr Rumpole have a look at that. Do you wish to borrow my glass, Mr Rumpole?'

'No, my Lord. I think I can manage with the naked eye.' I was brought the picture by the usher and sat staring at it, as though waiting for some sudden revelation.

'Tell us,' Erskine-Brown asked the witness. 'Is "Nancy" a model who appears in any of Cragg's works known to you?'

'In none, my Lord.' Gandolphini shook his head, almost sadly.

'Did Cragg paint most of his models many times?'

'Many, many times, my Lord.'

'Thank you, Mr Gandolphini.'

Erskine-Brown sat, apparently satisfied and I rose up slowly, and slowly turned the picture so the witness could see it. 'You said, did you not, Mr Gandolphini, that this is a beautiful painting.' I began in a way that I was pleased to see the witness didn't expect.

'It's very fine. Yes.'

'Has it not at least sixty thousand pounds' worth of beauty?' I asked and then gave the jury a look.

'I can't say.'

'Can you not? Isn't part of your trade reducing beauty to mere cash!'

'I value pictures, yes.' I could see that Gandolphini was consciously keeping his temper.

'And would you not agree that this is a valuable picture, no matter who painted it?'

'I have said . . .' I knew that he was going to try and avoid answering the question, and I interrupted him. 'You have said it's beautiful. Were you not telling this jury the truth, Mr Gandolphini?'

'Yes, but . . .'

> ' "Beauty is truth, truth beauty," – that is all
> Ye know on earth, and all ye need to know.'

I turned and gave the jury their two bobs' worth of Keats.

'Is that really all we need to know, Mr Rumpole?' said a voice from on high.

'In this case, yes, my Lord.'

'I think I'll want to hear legal argument about that, Mr Rumpole.' Featherstone appeared to be making some form of minor joke, but I answered him seriously. 'Oh, you shall. I promise you, your Lordship.' I turned to the witness. 'Mr Gandolphini, by "beauty" I suppose you mean that this picture brings joy and delight to whoever stands before it?'

'I suppose that would be a definition.'

'You suppose it would. And let us suppose it turned out to have been painted by an even more famous artist than Septimus Cragg. Let us suppose it had been done by Degas or Manet.'

'Who, Mr Rumpole?' I seemed to have gone rather too fast for his Lordship's pencil.

'Manet, my Lord. Edouard Manet,' I explained carefully. 'If it were painted by a more famous artist it wouldn't become more of a thing of beauty and a joy to behold, would it?'

'No . . . but . . .'

'And if it were painted by a less famous artist – Joe Bloggs, say, or my Lord the learned Judge, one wet Sunday afternoon . . .'

'Really, Mr Rumpole!' Featherstone, J, smiled modestly, but I was busy with the con-o-sewer. 'It wouldn't become *less* beautiful, would it, Mr Gandolphini? It would have the same colourful shadows, the same feeling of light and air and breeze from the harbour. The same warmth of the human body?'

'Exactly the same, of course, but . . .'

'I don't want to interrupt . . .' Erskine-Brown rose to his feet, wanting to interrupt.

'Then don't, Mr Erskine-Brown!' I suggested. The suggestion had no effect. Erskine-Brown made a humble submission to his Lordship. 'My Lord, in my humble submission we are not investigating the beauty of this work, but the value, and the value of this picture depends on its being a genuine Septimus Cragg. Therefore my learned friend's questions seem quite irrelevant.'

At which Erskine-Brown subsided in satisfaction, and his Lordship called on Rumpole to reply.

'My learned friend regards this as a perfectly ordinary criminal case,' I said. 'Of course it isn't. We are discussing the value of a work of art, a thing of beauty and a joy forever. We are not debating the price of fish!'

There was a sound of incipient applause from the dock, so I whispered to Myersy, and instructed him to remind Brittling that he was not in the pit at the Old Holborn Empire but in the dock at the Old Bailey. I was interrupted by the Judge saying that perhaps I had better pursue another line with the witness.

'My Lord,' I said. 'I think we have heard enough – from Mr Gandolphini.' So I sat and looked triumphantly at the jury, as though I had, in a way they might not have entirely understood, won a point. Then I noticed, to my displeasure, that the learned Judge was engaged in some sort of intimate *tête-à-tête* with the man Gandolphini, who had not yet left the witness-box.

'Mr Gandolphini, just one point,' said the Judge.

'Yes, my Lord.'

'I happen myself to be extremely fond of Claude Lorrain,' said Featherstone, pronouncing the first name 'Clode' in an exaggerated Frog manner of speaking.

'Oh, my Lord, I do *so* agree.' Gandolphini waxed effusive.

'Absolutely *super* painter, isn't he? Now, I suppose, if you saw a good, a beautiful picture which you were assured came from a reputable source, you might accept that as a "Clode" Lorrain, mightn't you?'

'Certainly, my Lord.'

'But if you were later to learn that the picture had been painted in the seventeenth century and not the eighteenth! Well, you might change your opinion, mightn't you?'

Featherstone looked pleased with himself, but the turn of the conversation seemed to be causing Gandolphini intense embarrassment. 'Well, not really, my Lord,' he murmured.

'Oh, I'm sorry. Will you tell us why not?' The learned Judge looked nettled and prepared to take a note.

Gandolphini hated to do it, but as a reputable art expert he had to say, 'Well. You see. Claude Lorrain *did* paint in the seventeenth century, my Lord.'

It was almost the collapse of the Judge's morale. However, he started to talk rather quickly to cover his embarrassment. 'Oh, yes. Yes, that's right. Of course he did. Perhaps some of the jury will know that . . . or not, as the case may be.' He smiled at the jury, who looked distinctly puzzled, and then at the witness. 'We haven't all got *your* expertise, Mr Gandolphini.'

All I could think of to say was a warning to Mr Justice Featherstone to avoid setting himself up as any sort of con-o-sewer. Wiser counsels prevailed and I didn't say it.

For our especial delight we then had an appearance in the witness-box by Mrs DeMoyne, a well-manicured lady in a dark, businesslike suit, with horn-rimmed glasses and a voice like the side of a nail file. Mrs DeMoyne spoke with the assurance of an art lover who weighs up a post-Impressionist to the nearest dollar, and gives you the tax advantage of a gift to the Museum of Modern Art without drawing breath. She gave a brief account of her visit to the auction room to preview the Cragg in question, of her being assured that the picture had a perfect pedigree, having come straight from the artist's niece with no dealers involved, and described her successful bidding against stiff competition from a couple of Bond Street galleries and the Italian agent of a collector in Kuwait.

Erskine-Brown asked the witness if she believed she had been buying a genuine Septimus Cragg. 'Of course I did,' rasped Mrs DeMoyne. 'I was terribly deceived.' So Erskine-Brown sat down, I'm sure, with a feeling of duty done.

'Mrs DeMoyne. Wouldn't you agree,' I asked as I rose to cross-examine, 'that you bought a very beautiful picture?'

'Yes,' Mrs DeMoyne admitted.

'So beautiful you were prepared to pay sixty thousand pounds for it?'

'Yes, I was.'

'And it is still the same beautiful picture? The picture hasn't changed since you bought it, has it, Mrs DeMoyne? Not by one drop of paint! Is the truth of the matter that you're not interested in art but merely in collecting autographs!'

Of course this made the jury titter and brought Erskine-Brown furiously to his hind legs. I apologized for any pain and suffering I might have caused, and went on. 'When did you first doubt that this was a Cragg?' I asked.

'Someone rang me up.'

'*Someone?* What did they say?'

'Do you want to let this evidence in, Mr Rumpole?' The learned Judge was heard to be warning me for my own good.

'Yes, my Lord. I'm curious to know,' I reassured him. So Mrs DeMoyne answered the question. 'That was what made me get in touch with the police,' she said. 'The man who called me said the picture wasn't a genuine Cragg, and it never had belonged to Cragg's niece. He also said that I'd got a bargain.'

'A bargain. Why?'

'Because it was better than a Cragg.'

'Did he give you his name?' It was a risky question, dangerous to ask because I didn't know the answer.

'He did, yes. But I was so upset I didn't pay too much attention to it. I don't think I can remember it.'

'Try,' I encouraged her.

'White. I think it had "white" in it.'

'Whiting? Whitehead?' I tried a few names on her.

'No.' Mrs DeMoyne shook her head defeated. 'I can't remember.'

'Thank you, Mrs DeMoyne.' When I sat down I heard a gentle voice in my ear whisper, 'You were wonderful! Harold said you would be.' It was the girl Pauline, who had left her seat to murmur comforting words to Rumpole.

'Oh nonsense,' I whispered back, but then had to add, for the sake of truthfulness, 'Well, just a bit wonderful, perhaps. How do you think it's going, Myersy?'

The knowing old legal executive in front of me admitted that we were doing better than he expected, which was high praise from such a source, but then he looked towards the witness-box and whispered, 'That's the one I'm afraid of.'

The fearful object in Mr Myers's eyes was a small, grey-haired lady with wind-brightened cheeks and small glittering eyes, wearing a tweed suit and sensible shoes, who took the oath in a clear voice and gave her name as Miss Marjorie Evangeline Price, of 31 Majuba Road, Worthing, and admitted that the late Cragg, RA, had been her Uncle Septimus.

'Do you know the defendant Brittling?' Erskine-Brown began his examination-in-chief, and I growled, '*Mister* Brittling,' insisting on a proper respect for the prisoner at the Bar. I don't think the jury heard me. They were all listening eagerly to Miss Marjorie Evangeline Price, who talked to them as though she were having a cup of afternoon tea with a few friends she'd known for years.

'He came to see me in Worthing. He said he had one of Uncle Septimus's paintings to sell and he wanted me to put it into the auction for him. The real seller didn't want his name brought into it.'

'Did Mr Brittling tell you why?'

'He said it was a businessman who didn't want it to be known that he was selling his pictures. People might have thought he was in financial trouble, apparently.'

'So did you agree to the picture being sold in your name?'

'I'm afraid it was very wrong of me, but he was going to give me a little bit of a percentage. An ex-schoolmistress does get a very small pension.' Miss Price smiled at the jury and they smiled back, as though of course they understood completely. She was, unhappily for old Brittling, the sort of witness that the jury love, a sweet old lady who's not afraid to admit she's wrong.

'Did you have any idea that the picture wasn't genuine?'

'Oh no, of course not. I had no idea of that. Mr Brittling was very charming and persuasive.'

At which Miss Price looked at my client in the dock and smiled. The jury also looked at him, but they didn't smile.

'And how much of the money did Mr Brittling allow you to keep?'

'I think, I'm not sure, I *think* it was ten per cent.'

'How very generous. Thank you, Miss Price.'

Erskine-Brown had shot his bolt and sat down. I rose and put on the sweetest, gentlest voice in the Rumpole repertoire. Cross-examining Miss Price was going to be like walking on eggs. I had to move towards any sort of favourable answer on tiptoe. 'Miss Price, do you remember your Uncle Septimus Cragg?' I started to move her gently down Memory Lane.

'I remember him coming to our house when I was a little girl. He had a red beard and a very hairy tweed suit. I remember sitting on his lap.'

His Lordship smiled at her – he was clearly pro-Price.

'Is that all you can remember about him?' I was still probing gently.

'I remember Uncle Septimus telling me that there were two sorts of people in the world – nurses and patients. He seemed to think I'd grow up to be a nurse.'

'Oh, really? And which was he?'

'My Lord, can this possibly be relevant?' Erskine-Brown seemed to think the question was fraught with danger, when I was really only making conversation with the witness.

'I can't see it at the moment, Mr Erskine-Brown,' the Judge admitted.

'Which did he say he was?' I went on, ignoring the unmannerly interruption.

'Oh, he said he could always find someone to look after him. I think he was a bit of a spoiled baby really.'

The jury raised a polite titter, and Erskine-Brown sat down. I looked as though I'd got an answer of great importance.

'Did he? Did he say that? Tell me, Miss Price, do you know who Nancy was?'

'Nancy?' Miss Price looked puzzled.

'This picture is of Nancy, apparently. In an hotel bedroom in Dieppe. Who was Nancy?'

'I'm afraid I have no idea. I suppose she must have been a' – she gave a small, meaningful pause – 'a friend of Uncle Septimus.'

'Yes. I suppose she must have been.' I pointed to the picture which had brought us all to the Old Bailey. 'You've never seen this picture before?'

'Oh no. I didn't ask to see it. Mr Brittling told me about it and, well, of course I trusted him, you see.' Miss Price smiled sweetly at the jury and I sat down. There's no doubt about it. There's nothing more like banging your head against a brick wall than cross-examining a witness who's telling nothing but the truth.

Later that afternoon the usher came to Counsel engaged on the case with a message. The learned Judge would be glad to see us for a cup of tea in his room. So we were received amongst the red leather armchairs, the Law Reports, the silver-framed photographs of Marigold and the Featherstone twins, Simon and Sarah.

The Judge was hovering over the bone china, dispensing the Earl Grey and petits beurres, and the Clerk of the Court was lurking in the background to make sure there was no hanky-panky, I suppose, or an attempt to drop folding money into the Judge's wig.

'Come along, Horace. Sit you down, Claude. Sit you down. You'll take a dish of tea, won't you? What I wanted to ask you fellows is . . . How long is this case going to last?'

'Well, Judge . . . Guthrie . . .' said Erskine-Brown, stirring his tea. 'That rather depends on Rumpole here. He has to put the defence. If there *is* a defence.'

'I don't want to hurry you, Horace. The point is, I may not be able to sit next Monday afternoon.' The Judge gave a secret sort of a smile and said modestly, 'Appointment at the Palace, you know what these things are . . .'

'Marigold got a new outfit for it, has she?' I couldn't resist asking.

'Well, the girls like all that sort of nonsense, don't they?' he said, as though the whole matter were almost too trivial to mention. 'It's not so much an invitation as a Royal command. You know the type of thing.'

'I *don't* know,' I assured him. 'My only Royal command was to join the RAF Ground Staff, as I remember it.'

'Yes, Horace, of course. You old warhorse!' There was a pause while we all had a gulp of tea and a nibble of biscuit. 'How much longer are you going to be?' the Judge asked.

'Well, not long, I suppose. It's rather an absurd little case, isn't it? Bit of a practical joke, really. Isn't that what it is? Just a prank, more or less.' I was working my way towards a small fine should the old idiot Brittling go down; but to my dismay Mr Justice Featherstone looked extremely serious.

'I can't pretend that I find it a joke, exactly,' he said, in his new-found judicial manner.

'Well, I don't suppose that the shades of the prison house begin to fall around the wretched Brittling, do they? I mean, all he did was to pull the legs of a few so-called con-o-sewers.'

'And made himself a considerable sum of money in the process,' said Erskine-Brown, who was clearly anxious to be no sort of help.

'It's deceit, Horace. And forgery for personal profit. If your client's convicted I'm afraid I couldn't rule out a custodial sentence.' The Judge bit firmly into the last petit beurre.

'You couldn't?' I sounded incredulous.

'How could I?'

'Not send him to prison for a little bit of "let's pretend"? For a bit of a joke on a pompous profession?' I put down my cup and stood. My outrage was perfectly genuine. 'No. I don't suppose you could.'

Tea with the Judge was over, and I was about to follow Erskine-Brown and the learned clerk out of his presence, when Mr Justice Featherstone called me back. 'Oh, Horace,' he said, 'a word in your ear.'

'Yes.'

'I've noticed you've fallen into rather a bad habit.'

'Bad habit?' What on earth, I wondered, was he about to accuse me of – being drunk in charge of a forgery case?

'Hands in pockets when you're addressing the Court. It looks so bad, Horace. Such a poor example to the younger men. Keep them out of the pockets, will you? I'm sure you don't mind me pulling you up about it?'

It was the old school prefect speaking. I left him without comment.

The hardest part of any case, I have always maintained, comes when your client enters the witness-box. Up until that moment you have been able to protect him by attacking those who give evidence against him, and by concealing from the jury the most irritating aspects of his personality. Once he starts to give evidence, however, the client is on his own. He is like a child who has left its family on the beach and is swimming, in a solitary fashion, out to sea, where no cries of warning can be heard.

I knew Harold Brittling was going to be a bad witness by the enormously confident way that he marched into the box, held the Bible up aloft and promised to tell the truth, the whole truth and nothing but the truth. He was that dreadful sort of witness, the one who can't wait to give evidence, and who has been longing, with unconcealed impatience, for his day in Court. He leant against the top of the box and surveyed us all with an expression of tolerant disdain, as though we had made a bit of a pig's breakfast of his case up to that moment, and it was now up to him to put it right.

I dug my hands as deeply as possible into my pockets, and asked what might prove to be the only really simple question.

'Is your name Harold Reynolds Gainsborough Brittling?'

'Yes, it is. You've got *that* perfectly right, Mr Rumpole.'

I didn't laugh; neither, I noticed, did the jury.

'You came of an artistic family, Mr Brittling?' It seemed a legitimate deduction.

'Oh yes,' said Brittling, and went on modestly, 'I showed an extraordinary aptitude, my Lord, right from the start. At the Slade School, which I entered at the ripe old age of sixteen, I was twice a gold medallist and by far the most brilliant student of my year.'

The jury appeared to be moderately nauseated by this glowing account of himself. I changed the subject. 'Mr Brittling, did you know the late Septimus Cragg?'

'I knew and loved him. There is a comradeship among artists, my Lord, and he was undoubtedly the finest painter of *his* generation. He came to a student exhibition and I think he recognized . . . well . . .'

I was hoping he wouldn't say 'a fellow genius'; he did.

'After that did you meet Cragg on a number of occasions?'

'You could say that. I became one of the charmed circle at Rottingdean.'

'Mr Brittling. Will you take in your hands Exhibit 1.'

The usher lifted *Nancy* and carried her to the witness-box. Harold Brittling gave me a look of withering scorn.

'This is a beautiful picture!' he said. 'Please don't call it "Exhibit 1", Mr Rumpole. "Exhibit 1" might be a blunt instrument or something.'

The witness chuckled at this; no one else in Court smiled. I prayed to God that he'd leave the funnies to his learned Counsel.

'Where did that picture come from, Mr Brittling?'

'I really don't remember very clearly.' He looked airily round the Court as though it were a matter of supreme unimportance.

'You don't remember?' The Judge didn't seem able to believe what he was writing down.

'No, my Lord. When one is leading the life of an artist, small details escape the memory. I suppose Septimus must have given it to me on one of my visits to him. Artists pay these little tributes to each other.'

'Why did you take it to Miss Price and ask her to sell it?' I asked as patiently as possible.

'I suppose I thought that the dealers would have more faith in it if it came from that sort of source. And I rather wanted the old puss to get her little bit of commission.'

One thing emerged clearly from that bit of evidence: the jury didn't approve of Miss Price being called an 'old puss'. In fact, Brittling was going down with them like a cup of cold cod liver oil.

'Mr Brittling. What is your opinion of that picture?' Of course I wanted him to say that it was a genuine Cragg. Instead he closed his eyes and breathed in deeply. 'I think it is the work of the highest genius . . .'

'Slowly please . . .' The Judge was writing this art criticism down.

'Just watch his Lordship's pencil,' I advised the witness.

'I think it is a work of great beauty, my Lord . . . The painting of the curtains, and of the *air* in the room . . . Quite miraculous!'

'Did Septimus Cragg paint it?' I tried to bring Brittling's attention back to the case.

'It's a lovely thing.' And then the little man actually shrugged his shoulders. 'What does it matter who painted it?'

'For the purposes of this case, you can take it from me – it matters,' I instructed him. 'Now, have you any doubts that it is a genuine Cragg?'

'Only one thing gives me the slightest doubt.' Like all bad witnesses Brittling was incapable of a simple answer.

'What's that?'

'It really seems to be too good for him. It exists beautifully on a height the old boy never reached before.'

'Did you paint that picture, Mr Brittling?' I tried to direct his attention to the charge he was facing.

'Me? Is someone suggesting I did it?' Brittling seemed flattered and delighted.

'Yes, Mr Brittling. Someone is.'

'Well, in all modesty, it really takes my breath away. You are suggesting that I could produce a masterpiece like that!' And Mr Brittling smiled triumphantly round the Court.

'I take it, Mr Rumpole, that the answer means "no".' The Judge was looking understandably confused.

'Yes, of course. If your Lordship pleases.'

Featherstone, J, had interpreted Brittling's answer as a denial of forgery. I thought that no further questions could possibly improve the matter, and I sat down. Erskine-Brown rose to cross-examine with the confident air of a hunter who sees his prey snoozing gently at a range of about two feet.

'Mr Brittling,' he began quietly. 'Did you say you "laundered" the picture through Miss Price?'

'He did *what*, Mr Erskine-Brown?' The Judge was not quite with him.

'*Sold* the picture through Miss Price, my Lord, because it seemed such an unimpeachable source.'

'Yes.' The witness didn't bother to deny it.

'Does that mean that the picture isn't entirely innocent?'

'Mr Erskine-Brown, all great art is innocent.' Brittling was outraged. It seemed that all we had left was the John Keats defence:

> '*Beauty is truth, truth beauty,*' – *that is all*
> *Ye know on earth, and all ye need to know.*

'Then why this elaborate performance of selling the picture through Miss Price?' Erskine-Brown raised his voice a little.

'Just to tease them a bit. Pull their legs . . .' The worst was happening. Brittling was chuckling again.

'Pull *whose* legs, Mr Brittling?'

'The art experts! The con-o-sewers. People like Teddy Gandolphini. I just wanted to twist their tails a little.'

'So we have all been brought here, to this Court, for a sort of a joke?' Erskine-Brown acted extreme amazement.

'Oh no. Not just a joke. Something very serious is at stake.' I didn't know what else Brittling was going to say, but I suspected it would be nothing helpful.

'What?' Erskine-Brown asked.

'My reputation.'

'Your reputation as an honest man, Mr Brittling?'

'Oh no. Far more important than that. My reputation as an artist! You see, if I did paint that picture, I must be a genius, mustn't I?'

Brittling beamed round the Court, but once again no one else was smiling. At the end of the day the Judge withdrew the defendant's bail, a bad sign in any case. Harold Brittling, however, seemed to feel he had had a triumph in the witness-box, and departed, with only a moderate show of irritation, for the nick.

When I left Court – a little late, as we had the argument about bail after the jury had departed – I saw a lonely figure on a bench in the marble hall outside Number 1 Court. It was Pauline, shivering slightly, wrapped in her ethnic clothing, clutching her holdall, and her undoubtedly beautiful face was, I saw when she turned it in my direction, wet with tears. Checking a desire to suggest that the temporary absence of the appalling Brittling might come as something of a relief to his nearest and dearest, I tried to put a cheerful interpretation on recent events.

'Don't worry.' I sat down beside her and groped for a small cigar. 'Bail's quite often stopped, once a defendant's given his evidence. The jury won't know about it. Personally, I think the Judge was just showing off. Well, he's young, and a bit wet round the judicial ears.' There was a silence. Young Pauline didn't seem to be at all cheered up. Then she said, very quietly, 'They'll find Harold guilty, won't they?' She was too bright to be deceived and I exploded in irritation. 'What the hell's the matter with old Harold? He's making his evidence as weak as possible. Does he want to lose this case?'

And then she said something I hadn't expected: 'You know he does, don't you?' She put her hand on my arm in a way I found distinctly appealing.

'Please,' she said, 'will you take me for a drink? I really need one. I'd love it if you would.'

In all the circumstances it seemed a most reasonable request. 'All right,' I said. 'We'll go to Pommeroy's Wine Bar. It's only just over the road.'

'No we won't,' Pauline decided. 'We'll go to the Old Monmouth in Greek Street. I want you to meet somebody.'

The Old Monmouth, to which we travelled by taxi at Pauline's suggestion, turned out to be a large, rather gloomy pub with a past which was considerably more interesting than its present. Behind the bar there were signed photographs, and even sketches by a number of notable artists who drank there before the war and in the forties and fifties. There were also photographs of boxers, dancers and music-hall performers, and many caricatures of 'Old Harry', the former proprietor, with a huge handlebar moustache, whose son, 'Young Harry', with a smaller moustache, still appeared occasionally behind the bar.

The habits of artists have changed. Perhaps they now spend their evenings sitting at home in Islington or Kew, drinking rare Burgundy and listening to Vivaldi on the music centre. The days when a painter started the evening with a couple of pints of Guinness and ended stumbling out into Soho with a bottle of whisky in his pocket and an art school model, wearing scarlet lipstick and a beret, on his arm have no doubt gone for ever. At the Old Monmouth pale young men with orange quiffs were engaged in computerized battles on various machines. There were some eager executives in three-piece suits buying drinks for their secretaries, and half-a-dozen large men loudly discussing the virtues of their motor cars. No one looked in the least like an artist.

'They all used to come here,' Pauline said, nostalgic for a past she never knew. 'Augustus John, Sickert, Septimus Cragg. And their women. All their women . . .'

'Wonder they found room for them all.' I handed her the rum she had requested, and took a gulp of a glass of red wine which made the taste of Pommeroy's plonk seem like Château Lafite. I couldn't quite imagine what I was doing, drinking in a Soho pub with an extraordinarily personable young woman, and I was thankful for the thought that the least likely person to come through the door was She Who Must Be Obeyed.

So I tossed back the rest of the appalling Spanish-style *vin ordinaire* with the sort of gesture which I imagine Septimus Cragg might have used on a similar occasion.

'It's changed a bit now,' Pauline said, looking round the bar regretfully. 'Space Invaders!' She gave a small smile, and then her smile faded. 'Horace . . . Can I call you Horace?'

'Please.'

She put a hand on my arm. I didn't avoid it.

'You've been very kind to me. You and Hilda. But it's time you knew the truth.'

I moved a little away from her, somewhat nervously, I must confess. When someone offers to tell you the truth in the middle of a difficult criminal trial it's rarely good news.

'No,' I said firmly.

'What?' She looked up at me, puzzled.

'The time for me to know the truth is when this case is over. Too much of the truth now and I'd have to give up defending that offbeat little individual you go around with. Anyway,' I pulled out my watch, 'I've got to get back to Gloucester Road.'

'Please! Please don't leave me!' Her hand was on my arm again, and her words came pouring out, as though she were afraid I'd go before she'd finished. 'Harold said he loved Septimus Cragg. He didn't. He hated him. You see, Septimus had everything Harold wanted – fame, money, women and a style of his own. Harold can paint brilliantly, but always like other people. So he wanted to get his own back on Septimus, to get his revenge.'

'Look. If you're trying to prove to me my client's guilty . . .' I was doing my best to break off this dangerous dialogue, but she held my arm now and wouldn't stop talking.

'Don't go. If you'll wait here, just a little while, I'll show you how to prove Harold's completely innocent.'

'Do you really think I care that much?' I asked her.

'Of course you do!'

'Why?'

'Patients and nurses. Septimus said that's how the world is divided. We're the nurses, aren't we, you and I? We've *got* to care, that's our business. Please!'

I looked at her. Her eyes were full of tears again. I cursed her for having said something true, about both of us.

'All right,' I said. 'But this time I'll join you in a rum. No more Château Castanets. Oh, and I'd better make a telephone call.'

I rang Hilda from a phone on the wall near the Space Invader machine. Although there was a good deal of noise in the vicinity, the voice of She Who Must Be Obeyed came over loud and clear.

'Well, Rumpole,' she said, 'I suppose you're going to tell me you were kept late working in Chambers.'

'No,' I said, 'I'm not going to tell you that.'

'Well, what *are* you going to tell me?'

'Guthrie Featherstone put Brittling back in the cooler and I'm with the girlfriend Pauline. Remember her? We're drinking rum together in a bar in Soho and I really have no idea when I'll be back, so don't wait up for me.'

'Don't talk rubbish, Rumpole! You know I don't believe a word of it!' and my wife slammed down the receiver. If such were the price of establishing my client's innocence, I supposed it would have to be paid. I returned to the bar, where Pauline had already lined up a couple of large rums and was in the act of paying for them.

'What did you tell your wife?' she asked, having some feminine instinct, apparently, which told her the nature of my call.

'The truth.'

'I don't suppose she believed it.'

'No. Here, let me do that.' I felt for my wallet.

'It's the least I can do.' She was scooping up the change. 'You were splendid in Court. You were, honestly. The way you handled that awful Gandolphini, and the Judge. You've got what Harold always wanted.'

'What's that?'

'A voice of your own.' We both drank and she swivelled round on her bar stool to survey the scene in the Old Monmouth pub, and smiled. 'Look,' she said. 'It's here.'

'What?'

'All you need to prove Harold's innocent.'

I looked to a corner of the bar, to where she was looking. An old woman, a shapeless bundle of clothes with a few bright cheap beads, had come in and was sitting at a table in the corner. She started to search in a chaotic handbag with the air of someone who has no real confidence that anything will be found. Pauline had slid off her stool and I followed her across to the new arrival. She didn't seem to notice our existence until Pauline said, quite gently, 'Hullo, Nancy.' Then the woman looked up at me. She seemed enormously old, her face was as covered with lines as a map of the railways. Her grey hair was tousled and untidy, her hands, searching in her handbag, were not clean. But there was still a sort of brightness in her eye as she smiled at me and said, in a voice pickled during long years in the Old Monmouth pub, 'Hullo, young man. I'll have a large port and lemon.'

It is, of course, quite improper for a barrister to talk to a potential witness, so I will draw a veil over the rest of the evening. It's not so difficult to draw the aforesaid veil, as my recollection of events is somewhat hazy. I know that I paid for a good many rums and ports with lemon, and that I learnt more than I can now remember about the lives and loves of many British painters. I can remember walking with two ladies, one old and fragile, one young and beautiful, in the uncertain direction of Leicester Square tube station, and it may be that we linked arms and sang a chorus of the 'Roses of Picardy' together. I can't swear that we didn't.

I had certainly left my companions when I got back to Gloucester Road, and then discovered that the bedroom door was obstructed by some sort of device, probably a lock.

'Is that you, Rumpole?' I heard a voice from within. 'If you find her so fascinating, I wonder you bothered to come home at all.'

'Hilda!' I called, rattling at the handle. 'Where on earth am I expected to sleep?'

'I put your pyjamas on the sofa, Rumpole. Why don't you join them?'

Before I fell asleep in our sitting room, however, I made a telephone call to his home number and woke up our learned prosecutor, Claude Erskine-Brown, and chattered to him, remarkably brightly, along the following lines: 'Oh, Erskine-Brown. Hope I haven't woken you up. I have? Well, isn't it time to feed the baby anyway? Oh, the baby's four now. How time flies. Look. Check something for me, will you? That Mrs DeMoyne. Yes. The purchaser. I don't want to drag her back to Court but could your officer ask if the man who rang her was called Blanco Basnet? Yes. "Blanco". It means white, you see. Sweet dreams, Erskine-Brown.'

After which, I stretched out, dressed as I was, on the sofa and dreamed a vivid dream in which I was appearing before Mr Justice Featherstone wearing pyjamas, waving a paintbrush and singing the 'Roses of Picardy' until he sent me to cool off in the cells.

'You look tired, Rumpole.' Erskine-Brown and I were sitting side by side in Court awaiting the arrival of Blind Justice in the shape of Featherstone, J. The sledgehammer inside my head was quietening a little, but I still had a remarkably dry mouth and a good deal of stiffness in the limbs after having slept rough in Froxbury Court.

'Damn hard work, La Vie de Bohème,' I told him. 'By the way, Erskine-Brown, what's the news from Mrs DeMoyne?'

'Oh, she remembered the name as soon as the Inspector put it to her. Blanco Basnet. Odd sort of name, isn't it?'

'Distinctly odd,' I agreed. But before he could ask for any further explanation the usher called, 'Be upstanding', and upstanding we all were, as the learned Judge manifested himself upon the Bench, was put in position by his learned clerk, supplied with a notebook and sharpened pencils, and then leant forward to ask me, with a brief wince at the sight of the hands in the Rumpole pockets, 'Is there another witness for the defence?'

'Yes, my Lord,' I said, as casually as possible. 'I will now call Mrs Nancy Brittling.'

As the usher left the Court to fetch the witness in question I heard sounds, as of a ginger-beer bottle exploding on a hot day, from the dock, to which Harold Brittling had summoned the obedient Myers.

Then the courtroom door opened and the extremely old lady with whom I had sung around Goodge Street made her appearance, not much smartened up for the occasion, although she did wear, as a tribute to the learned Judge, a small straw hat perched inappropriately upon her tousled grey curls. As she took the oath, Myers was whispering to me. 'The client doesn't want this witness called, Mr Rumpole.'

'Tell the client to belt up and draw a picture, Myersy. Leave me to do my work in peace.' Then I turned to the witness-box. 'Are you Mrs Nancy Brittling?'

'Yes, dear. You know that.' The old lady smiled at me and I went on in a voice of formal severity, to discourage any possible revelation about the night before.

'Please address yourself to the learned Judge. Were you married to my client, Harold Reynolds Gainsborough Brittling?'

'It seems a long time ago now, my Lordship.' Nancy confided to Featherstone, J.

'Did Mr Brittling introduce you to the painter Septimus Cragg at Rottingdean?'

'I remember *that*.' Nancy smiled happily. 'It was my nineteenth birthday. I had red hair then, and lots of it. I remember he said I was a stunner.'

'Who said you were a "stunner",' I asked for clarification, 'your husband or . . . ?'

'Oh, Septimus said that, of course.'

'Of course.'

'And Septimus asked me to pop across to Dieppe with him the next weekend,' Nancy said proudly.

'What did you feel about that?' The old lady turned to the jury and I could see them respond to a smile that still had in it, after more than half a century, some relic of the warmth of a nineteen-year-old girl.

'Oh,' she said, 'I was thrilled to bits.'

'And what was Harold Brittling's reaction to the course of events?'

'He was sick as a dog, my Lordship.' It was an answer which found considerable favour with the jury, so naturally Erskine-Brown rose to protest.

'My Lord, I don't know what the relevance of this is. We seem to be wandering into some rather sordid divorce matter.'

'Mr Erskine-Brown!' I gave it to him between the eyebrows. 'My client has already heard the cell door bang behind him as a result of this charge, of which he is wholly innocent. And when I am proving his innocence, I will *not* be interrupted!'

'My Lord, it's quite intolerable that Mr Rumpole should talk to the jury about cell doors banging!'

'Is it really? I thought that was what this case is all about.'

At which point the learned Judge came in to pour a little oil.

'I think we must let Mr Rumpole take his own course, Mr Erskine-Brown,' he said. 'It may be quicker in the end.'

'I am much obliged to your Lordship.' I gave a servile little bow, and even took my hands out of my pockets. Then I turned to the witness. 'Mrs Brittling, did you go to Dieppe with Septimus Cragg, and while you were there together, did he paint you in the bedroom of the Hôtel du Vieux Port?'

'He painted me in the nude, my Lordship. I tell you, I was a bit of something worth painting in those days.'

Laughter from the jury, and a discreet smile from the learned Judge, were accompanied by a pained sigh from Erskine-Brown. I asked the usher to take Exhibit 1 to the witness, and Nancy looked at the picture and smiled, happily lost, for a moment, in the remembrance of things past.

'Will you look at Exhibit 1, Mrs Brittling?'

'Yes. That's the picture. I saw Septimus paint that. In the bedroom at Dieppe.'

'And the signature . . . ?' Erskine-Brown had told the jury that all forged pictures carried large signatures, as this one did. But Nancy Brittling was there to prove him wrong.

'I saw Septimus paint his signature. And, we were so happy together, just for a bit of fun, he let me paint my name too.'

'Let his Lordship see.'

So the usher trundled up to the learned Judge with the picture, and once again Guthrie raised his magnifying glass respectfully to it.

'It's a bit dark. I did it in sort of purple, at the edge of the carpet. I just wrote "Nancy", that's all.'

'Mr Rumpole,' Featherstone, J, said, and I blessed him for it. 'I think she's right about that.'

'Yes, my Lord. I have looked and I think she is. Mrs Brittling, do you know how your husband got hold of that picture?'

Once again, the evidence was accompanied by popping and fizzing noises from the dock as the prisoner's wife explained, with some gentle amusement, 'Oh yes. Septimus gave it to *me*, but when I brought it home to Harold he fussed so much that in the end I let him have the picture. Well, after a time Harold and I separated and I suppose he kept hold of it until he wanted to pretend he'd painted it himself.'

'Thank you, Mrs Brittling.' I sat down, happy in my work. The sledgehammer had quietened and I stretched out my legs, preparing to watch Erskine-Brown beat his head against the brick wall of a truthful witness.

'Mrs Brittling,' he began. 'Why have you come here to give this evidence? It must be painful for you, to remember those rather sordid events.'

'Painful? Oh, no!' Nancy looked at him and smiled. 'It's a pure pleasure, my dear, to see that picture again and to remember what I looked like, when I was nineteen and happy.'

The next morning I addressed the jury, and I was able to offer them the solution to the mystery of Harold Brittling and the disputed Septimus Cragg. I started by reminding them of one of Nancy's answers: ' ". . . he kept hold of it until he wanted to pretend he'd painted it himself." Harold Brittling, you may think, ladies and gentlemen of the jury,' I said, 'had one driving passion in his life – his almost insane jealousy of Septimus Cragg. Cragg became his young wife's lover. But worse than that in Brittling's eyes, Cragg was a great painter and Brittling was second rate, with no style of his own. So now, years after Cragg's death, Brittling planned his revenge. He was going to prove that he could paint a better Cragg than Cragg ever painted. He would prove that this fine picture was his work and not Cragg's. That was his revenge for a weekend in Dieppe, and a lifetime's humiliation. To achieve that revenge Brittling was prepared to sell his Cragg in a devious way that would be bound to attract suspicion. He was prepared to get a friend of his named Blanco Basnet to telephone Mrs DeMoyne and claim that the picture was not a genuine Cragg, but something a great deal better. He was prepared to face a charge of forgery. He was prepared to go to prison. He was prepared to give his evidence to you in such a way as to lead you to believe that he was the true painter of a work of genius. Don't be deceived, members of the jury, Brittling is no forger. He is a fake criminal and not a real one. He is not guilty of the crime he is charged with.

He is guilty only of the bitterness felt for men of genius by the merely talented. You may think, members of the jury, as you bring in your verdict of "Not Guilty", that that is an understandable emotion. You may even feel pity for a poor painter who could not even produce a forgery of his own.'

As I sat down, the ginger-beer bottle in the dock finally exploded and Brittling shouted, in an unmannerly way, at his defending Counsel, 'You bastard, Rumpole!' he yelled, 'you've joined the con-o-sewers!'

'Good win, Horace. Of course, I always thought your client was innocent.'

'Did you now?'

The Judge had invited me in for a glass of very reasonable amontillado after the jury brought in their verdict and, as the case was now over, we were alone in his room.

'Oh yes. One gets a nose for these things. One can soon assess a witness and know if he's telling the truth. Have to do that all the time in this job. Oh, and Horace . . .'

'Yes, Judge?'

His Lordship continued in some embarrassment. 'That bit of a tizz I was in, about the great secret getting out. No need to mention that to anyone, eh?'

'Oh, I rang the Lord Chancellor's office about that. The day after we met in Pommeroy's,' I told him, and casually slipped my hands into my pockets.

'You *what*?' Featherstone looked at me in a wild surmise.

'I assured them you hadn't said a word to anyone and it was just a sort of silly joke put about by Claude Erskine-Brown. I mean, no one in the Temple ever dreamed that they'd make *you* a Judge.'

'Horace! Did you say that?'

'Of course I did.' He took time to consider the matter and then pronounced judgement. 'Then you got me out of a nasty spot! I was afraid Marigold had been a bit indiscreet. Horace, I owe you an immense debt of gratitude.'

'Yes. You do,' I agreed. His Lordship looked closely at me, and some doubt seemed to have crept into his voice as he said, 'Horace. *Did* you ring the Lord Chancellor's office? Are you telling me the truth?'

I looked at him with the clear eyes of a reliable witness. 'Can't you tell, Judge? I thought you had such an infallible judicial eye for discovering if a witness is lying or not. Not slipping a bit, are you?'

'What is it, Rumpole. Not flowers again?'

'Bubbly! Non-vintage. Pommeroy's sparkling – on special offer. And I paid for it myself!' I had brought Hilda a peace offering which I set about opening on the kitchen table as soon as I returned to the matrimonial home.

'Where's that girl now?' she asked suspiciously.

'God knows. Gone off into the sunset with the old chump. He'll never forgive me for getting him acquitted, so I don't suppose we'll be seeing either of them again.'

The cork came out with a satisfying pop, and I began to fill a couple of glasses with the health-giving bubbles.

'I should have thought you'd had quite enough to drink with her last night!' Hilda was only a little mortified.

'Oh, forget her. She was a girl with soft eyes, and red hair, who passed through the Old Bailey and then was heard no more.'

I handed Hilda a glass, and raised mine in a toast.

> ' "Beauty is truth, truth beauty," – that is all
> Ye know on earth, and all ye need to know.'

I looked at She Who Must Be Obeyed and then I said, 'It isn't, is it, though? We need to know a damn sight more than that!'

Rumpole and the Last Resort

I have almost caught up with myself. Decent crime has not been too thick on the ground recently, and time has been hanging a little heavily on the Rumpole hands. I have had a good deal of leisure to spend on these chronicles of the splendours and miseries of an Old Bailey Hack and, although I have enjoyed writing them, describing and remembering is something of a second-hand occupation. I am happiest, I must confess, with the whiff of battle in my nostrils, with the Judge and the prosecuting Counsel stacked against me, with the jury unconvinced, and everything to play for as I rear to my hind legs and start to cross-examine the principal witness for the Crown. There has been a notable decrease in the number of briefs in my tray in Chambers of late, and I have often set out for Number 3 Equity Court with nothing but *The Times* crossword and the notebook in which I have spent otherwise undemanding days recalling old murders and other offences. A barrister's triumphs are short-lived: a notable victory may provide gossip round the Temple for a week or two; a row with the Judge may be remembered a little longer; but those you have got off don't wish to be reminded of the cells where they met you, and those whose cases you have lost aren't often keen to share memories. By and large, trials are over and done with when you pack up your robes and leave Court after the verdict. For that reason it has been some satisfaction to me to write these accounts, although the truth of the matter is, as I have already hinted, that I haven't had very much else to do.

So up to date have I become that I can recount no more cases of sufficient interest and importance which have engaged my talents since my unexpected return from retirement. All I have left to do is something new to me – that is, to write about a case as I am doing it, in the hope that it will turn out to be sufficiently unusual to be included among these papers which will form some sort of memorial to the transient life of Horace Rumpole, barrister-at-law. I am soon to go into Court with one of my dwindling number of briefs, as Counsel for the defence of a young businessman named Frank Armstrong, Chairman and Managing Director of Sun-Sand Holidays Ltd, an organization which supplies mobile homes to holidaymakers in allegedly desirable sites in the West Country, the Lake District and other places which have every known inconvenience, including being much too far away from Pommeroy's Wine Bar. The case itself may have some points of interest, including the mysterious mobility of Sun-Sand Mobile Homes, and the period about which I am writing contains another minor mystery, that is to say, the disappearance of a Mr Perivale Blythe, solicitor of the Supreme Court, a fellow who, so far as I am concerned, is fully entitled to disappear off the face of the earth, were it not for the fact that he has, for longer than I care to remember, owed me money.

One of the many drawbacks of life at the Bar is the length of time it takes to get paid for services rendered. As the loyal punter may not appreciate, he pays the solicitor for the hire of a barrister and, in theory at any rate, the solicitor passes the loot on to the member of the Bar, the front-line warrior in the courtroom battle, with the greatest possible dispatch. In many cases, unhappily, the money lingers along the line and months, even years, may pass before it percolates into the barrister's bank account. There is really nothing much the average advocate can do about this. In the old days, when barristering was regarded as a gentlemanly pursuit for persons of private means, rather like fox hunting or collecting rare seaweed, the rule grew up that barristers couldn't sue for their fees, on the basis that to be seen suing a solicitor would be as unthinkable as to be found dancing with your cook.

So it was not only a decline in the number of briefs bearing the Rumpole name, but a considerable slowing down in the paying process, which caused my account at the Temple branch of the United Metropolitan Bank to blush an embarrassing red. One day I called in to cash a fifty-pound cheque, mainly to defray the costs of those luxuries Hilda indulges in, matters such as bread and soap powder, and I stood at the counter breathing a silent prayer that the cashier might see fit to pay me out. Having presented my cheque, I heard the man behind the grille say, to my considerable relief, 'How would you like the money, sir?'

'Oh, preferably in enormous quantities.' Of course it was a stupid thing to say. As soon as the words had passed my lips, I thought he'd take my cheque off to the back of the shop and discover the extent of the Rumpole debt. Why was he reading the thing so attentively? The art of cheque cashing is to appear totally unconcerned.

'How would I like the money?' I said rapidly. 'Oh, I'll take it as it comes. Nothing fancy, thank you. Not doubloons. Or pieces of eight. Just pour me out a moderate measure of pounds sterling.'

To my relief the notes came out on a little wheel under the glass window. I scooped up the boodle and told myself that the great thing was not to run. Break into any sort of jogtrot on the way to the door and they check up on the overdraft at once. The secret is to walk casually and even whistle in a carefree manner.

I was doing exactly that when I was stopped with a far from cheery good morning by Mr Medway, the Assistant Manager. I should have made a dash for it.

'Paying in or drawing out today, are we?' Medway looked at the money in my hand. 'Oh. Drawing out, I see. Could you step into my office, sir?'

'Not now. Got to get to Court. A money brief, of course.' I was hastily stuffing the notes into my pocket.

'Just a moment of your time, Mr Rumpole.' Medway was not to be put off. Within a trice I found myself closeted with him as I was grilled as to my financial position.

'Gone right over the limit of our overdraft, haven't we, Mr Rumpole?' The man smiled unpleasantly.

'My overdraft? A flea bite, compared with what you chaps are lending the Poles.'

I searched for a packet of cigars, feeling that I rather had him there.

'I don't think the Poles are making out quite so many cheques in favour of Jack Pommeroy of Pommeroy's Wine Bar.'

'Those are for the bare necessities of life. Look here, Medway. A fellow's got to live!'

'There's bound to come a time, Mr Rumpole, when that may not be necessary at the expense of the United Metropolitan Bank.' A peculiarly heartless financier, this Medway.

'"The Bank with the Friendly Ear".' I quoted his commercial, lit the cigar and blew out smoke.

'There comes a time, Mr Rumpole, when the United Metropolitan goes deaf.'

'That little overdraft of mine. Peanuts! Quite laughable compared to my outstanding fees.' It was my time to bring out the defence. 'My fees'll come in. Of course they will. You know how long solicitors keep owing us money? Why, there's one firm who still hasn't paid me for a private indecency I did for them ten years ago. No names, of course, but . . .'

'Is that Mr Perivale Blythe?' Medway was consulting my criminal record. 'Of Blythe, Winterbottom and Paisley?'

'Yes. I believe that's the fellow. Slow payer, but the money's there, of course.'

'Is it, Mr Rumpole?' Medway was a banker of little faith. 'Every time we've had one of these little chats, you've told me that you're owed a considerable amount in fees by Mr Perivale Blythe.'

'Can't remember how much, of course. But enough to pay off my overdraft and make a large contribution to the National Debt.' I stood up, anxious to bring this embarrassing interview to a conclusion. 'Must be scooting along,' I said. 'Got to earn both of us some money. Engaged in Court, you know.'

'My advice to you, Mr Rumpole,' Medway said darkly, 'is to take steps to make this Mr Perivale Blythe pay up. And without delay.'

'Of course. Get my clerk on to it at once. Now don't you worry, Medway.' I opened the door on my way to freedom. 'Having the Poles in next, are you? Hope you give them a good talking to.'

When I had told Medway that I had an engagement in Court it was a pardonable exaggeration. In fact I had nothing much to do but settle into my room at 3 Equity Court and write these memoirs. I had found the *tête-à-tête* in the bank somewhat depressing and I was in a low mood as I turned into the Temple and approached the entrance of our Chambers. There I met our demure Head, Sam Ballard, QC, who was standing on the step in conversation with a young man with dark hair, soft eyes and an expression of somewhat unjustified self-confidence which reminded me of someone. Ballard greeted me with 'Hullo there, Rumpole. How are you?'

'*Tir'd with all these, for restful death I cry*,' I told him candidly.

> '*As to behold desert a beggar born,*
> *And needy nothing trimm'd in jollity,*
> *And purest faith unhappily forsworn,*
> *And gilded honour shamefully misplac'd . . .*'

'What's this talk of death, Rumpole?' Ballard was brisk and disapproving. 'You know young Archie Featherstone, don't you? Mr Justice Featherstone's nephew.' He introduced the young man, who smiled vaguely.

'My God. More Featherstones!' I was amazed. '*What! will the line stretch out to the crack of doom?*'

'I'm sure he'd like your advice about starting out at the Bar.'

'My advice is, "Don't",' I told the young man.

'Don't?' he repeated, pained.

'Don't slog your heart out. Don't tramp for years round some pretty unsympathetic Courts. What'll you have to show at the end of it? You're up to your eyes in debt to the United Metropolitan Bank and they'll grudge you such basic nourishment as a couple of dozen non-vintage Château Thames Embankment.'

'Young Featherstone would love to get a seat in our Chambers, Rumpole.' Ballard had clearly not followed a word I'd said. 'I've told him that at the moment there's just not the accommodation available.'

'At the moment?' Was the man expecting a sudden departure from our little band of barristers?

'Well, I don't suppose you'll be in your room for ever.' Ballard didn't sound too regretful. 'The time must come when you take things a little more easily. Henry was saying how tired he thought you looked.'

'*Tir'd with all these, for restful death I cry . . .*' I repeated, and I looked at Ballard, remembering, '*And gilded honour shamefully misplac'd*. Oh yes, Ballard. The time's got to come. Cheer up, young Featherstone,' I told him. 'You'll soon be able to take over my overdraft.'

I left them there and went to report to the clerk's room. When I got there I found Henry in position at his desk and Dianne rattling her typewriter in a corner.

'Henry, how much does Perivale Blythe owe me in fees?' I asked at once.

'Two thousand, seven hundred and sixty-five pounds, ninety-three pence, Mr Rumpole,' Henry said, as if he knew it all by heart.

'You tell me of wealth undreamed of by the United Metropolitan Bank. It's a debt stretching back over a considerable time, eh, Henry?'

'Stretching back, Mr Rumpole, to the indecency at Swansea in April 1973.' Henry confirmed my suspicions.

'You have, I suppose, been on to him about it, Henry?'

'Almost daily, Mr Rumpole.'

'And what has this blighter Blythe to say for himself?'

'The last time his secretary told us a cheque was in the post.'

'Not true?' I guessed.

'Not unless it evaporated mysteriously between here and Cheapside.'

'Get after him, Henry, like a terrier. Get your teeth into the man Blythe, and don't let him go until he disgorges the loot.'

I looked at Henry's desk and my eyes were greeted with the unusual and welcome sight of a brief bearing the Rumpole name. 'Is that a set of papers for me you're fingering?' I asked with assumed indifference.

'Mr Myers brought it in, sir. It's a case at the Bailey.' Henry confirmed the good news.

'God bless old Myersy. A man who pays up from time to time.' I looked at the brief. 'What is it, Henry? Murder? Robbery? Sudden death?'

'Sorry, Mr Rumpole.' Henry realized that I would be disappointed. 'It seems to be about Sun-Sand Mobile Homes.'

When I went up to my room to familiarize myself with the brief Henry had given me, I threw my hat, as usual, on to the hatstand; but, the hatstand not being there, the Rumpole headgear thudded to the ground. Of course, I knew what had happened. Erskine-Brown had always coveted the old hatstand that had stood in my room for years and, when he had a big conference, he put it in his room to impress the clientele. Before I started work I crept along the passage, found Erskine-Brown's room empty and purloined the old article of furniture back again. Then I sat down, lit a small cigar, and studied the facts in the case of *R. v. Armstrong*.

The trouble had started at a Sun-Sand holiday site in Cornwall.

A family returned from a cold, wet day on the beach and had their mobile holiday home towed away before they could get at their high tea. Other punters were apparently sold holidays in mobile homes which were said to have existed only in the fertile imagination of my client, Frank Armstrong.

In due course police officers – Detective Inspector Limmeridge and Detective Sergeant Banks – called on Sun-Sand Holidays in North London. The premises were small and unimposing but the officers noticed that they were elaborately equipped with all the latest gadgets of computer technology. The young chairman of the company was there, busily pressing buttons and anxiously watching figures flash and hearing the bleeps and hiccoughs of such machines at work. When arrested, Mr Armstrong was given permission to telephone his solicitor, but when he did so he found that the gentleman in question had just slipped out of the office.

Eventually Frank Armstrong was allowed bail and turned up in my room at Chambers with old Myers, the solicitor's clerk (or legal executive, as such gentlemen are now called), whom I would rather have with me on a bad day at the Bailey than most of the learned friends I can think of. I had asked Miss Fiona Allways to join us and generally help with the sums.

'My brother Fred and I, we was born into the modern world, Mr Rumpole,' said Frank. 'And what is the name of the game, in the world today?'

'Space Invaders?' I hazarded a guess. My client looked at me seriously. In spite of a sharp business suit, his gaucho moustache, longish hair, gold watch and bracelet, Playboy Club tie and the manner of a tough young businessman, Frank Armstrong looked younger than I had expected, and both pained and puzzled by the turn of events.

'The name of the game is leisure interests and computer technology,' he told me seriously. 'You won't believe this, Mr Rumpole. You will not believe it.'

'Try me.'

'Our old dad kept a fruit barrow in the Shepherd's Bush Market.'

'Not incredible,' I assured him.

'Yes, indeed. Well, he made a few bob in his time and when he died my brother and I divided the capital. Fred went into hardware, right?'

'Ironmongery?'

'You're joking,' Frank said. 'Fred joined the microchip revolution. Looking round your office now, Mr Rumpole, I doubt it's fully automated. There are delays in sending your bills out, right?'

'Sometimes I think my bills are sent out by a carrier pigeon with a poor sense of direction,' I admitted.

'Trust in the computer, Mr Rumpole, and you'd have so much more time, leisure-wise. That's the . . .'

'Name of the game?' I hazarded.

'Yes, indeed. That's why I saw my future definitely in the leisure industry.'

' "Leisure industry". Sounds like a contradiction in terms.'

Frank didn't hear my murmur. He was clearly off on a favourite subject. 'Who wants hotel expenses these days? Who needs porters, tips, waiter service? All the hassle. The future, as I see it, is in self-catering mobile homes set in A3 and B1 popularity, mass appeal holiday areas. That's the vision, Mr Rumpole, and it's got me where I am today.'

'On bail, facing charges of fraud and fraudulent conversion,' I reminded him.

'Mr Rumpole. I want you to believe this . . .'

'Try me again.'

'I just don't understand it. I want to tell you that very frankly. I was doing my best to run a go-ahead service industry geared to the needs of the eighties. What went wrong exactly?' Frank asked plaintively. I got up, stretched the legs and lit a small cigar.

'I imagine a close study of the accounts might tell us that,' I said. 'By the way, that's one of the reasons I've asked you to give Miss Allways a little brief. She's got a remarkable head for figures.'

'And quite a figure for heads, I should think.' Frank gave our lady barrister one of his 'Playboy Club' leers and laughed. Fiona froze him with a look.

'Pardon me, Miss Allways. Probably out of place, right?' Our client apologized and Miss Allways ignored him and rattled out some businesslike instructions to old Myers. 'I'd like the accounts sent down to Chambers as soon as possible,' she said. 'There's a great deal of spadework to be done.'

'This is where we're in a certain amount of difficulty.' Myers coughed apologetically.

'Surely not?'

'You see, the accounts were all given to Mr Armstrong's previous solicitor. That was the firm that acted for his father back in the fruit barrow days and went on acting till after our client's arrest.'

'It's perfectly simple.' Fiona was impatient. 'You've only got to get in touch with the former solicitors.'

'Well, not quite as simple as all that, Miss Allways. We've tried writing but we never get an answer to our letters and when we telephone, well, the gentleman dealing with the matter always seems to have just slipped out of the office.'

'Really? What's the name of the firm?' Miss Allways asked, but I was ahead of her. 'Don't tell me, let me guess,' I said. 'What about Blythe, Winterbottom and Paisley?'

'Well,' our client admitted dolefully. 'This is it.'

At the end of the day I called into Pommeroy's Wine Bar and the first person I met was Claude Erskine-Brown on his way out. Of course I went straight into the attack.

'Erskine-Brown,' I said accusingly. 'Hatstand-pincher!'

'Rumpole. That's a most serious allegation.'

'Hatstand-pinching is a most serious crime,' I assured him.

'You don't need a hatstand in your room, Rumpole. Criminals hardly ever wear hats. I happened to have a conference yesterday with three solicitors all with bowlers.'

'That hatstand is a family heirloom, Erskine-Brown. It belonged to my old father-in-law. I value it highly,' I told him.

'Oh, very well, Rumpole. If that's the attitude.' He was leaving me.

'Goodnight, Erskine-Brown. And keep your hands off my furniture.'

As I penetrated the interior, I saw our clerk Henry, who is, far more effectively than the egregious Bollard, the true Head of our Chambers and ruler of our lives, in the company of the ever-faithful Dianne. I asked him to name his poison, which he did, in an unattractive manner, as Cinzano Bianco and lemonade.

'Dianne?' I included her in the invitation.

'I'll have the same.' She looked somewhat meltingly at Henry. 'It's what we used to have in Lanzarotte.'

'Did you really? Well, I won't inquire too deeply into that. And a large cooking claret, Jack, and no doubt you'd be happy to cash a small cheque?' I asked the host as he came past pushing a cloth along the counter.

'Well, not exactly happy, Mr Rumpole.' Pommeroy was not in one of his sunnier moods.

'Come on, you've got nothing to worry about. You haven't lent a penny to Poland, have you? This is a much safer bank than the United Metropolitan. Oh, give yourself one while you're about it,' I said, as Jack moved reluctantly to get the drinks and the money. Then I turned to my clerk in a businesslike manner. 'Now then, Henry, about this abominable Blythe. Not surfaced, by any stretch of the imagination?'

'No, Mr Rumpole. Not as yet, sir.'

'Not as yet. Lying in his hammock in some South Sea Island, is he, fondling an almond-eyed beauty and drinking up our brief fees and refreshers?'

'I've made inquiries around the Temple. Mr Brushwood in Queen Elizabeth's Buildings had the same problem, his clerk was telling me. Blythe owed well into four figures, and they couldn't find hide nor hair of him, sir.'

'But poor old Tommy Brushwood is . . .' The claret had come and I resorted to it.

'No longer with us. I know that, sir. And as soon as he'd gone, Blythe called on Mr Brushwood's widow and got her to give him some sort of release for a small percentage. She signed as executor, not quite knowing the form, I would imagine. Cheers, Mr Rumpole.'

'Oh, yes. Cheers everso.' Dianne smiled at me over the fizzy concoction.

'But Henry, why has this Blythe not been reported to the Law Society? Why hasn't he been clapped in irons,' I asked him, 'and transported to the colonies?'

'All the clerks have thought of reporting him, of course. But if we did that we'd never get paid, now would we?'

'Despite that drink you indulge in, which has every appearance of chilled Lucozade, I believe you still have your head screwed on, Henry. I have another solution.'

'Honestly, Mr Rumpole? I'd be glad to hear it.'

'We need Blythe as a witness in the Sun-Sand Mobile Homes case.'

'R. v. *Armstrong*?'

'Your memory serves you admirably. We'll get Newton the Private Dick to find Blythe so he can slap a subpoena on him. If "Fig" Newton can't find the little horror, no one can. Isn't that all we need?'

'I hope so, Mr Rumpole,' Henry said doubtfully. 'I really hope so.'

Ferdinand Ian Gilmour Newton, widely known in the legal profession as 'Fig' Newton, was a tall, gloomy man who always seemed to be suffering from a heavy cold. No doubt his work, forever watching back doors, peering into windows, following errant husbands in all weathers, was responsible for his pink nostrils and the frequent application of a crumpled handkerchief. I have known Fig Newton throughout my legal career. He appeared daily in the old-style divorce cases, when his evidence was invariably accepted. Since the bonds of matrimony can now be severed without old Fig having to inspect the sheets or observe male and female clothing scattered in a hotel bedroom, his work has diminished; but he can still be relied upon to serve a writ or unearth an alibi witness. He seems to have no interests outside his calling. His home life, if it exists at all, is a mystery. I believe he snatches what sleep he can while sitting in his battered Cortina watching the lights go on and off in the bedroom of a semi-detached, and he dines off a paper of fish and chips as he guards the door of a debtor who has gone to earth.

Fig Newton called at the offices of Blythe, Winterbottom and Paisley early one morning and asked to see Mr Perivale Blythe. He was greeted by a severe-looking secretary, a lady named Miss Claymore, with spectacles, a tweed skirt and cardigan, and a Scots accent. Despite her assuring him that Perivale Blythe was out of the office and not expected back that day, the leech-like Fig sat down and waited. He learned nothing of importance, except that round about noon Miss Claymore went into an inner office to make a telephone call. The detective was able to hear little of the conversation, but she did say something about the times of trains to Penzance.

When Miss Claymore left her office, Fig Newton followed her home. He sat in his Cortina in Kilburn outside the Victorian building, divided into flats, to which Miss Claymore had driven her small Renault. He waited for almost two hours, and when Miss Claymore finally emerged she had undergone a considerable change. She was wearing tight trousers of some satin-like material and a pink fluffy sweater. Her feet were crammed into high-heeled gold sandals and she was without her spectacles. She got into the Renault and drove to Soho, where she parked with considerable daring halfway up a pavement, and went into an Italian restaurant where she met a young man. Fig Newton kept observation from the street and was thus unable to share in the lasagne and the bottle of Valpolicella, which he carefully noted down. Later the couple crossed Frith Street and entered a Club known as the 'Pussy Cat A-Go-Go', where particularly loud music was being played. Fig Newton was later able to peer down into the basement of this Club, where, lit by sporadic, coloured lights, Miss Claymore was dancing with the same young man, whom he described as having the appearance of a young business executive with features very similar to those of our client.

On the evening that Mr Perivale Blythe's secretary went dancing, I was reading on the sofa at 25B Froxbury Court, smoking a small cigar and recovering from a hard day of writing this account in my Chambers. Suddenly, and without warning, my wife, She Who Must Be Obeyed, dropped a heavy load of correspondence on to my stomach.

'Hilda,' I protested. 'What are these?'

'Bills, Rumpole. Can't you recognize them?'

'Electricity. Gas. Rates. Water rates.' I gave them a glance. 'We really must cut down on these frivolities.'

'All gone red,' Hilda told me.

'It's only last month's telephone bill.' I looked at a specimen. 'We should lay that down for maturing. You don't have to rush into paying these things, you know. Mr Blythe hasn't paid me much of anything since 1972.'

'Well, you'd better tell Mr Perivale Blythe that the London Electricity Board aren't as patient as you are, Rumpole,' She said severely.

'Hilda. You know we can't sue anyone for our fees.'

'I can't think why ever not.' My wife has only a limited understanding of the niceties of legal etiquette.

'It wouldn't be a gentlemanly thing to do,' I explained. 'Against the finest traditions of the Bar.'

'Perhaps it's a gentlemanly thing to sit here in the dark with the gas cut off and no telephone and nasty looks every time you go into the butcher's. All I can say is, you can sit there and be gentlemanly on your own. I'm going away, Rumpole.'

I looked at Hilda with a wild surmise. Was I, at an advanced age, about to become the product of a broken home? 'Is that a threat or a promise,' I asked her.

'What did you say?'

'I said, "Of course, you'll be missed",' I assured her.

'Dodo's been asked to stay with a friend in the Lake District, Pansy Rawlins, whom we were both at school with, if you remember.'

'Well, I don't think I was there at the time.'

'And Pansy's lost her husband recently.'

'Careless of her,' I muttered, moving the weight of the bills off me.

'So it'll be a bachelor party. Of course, when Dodo first asked me I said I couldn't possibly leave *you*, Rumpole.'

'I am prepared to make the supreme sacrifice and let you go. Don't worry about me,' I managed to say bravely.

'I don't suppose I shall, unduly. But you'd better worry about yourself. My advice to you is, find this Colindale Blythe.'

'*Perivale*, Hilda.'

'Well, he sounds a bit of a twister, wherever he lives. Find him and get him to pay you. Make that your task.' She looked down at me severely. 'Oh, and while I'm away, Rumpole, try not to put your feet on the sofa.'

Today I arrived in good time at the Old Bailey. I like to give myself time to drink in the well-known atmosphere of floor polish and uniforms, to put on the fancy dress at leisure, and then go down to the public canteen for a cup of coffee and a go at the crossword. I needed to build up my strength particularly this morning, as Henry had let me know the name of our Judge the evening before. I therefore ordered a particularly limp sausage roll with the coffee, and I had just finished this and was lighting a small cigar, when Myers appeared carrying Newton's latest report, accompanied by Miss Fiona Allways, wigged and gowned and ready for the fray. Since the curious sighting of Blythe's secretary tripping the light fantastic at the Pussy Cat A-Go-Go, Fig had kept up a patient and thorough search for the elusive Perivale Blythe, with no result whatsoever.

'I still think Blythe's an essential witness.' Fiona was sticking to her guns.

'Of course he is,' I agreed.

'We just need more time for Newton to make inquiries. Can't we ask for an adjournment?' Myers suggested hopefully.

'We can ask.' I'm afraid my tone was not particularly encouraging.

'Surely, Mr Rumpole, any reasonable judge would grant it.'

Perhaps Myers was right; but it was then that I had to remind him that we'd been landed with his Honour Judge Roger Bullingham. I stood up in front of him, with the jury out of Court and Ward-Webster, our young and eager prosecutor, relaxing in his seat, and asked for an adjournment in no less than five distinct and well-considered ways. It was like trying to shift a mountain with a teaspoon. Finally his Honour said, in a distinctly testy tone of voice,

'Mr Rumpole! For the fifth time, I'm not adjourning this case. So far as I can see the defence has had all the time in the world.'

'Your Lordship may know how long it takes to find a solicitor.' I tried the approach jovial. 'If your Lordship remembers his time at the Bar.' The joke, if it can be dignified with such a title, went down like a lead balloon.

'Mr Rumpole, neither your so-called eloquence nor your alleged pleasantry are going to make me change my mind.' Bullingham was beginning to irritate me. I raised the Rumpole voice a couple of decibels. 'Then let me tell you an indisputable fact. For years my client's business life was in the hands of Mr Perivale Blythe.'

'Your client's business life, such as it was, was in his own hands, Mr Rumpole.' The Judge was unimpressed. 'And it's about time he faced up to his responsibilities. This case will proceed without any further delay. That is my final decision.'

There is a way of saying 'If your Lordship pleases' so that it sounds like dumb insolence. I said it like that and sat down.

'You did your best, sir,' Myers turned and whispered to me. Good old Myersy. That's what he always says when I fail dismally.

For the rest of the day I sat listening to prosecution evidence. From time to time my eyes wandered around the courtroom and, on one such occasion, I saw a severe-looking female in spectacles sitting in the front of the Public Gallery, taking notes.

It was a long day in Court. When I got back to the so-called mansion flat, I noticed something unusual. She Who Must Be Obeyed was conspicuous by her absence. I called, 'Hilda!' in various empty rooms and then I remembered that she had gone off, in none too friendly a mood, to stay with her old school chums, Dodo and Pansy, in the Lake District. So I poached a couple of eggs, buttered myself a slice of toast and sat down to a bottle of Pommeroy's plonk and this account. Now I am up to date with my life and with events in the Sun-Sand Mobile Holiday Homes affair. Tomorrow, I suppose, will bring new developments on all fronts. The only thing that can be said with any certainty about tomorrow is that I shan't become any younger, nor will Judge Bullingham prove any easier to handle. Now the bottle's empty and I've smoked the last of my small cigars. The washing-up can take care of itself. I'm going to bed.

THE NARRATIVE OF MISS FIONA ALLWAYS

I should never have taken this on. From the first day I met him in Chambers, after I had received a severe ticking-off from Mrs Erskine-Brown, QC, Rumpole was extremely decent to me. I'm still not absolutely sure how he managed to persuade the men at 3 Equity Court to take me on, but I have a feeling that he did something pretty devious for my sake. I took a note from him in quite a few of his cases and he was able to winkle a junior brief in *R. v. Armstrong* for me out of his instructing solicitor. So you see, although a lot of people found him absolutely impossible, and he could say the most appalling things quite unexpectedly, Rumpole was always extremely kind to me and, above all, he saved my sister Jennifer from doing a life sentence for murder.

So you can imagine my feelings about what happened to Rumpole in the middle of the Armstrong trial. Well, you'll have to imagine them, I'm afraid to say, because although I never got less than B+ for an essay at school, and although I can get a set of facts in order and open a case fairly clearly at Thames Mags' Court now, I'm never going to have Rumpole's talent for emotional speeches. All I can say is that the day *R. v. Armstrong* was interrupted, as it was, was a day I hope I never have to live through again. What I'm trying to say is, my feelings of gratitude to old Rumpole made that a pretty shattering experience.

All the same, I do realize that the records of one of Rumpole's more notable cases should be complete, and that's why I've agreed to give my own account of the closing stages of the Armstrong trial. I suppose my taking this on is the least I can do for him now. So, anyway, here goes.

I have to say that I never particularly liked our client, Frank Armstrong. He had doggy eyes and a good deal of aftershave and I got the feeling that he was trying to make some sort of a pass at me at our first conference; and that sort of thing, so far as I am concerned, is definitely not on. When he came to give evidence I think Rumpole soon realized that Armstrong wasn't going to be a particularly impressive witness, and he looked fairly gloomy as we sat listening to our client being cross-examined by Ward-Webster, who was doing a pretty competent job for the prosecution. I took a full note and, looking at it now, I see that the moment came when the witness was shown the photograph of the Sun-Sand Mobile Homes site in Cornwall, and Judge Bullingham, who didn't seem to like Rumpole, turned to the jury and said, 'Hardly looks like the Côte d'Azur, does it, members of the jury? It looks like an industrial tip.'

'Looking in the other direction, there's a view of the sea, my Lord.' I remember our client sounding distinctly pained.

'What, between the crane and the second lorry?' Bullingham was still smiling at the jury.

'A great deal of our patrons' time is spent on the beach,' Armstrong protested.

'Perhaps they want a quiet night!' The Judge suggested, and the jury laughed.

'Mr Armstrong. Do you agree that on no less than fifty occasions holidays on the site in Cornwall turned out to have been booked in non-existent mobile homes?' Ward-Webster went on with his cross-examination.

'Yes indeed, but . . .' the witness was sounding particularly hopeless.

'And that your firm was paid large deposits for such holidays?' Ward-Webster went on.

'Well, this is it, but . . .'

'And on one occasion at least a mobile home was actually removed from an unhappy mother just as she was about to enter it?'

'It was one of those things . . .'

'Instead of mother running away from home, the home ran away from mother?'

I remember that the Judge made his joke at that point, and Rumpole muttered to me, 'Oh well done, Bull. Quite the stand-up comic.'

'And that letters of protest from the losers and their legal advisers remained unanswered?' Ward-Webster went on when the laughter died down.

'If there were complaints, the information should have been fed into the office computer.'

'Perhaps the people in question would rather have had their money back than have their complaints consumed by your computer.'

'Quite frankly, Mr Ward-Webster, our office at Sun-Sand Holidays is equipped with the latest technology.' Our client sounded deeply offended. At this the Judge told him that it was a pity it wasn't also equipped with a little old-fashioned plain dealing.

Of course, Rumpole objected furiously and said that was the point the jury had to decide. My note reminds me that the Judge then smiled at the jury and said, 'Very well, members of the jury, you will have heard Mr Rumpole's objection. Now, shall we get on with the trial?'

'Mr Armstrong, are you telling us that these events are due to the inefficiency of your office?' Ward-Webster was only too glad to get on with it.

'My office is not in the least inefficient. My brother's business is computer hardware and . . .'

It was at about this point in the evidence that I saw Rumpole closely studying the report of Mr Newton, the inquiry agent.

'What's the relevance of that, Mr Armstrong?' Ward-Webster was asking.

'My brother supplies our office equipment,' our client told him proudly.

'Mr Ward-Webster,' said the Judge. 'This family story is no doubt extremely fascinating, but has it really anything to do with the case?'

'I agree, my Lord. And I will pass to another matter . . .'

While this was happening, Rumpole asked me in a whisper if I thought that our client had ever danced with Blythe's secretary. I told him that I had no idea. In fact, I couldn't see the point of the question. But Rumpole leaned forward and asked Mr Myers, of our instructing solicitor's office, to get Mr Newton down to the Old Bailey during the lunch adjournment.

Mr Newton came and we met him with our client in the public canteen. He took a look at Frank Armstrong and said that Blythe's secretary's dancing partner did look like our client but he was sure that he wasn't the same man. Rumpole, who seemed to have a great deal of confidence in this detective whom he always called 'Fig' Newton, seemed to accept this and asked Frank Armstrong if he had a photograph of his brother.

'Yes, indeed.' Frank Armstrong got out his wallet. 'Taken in Marbella. The summer before last.' He handed a photograph to Newton.

'That's the gentleman,' Mr Newton said. 'No doubt about it.'

'Fred's been dancing!' Rumpole laughed. 'Where is he now?'

'In the Gulf. Dubai. So far as I know. He's been asked to develop a computer centre,' Frank Armstrong answered vaguely.

'How long did you think he'd been away?'

'Six months. All of six months.'

'Since before you were arrested?' Rumpole was puzzled. 'You see, Newton saw him a couple of weeks ago in London.'

'Mr Rumpole, I don't know what you're getting at. I'm sure Fred would help me if he possibly could,' Mr Armstrong said.

'You've never quarrelled?'

'Only one little falling out, perhaps. When he wanted to buy the land in Cornwall.'

'Did he offer you much money?' That seemed to interest Rumpole.

'Enormous! Stupid sort of price, I called it. But I wasn't selling. Bit unbrotherly of me perhaps, but I wanted to build up my empire.'

'Perhaps Fred wanted to build up his,' Rumpole said, and then he turned to us and gave orders. He seemed, at that moment, quite determined and in charge of the case.

'There's a lot to be done,' he said. 'Newton's got to find brother Fred.'

'In Dubai?' Mr Newton protested.

'Keep a watch on the office of Sun-Sand Holidays after hours, late at night, early in the morning. Blythe, too. We *have* to get hold of Blythe. You may have to go to Cornwall,' he told Newton.

'I suppose you want all that before two o'clock?' Mr Myers was used to Rumpole's moments of decision.

'No. No, Myersy. Come on, Fiona. This time I've got to get the Mad Bull to give us an adjournment, or die in the attempt!'

So much of what Rumpole said that day sticks in my memory – that last sentence is one I shall never forget, as long as I live.

Of course, when Rumpole got to his feet after lunch Judge Bullingham was as unreceptive as ever.

'So what is the basis of this application, which you are now making for the fifth time since the start of this case?' the Judge asked, and when Mr Mason, the Clerk of the Court, rose to remind him of something, he was delighted to correct himself. 'Is it? Oh, thank you, Mason. For the *sixth* time, Mr Rumpole!'

'The basis should be clear, even to your Lordship,' Rumpole said; it was pretty typical of him, actually. 'It is vital that justice should be done to the gentleman I have the honour to represent.'

'Mr Rumpole. This case has been committed for six months. If Mr Blythe could have helped you he'd have come forward long ago.'

'That's an entirely unwarranted assumption! Perivale Blythe may have other reasons for his absence.'

'It seems you know very little about Mr Blythe. May I ask, have you a proof of his evidence?'

'No.'

'No?' The Judge raised his voice angrily.

'No, I haven't.' I remember Rumpole spoke casually and I remember he sounded quieter than usual.

'So you have no idea what this Mr Blythe is going to say?'

'No, but I know what I'm going to ask him. If he answers truthfully, I have no doubt that my client will be acquitted.'

'A pious hope, Mr Rumpole!' The Judge was smiling at the jury now.

'Of course, if your Lordship wishes to exclude this vital evidence, if you have no interest in doing justice in this case, then I have little more to say . . .' His voice was really tired and quiet by then, and I wondered if he was going to give up and sit down, but he was still on his feet.

'Well, I have a lot more to say. As you should know perfectly well, Mr Rumpole, getting through the work at the Old Bailey is a matter of considerable public importance . . .'

'Oh, of course. Far more important than justice!' Rumpole's voice was still faint and I thought he looked pale.

'In my view these constant applications by the defence are merely an attempt to put off the evil hour when the jury have to bring in a verdict,' the Judge went on, quite unnecessarily I thought. 'It's my duty to see that justice is done speedily. Mr Rumpole, I believe you have a taste for poetry. You will no doubt remember the quotation about the *law's delays.*'

'Oh yes, my Lord. It comes in the same passage which deals with *the insolence of office*. My Lord, if I might say . . .'

'Mr Rumpole!' the Judge barked at him. 'This application for an adjournment is refused. There is absolutely nothing you could say which would persuade me to grant it.'

Then Rumpole seemed to be swaying slightly. He raised a finger to loosen his collar. His voice was now hoarse and almost inaudible.

'Nothing, my Lord?'

'No, Mr Rumpole. Absolutely nothing!' The Judge had reached his decision. But Rumpole was swaying more dangerously. Judge Bullingham watched, astonished, and the whole Court was staring as Rumpole collapsed, apparently unconscious. The Judge spoke loudly over the gasps of amazement.

'I shall adjourn this case.' Judge Bullingham rose, and then bent to speak to Mr Mason, the Clerk of the Court. 'Send for matron!' he said.

In a while, when the Court had cleared, Mr Myers, the usher and I managed to get Rumpole, who seemed to have recovered a certain degree of consciousness, out into the corridor and sit him down. He was still looking terribly grey and ill and the usher went off to hurry up matron.

'Always thought I'd die with my wig on,' Rumpole just managed to murmur.

'Did he say die?' A woman in glasses, whom I had noticed in Court, asked the usher and, when he nodded at her, walked quietly away. I took his wig off then and stood holding it. 'Nonsense, Rumpole.' I tried to sound brisk. 'You're not going to die.'

'Fiona.' His voice was now a sort of low croak. I had to bend down to hear what came out like a last request. 'Air . . . Miss Allways . . . Must have air. Take me . . . Take me out . . .'

He was pulling feebly at his winged collar and bands. I managed to get them undone and then he rose to his feet and stood swaying. He looked absolutely ghastly. Mr Myers was supporting him under one arm. 'Just a breath of air . . . Want to smell Ludgate Circus . . . Your little runabout, Fiona . . . Is it outside? Can't spend my last moments outside Bullingham's Court.'

I suppose I shouldn't have done it, but he looked so pathetic. He whispered to me about not being taken to some hospital full of bedpans and piped Capital Radio, and promised that his wife would send for their own doctor – he could at least die with dignity. Myers and I helped him out to my battered Deux Chevaux and I drove Rumpole to his home.

It took a long time to help him up the stairs and into his flat, but he seemed happy to be home and managed a sort of fleeting smile. His wife wasn't there but he muttered something about her having only just slipped out – said that she'd be back in a moment from the shops and that Dr MacClintock would look after him – for so long, he murmured, as anything could be done. At least, I told him, I'd help him into bed. So we moved towards the bedroom, but at the door he seemed to have second thoughts.

'Perhaps . . . Better not. She Who Must Be Obeyed . . . Bound to stalk in . . . Just when I've lowered the garments . . . Gets some . . . funny ideas . . . does She.'

All the same, I helped him as he staggered into the bedroom and I hung his wig and gown, which I was carrying, over the bedrail as he lay down, still dressed. It was very cold in the mansion flat and I thought that the old couple must be extremely hardy. I covered Rumpole with the eiderdown and he was babbling, apparently delirious.

'Ever thought about . . . the hereafter, Fiona?' I heard him say. 'Hereafter's all right. Until Bollard gets there . . . He's bound to make it . . . Have to spend all eternity listening to Bollard . . . on the subject of "Lawyers for the Faith" . . . Difficult to make an excuse . . . and slip away. He'll have me buttonholed . . . in the hereafter. Go along now . . .'

'Are you sure?' I hated to leave him but I knew that our wretched client had been taken down to the cells when the trial was interrupted.

Someone would have to go and get him released until he was needed again.

'And bail,' Rumpole was muttering very faintly, echoing my thoughts. 'Ask bail . . . from the dotty Bull. For Frank. Suppose Bullingham'll be turning up there too . . . in the hereafter. Apply for bail . . . Fiona.'

'I'll ring you later,' I promised as I moved to the door.

'Later . . . Not too late . . .' Rumpole closed his eyes as I went out of the door; he was quite motionless, apparently asleep.

Judge Bullingham was looking at me, smiling, apparently deeply sympathetic, when I applied for bail. Mr Mason, the Court clerk, later told me that the Judge had taken something of a 'shine' to me and was considering sending me a box of chocolates. Life at the Bar can be absolute hell for a girl sometimes.

'Bail? Yes, of course, Miss Allways. By all means,' said the Judge. 'On the same terms. And what is the latest news of Mr Rumpole?'

'He is resting peacefully, my Lord,' I told him truthfully.

'Peacefully.' The Judge sounded very solemn. 'Yes, of course. Well, that comes to all of us in time. Nothing else for this afternoon, is there, Mason?'

The Judge went home early. But in the Old Bailey, round the other London Courts and in the Temple the news spread like wildfire. Rumpole had collapsed, the stories went, it was all over and the old boy had gone home at last. I heard that in the cells villains, with their trials due to come up, cursed because they wouldn't have Rumpole to defend them.

Some said he'd died with his wig on, others told how he'd been suddenly taken away before the matron could get at him. Quite a lot of people, from Detective Inspectors to safe-blowers, said that, if he had to go, Rumpole would have wanted it to come as it did, when he was on his feet and in the middle of a legal argument.

When I got back to Chambers I found a crowd gathered in our clerk's room. Henry had been trying the phone in Rumpole's flat over and over again and getting no reply.

'No reply from Rumpole's flat!' said Hoskins, a rather dreary sort of barrister who's always talking about his daughters.

'Probably no one at home,' Uncle Tom, our oldest inhabitant, hazarded a guess.

'That would appear to be the natural assumption, Uncle Tom.' Erskine-Brown was as sarcastic as usual.

'Surely, we've got absolutely no reason to think . . .' Hoskins said.

'I agree. All we know is that Rumpole suffered some sort of a stroke or a seizure,' Ballard told them.

'Rumpole often said Judge Bullingham had that effect on him,' Uncle Tom said.

'And that he's clearly been taken somewhere,' Erskine-Brown added.

' "Taken somewhere" expresses it rather well.' Uncle Tom shook his head. ' "Taken somewhere" is about the long and short of it.'

Then I told them I'd taken Rumpole home where his wife would be able to get their own doctor to look after him. In the pause that followed Henry gave me the good news that he had got me a porn job in Manchester and I'd have to travel up overnight.

'A porn job!' Our Head of Chambers looked shocked. 'I'd've thought this was hardly the moment for that sort of thing.'

'Mr Rumpole would want Chambers to carry on, sir, I'm sure. As usual,' Henry said solemnly.

'Poor old fellow. Yes,' Uncle Tom agreed. 'Well. One thing to be said for him. He went in harness.'

'I don't really think it's the sort of subject we should be discussing in the clerk's room,' Ballard decided. 'No doubt I shall be calling a Chambers meeting, when we have rather more detailed information.'

As they went, I lingered long enough to hear Dianne, our rather hit-and-miss typist, give a little sob as she pounded her machine.

'Oh, please, Dianne,' Henry protested. 'Didn't you hear what I said to Mr Ballard? Chambers must go on. That would have been *his* wishes.'

So I went to Manchester and read a lot of jolly embarrassing magazines in a dark corner of the railway carriage. Meanwhile Mr Newton, the inquiry agent, was still keeping a watch on the offices of Sun-Sand Holidays every night. Of course, I saw his reports eventually and it seemed that the office was visited, late at night and in a highly suspicious manner, by our client's brother Fred, who spent a long time working on the computers.

And there were other developments. Archie Featherstone, the Judge's nephew, was still very anxious to get into our Chambers and, when there was no news of Rumpole's recovery, I suppose the poor chap felt a bit encouraged in a horrible sort of way.

Perhaps I can understand how he felt because, although I never liked Archie Featherstone much (he'd danced with me at some pretty grue-some ball and his way of dancing was to close his eyes, suck in his teeth and bob up and down in the hope that he looked like Mick Jagger, which he didn't), I knew jolly well what it was like to be desperate to get a seat in Number 3 Equity Court.

It was while I was still in Manchester that Henry received a telemes-sage about Rumpole and immediately took it up to our Head of Chambers. Sometime later, when I bought him his usual Cinzano Bianco in Pommeroy's Wine Bar, Henry gave me a full account of how his meeting with Ballard went. First of all our Head read the message out aloud very carefully and slowly, Henry told me.

'"Please let firm of Blythe, Winterbottom and Paisley know sad news. Deeply regret Rumpole gone up to a Higher Tribunal. Signed Rumpole."' Ballard apparently looked puzzled. 'What *is* it, Henry?'

'It's a telemessage, sir. Telegrams having been abolished, *per se*,' Henry explained.

'Yes, I know it's a telemessage. But the wording. Doesn't it strike you as somewhat strange?'

'Mr Rumpole was always one for his joke. It caused us a good deal of embarrassment at times.'

'But presumably this can't be signed by Rumpole. Not in the circum-stances.' Ballard was working on the problem. 'On any reasonable interpretation, the word "Rumpole", being silent so far as sex is con-cerned, must surely be construed as referring to *Mrs* Rumpole?' He was being very legal, Henry told me, and behaving like a Chancery barrister.

'That's what I assumed, sir,' said Henry. 'Unfortunately I can't get through to the Gloucester Road flat on the telephone. It seems there's a "fault on the line".'

'Have you tried calling round?'

'I have, sir. No answer to my ring.'

'Well, of course, it's a busy time in any family. A busy and distressing time.' But Ballard was clearly worried. 'Does it strike you as rather odd, Henry?'

'Well, just a bit, sir.'

'As Head of Chambers I surely should be the first to be informed of any decease among members. Am I not entitled to that?'

'In the normal course of events, yes.' Henry told me he agreed to save any argument.

'In the normal course. But this message doesn't refer to me, or to his fellow members, or even to the Court where he was appearing when he was stricken down. This Blythe, Sidebottom and . . .'

'Winterbottom, sir. And Paisley.'

'Was it a firm to which old Rumpole was particularly attached?'

'I don't think so, Mr Ballard. They owed him money,' Henry said he told him frankly.

'They owed him money! Strange. Very strange.' Ballard was thoughtful, it seems. 'From the way he was talking the other day, I think the old fellow had a queer sort of premonition that the end was pretty close.' And then our Head of Chambers went back to the document Henry had given him. 'All the same, Henry. There is something hopeful in this telemessage.'

'Is there, sir?'

'I mean the reference to a "Higher Tribunal". You know, I'm afraid I'd always found Rumpole a bit of a scoffer. I couldn't get him interested in "Lawyers As Churchgoers". He wouldn't even come along to one meeting of L.A.C.! But his wife's message says he was thinking in terms of a "Higher Tribunal". It suggests he found faith in the end, Henry. It must have been a great comfort to him.'

As I say, Henry told me this after I got back from Manchester, when I was buying him a drink in Pommeroy's Wine Bar. As we were talking I noticed that the frumpy sort of woman in glasses, the one who'd been listening to the Armstrong trial, was doing her best to overhear our conversation. She carried on listening when Jack Pommeroy slid his counter cloth up to us and said to Henry,

'I say. Has old Rumpole really had it? I've got about twenty-three of his cheques!'

'My clerk's fees aren't exactly up to date either,' Henry said. 'You'll miss him round here, won't you, Jack?'

'Well, he did use to pass some pretty insulting remarks about our claret. Called it Château Thames Embankment!' Jack Pommeroy looked pained. 'Didn't exactly help our business. And when he wasn't paying cash . . .'

I wasn't really listening to him then. I was watching the woman in glasses. She was talking into the telephone on the wall and I distinctly heard her say, 'True? Yes, of course it's true.'

Mr Newton, the inquiry agent, later pointed her out to me as Blythe's secretary, whom he had once seen dancing in Soho wearing, incredibly enough, pink satin trousers.

Oddly enough I won my case in Manchester. My solicitor told me that an elderly man on the jury had been heard to say that if a nice girl like me read those sort of magazines there couldn't be much harm in them. It seems I'm to get a lot more dirty books from Manchester! Anyway, I was back in time for the Chambers meeting and all of us, except for Mrs Erskine-Brown who was apparently doing something extremely important in Wales, assembled in Ballard's room. I was taking the minutes so I can tell you more or less exactly what happened. It started when Ballard read out the telemessage again in a very sad and solemn sort of way.

'Bit rum, isn't it? What's he mean exactly, "Higher Tribunal"?' Uncle Tom said.

'I have no doubt he means that Great Court of Appeal before which we shall all have to appear eventually, Uncle Tom,' Ballard explained.

'I never got to the Court of Appeal. Never had a brief to go there, as a matter of fact. Probably just as well. I wouldn't've been up to it.' Uncle Tom smiled round at us all.

'Knowing Rumpole,' said Erskine-Brown, 'there must be a joke there somewhere.'

'It must have been sent by Mrs Rumpole. Poor Rumpole is clearly not in a position to send "telemessages",' our Head of Chambers told us.

'Not in a position? Oh. See what you mean. Quite so. Exactly.' Uncle Tom got the point.

'Now, of course, this sad event will mean consequent changes in Chambers.' Ballard moved the discussion on.

'So far as the furniture is concerned. Yes.' Erskine-Brown opened a favourite subject. 'I don't suppose anyone will have any particular use for the old hatstand which stood in Rumpole's room.'

'His *hatstand*, Erskine-Brown?' Ballard was surprised.

'I happen to have conferences, from time to time, with a number of solicitors. Naturally they have hats. Well, if no one else wants it . . .'

'I don't think there'll be a stampede for Rumpole's old hatstand,' Uncle Tom assured him.

'I was thinking that there ought to be a bit more work about,' Hoskins said. 'I mean, I suppose Henry can hang on to some of Rumpole's solicitors. Myers and people like that. Now the work may get spread around a bit.'

'I'm not sure I agree with Hoskins.' Erskine-Brown was doubtful. 'There's some part of Rumpole's work which we might be glad to lose. I mean the sort of thing you were doing in Manchester, Allways.'

'You mean porn?' I asked him brightly.

'Obscenity! That's exactly what I do mean. Or rape. Or indecent assault. Or possessing housebreaking instruments by night. I mean, this may be our opportunity, sad as the occasion is, of course, to improve the image of Chambers. I mean, do we *want* dirty-book merchants hanging about the clerk's room?'

'Speaking for myself,' Ballard agreed, 'I think there's a great deal in what Erskine-Brown says. If you're not *for* these moral degenerates, in my view, you should be *against* them. I'd like to see a great deal more prosecution work in Chambers.'

'Well, you are certain of the money, with prosecutions.' Hoskins was with him. 'Speaking as a man with daughters.'

'There is a young fellow who's a certainty for the Yard's list of prosecutors,' Ballard said. 'I think I've mentioned young Archie Featherstone to you, Erskine-Brown?'

'Of course. The Judge's nephew.'

'It may be, in the changed circumstances, we shall have a room to offer young Archie Featherstone.'

'He won't be taking work from us?' Hoskins was more than a bit nervous at the prospect.

'In my opinion he'll be bringing it in,' Ballard reassured him, 'in the shape of prosecutions. Now, there are a few arrangements to be discussed.'

'I hope "arrangements" doesn't mean a crematorium,' Uncle Tom said mournfully. 'I always think there's something terribly depressing about those little railway lines, passing out through the velvet curtain.'

'Of course, it is something of an event. I wonder if we'd get the Temple Church?' Hoskins seemed almost excited.

'Oh, I imagine not.' Erskine-Brown was discouraging. 'And, of course, we've seen nothing in *The Times* Obituaries. I'm afraid Rumpole never got the cases which made legal history.'

'I suppose they might hold some sort of memorial service in Pommeroy's Wine Bar,' Uncle Tom said thoughtfully. Our Head of Chambers looked a bit disapproving at that, as it didn't seem to be quite the right thing to say on a solemn occasion.

'I think we should send a modest floral tribute,' he suggested. 'Henry can arrange for that, out of Chambers expenses. Everyone agreed?' They all did, and Ballard went on, 'In view of the fact that at the eleventh hour he appeared to be reconciled to the deeper realities of our brief life on earth, you might all care to stand for a few minutes' silence, in memory of Horace Rumpole.'

So we all stood up, just a bit sheepishly, and bowed our heads. The silence seemed to last a long time, like it used to in Poppy Day services at school.

As I have been writing up this account for the completion of Rumpole's papers, I have got to know Mrs Rumpole and, in the course of a few teas, come to get on with her jolly well. As we all knew in Chambers, Rumpole used to call her She Who Must Be Obeyed and always seemed to be in tremendous awe of her, but I didn't find her all that alarming. In fact she always seemed grateful for someone to talk to. She told me a lot about the old days, when her father, C. H. Wystan, was Head of Chambers, and of how Rumpole always criticized him for not knowing enough about bloodstains; and she described how Rumpole proposed to her at a ball in the Temple, when he'd had, as she described it, 'quite enough claret cup to be going on with'. During one of our teas (she took me, which was very decent of her, to Fortnum's) she described the visit she had received at her flat in the Gloucester Road shortly before Mr Myers restored *R. v. Armstrong* for a further hearing before Judge Bullingham.

One afternoon there came a ring, so it seemed, at the doorbell of the Rumpole mansion flat. Mrs Rumpole – I'll call her 'Hilda' from now on since we've really become quite friendly – opened the door to see a small, fat, elderly man (Hilda described him to me as toad-like), who had a bald head, gold-rimmed spectacles and the cheek to put on a crêpe armband and a black tie. As he sort of oozed past her into her living room, he looked, Hilda told me, like a commercial traveller for a firm of undertakers. She wasn't entirely unprepared for this visit, however. The man had rung her earlier and explained that he was Mr Perivale Blythe, a solicitor of the Supreme Court and anxious to pay his respects to the Widow Rumpole.

When he had penetrated the living room, Mr Blythe sat on a sofa with his briefcase on his knee and began to talk in hushed, respectful tones, Hilda told me.

'I felt I had to intrude,' he said softly. 'Even at this sad, sad moment, Mrs Rumpole. I do not come as myself, not even as Blythe, Winterbottom and Paisley, but I come as a representative, if I may say so, of the entire legal profession. Your husband was a great gentleman, Mrs Rumpole. And a fine lawyer.'

'A fine lawyer?' Hilda was puzzled. 'He never told me.'

'And, of course, a most persuasive advocate.'

'Oh, yes. He told me *that*,' Hilda agreed.

'We all join you in your grief, Mrs Rumpole. And I have to tell you this! There are no smiling faces today in the firm of Blythe, Winterbottom and Paisley!'

'Thank you.' Hilda did her best to sound grateful.

'Nor anywhere, I suppose, from Inner London to Acton Magistrates. He will be sorely missed.'

'I have to tell you what will be sorely missed, Mr Blythe,' Hilda said then, and said it in a meaningful kind of way.

'What, Mrs Rumpole?'

I think she said she stood up then and looked down on her visitor's large, pale, bald head, 'All those fees you owe him. Since the indecency case, I believe, in 1973.'

Blythe was clearly taken aback. He cleared his throat and began to fiddle nervously with the catch on his briefcase. 'You have heard a little about that?'

'I've heard a lot about it!'

'Well, of course, a great deal of that money hasn't been completely recovered from the clients. Not in full. But I'm here to settle up,' he assured her. 'I imagine you're the late Mr Rumpole's executor?'

He opened his briefcase; Hilda looked into it and noticed a cheque-book. Blythe got out a document and shut the briefcase quickly.

'Of course I'm his executor,' Hilda told him.

'Then no doubt you're fully empowered to enter into what I think you'll agree is a perfectly fair compromise. Now, the sum involved is . . .'

'Two thousand, seven hundred and sixty-five pounds, ninety-three pence,' Hilda said quickly. She has a jolly good memory.

'Quite the businesswoman, Mrs Rumpole.' The beastly Blythe smiled in a patronizing manner. 'Now, would an immediate payment of . . . let's say ten per cent, be a nice little arrangement? Then it'll be over and done with.'

'Mr Blythe. I have to face the butcher!' Hilda told him.

'Yes, of course, but . . .' Blythe didn't seem to understand.

'And the water rates. And the London Electricity Board. And the telephone has actually been cut off during my visit to the Lake District. I can't offer them a nice little arrangement, can I?'

'Well. Possibly not,' Blythe admitted.

'But I will offer *you* one, Mr Perivale Blythe,' Hilda said firmly.

'Well, that's extremely obliging of you . . .' Blythe took out his fountain pen.

And then Hilda spoke to him along the following lines. It was undoubtedly her finest hour. 'I will offer you this,' she said. 'I won't report this conversation to the Law Society, although this year's President's father was a close personal friend of *my* father, C. H. Wystan. I will not take immediate steps to have you struck off, Mr Blythe, just provided you sit down and write out a cheque for two thousand, seven hundred and sixty-five pounds, ninety-three pence, in favour of Hilda Rumpole.'

The effect of this on the little creep on the sofa was apparently astonishing. For a moment his mouth sagged open. Then, in desperation, he patted his pockets. 'Unfortunately forgot my chequebook,' he lied. 'I'll slip one in the post.'

'Look in your briefcase, Mr Blythe. I think you'll find your chequebook there.' Hilda's words of command were interrupted by the sound of a ring at the door. As she went to open it she said, 'Excuse me. And don't try the window, Mr Blythe. It's really a great deal too far for you to jump.'

No doubt about it, she was a woman born to command. When she was out of the room, Blythe, with moist and trembling fingers, wrote out a cheque for the full amount. She returned with a tall, lugubrious figure who was scrubbing the end of his nose with a crushed pocket handkerchief.

'Thank you, Mr Blythe,' Hilda said politely as she took the cheque. 'And now there's a gentleman to see you.'

At which the new arrival whisked a paper out of his pocket and put it into the hand of the demoralized Perivale Blythe.

' "Fig" Newton!' he said. 'Whatever's this?'

'It's a subpoena, Mr Blythe,' Mr Newton explained patiently. 'They want you to give evidence in a case down the Old Bailey.'

The case was, of course, *R. v. Armstrong*. On the morning when it started again I sat in Rumpole's place, the only defending barrister. When the jury was reassembled the usher called for silence and his Honour Judge Bullingham came into Court, looked towards me, noticed the gap that used to be Rumpole and clearly decided that it would be in order to say a few words of tribute to the departed. They took the form of a speech to the jury in which his Lordship sounded confidential and really jolly sincere. 'Members of the jury,' he said, and they all turned their faces solemnly towards him. 'Before we start this case, there is something I have to say. In our Courts, warm friendships spring up between judges and counsel, between Bench and Bar. We're not superior beings as judges; we don't put on "side". We are the barristers' friends. And one of my oldest friends, over the years, was Horace Rumpole.' Both Ward-Webster for the prosecution and I looked piously up to the ceiling. We carefully hid our feelings of amazement.

'During the time he appeared before me, in many cases, I can truthfully say that there was never a cross word between us, although we may have had trivial disagreements over points of law,' Bullingham went on. 'We are all part of that great happy family, members of the jury, which is the Criminal Court.'

It was at that moment that I heard a sound beside me and smelt the familiar shaving soap and small cigar. The Judge and the jury were too busy with each other to notice, but Ward-Webster and almost everyone else in Court were looking towards us in silent stupefaction. Rumpole was, I must say, looking in astonishingly fine condition, pinker than usual and well rested. He was obviously enjoying the Judge's speech.

'Mr Horace Rumpole was one of the old brigade.' By now Judge Bullingham was clearly deeply moved. 'Not a leader, perhaps, not a general, but a reliable, hard-working and great-hearted old soldier of the line.'

Of course, Rumpole could resist it no longer. He got slowly to his feet and bowed deeply, saying, 'My Lord.' The jury's faces swivelled towards him. Bullingham looked away from the jury-box and into the Court. If people who see ghosts go dark purple, well, that's how Bullingham looked.

'My Lord,' Rumpole repeated, 'I am deeply touched by your Lordship's remarks.'

'Mr Rumpole . . . Mr Rumpole . . . ?' The Judge's voice rose incredulously. 'I heard . . .'

'Greatly exaggerated, my Lord, I do assure you.' Of course, Rumpole had to say it. 'May I say what a pleasure it is to be continuing this case before your Lordship.'

'Mason. What's this mean?' Bullingham leant forward and whispered hoarsely to the Clerk of the Court. We heard Mr Mason whisper back, 'Quite honestly, Judge, I haven't a clue.'

'Mr Rumpole. Have you some application?' The Judge was looking at Rumpole with something like fear. Perhaps he thought he was about to call someone from the spirit world.

'No application.' Rumpole smiled charmingly. 'Your Lordship kindly adjourned this case, if you remember. It's now been restored to your list. Our inquiries are complete and I will call Mr Perivale Blythe.'

After the sensation of Rumpole's return from the tomb, where Bullingham quite obviously thought he'd been, I'm afraid to say that the rest of *R. v. Armstrong* was a bit of an anticlimax. Perivale Blythe padded into the witness-box, took the oath in a plummy sort of voice, and I have the notes of Rumpole's examination-in-chief.

'Mr Blythe,' the resurrected old barrister asked. 'After their father's death, did you act for the two Armstrong brothers, my client Frank and his brother Frederick?'

'Yes, I did,' Blythe agreed.

'And did Fred supply the computers set up in the offices of Sun-Sand Holidays, my client Frank Armstrong's firm?'

'I believe he did.' Blythe sounded uninterested.

'Mr Blythe, would you take the photograph of the Cornish holiday site?'

As the usher took the photograph to the witness-box, Bullingham staged a bit of a comeback and said, 'The industrial area, Mr Rumpole?'

'Exactly, my Lord.' Rumpole bowed politely. 'Do you know what that industry is, Mr Blythe?'

'Tin mines, my Lord. I rather think.' Once again, Blythe sounded deliberately unconcerned.

'You *know*, don't you? Didn't you visit that site on behalf of your client Mr *Frederick* Armstrong?'

'I did. He was anxious to buy his brother Frank's site.'

'Because he knew tin would also be discovered there.'

'Yes, of course.' And then Blythe forgot his lack of interest. 'I don't believe he told his brother that.'

'I don't believe he did.' Rumpole was after him now. 'And when his brother refused, didn't Fred take every possible step to ruin his brother Frank's business, no doubt by interfering with the computers that he'd installed so that they constantly gave misleading information, booked non-existent holiday homes and gave false instructions for caravans to be towed away?'

'I never approved of that, my Lord. I am an officer of the Court. I wouldn't have any part of it.' Perivale Blythe was sweating. He patted his bald head with a handkerchief and protested his innocence. I'd say he made a pretty unattractive figure in the witness-box.

'Although you knew about it. Come, Mr Blythe. You must have known about it to disapprove.' Rumpole pressed his advantage but the Judge, back to his old form, was getting restless. 'Mr Rumpole! I take the gravest objection to this in examination-in-chief. It is quite outrageous!'

'A trivial objection, surely?' Rumpole gave a sweet smile. 'Your Lordship has told the jury we only have trivial disagreements.'

'You are putting an entirely new case to this witness, so far as I can see, on no evidence.'

'Oh, there will be evidence, my Lord.'

'I hope that my learned friend doesn't wish to conceal from the jury the fact that Detective Inspector Limmeridge arrested Frederick Armstrong when he had entered his brother's office by night and was reprogramming the computers. There has been a charge of Perverting the Course of Justice,' Rumpole said, looking hard at the jury. 'In fact, Mr Newton has given the results of all his observations to the Officer-in-Charge of the case.'

'Is that right, Mr Ward-Webster?' Bullingham asked incredulously.

'So I understand, my Lord.' Ward-Webster subsided.

'I shall be recalling the Detective Inspector, my Lord,' Rumpole said triumphantly, 'as a witness for the defence.'

Well in the end, of course, the jury saw the point. Brother Fred had set out to ruin brother Frank's business by interfering with the computers so that they sold non-existent holidays, or removed existing caravans. With Frank in prison Fred could have got hold of the Cornish mobile homes site and a great deal of tin. It wasn't one of Rumpole's greatest cases, but a jolly satisfying win. Horace Rumpole has taught me a lot about criminal procedure, but I don't think I'd ever dare try his way of getting an adjournment.

Well, I've written my bit. I hope it's all right and that someone will check it through for grammar. It tells what happened so far as I knew it at the time, or almost as far as I knew it.

(Signed) Fiona Patience Allways, barrister-at-law.

3 Equity Court

Temple

London, EC4

I'm extremely grateful to my learned friend, Miss Fiona Allways, for dealing with that part of the story. It had been necessary, as I expect you have guessed, to take her into my confidence (a little earlier than she divulges in her account) when I decided to lie doggo, to feign death and lure the wretched Perivale Blythe out of hiding. Of course I saw Hilda as soon as she got back from her 'bachelor holiday' in the Lake District and I had to let her in on the scheme. But I must say, She was something of a sport about the whole business and the way she dealt with the appalling Blythe, much of which I heard from a point of vantage near our bedroom door, seemed to me masterly. When She Who Must Be Obeyed is on form, no lawyer can possibly stand up to her.

On the whole the incident gave me enormous pleasure. One of the many drawbacks of actually snuffing it will be that you can't hear the things people say about you when they think you're safe in your box. I enormously enjoyed Fiona's account of the Chambers meeting and the silent prayer which marked my passing – just as I will never let Judge Bullingham forget his funeral oration.

Oh, and one other marvellous moment: Hilda and I were sitting at tea one afternoon when I was out of circulation and a ring came at the doorbell. Some boy was delivering Hilda a socking great wreath from Chambers, compliments of Sam Ballard and all the learned friends. The deeply respectful note to Hilda explained that the tribute was sent to her home as they didn't quite know when the interment was due to take place.

After I had won Frank Armstrong's case I walked up to Chambers and called on our learned Head. For some reason my appearance in the flesh seemed to irritate the man almost beyond endurance.

'Rumpole,' he said, 'I think you've behaved disgracefully.'

'I don't know why you should say that,' I told him. 'Isn't there a Biblical precedent for this sort of thing?'

'I suppose you're very proud of yourself,' Ballard boomed on.

'Well, it wasn't a bad win.' I lit a small cigar. 'Got the Sun-Sand Mobile Homes owner away and clear. Made the world safe for a few more ghastly holidays.'

'I am not referring to your case, Rumpole. You caused us all . . . You caused me personally . . . a great deal of unnecessary grief!'

'Oh, come off it, Bollard. I understand you couldn't wait to relet my room to young Archie Featherstone.

> 'A little month; or ere those shoes were old
> With which you follow'd poor old Rumpole's body,
> Like Niobe, all tears . . .'

I gave him a slice of *Hamlet* which he didn't appreciate.

'We had to plan for the future, Rumpole. Deeply distressed as we all were . . .'

'Deeply distressed indeed! I hear that Uncle Tom suggested a memorial service in Pommeroy's Wine Bar.'

Ballard had the decency to look a little embarrassed. 'I never approved of that,' he said.

'Well, it's not a bad idea. And I happen to be in funds at the moment. Why don't I invite you all to a piss-up at Pommeroy's?'

Ballard looked at me sadly. 'And I thought you had finally found faith!' he said. 'That's what I can never forgive.'

In due course the learned friends assembled in Pommeroy's at the end of a working day. I had invited Hilda to join us. We were on friendly terms at the time and, as a result of Blythe's cheque, her bank balance was in a considerably more healthy state than mine. So I got Jack Pommeroy to dispense the plonk with a liberal hand and during the celebrations I heard She Who Must Be Obeyed talking to our Head of Chambers.

'It was very naughty of Rumpole, of course,' She said, 'but there was just no other way of getting his fees from that appalling man, Perivale Blythe.'

'Mrs Rumpole. Can I get this clear? You were a knowing party to this extraordinary conspiracy?'

'Oh yes.' And Hilda sounded proud of it.

'I'll have you after my job, Mrs Rumpole,' Henry said. 'I couldn't get Mr Blythe to pay up. Not till we got this idea.'

'Henry! You're not saying *you* knew?'

'I'm not saying anything, Mr Ballard,' Henry answered with a true clerk's diplomacy. 'But perhaps I had an inkling.'

'Allways! You took Rumpole home. You must have thought . . .' Ballard clearly guessed that he was on to an appalling conspiracy.

'That he'd died?' Fiona smiled at him. 'Oh, I can't see how anyone could think that. He'd never die in the middle of a case, would he?'

'It was exactly the same when we believed he'd retired,' Uncle Tom told the world in general. 'Rumpole kept popping back, like a bloody opera singer!'

At which point I felt moved to address them and banged a glass on the bar for silence.

'Well, my learned friends!' I said in my final speech. 'Since no one else seems inclined to, it falls on me to say a few words. After the distressing news you have heard, it comes as a great pleasure to welcome Horace Rumpole back to the land of the living. When he was deceased he was constantly in your thoughts. Some of you wanted his room. Some of you wanted his work. Some, I know, couldn't wait to get their fingers on the old boy's hatstand. You are all nonetheless welcome to drink to his long life and continued success in a glass of Château Thames Embankment!'

I must say that they all raised their glasses and drank with every appearance of enjoyment. Then I went over to Jack Pommeroy and asked him to bring out, from behind the bar, the tribute from Ballard which I had concealed there before the party began.

'Bollard,' I said as I handed it to him, 'this came to my home address. I'm afraid you went to some expense over the thing. Never mind. As I shan't be needing it now, keep it for one of your friends.'

So, at the end of the day, Sam Ballard was left holding the wreath.

Rumpole and the Blind Tasting

'Rumpole! How could you drink that stuff?'

'Perfectly easy, Erskine-Brown. Raise the glass to the lips, incline the head slightly backwards and let the liquid flow gently past the tonsils.' I gave the man a practical demonstration. 'I admit I've had a good deal of practice, but even you may come to it in time.'

'Of course you *can* drink it, Rumpole. Presumably it's *possible* to drink methylated spirits shaken up with a little ice and a dash of Angostura bitters.' Erskine-Brown smiled at me from over the edge of the glass of Côte de Nuits Villages '79, which he had been ordering in his newly acquired wine-buff's voice from Jack Pommeroy, before he settled himself at the bar; I couldn't help noticing that his dialogue was showing some unaccustomed vivacity. 'I fully appreciate that you *can* drink Pommeroy's Very Ordinary. But the point is, Rumpole, why should you want to?'

'Forgetfulness, Erskine-Brown. The consignment of a day in front of his Honour Judge Bullingham to the Lethe of forgotten things. The Mad Bull,' I told him, as I drained the large glass of Château Fleet Street Jack Pommeroy had obligingly put on my slate until the next legal aid cheque came in, 'constantly interrupted my speech to the jury. I am defending an alleged receiver of stolen sugar bowls. With this stuff, not to put too fine a point on it, you have a reasonable chance of getting blotto.'

It is a good few years now since I adopted the habit of noting down the facts of some of my outstanding cases, the splendours and miseries of an Old Bailey Hack, and those of you who may have cast an eye over some of my previous works of reminiscence may well be muttering *'Plus ça change, plus c'est la même chose'* or words to the like effect. After so many cross-examinations, speeches to the jury, verdicts of guilty or not guilty, legal aid cheques long-awaited and quickly disposed of down the bottomless pit of the overdraft at the Caring Bank, no great change in the Rumpole fortunes had taken place, the texture of life remained much as it always had been and would, no doubt, do so until after my positively last case when I sit waiting to be called on in the Great Circuit Court of the Skies, if such a tribunal exists.

Take that evening as typical. I had been involved in the defence of one Hugh Snakelegs Timson. The Timsons, you may remember, are an extended family of South London villains who practise crime in the stolid, hard-working, but not particularly successful manner in which a large number of middle-of-the-road advocates practise at the Bar. The Timsons are not high-flyers; not for them the bullion raids or the skilled emptying of the Rembrandts out of ducal mansions. The Timsons inhabit the everyday world of purloined video recorders, bent log-books and stolen Cortinas. They also provide me and my wife Hilda (known to me, quite off the record, and occasionally behind the hand, as She Who Must Be Obeyed) with our bread and butter. When prospects are looking bleak, when my tray in the clerk's room is bare of briefs but loaded with those unpleasant-looking buff envelopes doshed out at regular intervals by Her Majesty the Queen, it is comforting to know that somewhere in the Greater London area, some Timson will be up to some sort of minor villainy and, owing to the general incompetence of the clan, the malefactor concerned will no doubt be in immediate need of legal representation.

Hugh Snakelegs Timson was, at that time, the family's official fence, having taken over the post from his Uncle Percy Timson,* who was getting a good deal past it, and had retired to live in Benidorm. Snakelegs, a thin, elegant man in his forties, a former winner of the Mr Debonair contest at Butlin's Holiday Camp, had earned his name from his talent at the tango. He lived with his wife, Hetty, in a semi-detached house in Bromley to which Detective Inspector Broome, the well-known terror of the Timsons, set out on a voyage of discovery with his faithful Detective Sergeant Cosgrove. At first Inspector 'New' Broome had drawn a blank at the Timson home; even the huge coffin-shaped freezer seemed to contain nothing but innumerable bags full of frozen vegetables. The eager Inspector had the bright idea of thawing some of these

* See 'Rumpole and the Age for Retirement' (*The First Rumpole Omnibus*).

provisions however, and was rewarded by the spectacle of articles of Georgian silver arising from the saucepans of boiling peas in the manner of Venus arising from the Sea.

The defence of Hugh Snakelegs Timson had not been going particularly well. The standard receiver's story, 'I got the whole lot from a bloke in a pub who was selling them off cheap, and whose name I cannot for the life of me recall', was treated with undisguised contempt by his Honour, Judge Roger Bullingham, who asked, with the ponderous cynicism accompanied by an undoubted wink at the jury, of which he is master, if I were not going to suggest that there had been a shower of sugar-sifters, cream jugs and the like from the back of a lorry? Anyway, if got innocently, why was the silverware in the deep freezer? I told the jury that an Englishman's freezer was his castle and that there was no reason on earth why a citizen shouldn't keep his valuables in a bag of Birds Eye peas at a low temperature. Indeed, I added, as I thought helpfully, I had an old aunt who kept odd pound notes in the tea caddy, and constantly risked boiling up her savings in a pot of Darjeeling. At this the Mad Bull went an even darker shade of purple, his neck swelled visibly so that it seemed about to burst his yellowing winged collar and he told the jury that my aunt was 'not evidence', and that they must in reaching a decision 'dismiss entirely anything Mr Rumpole may have said about his curious family', adding, with a whole battery of near-nudges and almost-winks, 'I expect our saner relatives know the proper place for their valuables. In the bank.'

At this point the Bull decided to interrupt my final speech by adjourning for tea and television in his private room, and I was left to wander disconsolately in the direction of Pommeroy's Wine Bar, where I met that notable opera buff and wine connoisseur, half-hearted prosecutor and inept defender, the spouse and helpmeet of Phillida Erskine-Brown, QC. Phillida Trant, as was, the Portia of our Chambers, had put his nose somewhat out of joint by taking silk and leaving poor old Claude, ten years older than she, a humble junior. So there I was, raising yet another glass of Château Thames Embankment to my lips and telling Claude that the only real advantage of this particular vintage was that it was quite likely to get you drunk.

'The purpose of drinking wine is not intoxication, Rumpole.' Erskine-Brown looked as pained as a prelate who is told that his congregation only came to church because of the central heating. 'The point is to get in touch with one of the major influences of western civilization, to taste sunlight trapped in a bottle and to remember some stony slope in Tuscany or a village by the Gironde.'

I thought with a momentary distaste of the bit of barren soil, no doubt placed between the cowshed and the *pissoir*, where the Château Pommeroy grape struggled for existence. And then, Erskine-Brown, long-time member of our Chambers in Equity Court, went considerably too far.

'You see, Rumpole,' he said, 'it's the terrible nose.'

Now I make no particular claim for my nose and I am far from suggesting that it's a thing of beauty and a joy forever. When I was in my perambulator it may, for all I can remember, have had a sort of tip-tilted and impertinent charm. In my youth it was no doubt pinkish and healthy-looking. In my early days at the Bar it had a sharp and inquisitive quality which made prosecution witnesses feel they could keep no secrets from it. Today it is perhaps past its prime, it has spread somewhat; it has, in part at least, gone mauve; it is, after all, a nose that has seen a considerable quantity of life. But man and boy it has served me well, and I had no intention of having my appearance insulted by Claude Erskine-Brown, barrister-at-law, who looks, in certain unfavourable lights, not unlike an abbess with a bad period.

'We may disagree about Pommeroy's plonk,' I told him, 'but that's no reason why you should descend to personal abuse.'

'No, I don't mean *your* nose, Rumpole. I mean the wine's nose.'

I looked suspiciously into the glass; did this wine possess qualities I hadn't guessed at? 'Don't babble, Erskine-Brown.'

'"Nose", Rumpole! The bouquet. That's one of the expressions you have to learn to use about wine. Together with the "length".'

'Length?' I looked down at the glass in my hand; the length seemed to be about one inch and shrinking rapidly.

'The "length" a great wine lingers in the mouth, Rumpole. Look, why don't you let me educate you? My friend, Martyn Vanberry, organizes tastings in the City. Terrifically good fun. You get to try about a dozen wines.'

'A dozen?' I was doubtful. 'An expensive business.'

'No, Rumpole. Absolutely free. They are blind tastings. He's got one on tomorrow afternoon, as it so happens.'

'You mean they make you blind drunk?' I couldn't resist asking. 'Sounds exactly what I need.' At that moment the promise of Martyn Vanberry and his blind tastings were a vague hope for the future. My immediate prospects included an evening drink with She Who Must Be Obeyed and finishing my speech for Snakelegs to the jury against the Mad Bull's barracking. I emptied Pommeroy's dull opiate to the drains and aimed Lethe-wards.

It might be said that the story of the unknown vendor of Georgian silver in the pub lacked originality, and that the inside of a freezer-pack was not the most obvious place for storing valuable antiques, but there was one point of significance in the defence of Hugh Snakelegs Timson. Detective Inspector Broome was, as I have already suggested, an enthusiastic officer and one who regarded convictions with as much pride as the late Don Giovanni regarded his conquests of the female sex. No doubt he notched them up on his braces. He had given evidence that there had been thefts of silver from various country houses in Kent, but all the Detective Inspector's industry and persistence had not produced one householder who could be called by the prosecution to identify the booty from the freezer as his stolen silverware. So where, I was able to ask, was the evidence that the property undoubtedly received by Snakelegs had been stolen? Unless the old idea that the burden lay on the prosecution to prove its case had gone out of fashion in his Lordship's Court (distant rumblings as of a volcano limbering up for an eruption from the Bull), then perhaps, I ventured to suggest, Snakelegs was entitled to squeeze his way out of trouble.

Whether it was this thought, or Judge Bullingham's frenzied eagerness to secure a conviction (Kane himself might have got off his murder rap if he'd only been fortunate enough to receive a really biased summing-up), the jury came back with a cheerful verdict of not guilty. After only a brief fit of minor apoplexy, and a vague threat to bring the inordinate length of defending Counsel's speeches to the attention of the legal aid authorities, the Bull released the prisoner to his semi-detached and his wife Hetty. I was strolling along the corridor, puffing a small cigar with a modest feeling of triumph, when a small, eager young lady, her fairly pleasing face decorated with a pair of steel-rimmed specs and a look of great seriousness, rather as though she was not quite certain which problem to tackle first, world starvation or nuclear war, came panting up alongside.

'Mr Rumpole,' she said, 'you did an absolutely first-class job!'

I paused in my tracks, looked at her more closely, and remembered that she had been sitting in Court paying close attention throughtout R. v. *Snakelegs Timson*.

'I just gave my usual service.'

'And I,' she said, sticking out her hand in a gesture of camaraderie, 'have just passed the Bar exams.'

'Then we don't shake hands,' I had to tell her, avoiding physical contact. 'Clients don't like it you see. Think we might be doing secret deals with each other. All the same, welcome to the treadmill.'

I moved away from her then, towards the lift, pressed the button, and as I waited for nothing very much to happen, she accosted me again.

'You don't stereotype that much, do you, Mr Rumpole?' She looked as though she were already beginning to lose a little faith in my infallibility.

'And you don't call me *Mister* Rumpole. Leave that to the dotty Bull,' I corrected her, perhaps a little sharply.

'I thought you were too busy fighting the class war to care about outdated behaviour patterns.'

'Fighting the *what?*'

'Protecting working people against middle-class judges.'

The lift was still dawdling away in the basement and I thought it would be kind now to put this recruit right on a few of the basic principles of our legal system. 'The Timsons would hate to be called "working people",' I told her. 'They're entirely middle-class villains. Very Conservative, in fact. They live by strict monetarist principles and the free market economy. They're also against the closed shop; they believe that shops should be open at all hours of the night. Preferably by jemmy.'

'My name's Liz Probert,' she said, failing to smile at the jest I was not making for the first time. At this point the lift arrived. 'Good day Mizz' – I took her for a definite Mizz – I said, as I stepped into it. Rather to my surprise she strode in after me, still chattering. 'I want to defend like you. But I must still have a lot to learn. I never noticed the point about the owners not identifying the stolen silver.'

'Neither did I,' I had to admit, 'until it was almost too late. And you know why they didn't?' I was prepared to tell this neophyte the secrets of my astonishing success. That, after all, is part of the Great Tradition of the Bar, otherwise known as showing off to the younger white-wigs. 'They'd all got the insurance money, you see, and done very nicely out of it, thank you. The last thing they wanted was to see their old sugar bowls back and have to return the money. Life's a bit more complicated than they tell you in the Bar exams.'

We had reached the robing-room floor and I made for the Gents with Mizz Probert following me like the hound, or at least the puppy, of heaven. 'I was wondering if you could possibly give me some counselling in my career area.'

'Not now, I'm afraid. I've got a blind date, with some rather attractive bottles.' I opened the door and saw the gleaming porcelain fittings which had been in my mind since I got out of Court. 'Men only in here, I'm afraid,' I had to tell Mizz Probert, who still seemed to be at my heels. 'It's one of the quaint old traditions of the Bar.'

The surprisingly rapid and successful conclusion of the *Queen* v. *Snakelegs* had liberated me, and I set off with some eagerness to Prentice Alley in the City of London, and the premises of Vanberry's Fine Wines & Spirits Ltd, where I was to meet Claude Erskine-Brown, and sample, for the first time in my life, the mysterious joys of a blind tasting. After my credentials had been checked, I was shown into a small drinks party which had about it all the gaiety of an assembly of the bereaved, when the corpse in question has left his entire fortune to the Cats' Home.

The meeting took place in a brilliantly lit basement room with glaring white tiles. It seemed a suitable location for a post-mortem, but, in place of the usual deceased person on the table, there were a number of bottles, all shrouded in brown-paper bags. It was there I saw my learned friend Erskine-Brown, already in place among the tasters, who were twirling minute quantities of wine in their glasses, holding them nervously up to the light, sniffing at them with deep suspicion and finally allowing a small quantity to pass their lips. They were mainly solemn-looking characters in dark three-piece suits, although there was one female in a tweed coat and skirt, a sort of white silk stock, sensible shoes and a monocle. She looked as though she'd be happier judging hunters at a country gymkhana than fine wines, and she was, so Erskine-Brown whispered to me, Miss Honoria Bird, the distinguished wine correspondent of the *Sunday Mercury*. Before the tasting competition began in earnest we were invited to sample a few specimens from the Vanberry claret collection. So I took my first taste and experienced what, without doubt, was a draft of vintage that hath been *'Cool'd a long age in the deep-delved earth, / Tasting of Flora and the country green, . . .'* And it was whilst I was enjoying the flavour of Dance, and Provençal song, and sunburnt mirth, mixed with a dash of wild strawberries, that a voice beside me boomed, 'What's the matter with you? Can't you spit?'

Miss Honoria Bird was at my elbow and in my mouth was what? Something so far above my price range that it seemed like some new concoction altogether, as far removed from Pommeroy's Very Ordinary as a brief for Gulf Oil in the House of Lords is from a small matter of indecency before the Uxbridge Magistrates.

'Over there, in case you're looking for it. Expectoration corner!' Miss Bird waved me to a wooden wine-box, half-filled with sawdust into which the gents in dark suitings were directing mouthfuls of purplish liquid. I moved away from her, reluctant to admit that the small quantity of the true, the blushful Hippocrene I had been able to win had long since disappeared down the little red lane.

'Collie brought you, didn't he?' Martyn Vanberry, the wine merchant, caught me as I was about to swallow a second helping. He was a thin streak of a chap, in a dark suit and a stiff collar, whose faint smile, I thought, was thin-lipped and patronizing. Beside him stood a pleasant enough young man who was in charge of the mechanics of the thing, brought the bottles and the glasses and was referred to as Ken.

'Collie?' The name meant nothing to me.

'Erskine-Brown. We called him Collie at school.'

'After the dog?' I saw my Chambers companion insert the tip of his pale nose into the aperture of his wine glass.

'No. After the Doctor. Collis-Brown. You know, the medicine? Old Claude was always a bit of a pill really. We used to kick him around at Winchester.'

Now I am far from saying that, in my long relationship with Claude

Erskine-Brown, irritation has not sometimes got the better of me, but as a long-time member of our Chambers at Equity Court he has, over the years, become as familiar and uncomfortable as the furniture. I resented the strictures of this public-school bully on my learned friend and was about to say so when the gloomy proceedings were interrupted by the arrival of an unlikely guest wearing tartan trousers, rubber-soled canvas shoes of the type which I believe are generally known as 'trainers', and a zipped jacket which bore on its back the legend MONTY MANTIS SERVICE STATION LUTON BEDS. Inside this costume was a squat, ginger-haired and youngish man who called out, 'Which way to the antifreeze? At least we can get warmed up for the winter.' This was a clear reference to recent scandals in the wine trade, and it was greeted, in the rarefied air of Vanberry's tasting room, with as much jollity as an advertisement for contraceptive appliances in the Vatican.

'One of your customers?' I asked Vanberry.

'One of my best,' he sighed. 'I imagine the profession of *garagiste* in Luton must be extremely profitable. And he makes a point of coming to *all* of our blind tastings.'

'Now I'm here,' Mr Mantis said, taking off his zipper jacket and displaying a yellow jumper ornamented with diamond lozenges, 'let battle commence.' He twirled and sniffed and took a mouthful from a tasting glass, made a short but somehow revolting gargling sound and spat into the sawdust. 'A fairly unpretentious Côte Rotie,' he announced, as he did so. 'But on the whole 1975 was a disappointing year on the Rhône.'

The contest was run like a game of musical chairs. They gave you a glass and if you guessed wrong, the chair, so to speak, was removed and you had to go and sit with the girls and have an ice cream. At my first try I got that distant hint of wild strawberries again from a wine that was so far out of the usual run of my drinking that I became tongue-tied, and when asked to name the nectar could only mutter 'damn good stuff' and slink away from the field of battle.

Erskine-Brown was knocked out in the second round, having confidently pronounced a Coonawarra to be Châteauneuf du Pape. 'Some bloody stuff from Wagga, Wagga,' he grumbled unreasonably – on most occasions Claude was a staunch upholder of the Commonwealth, 'one always forgets about the colonies.'

So we watched as, one by one, the players fell away. Martyn Vanberry was in charge of the bottles and after the contestants had made their guesses he had to disclose the labels. From time to time, in the manner of donnish quiz-masters on upmarket wireless guessing-games, he would give little hints, particularly if he liked the contender. 'A churchyard number' might indicate a Graves, or 'a macabre little item, somewhat skeletal' a Beaune. He never, I noticed, gave much assistance to the *garagiste* from Luton, nor did he need to because the ebullient Mr Monty Mantis had no difficulty in identifying his wines and could even make a decent stab at the vintage year, although perfect accuracy in that regard wasn't required.

Finally the challengers were reduced to two: Monty Mantis and the lady with the eyeglass, Honoria Bird or Birdie as she was known to all the pinstriped expectorating undertakers around her. It was their bottoms that hovered, figuratively speaking, over the final chair, the last parcelled bottle. Martyn Vanberry was holding this with particular reverence as he poured a taster into two glasses. Monty Mantis regarded the colour, lowered his nose to the level of the tide, took a mouthful and spat rapidly.

'Gordon Bennett!' He seemed somewhat amazed. 'Don't want to risk swallowing that. It might ruin me carburettor!'

Martyn Vanberry looked pale and extremely angry. He turned to the lady contestant, who was swilling the stuff around her dentures in a far more impressive way. 'Well, Birdie,' he said, as she spat neatly, 'let me give you a clue. It's not whisky.'

'I think I could tell that.' She looked impassive. 'Not whisky.'

'But think . . . just think . . .' Vanberry seemed anxious to bring the contest to a rapid end by helping her. 'Think of a whisky translated.'

'*Le quatre-star Esso?*' said the *garagiste*, but Vanberry was unamused.

'White Horse?' Birdie frowned.

'Very good. Something Conservative, of course. And keep to the right!'

'The right bank of the river? St Emilion. White Horse? Cheval Blanc . . .' Birdie arrived at her destination with a certain amount of doubt and hesitation.

'1971, I'm afraid, nothing earlier.' Vanberry was pulling away the brown paper to reveal a label on which the words Cheval Blanc and Appellation St Émilion Contrôlée were to be clearly read. There was a smatter of applause. 'Dear old Birdie! Still an unbeatable palate.' It was a tribute in which the Luton *garagiste* didn't join; he was laughing as Martyn Vanberry turned to him and said, icily polite, 'I'm sorry you were pipped at the post, Mr Mantis. You did jolly well. Now, Birdie, if you'll once again accept the certificate of *Les Grands Contestants du Vin* and the complimentary bottle which this time is a magnum of Gevrey Chambertin Claire Pau 1970 – a somewhat underrated vintage. Can you not stay with us, Mr Mantis?'

But Monty Mantis was on his way to the door, muttering about getting himself decarbonized. Nobody laughed, and no one seemed particularly sorry to see him go.

There must be no accounting, I reflected on this incident, for tastes. One man's antifreeze may be another's Mouton Rothschild, especially if you don't see the label. I was reminded of those embarrassing tests on television in which the puzzled housewife is asked to tell margarine from butter, or say which washing powder got young Ronnie's football shorts whitest. She always looks terrified of disappointing the eager interviewer and plumping for the wrong variety. But then I thought that as a binge, the blind tasting at Vanberry's Fine Wines had been about as successful as a picnic tea with the Clacton Temperance Society and the incident faded from my memory.

Other matters arose of more immediate concern. One was to be of some interest and entertainment value. To deal with the bad news first: my wife Hilda, whose very name rings out like a demand for immediate obedience, announced the imminent visit to our mansion flat (although the words are inept to describe the somewhat gloomy and cavernous interior of Casa Rumpole) in Froxbury Court, Gloucester Road, of her old school-friend Dodo Mackintosh.

Now Dodo may be, in many ways, a perfectly reasonable and indeed game old bird. Her watercolours of Lamorna Cove and adjacent parts of Cornwall are highly regarded in some circles, although they seem to me to have been executed in heavy rain. She is, I believe, a dab hand at knitting patterns and during her stays a great deal of fancywork is put in on matinée jackets and bootees for her younger relatives. Hilda tells me that she was, when they were both at school, a sturdy lacrosse player. My personal view, and this is not for publication to She Who

Must Be Obeyed, is that in any conceivable team sent out to bore for England, Dodo would have to be included. As you may have gathered, I do not hit it off with the lady, and she takes the view that by marrying a claret-drinking, cigar-smoking legal hack who is never likely to make a fortune, Hilda has tragically wasted her life.

The natural gloom that the forthcoming visit cast upon me was somewhat mitigated by the matter of Mizz Probert's application to enter 3 Equity Court, which allowed me a little harmless fun at the expense of Soapy Sam Bollard (or Ballard as *he* effects to call himself), the sanctimonious President of the Lawyers As Christians Society who, in his more worldly manifestation, has contrived to become Head of our Chambers.

Sometime after the end of *Regina* v. *Snakelegs* (not a victory to be mentioned in the same breath as the Penge Bungalow Murders, in which I managed to squeeze first past the post *alone and without a leader*, but quite a satisfactory win all the same), I wandered into the clerk's room and there was the eager face of Mizz Probert asking our clerk Henry if there was any news about her application to become a pupil in Chambers, and Henry was explaining to her, without a great deal of patience, that her name would come up for discussion by the learned friends in due course.

'Pupil? You want to be a pupil? Any good at putting, are you?' This was the voice of Uncle Tom – T. C. Rowley – our oldest member, who hadn't come by a brief for as long as any of us can remember, but who chooses to spend his days with us to vary the monotony of life with an unmarried sister. His working day consists of a long battle with *The Times* crossword – won by the setter on most days, a brief nap after the midday sandwich and a spell of golf practice in a corner of the clerk's room. Visiting solicitors occasionally complain of being struck quite smartly on the ankle by one of Uncle Tom's golf balls.

'Good at putting? No. Do you have to be?' Mizz Probert asked in all innocence.

'My old pupil master, C. H. Wystan,' Uncle Tom told her, referring to Hilda's Daddy, the long-time-ago Head of our Chambers, 'was a terribly nice chap, but he never gave me anything to do. So I became the best member at getting his balls into a waste-paper basket. Awfully good training, you know. I never had an enormous practice. Well, very little practice at all quite honestly, so I've been able to keep up my golf. If you want to become a pupil this is my advice to you. Get yourself a mashie niblick . . .'

As this bizarre advice wound on, I left our clerk's room in order to avoid giving vent to any sort of unseemly guffaw. I had a conference with Mr Bernard, the solicitor who appeared to have a retainer for the Timson family. The particular problem concerned Tony Timson, who had entered a shop with the probable intention of stealing three large television sets. Unfortunately the business had gone bankrupt the week before and was quite denuded of stock, thus raising what many barristers might call a nice point of law – I would call it nasty. Getting on for half a century knocking around the Courts has given me a profound distaste for the law. Give me a bloodstain or two, a bit of disputed typewriting or a couple of hairs on a cardigan, and I am happy as the day is long. I feel a definite sense of insecurity and unease when solicitors like Mr Bernard say, as he did on that occasion, 'Hasn't the House of Lords had something to say on the subject?'

Well, perhaps it had. The House of Lords is always having something to say; they're a lot of old chatterboxes up there, if you want my opinion. I was saved from an immediate answer by Mizz Probert entering with a cup of coffee which she must have scrounged from the clerk's room for the sole purpose of gaining access to the Rumpole sanctum. I thanked her and prepared to parry Bernard's next attack.

'It's the doctrine of impossible attempt of course,' he burbled on. 'You must know the case.'

'Must I?' I was playing for time, but I saw Mizz Probert darting to the shelves where the bound volumes of the law reports are kept mainly for the use of other members of our Chambers.

'I mean there have been all these articles in the *Criminal Law Review.*'

'My constant bedtime reading,' I assured him.

'So you do *know* the House of Lords decision?' Mr Bernard sounded relieved.

'Know it? Of course I know it. During those long evenings at Froxbury Court we talk of little else. The name's on the tip of my tongue . . .'

It wasn't, of course, but the next minute it was on the law report which Mizz Probert put in front of me. '"*Swinglehurst against the Queen . . .*" Of course. Ah, yes. I've got it at my fingertips, as always, Mr Bernard. "*Doctrine of impossible attempts examined – R.* v. *Dewdrop and Banister distinguished*".' I read him a few nuggets from the headnote of the case. 'All this is good stuff, Bernard, couched in fine rich prose . . .'

'So how does that affect Tony Timson trying to steal three non-existent telly sets?'

'How does it?' I stood then, to end the interview. 'I think it would be more helpful to you, Mr Bernard, if I gave you a written opinion. I may have to go into other authorities in some depth.'

So it became obvious that, as far as I was concerned, Mizz Liz Probert would be a valuable, perhaps an indispensable, member of Chambers. When I asked her to write the opinion I had promised Bernard, she told me that she had been the top student of her year and won the Cicero scholarship. With Probert's knowledge of the law and my irresistible way with a jury, we might, I felt, become a team which could have got the Macbeths off regicide.

A happy chance furthered my plans. Owing to the presence on the domestic scene of Dodo Mackintosh (not the sort of spectacle a barrister wishes to encounter early in the mornings), I was taking my breakfast in the Taste-Ee-Bite, one of the newer and more garish serve-yourself eateries in Fleet Street. I was just getting outside two eggs and bacon on a fried slice, when Soapy Sam Bollard plonked himself down opposite me with a cup of coffee.

'Do you read the *Church Times*, Rumpole?' he started improbably, waving a copy of that organ in the general direction of my full English breakfast.

'Only for the racing results.'

'There's a first-class fellow writing on legal matters. This week's piece is headed VENGEANCE IS MINE. I WILL REPAY. This is what Canon Probert says . . .'

'Canon who?'

'Probert.'

'That's what I thought you said.'

'Society is fully entitled to be revenged upon the criminal.' Ballard gave me a taste of the Canon's style. 'Even the speeding motorist is a fit object for the legalized vengeance of the outraged pedestrian.'

'What does the good Canon recommend? Bring back the thumb-screw for parking on a double yellow line?'

'"Too often the crafty lawyer frustrates the angel of retribution",' Ballard went on reading.

'Too often the angel of retribution makes a complete balls-up of the burden of proof.'

'You may mock, Rumpole. You may well mock!'

'Thank you.'

'What we need is someone with the spirit of Canon Probert in Chambers. Someone to convince the public that lawyers still have a bit of moral fibre.' Ballard's further mention of this name put quite a ruth-less scheme into my head. 'Probert,' I said thoughtfully, 'did you say Probert?'

'Canon Probert.' Ballard supplied the details.

'Odd, that,' I told him. 'The name seems strangely familiar . . .'

Later, when Mizz Probert handed in a highly expert and profound legal opinion in the obscure subject of impossible attempt, often known in the trade as 'stealing from an empty purse', I had a few words with her on the subject of her parentage.

'Is your father,' I asked, 'by any chance the Canon Probert who writes for the *Church Times*?' And then I gave her an appropriate warn-ing: 'Don't answer that.'

'Why ever not?'

'Because our Head of Chambers is quite ridiculously prejudiced against women pupils whose fathers aren't canons who write for the *Church Times*. You may go now, Mizz Probert. Thank you for the excellent work.' She left me then. Clearly I had given her much food for thought.

So, in due course, a meeting was called in Sam Ballard's room to con-sider the intake of new pupils into Chambers. Those present were Rumpole, Erskine-Brown and Hoskins, a grey and somewhat fussy bar-rister, much worried by the expensive upbringing of his numerous daughters.

'Elizabeth Probert,' Ballard, QC, being in the Chair, read out the next name on his list. 'Does anyone know her?'

'I have seen her hanging about the clerk's room,' Erskine-Brown admitted. 'Remove the glasses and she might have a certain elfin charm.' Poor old Claude was ever hopelessly susceptible to a whiff of beauty in a lady barrister. 'I wonder if she could help me with my County Court practice . . .'

'That's all you think about, Erskine-Brown!' Hoskins sounded disapproving. 'Wine, women and your County Court practice.'

'That is distinctly unfair!'

'So far as I remember your wife didn't care for Fiona Allways.' Hoskins reminded him of his moment of tenderness for a young lady barrister now married to a merchant banker and living in Cheltenham.

'Yes. Well. Of course, Phillida can't be here today. She's got a long firm fraud in Doncaster,' Claude apologized for his wife.

'She might not take to anyone who looked at all elfin without her glasses.' Hoskins struck a further warning note.

'It was just a casual observation . . .'

'And I'm not sure we want any new intake in Chambers. Even in the form of pupils. I mean, is there enough work to go round? I speak as a member with daughters to support,' Hoskins reminded us.

'Thinking the matter over' – Erskine-Brown was clearly losing his bottle – 'I'm afraid Philly might be rather against her.'

It was then that I struck my blow for the highly qualified Mizz. 'I would be against her too,' I said, 'if it weren't for the name. Ballard, isn't that canon you admire so tremendously, the one we all read in the *Church Times*, called Probert?'

'You mean she's some relation?' Ballard was clearly excited.

'She hasn't said she isn't.'

'Not his daughter.' By now he was positively awe-struck.

'She hasn't denied it.'

Then Ballard looked like one whose eyes had seen his and my salvation. 'Then Elizabeth Probert comes from a family with enormously sound views on the religious virtue of retribution as part of our criminal law. I see her as an admirable pupil for Rumpole!'

'You think he might teach her some of his courtroom antics?' Erskine-Brown sounded sceptical.

'I think she might' – Ballard spoke with deep conviction – 'just possibly save his soul!'

So it came about that I was driven to my next conference at Brixton Prison in a very small runabout, something like a swaying biscuit box, referred to by Mizz Probert as her Deux Chevaux, and I supposed there was something to be said for having a pupil on wheels. Apart from the matter of transport, there was nothing particularly new or unusual about the conference in question, for I had once again been summoned to the aid of Hugh Snakelegs Timson who had, once again, been found in possession of a quantity of property alleged to have been stolen. Once again, DI Broome and DC Cosgrove had called at the Bromley semi to find the Cortina parked out in the street, and the lock-up garage full of cases of a fine wine, none other than St Émilion Château Cheval Blanc 1971.

'Hugh Timson seems to be always getting into trouble.' Mizz Probert was steering us, with a good deal of dexterity, round the Elephant and Castle.

'I suppose he takes the usual business risks.'

'Have you ever found out the root of the problem?'

'The root of the problem would seem to be Detective Inspector Broome who's rapidly becoming the terror of the Timsons.'

'I bet you'll find that he comes from a broken home.'

'Inspector Broome? Probably.'

'No. I meant Hugh Timson. In an inner-city area. With an antisocial norm among his peer group, most likely. He must always have felt alienated from society.'

Was Mizz Probert right, and is it nurture and not nature that shapes our ends? I suppose I was brought up in appalling conditions, in an ice-cold vicarage with no mod cons or central heating. My old father, being a priest of the Church of England, had only the sketchiest notion of morality, and my mother was too occupied with jam-making and the Women's Institute to notice my existence. Is it any real wonder that I have taken to crime?

When we had met Mr Bernard at the gates of Brixton and settled down with the ex-Mr Debonair in the interview room, I thought I would put Mizz Probert's theories to the test. 'Come from a broken home, did you?' I asked Snakelegs.

'Broken home?' The client looked displeased. 'I don't know what you mean. Mum and Dad was married forty years, and he never so much as looked at another woman. Hetty and I, we're the same. What you on about, Mr Rumpole?'

'At least you were born in an inner-city area.'

'My old dad wouldn't have tolerated it. Bromley was really nice in those days. More green fields and that. What's it got to do with my case?'

'Not much. Just setting my pupil's mind at rest. Why was your garage being used as a cellar for fine wines?'

'Bit of good stuff, was it?' Snakelegs seemed proud of the fact.

'Didn't you try it?'

'Teetotal, me. You know that.' The client sounded shocked. 'Although the wife, she will take a drop of tawny port at Christmas. Not that I think it's right. It's drink that leads to crime. We all know that, don't we, Mr Rumpole?'

'So *how* . . . ?'

'Well, I got them all a bit cheap. Not for myself, you understand. They'd be no good for Hetty and me. But I thought it was a drop of stuff I might sell on to anyone having a bit of a wedding – anything like that.'

'And *where* did you get it? The Judge might be curious to know.' I felt a sudden weariness, such as whoever it was among the ancient Greeks who had just pushed a stone up a hill, and seen it come rolling down again for the three-millionth time, must have felt. It was one thing to win a case because the prosecution evidence wasn't strong enough for a conviction. It was another, and far more depressing matter, to be putting forward the same distinctly shopworn defence throughout a working life. I just hoped to God that Snakelegs wasn't going to babble on about a man in a pub.

'Well, there was this fellow what I ran into down the Needle Arms . . . What's the matter, Mr Rumpole?'

'Please, Snakelegs' – my boredom must have become evident – 'can't we have some sort of variation? Judge Bullingham's getting tremendously tired of that story.'

'Bullingham?' Snakelegs was understandably alarmed. 'We're not getting him again, are we?'

'Not if I can help it. This character in the Needle Arms – not anyone whose name you happen to remember?' I lit a small cigar and waited in hope.

'Afraid I can't help you there, Mr Rumpole.'

'You can't help me? And he sold you all these crates of stuff. Who's got the list of exhibits?' Mizz Probert handed it to me immediately. 'Cheval Blanc. St Émilion . . .'

'No. That wasn't the name. It was more like, something Irish . . .' Snakelegs looked at me. 'What's our chances, Mr Rumpole?'

'Our chances?' I gave him my considered opinion. 'Well, you've heard about snowballs in hell?'

'You saw me right last time.'

'Last time the losers didn't come forward to claim their property.'

'Because of the insurance.' Liz filled in the details.

'Mizz Probert remembers. This time the loser of the wine is principal witness for the prosecution.'

'Martyn Vanberry.' Bernard was looking at the prosecution witness statements. First among them was indeed the proprietor of Vanberry's – purveyors of fine wines, Prentice Alley in the City of London – not a specially attractive character, the highly respectable public-school bully.

Back in the Deux Chevaux, I felt a little guilty about disillusioning Liz Probert and depriving Snakelegs of an unhappy childhood. I complimented her on her runabout and asked if it weren't by any chance a present from her father, the Canon. It was then that she told me that her father was, in fact, the leader of the South-east London Council widely known as Red Ron Probert. He was a man, no doubt, whose own article of religion was the divine right of the local Labour Party to govern that area of London, and he frequently appeared on television chat-shows to speak up for minority rights. His ideal voter was apparently an immigrant Eskimo lesbian, who strongly supported the IRA.

'Is there anything wrong with Ron Probert being my father?'

'Nothing at all provided you don't chatter about it to our learned Head of Chambers. Do you think you could point this machine in the general direction of Luton? I'm going to take a nap.'

'What are we doing in Luton?'

'Seeing a witness.'

'I thought we weren't allowed to see witnesses.'

'This is an expert witness. We're allowed to see them.'

Luton is not exactly one of the Jewels of Southern England. American tourists don't brave the terrorists to loiter in its elegant parks or snap each other in the Cathedral Close, but its inhabitants seem friendly enough and the first police officer we met was delighted to direct us to the Monty Mantis Service Station. It was a large and clearly thriving concern, selling not only petrol but new and second-hand cars, cuddly toys, garden furniture, blow-up paddling pools, furry dice and anoraks. The proprietor remembered my face from Vanberry's, and when I gave him a hint of what we wanted, invited us into his luxuriously appointed office, where we sat on plastic zebra-skin covered furniture, gazing at pictures of peeing children and crying clowns, while he poured us out a couple of glasses of Cheval Blanc from his own cellar, so that I might understand the experience. When I made my delight clear, he said it was always a pleasure to meet a genuine enthusiast.

'And you, Mr Mantis,' I ventured to ask him, 'I've been wondering how *you* became so extraordinarily well informed in wine lore. I mean, where did you get your training?'

'Day trip to Boulogne. 1963. With the Luton Technical.' He refilled our glasses. 'Unattractive bunch of kids, we must have been. Full of terminal acne and lavatory jokes. Enough to drive "sir" what took us into the funny farm. We were all off giving him the slip. Trying to chase girls that didn't exist, or was even fatter and spottier than the local talent round the Wimpy. Anyway, I ended up in the station buffet for some reason, and spent what I'd been saving up for an unavailable knees' trembler, if you'll pardon my French, Miss Probert. I bought a half bottle. God knows what it was. *Ordinaire de la Gare*, French railways perpetual standby. And there was I, brought up on Tizer and Coke that tastes of old pennies, and sweet tea you could stand the spoon up in, and it came as a bit of a revelation to me, Mr Rumpole.'

'*Tasting of Flora and the country green . . . Dance, and Provençal song, and sunburnt mirth! . . .*'

'Shame you can't ever talk about the stuff without sounding like them toffee noses round Vanberry's. Well, I bought four bottles and kept a cellar under my bed and shared it out in toothmugs with a chosen few. Then when I started work at the garage, I didn't go round the pub Friday nights. I began investing . . .'

'And acquired your knowledge?'

'I don't know football teams, you see. Haven't got a clue about the Cup. But I reckon I know my vintages.'

'Such as the Cheval Blanc 1971.' I sampled it again.

'All right, is it?'

'It seems perfectly all right.'

'You're sure you won't, Miss Probert?'

'I never have.'

Liz Probert, I thought, a hard worker, with all the puritanism of youth.

'This is better, perhaps' – I held my glass to the light – 'than the Cheval Blanc round Vanberry's?'

Monty Mantis looked at me then and began to laugh. It was not unkind, but genuinely amused laughter, coming from a man who no doubt knew his wines.

Our clerk Henry is a star of his local amateur dramatic society, and is famous, as I understand it, for the Noël Coward roles he undertakes. Henry's life in the theatre has its uses for us as a fellow Thespian is Miss Osgood, who, when she is not appearing in some role made famous by the late Gertrude Lawrence, is in charge of the lists down the Old Bailey. Miss Osgood can exercise some sort of control on which case comes before which judge, and when the wheel of fortune spins to decide such matters, she can sometimes lay a finger on it. I had fortunately hit on a time when Henry and Miss Osgood were playing opposite each other in *Private Lives* and I asked our clerk to use his best endeavours with his co-star to see that *R. v. Snakelegs Timson* did not come up for trial before Judge Bullingham. On the night before the hearing, Henry rang Froxbury Court to give me the glad news that the case was fixed to come on before a judge known to his many friends and admirers as Moley Molesworth.

'A wonderful judge for us,' I told Bernard and Liz Probert as we assembled at the door of the Court the next morning. 'I'll have Moley eating out of my hand. Mildest-mannered chap that ever thought in terms of probation.'

'For receiving stolen wine?' Bernard sounded doubtful.

'Oh, yes. I shouldn't be at all surprised. Community service is his equivalent of dispatching chaps to the galleys.'

But just when everything seemed set fair, a cloud no bigger than a man's hand blew up in the shape of Miss Osgood, who came to announce that his Honour Judge Molesworth was confined to bed with a severe cold and would not, therefore, be trying Snakelegs.

'A severe cold? What's the matter with the old idiot, can't he wrap up warm?'

'It's all right, Mr Rumpole. We can transfer you to another Court immediately.' Miss Osgood smiled with the charm of the late Gertrude Lawrence. 'Judge Bullingham's free.'

Why is it that whoever dishes out severe colds invariably gives them to the wrong person?

'Mr Rumpole. Do you wish to detain this gentleman in the witness-box?'

The Bull had clearly recognized Snakelegs, and remembered the antiques in the frozen peas. He looked with equal disfavour at the dock and at defending Counsel. It was only when his eye lit upon young Tristram Paulet for the prosecution, or the chief prosecution witness, Martyn Vanberry, who was now standing, at the end of his evidence-in-chief, awaiting my attention, that he exposed his yellowing teeth in that appalling smirk which represents Bullingham's nearest approximation to moments of charm.

'I have one or two questions for Mr Vanberry,' I told him.

'Oh' – his Lordship seemed surprised – 'is there any dispute that your client, Timson, had this gentleman's wine in his possession?'

'No dispute about that, my Lord.'

'Then to what issue in this case can your questions possibly be directed?'

I was tempted to tell the old darling that if he sat very quietly and paid close attention he might, just possibly, find out. Instead, I said that my questions would concern my client's guilt or innocence, a matter which might be of some interest to the jury. And then, before the Bull could get his breath to bellow, I asked Mr Vanberry if the wine he lost was insured.

'Of course. I had it fully insured.'

'As a prudent businessman?'

'I hope I am that, my Lord,' Vanberry appealed to the Judge, who gave his ghastly smile and murmured as unctuously as possible, 'I'm sure you are, Mr Vanberry. I am perfectly sure you are.'

'And how long have you been trading as a wine merchant in Prentice Alley in the City of London?' I went on hacking away.

'Just three years, my Lord.'

'And done extremely well! In such a short time.' The Bull was still smirking.

'We have been lucky, my Lord, and I think we've been dependable.'

'Before that, where were you trading?' I interrupted the love duet between the witness and the Bench.

'I was selling pictures. As a matter of fact I had a shop in Chelsea; we specialized in nineteenth-century watercolours, my Lord.'

'The name of the business?'

'Vanberry Fine Arts.'

'Manage to find any insurance claims for Vanberry Fine Arts . . . ?' I turned to whisper to Bernard, but it seemed he was still making inquiries. Only one thing to do then, pick up a blank sheet of paper, study it closely and ask the next question looking as though you had all the answers in your hands. Sometimes, it was to be admitted, the old-fashioned ways are best.

'I must put it to you that Vanberry Fine Arts made a substantial insurance claim in respect of the King's Road premises.'

'We had a serious break-in and most of our stock was stolen. Of course I had to make a claim, my Lord.' Vanberry still preferred to talk to his friend, the Bull, but at least he had been forced by the information he thought I had to come out with some part of the truth.

'You seem to be somewhat prone to serious break-ins, Mr Vanberry,' I suggested, whereupon the Bull came in dead on cue with, 'It's the rising tide of lawlessness that is threatening to engulf us all. You should know that better than anyone, Mr Rumpole!'

I thought it best to ignore this, so I then called on the usher to produce Exhibit 34, which was, in fact, one of the bottles of allegedly stolen wine.

'You're not proposing to sample it, I hope, Mr Rumpole?' The Bull tried heavy sarcasm and the jury and the prosecution Counsel laughed obediently.

'I'm making no application to do so at the moment,' I reassured him. 'Mr Vanberry. You say this bottle contains vintage claret of a high quality?'

'It does, my Lord.'

'Retailing at what price?'

'I think around fifty pounds a bottle.'

'And insured for . . . ?'

'I believe we insured it for the retail price. Such a wine would be hard to replace.'

'Of course it would. It's a particularly fine vintage of the . . . What did you say it was?' The Bull charged into the arena.

'Cheval Blanc, my Lord.'

'And we all know what you have to pay for a really fine Burgundy nowadays, don't we, members of the jury?'

The members of the jury – an assortment of young unemployed blacks, puzzled old-age pensioners from Hackney and grey-haired cleaning ladies – looked at the Judge and seemed to find his question mystifying.

'It's a claret, my Lord. Not a Burgundy,' Vanberry corrected the Judge, as I thought unwisely.

'A claret. Yes, of course it is. Didn't I say that? Yes, well. Let's get on with it, Mr Rumpole.' Bullingham was not pleased.

'You lost some fifty cases. It was insured for six hundred pounds a case, you say?'

'That is so.'

'So you recovered some thirty thousand pounds from your insurers?'

'There was a considerable loss . . .'

'To your insurance company?'

'And a considerable profit to whoever dealt with it illegally,' the Bull couldn't resist saying, so I thought it about time he was given a flutter of the cape: 'My Lord, I have an application to make in respect of Exhibit 34.'

'Oh, very well. Make it then.' The Judge closed his eyes and prepared to be bored.

'I wish to apply to the Court to open this bottle of alleged Cheval Blanc.'

'You're not serious?' The Bull's eyes opened.

'Your Lordship seemed to have the possibility in mind . . .'

'Mr Rumpole!' – I watched the familiar sight of the deep purple falling on the Bullingham countenance – 'from time to time the weight of these grave proceedings at the Old Bailey may be lifted when the Judge makes a joke. One doesn't do it often. One seldom can. But one likes to do it whenever possible. I was making a *joke*, Mr Rumpole!'

'I'm sure we're all grateful for your Lordship's levity,' I assured him, 'but I'm entirely serious. My learned pupil, Mizz Probert, has come equipped with a corkscrew.'

'Mr Rumpole!' – the Judge was exercising almost superhuman self-control – 'may I get this quite clear. What would be your purpose in opening this bottle?'

'The purpose of tasting it, my Lord.'

It was then, of course, that the short Bullingham fuse set off the explosion. 'This is a Court of Law, Mr Rumpole,' he almost shouted. 'This is not a barroom! I have sat here for a long time, far too long in my opinion, listening to your cross-examination of this unfortunate gentleman who has, as the jury may well find, suffered at the hands of your client. But I do not intend to sit here, Mr Rumpole, while you drink the exhibits!'

'Not "drink" ' – I tried to calm the Bull – ' "taste", my Lord. And may I say this: if the defence is to be denied the opportunity of tasting a vital exhibit, that would be a breach of our fundamental liberties! The principles we have fought for ever since the days of Magna Carta. In that event I would have to make an immediate application to the Court of Appeal.'

'The Court of Appeal, did you say?' I had mentioned the only institution which can bring the Bull to heel – he dreads criticism by the Lords of Appeal in Ordinary which might well get reported in *The Times*. 'You would take the matter up to the Court of Appeal?' he repeated, somewhat aghast.

'This afternoon, my Lord.'

'That's what you'd do?'

'Without hesitation, my Lord.'

'What do you say about this, Mr Tristram Paulet?' The Judge turned for help to the prosecution.

'My Lord. I'm sure the Court would not wish my learned friend to have any cause for complaint, however frivolous. And it might be better not to delay matters by an application to the Court of Appeal.' Paulet is one of Nature's old Etonians, but I blessed him for his words which were also welcomed by the Bull. 'Exactly what was in *my* mind, Mr Tristram

Paulet!' the Judge discovered. 'Very well, Mr Rumpole. In the quite exceptional circumstances of this case, the Court is prepared to give you leave to taste . . .'

So, in a sense, the party was on. Mizz Probert produced a corkscrew from her handbag. I opened the bottle, a matter in which I have had some practice, and asked the Judge and my learned friend, Mr Paulet, to join me. The usher brought three of the thick tumblers which are used to carry water to hoarse barristers or fainting witnesses. While this operation was being carried out, my eye lighted on Martyn Vanberry in the witness-box – he looked suddenly older, his expensive tan had turned sallow and I saw his forehead shining with sweat. He opened his mouth, but no sound of any particular significance emerged. And so, in the ensuing silence, Tristram Paulet sniffed doubtfully at his glass, the Bull took a short swig and looked enigmatic, and I tasted and held the wine long enough in my mouth to be certain. It was with considerable relief that I realized that the label on the bottle was an unreliable witness, for the taste was all too familiar – that of Château Thames Embankment 1985, a particularly brutal year.

'Rumpole's got a pupil.'

'I hope he's an apt pupil.'

'It's not a he. It's a she.'

'A she. Oh, really, Rumpole?' Dodo Mackintosh clicked her knitting needles and looked at me with deep suspicion.

'A Mizz Liz Probert . . .'

'You call her Liz?' The cross-examination continued.

'No. I call her Mizz.'

'Is she a middle-aged person?'

'About twenty-three. Is that middle-aged nowadays?'

'And is Hilda quite happy about that, do you think?' Dodo asked me, and not my wife, the question.

'Hilda doesn't look for happiness.'

'Oh. What does she look for?'

'The responsibilities of command.' I raised a respectful glass of Château Fleet Street at She Who Must Be Obeyed. There was a brief silence broken only by the clicking of needles, and then Dodo said, 'Don't you want to know what this Liz Probert is like, Hilda?'

'Not particularly.'

It was at this moment that the telephone rang and I picked it up to hear the voice of a young man called Ken Eastham, who worked at Vanberry's. He wanted, it seemed, to ask my legal advice. I spoke to him whilst Hilda and her old friend, Dodo Mackintosh, speculated on the subject of my new pupil. When the call was over, I put down the telephone after thanking Mr Eastham from the bottom of my heart. It's rare, in any experience, for anyone to care enormously for justice.

'Well, Rumpole, you look extremely full of yourself,' Hilda said as I dialled Mr Bernard's number to warn him that we might be calling another witness.

'No doubt he is full of himself' – Dodo put in her two penn'orth – 'having a young pupil to trot around with.'

'Dodo's coming down to the Old Bailey tomorrow, Rumpole,' Hilda warned me. 'She's tremendously keen to see you in action.'

In fact Dodo Mackintosh's view of Rumpole in action was fairly short-lived. She arrived early at my Chambers, extremely early, and Henry told her that I was still breakfasting at the Taste-Ee-Bite in Fleet Street. Indeed I was then tucking into the full British with Mizz Probert, to whom I was explaining the position of the vagal nerve in the neck, which can be so pressed during a domestic fracas that death may ensue unintentionally. (I secured an acquittal for Gimlett, a Kilburn grocer, armed with this knowledge – the matter is described later in this very volume.) At any rate I had one hand placed casually about Mizz Probert's neck explaining the medical aspect of the matter when Dodo Mackintosh entered the Taste-Ee-Bite, took in the scene, put the worst possible construction on the events, uttered the words 'Rumpole in action! Poor Hilda' in a tragic and piercing whisper and made a hasty exit. This was, of course, a matter which would be referred to later.

I did not, as I think wisely, put Snakelegs Timson in the witness-box, but I had told Mr Bernard to get a witness summons delivered to the wine correspondent of the *Sunday Mercury* and took the considerable risk of calling her. When she was in the box I got the Bull's permission to allow her to taste a glass of the wine which the prosecution claimed was stolen Château Cheval Blanc, although I had it presented to her in an anonymous tumbler. She held it up to the light, squinted at it through her monocle and then took a mouthful, which I told her she would have to swallow, however painful she found it, as we had no 'expectoration corner'. At which point Tristram Paulet muttered a warning not to lead the witness.

'Certainly not! In your own words, would you describe the wine you have just tasted?'

'Is it worth describing?' Miss Bird asked, having swallowed with distaste.

'My client's liberty may depend on it,' I looked meaningfully at the jury.

'It's a rough and, I would say, crude Bordeaux-type of mixed origins. It may well contain some product of North Africa. It's too young and drinking it would amount to infanticide had its quality not made such considerations irrelevant.'

'Have you met such a wine before?'

'I believe it is served in certain bars in this part of London to the more poorly paid members of the legal profession.'

'Would you price it at fifty pounds a bottle?' this poorly paid member asked.

'You're joking!'

'It is not I that made the joke, Miss Bird.'

I could see Vanberry, who was looking even more depressed and anxious than he had the day before, pass a note to the prosecuting solicitor. Meanwhile, Birdie gave me her answer. 'It would be daylight robbery to charge more than two pounds.'

'Yes. Thank you, Miss Bird. Just wait there, will you?' I sat down and Tristram Paulet rose to cross-examine, armed with Vanberry's note.

'Miss Bird. The wine you have tasted came from a bottle labelled Cheval Blanc 1971. I take it you don't think that is its correct description.'

'Certainly not!' The admirable Birdie would have none of it.

'At a blind tasting which took place at Mr Vanberry's shop, did you not identify a Cheval Blanc 1971?' There was a considerable pause after this question, during which Miss Bird looked understandably uncomfortable.

'I had my doubts about it,' she explained at last.

'But did you not identify it?'

'Yes. I did.' The witness was reluctant, but Paulet had got all he wanted. He sat down with a 'thank you, Miss Bird', and I climbed to my hindlegs to repair the damage in re-examination.

'Miss Bird, on that occasion, were you competing against a Mr Monty Mantis, a garage owner of Luton, in the blind-tasting contest?'

'Yes. I was.'

'Did he express a poor opinion of the alleged Cheval Blanc?'

'He did.'

'But were you encouraged by Mr Martyn Vanberry to identify it as a fine claret by a number of hints and clues?'

'Yes. He was trying to help me a little.' Miss Bird looked doubtfully at the anxious wine merchant sitting in the well of the Court.

'To help you to call it Cheval Blanc?' I suggested.

'I suppose so. Yes.'

'Miss Bird. What was your opinion of Mr Monty Mantis?'

'I thought him a very vulgar little man who probably had no real knowledge of wine.' She had no doubt about it.

'And, thinking that about him, were you particularly anxious to disagree with his opinion?'

There was a pause while the lady faced up to the question and then said with some candour, 'I suppose I may have been.'

'And you were anxious to win the contest?' Paulet rose to make an objection, but I ploughed on before the Bull could interrupt. 'As Mr Vanberry was clearly helping you to do?'

'I may have wanted to win. Yes,' Miss Bird admitted, and Paulet subsided, discouraged by her answer.

'Looking back on that occasion, do you think you were tasting genuine Cheval Blanc?' It was the only important question in the case and Bullingham and Martyn Vanberry were both staring at the expert, waiting for her answer. When it came it was entirely honest.

'Looking back on it, my Lord, I don't think I was.'

'And today you have told us the truth?'

'Yes.'

'Thank you, Miss Honoria Bird.' And I sat down, with considerable relief.

★

With Honoria Bird's evidence we had turned the corner. Young Ken Eastham, who had rung me at home, went into the witness-box. He told the Court that Vanberry had a few dozen of the Cheval Blanc, and then a large new consignment arrived from a source he had not heard of before. Martyn Vanberry asked him to set the new bottles apart from the old, but he had already unpacked some of the later consignment, and put a few bottles with the wine already there. Later, almost all the recently delivered 'Cheval Blanc' was stolen, and Martyn Vanberry seemed quite unconcerned at the loss. Subsequently, and by mistake he thought, one of the new bottles of 'Cheval Blanc' must have been used for the blind tasting. When I asked Mr Eastham why he had agreed to give this evidence he said, 'I've done a long training in wine, and I suppose I love the subject. Well, there's not much point in that is there, if there's going to be lies told on the labels.'

'Mr Rumpole' – his Honour Judge Bullingham was now interested, but somewhat puzzled – 'I'm not absolutely sure I follow the effect of this evidence. If Mr Vanberry were in the business of selling the inferior stuff we have tasted, and Miss Honoria Bird has tasted, as highly expensive claret surely the deceit would be obvious to anyone drinking . . . ?'

'I'm not suggesting that the wine was in Mr Vanberry's possession for drinking, my Lord.' I was doing my best to help the Bull grasp the situation.

'Well, what on earth did he have it for?'

Of course Vanberry had fixed the burglary at his wine shop just as he had fixed the stealing of his alleged Victorian watercolours, so that he could claim the insurance money on the value of expensive Cheval Blanc, which he never had. No doubt, whoever was asked to remove the swag was instructed to dispose of it on some rubbish tip. Instead it got sold round the pubs in Bromley, where Snakelegs bought it, and was tricked, without his knowledge, into a completely honest transaction, because it was never, in any real sense of the word, stolen property. So I was able to enlighten Bullingham in the presence of the chief prosecution witness, who was soon to become the defendant, in a case of insurance fraud: 'Mr Vanberry didn't ever have this wine for anyone to drink, my Lord. He had it there for someone to steal.'

*

When the day's work was done I called into the Taste-Ee-Bite again and retired behind the *Standard* with a pot of tea and a toasted bun. At the next table I heard the monotonous tones of Soapy Sam Bollard, QC, our Head of Chambers. 'Your daughter's really doing very well. She's with Rumpole, a somewhat elderly member of our Chambers. Perhaps it's mixing with the criminal classes, but Rumpole seems somewhat lacking in a sense of sin. A girl with your daughter's background may well do him some good.'

I could recognize the man he was talking to as Red Ron Probert, Labour Chairman of the South-east London Council. Ballard, who never watches the telly, was apparently unable to recognize Red Ron. Liz's father, it seemed, had come to inquire as to his daughter's progress and our Head of Chambers had invited him to tea.

'I didn't realize who you were at first,' Ballard droned on. 'Of course, you're in mufti!'

'What?' Red Ron seemed surprised.

'Your collar.'

'What's wrong with my collar?'

'Nothing at all,' Ballard hastened to reassure him. 'I'm sure it's very comfortable. I expect you want to look just like an ordinary bloke.'

'Well, I am an ordinary bloke. And I represent thousands of ordinary blokes . . .' Ron was about to deliver one of his well-loved speeches.

'Of course you do! I must say, I'm a tremendous admirer of your work.'

'Are you?' Ron was surprised. 'I thought you lawyers were always Right . . .'

'Not always. Some of them are entirely wrong. But there are a few of us prepared to fight the good fight!'

'On with the revolution!' Ron slightly raised a clenched fist.

'You think it needs *that*' – Ballard was thoughtful – 'to awaken a real sense of morality . . . ?'

'Don't you?'

'A revolution in our whole way of thinking? I fear so. I greatly fear so.' Ballard shook his head wisely.

'Fear not, Brother Ballard! We're in this together!' Red Ron rallied our Head of Chambers.

'Of course.' Ballard was puzzled. 'Yes. Brother. Were you in some Anglican Monastic Order?'

'Only the Clerical Workers' Union.' Red Ron laughed at what he took to be a Ballard witticism.

'Clerical Workers? Yes, that, of course.' Ballard joined in the joke. 'Amusing way of putting it.'

'And most of them weren't exactly monastic!'

'Oh dear, yes. There's been a falling off, even among the clergy. I really must tell you . . .'

'Yes, Brother.' Red Ron was prepared to listen.

'Brother! I can't really . . . I should prefer to call you Father. It might be more appropriate.'

'Have it your own way.' Ron seemed to find the mode of address acceptable.

'Father Probert,' Ballard said, very sincerely, 'you have been, for me at any rate, a source of great inspiration!'

I folded my *Standard* then and crept away unnoticed. I felt no need to correct a misunderstanding which seemed to be so gratifying to both of them, and had had such a beneficial effect on Mizz Probert's legal career.

That night I carried home to Froxbury Court a not unusual treat, that is to say, a bottle of Pommeroy's Château Thames Embankment. I was opening it with a feeling of modified satisfaction when Hilda said, 'You look very full of yourself! I suppose you've won another case.'

'I'm afraid so.' I had the bottle open and was filling a couple of glasses: '*Oh, for a draught of vintage! that hath been/Cool'd a long age in the deep-delved earth, . . .*' And then I tasted the wine and didn't spit. 'A crude Bordeaux-type of mixed origins. On sale to the more poorly paid members of the legal profession.' I couldn't help laughing.

'What've you got to laugh about, Rumpole?'

'Bollard!'

'Your Head of Chambers.'

'He met Mizz Probert's father. Red Ron. And he still thought he was some Anglican Divine. He went entirely by the name on the label . . .' I lowered my nose once more to the glass. '*Tasting of Flora and the country green . . .* Isn't it remarkably quiet around here? I don't seem to hear the fluting tones of your old childhood chum, Dodo Mackintosh.'

'Dodo's gone home.'

'*Dance, and Provençal song, and sunburnt mirth.*'

'She's disgusted with you, Rumpole. As a matter of fact, I told her she'd better go.'

'You told Dodo that?' She Who Must Be Obeyed was usually clay in Miss Mackintosh's hands.

'She said she'd seen you making up to some girl, in a tea-room.'

'That's what she said?'

'I told her it was absolutely ridiculous. I really couldn't imagine a young girl wanting to be made up to by you, Rumpole!'

'Well. Thank you very much.' I refilled the glass which had mysteriously emptied:

> *O for a beaker full of the warm South,*
> *Full of the true, the blushful Hippocrene,*
> *With beaded bubbles winking at the brim,*
> *And purple-stained mouth . . .*'

'She said you were in some sort of embrace. I told her she was seeing things.'

> *That I might drink, and leave the world unseen,*
> *And with thee fade away into the forest dim:*

> *Fade far away, dissolve, and quite forget*
> *What thou among the leaves hast never known,*
> *The weariness, the fever and the fret . . .*'

I must say the words struck me as somewhat comical. At the idea of my good self and She dancing away into the mysterious recesses of some wood, the mind, as they say, boggled.

Rumpole and the Judge's Elbow

Up to now in these accounts of my most famous or infamous cases I have acted as a faithful historian, doing my best to tell the truth, the whole truth, about the events that occurred, and not glossing over the defeats and humiliations which are part of the daily life of an Old Bailey Hack, nor being ridiculously modest about my undoubted triumphs. When it comes to the matter of the Judge's elbow, however, different considerations arise. Many of the vital incidents in the history of the tennis injury to Mr Justice Featherstone, its strange consequences and near destruction of his peace of mind, necessarily happened when I was absent from the scene, nor did the Judge ever take me into his confidence over the matter. Indeed as most of his almost frenetic efforts during the trial of Dr Maurice Horridge were devoted to concealing the truth from the world in general, and old Horace Rumpole in particular, it is a truth which may never be fully known. I have been, however, able to piece together from the scraps of information at my disposal (a word or two from a retired usher, some conversations Marigold Featherstone had with She Who Must Be Obeyed) a pretty clear picture of what went on in the private and, indeed, sheltered life of one of the Judges of the Queen's Bench. I feel that I now know what led to Guthrie Featherstone's curious behaviour during the Horridge trial, but in reconstructing some of the scenes that led up to this, I have had, as I say for the first time in these accounts, to use the art of the fiction writer and imagine, to a large extent, what Sir Guthrie or Lady Marigold Featherstone, or the other characters involved, may have said at the time. Such scenes are based, however, on a long experience of how Guthrie Featherstone was accustomed to behave in the face of life's little difficulties, that is to say, with anxiety bordering on panic.

I think it is also important that this story should be told to warn others of the dangers involved in sitting in Judgement on the rest of erring humanity. However, to save embarrassment to anyone concerned, I have left strict instructions that this account should not be published until after the death of the main parties, unless Mr Truscott of the Caring Bank should become particularly insistent over the question of my overdraft.

Guthrie Featherstone, then plain Mr Guthrie Featherstone, QC, MP, became the Head of our Chambers in Equity Court on the retirement of Hilda's Daddy, old C. H. Wystan, a man who could never bring himself to a proper study of bloodstains. I had expected, as the senior member in practice, to take over Chambers from Daddy, but Guthrie Featherstone, a new arrival, popped in betwixt the election and my hopes.

I have forgotten precisely what brand of MP old Guthrie was; he was either right-wing Labour or left-wing Conservative until, in the end, he gave up politics and joined the SDP. He was dedicated to the middle of the road, and very keen on our Chambers 'image', which, on one occasion, he thought was being let down badly by my old hat. Finally, the Lord Chancellor, who was probably thinking of something else at the time, made Guthrie a Scarlet Judge, and the old darling went into a dreadful state of panic, fearing that there had been a premature announcement of this Great Event in the History of our Times.

From that time, Sir Guthrie Featherstone was entitled to scarlet and ermine and other variously coloured dressing-gowns, to be worn at different seasons of the year, and sat regularly in the seat of Judgement, dividing the sheep from the goats with a good deal of indecision and anxiety. When his day's work was done, he returned to the block of flats in Kensington, where he lived with his wife Marigold. The flats came equipped with a tennis court, and there the Judge and his good lady were accustomed to playing mixed doubles with their neighbours, the Addisons, during the long summer evenings. Mr Addison, I imagine, was excessively respectful of the sporting Guthrie and frequently called out 'Nice one, Judge', or 'Oh, I say, Judge, what frightfully bad luck', during the progress of the game.

What I see, doing my best to reconstruct the occasion which gave rise to the following chapter of accidents, is Guthrie and Marigold diving for the same ball with cries of 'Leave it, Marigold!' and 'Mine, Guthrie!' These two rapidly moving bodies were set on a collision course and, when it happened, the Judge fell heavily to the asphalt, his wife stood over his recumbent figure and the anxious Addisons came round the net with cries of 'Nothing broken I hope and trust?' From then on, perhaps, it went something like this:

'Nothing broken is there, Guthrie?' from Marigold.

'My elbow.' The Judge sat up nursing the afflicted part.

'Such terrible luck when it was going to be such a super shot!' said the ever-sycophantic Addison.

'Twiddle your fingers, Guthrie, and let's see if anything is broken.' When the Judge obeyed, Marigold was able to tell him: 'There you are, nothing broken at all!'

'There's an extraordinary shooting pain. Ouch!' Guthrie was clearly suffering.

'Oh, you poor man, you are in the wars, aren't you?' Mr Addison was sympathetic. 'It'll wear off.' Lady Featherstone was not.

'It shows absolutely no sign of wearing off.'

'Rub it then, Guthrie! And for heaven's sake don't be such a baby!'

The next day I was at my business at the Old Bailey, making my usual final appeal on the subject of the burden of proof, that great presumption of innocence, which has been rightly called the golden thread which runs through British justice, when Mr Justice Featherstone, presiding over the trial, interrupted my flow to say, 'Just a moment, Mr Rumpole. I am in considerable pain.' He was, in fact, still rubbing his elbow. 'I have suffered a serious accident.'

'Did your Lordship say "pain"?' I couldn't, for the moment, see how his Lordship's accident was relevant to the question of the burden of proof.

'It's not something one likes to comment about,' the Judge commented nobly, 'in the general course of events. I have, of course, had some experience of pain, even at a comparatively young age.'

'Did you say comparatively *young*, my Lord?' I thought he was knocking on a bit, for a youngster.

'And if I was the only person concerned I should naturally soldier on regardless . . .'

'Terribly brave, my Lord!' Leaving him to soldier on, I turned back to the jury. 'Members of the jury. The question you must ask about each one of these charges is "Are you certain sure?"'

'But I mustn't only think of myself,' the Judge interrupted me again. 'The point is, am I in too much pain to give your speech the attention it deserves, Mr Rumpole?'

'I don't know. Are you?' That was all the help I could give him.

'Exercising the best judgement I have, I have come to the conclusion that I am not. I will adjourn now.'

'At three o'clock?' I must confess I was surprised. 'Pain,' his Lordship told me solemnly, 'is no respecter of time. Till tomorrow morning, members of the jury.'

'Would your Lordship wish us to send for matron?' I was solicitous.

'I think not, Mr Rumpole. I'm afraid in this particular instance matters have gone rather beyond matron.' Norman, the tall, bald usher, called on us all to be upstanding. Guthrie rose, and nursing his elbow, and faintly murmuring 'Ouch', left us.

Norman the usher was well known to me as a man of the world, well used to judicial foibles and surprisingly accurate in forecasting the results of cases. He was a man who took pleasure in supplying the needs of others, often coming up to me during lulls in cases to say he knew where to lay his hands on some rubber-backed carpeting or a load of bathroom tiles. Although I felt no need of any of Norman's contacts, he was able, on this occasion, to put Mr Justice Featherstone in touch with a cure. Long after his retirement Norman returned to the Bailey to look up a few old friends and over a couple of pints of Guinness in the pub opposite he eventually told me of his part in the affair of the Judge's elbow. 'Muscular is it, your Lordship's affliction?' Norman asked when he had led Guthrie out of Court into the Judge's room, a leather and panelled sanctum furnished with law reports and silver-framed photographs of the children.

'Muscular, Norman,' the Judge admitted. 'One does not complain.'

'Only one thing for muscular pain, my Lord.'

'Aspirins?' The Judge winced as he started to unbutton his Court coat.

'Throw away the aspirins. It's a deep massage. That's what your Lordship needs. Here. Let me slip that off for you.' He removed Guthrie's coat delicately. 'Of course, your Lordship needs a massoose with strong fingers. One who can manipulate the fibres in depth.' At which point the usher grasped the Judge's elbow with strong fingers, causing another stab of pain, heroically borne. 'I can feel that the fibres are in need of deep, deep manipulation. If your Lordship would allow me. I know just the massoose as'd get to your fibres and release the tension!'

'You know someone, Norman?' The Judge sounded hopeful.

'The wife's sister's daughter, Elsie. Thoroughly respectable, and fingers on her like the grab of a crane . . .'

'A talented girl?'

'Precisely what the doctor ordered. Our Elsie has brought relief to thousands of sufferers.'

'Where . . . does she carry on her practice?' The Judge started tentative inquiries, rather as some fellow in classical times might have said, 'Who's got the key to Pandora's Box?'

'In a very hygienic health centre, my Lord. Only a stone's throw down the Tottenham Court Road, your Lordship.'

'Tottenham Court Road?' Guthrie was, at first, fearful. 'Not oriental in any way, this place, is it?'

'Bless you, no, my Lord. They're thoroughly reliable girls. Mostly drawn from the Croydon area. All medically trained, of course.' Norman had hung up the Court coat and was restoring the Judge to mufti.

'Medically trained? That's reassuring.'

'They have made a thorough study, my Lord, of the human anatomy. In all its aspects. Seeing as you've got no relief through the usual channels . . .'

'My doctor's absolutely useless!' The Chelsea GP had merely referred the Judge to time, the great healer. Guthrie lifted a brush and comb to his hair, and was again reminded of his plight. 'You're right, Norman. Why not try a little alternative medicine?'

'You wait, my Lord,' Norman told him. 'Just let our Elsie get her fingers on you.'

The address which Norman gave the Judge was situated in a small street running eastward from Tottenham Court Road. After a few days' more pain, Guthrie took a taxi there, got out and paid off the driver, wincing as he felt for his money. 'Had a bit of trouble with my elbow,' he said, as though to explain his visit to the Good Life Health Centre,

Sauna and Massage. At which point, the cabby drove away, no doubt thinking it was none of his business, and Guthrie entered the establishment in some trepidation. He was reassured to some extent by the cleanliness of the interior. There was a good deal of light and panelling, photographs of fit-looking young blond persons of both sexes, and a kindly receptionist behind a desk, filing her nails.

'I rang for an appointment,' Guthrie told her. 'The name's Featherstone.' 'Elsie,' the receptionist called out, 'your gentleman's here. You can go right in, dear' – she nodded towards a bead curtain – 'and take off your things.' Later, after a brief spell in an airless and apparently red-hot wooden cupboard, the Judge was stretched out on a table, clad in nothing but a towel, whilst Elsie, a muscular, but personable, young lady, who might have captained a hockey team, manipulated his elbow, and asked him if he was going anywhere nice for his holiday.

'Hope so. I'm tired out with sitting,' Guthrie told her.

'Are you really?' Elsie, no doubt, had heard all sorts of complaints in her time.

'In fact I've been sitting almost continuously this year.'

'Fancy!'

'It gets tiring.'

'I'm sure it does.'

'Not how I did my elbow in, though. Tennis. When I'm not sitting, my wife and I play a bit of tennis.'

'Well, it makes a change, dear. Doesn't it?'

When Elsie had finished her manipulations, Guthrie got dressed and came back into the reception area. Being a little short of cash, and seeing the American Express sign on the counter, he decided to pay with his credit card. 'It feels better already,' he told her, as he signed without an 'ouch'. The receptionist banged the paperwork into her machine. 'There you are then.' She tore off his part of the slip and handed it and the credit card back to Guthrie, who thanked her again, and put the card and the slip carefully into his wallet. After he had left, Elsie came out from behind her curtain. 'He says he's tired out, done a lot of sitting,' she told the receptionist, who smiled and said, 'Poor bloke.'

I was not, of course, among those present when Mr Justice Featherstone had his treatment, and I have had to invent, or attempt to reconstruct, the above dialogue. I may have got it wrong, but of one thing I am certain, the Judge's massage was given in strict accordance with the Queensberry rules, and there was nothing below the belt.

Whilst Guthrie had undergone this satisfactory cure and almost forgotten his old tennis injury, much had changed in our old Chambers at 3 Equity Court. I had been away for a week or two, doing a long firm fraud in Cardiff, a case which had absolutely no bloodstains and a great deal of adding up. I returned from exile to find our tattered old clerk's room, with its dusty files, abandoned briefs, out-of-date textbooks and faded photograph of C. H. Wystan over the fireplace, had been greatly smartened up. Someone had had it painted white, given Henry a new desk and Dianne a new typewriter, hung the sort of coloured prints on the walls which they buy by the yard for 'modernized' hotels and introduced a large number of potted plants, at which Dianne was, even as I arrived one morning in my old hat and mac, squirting with a green plastic spray.

'*Through the jungle very softly flits a shadow and a sigh*—': the shadow was Dianne, and the sigh came from Henry when I asked if this was indeed our old clerk's room or the tropical house at Kew.

'It's Mr Hearthstoke.' Henry pronounced the name as though it were some recently discovered malignant disease.

'Some old gardener?' I asked, clutching three weeks' accumulation of bills.

'The new young gentleman in Chambers. He reckons an office space needs a more contemporary look.'

'And I've been ticked off for putting.' Uncle Tom was in the corner as usual, trickling a golf ball across the carpet.

'Uncle Tom has been ticked off.' Dianne confirmed the seriousness of the situation.

'I've been asked to do it upstairs, but it isn't the same.' Uncle Tom sounded reasonable. 'Down here, you can see the world passing by.'

'Carry on putting, Uncle Tom,' I told him. 'Imagine you're on the fourth green at Kuala Lumpur.'

I forced my way through the undergrowth and went out into the passage; there I found that our clerk had followed me, and was whispering urgently, 'Could I have a word in confidence?'

'In the passage?'

'It's not only my clerk's room Mr Hearthstoke reckons should have a more contemporary look.' Henry started to outline his grievances. 'He says we could do with a smarter typist. Well, as you know, Mr Rumpole, Dianne has always been extremely popular with the legal executives.'

'A fine-looking girl, Dianne. A fine, sturdy girl. I always thought so.' I had the feeling that Henry felt a certain *tendresse* for our tireless typist, although I didn't think it right to inquire into such matters too deeply.

'Worse than that, Mr Rumpole, he wants to privatize the clerking.'

'To *what?*'

'Mr Hearthstoke's not over-enamoured, sir, with my ten per cent.'

For the benefit of such of my readers as may never have shared in the splendours and miseries of life at the Bar, I should explain that the senior clerk in a set of Chambers is usually paid ten per cent of the earnings of his stable of legal hacks. This system is frequently criticized by those who wish to modernize our profession, but I do not share their views. 'Good God!' I said, 'if barristers' clerks didn't get their ten per cent we'd have no one left to envy.'

'And he's got his criticism of you too, Mr Rumpole. That's why I thought, sir, we might be in the same boat on this one. Even if we'd had our differences in the past.'

'Of me?' I was surprised, and a little pained to hear it. 'What has this "Johnny Come Lately" got to criticize about me?'

'He's not enamoured of your old Burberry.'

Unreasonable I thought. My mac may not have been hand-tailored in Savile Row, but it has kept out the rain on journeys to some pretty unsympathetic Courts over the years. And then I looked at our clerk and saw a man apparently in the terminal stage of melancholia.

'Henry!' I asked him. 'Why this hangdog look? What on earth's the need for this stricken whisper? If, whatever his name is, has only been here a few weeks . . .'

'Voted in when you were in Cardiff, Mr Rumpole . . .'

'Why does our learned Head of Chambers take a blind bit of notice?'

'Quite frankly, it seems to Dianne and me, Mr Ballard thinks, with great respect, that the sun shines out of Mr Hearthstoke's —' Perhaps it was just as well that he was prevented from finishing this sentence by our learned Head of Chambers, Soapy Sam Ballard, who popped out of his door and instructed Henry to rally the chaps for a Chambers meeting. He didn't seem exactly overjoyed to see me back.

Charles Hearthstoke turned out to be a young man in his early thirties, dark, slender and surprisingly good-looking; he reminded me at once of Steerforth in the illustrations to *David Copperfield*. Despite his appearance of a romantic hero, he was one of those persons who took the view, one fashionable with our masters in government, that we were all set in this world to make money. He might have made an excellent accountant or merchant banker; he wasn't, in my view, cut out for work at the Criminal Bar. He had been at some Chambers where he hadn't hit it off with the clerk (a fact which didn't surprise me in the least) and now he sat at the right hand of Ballard and was clearly the apple of the eye of our pure-minded Head of Chambers.

'I've asked Hearthstoke to carry out an efficiency study into the working of Number 3 Equity Court, and I must say he's done a superb job!' My heart sank as Ballard told us this. 'Quite superb. Charles, would you speak to this paper?'

'He may speak to it,' I grumbled, 'but would it answer back?'

'What's that, Rumpole?'

'Oh, nothing, Ballard. Nothing at all . . .'

But Uncle Tom insisted on telling them. 'That was rather a good one! You heard what Rumpole said, Hoskins? Would it answer back?'

'Leave it, Uncle Tom,' I restrained him. Hearthstoke was now holding up some sort of document.

'In the first section of the report I deal with obvious reforms to the system. It's quite clear that our fees need to be computerized and I've made inquiries about the necessary software.'

'Oh, I'm all in favour of that.'

'Yes, Rumpole?' Ballard allowed my interruption with a sigh.

'Soft wear! Far too many stiff collars in the legal profession. Makes your neck feel it's undergoing a blunt execution.'

'Has Rumpole done another joke . . . ?' Uncle Tom didn't seem to be sure about it.

'Do please carry on, Charles.' Ballard apologized to Hearthstoke for the crasser element in Chambers.

'I'm also doing a feasibility study in putting our clerking out to private tender,' Hearthstoke told the meeting. 'I'm sure we can find a young up-thrusting group of chartered accountants who'd take on the job at considerably less than Henry's ten per cent.'

'Brilliant!' I told him.

'So glad you agree, Rumpole.'

'Wonderful thing, privatization. Why not privatize the judges while you're about it? I mean, they're grossly inefficient. Only give out about a hundred years' imprisonment a month, on the average. Why not sell them off to the Americans and step up production?'

'That, if I may say so,' – Hearthstoke gave a small, wintry smile – 'is the dying voice of what may well become a dying profession.'

'We've got to move with the times, Rumpole, as Charles has pointed out.' Ballard was clearly exercising a great self-control in dealing with the critics.

'As a matter of fact I'm entirely in favour of the privatization of Henry.' This was the colourless barrister Hoskins. 'Speaking as a chap with daughters, I can ill afford ten per cent.'

'Those of us who have a bit of practice at the Bar, those of us who can't spend all our days doing feasibility studies on the price of paper-clips, know how important it is to keep our clerk's room happy.' That, at any rate, was my considered opinion. 'Besides, I don't want to go in there in the morning and find the place full of up-thrusting young chartered accountants. It'd put me off my breakfast.'

'Is that all you have to say on the subject?' Ballard looked as though he couldn't take much more.

'Absolutely. I'm going to work. Come along, Mizz Probert' – I rose to my feet – 'I believe you've got a noting brief.'

'There's a dingy-looking character in a dirty mac hanging about the waiting-room for you, Rumpole,' Erskine-Brown was at pains to tell me. 'And talking of dirty macs' – Hearthstoke looked at me in a meaningful fashion – 'There is one other point I have to raise,' he said, but I left him to raise it on his own. I was busy.

The client who was waiting for me was separated from his mac; all the same he cut a somewhat depressing figure. He wore thick, pebble glasses, a drooping bow tie and a cardigan which had claimed its fair share of soup. A baggy grey suit completed the get-up of a man who seemed to have benefited not at all from the programme of physical fitness which he sold to the public; neither did he seem to enjoy the prosperity which the prosecution had suggested. He had a curiously high voice and the pained expression of a man who at least pretended not to understand why he was due to be tried at the Old Bailey.

'Dr Maurice Horridge. Where does the "Doctor" come from, by the way?' I asked him.

'New Bognor. A small seat of learning, Mr Rumpole. In the shadow of the Canadian Rockies . . .'

'You know Canada well?'

'I was never out of England, Mr Rumpole. Alas.'

'So this degree of yours. You wrote up for it?'

'I obtained my diploma by correspondence,' he corrected me. 'None the less valuable for that.'

'And it is a doctorate in . . . ?'

'Theology, Mr Rumpole. I trust you find that helpful.' I got up and stood at the window, looking out at some nice, clean rain. 'Oh, very helpful, I'm sure. If you want to be well up in the Book of Job or if you want to carry on an intelligent chat on the subject of Ezekiel. I just don't see how it helps with the massage business.'

'The line of the body, Mr Rumpole, is the line of God.' My client spoke reverently. 'We are all of us created in His image.'

'Yes. I've often thought He must be quite a strange-looking chap.'

'Pardon me, Mr Rumpole?' Dr Horridge looked pained.

'Forget I spoke. But massage . . .'

'Spiritual, Mr Rumpole! Entirely spiritual. I could stretch you flat on the floor, with your head supported by a telephone directory, and lay your limbs out spiritually. All your aches and pains would be relieved at once. I don't know if you'd care to stretch out?'

'The girls in these massage parlours you run . . .' I got to the nub of the case.

'Trained! Mr Rumpole. All fully trained.'

'Medically?'

'In my principles, of course. The principles of the spiritual alignment of the bones.'

'What's alleged is that they so far forgot their spiritual mission as to indulge in a little hanky-panky with the customers.' I explained the nature of the charges to the good doctor; roughly it was alleged that he was living on immoral earnings and keeping a large number of disorderly houses. 'I cannot believe it, Mr Rumpole! I simply cannot believe it of my girls.' He spoke like a priest who has heard of group sex among the vestal virgins.

'So that your defence,' I asked him as patiently as possible, 'is that entirely without your knowledge your girls turned from sacred to profane massage?'

Dr Horridge nodded his head energetically. He seemed to think that I had put his case extremely well.

Now I must try to tell you how the troubles of Dr Maurice Horridge became connected with the painful matter of the Judge's elbow. Meeting his wife at the tennis court one night – he had so far improved in his health, thanks to Elsie, that he felt fit enough to resume mixed doubles with the Addisons – Guthrie found Marigold reading the *Standard*. 'Massage parlours,' she almost spat out the words with disgust.

'Well. Yes. In fact . . .' Guthrie hadn't yet confided the full facts of his visit to the Good Life Health Centre to his wife, who read aloud to him from the paper.

' "Doctor of Theology charged with running massage parlours as disorderly houses." How revolting! What was it you wanted to tell me, Guthrie?'

'Well, nothing really. Just that my elbow seems much better. I can really swing a racket now.'

'Well, just don't dislocate anything else.' She gave him more of the news. ' "Thirty-five massage parlours alleged to offer immoral services in the Greater London area." Pathetic! Grown men having to go to places like that!'

'I'm quite sure some of them just needed a massage,' Guthrie tried to persuade her.

'If you'd believe that, Guthrie, you'd believe anything!' She read on regardless. ' "Arab oil millionaires, merchant bankers and well-known names from television are said to be among those who used the cheap sex provided at Dr Horridge's establishments and paid by *credit card*"!' Guthrie stifled an agonized exclamation of terror. 'What on earth's the matter? That elbow playing you up again?'

The next thing Guthrie did was to visit the tennis club Gents, and flush away the American Express slip which he had retained for the monthly check-up. He didn't want Marigold, searching for a bit of cash, to find the dreaded words 'Massage and Sauna' stamped on a bit of blue paper. The next day, in the privacy of the Judge's room, he made a telephone call, which I imagine went something like this.

'American Express? The name is Featherstone. Mr Justice Featherstone. No, not Justice-Featherstone with a hyphen. My name is Featherstone and I'm a justice. I'm a Judge, that is. Yes. Well, actually I got into a bit of a muddle and paid someone with a credit card when I should have paid cash and if I could go and pay them now, could I get my credit-card slip back and you wouldn't need to have any record of it at all if it's a purely private matter, just a question of my own personal accounting? . . . Do I make myself clear? What's that? Oh. I don't . . .'

It is never easy to recall the past and rectify our mistakes. In this case, Guthrie was to find it impossible. Norman the usher, who started all the trouble, had suddenly retired and gone to live in the North of England, and when Guthrie revisited the address near Tottenham Court Road, in the hope that his credit-card transaction could be expunged from the records, he found that the Health Centre had sold up and the premises taken over by Luxifruits Ltd. He was offered some nice juicy satsumas by the greengrocer now in charge, but all traces of Elsie and the receptionist had vanished away.

Guthrie's cup of anxiety ran over when he bumped into Claude Erskine-Brown walking up from the Temple tube station. 'Always so good to see some of the chaps from my old Chambers,' the Judge was gracious enough to observe after Claude had removed his hat and then restored it to its position. 'See your wife was in the Court of Appeal again the other day. And Rumpole! What's old Horace doing?'

'Something sordid as usual,' Claude told him.

'Distasteful?'

'Downright disgusting. Rumpole's cases do tend to lower the tone of 3 Equity Court. This time it's massage parlours! Rumpole's acting for the King of the massage parlours. Of course, he thinks it's a huge joke.'

'But it's not, Erskine-Brown, is it?' The Judge was serious. 'In fact, it's not a joke at all!'

'I can't pretend my marriage is all champagne and opera. We've had our difficulties, Philly and I, from time to time, as I'd be the first to admit. But thank heavens I've never had to resort to massage parlours! I simply can't understand it.'

'No. It's a mystery to me, of course.'

'Anyway. That sort of thing simply lets down the tone of Chambers.'

'Yes. Of course, Claude. Of course it does. The honour of Equity Court is still extremely important to me, as you well know. Perhaps I should invite Horace Rumpole to lunch at the Sheridan. Have a word with him on the subject?'

'What subject?' Claude was apparently a little mystified.

'Massage . . . No,' the Judge corrected himself, 'I mean Chambers, of course.'

'Oysters for Mr Rumpole . . . and I'll take soup of the day. And Mr Rumpole will be having the grouse and I – I'll settle for the Sheridan Club Hamburger. I thought a Chablis Premier Cru to start with and then, would the Château Talbot '77 appeal to you at all, Horace?' The autumn sunlight filtered through the tall windows that badly needed cleaning and glimmered on the silver and portraits of old judges. Around us, actors hobnobbed with politicians and publishers. I sat in the Sheridan Club, amazed at the Judge's hospitality. As the waitress left us with my substantial order, I asked him if he'd won the pools.

'No. It's just that one gets so few opportunities to entertain the chaps from one's old Chambers. And now Claude Erskine-Brown tells me you're doing this case about what was it . . . beauty parlours?'

'Massage parlours. Or, as I prefer to call them, Health Centres.'

'Oh, yes, of course. Massage parlours.' The Judge seemed to choke on the words and then recovered. 'Well, I suppose some of these places are quite respectable and above board, aren't they? I mean, people might just drop in because they'd got . . .'

'A touch of housemaid's knee?' I was incredulous.

'That sort of thing, yes.'

'Someone who was as innocent and unsuspecting as that, they shouldn't be let off the lead.'

'Why do you say that?'

The waitress came with the white wine. Guthrie tasted it and she then poured. I tasted a cold and stony Chablis, no doubt at a price that seldom passes my lips. 'Well, to your average British jury, the words massage parlour mean only one thing,' I told Guthrie, without cheering him up.

'What?'

'Hanky-panky!'

'Oh. You think that, do you?'

'Everyone does.'

'Hanky-panky?' The words stuck in the Judge's throat.

'In practically every case.'

'Rumpole! Horace . . . Look, do let me top you up.' He poured more Chablis. 'You're defending in this case, I take it?'

'What else should I be doing?'

'And as such, as defending Counsel, I mean, you'll get to see the prosecution evidence . . .'

'Oh, I've seen most of that already,' I assured him cheerfully.

'Have you?' He looked as though I'd already passed sentence on him. 'How extraordinarily interesting.'

'It's funny, really.'

'Funny?'

'Yes. Extremely funny. You know, all sorts of Very Important People visited my client's establishments. Nobs. Bigwigs.'

'Big *wigs*, Horace?' Guthrie seemed to take the expression personally.

'Most respectable citizens. And you know what? They actually paid with their credit cards! Can you imagine anything so totally dotty . . .'

'Dotty? No! Nothing.' The Judge laughed mirthlessly. 'So their names are all . . . in the evidence? Plain for all the world to see?' He broke off as the soup and the oysters were brought by the waitress, and then said thoughtfully, 'I don't suppose that *all* the evidence will necessarily be put before the jury.'

'Oh no. Only a few little nuggets. The cream of the collection. It should provide an afternoon of harmless fun.'

'Not fun for the . . . big . . . big wigs involved . . .' He looked appalled.

'Well, if they were so idiotic as to use their *credit cards*!' There was a long pause during which my host seemed sunk in the deepest gloom.

He then rallied a little, smiled in a somewhat ghastly manner and addressed me with all his judicial charm and deep concern. 'Horace,' he said, 'don't you find this criminal work rather exhausting?'

'It's a killer!' I admitted. 'Only sometimes a bit of evidence turns up and makes it all worthwhile.'

'Have you ever considered relaxing a little?' He ignored any further reference to big wigs in massage parlours. 'Perhaps on the Circuit Bench?'

'You're joking!' He had amazed me. 'Anyway, I'm far too old.'

'I don't know. I could have a word with the powers that be. They might ask you to sit as a deputy, Rumpole. On a more or less permanent basis. A hundred and fifty quid a day and absolutely no worries.'

'Deputy Circus Judge?' I was still in a state of shock. 'Why should they offer me that?'

'As a little tribute, perhaps, to the tactful way you've always conducted your defences.'

'Tactful? No one's ever called me that before.' I squeezed lemon on an oyster and sent it sliding down.

'I've always found you extremely tactful in Court, Horace. And discreet. Oysters all right, are they?'

'Oh, yes, Judge.' I looked at him with some suspicion. 'Absolutely nothing wrong with the oysters.'

Walking back from the Sheridan Club to Chambers, I thought about Guthrie's strange suggestion and felt even more surprised. Deputy Circuit Judge! Why on earth should I want that? These thoughts flitted through my head. Judging people is not my trade. I defend them. All the same . . . One hundred and fifty smackers a day, the old darling did say a hundred and fifty, and you didn't even have to stand up for it. It could all be earned sitting down. With hacks constantly flattering you and saying 'If your Honour pleases', 'If your Honour would be so kind as to look at the fingerprint evidence.' No one has ever spoken to me like that. But what was the Judge up to exactly? Offering me grouse and oysters and Deputy Circus Judge. What, precisely, was Guthrie's game?

I could find no answer to these questions as I walked along the Strand. Then a voice hailed me and I turned to see a tall, bald man familiar to me from the Bailey. It was Norman the ex-usher, who had apparently called down to the old shop to collect his cards. He asked if Mr Justice Featherstone's elbow had improved.

'It seems to be remarkably recovered,' I told him.

'In terrible pain, he was,' Norman clucked sympathetically. 'Don't you remember? I was able to put him on to a place where they could give him a bit of relief. Get down to the deep fibres, you know. Have the Judge's bones stretched out properly . . .'

'You recommended a place?' I was suddenly interested.

'The wife's niece worked there. Nice type of establishment, it was really. Very hygienically run.' He looked down the road. 'Here comes a number 11. I'll be seeing you, Mr Rumpole. I don't know if you've got any use for a nice length of garden hose.'

'What place? What place did you recommend exactly?' I tried to ask him, but he skipped lightly on to his number 11 and left me.

The prosecutor in *R.* v. *Dr Maurice Horridge* was a perfectly decent fellow called Brinsley Lampitt. I called on him at his Chambers and he let me have a large cardboard box of documents, bank statements, accounts and credit-card slips all connected with the questioned massage parlours. My meetings with Guthrie Featherstone and Norman the usher had given me the idea of a defence which seemed so improbable that at least it had to be tried. I carried the box of exhibits back to Chambers, and set Mizz Liz Probert to sift through them, with particular reference to the credit-card transactions. Then I went down to see Henry.

I found Charles Hearthstoke in the clerk's room asking for PAYE forms and petty-cash vouchers for coffee consumed over the last two years. Henry was looking furious and Dianne somewhat flustered. I discovered much later that they had been surprised in a flagrant kiss behind a potted plant when Hearthstoke entered. On my arrival, he turned his unwelcome attentions on me. 'Sorry you had to slip away from the Chambers meeting, Rumpole.' 'What did I miss, Hearthrug?' I asked him. 'Have you replaced me with a reliable computer?'

'Not yet. But we did pass a resolution on the general standards of appearance in Chambers. Old macs are not acceptable now, over a black jacket and striped trousers.' The Pill then left us, and I looked after him with some irritation and contempt. 'I quite agree with you, Mr Rumpole,' Henry said, and I told him we stood together on the matter. 'Together,' I told him, 'we shall contrive to scupper Hearthrug.'

'It'll need a bit of working out,' Henry said, 'Mr Ballard being so pro . . .'

'Bollard? Leave Bollard to me! Providing, Henry, I can leave something to you.'

'I'll do my best, sir. What exactly?'

'Miss Osgood. The lady who arranges the lists down the Bailey. You know, your co-star from the Bromley amateur dramatics.'

'We're playing opposite each other, Mr Rumpole. In *Brief Encounter*.'

'Encounter her, Henry! Drop a word in her shell-like ear about the massage parlour case. What we need, above all things, is a sympathetic judge . . . *There is a tide in the affairs of barristers*, Henry, *Which, taken at the flood, leads on to fortune;/ Omitted, all the voyage of their life/ Is bound in shallows and in miseries* . . .' On such a full tide were we now afloat, and I took charge of the helm and suggested the name of the Judge whom I thought Miss Osgood would do well to assign to *R. v. Horridge*.

So it came about that when Guthrie Featherstone arrived for his next stint of work down the Bailey, and Harold the new usher brought him coffee in his room, he found the Judge staring, transfixed with horror, at the papers in the case he was about to try and muttering the words 'massage parlours' in a voice of deep distress. Not even the offer of a few nice biscuits could cheer him up. And when he entered Court and saw Dr Horridge in the dock, Rumpole smiling up at him benignly and the table of proposed exhibits loaded with credit-card slips, the Judge looked like a man being led to the place of execution.

'Mr Lampitt, Mr Rumpole.' His Lordship addressed us both in deeply serious tones before the jury was summoned into Court. 'I feel I have a duty to raise a matter of a personal nature.' I said I hoped he wasn't in pain.

'No. Not that, Mr Rumpole . . . Not that . . . The fact is, Mr Lampitt . . . Mr Rumpole . . . Gentlemen. I feel very strongly that I should *not* try this case. I should retire and leave the matter to some other judge.'

'Of course, we should be most reluctant to lose your Lordship,' I flattered Guthrie, and Brinsley Lampitt chimed in with 'Most reluctant.'

'Well, there it is. I'll rise now and . . .' Guthrie started to make his escape.

'May we ask . . . why?' I stopped him.

'May you ask what?'

'*Why*, my Lord. I mean, it's nothing about my client, I hope.'

'Oh no, Mr Rumpole. Nothing at all to do with him.' The Judge was back, despondently, in his seat.

'I can't imagine that your Lordship *knows* my client.'

'Know him? Certainly not!' The Judge was positive. 'Not that I'm suggesting I'd have anything against knowing your client. If I did, I mean. Which I most certainly don't!'

'Then, with the greatest respect, my Lord, where's the difficulty?'

'Where's the *what*, Mr Rumpole?' The Judge was clearly in some agony of mind.

'The difficulty, my Lord.'

'You wish to know where the difficulty is?'

'If your Lordship pleases!'

'And you, Mr Lampitt. You wish to know where the difficulty is?'

'If your Lordship pleases,' said the old darling for the Crown.

'It's a private matter. As you know, Mr Rumpole,' was the best the Judge could manage after a long pause.

'As *I know*, my Lord? Then it can't be exactly private.'

'Perhaps I should make this clear in open Court. I happened to have lunch at my club with Counsel for the defence.'

'The oysters were excellent! I'm grateful to your Lordship.'

There was a flutter of laughter and Harold called for silence as the Judge went on: 'And I happened to discuss this case, in purely general terms, with Counsel for the defence.' In the ensuing silence Lampitt was whispering to the police. I asked, 'Is that all, my Lord?'

'Yes. Isn't it enough?' The Judge sounded deeply depressed. Lampitt didn't cheer him up by telling him that he'd spoken to the Officer-in-Charge of the case, who had no objection whatever to the Judge trying Dr Horridge. He was sure that no lunchtime conversation with Mr Rumpole could possibly prejudice his Lordship in any way. 'In fact,' Brinsley Lampitt ended, to the despair of the Judge, 'the prosecution wish your Lordship to retain this case.'

'And so do the defence.' I drove in another nail.

'In fact I urge your Lordship to do so,' Lampitt urged.

'So do I, my Lord,' from Rumpole. 'It would be a great waste of public money if we had to fix a new date before a different judge. And in view of the Lord Chancellor's recent warnings about the high cost of legal aid cases . . .'

The Judge clearly felt caught then. He looked with horror at the exhibits and thought with terror of the Lord Chancellor. 'Mr Lampitt, Mr Rumpole,' he asked us without any real hope, 'are you *insisting* I try this case?'

'With great respect, yes,' from Lampitt.

'That's what it comes to, my Lord,' from me.

So the twelve honest citizens were summoned in and one of the strangest trials I have ever known began, because I could not tell who was more fearful of the outcome, the prisoner at the Bar, or the learned Judge.

Picture Guthrie after the first day in Court, returning to play a little autumn tennis with his wife. Unfortunately the game was rained off, and he sat with Marigold in the bar of the tennis club and told her, when she asked if he'd had a good day, that he was sorry to say he had not. Then he looked out of the window at the grey sky and asked her if she didn't sometimes long to get away from it all. 'Fellow I was at school with runs a little bar in Ibiza. Wouldn't you like to run a little bar in Ibiza, Marigold?'

'I think I should hate it.'

'But you don't want to hang about around Kensington, in the rain, married to a Judge who's away all day, sitting.'

'I like you being a Judge, Guthrie,' Marigold explained patiently. 'I like you being away all day, sitting. And what's wrong with Kensington? It's handy for Harrods.'

'Marigold,' he started again after a thoughtful silence.

'Yes, Guthrie.'

'I was just thinking about that Cabinet Minister. You know. The fellow who had to resign. Over some scandal.'

'Did he run a little bar in Ibiza?'

'No. But what I remember about him is his wife stood by him. Through thick and thin. Would you stand by me, Marigold? Through thick and thin?'

'What's the scandal, Guthrie?' She was curious to know, but he answered, 'Nothing. Oh, no. Just a theoretical question. I just wondered if you'd stand by me. That's all.'

'Don't count on it, Guthrie,' she told him. 'Don't ever count on it.'

Meanwhile, back at 3 Equity Court, Liz Probert was working late, sorting through the prosecution exhibits of which we had not yet made a full list. Hearthstoke saw the light on in my room and, suspecting me of wasting electricity, called in to inspect. He apparently offered to help Liz with her task and, sitting beside her, started to sort out the credit-card slips. She remembered asking him why he was helping her, and hoping it had nothing to do with her eyes. She told him that Claude Erskine-Brown had taken her to the opera and complimented her on her eyes, a moment she had found particularly embarrassing.

'Erskine-Brown's old-fashioned, like everything else in these Chambers,' he told her.

'Just because I'm a woman! I mean, I bet no one mentions *your* eyes. And Hoskins told me I could only do petty larceny and divorce; quite honestly he thinks that's all women are fit for.'

'Out of the ark, Hoskins. Liz, I know we'd disagree about a lot of things.'

'Do you?' She looked at him; I suppose it was not an entirely hostile gaze.

'I'm standing as a Conservative for Battersea Council,' he told her. 'And your father's Red Ron of South-east London! But we're both young. We both want things changed. When we've finished this, why don't you buy yourself a Chinese at the Golden Gate in Chancery Lane?'

'Why on earth?'

'I could buy one too. And we might even eat them at the same table. Oh, and I do promise you not to mention your eyes.'

'You can if you want to.'

'Mention your eyes?'

'No, you fool! Eat your Chinese at my table.' She was laughing as I came in after a little refreshment at Pommeroy's Wine Bar. I took in the scene with some surprise. 'Hearthrug! What's this, another deputation about my tailoring?'

'I was helping out your pupil, Rumpole.' He was staring, with some distaste, at my old mac.

'Very considerate of you. I can take over now, after a pit stop at Pommeroy's for refuelling. Why don't you two young things go home?' Liz Probert went, after Hearthstoke told her to wait for him downstairs. And then he revealed some of the results of his snooping round our Chambers. 'I was just going to ask you about Henry.'

'*What* about Henry?' I lit a small cigar.

'I was looking at his PAYE returns. He *is* married, isn't he?'

'To a lady tax inspector in Bromley. That's my belief.'

'So what exactly is his relationship with Dianne, the typist?'

'Friendly, I imagine.'

'Just friendly?'

'That is a question I have never cared to ask.'

'There are lots of questions like that, aren't there, Rumpole?' With that, the appalling Hearthrug left me. I pulled the box of documents towards me and started working on them angrily. In the morning I would have to deal with further snoopers: police officers in plain clothes, or rather, in no clothes at all, as they lay on various massage tables and pretended to be in need of affection.

'Detective Constable Marten,' I asked the solid-looking copper with the moustache, 'that is not a note you made at the time?'

'No, sir.'

'Of course not! At the time this incident occurred, you were deprived of your clothing and no doubt of your notebook also?'

'I made the note on my return to the station.'

'After these exciting events had taken place?'

'After the incident complained of, yes.'

'And your recollection was still clear?'

'Quite clear, Mr Rumpole.'

'It started off with the lady therapist.'

'The masseuse, yes.'

'Passing an entirely innocent remark.'

'She asked me if I was going anywhere nice on holiday.'

'She asked you *that*?' The evidence seemed to have awakened disturbing memories in the Judge.

'Yes, my Lord.'

'Up to that time it appeared to be a perfectly routine, straight-forward massage?' I put it to the officer.

'I informed the young lady that I had a certain pain in the knee from playing football.'

'Was that the truth?' I asked severely.

'No, my Lord,' DC Marten told the Judge reluctantly.

'So you were lying, Officer?'

'Yes. If you put it that way.'

'What other way is there of putting it? You are an Officer who is prepared to lie?'

'In the course of duty, yes.'

'And submit to sexual advances in massage parlours. In the course of duty.' I was rewarded by a ripple of laughter from the jury, and a shocked sign from the Judge. 'Mr Rumpole,' he said politely, 'can I help?'

'Of course, my Lord.' I was suitably grateful.

'When the massage started, you told the young lady you had a pain in your knee?' The Judge recapped, rubbing in the point.

'Yes, my Lord.'

'From playing tennis?'

'Football, my Lord.'

'Yes. Of course. Football. I'm much obliged.' His Lordship made a careful note. 'So far as the lady masseuse was concerned, that might have been the truth?'

'She might have believed it, my Lord,' the Detective Constable admitted grudgingly.

'And so far as you know, quite a number of perfectly decent, respectable, happily married men may visit these . . . health centres simply because they have received injuries in various sporting activities. Football . . . tennis and the like!' The Judge was moved to express his indignation.

'Some may, I suppose, my Lord.' DC Marten was still grudging.

'Many may!'

'Yes.'

'Very well.' The Judge turned from the officer with distaste. 'Yes, Mr Rumpole. Thank you.'

'Oh, thank *you*, my Lord. If your Lordship pleases.' I stopped smiling then and turned to the witness. 'So at first sight this appeared to be an entirely genuine health centre?'

'At first sight. Yes.'

'An entirely genuine health centre.' The Judge was actually writing it down, paying a quite unusual compliment to the defence. 'Those were your words, Mr Rumpole?'

'My exact words, your Lordship. No doubt your Lordship is writing them down for the benefit of the jury.'

'I am, Mr Rumpole. I am indeed.'

I saw Lampitt looking bewildered. Judges who brief themselves for the accused are somewhat rare birds down the Bailey.

'And the whole thing was as pure as the driven snow. In fact it was the normal treatment of a football injury until you made a somewhat distasteful suggestion?'

'Distasteful?' DC Marten appeared to resent the adjective.

'Just remind the jury of what you said, Officer. As you lay on that massage table, clad only in a towel.'

'I said, "Well, my dear"' – the officer read carefully from his notebook – ' "How about a bit of the other?" '

'The *what*, Officer?' The Judge was puzzled.

'The other, my Lord.'

'The other what?'

'Just. The other . . .'

'I must confess I don't understand.' His Lordship turned to me for assistance.

'You were using an expression taken from the vernacular,' I suggested to the Detective Constable.

'Meaning what, Mr Rumpole?' The Judge was still confused.

'Hanky-panky, my Lord.'

'I'm much obliged. I hope that's clear to the jury?' Guthrie turned to the twelve honest citizens, who nodded wisely.

'You suggested some form of sexual intimacy might be possible?' The Judge was now master of the facts.

'I did, my Lord. Putting it in terms I felt the young lady would understand.'

'And if you hadn't made this appalling suggestion, the massage might have continued quite inoffensively?'

'It might have done.'

'To the considerable benefit of your knee!'

'There was nothing wrong with my knee, my Lord.'

'No. No, of course not! You were lying about that!' And then, high on his success, Guthrie asked the question that would have been better to leave unsaid. 'When you asked the young lady about "the other", what did she reply?'

'Her answer was, my Lord, "That'll be twenty pounds."'

'Very well, Officer,' Guthrie said hastily. 'No one wants to keep this officer, do they? The witness may be released.'

And as DC Marten left the box, Brinsley Lampitt whispered to me, 'Have you any idea why the Judge is batting so strenuously for the defence?'

'Oh, yes,' I whispered back, 'it must be my irresistible charm.'

Two wives, Marigold Featherstone and Hilda 'She Who Must Be Obeyed' Rumpole, bumped into each other in Harrods, and had tea together, swapping news of their married lives. Hilda said she had been after a hat to wear when Rumpole was sitting. 'I thought I might be up beside him on the Bench occasionally.'

'Rumpole sitting?' For some reason Marigold appeared surprised.

'Yes. It was your Guthrie that mentioned it to him actually, when they took a spot of lunch together at the Sheridan Club. Rumpole said that it rather depended on his behaving himself in this case that's going on. But if he's a bit careful . . . well, Deputy County Court Judge! For all the world to see. It'll be one in the eye for Claude Erskine-Brown. That's what he's always wanted.'

'Guthrie seems to want to give up sitting.' Marigold told Hilda of their mysterious conversation. 'He speaks of going to Ibiza and opening a bar.'

'Ibiza!'

'Terrible place. Full of package tours and Spaniards.'

'Oh dear. I don't think Rumpole and I would like that at all.'

'Tell me, Mrs Rumpole. May I call you Helen?'

'Hilda, Marigold. And you and Guthrie always have.'

'Guthrie's been most peculiar lately. I wonder if I should take him to the doctor.'

'Oh dear. Nothing terribly serious, I hope.'

'He keeps asking me if I'd stand by him. Through thick and thin. Would you do that for Rumpole?'

'Well. Rumpole and I've been together nearly forty years . . .' she began judicially.

'Yes.'

'And I'd stand by him, of course.'

'Would you?'

'But thick and thin. No, I'm not sure about that.'

'Neither am I, Hilda. I'm not sure at all.'

'Have another scone, dear' – my wife passed the comforting plate – 'and let's hope it never comes to that.'

The next morning, Marigold's husband asked Rumpole (for the defence) and Brinsley Lampitt (for the prosecution) to see him in his room. 'I thought I'd just ask you fellows in to find out how much longer this case is going to last. Time's money you know. I don't think we should delay matters by going into a lot of unnecessary documents. Will you be producing documents, Lampitt?'

'Just Dr Horridge's bank accounts. Nothing else.' The words clearly brought great comfort to his Lordship. 'I don't think anything else is necessary.'

'Oh no. Absolutely right! I do so agree. I seem to remember hearing something about customers using credit cards. You won't be putting in any of the credit-card slips? Nothing of that nature?'

'No, Judge. I don't think we need bother with that evidence.'

'No. Of course not. That'd just be wasting the jury's time. I'm sure you agree, don't you, Rumpole?'

'Well, yes.' I was more doubtful. 'That is. Not quite.'

'Not quite?'

'About the credit-card evidence.'

'Yes?' The Judge's spirits seemed to have sunk to a new low.

'I think I'd like to keep my options open.'

'Keep them . . . open?'

'You see, my argument is that no one who wasn't completely insane would pay by credit card in a disorderly house.'

'That's your argument?'

'So the fact that credit cards were used *may* indicate my client's innocence. It's a matter I'll have to consider, Judge. Very carefully.'

'Yes. Oh, yes. I suppose you will.' His Lordship seemed to have resigned himself to certain disaster.

'Was that all you wanted to see us about?' I asked cheerfully.

'How much longer?' was all the Judge could bring himself to say.

'Oh, don't worry, Judge. It'll soon be over!'

After we left, I imagined that Mr Justice Featherstone got out his Spanish Phrase Book and practised saying, '*Este vaso no esta limpio*. This glass is not clean.'

It must have been after the prosecution case was closed, and immediately before I had to put my client in the witness-box, that Guthrie Featherstone's view of life underwent a dramatic change. He had brought in the envelope containing his American Express accounts, a document that he had not dared to open. But, in the privacy of his room and after a certain amount of sherry and claret at the Judge's luncheon, he steeled himself to open it. Summoning up a further reserve of courage, he looked and found the entry, his payment to the Good Life Health Centre. 'Good Life'? A wild hope rose in an unhappy Judge, and he snatched up the papers in the case he was trying. There was no doubt about it. Maurice Horridge was charged with running a number of disorderly houses known as the Good Line Health Centre. It was clearly a different concern entirely. Guthrie felt like a man given six months to live, who discovers there's been a bit of a mix-up down the lab and all he's had is a cold in the head. He had never been to one of Dr Horridge's establishments, and there was no record of any judicial payment among the prosecution exhibits. 'I have no doubt,' he shouted, 'I'm in the clear', and down the Bailey they still speak of the little dance of triumph Guthrie was executing when Harold the new usher came to take him into Court.

Installed, happy now, on his Bench, Guthrie was treated to the Rumpole examination-in-chief of my distinctly shifty-looking client 'Dr Horridge'. I was saying, 'If any of these young ladies misconducted themselves in your Health Centres . . .'

'They wouldn't,' the witness protested, 'I'm sure they wouldn't. They were spiritually trained, Mr Rumpole.'

'All the same, if by any chance they did, was it with your knowledge and approval?'

'Certainly not, my Lord. Quite certainly not!' Horridge turned to Guthrie, from whom I expected a look of sympathy. Instead, the Judge uttered a sharpish, 'Come now, Dr Horridge!'

'Yes, my Lord?' The theological doctor blinked.

'Come, come! We have had the evidence from that young officer, Detective Constable Marten, that he suggested to one of your masseuses . . . something of "the other"!'

'Something or other, my Lord?'

'No, Dr Horridge.' The Judge sounded increasingly severe. 'Something *of* the other. I'm sure you know perfectly well what that means. To which the masseuse replied, "That will be twenty pounds." A pretty scandalous state of affairs, I'm sure you'll agree?'

'Yes, my Lord.' What else could the wretched massage pedlar say?

'Are you honestly telling this jury that you had no idea whatever that was going on, in your so-called Health Centre?'

'No idea at all, my Lord.'

'And you didn't make it your business to find out?' Guthrie was now well and truly briefed for the prosecution.

'Not specifically, my Lord.' It wasn't a satisfactory answer and the Judge met it with rising outrage. 'Not specifically! Didn't you realize that decent, law-abiding citizens, husbands and *ratepayers* might be trapped into the most ghastly trouble just by injuring an elbow – I mean, a knee?'

'I suppose so, my Lord,' came the abject reply.

'You suppose so! Well. The jury will have heard your answer. What *are* you doing, Mr Rumpole?' His Lordship had some reason to look at me. I had wet my forefinger and now held it up in the air.

'Just testing the wind, my Lord.'

'The wind?' The Judge was puzzled.

'Yes. It seems to have completely changed direction.'

When the case was concluded, I returned to Chambers exhausted. Thinking I might try my client's recipe, I lay flat on the floor with my eyes closed. I heard the door open, and the voice of the Hearthrug from far away asking, 'Rumpole! What's the matter? Are you dead or something?'

'Not dead. Just laid out spiritually.' I opened my eyes. 'Losing a case is always a tiring experience.'

'I'm trying to see Ballard,' Hearthstoke alleged.

'Well, look somewhere else.'

'He always seems to be busy. I wanted to tell him about Henry.'

I rose slowly, and with some difficulty, to a sitting position, and thence to my feet. 'What about Henry?'

'Kissing Dianne in the clerk's room.' The appalling Hearthrug did his best to look suitably censorious. 'It's just not on.'

'Oh, I agree.' I was upright by now, but panting slightly.

'Do you?' He seemed surprised. 'I thought you'd say it was all just part of the freedom of the subject, or whatever it is you're so keen on.'

'Oh, good heavens, no! I really think he should stop rehearsing in his place of work.'

'Rehearsing?' He seemed surprised.

'Didn't you know? Henry's a pillar of the Bromley amateur dramatics. He's playing opposite Dianne in some light comedy or other. Of course, they both work so hard they get hardly any time to rehearse. I'll speak to them about it. By the way, how's the housemaid's knee?'

'The what?' Clearly, my words had no meaning for the man.

'The dicky ankle, dislocated elbow, bad back, tension in the neck. In a lot of pain, are you?'

'Rumpole! What *are* you talking about? I am perfectly fit, thank you!'

'No aches and pains of any sort?' It was my turn to sound surprised.

'None whatever.'

'How very odd! And you've been having such a lot of massage lately.'

'What on *earth* do you mean?' Hearthrug, I was delighted to note, was starting to bluster.

'Unfortunate case. The poor old theologian got two years, once the Judge felt he had a free hand in the matter. But we were looking through the evidence. Of course, you knew that. That was why you came in to give Mizz Probert a helping hand. I was after another name, as it so happens. But I kept finding yours, Charles Hearthstoke. In for a weekly massage at the Battersea Health Depot and Hanky-Panky Centre.'

'It was entirely innocent!' he protested.

'Oh, good. You'll be able to explain that to our learned Head of Chambers. *When* you can find him.'

But Hearthrug looked as though he was no longer eager to find Soapy Sam Ballard, or level his dreadful accusations against Henry and Dianne.

From time to time, and rather too often for my taste, we have Chambers parties, and shortly after the events described previously, Claude Erskine-Brown announced that he was to finance one such shindig; he had some particular, but unknown, cause for celebration. So we were all assembled in Ballard's room, where Pommeroy's most reasonably priced Méthode Champenoise was dished out by Henry and Dianne to the members of Chambers with their good ladies and a few important solicitors and such other distinguished guests as Mr Justice Featherstone, now fully restored to health both of mind and elbow. 'Hear you potted Rumpole's old brothel-keeper,' Uncle Tom greeted Sir Guthrie, making a gesture as though playing snooker, 'straight into the pocket!'

'It was a worrying case,' Guthrie admitted.

'It must have been for you, Judge. Extremely worrying.' I saw his point.

'There used to be a rumour about the Temple' – Uncle Tom was wandering down Memory Lane – 'that old Helford-Davis's clerk was running a disorderly house over a sweet shop in High Holborn. Trouble was, no one could ever find it!' At which point, Hilda, in a new hat, came eagerly up to Guthrie and said, 'Oh, Judge. How we're going to envy you all that sunshine!' And she went on in spite of my warning growl. 'Of course, we'd love to retire to a warmer climate. But Rumpole's got all these new responsibilities. He feels he won't be able to let the Lord Chancellor down.'

'The Lord Chancellor?' Guthrie didn't seem quite to follow her drift.

'He's expecting great things, apparently, of Rumpole. Well' – she raised her glass – 'happy retirement.'

'Mrs Rumpole. I'm not retiring.'

'But Marigold distinctly told me that it was to be Ibiza.'

'Well. I had toyed with the idea of loafing about all day in an old pair of shorts and an old straw hat. Soaking up the sun. Drinking Sangria. But no. I feel it's my duty to go on sitting.'

'Ibiza is no longer necessary,' I explained to Hilda, but she had to say, 'Your duty! Yes, of course. Rumpole is going to be doing his duty too.' At which point, our Head of Chambers banged a glass on his desk for silence. 'I think we are going to hear about Rumpole's future now,' Hilda said, and Ballard addressed the assembled company. 'Welcome! Welcome everyone. Welcome Judge. It's delightful to have you with us. Well, in the life of every Chambers, as in every family, changes take place. Some happy, others not so happy. To get over the sadness first. Young Charles Hearthstoke has not been with us long, only three months in fact.' 'Three months too long, if you want my opinion,' I murmured to Uncle Tom, and Bollard swept on with his ill-deserved tribute. 'But I'm sure we all came to respect his energy and drive. Charles has told me that he found the criminal side of our work here somewhat distasteful, so he is joining a commercial set in the Middle Temple.' At this news, Henry applauded with enthusiasm. 'I'm sure we're all sorry that Charles had to leave us before he could put some of his most interesting ideas for the reform of Chambers into practice . . .'

At this point, I looked at Mizz Probert. I have no idea what transpired when she and Hearthrug had their Chinese meal together, but I saw Liz's eyes wet with what I took for tears. Could she have been sorry to see the blighter go? I handed her the silk handkerchief from my top pocket, but she shook her head violently and preferred to sniff.

'Now I come to happier news,' Ballard told us. 'From time to time, the Lord Chancellor confers on tried and trusty members of the Bar . . .'

'Like Rumpole!' This was from Hilda, *sotto voce.*

'The honour of choosing them to sit as Deputy Circuit Judge.'

'We know he does!' Hilda again, somewhat louder.

'So we may find ourselves appearing before one of our colleagues and be able to discover his wisdom and impartiality on the Bench.'

'You may have Ballard before you, Rumpole,' Hilda called out in triumph, to my deep embarrassment.

'This little party, financed I may say,' Ballard smiled roguishly, 'by Claude Erskine-Brown . . .'

'So kind of Claude to do this for Rumpole,' was my wife's contribution.

'. . . Is to announce that he will be sitting, from time to time, at Snaresbrook and Inner London, where we wish him every happiness.'

Ballard raised his glass to Erskine-Brown, as did the rest of us, except for Hilda, who adopted a sort of stricken whisper to ask, '*Claude Erskine-Brown* will be sitting? Rumpole, what happened?' 'My sitting,' I tried to explain to her, 'like Guthrie Featherstone's Ibiza, is no longer necessary.' And then I moved over to congratulate the new Deputy Circus Judge.

'Well done, Claude.' And I told him, 'I've only got one word of advice for you.'

'What's that, Rumpole? Let everyone off?'

'Oh, no! Much more important than that. Always pay in cash.'

Rumpole's Last Case

Picture, if you will, a typical domestic evening, *à côté de Chez* Rumpole, in the 'mansion' flat off the Gloucester Road. I am relaxed in a cardigan and slippers, a glass of Jack Pommeroy's Very Ordinary perched on the arm of my chair, a small cigar between my fingers, reading a brief which, not unusually, was entitled, *R. v. Timson*. She Who Must Be Obeyed was staring moodily at the small hearthrug, somewhat worn over the ages I must admit, that lay in front of our roaring gas-fire.

'The Timsons carrying a shooter!' I was shocked at what I had just read. 'Whatever's the world coming to?'

'We need a new one urgently,' Hilda was saying, 'and we need it *now.*' She was still gazing at our hearthrug, scarred by the butt ends of the small cigars I was aiming at the bowl of water that stood in front of the fire.

'It's like music in lifts and wine in boxes.' I was lamenting the decline of standards generally. 'We'll be having Star Wars machines in Pommeroy's Wine Bar next. Decent, respectable criminals like the Timsons never went tooled up.'

'Rumpole, you've done it again!' Hilda recovered the end of my cigar from the rug and ground it ostentatiously out in an ashtray as I told her a bit of ash never did a carpet any harm, in fact it improved the texture.

'There's a perfectly decent little hearthrug going in Debenhams for £100,' Hilda happened to mention.

'Going to someone who isn't balancing precariously on the rim of their overdraft.'

'Rumpole, what on earth's the use of all these bank robberies and the rising crime-rate they're always talking about if we can't even get a decent little hearthrug out of it?' Hilda was clearly starting one of her campaigns, and I got up to recharge my glass from the bottle on the sideboard. 'Remember what they're paying for legal aid cases nowadays,' I told her firmly. 'It hardly covers the fare to Temple station. And there's Henry's ten per cent and the cost of a new briefcase . . .'

'You're never buying a new briefcase!' She was astonished.

'No. No, of course not. I can't afford it.' I took a quick sustaining gulp and carried the glass back to my armchair. '. . . And there's a small claret at Pommeroy's to recover from the terrors of the day.'

'That's your trouble, isn't it, Rumpole.' She looked at me severely. 'If it weren't for the "small claret" at Pommeroy's we'd have no trouble buying a nice new hearthrug, and if it weren't for those awful cheroots of yours we shouldn't need one anyway. I warn you I shall call in at Debenhams tomorrow; it's up to you to deal with the bank.'

'How do you suggest I deal with the bank?' I asked her. 'Tunnel in through the drains and rob the safe? Not carrying a shooter, though. A Timson carrying a shooter! It's the end of civilization as we know it.'

Counsel is briefed for Mr Dennis Timson. He will 'know the Timson family of old'. It appears that Dennis and his Cousin Cyril entered the premises of the 'Penny-Wise Bank' in Tooting by masquerading as workers from British Telecom inspecting underground cables that were laid in Abraham Avenue. Whilst working underground the two defendants contrived to burrow into the 'strongroom' of the 'Penny-Wise' and open the safe, abstracting therefrom a certain quantity of cash and valuables. As they were doing so, they were surprised by a Mr Huggins, a middle-aged bank guard. It is clear from the evidence that Huggins was shot and wounded by a revolver, which was then left at the scene of the crime. The alarm had been given and the two Timson cousins were arrested by police officers who arrived at the scene of the crime.

Mr Dennis Timson admits the break-in and the theft. He says, however, that he had no idea that his Cousin Cyril was carrying a 'shooter', and is profoundly shocked at such behaviour in a member of the family. He is most anxious to avoid the 'fourteen', which he believes would be the sentence if the jury took the view he was party to the wounding of Mr Huggins. Cyril Timson, who, instructing solicitors understand, is represented by Mrs Phillida Erskine-Brown, QC, as 'silk' with Mr Claude

Erskine-Brown as her 'learned junior', will, it seems likely, say that it is all 'down to' our client, Dennis. He has told the police (DI Broome) that he had no idea Dennis came to the scene 'tooled up', and that he was horrified when Dennis shot the bankguard. It seems clear to those instructing that Cyril is also anxious to avoid the 'fourteen' at all costs.

Counsel will see that he is faced with a 'cut-throat' defence with the defendants Timson blaming each other. Counsel will know from his long experience that in such circumstances the prosecution is usually successful, and both 'throat-cutters' tend to 'go down'. Counsel may think it well to have a word or two with Mr Cyril Timson's 'silk', Mrs Phillida Erskine-Brown, who happens to be in Counsel's Chambers, to see if Cyril will 'see sense' and stop 'putting it all down' to Mr Dennis Timson.

Counsel is instructed to appear for Mr Dennis Timson at the Old Bailey, and secure his acquittal on the charges relating to the firearm. Those instructing respectfully wish learned Counsel 'the best of British luck'.

Dear old Bernard, the Timsons' regular solicitor, was a great one for the inverted comma. He had put the matter clearly enough in his instructions with my brief in *R. v. Timson*, and the case as he described it had several points of interest as well as a major worry. Both Cyril and Dennis were well into middle age and, at least so far as Cyril was concerned, somewhat overweight. The whole enterprise, setting up a tent over a manhole in the road and carrying out a great deal of preliminary work in the guise of men from British Telecom, seemed ambitious for men whom I should never have thought of as bank robbers. It was rather as though the ends of a pantomime horse had decided to get together and play Hamlet. Den and Cyril Timson, I thought, should have stuck to thieving frozen fish from the Cash & Carry. The Penny-Wise affair seemed distinctly out of their league.

The fly in the ointment of our case had been accurately spotted by the astute and experienced Bernard. In a cut-throat defence, two prisoners at the Bar blame each other. The prosecutor invariably weighs in with titbits of information designed to help the mutual mayhem of the two defendants and the jury pot them both. The prospects were not made brighter by the fact that his Honour Judge Bullingham was selected to preside over this carnage. On top of all this anxiety, I was expecting my overdraft, already bursting at the seams constructed for it by Mr Truscott of the Caring Bank, to be swollen by Hilda's extravagant purchase of a new strip of floor covering.

And then an event occurred which set me on the road to fortune and so enabled me to call this particular account 'Rumpole's Last Case'.

My luck began when I called in at the clerk's room on the first morning of *R. v. Timson* and found, as usual, Uncle Tom getting a chip shot into the waste-paper basket, Dianne brewing up coffee and Henry greeting me with congratulations such as I had never received from him after my most dramatic wins in Court (barristers, according to Henry, don't win or lose cases, they just 'do' them and he collects his ten per cent). 'Well done, indeed, Mr Rumpole,' he said. 'You remember investing in the barristers clerks' sweepstake on the Derby?' In fact I remembered his twisting my arm to part with two quid, much better spent over the bar at Pommeroy's. 'You drew that Dire Jeans,' Henry told me.

'I drew what?'

'Diogenes, Rumpole.' Uncle Tom translated from the original Greek. 'Do you know nothing about the turf? It came in at a canter. I said to myself, "That's old Rumpole for you. He has all the luck!"'

'Oh. Got a winner, did I?' I tried to remain cool when Henry handed me a bundle and told me that it was a hundred of the best and asked if I wanted to count them. I told him I trusted him implicitly and counted off twenty crisp fivers. It was an excellent start to the day.

'You know what they say!' Uncle Tom looked on with interest and envy. 'Lucky on the gee-gees, unlucky in love. You've never been tremendously lucky in love, have you, Rumpole?'

'Oh, I don't know, Uncle Tom. I've had my moments. One hundred smackers!' I put the loot away in my hip pocket. 'It's not every day that a barrister gets folding money out of his clerk.' Uncle Tom looked at me a little sceptically. Perhaps he wondered what sort of moments I had had; after all he had enjoyed the privilege of meeting Mrs Hilda Rumpole at our Chambers parties.

> As I sat in the café I said to myself,
> They may talk as they please about what they call 'pelf',
> They may sneer as they like about eating and drinking,
> But I cannot help it, I cannot help thinking . . .

How pleasant it is to have money, heigh ho!
How pleasant it is to have money . . .
So pleasant it is to have money . . .

The lines went through my head as I took my usual walk down Fleet Street to Ludgate Circus and then up to the Old Bailey. As I walked I could feel the comforting and unusual bulge of notes in my hip pocket. As I marched up the back lanes to the Palais de Justice, I passed a newspaper kiosk which, I had previously noticed, seemed to mainly cater to the racing fraternity. There were a number of papers and posters showing jockeys whose memoirs were printed and horses whose exploits were described, and I noticed that morning the advertisement for a publication entitled *The Punter's Guide to the Turf* which carried a story headed FOUR-HORSE WINNER FATHER OF THREE TELLS HOW HE HIT QUARTER OF A MILLION JACKPOT.

Naturally, as a successful racing man (a status I had achieved in the last ten minutes), I took a greater interest in the familiar kiosk. I had, clearly, something of a talent for the turf. The Derby one day, perhaps the Grand National the next – was it the Grand National or the Oaks? With a few winners, I thought, a fellow could live pretty high on the hog – I took a final turning and the Old Bailey hoved into view – a fellow might even be able to consider giving up the delights of slogging down the Bailey for the dubious pleasure of doing a cut-throat defence before his unpredictable Honour Judge Roger Bullingham.

And then, walking on towards the old verdict factory, I heard the familiar voices of Phillida Erskine-Brown, QC, and her spouse; fragments of conversation floated back to me on the wind.

'Rumpole's got Probert taking a note for him,' our Portia said. 'Do try not to dream about taking her to the opera again.'

'I only took her once. And then she didn't enjoy it.' This was Claude's somewhat half-hearted defence.

'I bet she didn't. You would have been better off inviting her to a Folk Festival at the Croydon Community Centre. *Much* more her style.'

'Philly! Look, aren't you ever going to forget it?'

'Frankly, Claude, I don't think I ever am.'

They crossed the road in front of me and their voices were lost, but I had heard enough to know that all was not sweetness and light in the

Erskine-Brown household. I hoped that our Portia's natural irritation with her errant husband would not lead her to sharpen her scalpel for the cut-throat defence.

Half an hour later I knew the answer to that question. I was robed up with Liz Probert and Mr Bernard in tow on my way to a pre-trial conference with my client Dennis Timson, when we met Phillida Erskine-Brown and her husband on a similar mission to Den's cousin, Cyril.

'*Ill met by moonlight, proud Titania.*' I thought this was a suitable greeting to the lady silk in the lift.

'Rumpole! What's all this about proud Titania?'

'You're not going to listen to me?'

'I'll certainly listen, Rumpole. What've you got to say?'

'You know it's always fatal when two accused persons start blaming each other! A cut-throat defence with the prosecutor chortling in his joy and handing out the razors. That's got to be avoided at all costs.'

'Why don't you admit it then?'

'Admit *what*?'

'Admit you had the shooter? Accept the facts.'

'Plead guilty?' I must admit I was hurt by the suggestion. 'And break the habit of a lifetime?' We were out of the lift now and waiting, at the gateway of the cells in the basement, for a fat and panting screw, who had just put down a jumbo-sized sandwich, to unlock the oubliettes. 'Who's prosecuting?' I asked Phillida.

'Young fellow who was in our Chambers for about five minutes,' she told me. 'Charles Hearthstoke.'

'My life seems to be dominated by hearthrugs,' I told her.

'He's rather sweet.'

'If you can possibly think Hearthrug's sweet' – I must say I was astonished – 'no wonder you suspect Dennis Timson of carrying a shooter.'

'Dennis Timson was tooled up.' She was positive of the fact.

'Cyril was!' I knew my Dennis.

'Moreover, he shot the bank guard extremely inefficiently – in the foot.'

'Come on, proud Titania. Plead guilty . . .' I tried a winsome smile to a minus effect.

'*Not for thy fairy kingdom*, Rumpole!'

'What *do* you mean?'

'Isn't that what Titania tells him. At the end of the scene? I suppose it means "no deal".' We parted then, to interview our separate clients, and I was left wondering if, when she was a white-wig, I had not taught young Phillida Trant, as she then was, far too much.

We, that is to say, Liz, Mr Bernard and I, found Dennis in one of the small interview rooms, smoking a little snout and reading *The Punter's Guide to the Turf*. I thought I should do best by an appeal to our old friendship and business association. 'You and I, Dennis,' I reminded him, 'have known each other for a large number of years and I've never heard of you carrying a shooter before.'

'You're a sporting man, Mr Rumpole,' the client said unexpectedly. I had to admit that I had enjoyed some recent success on the turf.

'Bloke in here cleared quarter of a million on the horses.' And Dennis was good enough to show me his *Punter's Guide*. 'Well,' I told him, 'I've had handsome wins in my time, but nothing to equal . . .'

'He's seen boarding an aeroplane for the Seychelles.' Dennis showed me the picture in his *Punter's*.

'The Seychelles, eh?' I was thoughtful. 'Far from Judge Bullingham and the Old Bailey.'

'I could make more than that on a four-horse accumulator. If I had a ton,' our client claimed.

'A ton of what?'

'A hundred pound stake.'

'A hundred pounds?' That very sum was swelling in my back pocket.

'I reckon I could top three hundred grand in the next few days.'

I pulled myself together and reluctantly came back to the matter in hand. 'You know what's going to happen when you and Cyril blame each other for carrying the shooter? The Mad Bull's going to tell the jury you agreed to go on an armed robbery together. He'll say that it doesn't really matter who was in charge of the equipment. You're *both* guilty! Did you say . . . three hundred thousand pounds?'

'From a four-horse accumulator.' Dennis made the point again.

'Four-horse what?'

'Accumulator.' He consulted his paper again. 'I could get 9 to 1 about Pretty Balloon at Goodwood this afternoon.'

'Do you want me to take this down?' Mizz Probert was puzzled at the course the conference was taking. I told her to relax but I pulled out a pencil and made a few notes on the back of my brief. I am ashamed to have to tell you they were not about the case.

'So there'd be a grand to go on Mother's Ruin at Redcar. 5 to 1, I reckon. That'd give us six thou.' Dennis went on as though it were peanuts. 'And that'd be on Ever So Grateful . . . which should get you fours at Yarmouth. So that's thirty grand!'

'Ever So Grateful, sounds a polite little animal.' I was taking a careful note.

'Now we need 10 to 1 for a bit of a gamble.' Dennis was studying the forecasts.

'What's it been up to now?'

'A doddle,' he told me calmly.

'Easy as tunnelling into a bank vault?' I couldn't help it.

'Do me a favour, Mr Rumpole, don't bring that up again.' His pained expression didn't last long. 'Kissogram at Newbury on Wednesday,' he read out in triumph. 'Ante-post price should bring you, let's say three hundred and thirty grand! Give or take a fiver.'

'In round figures?'

'Oh, yes. In round figures.'

I put away my pen and looked at Dennis. 'Just tell me one thing.'

'About the shooter?' His cheerfulness was gone.

'We'll come back to the shooter in a minute; I was thinking that you've been in custody since that eventful night.'

'Six months, Mr Rumpole,' Bernard told me and Liz Probert added, 'We should get that off the sentence.'

'I suppose, being in Brixton and now here, it's difficult to place a small bet or two? Not to mention a four-horse accumulator?'

'Bless your heart, Mr Rumpole. There's always screws that'll do it for you, even down the Old Bailey cells.'

'Screws that'll put on bets?' I was surprised to hear it.

'You know Gerald, the fat one at the gate, the one that's always got his face in a bacon sarny?'

'Gerald.' I was grateful for the information. And then I stood up; we seemed to have covered all the vital points. 'Well, I think that's about all on the legal aspect of the case. Just remember one thing, Dennis. The Timsons don't carry weapons and they don't grass on each other.'

'That's true, Mr Rumpole. That has always been our point of honour.'

'So don't you go jumping into that witness-box and blame it all on your Cousin Cyril. Let the prosecution try and prove which of you had the gun; don't you two start cutting each other's throats.'

'Cyril goes in the first, don't he?' Dennis had a certain amount of legal knowledge gained in the hard school of experience.

'If he goes in at all, yes. You're second on the indictment.'

'I'll have to see what he says, won't I?'

'But you wouldn't grass on him?'

'Not unless I have to.' Dennis didn't sound so sure.

'What is honour? A word. What is that word, honour? Air!' Happily the allusion was lost on my client, so I went off to try a few passes at the Mad Bull after a word in confidence with the stout warder at the gate.

'Gerald.' I accosted him after I had told Liz and Mr Bernard to go on up and keep my place warm in Court. 'Yes, Mr Rumpole. Got a busy day in Court ahead, have you?' The man's voice came muffled by a large wadge of sandwich.

'I am a little hard-pressed; in fact I'm too busy to get to my usual bookmakers.' 'Want me to put something on for you?' Gerald seemed to follow my drift at once.

'A hundred pounds. Four-horse accumulator. Start this afternoon at Goodwood' – I consulted the notes on my brief – 'with Pretty Balloon. I reckon you can get 9 to 1 about it.'

'Will do, Mr Rumpole. I'll be slipping out soon, for a bit of dinner.'

'And I'm sure you'll need it . . .' I looked at the man with something akin to awe and gave him the name of my four hopeful horses. Then I put my hand in my back pocket, lugged out the hundred pounds and handed it all to Gerald. As some old gambler put it:

> He either fears his fate too much,
> Or his deserts are small,
> That puts it not unto the touch,
> To win or lose it all.

It was after I had placed the great wager with Gerald that I went upstairs. Outside Judge Bullingham's Court, I found three large figures awaiting me. I recognized Fred Timson, a grey-haired man, his face bronzed by the suns of Marbella, wearing a discreet sports jacket, cavalry-twill trousers and an MCC tie. He was the acknowledged head of the family, always called on for advice in times of trouble, and with him I had also a long-standing business relationship. Fred was flanked by two substantial ladies who had clearly both been for a recent tint and set at the hairdressers; they were brightly dressed as though for a wedding or some celebration other than their husbands' day in Court. They, as I was reminded, were Den's Doris and Cyril's Maureen. Fred hastily told me of the family troubles. 'We're being made a laughing stock, Mr Rumpole. There's Molloys making a joke of this all over South London.' Of course, I knew the numerous clan Molloy, rival and perhaps more deft and successful villains, who were to the Timsons what the Montagues were to the Capulets, York to Lancaster or the Guelphs to the Ghibellines of old.

'I've been called out to in the street by Molloy women,' Den's Doris complained. 'Maureen's been called out to in Tesco on several occasions.'

'They're laughing at our husbands' – this, from Cyril's Maureen – 'grassing on each other.'

'Is *that* what they're laughing at?' I wondered.

'Oh, the Molloys is doing very nicely, that's what we hear. They pulled off something spectacular.' Fred had the latest information.

'They got away with something terrific, they reckon,' Maureen and Doris added. 'And they calls out that all the Timsons can do is get nicked and then grass on each other.'

'These Molloys aren't ever going to let us hear the last of it.' Fred was gloomy. 'Young Peanuts Molloy, he called out that all the Timsons is good for is to use as ferrets.'

'Ferrets?' I looked at him with some interest. 'Why on earth did he say *that*, I wonder?'

'You know the way they talk.' Fred was full of contempt for Molloy boasting. 'We wants you to go in there, Mr Rumpole. And save our reputation.'

'I'll do my best,' I had to promise. After all, the Timson family had done more for the legal profession than a hundred Lord Chancellors.

A standard opening gambit, when faced with the difficulties of a cut-throat defence, is to apply to the Court, before the jury is let in and sworn, for separate trials for the defendants. If they are tried on different occasions they cannot then give evidence which will be harmful to each other. Such applications are usually doomed, as the Judge is as keen as the prosecution to see a couple of customers convicting each other without the need for outside assistance.

'A separate trial,' the Bull growled when I stood on my feet to make the application, 'for Dennis Timson? Any *reason* for that, Mr Rumpole, apart from your natural desire to spin out these proceedings as long as possible? I assume your client's on legal aid?'

I am sorry to say that not only the handsome young Hearthstoke but Phillida laughed at Bullingham's 'joke', and I thought that if I were to win the four-horse accumulator, I could tell his Lordship to shut up and not be so mercenary.

'The reason, my Lord,' I told him, 'is my natural desire to see that justice is done to my client.'

'Provided it's paid for by the unfortunate ratepayers of the City of London.' The Bull glared at me balefully. 'Go on, Mr Rumpole.'

'I understand that my co-defendant, Mr Cyril Timson, may give evidence accusing my client of having the gun.'

'And you, no doubt, intend to return the compliment?'

'I'm not prepared to say at this stage what my defence will be,' I said with what remained of my dignity.

'But it may be a cut-throat?' the Bull suggested artlessly.

'That is possible, my Lord.'

'These two . . .' – he looked at the dock with undisguised contempt – '*gentry*! Are going to do their best to cut each other's throats?'

Gazing at his Lordship, I knew how the Emperor Nero looked when he settled down in the circus to watch a gladiator locked in hopeless combat with a sabre-toothed tiger. I glanced away and happened to catch sight of a pale, weaselly-faced young man with lank hair and a leather jacket leaning over the rail of the Public Gallery, listening to the proceedings with interest and amusement. I immediately recognized the face, well known in criminal circles, of Peanuts Molloy, who also appeared to enjoy the circus. I averted my eyes and once more addressed the learned Judge, 'Of course,' I told him, 'the statements the defendants made to the police wouldn't be evidence against each other.'

'But once they go into the witness-box in the same trial and repeat them on oath, then they become evidence on which the jury could convict!' Bullingham added with relish.

'Your Lordship has my point.'

'Of course I do. You don't want your client sent down for armed robbery and grievous bodily harm, do you, Mr Rumpole?'

'I don't want my client sent down on evidence which may well be quite unreliable!' At that I sat down in as challenging a manner as possible and his Honour Judge Bullingham directed a sickly smile at Phillida. 'Mrs Erskine-Brown. Do you support Mr Rumpole's application?' he asked her in a voice like Guinness and treacle.

'My Lord. I do not!' Phillida rose to put her small stiletto heel into Rumpole. 'I'm sure that under your Lordship's wise guidance justice will be done to both the defendants. Your Lordship will no doubt direct the jury with your Lordship's usual clarity.' When it came to buttering up the Bull our Portia could lay it on with a trowel. 'You may well warn them of the danger of convicting Mr Dennis Timson on the evidence of an accomplice. But, of course, they *can* do so if they think it right.'

'Oh yes, Mrs Erskine-Brown.' The Bull was purring like a kitten. 'I shall certainly tell them that. The Court is grateful for your most valuable contribution.'

So the two Timsons were ordered to be tried together and I thought that if only certain horses managed their races better than I was managing my case I might, in the not too distant future, be boarding an aeroplane for the Seychelles. In fact, that first day in Court was not an unmitigated disaster. As Hearthrug was drawing to the end of a distinctly unsporting address to the jury, in the course of which he told them that the bank guard, Huggins, 'a family man, a man of impeccable character, who has sat upon his local Church Council, was wounded by these two desperate robbers, albeit in the foot', my client scribbled a note which was delivered to me by a helpful usher. I opened it and read the glad tidings: THE SCREWS TOLD ME, MR RUMPOLE. PRETTY BALLOON WON BY A SHORT HEAD AT GOODWOOD. One up, I thought as I crumpled the note and looked up at Bullingham like a man who might not be in his clutches for ever – one up and three to go.

I have it on the good authority of Harry Shrimpton, the Court Clerk, that after he rose, Bullingham said to him, 'A really most attractive advocate, Mrs Erskine-Brown. Do you think it would be entirely inappropriate if I sent her down a box of chocolates?'

'Yes, Judge,' Shrimpton felt it his duty to tell him.

'You mean, "Yes", I can?'

'No. I mean "Yes", it would be entirely inappropriate.'

'Hm. She hasn't a sweet tooth?' The Bull was puzzled.

'The Lord Chancellor wouldn't like it.' The Court Clerk was expert on such matters, but the Judge merely growled, 'I wasn't going to send chocolates to the Lord Chancellor.'

Whilst the learned female QC was being threatened by unsolicited chocolates from the Judge, she was sitting, at his express invitation, with Charlie Hearthstoke, in a quiet corner of Pommeroy's Wine Bar in the company of two glasses and a gold-paper-necked bottle in an ice bucket. The ruthless Counsel for the prosecution, she was able to tell me much later, had invited her there so that he could tell her that my client, Dennis, possessed a firearm without a licence, although it was unfortunately a shotgun and not a revolver, and that he had done malicious damage with an air rifle when he was fourteen. It was also thought that he had rung the hospital to inquire about Huggins's health; an event which, as interpreted by Hearthrug, showed not natural sympathy, but a desire to discover if he were likely to be charged with murder. All these facts were put at Phillida's disposal, so that she might be the better able to cut my client's throat. Then Charlie Hearthstoke told Phillida what a superb 'Courtroom technician' she was. 'The way you handled Bullingham was superb. He's dotty about you, naturally. Well, I can't blame him. I suppose everyone is.'

There was more of such flattery, apparently, and Hearthstoke made it clear that he wished he'd got to know Phillida better when he was in our Chambers, but of course she was always doing such important cases, and was 'very much married, naturally'.

'Not all *that* married,' Phillida now agrees she replied, and who knows what course the conversation might not have taken had I not hoved to with Liz Probert, seen the bottle in the bucket and asked Jack Pommeroy's girl Barbara to bring us another couple of glasses. 'Champagne all round, eh, Hearthrug?' I said, as we settled in our places. 'And I know exactly what you're celebrating.'

'I can't imagine what that could be.' Phillida tried to sound innocent.

'Come off it,' I told her. 'You're celebrating the unholy alliance between Cyril Timson and the prosecution, with a full exchange of information designed to send poor old Dennis away for at least fourteen years.'

'That's not fair!'

'Of course it's not fair, Portia. But it's true. And as the quality of mercy doesn't seem to be dropping like the gentle rain from heaven around here, we'll have to make do with Pommeroy's bubbly.' I pulled the bottle out of the bucket and looked at it with dismay. 'Méthode Champenoise. Oh, Hearthrug. You disappoint me.'

'Actually, Charles, it's quite delicious.' I saw Phillida smile at the odious prosecutor.

'Grape juice and gas,' I warned her. 'Wait for the headache. You know Mizz Probert, of course?' Of course she knew Liz only too well, but I wasn't in a mood to make life easy for Cyril Timson's silk.

'Of course,' Phillida spoke from the deep freeze.

'There's one thing I've always wanted to ask you, Phillida.' Liz being extremely nervous, started to chatter. 'Now you're a QC and all that. But when you started at the Bar, wasn't it terribly difficult being a woman?'

'Oh, no. Being a woman comes quite naturally, to some of us.' She smiled at Hearthstoke who laughed encouragingly. 'Not that I had much choice in the matter.'

'But didn't you come up against a load of fixed male attitudes?' Liz stumbled on, doing herself no good at all. 'That's what made it all such tremendous fun,' Phillida told her. 'If you really want to know, I didn't get a particularly brilliant law degree but I never had the slightest trouble getting on with men.'

'Clearly not.' Hearthrug was prepared to corroborate her story. 'Oh, yes' – Phillida smiled at Liz in a particularly lethal way – 'and there's one question I wanted to ask *you*.'

'About the exploitation of women at the Bar?' A simple-minded girl, Mizz Probert.

'No. Just . . . seen any good operas lately?' A deep old-fashioned blush spread across the face of that liberated lady Liz Probert, and I tried to help her by saying, 'You could have learned a great lesson from Portia today, Mizz Probert. How to succeed at the Bar by reducing

Judge Bullingham to a trembling blob of sexual excitement. I've never been able to manage it myself.' Gazing idly about me, I saw Claude enter Pommeroy's, and I happened to tell his wife that he looked as though he'd lost her, a remark not lost on the egregious Hearthrug.

'Rumpole, lay off!' Phillida's aside was unusually angry. 'Are you going to lay off Dennis?' I was prepared to strike a bargain with her, but as she made no response, I invited Erskine-Brown to draw up a chair and sit next to Mizz Probert. He declined to do this, but squeezed himself, in a way welcomed by neither of the parties, between his wife and Hearthstoke. When we were all more or less uncomfortably settled, I asked Claude if I could borrow the copy of the *Standard*, which he was holding much as a drowning man clings to a raft.

'I went back to Chambers, Philly,' the unhappy man was saying. 'They said you hadn't been in.'

'No. I came straight here. I was discussing the case with prosecuting Counsel.'

'Oh, yes.' Erskine-Brown was clearly cowed. 'Oh, yes. Of course.'

I wasn't listening to them. I was gazing like a man entranced at a stop-press item on the back of the *Standard*. The golden words read LATE RESULT FROM REDCAR. NUMBER ONE, MOTHER'S RUIN. Two down and two to go! Things were going so well that I suggested to Hearthrug he might order a bottle of the real stuff.

'Why? What are *you* celebrating?' Phillida asked.

'I don't know about you fellows,' I told them. 'But I've made a few investments which seem to have turned out rather well. In fact, my future is almost entirely secure. Perhaps I won't have to do this job any more.' I looked round the table, smiling. 'Suppose this should turn out to be Rumpole's positively last case!' At which point my learned friends, and one of my learned enemies, looked at me with a wild surmise, silent at a table in Pommeroy's Wine Bar, faced with what might well count as the most significant moment in recent legal history.

Events were moving quickly. Diogenes had won the Derby the previous Wednesday, and on Monday morning Henry had paid out my little bit of capital when I called into Chambers on my way to participate in *R. v. Timson*. By Monday night, two of my favoured horses had brought home the bacon: Pretty Balloon at Goodwood, and Mother's Ruin most recently at Redcar. The speed of my success had somewhat stunned me, but I began to feel, as anyone must halfway through a successful four-horse accumulator, that I had the Midas touch. I had listened to Dennis's advice perhaps, but I could certainly pick them. As I settled in my armchair at the gas fireside in the Gloucester Road area that Monday evening I had no real doubt that Hilda and I were bound for some easy retirement by a sun-kissed lagoon. We should soon, I thought, be boarding an aeroplane for the Seychelles. 'I've got it, Rumpole.' She broke into my reverie.

'What've you got, Hilda?'

'What I've been wanting for a long time, that little hearthrug. It looks smart, doesn't it?'

'If that's what you always wanted, I think you might be rather more ambitious!' The new arrival at our 'mansion' flat seemed hardly appropriate to our new-found wealth.

'Just don't you dare throw your cigar ends at it!'

'Don't you worry,' I told her. 'I shall be chucking my cigar ends, my Havana cigar ends, my Romeo y Julieta cigar ends, at the sparkling ocean, as I wander barefoot along the beach in a pair of old white ducks and knock the sweet oysters off the rocks.'

'You're hardly going to do that in the Gloucester Road.' Hilda seemed not to be following my drift.

'Forget the Gloucester Road! We'll move somewhere far away from Gloucester Road and the Old Bailey.' I rose to get a glass of Château Fleet Street from the bottle on the sideboard. 'It's not *real* Persian, of course, but I think it's a traditional pattern,' Hilda told me.

' "*Courage!*" he said,' – I gave her a taste of 'The Lotos-Eaters':

> '*and pointed toward the land,*
> "*This mounting wave will roll us shoreward soon.*"
> *And in the afternoon they came unto a land*
> *In which it seemed always afternoon.*
> *All round the coast the languid air did swoon,*
> *Breathing like one that hath a weary dream.*'

'I have absolutely no idea what you mean,' Hilda sighed and turned her attention to the *Daily Telegraph*.

'It's not the *meaning*, Hilda, it's the sounds we shall hear: the chatter of monkeys, the screech of parrots in the jungle, the hum of dragon-flies, the rattle of grasshoppers rubbing their little legs together, the boom of breakers on the coral reef. And we shall sit out on the hotel verandah, drinking Planter's Punch and never having to wear a bloody winged collar again.'

'I don't wear a winged collar now.' Hilda tends to think first of her-self. Then she said, as I thought, a little sharply, 'I wonder if the bank manager will have anything to say about the hearthrug.'

'Hardly, Hilda!' I reassured her. 'I rather suspect that when I next run into Mr Truscott of the Caring Bank, he'll be inviting me for a light lunch at the Savoy Grill. I just hope I can make time for him.'

'The bank manager inviting *you* to lunch? That'll be the day!' She suddenly looked at me. 'You have *got* the hundred pounds for our hearthrug, haven't you, Rumpole?'

'*Fear not*, Hilda . . . *I do expect return / Of thrice three times the value of this bond.*'

'That's all very well. But have you got the hundred pounds?'

Tuesday dawned with only the case and Yarmouth races to worry about, but soon a new drama was unfolding itself before my eyes. I got to Chambers a little too late for my breakfast at the Taste-Ee-Bite in Fleet Street, so, once trapped again in the robes and the winged collar, I went down to the Old Bailey canteen, took my solitary coffee and bun to a corner table and sank behind *The Times*. I was soon aware of voices at the next table. It was Phillida again, but this time her companion was Charlie Hearthrug, and they both seemed blissfully unaware of old Rumpole at the table behind them.

'You might come back into the fold?' I heard Phillida say, and Hearth-stoke answered, 'Well, without Rumpole there, I don't see why I shouldn't find my way back into your Chambers at Equity Court.'

'That'd be something to look forward to. I used to think nothing would ever change. Marriage and building up the practice and having the kids and taking silk and perhaps becoming one of the statutory women on the Circuit Bench – Circus Bench, Rumpole calls it . . .' Phillida was clearly choosing this unlikely time and place to pour out her heart to Hearthstoke, who encouraged her by asking in soft and meaningful tones, like a poorish actor, 'Doesn't that seem enough for you now?'

'Not really. You know' – more confidences were clearly to come from Mrs Erskine-Brown – 'sometimes I envy my clients getting into trouble and leaving home and doing extraordinary things, dreadful things sometimes. But their lives aren't dull. Nothing happens to us! Nothing adventurous, really.'

'Perhaps it will if this is really Rumpole's last case and we're in Chambers together. Almost anything can happen then.'

'Almost anything?' I saw Phillida's elegant hand, with its rosy nails and sparkling cuff, descend gently on to Hearthrug's. It was time to clear the throat, stand up and approach the couple.

'How are you enjoying our duel to the death, Portia?'

'Fighting you, Rumpole' – she withdrew her hand as casually as possible – 'is always a pleasure.'

'Of course, you've got one great advantage,' I told her.

'Have I?'

'Oh yes. You've got an excellent junior. Good old Claude. He's always behind you. Working hard. I think you should remember that.' And with a brief nod to both of them, I swept on towards the corrida for another day's battle with the Bull.

When I rose to cross-examine Inspector Broome, the Officer-in-Charge of the case, a glance up at the Public Gallery told me that Peanuts Molloy was still *in situ* and apparently enjoying the proceedings. My gaze lingered on him for but a moment and then I turned my attention to the Inspector as I had done over so many cases and confronted a middle-aged, somewhat sardonic man who was capable of rare moments of humour and even rarer moments of humanity. He looked back at me, as always, with a sort of weary patience. Defence barristers in general, and Horace Rumpole in particular, were not among the Inspector's favourite characters.

'Inspector Broome,' I began my cross-examination. 'I understand that no fingerprints were found on the gun.' At which point the Bull couldn't resist weighing in with 'I imagine, Mr Rumpole, that these gentry would be too . . .' – for a wild moment I hoped he was going to say 'experienced' and then I'd have him on toast in the Court of Appeal, but his dread of that unjust tribunal made him say 'too *intelligent* to leave fingerprints?'

Something, perhaps it was the success I was enjoying with the horses, emboldened me to protest at the Judge's constant interruptions at the expense of my client. 'My Lord,' I ventured to point out, 'the prosecution in this case is in the hands of my learned friend, Mr Hearthrug.'

'Hearthstoke.' The young gentleman in question rose to correct me. 'Beg his pardon. Hearthstone. I'm sure he needs no assistance from your Lordship.'

There was the usual pause while the Bull lowered his head, snorted, pawed the ground and so on. Then he charged in with 'Mr Rumpole. That was an outrageous remark! It is one I may have to consider reporting as professional misconduct!'

Of course, by the time he did that, I might be safely on my way to the Seychelles, but I still had to get through Yarmouth that day and Newbury the next. I thought it best to return the retort courteous. 'I'm sorry if anything I might have said could possibly be construed as critical of your Lordship . . .'

'Very well! Let's get on with it.' Bullingham suspended his attack for the moment and I returned to the witness. 'Were the other areas of the strongroom examined for fingerprints, in particular the safe?'

'Yes, they were,' the Inspector told me.

'And again no fingerprints of either Mr Cyril or Mr Dennis Timson were found?' Bullingham roused himself to interrupt again, so I went on quickly, 'My Lord is about to say, of course, that they'd still be wearing their gloves when they opened the safe and that is a perfectly fair point. I needn't trouble your Lordship to make that interjection.'

'Isn't Rumpole going rather over the top?' I heard Phillida whispering to her husband, and she got the sensible reply, 'He's behaving like a chap who's got a secure future from investments.'

'No fingerprints identifiable as the defendant's were found, my Lord. That is true,' Broome told the Court.

'But no doubt a number of fingerprints *were* found on the door of the safe?' I asked.

'Of course.'

'And they were photographed?'

'Yes.'

'No doubt many of them came from bank employees?'

'No doubt about that, my Lord.'

'But did you take the trouble to check any of those fingerprints with criminal records?'

'Why should we have done that?' The Inspector looked somewhat pained at the suggestion.

'To see if they corresponded to the fingerprints of any known criminal, other than the two Mr Timsons.'

'No. We didn't.'

'Why not?'

'The two Mr Timsons were the only men we found at the scene of the crime and we had established that they were wearing gloves.'

'Because they had gloves on them when you caught them,' Bullingham explained to me as though I were a child, for the benefit of the jury.

'We are so much obliged to the learned Judge for his most helpful interjection, aren't we, Inspector? Otherwise you might have had to think of the answer for yourself.'

Of course that brought the usual warning rumble from the Bench, but I pressed on, more or less regardless, with, 'Let me ask you something else, Inspector. When the defendants were apprehended, they were carrying about three-thousand-pounds-worth of cash and other valuables from various deposit boxes?'

'That is so.'

'Was that the total amount missing from the safe?'

'No. No, as a matter of fact, it wasn't.' For the first time Broome sounded puzzled. 'That particular safe had been almost entirely emptied when we came to inspect it.'

'Were its entire contents valued at something over sixty thousand pounds?'

'Well over that, my Lord.'

'Well over that . . .' The Judge made a grateful note.

'You have no idea when the sixty-thousand-pound-worth was taken?' I heard Bullingham start with a menacing 'Perhaps . . .' and went on, 'My Lord is about to say perhaps they took it first and carried it out by the tunnel. That would be a sound point for my Lord to make.'

'Thank *you*, Mr Rumpole.' The Judge tried the retort ironical.

'Not at all, my Lord. I'm only too glad to be of assistance.' I smiled at him charmingly. 'But let me ask you this, Inspector. Your men came to the bank because an alarm went off in the strongroom?'

'That is so. The signal was received at Tooting Central at . . .'

'About 3 a.m. We know that. But it's clear, isn't it, that when your men invaded the bank they knew nothing about the tunnel?'

'That is quite right.'

'So they were admitted by the second guard on duty and went down to the vaults.'

'Yes.'

'No police officer ever entered by the tunnel?'

'Not so far as I am aware.'

'We all heard that evidence, Mr Rumpole. Or perhaps you weren't listening?' Nothing subtle, you see, about Judge Bullingham's little sallies.

'On the contrary, my Lord. I was listening most intently.' I turned back to the Inspector. 'And when your officers entered the vaults they found there two men running down a passage towards them?'

'That's what they reported.'

'Running *away* from the entrance to the tunnel.'

'Yes, indeed.'

'That is all I have to ask' – I gave Bullingham another of my smiles – 'unless your Lordship wishes to correct any of those answers . . .'

'Hadn't you better sit down, Mr Rumpole?'

'Sit down? Yes, of course. I'd be glad to. Your Lordship is most kind and considerate as always . . .' As I sat I thought that dear old Ever So Grateful had better get a spurt on or I would find myself up on a charge of professional misconduct. These thoughts were interrupted by Charlie Hearthstoke's re-examination of the witness.

'Mr Rumpole has asked you if you consulted criminal records on any of the fingerprints you *did* find on the safe.'

'Yes. I remember him asking me that,' Broome answered.

'Mr Rumpole no doubt felt that he had to ask a large number of questions in order to justify his fee from the legal aid.' Bullingham did one of his usual jokes to the jury; it was a moderate success only with the twelve honest citizens.

'I suppose you *could* compare the photographs of fingerprints you have with criminal records, couldn't you?' Hearthstoke suggested, greatly to my relief.

'I could, my Lord. If the Court wishes it.' Inspector Broome turned politely to the Bench for guidance and the Judge did his best to sound judicial. 'Mr Hearthstoke has made a very fair suggestion, Inspector, as one would expect of a totally impartial prosecutor.' He said graciously, 'Perhaps you would be so kind as to make the inquiry. We don't want to give Mr Rumpole any *legitimate* cause for complaint.'

When we left Court at lunchtime, I followed the Inspector down the corridor in pursuit of the line of defence I had decided to adopt for Dennis Timson. When I caught up with him, I ventured to tell Inspector 'New' Broome what a thoroughly dependable and straightforward officer I had always found him. Quite rightly he suspected that I wanted something out of him and he asked me precisely what I had in my mind.

'A small favour,' I suggested.

'Why should I do you a favour, Mr Rumpole? You have been a bit of a thorn in my flesh over the years, if I have to be honest.'

'Oh yes, you have to be honest. But if I promised never to be a thorn in your flesh ever again?'

'Not making me and my officers look Charlies in front of the jury?' Broome asked suspiciously.

'Never again.'

'Not letting the Timsons get away with murder?'

'Never murder, Inspector! Perhaps, occasionally, stolen fish.'

'Not getting my young DCs tied up in their own notebooks?' He pressed for specific assurances.

'If I swore on my old wig never to do anything of the sort again. In fact, Inspector Broome, if I were to promise you that this would be positively my last case!'

'Your last case, Mr Rumpole?' The Inspector was clearly reluctant to believe his ears.

'My positively last case!'

'You'd be leaving the Bailey after this for good?' Hope sprang in the officer's breast.

'I was thinking in terms of a warmer climate. So if I were to leave and never trouble you again . . .'

'Then I suppose I might be more inclined to help out,' Inspector Broome conceded. 'But if it's that fingerprint business!'

'Oh, you won't get anything out of that. I just wanted to get somebody worried. No respectable thief's ever going to leave their prints on a Peter. No, what I was going to suggest, old darling, is something entirely different.'

'Nothing illegal, of course?'

'Illegal! Ask Detective Inspector Broome to do anything illegal?' I hope I sounded suitably appalled at the idea. 'Certainly not. This is only guaranteed to serve the interests of justice.'

After lunch, and after I had made my most respectful suggestions to the Inspector, Hearthstoke closed the prosecution case and Phillida called Cyril Timson to the witness-box. He agreed with most of the prosecution case and accepted the evidence, which we had heard, of Mr Huggins of having been shot at by some person and wounded in the foot. Phillida held the revolver in her hand and asked in her most solemn tones, 'Cyril Timson. Did you take this weapon with you when you tunnelled into the Penny-Wise Bank?' When he had, not unexpectedly, answered, 'No. I never,' I whispered a request to her to sit down and resist the temptation of cutting Dennis's throat. She was not in a temptation resisting mood.

'Did you ever,' she asked Cyril, 'have any idea that your cousin, the co-defendant, Dennis Timson, was armed with a pistol?'

'My Lord,' I objected, 'there is absolutely no evidence that Dennis was armed with anything!'

'The pistol was there at the scene of the crime, Mr Rumpole. *Some-one* must have brought it,' Bullingham reasoned.

'Someone perhaps. But the question assumes . . .'

'Please continue, Mrs Erskine-Brown.' The Judge, ignoring me, almost simpered at Phillida, 'You may ask your question.'

'But you don't have to, Portia,' I whispered to her as I sat down. 'Remember the quality of mercy!'

'Did you have any idea that Dennis was armed?' She forgot it.

'No idea at all.' Cyril looked pained.

'And what would you have said if you had known?'

'My Lord' – I had another go – 'how can this be evidence? It's pure speculation!'

'Please, Mrs Erskine-Brown.' Again, I was ignored. 'Do ask the question.'

'What would you have said?'

'Leave that thing at home, Den.' Cyril sounded extraordinarily right-eous. 'That's not the way we carry on our business.'

'Can you tell us if Dennis ever owned a firearm?'

'I don't object, my Lord. All objections are obviously perfectly use-less.' I rose to tell the Court and got a look from the Judge which meant 'And that's another one for the report.' But now Cyril was saying, 'Den-nis was always pretty keen on shooters. When he was a kid he had an airgun.'

'And probably a catapult as well,' I whispered as I subsided.

'Did you say something, Mr Rumpole?' The Judge was kind enough to ask.

'Nothing whatever, my Lord.'

'In his later years he bought a shotgun.' Cyril added to the indict-ment of his cousin.

'Did you know what he used that for?' Phillida asked.

'He said clay pigeons, my Lord.'

'He said clay pigeons. Did you believe him?' the Judge asked and, looking up at the Public Gallery, I again saw Peanuts Molloy smiling.

'I had no means of checking the veracity of Cousin Den's statement.'

'Thank you, Mr Timson, just wait there.' Phillida sat down, happily conscious of having done her worst, and I rose to cross-examine the witness. Bullingham sat back to enjoy further bloodshed.

'Mr Timson. When you were removing some of the property from the safe, you suddenly ran out of the strongroom into the corridor. Why was that?'

'We thought we heard a noise behind us.' Cyril frowned, as though he still found the situation puzzling.

'Coming from where?'

'He said "behind us", Mr Rumpole,' Bullingham reminded me.

'Thank you, your Lordship, so much! And it was that sound that made you retreat?'

'We thought we was being copped, like.'

'Why didn't you retreat back into the tunnel you came from? Was it by any chance because the sound was coming from that direction?'

'Yes. It might have been,' Cyril admitted.

'When you ran out into that corridor you were holding some boxes containing money and valuables.'

'Yes, I was.'

'And so was your Cousin Dennis?'

'Yes.'

'You saw that?'

'Yes.'

'You never saw him with a gun in his hand?'

'No. I never saw it, like. But I knew *I* didn't have it.'

'Mr Cyril Timson, may I say at once that I accept the truth of that statement . . .' The Court went strangely silent; Bullingham looked disappointed, as though I had announced that throat-cutting was off and the afternoon would be devoted to halma. Phillida whispered to me, 'Rumpole, have you gone soft in your old age?'

'Not soft, Portia, I just thought it might be nice to win my last case,' I whispered back. Then I spoke to the witness, 'I agree that you didn't have the gun, and Dennis certainly didn't.'

'So where did it come from, Mr Rumpole?' The Judge gave me the retort sarcastic. 'Did it drop from the sky?'

'Yes, my Lord. In a manner of speaking, it did. Thank you, Mr Cyril Timson.'

I shot out of the Old Bailey, when Judge Bullingham rose at the end of that day, like a bat leaving hell. That was not my usual manner of departure, but careful inquiry at the sporting kiosk in the alley off Ludgate Circus had led me to believe that *The Punter's Guide*, out late on Tuesday afternoon, carried a full printout of that very afternoon's results. If you can make one heap of all your winnings and risk it on one turn of pitch and toss, you will have some idea what I felt like as I hastened towards the news-stand and to what had rapidly become my favourite reading.

Meanwhile as Peanuts Molloy came out of the entrance of the Public Gallery, DS Garsington, an officer in plain clothes, peeled himself off a wall and followed at a discreet distance. When Peanuts mounted a bus going south of the river, the Detective Sergeant was also in attendance. This close watch on Peanuts's movements was something that the Detective Inspector had authorized on the understanding that I would be leaving the Bar after the present case and so would trouble the authorities no more.

While Peanuts was off on his bus journey with DS Garsington in attendance, I was watching the elderly, partially blind lady with the bobble hat try to undo the newly arrived parcel of *The Punter's Guide*, with swollen and arthritic fingers. At last I could bear it no longer. I seized the string and broke it for her. I fluttered *The Punter's* pages for the fly-away leaf of that afternoon's results, and there was the printout from Yarmouth: 1.30 FIRST EVER SO GRATEFUL. 'Oh, my God,' I said devoutly as I paid the old lady. 'Thanks most awfully!'

At about opening time Peanuts Molloy was in a gym used to train young boxers over the Venerable Bede pub along the Old Kent Road. Peanuts was neither sparring nor skipping; he was reporting back to another deeply interested member of the clan Molloy. What he said, as later recalled by DS Garsington, went something like this: 'Like I told you. No sweat. They're still just blaming it on each other. There's one old brief that thinks different, but the Judge don't take a blind bit of notice. Not of him.' At which point the Detective Sergeant intruded and asked, 'Are you Peter James Molloy?'

'What if I am?' said Peanuts.

'I must ask you to accompany me. My Inspector would like to ask you some questions.'

'Oh yes. What about?'

'I believe . . .' – DS Garsington was suitably vague – 'it's about a fingerprint.'

Wednesday morning passed as slowly as a discourse on the Christian attitude to Tort from Soapy Sam Ballard, or an afternoon in a rain-soaked holiday hotel with She Who Must Be Obeyed.

First of all, Judge Bullingham had some applications in another case to deal with and so we started late, and then Phillida had some other evidence of a particularly unimportant nature to call. At last it was lunchtime and I was ready for the final throw; this was the crunch, the crisis, the moment to win or lose it all. I couldn't get away to Newbury to cheer Kissogram on, but I had decided to do the next best thing. Discreet inquiries from the ushers at the Bailey had revealed the fact that there was a betting shop recently opened by Blackfriars Station. I found it a curious establishment with painted-over windows and only a few visitors, who looked to be of no particular occupation, watching the television at lunchtime. They were joined by an ageing barrister in bands and a winged collar, who put a small cigar into his mouth but forgot to light it while watching the one-thirty.

I find it hard to recall my exact feelings while the race was going on and I supposed I have had worse times waiting for juries to come back with a verdict. Somewhere in the depths of my being I felt that I had come so far that nothing could stop me now, nor could it – Kissogram pulled it off by three lengths.

I hurried back to the Bailey repeating Dennis's magic figure: 'Let's say, three hundred and thirty grand! Give or take a fiver.' It was, of course, an extraordinary happening, and one which I intended to keep entirely to myself for the moment or God only knew how many learned friends would remember old Rumpole and touch him for a loan. Uppermost in my mind was the opening speech I was due to make of Dennis Timson's defence when the Bull, full of the City of London's roast beef and claret, returned to the seat of Judgement. It would be the last time I opened a defence in my positively last case. Why should I not do what a barrister who has his future at the Bar to think of can never do? Why should I not say exactly what I thought?

As I took the lift up to the robing room, the idea appealed to me more and more; it became even more attractive than the prospect of wandering along palm-fringed beaches beside the booming surf, although, of course, I meant to do that as well. Phrases, heartfelt sentiments, began to form in my mind. I was going to make the speech of a lifetime, Rumpole's last opening, and the Bull would have to listen. So, at exactly ten past two, I rose to my feet, glanced up at the Public Gallery, found that 'Peanuts' Molloy was no longer in his place and began.

'Members of the jury. You heard the prosecution case opened by my learned friend Mr Hearth—*stoke*. And I wish, now, to make a few remarks of a general nature before calling Mr Dennis Timson into the witness-box. I hope they will be helpful.'

'I hope so, too, Mr Rumpole. The defence doesn't *have* to indulge in opening speeches.' The Judge was scarcely encouraging, but no power on earth was going to stop me now.

'Members of the jury. You have no doubt heard of the presumption of innocence, the golden thread that runs through British justice. Everyone in this fair land of ours is presumed to be innocent until they're proved to be guilty, but against this presumption there is another mighty legal doctrine,' I told them. 'It is known as the Bullingham factor. Everyone who is put into that dock before this particular learned Judge is naturally assumed to have done the deed, otherwise they wouldn't be there. Not only are those in the dock presumed to be guilty, defending barristers are assumed to be only interested in wasting time so they can share in the rich pickings of the legal aid system, an organization which allows criminal advocates to live almost as high on the hog as well-qualified shorthand typists. For this princely remuneration, members of the jury, we are asked to defend the liberty of the subject, carry on the fine traditions of Magna Carta, make sure that all our citizens are tried by their peers and no man nor woman suffers unjust imprisonment, and knock our heads, day in day out, against the rock solid wall of the Bullingham factor! For this we have to contend with a Judge who invariably briefs himself for the prosecution . . .'

During the flow of my oratory, I had been conscious of two main events in Court. One was the arrival of Detective Inspector Broome, who was in urgent and whispered consultation with Charlie Hearthstoke. The other was the swelling of the Bull like a purple gas balloon, which I had been pumping up to bursting point. Now he exploded with a deafening '*Mr Rumpole!*' But before he could deliver the full fury of his Judgement against me, Hearthstoke had risen and was saying, 'My Lord. I wonder if I may intervene? With the greatest respect . . .'

'Certainly, Mr Hearthstoke.' The Judge subsided with a gentle hiss of escaping air. 'Certainly you may. Perhaps you have a suggestion to offer on how I might best deal with this outrageous contempt?'

'I was only about to say, my Lord, that what I am going to tell your Lordship may make the rest of Mr Rumpole's opening speech unnecessary.'

'I have no doubt that *all* of his opening speech is unnecessary!' Judge Bullingham glared in my general direction.

'I am informed by Detective Inspector Broome, my Lord, that, after further inquiries, we should no longer proceed on the allegation that either Cyril or Dennis Timson used, or indeed carried, the automatic pistol which wounded Mr Huggins the bank guard.'

'*Neither* of them?' The Bull looked as though his constitution might not stand another shock.

'It seems that further charges will be brought, with regard to that offence, against another "firm", if I may use that expression,' Hearth-stoke explained. 'In those circumstances, the only charge is one of theft.'

'To which Mr Cyril Timson has always been prepared to plead guilty,' Phillida stood up and admitted charmingly.

'Thank *you*, Mrs Erskine-Brown,' the Judge cooed, and then turned reluctantly to me. '*Mister* Rumpole?'

'Oh yes. Guilty to the theft, my Lord. With the *very greatest respect!*' I had said most of what I had always longed to say in Bullingham's Court, and my very last case was over.

'Ferrets! The Molloys said the Timsons were ferrets. They called it out after your wives in the street.' I was in the interview room again with Liz Probert and Mr Bernard, saying goodbye to our client Dennis Timson. 'I wonder why he used that particular expression. Ferrets are little animals you send down holes in the ground. Of course, the Molloys found out what you were up to and they simply followed you down the burrow. And after you'd got through the wall, what were they going to do? Use the gun to get the money off you and Cyril when you'd opened the safe? Anyway, it all ended in chaos and confusion, as most crimes do, I'm afraid, Dennis. You heard the Molloys and thought they were the Old Bill and ran towards the passage. The Molloys got their hands on the rest of the booty. Then Mr Huggins, the bank guard, appeared, some Molloy shot at him and dropped the gun and they scarpered back down the tunnel, leaving you and Cyril in hopeless ignorance, blaming each other.'

'But there weren't any fingerprints.' Liz Probert wondered about my cross-examination of Broome.

'Oh no. But the DI told Peanuts Molloy he'd found his and got him talking. In fact, Peanuts grassed on the rest of the Molloys.'

'Grassed on his family, did he?' Dennis was shocked. 'Bastard!'

'I'm afraid things aren't what they were in our world, Dennis. Standards are falling. When you've got this little stretch under your belt you'd do far better give it all up.'

'Never. I'd miss the excitement. You're all right, though, aren't you, Mr Rumpole?'

'What?' I was wondering whether I would miss the excitement, and decided that I could live without the thrills and spills of life with Judge Bullingham. 'I said *you're* all right,' Dennis repeated. 'On the old four-horse accumulator.'

'Oh yes, Dennis. I think I shall be all right. Thanks entirely to you. I shan't forget it. You were my last case.' I stood up and moved towards the door. 'Give me a ring when you get out, if you're ever passing through Lotos land.'

I had looked for Gerald as I arrived down the cells, but the gate had been opened by a thin turnkey without a sandwich. On my way out I asked for Gerald, anxious to collect my fortune, but was told, 'It's Gerald's day off, Mr Rumpole. He'll be back tomorrow for sure.'

'Back tomorrow? You don't know the name of his bookmaker by any chance?'

'Oh no, Mr Rumpole. Gerald don't take us into his confidence, not as far as that's concerned.'

'Well, all right. I'll be back tomorrow too.'

'Dennis Timson well satisfied with his four years, was he?' the thin warder said as he sprang me from the cells.

'He seemed considerably relieved.'

'I don't know how you do it, Mr Rumpole. Honest, I don't.'

'Well,' I told him. 'I'm not going to do it any more.'

I gave the same news to Henry when I got back to our clerk's room and he looked unexpectedly despondent. 'I've done my positively last case, Henry,' I told him. 'I shan't ever be putting my head round the door again asking if you've got a spare committal before the Uxbridge Magistrates.'

'It's a tragedy, Mr Rumpole,' my former clerk said, and I must say I was touched. A little later he came up to see me in my room and explained the nature of his anxiety. 'If you leave, Mr Rumpole, we're going to have that Mr Hearthstoke back again. He's going to get your room, sir. Mr Ballard's already keen on the idea. It'll be a disaster for Chambers. And my ten per cent.' His voice sank to a note of doom. 'And Dianne's threatened to hand in her notice.'

'I delivered you from Hearthrug once before, Henry.' I reminded him of the affair of the Massage Parlours.

'You did, Mr Rumpole, and I shall always thank you for it. But he's due here at five o'clock, sir, for an appointment with Mr Ballard. I think they're going to fix up the final details.'

Well, why should I have cared? By tomorrow, after a brief bit of business with Gerald and a word in the ear of my man of affairs at the Caring Bank, I would be well shot of the whole pack of them. And yet, just as a colonial administrator likes to leave his statue in a public park, or a university head might donate a stained-glass window to the Chapel, I felt I might give something to my old Chambers by which I would always be remembered. My gift to the dear old place would be the complete absence of Hearthrug. 'Five o'clock, eh?' I said. 'Courage, Henry! We'll see what we can do!'

Henry left me with every expression of confidence and gratitude, and at five o'clock precisely I happened to be down in our entrance hall when Hearthstoke arrived to squeeze Ballard and re-enter Equity Court.

'Well, Hearthrug,' I greeted him. 'Good win, that. An excellent win!'

'Who won?' He sounded doubtful.

'You did, of course. You were prosecuting. We pleaded guilty and you secured a conviction. Brilliant work! So you're going to have my old room in Chambers.'

'You *are* leaving, aren't you?' He seemed to need reassurance.

'Oh, yes, of course. Off to Lotos land! In fact, I only called in to pack up a few things.' I started up the stairs towards my room, calling to him over my shoulder, 'Your life's going to change too, I imagine. Have you had much experience as a father?'

'A father? No, none at all.'

'Pity. Ah, well, I expect you'll pick it up as you go along. That's the way you've picked up most things.'

I legged it up to the room then and had the satisfaction of knowing that he was in hot pursuit. Once in my sanctum, he closed the door and said, 'Now, Rumpole. Suppose you tell me exactly what you mean?'

'I mean it's clear to all concerned that you've fallen for Mrs Erskine-Brown hook, line and probably sinker. When you move into Chambers she'll be expecting to move into your bachelor pad in Battersea, bringing her children with her. Jolly brave of you to take her on, as well as little Tristan and Isolde.'

'Her children?' he repeated, dazed. The man was clearly in a state of shock.

'I suppose Claude will be round to take the kids off to the *Ring* occasionally. They'll probably come back whistling all the tunes.'

There was a long pause during which Hearthrug considered his position. Finally, he said, 'Perhaps, all things considered, these Chambers might not be *just* what I'm looking for . . .'

'Why don't you slip next door, old darling,' I suggested, 'and tell Bollard exactly that?'

I must now tell you something which is entirely to the credit of Mrs Phillida Erskine-Brown. She was determined, once the case was over, to save the neck of her old friend and one-time mentor, Horace Rumpole, despite the fact that she had only recently been merrily engaged in cutting his throat. She had no idea of my stunning success with the horses, so she took it upon herself to call on the Bull in his room, just as he was changing his jacket and about to set off for Wimbledon to terrorize his immediate family. When she was announced by Shrimpton, the Court Clerk, the learned Judge brushed his eyebrows, shot his cuffs and generally tried vainly to make himself look a little more appetizing.

When Phillida entered, and was left alone in the presence, an extraordinary scene transpired, the details of which our Portia only told me long after this narrative comes to an end. The, no doubt, ogling Judge told her that her conduct of the defence had filled him with admiration, and said, 'I'm afraid I can't say the same for Rumpole. In fact, I shall have to report him for gross professional misconduct.' And the old hypocrite added, 'After such a long career too. It's a tragedy, of course.'

'A tragedy he was interrupted,' Phillida told him. She clearly had the Judge puzzled, so she pressed on. 'I read the second half of that speech, Judge. Rumpole was extremely flattering, but I think the things he said about you were no less than the truth.'

'Flattering?' The Bull couldn't believe his ears.

' "One of the fairest and most compassionate judges ever to have sat in the Old Bailey"; "Combines the wisdom of Solomon with the humanity of Florence Nightingale" – that's only a couple of quotations from the rest of his speech.'

'But . . . but that's not how he started off!'

'Oh, he was describing the sort of mistaken view the jury might have of an Old Bailey Judge. Then he was about to put them right, but of course the case collapsed and he never gave the rest of that marvellous speech!'

'Florence Nightingale, eh? Can you tell me anything else' – the Bull was anxious to know – 'that Rumpole was *about* to say?'

' "With Judge Bullingham *the quality of mercy is not strain'd, / It droppeth as the gentle rain from heaven.*" Rather well put, I thought. Will you still be reporting Rumpole for professional misconduct?'

The Bull was silent then and appeared to reserve judgement. 'I shall have to reconsider the matter,' he said, 'in the light of what you've told me, Mrs Erskine-Brown.' And then he approached her more intimately: 'Phillida, may I ask you one question?'

'Certainly, Judge,' our Portia answered with considerable courage, and the smitten Bull asked, 'Do you prefer the hard or the creamy centres? When it comes to a box of chocolates?'

After this strange and in many ways heroic encounter, Phillida turned up, in due course, at Pommeroy's Wine Bar, and sat at the table in the corner where she had formerly been drinking with Hearthrug. She was there by appointment, but she didn't expect to meet me. I spotted her as soon as I came in, fresh from my encounter with the young man concerned, and determined to celebrate my amazing good fortune in an appropriate manner. I sat down beside her and, if she was disappointed that it was not someone else, she greeted me with moderate hospitality.

'Rumpole, have a choc?' I saw at once that she had a somewhat ornate box on the table in front of her. I was rash enough to take one with a mauve centre.

'Bullingham gave them to me,' she explained.

'The Mad Bull's in love! You're a *femme fatale*, Portia.'

'Don't ask me to explain yet, I'm not sure how it'll turn out,' she warned me. 'But I went to see him entirely in your interests.'

'And I've just been seeing someone entirely in yours. What are you doing here, anyway, alone and palely loitering?'

'I was just waiting for someone.' Phillida was non-committal.

'He's not coming.' I was certain.

'What?'

'Hearthrug's not coming. He's not coming into Chambers, either.' She looked at me, puzzled and not a little hurt. 'Why not?'

'Henry doesn't want him.'

'Rumpole! What've you done?' She suspected I had been up to something.

'Sorry, Portia. I told him you wanted to move into his bachelor pad in Battersea and bring Tristan and Isolde with you. I'm afraid he went deathly pale and decided to cancel his subscription.'

There was a longish silence and I didn't know whether to expect tears, abuse or a quick dash out into the street. I was surprised when at long last, she gave me a curious little half-smile and said, 'The rat!'

'I could have told you that before you started spooning with him all round the Old Bailey,' I assured her and added, 'Of course, I shouldn't have done that.'

'No, you shouldn't. You'd got no right to say any such thing.'

'It was Henry and Dianne I was thinking about.'

'Thank you very much!'

'They don't deserve Hearthrug. None of you deserve him.'

'I was only considering a small adventure . . .' she began to explain herself, a little sadly. But it was no time for regrets. 'Cheer up, Portia,' I told her. 'In all the circumstances, I think this is the moment for me to buy the Dom Perignon. Méthode Champenoise is a thing of the past.'

She agreed and I went over to the bar where Jack Pommeroy was dealing with the arrival of the usual evening crowd. 'A bottle of your best bubbles, Jack.' I placed a lavish order. 'Nothing less than the dear old Dom to meet this occasion.' And whilst he went about fulfilling it, I saw Erskine-Brown come in and look around the room. 'Ah, Claude,' I called to him. 'I'm in the chair. Care for a glass of vintage bubbly?'

'There you are!' he said, stating the obvious I thought. 'I took a telephone message for you in the clerk's room.'

'If it's about a murder tomorrow, I'm not interested.' My murdering days were over.

'No, this was rather a strange-sounding chap. I wouldn't have thought he was completely sober. Said his name was Gerald.'

'Gerald?' I was pleased to hear it. 'Yes, of course. Gerald . . .'

'Said he was calling from London airport.'

'From where?'

'He said would I give his thanks to Mr Rumpole for the excellent tips, and he was just boarding a plane for a warmer climate.'

'Gerald said that?' I have had some experience of human perfidy, but I must say I was shocked and, not to put too fine a point on it, stricken.

'Words to that effect. Oh, then he said he had to go. They were calling his flight.'

What do you do if your hopes, built up so bravely through the testing time of a four-horse accumulator, are dashed to the ground? What do you do if the doors to a golden future are suddenly slammed in your face and you're told to go home quietly? I called for Jack Pommeroy and told him to forget the Dom Perignon and pour out three small glasses of the Château Thames Embankment. Then I looked at Phillida sitting alone, and from her to Erskine-Brown. 'Claude,' I told him, 'I have an idea. I think there's something you should do urgently.'

'What's that, Rumpole?'

'For God's sake, take your wife to the opera!'

During the course of these memories I have stressed my article of faith: never plead guilty. Like all good rules this is, of course, subject to exceptions. For instance, readers will have noticed that having got Dennis Timson off the firearm charges, I had no alternative but to plead to the theft. So it was with my situation before She Who Must Be Obeyed. I knew that she would soon learn of my announced retirement from the Bar. If I wished to avoid prolonged questioning on this subject, no doubt stretching over several months, I had no alternative but to come clean and throw myself on the mercy of the Court. And so, that night, before the domestic gas-fire I gave Hilda a full account of the wager I had placed with Gerald, and of the fat screw's appalling treachery. 'But Rumpole,' she asked, and it was by no means a bad question, 'do you mean to say you've got no record of the transaction?'

'Nothing,' I had to admit. 'Not even a betting slip. I trusted him. So bloody innocent! We look after our clients and we're complete fools about ourselves.'

'You mean' – and I could see that things weren't going to be easy – 'you lost my hundred pounds?'

'I'm afraid it's on its way to a warmer climate. With about three hundred thousand friends.'

'The hundred pounds I spent on the new hearthrug!' She was appalled.

'*That* hundred pounds is still in the account of the Caring Bank, Hilda. Coloured red,' I tried to explain.

'You'll have to go and talk to Mr Truscott about it,' she made the order. 'I don't suppose he'll be inviting you to the Savoy Grill now, Rumpole?'

'No, Hilda. I don't suppose he will.' I got up then to recharge our glasses, and, after a thoughtful sip, Hilda spoke more reasonably.

'I'm not sure,' she told me, 'that I ever wanted to sit with you on a hotel verandah all day, drinking Planter's Punch.'

'Well. Perhaps not.'

'We might have run out of conversation.'

'Yes. I suppose we might.'

She had another sip or two and then, much to my relief, came out with 'So things could be worse.'

'They are,' I had to break it to her.

'What?'

'They are worse, Hilda.'

'What've you done now?' She sighed over the number of offences to be taken into consideration.

'Only promised Detective Inspector Broome that I'd done my last case. Oh, and told the jury exactly what I thought of the Mad Bull. In open Court! I'll probably be reported to the Bar Council. For disciplinary action to be considered.'

'Rumpole!' Of course she was shocked. 'Daddy would be ashamed of you.'

'That's one comfort.'

'What did you say?'

'Your Daddy, Hilda, has already been called to account by the Great Benchers of the Sky. I hope he was able to explain his hopeless ignorance of bloodstains.'

There was a long silence and then She said, 'Rumpole.'

'Yes.'

'What are you going to be doing tomorrow?'

'Tomorrow?'

'I mean' – and Hilda made this clear to me – 'I hope you're not really going to retire or anything. I hope you're not going to be hanging round the flat all day. You will be taking your usual tube. Won't you? At 8.45?'

'To hear is to obey.' I lifted my glass of Pommeroy's Ordinary to the light, squinted at it, and noted its somewhat murky appearance. ' "*Courage!*" he said, and pointed towards the Temple tube station.'

So it came about that at my usual hour next morning I opened the door of our clerk's room. Henry was telephoning, Dianne was brightening up her nails and Uncle Tom was practising chip shots into the waste-paper basket. Nothing had changed and nobody seemed particularly surprised to see me.

'Henry,' I said, when our clerk put down the telephone.

'Yes, Mr Rumpole?'

'Any chance of a small brief going today, perhaps a spot of indecency at the Uxbridge Magistrates' Court?'

Rumpole and the Tap End

There are many reasons why I could never become one of Her Majesty's judges. I am unable to look at my customer in the dock without feeling, 'There but for the Grace of God goes Horace Rumpole.' I should find it almost impossible to order any fellow citizen to be locked up in a Victorian slum with a couple of psychopaths and three chamber pots, and I cannot imagine a worse way of passing your life than having to actually listen to the speeches of the learned friends. It also has to be admitted that no sane Lord Chancellor would ever dream of the appointment of Mr Justice Rumpole. There is another danger inherent in the judicial office: a judge, any judge, is always liable to say, in a moment of boredom or impatience, something downright silly. He is then denounced in the public prints, his resignation is called for, he is stigmatized as malicious or at least mad and his Bench becomes a bed of nails and his ermine a hair shirt. There is, perhaps, no judge more likely to open his mouth and put his foot in it than that, on the whole well-meaning, old darling, Mr Justice Featherstone, once Guthrie Featherstone, QC, MP, a Member of Parliament so uninterested in politics that he joined the Social Democrats and who, during many eventful years of my life, was Head of our Chambers in Equity Court. Now, as a Judge, Guthrie Featherstone had swum somewhat out of our ken; but he hadn't lost his old talent for giving voice to the odd uncalled-for and disastrous phrase. He, I'm sure, will never forget the furore that arose when, in passing sentence in a case of attempted murder in which I was engaged for the defence, his Lordship made an unwise reference to the 'tap end' of a matrimonial bathtub. At least the account which follows may serve as a terrible warning to anyone contemplating a career as a judge.

I have spoken elsewhere, and on frequent occasions, of my patrons the Timsons, that extended family of South London villains for whom, over the years, I have acted as Attorney-General. Some of you may remember Tony Timson, a fairly mild-mannered receiver of stolen video recorders, hi-fi sets and microwave ovens, married to that April Timson who once so offended her husband's male chauvinist prejudices by driving a getaway car at a somewhat unsuccessful bank robbery.* Tony and April lived in a semi on a large housing estate with their offspring, Vincent Timson, now aged eight, who I hoped would grow up in the family business and thus ensure a steady flow of briefs for Rumpole's future. Their house was brightly, not to say garishly, furnished with mock tiger-skin rugs, Italian-tile-style linoleum and wallpaper which simulated oak panelling. (I knew this from a large number of police photographs in various cases.) It was also equipped with almost every labour-saving device which ever dropped off the back of a lorry. On the day when my story starts this desirable home was rent with screams from the bathroom and a stream of soapy water flowing out from under the door. In the screaming, the word 'murderer' was often repeated at a volume which was not only audible to young Vincent, busy pushing a blue-flashing toy police car round the hallway, but to the occupants of the adjoining house and those of the neighbours who were hanging out their washing. Someone, it was not clear who it was at the time, telephoned the local cop shop for assistance.

In a surprisingly short while a real, flashing police car arrived and the front door was flung open by a wet and desperate April Timson, her leopard-skin-style towelling bathrobe clutched about her. As Detective Inspector Brush, an officer who had fought a running battle with the Timson family for years, came up the path to meet her she sobbed out, at the top of her voice, a considerable voice for so petite a redhead, 'Thank God, you've come! He was only trying to bloody murder me.' Tony Timson emerged from the bathroom a few seconds later, water dripping from his ear-lobe-length hair and his gaucho moustache. In spite of the word RAMBO emblazoned across his bathrobe, he was by no means a man of formidable physique. Looking down the stairs, he saw his wife in hysterics and his domestic hearth invaded by the Old Bill. No sooner had he reached the hallway than he was arrested and charged with attempted murder of his wife, the particulars being, that, while

* See 'Rumpole and the Female of the Species' (*The Second Rumpole Omnibus*).

sharing a bath with her preparatory to going to a neighbour's party, he had tried to cause her death by drowning.

In course of time I was happy to accept a brief for the defence of Tony Timson and we had a conference in Brixton Prison where the alleged wife-drowner was being held in custody. I was attended, on that occasion, by Mr Bernard, the Timsons' regular solicitor, and that up-and-coming young radical barrister, Mizz Liz Probert, who had been briefed to take a note and generally assist me in the *cause célèbre*.

'Attempted murderer, Tony Timson?' I opened the proceedings on a somewhat incredulous note. 'Isn't that rather out of your league?'

'April told me,' he began his explanation, 'she was planning on wearing her skintight leatherette trousers with the revealing halterneck satin top. That's what she was planning on wearing, Mr Rumpole!'

'A somewhat tasteless outfit, and not entirely *haute couture*,' I admitted. 'But it hardly entitles you to drown your wife, Tony.'

'We was both invited to a party round her friend Chrissie's. And that was the outfit she was keen on wearing . . .'

'She says you pulled her legs and so she became submerged.' Bernard, like a good solicitor, was reading the evidence.

' "The Brides in the Bath"!' My mind went at once to one of the classic murders of all times. 'The very method! And you hit on it with no legal training. How did you come to be in the same bath, anyway?'

'We always shared, since we was courting.' Tony looked surprised that I had asked. 'Don't all married couples?'

'Speaking for myself and She Who Must Be Obeyed the answer is, thankfully, no. I can't speak for Mr Bernard.'

'Out of the question.' Bernard shook his head sadly. 'My wife has a hip.'

'Sorry, Mr Bernard. I'm really sorry.' Tony Timson was clearly an attempted murderer with a soft heart.

'Quite all right, Mr Timson,' Bernard assured him. 'We're down for a replacement.'

'April likes me to sit up by the taps.' Tony gave us further particulars of the Timson bathing habits. 'So I can rinse off her hair after a shampoo. Anyway, she finds her end that much more comfortable.'

'She makes you sit at the tap end, Tony?' I began to feel for the fellow.

'Oh, I never made no objection,' my client assured me. 'Although you can get your back a bit scalded. And those old taps does dig into you sometimes.'

'So were you on friendly terms when you both entered the water?' My instructing solicitor was quick on the deductions. 'She was all right then. We was both, well, affectionate. Looking forward to the party, like.'

'She didn't object to what you planned on wearing?' I wanted to cover all the possibilities.

'My non-structured silk-style suiting from Toy Boy Limited!' Tony protested. 'How could she object to that, Mr Rumpole? No. She washed her hair as per usual. And I rinsed it off for her. Then she told me who was going to be at the party, like.'

'Mr Peter Molloy,' Bernard reminded me. 'It's in the brief, Mr Rumpole.' Now I make it a rule to postpone reading my brief until the last possible moment so that it's fresh in my mind when I go into Court, so I said, somewhat testily, 'Of course I know that, but I thought I'd like to get the story from the client. Peanuts Molloy! Mizz Probert, we have a defence. Tony Timson's wife was taking him to a party attended by Peanuts Molloy.'

The full implications of this piece of evidence won't be apparent to those who haven't made a close study of my previous handling of the Timson affairs. Suffice it to say the Molloys are to the Timsons as the Montagues were to the Capulets or the Guelphs to the Ghibellines, and their feud goes back to the days when the whole of South London was laid down to pasture, and they were quarrelling about stolen sheep. The latest outbreak of hostilities occurred when certain Molloys, robbing a couple of elderly Timsons as *they* were robbing a bank, almost succeeded in getting Tony's relatives convicted for an offence they had not committed. Peter, better known as 'Peanuts', Molloy was the young hopeful of the clan Molloy and it was small wonder that Tony Timson took great exception to his wife putting on her leatherette trousers for the purpose of meeting the family enemy.

Liz Probert, however, a white-wig at the Bar who knew nothing of such old legal traditions as the Molloy–Timson hostility, said, 'Why should Mrs Timson's meeting Molloy make it all right to drown her?' I have to remind you that Mizz Liz was a pillar of the North Islington Women's Movement.

'It wasn't just that she was meeting him, Mr Rumpole,' Tony explained. 'It was the words she used.'

'What did she say?'

'I'd rather not tell you if you don't mind. It was humiliating to my pride.'

'Oh, for heaven's sake, Tony. Let's hear the worst.' I had never known a Timson behave so coyly.

'She made a comparison like, between me and Peanuts.'

'What comparison?'

Tony looked at Liz and his voice sank to a whisper. 'Ladies present,' he said.

'Tony,' I had to tell him, 'Mizz Liz Probert has not only practised in the Criminal Courts, but in the family division. She is active on behalf of gay and lesbian rights in her native Islington. She marches, quite often, in aid of abortion on demand. She is a regular reader of the woman's page of the *Guardian*. You and I, Tony, need have no secrets from Mizz Probert. Now, what was this comparison your wife made between you and Peanuts Molloy?'

'On the topic of virility. I'm sorry, Miss.'

'That's quite all right.' Liz Probert was unshocked and unamused.

'What we need, I don't know if you would agree, Mr Rumpole,' Mr Bernard suggested, 'is a predominance of *men* on the jury.'

'Underendowed males would condone the attempted murder of a woman, you mean?' The Probert hackles were up.

'Please. Mizz Probert.' I tried to call the meeting to order. 'Let us face this problem in a spirit of detachment. What we need is a sympathetic judge who doesn't want to waste his time on a long case. Have we got a fixed date for this, Mr Bernard?'

'We have, sir. Before the Red Judge.' Mr Bernard meant that Tony Timson was to be tried before the High Court Judge visiting the Old Bailey.

'They're pulling out all the stops.' I was impressed.

'It *is* attempted murder, Mr Rumpole. So we're fixed before Mr Justice Featherstone.'

'Guthrie Featherstone.' I thought about it. 'Our one-time Head of Chambers. Now, I just wonder . . .'

We were in luck. Sir Guthrie Featherstone was in no mood to try a long case, so he summoned me and Counsel for the prosecution to his room before the start of the proceedings. He sat robed but with his wig on the desk in front of him, a tall, elegant figure who almost always wore the slightly hunted expression of a man who's not entirely sure what he's up to – an unfortunate state of mind for a fellow who has to spend his waking hours coming to firm and just decisions. For all his indecision, however, he knew for certain that he didn't want to spend the whole day trying a ticklish attempted murder.

'Is this a long case?' the Judge asked. 'I am bidden to take tea in the neighbourhood of Victoria. Can you fellows guess where?'

'Sorry, Judge. I give up.' Charles Hearthstoke, our serious-minded young prosecutor, seemed in no mood for party games.

'The station buffet?' I hazarded a guess.

'The station buffet!' Guthrie enjoyed the joke. 'Isn't that you all over, Horace? You will have your joke. Not far off, though.' The joke was over and he went on impressively. 'Buck House. Her Majesty has invited me – no, correction – "commanded" me to a Royal Garden Party.'

'God Save The Queen!' I murmured loyally.

'Not only Her Majesty,' Guthrie told us, 'more seriously one's lady wife, would be extremely put out if one didn't parade in grey top-hat order!'

'He's blaming it on his wife!' Liz Probert, who had followed me into the presence, said in a penetrating aside.

'So naturally one would have to be free by lunchtime. Hearthstoke, is this a long case from the prosecution point of view?' The Judge asked.

'It is an extremely serious case, Judge.' Our prosecutor spoke like a man of twice his years. 'Attempted murder. We've put it down for a week.' I have always thought young Charlie Hearthstoke a mega-sized pill ever since he joined our Chambers for a blessedly brief period and tried to get everything run by a computer.

'I'm astonished,' I gave Guthrie a little comfort, 'that my learned friend Mr Hearthrug should think it could possibly last so long.'

'Hearth*stoke*,' young Charlie corrected me.

'Have it your own way. With a bit of common sense we could finish this in half an hour.'

'Thereby saving public time and money.' Hope sprang eternal in the Judge's breast.

'Exactly!' I cheered him up. 'As you know, it is an article of my religion never to plead guilty. But, bearing in mind all the facts in this case, I'm prepared to advise Timson to put his hands up to common assault. He'll agree to be bound over to keep the peace.'

'Common assault?' Hearthstoke was furious. 'Binding over? Hold on a minute. He tried to drown her!'

'Judge.' I put the record straight. 'He was seated at the tap end of the bath. His wife, lying back comfortably in the depths, passed an extremely wounding remark about my client's virility.'

It was then I saw Mr Justice Featherstone looking at me, apparently shaken to the core. 'The *tap end*,' he gasped. 'Did you say he was seated at the *tap end*, Horace?'

'I'm afraid so, Judge.' I confirmed the information sorrowfully.

'This troubles me.' Indeed the Judge looked extremely troubled. 'How does it come about that he was seated at the tap end?'

'His wife insisted on it.' I had to tell him the full horror of the situation.

'This woman insisted that her husband sat with his back squashed up against the taps?' The Judge's voice rose in incredulous outrage.

'She made him sit in that position so he could rinse off her hair.'

'At the *tap end*?' Guthrie still couldn't quite believe it.

'Exactly so.'

'You're sure?'

'There can be no doubt about it.'

'Hearthrug . . . I mean, *stoke*. Is this one of the facts agreed by the prosecution?'

'I can't see that it makes the slightest difference.' The prosecution was not pleased with the course its case was taking.

'You can't see! Horace, was this conduct in any way typical of this woman's attitude to her husband?'

'I regret to say, entirely typical.'

'Rumpole . . .' Liz Probert, appalled by the chauvinist chatter around her, seemed about to burst, and I calmed her with a quiet 'Shut up, Mizz.'

'So you are telling me that this husband deeply resented the position in which he found himself.' Guthrie was spelling out the implications exactly as I had hoped he would.

'What married man wouldn't, Judge?' I asked mournfully.

'And his natural resentment led to a purely domestic dispute?'

'Such as might occur, Judge, in the best bathrooms.'

'And you are content to be bound over to keep the peace?' His Lordship looked at me with awful solemnity.

'Reluctantly, Judge,' I said after a suitable pause for contemplation, 'I would agree to that restriction on my client's liberty.'

'Liberty to drown his wife!' Mizz Probert had to be 'shushed' again.

'Hearth*stoke*.' The Judge spoke with great authority. 'My compliments to those instructing you and in my opinion it would be a gross waste of public funds to continue with this charge of attempted murder. We should be finished by half past eleven.' He looked at his watch with the deep satisfaction of a man who was sure that he would be among those present at the Royal Garden Party, after the ritual visit to Moss Bros to hire the grey topper and all the trimmings. As we left the sanctum, I stood aside to let Mizz Probert out of the door. 'Oh, no, Rumpole, you're a man,' she whispered with her fury barely contained. 'Men always go first, don't they?'

So we all went into Court to polish off *R.* v. *Timson* and to make sure that Her Majesty had the pleasure of Guthrie's presence over the tea and strawberries. I made a token speech in mitigation, something of a formality as I knew that I was pushing at an open door. Whilst I was speaking, I was aware of the fact that the Judge wasn't giving me his full attention. That was reserved for a new young shorthand writer, later to become known to me as a Miss (not, I'm sure in her case, a Mizz) Lorraine Frinton. Lorraine was what I believe used to be known as a 'bit of an eyeful', being young, doe-eyed and clearly surrounded by her own special fragrance. When I sat down, Guthrie thanked me absent-mindedly and reluctantly gave up the careful perusal of Miss Frinton's beauty. He then proceeded to pass sentence on Tony Timson in a number of peculiarly ill-chosen words.

'Timson,' his Lordship began harmlessly enough. 'I have heard about you and your wife's habit of taking a bath together. It is not for this Court to say that communal bathing, in time of peace when it is not in the national interest to save water, is appropriate conduct in married life. *Chacun à son goût*, as a wise Frenchman once said.' Miss Frinton, the shorthand writer, looked hopelessly confused by the words of the wise Frenchman. 'What throws a flood of light on this case,' the Judge went on, 'is that you, Timson, habitually sat at the tap end of the bath. It seems you had a great deal to put up with. And your wife, she, it appears from the evidence, washed her hair in the more placid waters of the other end. I accept that this was a purely domestic dispute. For the common assault to which you have pleaded guilty you will be bound over to keep the peace . . .' And the Judge added the terrible words, '. . . in the sum of fifty pounds.'

So Tony Timson was at liberty, the case was over and a furious Mizz Liz Probert banged out of Court before Guthrie was halfway out of the door. Catching up with her, I rebuked my learned junior. 'It's not in the best traditions of the Bar to slam out before the Judge in any circumstances. When we've just had a famous victory it's quite ridiculous.'

'A famous victory.' She laughed in a cynical fashion. 'For men!'

'Man, woman or child, it doesn't matter who the client is. We did our best and won.'

'Because he was a man! Why shouldn't he sit at the tap end? I've got to do something about it!' She moved away purposefully. I called after her. 'Mizz Probert! Where're you going?'

'To my branch of the women's movement. The protest's got to be organized on a national level. I'm sorry, Rumpole. The time for talking's over.'

And she was gone. I had no idea, then, of the full extent of the tide which was about to overwhelm poor old Guthrie Featherstone, but I had a shrewd suspicion that his Lordship was in serious trouble.

The Featherstones' two children were away at university, and Guthrie and Marigold occupied a flat which Lady Featherstone found handy for Harrods, her favourite shopping centre, and a country cottage near Newbury. Marigold Featherstone was a handsome woman who greatly enjoyed life as a Judge's wife and was full of that strength of character and quickness of decision his Lordship so conspicuously lacked. They went to the Garden Party together with three or four hundred other pillars of the establishment: admirals, captains of industry, hospital matrons and drivers of the Royal Train. Picture them, if you will, safely back home with Marigold kicking off her shoes on the sofa and Guthrie going out to the hall to fetch that afternoon's copy of the *Evening Sentinel*, which had just been delivered. You must, of course, understand that I was not present at the scene or other similar scenes which are necessary to this narrative. I can only do my best to reconstruct it from what I know of subsequent events and what the participants told me afterwards. Any gaps I have been able to fill in are thanks to the talent for fiction which I have acquired during a long career acting for the defence in criminal cases.

'There might just be a picture of us arriving at the Palace.' Guthrie brought back the *Sentinel* and then stood in horror, rooted to the spot by what he saw on the front page.

'Well, then. Bring it in here.' Marigold, no doubt, called from her reclining position.

'Oh, there's absolutely nothing to read in it. The usual nonsense. Nothing of the slightest interest. Well, I think I'll go and have a bath and get changed.' And he attempted to sidle out of the room, holding the newspaper close to his body in a manner which made the contents invisible to his wife.

'Why're you trying to hide that *Evening Sentinel*, Guthrie?'

'Hide it? Of course I'm not trying to hide it. I just thought I'd take it to read in the bath.'

'And make it all soggy? Let me have it, Guthrie.'

'I told you . . .'

'Guthrie. I want to see what's in the paper.' Marigold spoke in an authoritative manner and her husband had no alternative but to hand it over, murmuring the while, 'It's completely inaccurate, of course.'

And so Lady Featherstone came to read, under a large photograph of his Lordship in a full-bottomed wig, the story which was being enjoyed by every member of the legal profession in the Greater London area. CARRY ON DROWNING screamed the banner headline. TAP END JUDGE'S AMAZING DECISION. And then came the full denunciation:

Wives who share baths with their husbands will have to be careful where they sit in the future. Because 29-year-old April Timson of Bexley Heath made her husband Tony sit at the tap end the Judge dismissed a charge of attempted murder against him. 'It seems you had a good deal to put up with,' 55-year-old Mr Justice Featherstone told Timson, a 36-year-old window cleaner. 'This is male chauvinism gone mad,' said a spokesperson of the Islington Women's Organization. 'There will be protests up and down the country and questions asked in Parliament. No woman can sit safely in her bath while this Judge continues on the bench.'

'It's a travesty of what I said, Marigold. You know exactly what these Court reporters are. Head over heels in Guinness after lunch,' Guthrie no doubt told his wife.

'This must have been in the morning. We went to the Palace after lunch.'

'Well, anyway. It's a travesty.'

'What do you mean, Guthrie? Didn't you say all that about the tap end?'

'Well, I may just have mentioned the tap end. Casually. In passing. Horace told me it was part of the evidence.'

'Horace?'

'Rumpole.'

'I suppose he was defending.'

'Well, yes . . .'

'You're clay in the hands of that little fellow, Guthrie. You're a Red Judge and he's only a junior, but he can twist you round his little finger,' I rather hope she told him.

'You think Horace Rumpole led me up the garden?'

'Of course he did! He got his chap off and he encouraged you to say something monumentally stupid about tap ends. Not, I suppose, that you needed much encouragement.'

'This gives an entirely false impression. I'll put it right, Marigold. I promise you. I'll see it's put right.'

'I think you'd better, Guthrie.' The Judge's wife, I knew, was not a woman to mince her words. 'And for heaven's sake try not to put your foot in it again.'

So Guthrie went off to soothe his troubles up to the neck in bathwater and Marigold lay brooding on the sofa until, so she told Hilda later, she was telephoned by the Tom Creevey Diary Column on the *Sentinel* with an inquiry as to which end of the bath she occupied when she and her husband were at their ablutions. Famous couples all over London, she was assured, were being asked the same question. Marigold put down the instrument without supplying any information, merely murmuring to herself, 'Guthrie! What have you done to us now?'

Marigold Featherstone wasn't the only wife appalled by the Judge's indiscretions. As I let myself into our mansion flat in the Gloucester Road, Hilda, as was her wont, called to me from the living room, 'Who's that?'

'*I am thy father's spirit,*' I told her in sepulchral tones.

> '*Doomed for a certain term to walk the night,*
> *And for the day confined to fast in fires,*
> *Till the foul crimes done in my days of nature*
> *Are burnt and purged away.*'

'I suppose you think it's perfectly all right.' She was, I noticed, reading the *Evening Sentinel*.

'What's perfectly all right?'

'Drowning wives!' She said in the unfriendliest of tones. 'Like puppies. I suppose you think that's all perfectly understandable. Well, Rumpole, all I can say is, you'd better not try anything like that with me!'

'Hilda! It's never crossed my mind. Anyway, Tony Timson didn't drown her. He didn't come anywhere near drowning her. It was just a matrimonial tiff in the bathroom.'

'Why should *she* have to sit at the tap end?'

'Why indeed?' I made for the sideboard and a new bottle of Pommeroy's plonk. 'If she had, and if she'd tried to drown him because of it, I'd have defended her with equal skill and success. There you are, you see. Absolutely no prejudice when it comes to accepting a brief.'

'You think men and women are entirely equal?'

'Everyone is equal in the dock.'

'And in the home?'

'Well, yes, Hilda. Of course. Naturally. Although I suppose some are born to command.' I smiled at her in what I hoped was a soothing manner, well designed to unruffle her feathers, and took my glass of claret to my habitual seat by the gas-fire. 'Trust me, Hilda,' I told her. 'I shall always be a staunch defender of Women's Rights.'

'I'm glad to hear that.'

'I'm glad you're glad.'

'That means you can do the weekly shop for us at Safeway.'

'Well, I'd really love that, Hilda,' I said eagerly. 'I should regard that as the most tremendous fun. Unfortunately I have to earn the boring stuff that pays for our weekly shop. I have to be at the service of my masters.'

'Husbands who try to drown their wives?' she asked unpleasantly.

'And vice versa.'

'They have late-night shopping on Thursdays, Rumpole. It won't cut into your work time at all. Only into your drinking time in Pommeroy's Wine Bar. Besides which I shall be far too busy for shopping from now on.'

'Why, Hilda? What on earth are you planning to do?' I asked innocently. And when the answer came I knew the sexual revolution had hit Froxbury mansions at last.

'Someone has to stand up for Women's Rights,' Hilda told me, 'against the likes of you and Guthrie Featherstone. I shall read for the Bar.'

Such was the impact of the decision in *R. v. Timson* on life in the Rumpole home. When Tony Timson was sprung from custody he was not taken lovingly back into the bosom of his family. April took her baths alone and frequently left the house tricked out in her skin-tight, wet-look trousers and the exotic halterneck. When Tony made so bold as to ask where she was going, she told him to mind his own business. Vincent, the young hopeful, also treated his father with scant respect and, when asked where he was off to on his frequent departures from the front door, also told his father to mind his own business.

When she was off on the spree, April Timson, it later transpired, called round to an off-licence in neighbouring Morrison Avenue. There she met the notorious Peanuts Molloy, also dressed in alluring leather, who was stocking up from Ruby, the large black lady who ran the 'offey', with raspberry crush, Champanella, crème de cacao and three-star cognac as his contribution to some party or other. He and April would embrace openly and then go off partying together. On occasion Peanuts would ask her how 'that wally of a husband' was getting on, and express his outrage at the lightness of the sentence inflicted on him. 'Someone ought to give that Tony of yours a bit of justice,' was what he was heard to say.

Peanuts Molloy wasn't alone in feeling that being bound over in the sum of fifty pounds wasn't an adequate punishment for the attempted drowning of a wife. This view was held by most of the newspapers, a large section of the public and all the members of the North Islington Women's Movement (Chair, Mizz Liz Probert). When Guthrie arrived for business at the judges' entrance of the Old Bailey, he was met by a vociferous posse of women, bearing banners with the following legend: WOMEN OF ENGLAND, KEEP YOUR HEADS ABOVE WATER. GET JUSTICE FEATHERSTONE SACKED. As the friendly police officers kept these angry ladies at bay, Guthrie took what comfort he might from the thought that a High Court Judge can only be dismissed by a Bill passed through both Houses of Parliament.

Something, he decided, would have to be done to answer his many critics. So Guthrie called Miss Lorraine Frinton, the doe-eyed shorthand writer, into his room and did his best to correct the record of his ill-considered judgement. Miss Frinton, breathtakingly decorative as ever, sat with her long legs neatly crossed in the Judge's armchair and tried to grasp his intentions with regard to her shorthand note. I reconstruct this conversation thanks to Miss Frinton's later recollection. She was, she admits, very nervous at the time because she thought that the Judge had sent for her because she had, in some way, failed in her duties. 'I've been living in dread of someone pulling me up about my shorthand,' she confessed. 'It's not my strongest suit, quite honestly.'

'Don't worry, Miss Frinton,' Guthrie did his best to reassure her. 'You're in no sort of trouble at all. But you are a shorthand writer, of course you are, and if we could just get to the point when I passed sentence. Could you read it out?'

The beautiful Lorraine looked despairingly at her notebook and spelled out, with great difficulty, 'Mr Hearthstoke has quite wisely . . .'

'A bit further on.'

'Jackie a saw goo . . . a wise Frenchman . . .' Miss Frinton was decoding.

'*Chacun à son goût!*'

'I'm sorry, my Lord. I didn't quite get the name.'

'*Ça ne fait rien.*'

'How are you spelling that?' She was now lost.

'Never mind.' The Judge was at his most patient. 'A little further on, Miss Frinton. Lorraine. I'm sure you and I can come to an agreement. About a full stop.'

After much hard work, his Lordship had his way with Miss Frinton's shorthand note, and Counsel and solicitors engaged in the case were assembled in Court to hear, in the presence of the gentlemen of the Press, his latest version of his unfortunate judgement.

'I have had my attention drawn to the report of the case in *The Times*,' he started with some confidence, 'in which I am quoted as saying to Timson, "It seems you had a great deal to put up with. And your wife, she, it appears from the evidence, washed her hair in the more placid waters" etc. It's the full stop that has been misplaced. I have checked this carefully with the learned shorthand writer and she agrees with me. I see her nodding her head.' He looked down at Lorraine who nodded energetically, and the Judge smiled at her. 'Very well, yes. The sentence in my judgement in fact read, "It seems you had a great deal to put up with, and your wife." Full stop! What I intended to convey, and I should like the press to take note of this, was that both Mr and Mrs Timson had a good deal to put up with. At different ends of the bath, of course. Six of one and half a dozen of the other. I hope that's clear?' It was, as I whispered to Mizz Probert sitting beside me, as clear as mud.

The Judge continued. 'I certainly never said that I regarded being seated at the tap end as legal provocation to attempted murder. I would have said it was one of the facts that the jury might have taken into consideration. It might have thrown some light on this wife's attitude to her husband.'

'What's he trying to do?' *sotto voce* Hearthstoke asked me.

'Trying to get himself out of hot water,' I suggested.

'But the attempted murder charge was dropped,' Guthrie went on.

'He twisted my arm to drop it,' Hearthstoke was muttering.

'And the entire tap end question was really academic,' Guthrie told us, 'as Timson pleaded guilty to common assault. Do you agree, Mr Rumpole?'

'Certainly, my Lord.' I rose in my most servile manner. 'You gave him a very stiff binding over.'

'Have you anything to add, Mr Hearthstoke?'

'No, my Lord.' Hearthstoke couldn't very well say anything else, but when the Judge had left us he warned me that Tony Timson had better watch his step in future as Detective Inspector Brush was quite ready to throw the book at him.

Guthrie Featherstone left Court well pleased with himself and instructed his aged and extremely disloyal clerk Wilfred to send a bunch of flowers, or, even better, a handsome pot plant to Miss Lorraine Frinton in recognition of her loyal services. So Wilfred told me he went off to telephone Interflora and Guthrie passed his day happily trying a perfectly straightforward robbery. On rising he retired to his room for a cup of weak Lapsang and a glance at the *Evening Sentinel*. This glance was enough to show him that he had achieved very little more, by his statement in open Court, than inserting his foot into the mud to an even greater depth.

BATHTUB JUDGE SAYS IT AGAIN screamed the headline. *Putting her husband at the tap end may be a factor to excuse the attempted murder of a wife.* 'Did I say that?' the appalled Guthrie asked old Wilfred who was busy pouring out the tea.

'To the best of my recollection, my Lord. Yes.'

There was no comfort for Guthrie when the telephone rang. It was old Keith from the Chancellor's office saying that the Lord Chancellor, as Head of the Judiciary, would like to see Mr Justice Featherstone at the earliest available opportunity.

'A Bill through the Houses of Parliament.' A stricken Guthrie put down the telephone. 'Would they do it to me, Wilfred?' he asked, but answer came there none.

'You do look, my clerk, in a moved sort, as if you were dismayed.' In fact, Henry, when I encountered him in the clerk's room, seemed distinctly rattled. 'Too right, sir. I am dismayed. I've just had Mrs Rumpole on the telephone.'

'Ah. She Who Must wanted to speak to me?'

'No, Mr Rumpole. She wanted to speak to me. She said I'd be clerking for her in the fullness of time.'

'Henry,' I tried to reassure the man, 'there's no immediate cause for concern.'

'She said as she was reading for the Bar, Mr Rumpole, to make sure women get a bit of justice in the future.'

'Your missus coming into Chambers, Rumpole?' Uncle Tom, our oldest and quite briefless inhabitant, was pursuing his usual hobby of making approach shots to the waste-paper basket with an old putter.

'Don't worry, Uncle Tom.' I sounded as confident as I could. 'Not in the foreseeable future.'

'My motto as a barrister's clerk, sir, is anything for a quiet life,' Henry outlined his philosophy. 'I have to say that my definition of a quiet life does not include clerking for Mrs Hilda Rumpole.'

'Old Sneaky MacFarlane in Crown Office Row had a missus who came into his Chambers.' Uncle Tom was off down Memory Lane. 'She didn't come in to practice, you understand. She came in to watch Sneaky. She used to sit in the corner of his room and knit during all his conferences. It seems she was dead scared he was going to get off with one of his female divorce petitioners.'

'Mrs Rumpole, Henry, has only just written off for a legal course in the Open University. She can't yet tell provocation from self-defence or define manslaughter.' I went off to collect things from my tray and Uncle Tom missed a putt and went on with his story. 'And you know what? In the end Mrs MacFarlane went off with a co-respondent she'd met at one of these conferences. Some awful fellow, apparently, in black and white shoes! Left poor old Sneaky high and dry. So, you see, it doesn't do to have wives in Chambers.'

'Oh, I meant to ask you, Henry. Have you seen my Ackerman on *The Causes of Death*?' One of my best-loved books had gone missing.

'I think Mr Ballard's borrowed it, sir.' And then Henry asked, still anxious, 'How long do they take then, those courses at the Open University?'

'Years, Henry,' I told him. 'It's unlikely to finish during our lifetime.'

When I went up to Ballard's room to look for my beloved Ackerman, the door had been left a little open. Standing in the corridor I could hear the voices of those arch-conspirators, Claude Erskine-Brown and Soapy Sam Ballard, QC. I have to confess that I lingered to catch a little of the dialogue.

'Keith from the Lord Chancellor's office sounded *you* out about Guthrie Featherstone?' Erskine-Brown was asking.

'As the fellow who took over his Chambers. He thought I might have a view.'

'And have you? A view, I mean.'

'I told Keith that Guthrie was a perfectly charming chap, of course.' Soapy Sam was about to damn Guthrie with the faintest of praise.

'Oh, perfectly charming. No doubt about that,' Claude agreed.

'But as a Judge, perhaps, he lacks judgement.'

'Which is a pretty important quality in a Judge,' Claude thought.

'Exactly. And perhaps there is some lack of . . .'

'Gravitas?'

'The very word I used, Claude.'

'There was a bit of lack of gravitas in Chambers, too,' Claude remembered, 'when Guthrie took a shine to a temporary typist . . .'

'So the upshot of my talk with Keith was . . .'

'What was the upshot?'

'I think we may be seeing a vacancy on the High Court Bench.' Ballard passed on the sad news with great satisfaction. 'And old Keith was kind enough to drop a rather interesting hint.'

'Tell me, Sam?'

'He said they might be looking for a replacement from the same stable.'

'Meaning these Chambers in Equity Court?'

'How could it mean anything else?'

'Sam, if you go on the Bench, we should need another silk in Chambers!' Claude was no doubt licking his lips as he considered the possibilities.

'I don't see how they could refuse you.' These two were clearly hand in glove.

'There's no doubt Guthrie'll have to go.' Claude pronounced the death sentence on our absent friend.

'He comes out with such injudicious remarks.' Soapy Sam put in another drop of poison. 'He was just like that at Marlborough.'

'Did you tell old Keith that?' Claude asked and then sat open-mouthed as I burst from my hiding-place with 'I bet you did!'

'Rumpole!' Ballard also looked put out. 'What on earth have you been doing?'

'I've been listening to the Grand Conspiracy.'

'You must admit, Featherstone, J, has made the most tremendous boo-boo.' Claude smiled as though he had never made a boo-boo in his life.

'In the official view,' Soapy Sam told me, 'he's been remarkably stupid.'

'He wasn't stupid.' I briefed myself for Guthrie's defence. 'As a matter of fact he understood the case extremely well. He came to a wise decision. He might have phrased his judgement more elegantly, if he hadn't been to Marlborough. And let me tell you something, Ballard. My wife Hilda is about to start a law course at the Open University. She is a woman, as I know to my cost, of grit and determination. I expect to see her Lord Chief Justice of England before you get your bottom within a mile of the High Court Bench!'

'Of course you're entitled to your opinion.' Ballard looked tolerant. 'And you got your fellow off. All I know for certain is that the Lord Chancellor has summoned Guthrie Featherstone to appear before him.'

The Lord Chancellor of England was a small, fat, untidy man with steel-rimmed spectacles which gave him the schoolboy look which led to his nickname 'The Owl of the Remove'. He was given to fits of teasing when he would laugh aloud at his own jokes and unpredictable bouts of biting sarcasm during which he would stare at his victims with cold hostility. He had been, for many years, the Captain of the House of Lords croquet team, a game in which his ruthless cunning found full scope. He received Guthrie in his large, comfortably furnished room overlooking the Thames at Westminster, where his long wig was waiting on its stand and his gold-embroidered purse and gown were ready for his procession to the woolsack. Two years after this confrontation, I found myself standing with Guthrie at a Christmas party given in our Chambers to members past and present, and he was so far gone in Brut (not to say Brutal) Pommeroy's Méthode Champenoise as to give me the bare bones of this historic encounter. I have fleshed them out from my knowledge of both characters and their peculiar habits of speech.

'Judgeitis, Featherstone,' I hear the Lord Chancellor saying. 'It goes with piles as one of the occupational hazards of the judicial profession. Its symptoms are pomposity and self-regard. It shows itself by unnecessary interruptions during the proceedings or giving utterance to private thoughts far, far better left unspoken.'

'I did correct the press report, Lord Chancellor, with reference to the shorthand writer.' Guthrie tried to sound convincing.

'Oh, I read that.' The Chancellor was unimpressed. 'Far better to have left the thing alone. Never give the newspapers a second chance. That's my advice to you.'

'What's the cure for judgeitis?' Guthrie asked anxiously.

'Banishment to a golf club where the sufferer may bore the other members to death with recollections of his old triumphs on the Western Circuit.'

'You mean, a Bill through two Houses of Parliament?' The Judge stared into the future, dismayed.

'Oh, that's quite unnecessary!' The Chancellor laughed mirthlessly. 'I just get a Judge in this room and say, "Look here, old fellow. You've got it badly. Judgeitis. The press is after your blood and quite frankly you're a profound embarrassment to us all. Go out to Esher, old boy," I say, "and improve your handicap. I'll give it out that you're retiring early for reasons of health." And then I'll make a speech defending the independence of the Judiciary against scurrilous and unjustified attacks by the press.'

Guthrie thought about this for what seemed a silent eternity and then said, 'I'm not awfully keen on golf.'

'Why not take up croquet?' The Chancellor seemed anxious to be helpful. 'It's a top-hole retirement game. The women of England are against you. I hear they've been demonstrating outside the Old Bailey.'

'They were only a few extremists.'

'Featherstone, all women are extremists. You must know that, as a married man.'

'I suppose you're right, Lord Chancellor.' Guthrie now felt his position to be hopeless. 'Retirement! I don't know how Marigold's going to take it.'

The Lord Chancellor still looked like a hanging judge, but he stood up and said in businesslike tones, 'Perhaps it can be postponed in your case. I've talked it over with old Keith.'

'Your right-hand man?' Guthrie felt a faint hope rising.

'Exactly.' The Lord Chancellor seemed to be smiling at some private joke. 'You may have an opportunity some time in the future, in the not-too-distant future, let us hope, to make your peace with the women of England. You may be able to put right what they regard as an injustice to one of their number.'

'You mean, Lord Chancellor, my retirement is off?' Guthrie could scarcely believe it.

'Perhaps adjourned. *Sine die.*'

'Indefinitely?'

'Oh, I'm so glad you keep up with your Latin.' The Chancellor patted Guthrie on the shoulder. It was an order to dismiss. 'So many fellows don't.'

So Guthrie had a reprieve and, in the life of Tony Timson also, dramatic events were taking place. April's friend Chrissie was once married to Shaun Molloy, a well-known safe breaker, but their divorce seemed to have severed her connections with the Molloy clan and Tony Timson had agreed to receive and visit her. It was Chrissie who lived on their estate and had given the party before which April and Tony had struggled in the bath together; but it was at Chrissie's house, it seemed, that Peanuts Molloy was to be a visitor. So Tony's friendly feelings had somewhat abated, and when Chrissie rang the chimes on his front door one afternoon when April was out, he received her with a brusque 'What you want?'

'I thought you ought to know, Tony. It's not right.'

'What's not right?'

'Your April and Peanuts. It's not right.'

'You're one to talk, aren't you, Chrissie? April was going round yours to meet Peanuts at a party.'

'He just keeps on coming to mine. I don't invite him. Got no time for Peanuts, quite honestly. But him and your April. They're going out on dates. It's not right. I thought you ought to know.'

'What you mean, dates?' As I have said, Tony's life had not been a bed of roses since his return home, but now he was more than usually troubled.

'He takes her out partying. They're meeting tonight round the offey in Morrison Avenue. Nine-thirty-time, she told me. Just thought you might like to know, that's all,' the kindly Chrissie added.

So it happened that at 9.30 that night, when Ruby was presiding over an empty off-licence in Morrison Avenue, Tony Timson entered it and stood apparently surveying the tempting bottles on display but really waiting to confront the errant April and Peanuts Molloy. He heard a door bang in some private area behind Ruby's counter and then the strip lights stopped humming and the off-licence was plunged into darkness. It was not a silent darkness, however; it was filled with the sound of footsteps, scuffling and heavy blows.

Not long afterwards a police car with a wailing siren was screaming towards Morrison Avenue; it was wonderful with what rapidity the Old Bill was summoned whenever Tony Timson was in trouble. When Detective Inspector Brush and his sergeant got into the off-licence, their torches illuminated a scene of violence. Two bodies were on the floor. Ruby was lying by the counter, unconscious, and Tony was lying beside some shelves, nearer to the door, with a wound in his forehead. The Sergeant's torch beam showed a heavy cosh lying by his right hand and pound notes scattered around him. 'Can't you leave the women alone, boy?' the Detective Inspector said as Tony Timson slowly opened his eyes.

So another Timson brief came to Rumpole, and Mr Justice Featherstone got a chance to redeem himself in the eyes of the Lord Chancellor and the women of Islington.

Like two knights of old approaching each other for combat, briefs at the ready, helmeted with wigs and armoured with gowns, the young black-haired Sir Hearthrug and the cunning old Sir Horace, with his faithful page Mizz Liz in attendance, met outside Number 1 Court at the Old Bailey and threw down their challenges.

'Nemesis,' said Hearthrug.

'What's that meant to mean?' I asked him.

'Timson's for it now.'

'Let's hope justice will be done,' I said piously.

'Guthrie's not going to make the same mistake twice.'

'Mr Justice Featherstone's a wise and upright Judge,' I told him, 'even if his foot does get into his mouth occasionally.'

'He's a judge with the Lord Chancellor's beady eye upon him, Rumpole.'

'I wasn't aware that this case was going to be decided by the Lord Chancellor.'

'By him and the women of England.' Hearthstoke smiled at Mizz Probert in what I hoped she found a revolting manner. 'Ask your learned junior.'

'Save your breath for Court, Hearthrug. You may need it.' So we moved on, but as we went my learned junior disappointed me by saying, 'I don't think Tony Timson should get away with it again.' 'Happily, that's not for you to decide,' I told her. 'We can leave that to the good sense of the jury.'

However, the jury, when we saw them assembled, were not a particularly cheering lot. For a start, the women outnumbered the men by eight to four and the women in question looked large and severe. I was at once reminded of the mothers' meetings that once gathered round the guillotine and I seemed to hear, as Hearthstoke opened the prosecution case, the ghostly click of knitting needles.

His opening speech was delivered with a good deal of ferocity and he paused now and again to flash a white-toothed smile at Miss Lorraine Frinton, who sat once more, looking puzzled, in front of her shorthand notebook.

'Members of the jury,' Hearthrug intoned with great solemnity. 'Even in these days, when we are constantly sickened by crimes of violence, this is a particularly horrible and distressing event. An attack with this dangerous weapon' – here he picked up the cosh, Exhibit 1, and waved it at the jury – 'upon a weak and defenceless woman.'

'Did you say a *woman*, Mr Hearthstoke?' Up spoke the anxious figure of the Red Judge upon the Bench. I cannot believe that pure chance had selected Guthrie Featherstone to preside over Tony Timson's second trial.

Our Judge clearly meant to redeem himself and appear, from the outset, as the dedicated protector of that sex which is sometimes called the weaker by those who have not the good fortune to be married to She Who Must Be Obeyed.

'I'm afraid so, my Lord,' Hearthstoke said, more in anger than in sorrow.

'This man Timson attacked a *woman*!' Guthrie gave the jury the benefit of his full outrage. I had to put some sort of a stop to this so I rose to say, 'That, my Lord, is something the jury has to decide.'

'Mr Rumpole,' Guthrie told me, 'I am fully aware of that. All I can say about this case is that should the jury convict, I take an extremely serious view of any sort of attack on a woman.'

'If they were bathing it wouldn't matter,' I muttered to Liz as I subsided.

'I didn't hear that, Mr Rumpole.'

'Not a laughing matter, my Lord,' I corrected myself rapidly.

'Certainly not. Please proceed, Mr Heart*stoke*.' And here his Lordship whispered to his clerk Wilfred, 'I'm not having old Rumpole twist me round his little finger in *this* case.'

'Very wise, if I may say so, my Lord,' Wilfred whispered back as he sat beside the Judge, sharpening his pencils.

'Members of the jury,' an encouraged Hearthstoke proceeded. 'Mrs Ruby Churchill, the innocent victim, works in an off-licence near the man Timson's home. Later we shall look at a plan of the premises. The prosecution does not allege that Timson carried out this robbery alone. He no doubt had an accomplice who entered by an open window at the back of the shop and turned out the lights. Then, we say, under cover of darkness, Timson coshed the unfortunate Mrs Churchill, whose evidence you will hear. The accomplice escaped with most of the money from the till. Timson, happily for justice, slipped and struck his head on the corner of the shelves. He was found in a half-stunned condition, with the cosh and some of the money. When arrested by Detective Inspector Brush he said, "You got me this time, then." You may think that a clear admission of guilt.' And now Hearthstoke was into his peroration. 'Too long, members of the jury,' he said, 'have women suffered in our Courts. Too long have men seemed licensed to attack them. Your verdict in this case will be awaited eagerly and hopefully by the women of England.'

I looked at Mizz Liz Probert and I was grieved to note that she was receiving this hypocritical balderdash with starry-eyed attention. During the mercifully short period when the egregious Hearthrug had been a member of our Chambers in Equity Court, I remembered, Mizz Liz had developed an inexplicably soft spot for the fellow. I was pained to see that the spot remained as soft as ever.

Even as we sat in Number 1 Court, the Islington women were on duty in the street outside bearing placards with the legend JUSTICE FOR WOMEN. Claude Erskine-Brown and Soapy Sam Ballard passed these demonstrators and smiled with some satisfaction. 'Guthrie's in the soup again, Ballard,' Claude told his new friend. 'They're taking to the streets!'

Ruby Churchill, large, motherly and clearly anxious to tell the truth, was the sort of witness it's almost impossible to cross-examine effectively. When she had told her story to Hearthstoke, I rose and felt the silent hostility of both Judge and jury.

'Before you saw him in your shop on the night of this attack,' I asked her, 'did you know my client, Mr Timson?'

'I knew him. He lives round the corner.'

'And you knew his wife, April Timson?'

'I know her. Yes.'

'She's been in your shop?'

'Oh, yes, sir.'

'With her husband?'

'Sometimes with him. Sometimes without.'

'Sometimes without? How interesting.'

'Mr Rumpole. Have you many more questions for this unfortunate lady?' Guthrie seemed to have been converted to the view that female witnesses shouldn't be subjected to cross-examination.

'Just a few, my Lord.'

'Please. Mrs Churchill,' his Lordship gushed at Ruby. 'Do take a seat. Make yourself comfortable. I'm sure we all admire the plucky way in which you are giving your evidence. *As a woman.*'

'And as a woman,' I made bold to ask, after Ruby had been offered all the comforts of the witness-box, 'did you know that Tony Timson had been accused of trying to drown his wife in the bath? And that he was tried and bound over?'

'My Lord. How can that possibly be relevant?' Hearthrug arose, considerably narked.

'I was about to ask the same question.' Guthrie sided with the prosecution. 'I have no idea what Mr Rumpole is driving at!'

'Oh, I thought your Lordship might remember the case,' I said casually. 'There was some newspaper comment about it at the time.'

'Was there really?' Guthrie affected ignorance. 'Of course, in a busy life one can't hope to read every little paragraph about one's cases that finds its way into the newspapers.'

'This found its way slap across the front page, my Lord.'

'Did it really? Do you remember that, Mr Hearthstoke?'

'I think I remember some rather ill-informed comment, my Lord.' Hearthstoke was not above buttering up the Bench.

'Ill-informed. Yes. No doubt it was. One has so many cases before one . . .' As Guthrie tried to forget the past, I hastily drew the witness back into the proceedings. 'Perhaps your memory is better than his Lordship's?' I suggested to Ruby. 'You remember the case, don't you, Mrs Churchill?'

'Oh, yes. I remember it.' Ruby had no doubt.

'Mr Hearthstoke. Are you objecting to this?' Guthrie was looking puzzled.

'If Mr Rumpole wishes to place his client's previous convictions before the jury, my Lord, why should I object?' Hearthstoke looked at me complacently, as though I were playing into his hands, and Guthrie whispered to Wilfred, 'Bright chap, this prosecutor.'

'And can you remember what you thought about it at the time?' I went on plugging away at Ruby.

'I thought Mr Timson had got away with murder!'

The jury looked severely at Tony, and Guthrie appeared to think I had kicked a sensational own goal. 'I suppose that was hardly the answer you wanted, Mr Rumpole,' he said.

'On the contrary, my Lord. It was exactly the answer I wanted! And having got away with it then, did it occur to you that someone . . . some avenging angel, perhaps, might wish to frame Tony Timson on this occasion?'

'My lord. That is pure speculation!' Hearthstoke arose, furious, and I agreed with him. 'Of course it is. But it's a speculation I wish to put in the mind of the jury at the earliest possible opportunity.' So I sat down, conscious that I had at least chipped away at the jury's certainty. They knew that I should return to the possibility of Tony having been framed and were prepared to look at the evidence with more caution.

That morning two events of great pith and moment occurred in the case of the Queen against Tony Timson. April went shopping in Morrison

Avenue and saw something which considerably changed her attitude. Peanuts Molloy and her friend Chrissie were coming out of the off-licence with a plastic bag full of assorted bottles. As Peanuts held his car door open for Chrissie they engaged in a passionate and public embrace, unaware that they were doing so in the full view of Mrs April Timson, who uttered the single word 'Bastard!' in the hearing of the young hopeful Vincent who, being on his school holidays, was accompanying his mother. The other important matter was that Guthrie, apparently in a generous mood as he saw a chance of re-establishing his judicial reputation, sent a note to me and Hearthstoke asking if we would be so kind as to join him, and the other judges sitting at the Old Bailey, for luncheon.

Guthrie's invitation came as Hearthstoke was examining Miss Sweating, the schoolmistress-like scientific officer, who was giving evidence as to the bloodstains found about the off-licence on the night of the crime. As this evidence was of some importance I should record that blood of Tony Timson's group was traced on the floor and on the corner of the shelf by which he had fallen. Blood of the same group as that which flowed in Mrs Ruby Churchill's veins was to be found on the floor where she lay and on the cosh by Tony's hand. Talk of blood groups, as you will know, acts on me like the smell of greasepaint to an old actor, or the cry of hounds to John Peel. I was pawing the ground and snuffling a little at the nostrils as I rose to cross-examine.

'Miss Sweating,' I began. 'You say there was blood of Timson's group on the corner of the shelf?'

'There was. Yes.'

'And from that you assumed that he had hit his head against the shelf?'

'That seemed the natural assumption. He had been stunned by hitting his head.'

'Or by someone else hitting his head?'

'But the Detective Inspector told me . . .' the witness began, but I interrupted her with 'Listen to me and don't bother about what the Detective Inspector told you!'

'Mr Rumpole!' That grave protector of the female sex on the Bench looked pained. 'Is that the tone to adopt? The witness is a woman!'

'The witness is a scientific officer, my Lord,' I pointed out, 'who pretends to know something about bloodstains. Looking at the photograph of the stains on the corner of the shelf, Miss Sweating, might not they be splashes of blood which fell when the accused was struck in that part of the room?'

Miss Sweating examined the photograph in question through her formidable horn-rims and we were granted two minutes' silence which I broke into at last with 'Would you favour us with an answer, Miss Sweating? Or do you want to exercise a woman's privilege and not make up your mind?'

'Mr Rumpole!' The newly converted feminist Judge was outraged. But the witness admitted, 'I suppose they might have got there like that. Yes.'

'They are consistent with his having been struck by an assailant. Perhaps with another weapon similar to this cosh?'

'Yes,' Miss Sweating agreed, reluctantly.

'Thank you. *Trip no further, pretty sweeting . . .*' I whispered as I sat down, thereby shocking the shockable Mizz Probert.

'Miss Sweating' – Guthrie tried to undo my good work – 'you have also said that the bloodstains on the shelf are consistent with Timson having slipped when he was running out of the shop and striking his head against it?'

'Oh, yes,' Miss Sweating agreed eagerly. 'They are consistent with that, my Lord.'

'Very well.' His Lordship smiled ingratiatingly at the women of the jury. 'Perhaps the ladies of the jury would like to take a little light luncheon now?' And he added, more brusquely, 'The gentlemen too, of course. Back at five past two, members of the jury.'

When we got out of Court, I saw my learned friend Charles Hearthstoke standing in the corridor in close conversation with the beautiful shorthand writer. He was, I noticed, holding her lightly and unobtrusively by the hand. Mizz Probert, who also noticed this, walked away in considerable disgust.

A large variety of judges sit at the Old Bailey. These include the Old Bailey regulars, permanent fixtures such as the Mad Bull Bullingham and the sepulchral Graves, Judges of the lower echelon who wear black gowns. They also include a Judge called the Common Sergeant, who is neither common nor a sergeant, and the Recorder who wears red and is the senior Old Bailey Judge – a man who has to face, apart from the usual diet of murder, robbery and rape, a daunting number of City dinners. These are joined by the two visiting High Court Judges, the Red Judges of the Queen's Bench, of whom Guthrie was one, unless and until the Lord Chancellor decided to put him permanently out to grass. All these judicial figures trough together at a single long table in a back room of the Bailey. They do it, and the sight comes as something of a shock to the occasional visitor, wearing their wigs. The sight of Judge Bullingham's angry and purple face ingesting stew and surmounted with horsehair is only for the strongest stomachs. They are joined by various City aldermen and officials wearing lace jabots and tailed coats and other guests from the Bar or from the world of business.

Before the serious business of luncheon begins, the company is served sherry, also taken whilst wearing wigs, and I was ensconced in a corner where I could overhear a somewhat strange preliminary conversation between our Judge and Counsel for the prosecution.

'Ah, Hearth*stoke*,' Guthrie greeted him. 'I thought I'd invite both Counsel to break bread with me. Just want to make sure neither of you had anything to object to about the trial.'

'Of course not, Judge!' Hearthstoke was smiling. 'It's been a very pleasant morning. Made even more pleasant by the appearance of the shorthand writer.'

'The . . . ? Oh, yes! Pretty girl, is she? I hadn't noticed,' Guthrie fibbed.

'Hadn't you? Lorraine said you'd been extraordinarily kind to her. She so much appreciated the beautiful pot plant you sent her.'

'Pot plant?' Guthrie looked distinctly guilty, but Hearthstoke pressed on with 'Something rather gorgeous she told me. With pink blooms. Didn't she help you straighten out the shorthand note in the last Timson case?'

'She corrected her mistake,' Guthrie said carefully.

'*Her* mistake, was it?' Hearthstoke was looking at the Judge. 'She said it'd been yours.'

'Perhaps we should all sit down now.' Guthrie was keen to end this embarrassing scene. 'Oh and, Hearthstoke, no need to mention that business of the pot plant around the Bailey. Otherwise they'll all be wanting one.' He gave a singularly unconvincing laugh. 'I can't give pink blooms to everyone, including Rumpole!'

'Of course, Judge.' Hearthstoke was understanding. 'No need to mention it at all *now*.'

'*Now?*'

'Now,' the prosecutor said firmly, 'justice is going to be done to Timson. At last.'

Guthrie seemed thankful to move away and find his place at the table, until he discovered that I had been put next to him. He made the best of it, pushed one of the decanters in my direction and hoped I was quite satisfied with the fairness of the proceedings.

'Are *you* content with the fairness of the proceedings?' I asked him.

'Yes, of course. I'm the Judge, aren't I?'

'Are you sure?'

'What on earth's that meant to mean?'

'Haven't you asked yourself why you, a High Court Judge, a Red Judge, have been given a paltry little robbery with violence?' I refreshed myself with a generous gulp of the City of London's claret.

'I suppose it's the luck of the draw.'

'Luck of the draw, my eye! I detect the subtle hand of old Keith from the Lord Chancellor's office.'

'Keith?' His Lordship looked around him nervously.

'Oh, yes. "Give Guthrie *Timson*," he said. "Give him a chance to redeem himself by potting the fellow and sending him down for ten years. The women of England will give three hearty cheers and Featherstone will be the Lord Chancellor's blue-eyed boy again." Don't fall for it! You can be better than that, if you put your mind to it. Sum up according to the evidence and the hell with the Lord Chancellor's office!'

'Horace! I don't think I've heard anything you've been saying.'

'It's up to you, old darling. Are you a man or a rubber stamp for the Civil Service?'

Guthrie looked round desperately for a new subject of conversation and his eye fell on our prosecutor who was being conspicuously bored by an elderly alderman. 'That young Hearthstoke seems a pretty able sort of fellow,' he said.

'Totally ruthless,' I told him. 'He'd stop at nothing to win a case.'

'Nothing?'

'Absolutely nothing.'

Guthrie took the decanter and started to pour wine into his own glass. His hand was trembling slightly and he was staring at Hearthstoke in a haunted way.

'Horace,' he started confidentially, 'you've been practising at the Old Bailey for a considerable number of years.'

'Almost since the dawn of time.'

'And you can see nothing wrong with a Judge, impressed by the hard work of a Court official, say a shorthand writer, for instance, sending that official some little token of gratitude?'

'What sort of token are you speaking of, Judge?'

'Something like' – he gulped down wine – 'a pot plant.'

'A plant?'

'In a pot. With pink blossoms.'

'Pink blossoms, eh?' I thought it over. 'That sounds quite appropriate.'

'You can see nothing in any way improper in such a gift, Horace?' The Judge was deeply grateful.

'Nothing improper at all. A "Busy Lizzie"?'

'I think her name's Lorraine.'

'Nothing wrong with that.'

'You reassure me, Horace. You comfort me very much.' He took another swig of the claret and looked fearfully at Hearthstoke. Poor old Guthrie Featherstone, he spent most of his judicial life painfully perched between the horns of various dilemmas.

'In the car after we arrested him, driving away from the off-licence, Tony Timson said, "You got me this time, then."' This was the evidence of that hammer of the Timsons, Detective Inspector Brush. When he had given it, Hearthstoke looked hard at the jury to emphasize the point, thanked the officer profusely and I rose to cross-examine.

'Detective Inspector. Do you know a near neighbour of the Timsons named Peter, better known as "Peanuts", Molloy?'

'Mr Peter Molloy is known to the police, yes,' the Inspector answered cautiously.

'He and his brother Greg are leading lights of the Molloy firm? Fairly violent criminals?'

'Yes, my Lord,' Brush told the Judge.

'Have you known both Peanuts and his brother to use coshes like this one in the course of crime?'

'Well. Yes, possibly . . .'

'My Lord, I really must object!' Hearthstoke was on his feet and Guthrie said, 'Mr Rumpole. Your client's own character . . .'

'He is a petty thief, my Lord.' I was quick to put Tony's character before the jury. 'Tape recorders and freezer-packs. No violence in his record, is there, Inspector?'

'Not up to now, my Lord,' Brush agreed reluctantly.

'Very well. Did you think he had been guilty of that attempted murder charge, after he and his wife quarrelled in the bathroom?'

'I thought so, yes.'

'You were called to the scene very quickly when the quarrel began.'

'A neighbour called us.'

'Was that neighbour a member of the Molloy family?'

'Mr Rumpole, I prefer not to answer that question.'

'I won't press it.' I left the jury to speculate. 'But you think he got off lightly at his first trial?' I was reading the note Tony Timson had scribbled in the dock while listening to the evidence as DI Brush answered, 'I thought so, yes.'

'What he actually said in the car was "I suppose you think you got me this time, then?"'

'No.' Brush looked at his notebook. 'He just said, "You got me this time, then."'

'You left out the words "I suppose you think" because you don't want him to get off lightly this time?'

'Now would I do a thing like that, sir?' Brush gave us his most honestly pained expression.

'That, Inspector Brush, is a matter for this jury to decide.' And the jury looked, by now, as though they were prepared to consider all the possibilities.

Lord Justice MacWhitty's wife, it seems, met Marigold Featherstone in Harrods, and told her she was sorry that Guthrie had such a terrible attitude to women. There was one old Judge, apparently, who made his wife walk behind him when he went on circuit, carrying the luggage, and Lady MacWhitty said she felt that poor Marigold was married to just such a tyrant. When we finally discussed the whole history of the Tony Timson case at the Chambers party, Guthrie told me that Marigold had said that she was sick and tired of women coming up to her and feeling sorry for her in Harrods.

'You see,' Guthrie had said to his wife, 'if Timson gets off, the Lord Chancellor and all the women of England will be down on me like a ton of bricks. But the evidence isn't entirely satisfactory. It's just possible he's innocent. It's hard to tell where a fellow's duty lies.'

'Your duty, Guthrie, lies in keeping your nose clean!' Marigold had no doubt about it.

'My nose?'

'Clean. For the sake of your family. And if this Timson has to go inside for a few years, well, I've no doubt he richly deserves it.'

'Nothing but decisions!'

'I really don't know what else you expected when you became a Judge.' Marigold poured herself a drink. Seeking some comfort after a hard day, the Judge went off to soak in a hot bath. In doing so, I believe Lady Featherstone made it clear to him, he was entirely on his own.

Things were no easier in the Rumpole household. I was awakened at some unearthly hour by the wireless booming in the living room and I climbed out of bed to see Hilda, clad in a dressing-gown and hairnet, listening to the device with her pencil and notebook poised whilst it greeted her brightly with 'Good morning, students. This is first-year Criminal Law on the Open University. I am Richard Snellgrove, law teacher at Hollowfield Polytechnic, to help you on this issue . . . Can a wife give evidence against her husband?'

'Good God!' I asked her, 'what time does the Open University open?'

'For many years a wife could not give evidence against her husband,' Snellgrove told us. 'See *R.* v. *Boucher* 1952. Now, since the Police and Criminal Evidence Act 1984, a wife can be called to give such evidence.'

'You see, Rumpole.' Hilda took a note. 'You'd better watch out!' I found and lit the first small cigar of the day and coughed gratefully. Snellgrove continued to teach me law. 'But she can't be compelled to. She has been a competent witness for the defence of her husband since the Criminal Evidence Act 1898. But a judgement in the House of Lords suggests she's not compellable . . .'

'What's that mean, Rumpole?' She asked me.

'Well, we could ask April Timson to give evidence for Tony. But we couldn't make her,' I began to explain, and then, perhaps because I was in a state of shock from being awoken so early, I had an idea of more than usual brilliance. 'April Timson!' I told Hilda, 'She won't know she's not compellable. I don't suppose she tunes into the "Open at Dawn University". Now I wonder . . .'

'What, Rumpole. What do you wonder?'

'Quarter to six.' I looked at the clock on the mantelpiece. 'High time to wake up Bernard.' I went to the phone and started to dial my instructing solicitor's number.

'You see how useful I'll be to you' – Hilda looked extremely pleased with herself – 'when I come to work in your Chambers.'

'Oh, Bernard,' I said to the telephone, 'wake you up, did I? Well, it's time to get moving. The Open University's been open for hours. Look, an idea has just crossed my mind . . .'

'It crossed *my* mind, Rumpole,' Hilda corrected me. 'And I was kind enough to hand it on to you.'

When Mr Bernard called on April Timson an hour later, there was no need for him to go into the nice legal question of whether she was a compellable witness or not. Since she had seen Peanuts and her friend Chrissie come out of the 'offey' she was, she made it clear, ready and willing to come to Court and tell her whole story.

'Mrs April Timson,' I asked Tony's wife when, to the surprise of most people in Court including my client, she entered the witness-box, as a witness for the defence, 'some while ago you had a quarrel with your husband in a bathtub. What was that quarrel about?'

'Peanuts Molloy.'

'About a man called Peter "Peanuts" Molloy. What did you tell your husband about Peanuts?'

'About him as a man, like . . . ?'

'Did you compare the virility of these two gentlemen?'

'Yes, I did.' April was able to cope with this part of the evidence without embarrassment.

409

'And who got the better of the comparison?'

'Peanuts.' Tony, lowering his head, got his first look of sympathy from the jury.

'Was there a scuffle in your bath then?'

'Yes.'

'Mrs April Timson, did your husband ever try to drown you?'

'No. He never.' Her answer caused a buzz in Court. Guthrie stared at her, incredulous.

'Why did you suggest he did?' I asked. 'My Lord. I object. What possible relevance?' Hearthrug tried to interrupt but I and everyone else ignored him. 'Why did you suggest he tried to murder you?' I repeated.

'I was angry with him, I reckon,' April told us calmly, and the prosecutor lost heart and subsided. The Judge, however, pursued the matter with a pained expression. 'Do I understand,' he asked, 'you made an entirely false accusation against your husband?'

'Yes.' April didn't seem to think it an unusual thing to do.

'Don't you realize, madam,' the Judge said, 'the suffering that accusation has brought to innocent people?' 'Such as you, old cock,' I muttered to Mizz Liz.

'What was that, Rumpole?' the Judge asked me. 'Such as the man in the dock, my Lord,' I repeated.

'And other innocent, innocent people.' His Lordship shook his head sadly and made a note.

'After your husband's trial did you continue to see Mr Peanuts Molloy?' I went on with my questions to the uncompellable witness.

'We went out together. Yes.'

'Where did you meet?'

'We met round the offey in Morrison Avenue. Then we went out in his car.'

'Did you meet him at the off-licence on the night this robbery took place?'

'I never.' April was sure of it.

'Your husband says that your neighbour Chrissie came round and told him that you and Peanuts Molloy were going to meet at the off-licence at 9.30 that evening. So he went up there to put a stop to your affair.'

'Well, Chrissie was well in with Peanuts by then, wasn't she?' April smiled cynically. 'I reckon he sent her to tell Tony that.'

'Why do you reckon he sent her?'

Hearthstoke rose again, determined. 'My Lord, I must object,' he said. 'What this witness "reckons" is entirely inadmissible.' When he had finished, I asked the Judge if I might have a word with my learned friend in order to save time. I then moved along our row and whispered to him vehemently, 'One more peep out of you, Hearthrug, and I lay a formal complaint on your conduct!'

'What conduct?' he whispered back.

'Trying to blackmail a learned Judge on the matter of a pot plant sent to a shorthand writer.' I looked across at Lorraine. 'Not in the best traditions of the Bar, that!' I left him thinking hard and went back to my place. After due consideration he said, 'My Lord. On second thoughts, I withdraw my objection.'

Hearthstoke resumed his seat. I smiled at him cheerfully and continued with April's evidence. 'So why do you think Peanuts wanted to get your husband up to the off-licence that evening?'

'Pretty obvious, innit?'

'Explain it to us.'

'So he could put him in the frame. Make it look like Tony done Ruby up, like.'

'So he could put him in the frame. An innocent man!' I looked at the jury. 'Had Peanuts said anything to make you think he might do such a thing?'

'After the first trial.'

'After Mr Timson was bound over?'

'Yes. Peanuts said he reckoned Tony needed a bit of justice, like. He said he was going to see he got put inside. 'Course, Peanuts didn't mind making a bit hisself, out of robbing the offey.'

'One more thing, Mrs Timson. Have you ever seen a weapon like that before?'

I held up the cosh. The usher came and took it to the witness.

'I saw that one. I think I did.'

'Where?'

'In Peanuts's car. That's where he kept it.'

'Did your husband ever own anything like that?'

'What, Tony?' April weighed the cosh in her hand and clearly found the idea ridiculous. 'Not him. He wouldn't have known what to do with it.'

When the evidence was complete and we had made our speeches, Guthrie had to sum up the case of *R. v. Timson* to the jury. As he turned his chair towards them, and they prepared to give him their full attention, a distinguished visitor slipped unobtrusively into the back of the Court. He was none other than old Keith from the Lord Chancellor's office. The Judge must have seen him, but he made no apology for his previous lenient treatment of Tony Timson.

'Members of the jury,' he began. 'You have heard of the false accusation of attempted murder that Mrs Timson made against an innocent man. Can you imagine, members of the jury, what misery that poor man has been made to suffer? Devoted to ladies as he may be, he has been called a heartless "male chauvinist". Gentle and harmless by nature, he has been thought to connive at crimes of violence. Perhaps it was even suggested that he was the sort of fellow who would make his wife carry heavy luggage! He may well have been shunned in the streets, hooted at from the pavements, and the wife he truly loves has perhaps been unwilling to enter a warm, domestic bath with him. And then, consider,' Guthrie went on, 'if the unhappy Timson may not have also been falsely accused in relation to the robbery with violence of his local "offey". Justice must be done, members of the jury. We must do justice even if it means we do nothing else for the rest of our lives but compete in croquet competitions.' The Judge was looking straight at Keith from the Lord Chancellor's office as he said this. I relaxed, lay back and closed my eyes. I knew, after all his troubles, how his Lordship would feel about a man falsely accused, and I had no further worries about the fate of Tony Timson.

When I got home, Hilda was reading the result of the trial in the *Evening Sentinel*. 'I suppose you're cock-a-hoop, Rumpole,' she said.

'Hearthrug routed!' I told her. 'The women of England back on our side and old Keith from the Lord Chancellor's office looking extremely foolish. And a miraculous change came over Guthrie.'

'What?'

'He suddenly found courage. It's something you can't do without, not if you concern yourself with justice.'

'That April Timson!' Hilda looked down at her evening paper. 'Making it all up about being drowned in the bathwater.'

'*When lovely woman stoops to folly*' – I went to the sideboard and poured a celebratory glass of Château Thames Embankment – '*And finds too late that men betray,/ What charm can soothe her melancholy . . .*'

'I'm not going to the Bar to protect people like her, Rumpole.' Hilda announced her decision. 'She's put me to a great deal of trouble. Getting up at a quarter to six every morning for the Open University.'

'*What art can wash her guilt away?* What did you say, Hilda?'

'I'm not going to all that trouble, learning Real Property and Company Law and eating dinners and buying a wig, not for the likes of April Timson.'

'Oh, Hilda! Everyone in Chambers will be extremely disappointed.'

'Well, I'm sorry.' She had clearly made up her mind. 'They'll just have to do without me. I've really got better things to do, Rumpole, than come home cock-a-hoop just because April Timson changes her mind and decides to tell the truth.'

'Of course you have, Hilda.' I drank gratefully. 'What sort of better things?'

'Keeping you in order for one, Rumpole. Seeing you wash-up properly.' And then she spoke with considerable feeling. 'It's disgusting!'

'The washing-up?'

'No. People having baths together.'

'Married people?' I reminded her.

'I don't see that makes it any better. Don't you ever ask me to do that, Rumpole.'

'Never, Hilda. I promise faithfully.' To hear, of course, was to obey.

That night's *Sentinel* contained a leading article which appeared under the encouraging headline BATHTUB JUDGE PROVED RIGHT. *Mrs April Timson*, it read, *has admitted that her husband never tried to drown her and the jury have acquitted Tony Timson on a second trumped-up charge. It took a Judge of Mr Justice Featherstone's perception and experience to see through this woman's inventions and exaggerations and to uphold the law without fear or favour. Now and again the British legal system produces a Judge of exceptional wisdom and integrity who refuses to yield to pressure groups and does justice though the heavens fall. Such a one is Sir Guthrie Featherstone.*

Sir Guthrie told me later that he read these comforting words whilst lying in a warm bath in his flat near Harrods. I have no doubt at all that Lady Featherstone was with him on that occasion, seated at the tap end.

Rumpole and the Bubble Reputation

It is now getting on for half a century since I took to crime, and I can honestly say I haven't regretted a single moment of it.

Crime is about life, death and the liberty of the subject; civil law is entirely concerned with that most tedious of all topics, money. Criminal law requires an expert knowledge of bloodstains, policemen's notebooks and the dark flow of human passion, as well as the argot currently in use round the Elephant and Castle. Civil law calls for a close study of such yawn-producing matters as bills of exchange, negotiable instruments and charter parties. It is true, of course, that the most enthralling murder produces only a small and long-delayed legal aid cheque, sufficient to buy a couple of dinners at some Sunday supplement eaterie for the learned friends who practise daily in the commercial Courts. Give me, however, a sympathetic jury, a blurred thumbprint and a dodgy confession, and you can keep *Mega-Chemicals Ltd* v. *The Sunshine Bank of Florida* with all its fifty days of mammoth refreshers for the well-heeled barristers involved.

There is one drawback, however, to being a criminal hack; the judges and the learned friends are apt to regard you as though you were the proud possessor of a long line of convictions. How many times have I stood up to address the tribunal on such matters as the importance of intent or the presumption of innocence only to be stared at by the old darling on the Bench as though I were sporting a black mask or carrying a large sack labelled SWAG? Often, as I walk through the Temple on my way down to the Bailey, my place of work, I have seen bowler-hatted commercial or revenue men pass by on the other side and heard them mutter, 'There goes old Rumpole. I wonder if he's doing a murder or a rape this morning?' The sad truth of the matter is that civil law is regarded as the Harrods and crime the Tesco of the legal profession.

And of all the varieties of civil action the most elegant, the smartest, the one which attracts the best barristers like bees to the honeypot, is undoubtedly the libel action. Star in a libel case on the civilized stage of the High Court of Justice and fame and fortune will be yours, if you haven't got them already.

It's odd, isn't it? Kill a person or beat him over the head and remove his wallet, and all you'll get is an Old Bailey Judge and an Old Bailey Hack. Cast a well-deserved slur on his moral character, ridicule his nose or belittle his bank balance and you will get a High Court Judge and some of the smoothest silks in the business. I can only remember doing one libel action, and after it I asked my clerk Henry to find me a nice clean assault or an honest break and entering. Exactly why I did so will become clear to you when I have revealed the full and hitherto unpublished details of *Amelia Nettleship* v. *The Daily Beacon and Maurice Machin*. If, after reading what went on in that particular defamation case, you don't agree that crime presents a fellow with a more honourable alternative, I shall have to think seriously about issuing a writ for libel.

You may be fortunate enough never to have read an allegedly 'historical' novel by that much-publicized authoress Miss Amelia Nettleship. Her books contain virginal heroines and gallant and gentlemanly heroes and thus present an extremely misleading account of our rough island story. She is frequently photographed wearing cotton print dresses, with large spectacles on her still pretty nose, dictating to a secretary and a couple of long-suffering cats in a wistaria-clad Tudor cottage somewhere outside Godalming. In the interviews she gives, Miss Nettleship invariably refers to the evils of the permissive society and the consequences of sex before marriage. I have never, speaking for myself, felt the slightest urge to join the permissive society; the only thing which would tempt me to such a course is hearing Amelia Nettleship denounce it.

Why, you may well ask, should I, whose bedtime reading is usually confined to *The Oxford Book of English Verse* (the Quiller-Couch edition), Archbold's *Criminal Law* and Professor Ackerman's *Causes of Death*, become so intimately acquainted with Amelia Nettleship? Alas, she shares my bed, not in person but in book form, propped up on the bosom of She Who Must Be Obeyed, alias my wife Hilda, who insists on reading her far into the night. While engrossed in *Lord Stingo's Fancy*, I distinctly heard her sniff, and asked if she had a cold coming on. 'No, Rumpole,' she told me. 'Touching!'

'Oh, I'm sorry.' I moved further down the bed.

'Don't be silly. The book's touching. Very touching. We all thought Lord Stingo was a bit of a rake but he's turned out quite differently.'

'Sounds a sad disappointment.'

'Nonsense! It's ending happily. He swore he'd never marry, but Lady Sophia has made him swallow his words.'

'And if they were written by Amelia Nettleship I'm sure he found them extremely indigestible. Any chance of turning out the light?'

'Not yet. I've got another three chapters to go.'

'Oh, for God's sake! Can't Lord Stingo get on with it?' As I rolled over, I had no idea that I was soon to become legally involved with the authoress who was robbing me of my sleep.

My story starts in Pommeroy's Wine Bar to which I had hurried for medical treatment (my alcohol content had fallen to a dangerous low) at the end of a day's work. As I sipped my large dose of Château Thames Embankment, I saw my learned friend Erskine-Brown, member of our Chambers at Equity Court, alone and palely loitering. 'What can ail you, Claude?' I asked, and he told me it was his practice.

'Still practising?' I raised an eyebrow. 'I thought you might have got the hang of it by now.'

'I used to do a decent class of work,' he told me sadly. 'I once had a brief in a libel action. You were never in a libel, Rumpole?'

'Who cares about the bubble reputation? Give me a decent murder and a few well-placed bloodstains.'

'Now, guess what I've got coming up?' The man was wan with care.

'Another large claret for me, I sincerely hope.'

'Actual bodily harm and affray in the Kitten-A-Go-Go Club, Soho.' Claude is married to the Portia of our Chambers, the handsome Phillida Erskine-Brown, QC, and they are blessed with issue rejoicing in the names of Tristan and Isolde. He is, you understand, far more at home in the Royal Opera House than in any Soho Striperama. 'Two unsavoury characters in leather jackets were duelling with broken Coca-Cola bottles.'

'Sounds like my line of country,' I told him.

'Exactly! I'm scraping the bottom of your barrel, Rumpole. I mean, you've got a reputation for sordid cases. I'll have to ask you for a few tips.'

'Visit the *locus in quo*' was my expert advice. 'Go to the scene of the crime. Inspect the geography of the place.'

'The geography of the Kitten-A-Go-Go? Do I have to?'

'Of course. Then you can suggest it was too dark to identify anyone, or the witness couldn't see round a pillar, or . . .'

But at that point we were interrupted by an eager, bespectacled fellow of about Erskine-Brown's age who introduced himself as Ted Spratling from the *Daily Beacon*. 'I was just having an argument with my editor over there, Mr Rumpole,' he said. 'You do libel cases, don't you?'

'Good heavens, yes!' I lied with instant enthusiasm, sniffing a brief. 'The law of defamation is mother's milk to me. I cut my teeth on hatred, ridicule and contempt.' As I was speaking, I saw Claude Erskine-Brown eyeing the journalist like a long-lost brother. 'Slimey Spratling!' he hallooed at last.

'Collywobbles Erskine-Brown!' The hack seemed equally amazed. There was no need to tell me that they were at school together.

'Look, would you join my editor for a glass of Bolly?' Spratling invited me.

'What?'

'Bollinger.'

'I'd love to!' Erskine-Brown was visibly cheered.

'Oh, you too, Colly. Come on, then.'

'Golly, Colly!' I said as we crossed the bar towards a table in the corner. 'Bolly!'

So I was introduced to Mr Maurice – known as 'Morry' – Machin, a large silver-haired person with distant traces of a Scots accent, a blue silk suit and a thick gold ring in which a single diamond winked sullenly. He was surrounded with empty Bolly bottles and a masterful-looking woman whom he introduced as Connie Coughlin, the features editor. Morry himself had, I knew, been for many years at the helm of the tabloid *Daily Beacon*, and had blasted many precious reputations with well-aimed scandal stories and reverberating 'revelations'. 'They say you're a fighter, Mr Rumpole, that you're a terrier, sir, after a legal rabbit,' he started, as Ted Spratling performed the deputy editor's duty of pouring the bubbly.

'I do my best. This is my learned friend, Claude Erskine-Brown, who specializes in affray.'

'I'll remember you, sir, if I get into a scrap.' But the editor's real business was with me. 'Mr Rumpole, we are thinking of briefing you. We're in a spot of bother over a libel.'

'Tell him,' Claude muttered to me, 'you can't do libel.'

'I never turn down a brief in a libel action.' I spoke with confidence, although Claude continued to mutter, 'You've never been offered a brief in a libel action.'

'I don't care,' I said, 'for little scraps in Soho. Sordid stuff. Give me a libel action, when a reputation is at stake.'

'You think that's important?' Morry looked at me seriously, so I treated him to a taste of *Othello*. '*Good name in man or woman, dear my lord*' (I was at my most impressive),

> '*Is the immediate jewel of their souls;*
> *Who steals my purse steals trash; 'tis something, nothing.*
> *'Twas mine, 'tis his, and has been slave to thousands;*
> *But he that filches from me my good name*
> *Robs me of that which not enriches him,*
> *And makes me poor indeed.*'

Everyone, except Erskine-Brown, was listening reverently. After I had finished there was a solemn pause. Then Morry clapped three times.

'Is that one of your speeches, Mr Rumpole?'

'Shakespeare's.'

'Ah, yes . . .'

'Your good name, Mr Machin, is something I shall be prepared to defend to the death,' I said.

'Our paper goes in for a certain amount of fearless exposure,' the *Beacon* editor explained.

'The "*Beacon* Beauties".' Erskine-Brown was smiling. 'I catch sight of it occasionally in the clerk's room.'

'Not that sort of exposure, Collywobbles!' Spratling rebuked his old school friend. 'We tell the truth about people in the public eye.'

'Who's bonking who and who pays,' Connie from features explained. 'Our readers love it.'

'I take exception to that, Connie. I really do,' Morry said piously. 'I don't want Mr Rumpole to get the idea that we're running any sort of a cheap scandal-sheet.'

'Scandal-sheet? Perish the thought!' I was working hard for my brief.

'You wouldn't have any hesitation in acting for the *Beacon*, would you?' the editor asked me.

'A barrister is an old taxi plying for hire. That's the fine tradition of our trade,' I explained carefully. 'So it's my sacred duty, Mr Morry Machin, to take on anyone in trouble. However repellent I may happen to find them.'

'Thank you, Mr Rumpole.' Morry was genuinely grateful.

'Think nothing of it.'

'We are dedicated to exposing hypocrisy in our society. Wherever it exists. High or low.' The editor was looking noble. 'So when we find this female pretending to be such a force for purity and parading her morality before the Great British Public . . .'

'Being all for saving your cherry till the honeymoon,' Connie Coughlin translated gruffly.

'Thank you, Connie. Or, as I would put it, denouncing premarital sex,' Morry said.

'She's even against the *normal* stuff!' Spratling was bewildered.

'Whereas her own private life is extremely steamy. We feel it our duty to tell our public. Show Mr Rumpole the article in question, Ted.'

I don't know if they had expected to meet me in Pommeroy's but the top brass of the *Daily Beacon* had a cutting of the alleged libel at the ready. THE PRIVATE LIFE OF AMELIA NETTLESHIP BY BEACON GIRL ON THE SPOT, STELLA JANUARY I read, and then glanced at the story that followed. 'This wouldn't be *the* Amelia Nettleship?' I was beginning to warm to my first libel action. 'The expert bottler of pure historical bilge water?'

'The lady novelist and hypocrite,' Morry told me. 'Of course I've never met the woman.'

'She robs me of my sleep. I know nothing of her morality, but her prose style depraves and corrupts the English language. We shall need a statement from this Stella January.' I got down to business.

'Oh, Stella left us a couple of months ago,' the editor told me.

'And went where?'

'God knows. Overseas, perhaps. You know what these girls are.'

'We've got to find her,' I insisted and then cheered him up with 'We shall fight, Mr Machin – Morry. And we shall conquer! Remember, I never plead guilty.'

'There speaks a man who knows damn all about libel.' Claude Erskine-Brown had a final mutter.

It might be as well if I quoted here the words in Miss Stella January's article which were the subject of legal proceedings. They ran as follows: *Miss Amelia Nettleship is a bit of a puzzle. The girls in her historical novels always keep their legs crossed until they've got a ring on their fingers. But her private life is rather different. Whatever lucky young man leads the 43-year-old Amelia to the altar will inherit a torrid past which makes Mae West sound like Florence Nightingale. Her home, Hollyhock Cottage, near Godalming, has been the scene of one-night stands and longer liaisons so numerous that the neighbours have given up counting. There is considerably more in her jacuzzi than bath salts. Her latest Casanova, so far unnamed, is said to be a married man who's been seen leaving in the wee small hours.* From the style of this piece of prose you may come to the conclusion that Stella January and Amelia Nettleship deserved each other.

One thing you can say for my learned friend Claude Erskine-Brown is that he takes advice. Having been pointed in the direction of the Kitten-A-Go-Go, he set off obediently to find a cul-de-sac off Wardour Street with his instructing solicitor. He wasn't to know, and it was entirely his bad luck, that Connie Coughlin had dreamt up a feature on London's Square Mile of Sin for the *Daily Beacon* and ordered an ace photographer to comb the sinful purlieus between Oxford Street and Shaftesbury Avenue in search of nefarious goings-on.

Erskine-Brown and a Mr Thrower, his sedate solicitor, found the Kitten-A-Go-Go, paid a sinister-looking myrmidon at the door ten quid each by way of membership and descended to a damp and darkened basement where two young ladies were chewing gum and removing their clothes with as much enthusiasm as they might bring to the task of licking envelopes. Claude took a seat in the front row and tried to commit the geography of the place to memory. It must be said, however, that his eyes were fixed on the plumpest of the disrobing performers when a sudden and unexpected flash preserved his face and more of the stripper for the five million readers of the *Daily Beacon* to enjoy with their breakfast. Not being a particularly observant barrister, Claude left the strip joint with no idea of the ill luck that had befallen him.

Whilst Erskine-Brown was thus exploring the underworld, I was closeted in the Chambers of that elegant Old Etonian civil lawyer Robin Peppiatt, QC, who, assisted by his junior, Dick Garsington, represented the proprietor of the *Beacon*. I was entering the lists in the defence of Morry Machin, and our joint solicitor was an anxious little man called Cuxham, who seemed ready to pay almost any amount of someone else's money to be shot of the whole business. Quite early in our meeting, almost as soon, in fact, as Peppiatt had poured Earl Grey into thin china cups and handed round the petits beurres, it became clear that everyone wanted to do a deal with the other side except my good self and my client, the editor.

'We should work as a team,' Peppiatt started. 'Of which, as leading Counsel, I am, I suppose, the Captain.'

'Are we playing cricket, old chap?' I ventured to ask him.

'If we were it would be an extremely expensive game for the *Beacon*.' The QC gave me a tolerant smile. 'The proprietors have contracted to indemnify the editor against any libel damages.'

'I insisted on that when I took the job,' Morry told us with considerable satisfaction.

'Very sensible of your client, no doubt, Rumpole. Now, you may not be used to this type of case as you're one of the criminal boys . . .'

'Oh, I know' – I admitted the charge – 'I'm just a juvenile delinquent.'

'But it's obvious to me that we mustn't attempt to justify these serious charges against Miss Nettleship's honour.' The Captain of the team gave his orders and I made bold to ask, 'Wouldn't that be cricket?'

'If we try to prove she's a sort of amateur tart the jury might bump the damages up to two or three hundred grand,' Peppiatt explained as patiently as he could.

'Or four.' Dick Garsington shook his head sadly. 'Or perhaps half a million.' Mr Cuxham's mind boggled.

'But you've filed a defence alleging that the article's a true bill.' I failed to follow the drift of these faint-hearts.

'That's our bargaining counter.' Peppiatt spoke to me very slowly, as though to a child of limited intelligence.

'Our what?'

'Something to give away. As part of the deal.'

'When we agree terms with the other side we'll abandon all our allegations. Gracefully,' Garsington added.

'We put up our hands?' I contemptuously tipped ash from my small cigar on to Peppiatt's Axminster. Dick Garsington was sent off to get 'an ashtray for Rumpole'.

'Peregrine Landseer's agin us.' Peppiatt seemed to be bringing glad tidings of great joy to all of us. 'I'm lunching with Perry at the Sheridan Club to discuss another matter. I'll just whisper the thought of a quiet little settlement into his ear.'

'Whisper sweet nothings!' I told him. 'I'll not be party to any settlement. I'm determined to defend the good name of my client, Mr Maurice Machin, as a responsible editor.'

'At our expense?' Peppiatt looked displeased.

'If neccessary. Yes! He wouldn't have published that story unless there was some truth in it. Would you?' I asked Morry, assailed by some doubt.

'Certainly not' – my client assured me – 'as a fair and responsible journalist.'

'The trouble is that there's no evidence that Miss Nettleship has done any of these things.' Clearly Mr Cuxham had long since thrown in the towel.

'Then we must find some! Isn't that what solicitors are for?' I asked, but didn't expect an answer. 'I'm quite unable to believe that anyone who writes so badly hasn't got *some* other vices.'

A few days later I entered the clerk's room of our Chambers in Equity Court to see our clerk Henry seated at his desk looking at the centre pages of the *Daily Beacon*, which Dianne, our fearless but somewhat hit-and-miss typist, was showing him. As I approached, Dianne folded the paper, retreated to her desk and began to type furiously. They both straightened their faces and the smiles of astonishment I had noticed when I came in were replaced by looks of legal seriousness. In fact Henry spoke with almost religious awe when he handed me my brief in *Nettleship* v. *The Daily Beacon and anor.* Not only was a highly satisfactory fee marked on the front but refreshers, that is the sum required to keep a barrister on his feet and talking, had been agreed at no less than five hundred pounds a day.

'You *can* make the case last, can't you, Mr Rumpole?' Henry asked with understandable concern.

'Make it last?' I reassured him. 'I can make it stretch on till the trump of doom! We have serious and lengthy allegations, Henry. Allegations that will take days and days, with any luck. For the first time in a long career at the Bar I begin to see . . .'

'See what, Mr Rumpole?'

'A way of providing for my old age.'

The door then opened to admit Claude Erskine-Brown. Dianne and Henry regarded him with solemn pity, as though he'd had a death in his family.

'Here comes the poor old criminal lawyer,' I greeted him. 'Any more problems with your affray, Claude?'

'All under control, Rumpole. Thank you very much. Morning, Dianne. Morning, Henry.' Our clerk and secretary returned his greeting in mournful voices. At that point, Erskine-Brown noticed Dianne's copy of the *Beacon*, wondered who the 'Beauty' of that day might be and picked it up before she could stop him.

'What've you got there? The *Beacon*! A fine crusading paper. Tells the truth without fear or favour.' My refreshers had put me in a remarkably good mood. 'Are you feeling quite well, Claude?'

Erskine-Brown was holding the paper in trembling hands and had gone extremely pale. He looked at me with accusing eyes and managed to say in strangled tones, '*You* told me to go there!'

'For God's sake, Claude! Told you to go where?'

'The *locus in quo*!'

I took the *Beacon* from him and saw the cause of his immediate concern. The *locus in quo* was the Kitten-A-Go-Go, and the blown-up snap on the centre page showed Claude closely inspecting a young lady who was waving her underclothes triumphantly over her head. At that moment, Henry's telephone rang and he announced that Soapy Sam

Ballard, our puritanical Head of Chambers, founder member of the Lawyers As Christians Society (L.A.C.) and the Savonarola of Equity Court, wished to see Mr Erskine-Brown in his room without delay. Claude left us with the air of a man climbing up into the dock to receive a stiff but inevitable sentence.

I wasn't, of course, present in the Head of Chambers' room where Claude was hauled up. It was not until months later, when he had recovered a certain calm, that he was able to tell me how the embarrassing meeting went and I reconstruct the occasion for the purpose of this narrative.

'You wanted to see me, Ballard?' Claude started to babble. 'You're looking well. In wonderful form. I don't remember when I've seen you looking so fit.' At that early stage he tried to make his escape from the room. 'Well, nice to chat. I've got a summons, across the road.'

'Just a minute!' Ballard called him back. 'I don't read the *Daily Beacon*.'

'Oh, don't you? Very wise,' Claude congratulated him. 'Neither do I. Terrible rag. Half-clad beauties on page four and no law reports. So they tell me. Absolutely no reason to bother with the thing!'

'But, coming out of the Temple tube station, Mr Justice Fishwick pushed this in my face.' Soapy Sam lifted the fatal newspaper from his desk. 'It seems he's just remarried and his new wife takes in the *Daily Beacon*.'

'How odd!'

'What's odd?'

'A Judge's wife. Reading the *Beacon*.'

'Hugh Fishwick married his cook,' Ballard told him in solemn tones.

'Really? I didn't know. Well, that explains it. But I don't see why he should push it in your face, Ballard.'

'Because he thought I ought to see it.'

'Nothing in that rag that could be of the slightest interest to you, surely?'

'Something is.'

'What?'

'You.'

Ballard held out the paper to Erskine-Brown, who approached it gingerly and took a quick look.

'Oh, really? Good heavens! Is that me?'

'Unless you have a twin brother masquerading as yourself. You feature in an article on London's Square Mile of Sin.'

'It's all a complete misunderstanding!' Claude assured our leader.

'I'm glad to hear it.'

'I can explain everything.'

'I hope so.'

'You see, I got into this affray.'

'You got into what?' Ballard saw even more cause for concern.

'This fight' – Claude wasn't improving his case – 'in the Kitten-A-Go-Go.'

'Perhaps I ought to warn you, Erskine-Brown.' Ballard was being judicial. 'You needn't answer incriminating questions.'

'No, *I* didn't get into a fight.' Claude was clearly rattled. 'Good heavens, no. I'm doing a case, about a fight. An affray. With Coca-Cola bottles. And Rumpole advised me to go to this club.'

'Horace Rumpole is an habitué of this house of ill-repute? At *his* age?' Ballard didn't seem to be in the least surprised to hear it.

'No, not at all. But he said I ought to take a view. Of the scene of the crime. This wretched scandal-sheet puts the whole matter in the wrong light. Entirely.'

There was a long and not entirely friendly pause before Ballard proceeded to judgement. 'If that is so, Erskine-Brown,' he said, 'and I make no further comment while the matter is *sub judice*, you will no doubt be suing the *Daily Beacon* for libel?'

'You think I should?' Claude began to count the cost of such an action.

'It is quite clearly your duty. To protect your own reputation and the reputation of this Chambers.'

'Wouldn't it be rather expensive?' I can imagine Claude gulping, but Ballard was merciless.

'What is money,' he said, 'compared to the hitherto unsullied name of number 3, Equity Court?'

Claude's next move was to seek out the friend of his boyhood, 'Slimey' Spratling, whom he finally found jogging across Hyde Park. When he told the *Beacon* deputy editor that he had been advised to issue a writ, the man didn't even stop and Erskine-Brown had to trot along beside him. 'Good news!' Spratling said. 'My editor seems to enjoy libel actions. Glad you liked your pic.'

'Of course I didn't like it. It'll ruin my career.'

'Nonsense, Collywobbles.' Spratling was cheerful. 'You'll get briefed by all the clubs. You'll be the strippers' QC.'

'However did they get my name?' Claude wondered.

'Oh, I recognized you at once,' Slimey assured him. 'Bit of luck, wasn't it?' Then he ran on, leaving Claude outraged. They had, after all, been to Winchester together.

When I told the helpless Cuxham that the purpose of solicitors was to gather evidence, I did so without much hope of my words stinging him into any form of activity. If evidence against Miss Nettleship were needed, I would have to look elsewhere, so I rang up that great source of knowledge, 'Fig' Newton, and invited him for a drink at Pommeroy's.

Ferdinand Isaac Gerald, known to his many admirers as 'Fig' Newton, is undoubtedly the best in the somewhat unreliable band of professional private eyes. I know that Fig is now knocking seventy; that, with his filthy old mackintosh and collapsing hat, he looks like a scarecrow after a bad night; that his lantern jaw, watery eye and the frequently appearing drip on the end of the nose don't make him an immediately attractive figure. Fig may look like a scarecrow but he's a very bloodhound after a clue.

'I'm doing civil work now, Fig,' I told him when we met in Pommeroy's. 'Just got a big brief in a libel action which should provide a bit of comfort for my old age. But my instructing solicitor is someone we would describe, in legal terms, as a bit of a wally. I'd be obliged if you'd do his job for him and send him the bill when we win.'

'What is it that I am required to do, Mr Rumpole?' the great detective asked patiently.

'Keep your eye on a lady.'

'I usually am, Mr Rumpole. Keeping my eye on one lady or another.'

'This one's a novelist. A certain Miss Amelia Nettleship. Do you know her works?'

'Can't say I do, sir.' Fig had once confessed to a secret passion for Jane Austen. 'Are you on to a winner?'

'With a bit of help from you, Fig. Only one drawback here, as in most cases.'

'What's that, sir?'

'The client.' Looking across the bar I had seen the little group from the *Beacon* round the Bollinger. Having business with the editor, I left Fig Newton to his work and crossed the room. Sitting myself beside my client I refused champagne and told him that I wanted him to do something about my learned friend, Claude Erskine-Brown.

'You mean the barrister who goes to funny places in the afternoon? What're you asking me to do, Mr Rumpole?'

'Apologize, of course. Print the facts. Claude Erskine-Brown was in the Kitten-A-Go-Go purely in pursuit of his legal business.'

'I love it!' Morry's smile was wider than ever. 'There speaks the great defender. You'd put up any story, wouldn't you, however improbable, to get your client off.'

'It happens to be true.'

'So far as we are concerned' – Morry smiled at me patiently – 'we printed a pic of a gentleman in a pinstriped suit examining the goods on display. No reason to apologize for that, is there, Connie? What's your view, Ted?'

'No reason at all, Morry.' Connie supported him and Spratling agreed.

'So you're going to do nothing about it?' I asked with some anger.

'Nothing we *can* do.'

'Mr Machin.' I examined the man with distaste. 'I told you it was a legal rule that a British barrister is duty-bound to take on any client however repellent.'

'I remember you saying something of the sort.'

'You are stretching my duty to the furthest limits of human endurance.'

'Never mind, Mr Rumpole. I'm sure you'll uphold the best traditions of the Bar!'

When Morry said that I left him. However, as I was wandering away from Pommeroy's towards the Temple station, Gloucester Road, home and beauty, a somewhat breathless Ted Spratling caught up with me and asked me to do my best for Morry. 'He's going through a tough time.' I didn't think the man was entirely displeased by the news he had to impart. 'The proprietor's going to sack him.'

'Because of this case?'

'Because the circulation's dropping. Tits and bums are going out of fashion. The wives don't like it.'

'Who'll be the next editor?'

'Well, I'm the deputy now . . .' He did his best to sound modest.

'I see. Look' – I decided to enlist an ally – 'would you help me with the case? In strict confidence, I want some sort of a lead to this Stella January. Can you find how her article came in? Get hold of the original. It might have an address. Some sort of clue . . .'

'I'll have a try, Mr Rumpole. Anything I can do to help old Morry.' Never had I heard a man speak with such deep insincerity.

The weather turned nasty, but, in spite of heavy rain, Fig Newton kept close observation for several nights on Hollyhock Cottage, home of Amelia Nettleship, without any particular result. One morning I entered our Chambers early and on my way to my room I heard a curious buzzing sound, as though an angry bee were trapped in the lavatory. Pulling open the door, I detected Erskine-Brown plying a cordless electric razor.

'Claude,' I said, 'you're shaving!'

'Wonderful to see the workings of a keen legal mind.' The man sounded somewhat bitter.

'I'm sorry about all this. But I'm doing my best to help you.'

'Oh, please!' He held up a defensive hand. 'Don't try and do anything else to help me. "Visit the scene of the crime," you said. "Inspect the *locus in quo!*" So where has your kind assistance landed me? My name's mud. Ballard's as good as threatened to kick me out of Chambers. I've got to spend my life's savings on a speculative libel action. And my marriage is on the rocks. Wonderful what you can do, Rumpole, with a few words of advice. Your clients must be everlastingly grateful.'

'Your marriage, on the rocks, did you say?'

'Oh, yes. Philly was frightfully reasonable about it. As far as she was concerned, she said, she didn't care what I did in the afternoons. But we'd better live apart for a while, for the sake of the children. She didn't want Tristan and Isolde to associate with a father dedicated to the exploitation of women.'

'Oh, Portia!' I felt for the fellow. 'What's happened to the quality of mercy?'

'So, thank you very much, Rumpole. I'm enormously grateful. The next time you've got a few helpful tips to hand out, for God's sake keep them to yourself!'

He switched on the razor again. I looked at it and made an instant deduction. 'You've been sleeping in Chambers. You want to watch that, Claude. Bollard nearly got rid of me for a similar offence.'*

'Where do you expect me to go? Phillida's having the locks changed in Islington.'

'Have you no friends?'

'Philly and I have reached the end of the line. I don't exactly want to advertise the fact among my immediate circle. I seem to remember, Rumpole, when you fell out with Hilda you planted yourself on us!' As he said this I scented danger and tried to avoid what I knew was coming.

'Oh. Now. Erskine-Brown. Claude. I was enormously grateful for your hospitality on that occasion.'

'Quite an easy run in on the Underground, is it, from Gloucester Road?' He spoke in a meaningful way.

'Of course. My door is always open. I'd be delighted to put you up, just until this mess is straightened out. But . . .'

'The least you could do, I should have thought, Rumpole.'

'It's not a sacrifice I could ask, old darling, even of my dearest friend. I couldn't ask you to shoulder the burden of daily life with She Who Must Be Obeyed. Now I'm sure you can find a very comfortable little hotel, somewhere cheap and cosy, around the British Museum. I promise you, life is by no means a picnic, in the Gloucester Road.'

Well, that was enough, I thought, to dissuade the most determined visitor from seeking hospitality under the Rumpole roof. I went about my daily business and, when my work was done, I thought I should share some of the good fortune brought with my brief in the libel action with She Who Must Be Obeyed. I lashed out on two bottles of Pommeroy's bubbly, some of the least exhausted flowers to be found outside the tube station and even, such was my reckless mood, lavender water for Hilda.

'All the fruits of the earth,' I told her. 'Or, let's say, the fruits of the first cheque in *Nettleship* v. *The Beacon*, paid in advance. The first of many, if we can spin out the proceedings.'

* See 'Rumpole and the Old, Old Story' (*The Second Rumpole Omnibus*).

'You're doing that awful case!' She didn't sound approving.

'That awful case will bring us in five hundred smackers a day in refreshers.'

'Helping that squalid newspaper insult Amelia Nettleship.' She looked at me with contempt.

'A barrister's duty, Hilda, is to take on all comers. However squalid.'

'Nonsense!'

'What?'

'Nonsense. You're only using that as an excuse.'

'Am I?'

'Of course you are. You're doing it because you're jealous of Amelia Nettleship!'

'Oh, I don't think so,' I protested mildly. 'My life has been full of longings, but I've never had the slightest desire to become a lady novelist.'

'You're jealous of her because she's got high principles.' Hilda was sure of it. 'You haven't got high principles, have you, Rumpole?'

'I told you. I will accept any client, however repulsive.'

'That's not a principle, that's just a way of making money from the most terrible people. Like the editor of the *Daily Beacon*. My mind is quite made up, Rumpole. I shall not use a single drop of that corrupt lavender water.'

It was then that I heard a sound from the hallway which made my heart sink. An all-too-familiar voice was singing '*La donna e mobile*' in a light tenor. Then the door opened to admit Erskine-Brown wearing my dressing-gown and very little else. 'Claude telephoned and told me all his troubles.' Hilda looked at the man with sickening sympathy. 'Of course I invited him to stay.'

'You're wearing my dressing-gown!' I put the charge to him at once.

'I had to pack in a hurry.' He looked calmly at the sideboard. 'Thoughtful of you to get in champagne to welcome me, Rumpole.'

'Was the bath all right, Claude?' Hilda sounded deeply concerned.

'Absolutely delightful, thank you, Hilda.'

'What a relief! That geyser can be quite temperamental.'

'Which is your chair, Horace?' Claude had the courtesy to ask.

'I usually sit by the gas-fire. Why?'

'Oh, do sit there, Claude,' Hilda urged him and he gracefully agreed to pinch my seat. 'We mustn't let you get cold, must we. After your bath.'

So they sat together by the gas-fire and I was allowed to open champagne for both of them. As I listened to the rain outside the window my spirits, I had to admit, had sunk to the lowest of ebbs. And around five o'clock the following morning, Fig Newton, the rain falling from the brim of his hat and the drop falling off his nose, stood watching Hollyhock Cottage. He saw someone – he was too far away to make an identification – come out of the front door and get into a parked car. Then he saw the figure of a woman in a nightdress, no doubt Amelia Nettleship, standing in the lit doorway waving goodbye. The headlights of the car were switched on and it drove away.

When the visitor had gone, and the front door was shut, Fig moved nearer to the cottage. He looked down at the muddy track on which the car had been parked and saw something white. He stooped to pick it up, folded it carefully and put it in his pocket.

On the day that *Nettleship* v. *The Beacon* began its sensational course, I breakfasted with Claude in the kitchen of our so-called 'mansion' flat in the Gloucester Road. I say breakfasted, but Hilda told me that bacon and eggs were off as our self-invited guest preferred a substance, apparently made up of sawdust and bird droppings, which he called muesli. I was a little exhausted, having been kept awake by the amplified sound of grand opera from the spare bedroom, but Claude explained that he always found that a little Wagner settled him down for the night. He then asked for some of the goat's milk that Hilda had got in for him specially. As I coated a bit of toast with Oxford marmalade, the man only had to ask for organic honey to have it instantly supplied by She Who Seemed Anxious to Oblige.

'And what the hell,' I took the liberty of asking, 'is organic honey?'

'The bees only sip from flowers grown without chemical fertilizers,' Claude explained patiently.

'How does the bee know?'

'What?'

'I suppose the other bees tell it. "Don't sip from that, old chap. It's been grown with chemical fertilizers." '

So, ill-fed and feeling like a cuckoo in my own nest, I set off to the Royal Courts of Justice, in the Strand, that imposing turreted château which is the Ritz Hotel of the legal profession, the place where a gentleman is remunerated to the tune of five hundred smackers a day. It is also the place where gentlemen prefer an amicable settlement to the brutal business of fighting their cases.

I finally pitched up, wigged and robed, in front of the Court which would provide the battleground for our libel action. I saw the combatants, Morry Machin and the fair Nettleship, standing a considerable distance apart. Peregrine Landseer, QC, Counsel for the plaintiff, and Robin Peppiatt, QC, for the proprietor of the *Beacon*, were meeting on the central ground for a peace conference, attended by assorted juniors and instructing solicitors.

'After all the publicity, my lady couldn't take less than fifty thousand.' Landseer, Chairman of the Bar Council and on the brink of becoming a judge, was nevertheless driving as hard a bargain as any second-hand car dealer.

'Forty and a full and grovelling apology.' And Peppiatt added the bonus. 'We could wrap it up and lunch together at the Sheridan.'

'It's steak-and-kidney pud day at the Sheridan,' Dick Garsington remembered wistfully.

'Forty-five.' Landseer was not so easily tempted. 'And that's my last word on the subject.'

'Oh, all right,' Peppiatt conceded. 'Forty-five and a full apology. You happy with that, Mr Cuxham?'

'Well, sir. If you advise it.' Cuxham clearly had no stomach for the fight.

'We'll chat to the editor. I'm sure we're all going to agree' – Peppiatt gave me a meaningful look – 'in the end.'

While Landseer went off to sell the deal to his client, Peppiatt approached my man with 'You only have to join in the apology, Mr Machin, and the *Beacon* will pay the costs and the forty-five grand.'

'*Who steals my purse steals trash*,' I quoted thoughtfully. '*But he that filches from me my good name* . . . You're asking my client to sign a statement admitting he printed lies.'

'Oh, for heaven's sake, Rumpole!' Peppiatt was impatient. 'They gave up quoting that in libel actions fifty years ago.'

'Mr Rumpole's right.' Morry nodded wisely. 'My good name – I looked up the quotation – it's the immediate jewel of my soul.'

'Steady on, old darling,' I murmured. 'Let's not go *too* far.' At which moment Peregrine Landseer returned from a somewhat heated discussion with his client to say that there was no shifting her and she was determined to fight for every penny she could get.

'But Perry . . .' Robin Peppiatt lamented, 'the case is going to take two weeks!' At five hundred smackers a day I could only thank God for the stubbornness of Amelia Nettleship.

So we went into Court to fight the case before a jury and Mr Justice Teasdale, a small, highly opinionated and bumptious little person who is unmarried, lives in Surbiton with a Persian cat and was once an unsuccessful Tory candidate for Weston-super-Mare North. It takes a good deal of talent for a Tory to lose Weston-super-Mare North. Worst of all, he turned out to be a devoted fan of the works of Miss Amelia Nettleship.

'Members of the jury,' Landseer said in opening the plaintiff's case, 'Miss Nettleship is the authoress of a number of historical works.'

'Rattling good yarns, Members of the jury,' Mr Justice Teasdale chirped up.

'I beg your Lordship's pardon.' Landseer looked startled.

'I said "rattling good yarns", Mr Peregrine Landseer. The sort your wife might pick up without the slightest embarrassment. Unlike so much of the distasteful material one finds between hard covers today.'

'My Lord.' I rose to protest with what courtesy I could muster.

'Yes, Mr Rumbold?'

'Rum*pole*, my Lord.'

'I'm so sorry.' The Judge didn't look in the least apologetic. 'I understand you are something of a stranger to these Courts.'

'Would it not be better to allow the jury to come to their own conclusions about Miss Amelia Nettleship?' I suggested, ignoring the Teasdale manners.

'Well. Yes. Of course. I quite agree.' The Judge looked serious and then cheered up. 'And when they do they'll find she can put together a rattling good yarn.'

There was a sycophantic murmur of laughter from the jury, and all I could do was subside and look balefully at the Judge. I felt a pang of nostalgia for the Old Bailey and the wild stampede of the mad Judge Bullingham.

As Peregrine Landseer bored on, telling the jury what terrible harm the *Beacon* had done to his client's hitherto unblemished reputation, Ted Spratling, the deputy editor, leant forward in the seat behind me and whispered in my ear. 'About that Stella January article,' he said. 'I bought a drink for the systems manager. The copy's still in the system. One rather odd thing.'

'Tell me . . .'

'The logon – that's the identification of the word processor. It came from the editor's office.'

'You mean it was written there?'

'No one writes things any more.'

'Of course not. How stupid of me.'

'It looks as if it had been put in from his word processor.'

'That is extremely interesting.'

'If Mr Rum*pole* has quite finished his conversation!' Peregrine Landseer was rebuking me for chattering during his opening speech.

I rose to apologize as humbly as I could. 'My Lord, I can assure my learned friend I was listening to every word of his speech. It's such a rattling good yarn.'

So the morning wore on, being mainly occupied by Landseer's opening. The luncheon adjournment saw me pacing the marble corridors of the Royal Courts of Justice with that great source of information, Fig Newton. He gave me a lengthy account of his observation on Hollyhock Cottage, and when he finally got to the departure of Miss Nettleship's nocturnal visitor, I asked impatiently, 'You got the car number?'

'Alas. No. Visibility was poor and weather conditions appalling.' The sleuth's evidence was here interrupted by a fit of sneezing.

'Oh, Fig!' I was, I confess, disappointed. 'And you didn't see the driver?'

'Alas. No, again.' Fig sneezed apologetically. 'However, when Miss Nettleship had closed the door and extinguished the lights, presumably in order to return to bed, I proceeded to the track in front of the house where the vehicle had been standing. There I retrieved an article which I thought might just possibly have been dropped by the driver in getting in or out of the vehicle.'

'For God's sake, show me!'

The detective gave me his treasure trove, which I stuffed into a pocket just as the usher came out of Court to tell me that the Judge was back from lunch, Miss Nettleship was entering the witness-box and the world of libel awaited my attention.

If ever I saw a composed and confident witness, that witness was Amelia Nettleship. Her hair was perfectly done, her black suit was perfectly discreet, her white blouse shone, as did her spectacles. Her features, delicately cut as an intaglio, were attractive, but her beauty was by no means louche or abundant. So spotless did she seem that she might well have preserved her virginity until what must have been, in spite of appearances to the contrary, middle age. When she had finished her evidence-in-chief the Judge thanked her and urged her to go on writing her 'rattling good yarns'. Peppiatt then rose to his feet to ask her a few questions designed to show that her books were still selling in spite of the *Beacon* article. This she denied, saying that sales had dropped off. The thankless task of attacking the fair name of Amelia was left to Rumpole.

'Miss Nettleship,' I started off with my guns blazing, 'are you a truthful woman?'

'I try to be.' She smiled at his Lordship, who nodded encouragement.

'And you call yourself an historical novelist?'

'I try to write books which uphold certain standards of morality.'

'Forget the morality for a moment. Let's concentrate on the history.'

'Very well.'

One of the hardest tasks in preparing for my first libel action was reading through the works of Amelia Nettleship. Now I had to quote from Hilda's favourite. 'May I read you a short passage from an alleged historical novel of yours entitled *Lord Stingo's Fancy*?' I asked as I picked up the book.

'Ah, yes.' The Judge looked as though he were about to enjoy a treat. 'Isn't that the one which ends happily?'

'Happily, all Miss Nettleship's books end, my Lord,' I told him. 'Eventually.' There was a little laughter in Court, and I heard Landseer whisper to his junior, 'This criminal chap's going to bump up the damages enormously.'

Meanwhile I started quoting from *Lord Stingo's Fancy*. ' "Sophia had first set eyes on Lord Stingo when she was a dewy eighteen-year-old and he had clattered up to her father's castle, exhausted from the Battle of Nazeby," ' I read. ' "Now at the ball to triumphantly celebrate the gorgeous, enthroning coronation of the Merry Monarch King Charles II they were to meet again. Sophia was now in her twenties but, in ways too numerous to completely describe, still an unspoilt girl at heart." You call that an *historical* novel?'

'Certainly,' the witness answered unashamed.

'Haven't you forgotten something?' I put it to her.

'I don't think so. What?'

'Oliver Cromwell.'

'I really don't know what you mean.'

'Clearly, if this Sophia . . . this girl . . . How do you describe her?'

' "Dewy", Mr Rumpole.' The Judge repeated the word with relish.

'Ah, yes. "Dewy". I'm grateful to your Lordship. I had forgotten the full horror of the passage. If this dew-bespattered Sophia had been eighteen at the time of the Battle of Naseby in the reign of Charles I, she would have been thirty-three in the year of Charles II's coronation. Oliver Cromwell came in between.'

'I am an artist, Mr Rumpole.' Miss Nettleship smiled at my pettifogging objections.

'What kind of an artist?' I ventured to ask.

'I think Miss Nettleship means an artist in words,' was how the Judge explained it.

'Are you, Miss Nettleship?' I asked. 'Then you must have noticed that the short passage I have read to the jury contains two split infinitives and a tautology.'

'A what, Mr Rumpole?' The Judge looked displeased.

'Using two words that mean the same thing, as in "the enthroning coronation". My Lord, t–a–u . . .' I tried to be helpful.

'I can *spell*, Mr Rumpole.' Teasdale was now testy.

'Then your Lordship has the advantage of the witness. I notice she spells Naseby with a "z".'

'My Lord. I hesitate to interrupt.' At least I was doing well enough to bring Landseer languidly to his feet. 'Perhaps this sort of cross-examination is common enough in the criminal courts, but I cannot see how it can possibly be relevant in an action for libel.'

'Neither can I, Mr Landseer, I must confess.' Of course the Judge agreed.

I did my best to put him right. 'These questions, my Lord, go to the heart of this lady's credibility.' I turned to give the witness my full attention. 'I have to suggest, Miss Nettleship, that as an historical novelist you are a complete fake.'

'My Lord. I have made my point.' Landseer sat down then, looking well pleased, and immediately whispered to his junior, 'We'll let him go on with that line and they'll give us four hundred thousand.'

'You have no respect for history and very little for the English language.' I continued to chip away at the spotless novelist.

'I try to tell a story, Mr Rumpole.'

'And your evidence to this Court has been, to use my Lord's vivid expression, "a rattling good yarn"?' Teasdale looked displeased at my question.

'I have sworn to tell the truth.'

'Remember that. Now let us see how much of this article is correct.' I picked up Stella January's offending contribution. 'You do live at Hollyhock Cottage, near Godalming, in the county of Surrey?'

'That is so.'

'You have a jacuzzi?'

'She has *what*, Mr Rumpole?' I had entered a world unknown to a Judge addicted to cold showers.

'A sort of bath, my Lord, with a whirlpool attached.'

'I installed one in my converted barn,' Miss Nettleship admitted. 'I find it relaxes me, after a long day's work.'

'You don't twiddle round in there with a close personal friend occasionally?'

'That's worth another ten thousand to us,' Landseer told his junior, growing happier by the minute. In fact the jury members were looking at me with some disapproval.

'Certainly not. I do not believe in sex before marriage.'

'And have no experience of it?'

'I was engaged once, Mr Rumpole.'

'Just once?'

'Oh, yes. My fiancé was killed in an air crash ten years ago. I think about him every day, and every day I'm thankful we didn't—' she looked down modestly – 'do anything before we were married. We were tempted, I'm afraid, the night before he died. But we resisted the temptation.'

'Some people would say that's a very moving story,' Judge Teasdale told the jury after a reverent hush.

'Others might say it's the story of *Sally on the Somme*, only there the fiancé was killed in the war.' I picked up another example of the Nettleship *œuvre*.

'That, Mr Rumpole,' Amelia looked pained, 'is a book that's particularly close to my heart. At least I don't do anything my heroines wouldn't do.'

'He's getting worse all the time,' Robin Peppiatt, the *Beacon* barrister, whispered despairingly to his junior, Dick Garsington, who came back with 'The damages are going to hit the roof!'

'Miss Nettleship, may I come to the last matter raised in the article?'

'I'm sure the jury will be grateful that you're reaching the end, Mr Rumpole,' the Judge couldn't resist saying, so I smiled charmingly and told him that I should finish a great deal sooner if I were allowed to proceed without further interruption. Then I began to read Stella January's words aloud to the witness. ' "Her latest Casanova, so far unnamed, is said to be a married man who's been seen leaving in the wee small hours." '

'I read that,' Miss Nettleship remembered.

'You had company last night, didn't you? Until what I suppose might be revoltingly referred to as "the wee small hours"?'

'What are you suggesting?'

'That someone was with you. And when he left at about 5.30 in the morning you stood in your nightdress waving goodbye and blowing kisses. Who was it, Miss Nettleship?'

'That is an absolutely uncalled-for suggestion.'

'You called for it when you issued a writ for libel.'

'Do I have to answer?' She turned to the Judge for help. He gave her his most encouraging smile and said that it might save time in the end if she were to answer Mr Rumpole's question.

'That is absolutely untrue!' For the first time Amelia's look of serenity vanished and I got, from the witness-box, a cold stare of hatred. 'Absolutely untrue.' The Judge made a grateful note of her answer.

'Thank you, Miss Nettleship. I think we might continue with this tomorrow morning, if you have any further questions, Mr Rumpole?'

'I have indeed, my Lord.' Of course I had more questions and by the morning I hoped also to have some evidence to back them up.

I was in no hurry to return to the alleged 'mansion' flat that night. I rightly suspected that our self-invited guest, Claude Erskine-Brown, would be playing his way through *Die Meistersinger* and giving Hilda a synopsis of the plot as it unfolded. As I reach the last of a man's Seven Ages I am more than ever persuaded that life is too short for Wagner, a man who was never in a hurry when it came to composing an opera. I paid a solitary visit to Pommeroy's well-known watering-hole after Court in the hope of finding the representatives of the *Beacon*; but the only one I found was Connie Coughlin, the features editor, moodily surveying a large gin and tonic. 'No champagne tonight?' I asked as I wandered over to her table, glass in hand.

'I don't think we've got much to celebrate.'

'I wanted to ask you' – I took a seat beside the redoubtable Connie – 'about Miss Stella January. Our girl on the spot. Bright, attractive kind of reporter, was she?'

'I don't know,' Connie confessed.

'But surely you're the features editor?'

'I never met her.' She said it with the resentment of a woman whose editor had been interfering with her page.

'Any idea how old she was, for instance?'

'Oh, young, I should think.' It was the voice of middle age speaking. 'Morry said she was young. Just starting in the business.'

'And I was going to ask you . . .'

'You're very inquisitive.'

'It's my trade.' I downed what was left of my claret. '. . . About the love life of Mr Morry Machin.'

'Good God. Whose side are you on, Mr Rumpole?'

'At the moment, on the side of the truth. Did Morry have some sort of romantic interest in Miss Stella January?'

'Short-lived, I'd say.' Connie clearly had no pity for the girl if she'd been enjoyed and then sacked.

'He's married?'

'Oh, two or three times.' It occurred to me that at some time, during one or other of these marriages, Morry and La Coughlin might have been more than fellow hacks on the *Beacon*. 'Now he seems to have got some sort of steady girlfriend.' She said it with some resentment.

'You know her?'

'Not at all. He keeps her under wraps.'

I looked at her for a moment. A woman, I thought, with a lonely evening in an empty flat before her. Then I thanked her for her help and stood up.

'Who are you going to grill next?' she asked me over the rim of her gin and tonic.

'As a matter of fact,' I told her, 'I've got a date with Miss Stella January.'

Quarter of an hour later I was walking across the huge floor, filled with desks, telephones and word processors, where the *Beacon* was produced, towards the glass-walled office in the corner, where Morry sat with his deputy Ted Spratling, seeing that all the scandal that was fit to print, and a good deal of it that wasn't, got safely between the covers of the *Beacon*. I arrived at his office, pulled open the door and was greeted by Morry, in his shirtsleeves, his feet up on the desk. 'Working late, Mr Rumpole? I hope you can do better for us tomorrow,' he greeted me with amused disapproval.

'I hope so too. I'm looking for Miss Stella January.'

'I told you, she's not here any more. I think she went overseas.'

'I think she's here,' I assured him. He was silent for a moment and then he looked at his deputy. 'Ted, perhaps you'd better leave me to have a word with my learned Counsel.'

'I'll be on the back bench.' Spratling left for the desk on the floor which the editors occupied.

When he had gone, Morry looked up at me and said quietly, 'Now then, Mr Rumpole, sir. How can I help you?'

'Stella certainly wasn't a young woman, was she?' I was sure about that.

'She was only with us a short time. But she was young, yes,' he said vaguely.

'A quotation from her article that Amelia Nettleship "makes Mae West sound like Florence Nightingale". No young woman today's going to have heard of Mae West. Mae West's as remote in history as Messa-lina and Helen of Troy. That article, I would hazard a guess, was written by a man well into his middle age.'

'Who?'

'You.'

There was another long silence and the editor did his best to smile. 'Have you been drinking at all this evening?'

I took a seat then on the edge of his desk and lit a small cigar. 'Of course I've been drinking *at all*. You don't imagine I have these brilliant flashes of deduction when I'm perfectly sober, do you?'

'Then hadn't you better go home to bed?'

'So you wrote the article. No argument about that. It's been found in the system with your word processor number on it. Careless, Mr Machin. You clearly have very little talent for crime. The puzzling thing is, why you should attack Miss Nettleship when she's such a good friend of yours.'

'Good friend?' He did his best to laugh. 'I told you. I've never even met the woman.'

'It was a lie, like the rest of this pantomime lawsuit. Last night you were with her until past five in the morning. And she said goodbye to you with every sign of affection.'

'What makes you say that?'

'Were you in a hurry? Anyway, this was dropped by the side of your car.' Then I pulled out the present Fig Newton had given me outside Court that day and put it on the desk.

'Anyone can buy the *Beacon*.' Morry glanced at the mud-stained exhibit.

'Not everyone gets the first edition, the one that fell on the editor's desk at ten o'clock that evening. I would say that's a bit of a rarity around Godalming.'

'Is that all?'

'No. You were watched.'

'Who by?'

'Someone I asked to find out the truth about Miss Nettleship. Now he's turned up the truth about both of you.'

Morry got up then and walked to the door which Ted Spratling had left half open. He shut it carefully and then turned to me. 'I went down to ask her to drop the case.'

'To use a legal expression, pull the other one, it's got bells on it.'

'I don't know what you're suggesting.'

And then, as he stood looking at me, I moved round and sat in the editor's chair. 'Let me enlighten you.' I was as patient as I could manage. 'I'm suggesting a conspiracy to pervert the course of justice.'

'What's that mean?'

'I told you I'm an old taxi, waiting on the rank, but I'm not prepared to be the getaway driver for a criminal conspiracy.'

'You haven't said anything? To anyone?' He looked older and very frightened.

'Not yet.'

'And you won't.' He tried to sound confident. 'You're my lawyer.'

'Not any longer, Mr Machin. I don't belong to you any more. I'm an ordinary citizen, about to report an attempted crime.' It was then I reached for the telephone. 'I don't think there's any limit on the sentence for conspiracy.'

'What do you mean, "conspiracy"?'

'You're getting sacked by the *Beacon*; perhaps your handshake is a bit less than golden. Sales are down on historical virgins. So your steady girlfriend and you get together to make half a tax-free million.'

'I wish I knew how.' He was doing his best to smile.

'Perfectly simple. You turn yourself into Stella January, the unknown girl reporter, for half an hour and libelled Amelia. She sues the paper and collects. Then you both sail into the sunset and share the proceeds. There's one thing I shan't forgive you for.'

'What's that?'

'The plan called for an Old Bailey Hack, a stranger to the civilized world of libel who wouldn't settle, an old warhorse who'd attack La Nettleship and inflame the damages. So you used me, Mr Morry Machin!'

'I thought you'd be accustomed to that.' He stood over me, suddenly looking older. 'Anyway, they told me in Pommeroy's that you never prosecute.'

'No, I don't, do I? But on this occasion, I must say, I'm sorely tempted.'

I thought about it and finally pushed away the telephone. 'Since it's a libel action I'll offer you terms of settlement.'

'What sort of terms?'

'The fair Amelia to drop her case. You pay the costs, including the fees of Fig Newton, who's caught a bad cold in the course of these proceedings. Oh, and in the matter of my learned friend, Claude Erskine-Brown . . .'

'What's he got to do with it?'

'. . . Print a full and grovelling apology on the front page of the *Beacon*. And get them to pay him a substantial sum by way of damages. And that's my last word on the subject.' I stood up then and moved to the door.

'What's it going to cost me?' was all he could think of saying.

'I have no idea, but I know what it's going to cost me. Two weeks at five hundred a day. A provision for my old age.' I opened the glass door and let in the hum and clatter which were the birth pangs of the *Daily Beacon*. 'Goodnight, Stella,' I said to Mr Morry Machin. And then I left him.

So it came about that next morning's *Beacon* printed a grovelling apology to 'the distinguished barrister Mr Claude Erskine-Brown' which accepted that he went to the Kitten-A-Go-Go Club purely in the interests of legal research and announced that my learned friend's hurt feelings would be soothed by the application of substantial, and tax-free, damages. As a consequence of this, Mrs Phillida Erskine-Brown rang Chambers, spoke words of forgiveness and love to her husband, and he arranged, in his new-found wealth, to take her to dinner at Le Gavroche. The cuckoo flew from our nest, Hilda and I were left alone in the Gloucester Road, and we never found out how *Die Meistersinger* ended.

In Court my one and only libel action ended in a sudden outburst of peace and goodwill, much to the frustration of Mr Justice Teasdale, who had clearly been preparing a summing-up which would encourage the jury to make Miss Nettleship rich beyond the dreams of avarice. All the allegations against her were dropped; she had no doubt been persuaded by her lover to ask for no damages at all and the *Beacon*'s editor accepted the bill for costs with extremely bad grace. This old legal taxi moved off to ply for hire elsewhere, glad to be shot of Mr Morry Machin. 'Is there a little bit of burglary around, Henry?' I asked our clerk, as I have recorded. 'Couldn't you get me a nice little gentle robbery? Something which shows human nature in a better light than civil law?'

'Good heavens!' Hilda exclaimed as we lay reading in the matrimonial bed in Froxbury mansions. I noticed that there had been a change in her reading matter and she was already well into *On the Make* by Suzy Hutchins. 'This girl's about to go to Paris with a man old enough to be her father.'

'That must happen quite often.'

'But it seems he *is* her father.'

'Well, at least you've gone off the works of Amelia Nettleship.'

'The way she dropped that libel action. The woman's no better than she should be.'

'Which of us is? Any chance of turning out the light?' I asked She Who Must Be Obeyed, but she was too engrossed in the doings of her delinquent heroine to reply.

Rumpole and Portia

This is a story of family life, of parents and children, and, like many such stories, it began with a quarrel. There was I, ensconced one evening in a quiet corner of Pommeroy's Wine Bar consuming a lonely glass of Château Thames Embankment at the end of a day's labours, when the voices of a couple in dispute came drifting over from the other side of one of Jack Pommeroy's high-backed pews which give such an ecclesiastical air to his distinguished legal watering-hole. The voices I heard were well known to me, being those of my learned friend, Claude Erskine-Brown, and of his spouse, Mrs Phillida Erskine-Brown, née Trant, the Portia of our Chambers, whom I befriended and advised when she was a white-wig, and who, no doubt taking advantage of that advice, rose to take silk and become a Queen's Counsel when Claude was denied that honour, and thus had his nose put seriously out of joint. The union of Claude and Phillida has been blessed with a girl and a boy named, because of Claude's almost masochistic addiction to the lengthier operas of Richard Wagner (and an opera isn't by Richard Wagner if it's not lengthy), Tristan and Isolde. It was the subject of young Tristan which was causing dissension between his parents that evening.

'Tristan was still in bed at quarter to eight this morning,' Claude was complaining. 'He won't be able to do that when he goes away to Bogstead.'

'Please, Claude' – Phillida sounded terminally bored – 'don't go on about it.'

'You know when I was at Bogstead' – no Englishman can possibly resist talking about his boarding school – 'we used to be woken up at half past six for early class, and we had to break the ice in the dormy washbasins.'

'You have told me that, Claude, quite often.'

446

'We had to run three times round Tug's Patch before early church on saints' days.'

'Did you enjoy that?'

'Of course not! I absolutely hated it.' Claude was looking back, apparently on golden memories.

'Why do you imagine Tristan would enjoy it then?'

'You don't *enjoy* Bogstead,' Claude was pointing out patiently. 'You're not meant to enjoy it. But if I hadn't gone there I wouldn't have got into Winchester and if I hadn't got into Winchester I'd never have been to New College. And I'll tell you something, Philly. If I hadn't been to Bogstead, Winchester and New College, I'd never be what I am.'

'Which might be just as well.' Our Portia sounded cynical.

'Whatever do you mean by that?' Claude was nettled. I strained my ears to listen; things were obviously getting nasty.

'It might be just as well if you weren't the man you are,' Claude's wife told him. 'If you hadn't been at Bogstead you might not make such a terrible fuss about losing that gross indecency today. I mean, the way you carried on about that, you must still be in the fourth form at Boggers. I notice you don't talk about sending Isolde to that dump.'

'Bogstead is not a dump,' Claude said proudly. 'And you may not have noticed this, Philly, but Isolde is a girl. They don't *have* girls there.'

'Oh, I see. It's a boy's world, is it?'

'I didn't say that.'

'Poor old Isolde. She's going to miss all the fun of breaking the ice at 6.30 in the morning and running three times round Tug's Patch on saints' days. Poor deprived child. She might even grow up to be a Queen's Counsel.'

'Come on, Philly. Isn't that a bit . . . ?'

'A bit what?' I had taught Phillida to be dead sharp on her cross-examination.

'Well, not quite the thing to say. Of course I'm terrifically glad you've been made a QC. I think you've done jolly well.'

'For a woman!' A short, somewhat bitter laugh from Mrs Erskine-Brown emphasized her point.

'But it's just not "the thing" to crow about it.' Erskine-Brown spoke with the full moral authority of his prep school and Winchester.

'Sorry, Claude! I don't know what "the thing" is. Such a pity I never went to Boggers. Anyway, I don't see the point of having children if you're going to send them away to boarding school.'

At that point, and much to my regret, the somewhat grey and tedious barrister named Hoskins of our Chambers, a man weighed down with the responsibility of four daughters, sat down at my table in order to complain about the extortionate price of coffee in our clerk's room, and I lost the rest of the Erskine-Brown family dispute. However, I have given you enough of it to show the nature of their disagreement and Phillida's reluctance to part with her young hopeful. These were matters which were to assume great importance in the defence of Stanley Culp on a charge of illicit arms dealing, for Stanley was a father who would have found our Portia's views entirely sympathetic.

In most other respects, the home life of the Culps and the Erskine-Browns was as different as chalk and cheese. Stanley Culp was a plump, remorselessly cheerful, disorganized dealer in second-hand furniture – bits of junk and dubious antiques – in a jumbled shop near Notting Hill Gate. Unlike the Erskine-Browns, the Culps were a one-parent family, for Stanley was in sole charge of his son, Matthew, a scholarly, bespectacled little boy of about Tristan's age. Some three and a half years before, Mrs Culp, so Stanley informed me when we met in Brixton Prison, had told her husband that he had 'nothing romantic in his nature whatever'. 'So she took off with the manager of Tesco, twenty years older than me if he was a day. Can you understand that, Mr Rumpole?'

I have long given up trying to understand the inscrutable ways of women in love, but I did come to understand Stanley Culp's attachment to his son. My son Nicky and I enjoyed a similar rapport when we used to walk in the park together and I would tell him the Sherlock Holmes stories in the days before he took up the mysterious study of sociology and went to teach in Florida. It was for young Matthew's sake, Stanley Culp told me, that he preferred to work at home in his antique business. 'We are good companions, Mr Rumpole. And I have to be there when he comes home from school. I don't approve of these latchkey children, left alone to do their homework until Mum and Dad come back from the office.'

The events which drew me and Stanley Culp together took place early one morning, not long before I heard the Erskine-Browns arguing in Pommeroy's. Young Matthew, a better cook and housekeeper than his father, was making the breakfast in the kitchen upstairs whilst Stanley was engaged in some business with an early caller in the shop below. Matthew put bread in the antique electric toaster, heard a car door slam, and then looked out of the window. What he saw was an unmarked car which in fact contained three officers of the Special Branch in plain clothes. A fourth man, wearing slightly tinted gold-rimmed glasses, who will have some importance in this account, was walking away from the car and paused to look up at the shop. Then the toast popped up and Matthew transferred it to a tarnished 'Georgian' rack and went to the top of the staircase which led down to the shop to call his father up for breakfast.

From his viewpoint at the top of the stairs Matthew saw the familiar jumble of piled tables, chairs and other furniture, and he saw Stanley talking to a thick-set, ginger-haired man who was carrying a briefcase. Matthew said, 'Breakfast, Dad!', at which moment the shop door was kicked open and two of the men from the car, Superintendent Rodney and Detective Inspector Blake, were among the junk and informing Stanley that they were officers of the Special Branch who had come to arrest him. As they said this, the thick-set, ginger-haired man, whose name turned out to be MacRobert, made a bolt for the back door and was out in the untidy patch of walled garden behind the building. He was there pursued by a third officer from the car, Detective Sergeant Trump, and shot dead in what Trump took to be the act of pulling out a gun. MacRobert, it transpired at the trial, was an important figure in a Protestant paramilitary group dedicated to open warfare in Northern Ireland.

Stanley was removed in the car and a subsequent search revealed, in a large storeroom behind his shop, a number of packing cases filled with repeating rifles of a forbidden category. Matthew didn't go to school that day, but a woman police constable and a social worker arrived for him and he was taken into the care of the local council. His fate was that which Phillida feared for young Tristan; he was sent away from home to be brought up by strangers.

Unhappiness, you see, was getting in everywhere, not only *à côté de Chez* Erskine-Brown, but also among the Culps. And things had also taken an unfortunate turn in the Rumpole household. I came back one evening to the mansion flat in the Gloucester Road, and, as I unlocked the front door, I heard the usual cry of 'Is that you, Rumpole?'

'Good heavens, no!' I called back. 'It's the Lord High Chancellor of England just dropped in to read the meter. What're you talking about, Hilda?'

'Ssh, Rumpole,' Hilda said mysteriously. 'It's Boxey!'

'Is it? Just a little fresh, I noticed, coming out of the Underground.'

'No. It's Boxey Horne. You must have heard me speak of my second cousin. Cousin Nancy's youngest.' We had spent many hours discussing the complexities of Hilda's family tree, but I couldn't immediately recollect the name. 'We were so close when we were youngsters but Boxey felt the call of Africa. He rang up this afternoon from Paddington Station.'

A masculine voice called through the open sitting-room door, 'Is that old Horace, back from the treadmill?'

'Boxey?' I was perplexed. 'Yes, of course.' And Hilda warned me, 'You try and behave yourself, won't you, Rumpole?'

With that she led me into our sitting room where a skinny, elderly and, I thought, cunning-looking cove was sitting in my chair nursing a glass of my Château Fleet Street and smiling at me in the slightly lopsided manner which I was to know as characteristic of Mr Boxey Horne. He wore a travel-stained tropical suiting, scuffed suede shoes and an MCC tie which had seen better days. When Hilda introduced me, he rose and gripped me quite painfully by the hand. 'Good old Horace,' he said. 'Back from the office same time every evening. I bet you can set your watch by the old fellow, can't you, Hilda?'

'Well. Not exactly,' Hilda told him.

'Your wife gave me some of this plonk of yours, Horace.' Boxey raised his glass to me. 'We'd have been glad of this back on the farm in Kenya. We might have run a couple of tractors on it!'

'Get Boxey a whisky, Rumpole,' Hilda instructed me. 'I expect you'd like a nice strong one, wouldn't you? Boxey couldn't get into the Travellers' Club.'

'Blackballed?' I asked on my way to the sideboard.

'Full up.' Boxey grinned cheerfully. 'Hilda was good enough to say I might camp here for a couple of weeks.' It seemed an infinity. I poured a very small whisky, hoping the bottle would last him out, and drowned it in soda.

'I've been knocking around the world, Horace,' Boxey told me. 'While you were off on your nine to five in a lawyers' office.'

'Not office,' I corrected him as I handed him his pale drink, 'Chambers.'

'That sort of life would never have suited old Boxey,' he told me, and I wondered if his name might be short for anything. 'Oh no,' Hilda laughed at my ignorance. 'We called him that because of the beautiful brass-bound box he had when he set off to Darkest Africa.'

'Always been a rover, Horace.' Boxey was in a reminiscing mood. 'All my worldly goods were in that old box. Tropical kit. Mosquito net. Dinner jacket to impress the natives. Family photographs, including one of Cousin Hilda looking young and alluring.' He drank and looked suitably disappointed, but Hilda, clearly entranced, said, 'You took me to Kenya? In your box?'

'Many a time I've sat alone,' he assured her, 'listening to the strange sounds of an African night and gazing at your photograph. You have been looking after Cousin Hilda, haven't you, Horace?'

'Looking after her?' I poured myself a bracing Pommeroy's plonk and confessed myself puzzled. 'Hilda's in charge.'

'A sweet, sweet girl, Cousin Hilda. I always thought she needed looking after but I suppose I had itchy feet and couldn't resist the call of Africa.' He propelled himself to the sideboard then, and with his back towards us, poured himself a straight whisky and then made a slight hissing noise imitating a siphon.

'What were you doing in Africa?' I asked him. 'Something like discovering the source of the Zambesi?'

'Well, not exactly. I was in coffee.'

'All your life?'

'Most of it.' Boxey returned to my chair to enjoy his drink.

'Working for the same firm?'

'Well, one has certain loyalties. You've never seen dawn over Kilimanjaro, Horry? Pink light on the snow. Zebra stampeding.'

'What time did you start work?' I was pursuing my own line of cross-examination.

'Well,' Boxey remembered, 'after my boy had got my bacon and eggs, coffee and Oxford marmalade . . . then I'd ride round the plantation.'

'Starting at nine o'clock?'

'About then, I suppose.'

'And knocking off?'

'Around sundown. Get a chair on the verandah and shout for a whisky.'

'At about five o'clock?'

'Why do you ask?'

'The old routine!' I muttered and the defence rested.

'What was that?'

'What a rover you've been,' I said without envy.

'Well, I had itchy feet.' Boxey slapped my knee. 'But thank God for chaps like you who're prepared to slog it out in the old country, and look after girls like Hilda.' Then he leant back in his chair, took a sizeable swig and prepared to give us another chapter of his memories. 'Ever been tiger-shooting, Horace?'

'Not unless you could call my frequent appearances before Judge Bullingham tiger-shooting,' I assured him.

'Best sport in the world! Tie an old goat to a tree and lie doggo. Your loader says, "Bwana. Tiger coming." There she is, eyes glittering through the undergrowth. She starts to eat the goat and . . .' – he raised an imaginary rifle – 'aim just above the shoulder. Pow!'

'What do you think of that, Rumpole?' Hilda was starry-eyed.

'I think it sounds bad luck on the goat.' We had a short silence while Boxey renewed his whisky. Then he said, 'I suppose it's another long day in Court for you tomorrow.'

'Oh, yes,' I agreed, 'dusty old law.'

'I don't know how you put up with it!'

'Tedious case about an Ulster terrorist shot by the police in Notting Hill,' I told him – by then I had received the brief for the defence in *R. v. Culp* – 'an inefficient gunrunner who acts as mother and father to his twelve-year-old son, and the curious activities of the Special Branch. Not nearly so exciting as nine to five on the old coffee plantation.'

That night, Hilda lay for a long time with the light on, when I was in dire need of sleep, staring into space. She was also in a reminiscing mood. 'I remember when we used to go to dances at Uncle Jacko's,' she said. 'Boxey was quite young, then. He brought his dancing pumps along in a paper bag. He was simply marvellous at the veleta.'

'It's a wonder he didn't join the Royal Ballet.'

'Rumpole. You *are* jealous!'

'I just thought he might've found *Casse Noisette* a good deal more interesting than coffee.'

'In those days I got the feeling that Boxey had taken a bit of a shine to me.' It wasn't, I thought, much to boast about, but Hilda seemed delighted. 'A definite shine! How different my life might have been if I'd married Boxey and gone to Africa!'

'My life would have been a bit different too,' I told her. 'With no one to make sure I didn't linger too long in Pommeroy's after work. No one to make sure I didn't take a second helping of mashed potatoes. And,' I added, *sotto voce*, 'magical!'

'What did you say, Rumpole?'

'Tragical, of course. Is there any chance of turning out the light?'

Mr Bernard, my favourite instructing solicitor, had briefed me in the Culp case, and we went together to Brixton, where, in the cheerfully painted interview room with its pot plants and reasonably tolerant screws, I made the acquaintance of Stanley. His first request was to get him out of confinement so that he could be with his son, to which I made not very encouraging noises, reminding him that he'd been charged with delivering automatic rifles to a known Irish terrorist and that my name was Rumpole and not Houdini.

The story he told me went roughly as follows. He dealt, he said, in bric-à-brac, *objects d' art*, old furniture – anything he could make a few bob out of. Asked where this property came from, he said we'd find it wise not to ask too many questions. (Well, I sometimes feel the same about my practice at the Bar.) He had a certain amount of space at the back of his shop and he put an advertisement in the local newsagent's window offering to store people's furniture for a modest fee. Some months previously a man had telephoned Stanley saying he was a Mr Banks, from the Loyalist League of Welfare and Succour for Victims of Terrorist Attack, and he wanted storage space for a number of packing cases which contained medical supplies for his organization in Northern Ireland. As a result, he received a visit from Mr Banks who paid him three months' rent in advance, a sum of money which Stanley found extremely welcome. Asked to describe this mysterious Banks he could only remember a man of average age and height, wearing a dark business suit and a white shirt. His sole distinguishing mark was apparently a large pair of gold-rimmed, slightly tinted spectacles. Stanley never saw Mr Banks again, but in due course a lorry arrived with the packing cases which it took a couple of blokes to lift. When I put the point to him he said they did seem heavy for sticking plaster and bandages.

Later Mr Banks telephoned and said that a man called MacRobert, a name which Stanley assured me meant nothing to him, would be calling to arrange the collection of the cases. MacRobert called whilst Matthew was preparing the breakfast and had wanted to see the goods inside, but before he could do so their conversation was interrupted by the Special Branch in the way I have described. Stanley was arrested and, while trying to escape across the garden wall, MacRobert was shot, so he was not in a position to tell us anything about the mysterious Mr Banks.

When he had finished his account Stanley looked at me beseechingly. 'You've got to get me out, Mr Rumpole,' he said. 'It's where they've put my Matthew.'

'Don't worry,' Bernard tried to console the client. 'He's being well looked after, Mr Culp. He's been put into care.'

'Me too. We're both in care.' Stanley managed a smile. 'That's it, isn't it? And it won't suit either of us. As I say, we've always been used to looking after each other.'

I looked at him, wondering what sort of a client I'd got hold of. If Stanley wasn't innocent, he was a tender-hearted gunrunner, so keen to be at home with Master Matthew that he flogged automatic rifles to political terrorists to fire off at other people's sons. It didn't make sense, but then not very much did in crime or politics.

Whilst I exercised my legal skills on a bit of gunrunning in Notting Hill Gate, Portia's practice went on among the jet-setters. Cy Stratton, it seems – I have to confess his name was unknown to me – was an international film star for whom Hilda, who pays more attention to the television set than I can manage, has a soft spot. He had been detected, as well-known film stars too often are, carrying exotic smoking materials through the customs at London Airport. In the consequent proceedings he hired, at a suitable fee, Mrs Phillida Erskine-Brown to make his apologies for him. She was ably assisted in this task by Mizz Liz Probert, to whom I am grateful for an account of the proceedings. Picture then the West Middlesex Magistrates' Court, unusually filled with reporters and spectators. On the Bench sat three serious-minded amateurs: a grey-haired schoolmaster Chairman, a forbidding-looking woman in a hat and a stout party with a toothbrush moustache and a Trades Union badge. In the dock, Mr Cy Stratton, a carefully suntanned specimen, whose curls were now greying, sat wearing a contrite expression and a suit and tie in place of his usual open-necked shirt and gold chain. On his behalf, our Portia, sincere and irresistible, spoke words which, when Liz Probert reported them to me, seemed to come straight out of Rumpole's first lesson on getting round to the soft side of the West Middlesex Magistrates as taught by me to Mrs Erskine-Brown in her white-wigged years.

'Cy Stratton is, of course,' she ended, 'a household name, known throughout the world from a string of successful films.' The star in the dock looked gratified. 'The Bench won't, I'm sure, punish him for his fame. He is entitled to be treated as anyone else found at London Airport with a small amount of cannabis for his own personal use. At the time he was under considerable personal strain, having just completed a new film, *Galaxy Wives*.' The Trades Union official, clearly a fan, nodded wisely. 'And, may I say this, Mr Stratton is absolutely opposed to hard drugs. He is a prominent member of the Presidential "Say No to Coke" Committee of Los Angeles. In these circumstances, I do most earnestly appeal to you, sir, and to your colleagues. You will do justice to Cy Stratton.' And here Portia used a gambit which even I have long since rejected as being overripe ham. 'But let it be justice tempered with that mercy which is the hallmark of the West Middlesex Magistrates' Court!'

Well, sometimes the old ones work best. Much moved, Cy Stratton looked as though he were about to applaud; even the lady in the hat seemed mollified. The Chairman smiled his thanks at Phillida and, after a short retirement and a warning to Cy to set a good example to his huge army of fans, imposed a fine of three hundred pounds.

'And I had that,' said Cy to his learned Counsel and Liz outside the Court, 'in my pants pocket.'

'They might have given you two months,' Phillida told him, 'and you wouldn't have had *that* in your pants pocket.'

On that occasion Cy told Phillida he had a proposition to put to her and invited her to share a celebratory bottle of Dom Perignon with him in some private place. However, she declined politely, gathered her legal team about her, and saying, 'We do have to work, you know, at the Bar,' drove back to the Temple, doing so, Liz thought, in a sort of reverie brought on by an impulsive kiss from her grateful client.

I was in our clerk's room a few days later, with Claude and Phillida, sorting out our business affairs when a messenger arrived with a huge cellophane-wrapped bouquet and called out, 'Flowers for Erskine-Brown!' I asked Claude if he had an admirer, but they appeared to be for his wife and he asked, somewhat nervously, I thought, as she read the card attached, if they were from anyone in particular.

'Oh, no. Flowers just drop on me by accident, from the sky.' Phillida sounded testy. 'Do try not to be silly, Claude.'

'Perhaps they're from a satisfied client,' I suggested.

'Yes, they are!'

'Really, Portia? Who was that?'

'Oh, someone I kept out of prison. Nothing tremendously important.' She sounded casual, and Uncle Tom, our oldest inhabitant, who was as usual practising approach shots at the waste-paper basket, began to reminisce. 'I've never had a present from a satisfied client,' he told us. 'Not that I've had many clients at all, come to that, satisfied or not. I suppose it's better to have no clients than those that aren't satisfied. Damn! I seem to be in a bunker.' His golf ball had taken refuge behind Dianne's desk.

'What've I got this afternoon, Henry?' Phillida asked. And when he told her she had a 3.30 conference she supposed, after some thought, that she could be back in time. Meanwhile Uncle Tom was off down Memory Lane in pursuit of presents from satisfied clients. 'Old Dickie Duckworth once had a satisfied client,' he told us. 'Some sort of a Middle Eastern Prince who was supposed to have got a Nippy from Lyons Corner House in pod and Dickie turned up at Bow Street and got him off. So you know what this fellow sent as a token of his appreciation? An Arab stallion! Well, Dickie Duckworth only had a small flat in Lincoln's Inn. No one ever sent me an Arab stallion. Chip shot out of the bunker!'

At that moment, Superintendent Rodney of the Special Branch, together with an official from the prosecution service, entered our clerk's room. Soapy Sam Ballard, QC, the Head of our Chambers, had been briefed to prosecute Stanley Culp and they were to see him in conference. Unfortunately Uncle Tom's chip shot was rather too successful; his golf ball rose into the air and struck the Superintendent smartly on the kneecap, producing a cry of pain and dire consequences for Uncle Tom.

The note on Phillida's bouquet was a pressing invitation to meet Cy Stratton for lunch at the Savoy Hotel. I suppose the suntanned and ageing Adonis had figured too largely in her thoughts since the trial for her to pass up the invitation, and when they met he surprised her by suggesting that they share a bottle of champagne and a surprise packet from the delicatessen on a bench in the Embankment Gardens. So Phillida found herself eating pastrami on rye and drinking Dom Perignon out of a plastic cup, both excited by the adventure and nervous at the amount of public exposure she was receiving. I learnt, long after the event, and when certain decisions had been made, the gist of Cy's conversation on that occasion from my confiding ex-pupil. It seems that after complimenting her on looking great – 'Great hair, great shape. Classy nose. Great legal mind' – Cy informed her that their 'vibes' were good and that they should spend more time together. He had, he said, 'A proposition to put'.

'Perhaps you shouldn't.' Phillida was flattered but nervous.

'What?'

'You shouldn't put a proposition to me.'

'Can't a guy ask?'

'It might be a great deal better if a guy didn't.'

'I need you, Phillida.' The actor was at his most intense, and he moved himself and the sandwiches closer to her.

'You may think you do.'

'I know I do. Desperately.'

'Don't exaggerate.' There has always been a strong streak of common sense in our Portia.

'I swear to you. I can't find anyone to do what I'd expect of you.'

'You can't?'

'Not a soul. They haven't the versatility.'

'What would you expect of me exactly?' Phillida was still nervous, but interested. His answer, she confessed, came as something of a surprise. 'Only, to take over the entire legal side of Cy Stratton Enterprises. Real estate. Audio-visual exploitations. Cable promotions. I want your cool head, Phillida, and your legal know-how.'

'Oh, is that what you want?' She tried not to sound in the least disappointed.

'Come to the sunshine. I'll find you a house on the beach.'

'I *have* got two children,' she told him.

'The kids'll love it.'

'And a husband,' she admitted. 'He's a lawyer too.'

'Maybe we could use him, as your assistant?'

'You don't send children away from home in California?' The idea was beginning to appeal to Portia.

'Summer camps, maybe. Think about it, Phillida. Our vibes are such we should spend more time together.'

'I'll think about it. Can I have another sandwich?' She put out her hand and Cy held it and looked into her eyes. And then Liz Probert, walking through the Gardens, stopped in front of them as Cy was saying, 'Find our own space together. That's all it takes!'

'Good afternoon. Having a picnic?' Liz's greeting was somewhat cold. Phillida quickly released her hand. 'Oh, Probert,' she greeted her colleague formally. 'You remember Cy Stratton?'

'Of course. Illegal possession.' Liz looked at Phillida. 'A satisfied client?'

The Erskine-Browns' private life was, you see, not exactly private – either they were spied on by Liz Probert or overheard by Rumpole. A few evenings later I was at my corner table in Pommeroy's trying to raise my alcohol level from the dangerous low to which it had sunk, when I heard their raised voices once again from the pew behind me. 'Haven't we been getting into a bit of a rut lately, Claude?' was the far from original remark which collared my attention.

'It's hardly fair to say that.' Claude sounded pained. 'When I got us tickets for *Tannhäuser*.'

'It's like Tristan's education. You want him to go to Bogstead and

Winchester and New College. Because you went to Winchester and New College and your father went to Winchester . . .'

'And Balliol. There was an unconventional streak in Daddy.'

'Claude. Don't you ever long to go to work in an open-necked shirt and cotton trousers?'

'Of course not, Philly.' The man was shocked. 'In an open-necked shirt and cotton trousers, the Judges at the Old Bailey can't even hear you. You'd be quite inaudible and sent up to the Public Gallery.'

'Oh, I don't mean that, Claude. Don't you ever long for the sun?'

'You want me to book up for Viareggio again?' Claude clearly thought he'd solved it, but his wife disillusioned him.

'Not just a holiday, Claude. I mean a change in our lives. It's only fair I should tell you this. There's someone I might want to spend time with in, well, a different sort of life. It's not that I'm in love in the least. Nothing to do with that. I just want a complete change. I sometimes feel I never want to go back to Chambers.'

This fascinating dialogue was interrupted again by the arrival of Ballard at their table. He had come to report the disgraceful occurrence of a superintendent of the Special Branch smitten by a golf ball, a blow from which, it seemed, he didn't think Chambers would ever recover. I didn't know then how the differences of the Erskine-Browns were to be resolved, but Phillida did come into Chambers the next morning, and there found an official-looking letter from the Lord Chancellor which was to have some considerable effect on the case of *R. v. Culp*.

In due course, Miss Sturt, his social worker, brought young Matthew Culp to visit his father in Brixton Prison. A special room was set aside for visits by prisoners' children, and the two Culps sat together trying to cheer each other up, Matthew being, by all accounts, the more decisive of the two. He told his father that he was determined to help him and that he meant to see to it that they were soon able to renew their contented domestic life together. He also asked Stanley to pass on certain information to me, his brief, as a consequence of which Mr Bernard made another appointment for me to visit the alleged gunrunner.

'My Matthew saw him, Mr Rumpole,' Stanley told me as soon as we were ensconced in the interview room. 'He says he saw that Mr Banks you were so interested in.'

'He did?'

'Oh, yes. Once when he came about leaving the packing cases, what he said were medical supplies for his charitable organization. Matthew can tell them all about it. And that last morning, my Matthew'll say, he saw the same man in gold-rimmed glasses get out of the police car.'

'So that's the trap you walked into?' If Stanley were a criminal, he was clearly incompetent.

'Trap?' He looked at me, puzzled.

'Oh, yes. Isn't that the way they shoot tigers? Tie a goat to a tree, wait for the tiger to come hunting, and then shoot. In this case, Mr Culp, you were the bait. Possibly innocent. The only question is . . .' I looked thoughtfully at Stanley. 'How much did the goat know?'

'I didn't know anything, Mr Rumpole,' he protested. 'Medical supplies they were, as far I was concerned. But Matthew will tell you all about it.'

'Your boy's prepared to give evidence?' Mr Bernard looked encouraged.

'Ready and willing. He wants to help all he can.'

'And you want me to put him in the witness-box? How old is he? Twelve?'

'But such an old head on his shoulders, Mr Rumpole. I told you how he masters his geometry.'

'He may be a demon on equilateral triangles, but he's a bit young for a starring role, down the Old Bailey.'

'Please, Mr Rumpole,' my client begged me. 'He'd never forgive me if we didn't let him have his say. We make it a rule, you see, to look after each other.'

The man was so eager, and obviously proud of the son he trusted to save him. But I was still not convinced of the wisdom of calling young Matthew to give evidence in the daunting atmosphere of the Central Criminal Court.

When Phillida had opened her official-looking envelope she spread the news it contained around Chambers. Ballard then called a meeting, and opened the agenda in his usual ponderous, not to say pompous, fashion.

'The first business today,' he began, 'is to congratulate Phillida Erskine-Brown, who has received gratifying news from the Lord

Chancellor's office. She has been made a Recorder and so will sit in as a criminal judge from time to time, in the intervals of her busy practice.'

'A Daniel come to justice!' I saluted her.

'How do you feel about having your wife sit in judgement, Claude?' Hoskins asked.

'I'd say, used to it by now,' Claude gave him the reply jocular.

'Thank you very much.' Phillida looked becomingly modest. 'Quite honestly, it's come as a bit of a shock.'

'Of course, we all know that the Lord Chancellor is anxious to promote women, so perhaps, Phillida, you've found the way to the Bench a little easier than it's been for some of us.' Ballard was never of a generous nature and he found congratulating other learned friends very hard.

'I suppose we'd see you Lord Chancellor by now, Bollard, if only you'd been born Samantha and not Sam,' was my comment.

'My second duty is a less pleasant one.' Soapy Sam ignored me. 'Which is why I have asked Uncle Tom not to join this meeting. Something quite inexcusable in a respectable barristers' Chambers has occurred. An officer of the Special Branch arrived to see me in conference. Rather a big matter. Gunrunning to Ulster. You may have read about *R. v. Culp* in the newspapers? Terrorist got shot in Notting Hill Gate . . . Well, you can see it's an extremely heavy case.'

'Oh, I'm in that,' I told him casually. 'Storm in a teacup, I think you'll find.'

'Superintendent Rodney came here for a consultation with myself,' Ballard continued with great seriousness. 'He walked into the clerk's room and was struck on the knee by a golf ball! I need hardly say who was responsible.'

'Uncle Tom!' Hoskins guessed the answer.

'He's been playing golf in there as long as I can remember.' Erskine-Brown was querulous.

'It wasn't Uncle Tom's fault,' I told them. 'I clearly heard him shouting, "Fore!"'

'He shouldn't have been shouting "fore" or anything else.' Ballard showed a very judicial irritation. 'A clerk's room is for collecting briefs, and discussing a chap's availability with Henry. A clerk's room isn't for shouting "fore" and driving off into superintendents' kneecaps!'

'He wasn't driving off,' I insisted.

'Oh. What was he doing then, Rumpole?'

'He was getting out of a bunker.'

'Sometimes you defeat me! I have no idea what you're talking about; there are no bunkers in our clerk's room!' Ballard seemed to think that decided the matter.

'It was an imaginary bunker.'

'I don't understand.'

'That's because you have no imagination.'

'Perhaps I haven't. In any event I can't see why Uncle Tom has to play golf in our clerk's room. It's quite unnecessary.'

'Of course it is,' I agreed.

'I'm glad you admit it, Rumpole.'

'Just as poetry is unnecessary,' I pointed out. 'You can't eat it. It doesn't make you money. I suppose people like you, Bollard, can get through life without Wordsworth's sonnet "Upon Westminster Bridge". What we are discussing is the quality of life. Uncle Tom adds an imaginative touch to what would otherwise be a fairly dreary, dusty little clerk's room, littered with biscuits, briefs and barristers.'

'Personally I don't understand why Uncle Tom comes into Chambers every day; he never gets any work.' Now Erskine-Brown showed his lack of imagination. If he lived with Uncle Tom's sister he'd come into Chambers every day whether there was any work for him there or not. Not that there was anything wrong with Uncle Tom's sister, she'd just worked her way through the entire medical directory without having had a day's illness in her life. Uncle Tom also, strange as it may have seemed, enjoyed our company.

Ballard now proceeded to judgement. 'Uncle Tom and his golf balls are,' he said, 'in my considered opinion, a quite unnecessary health hazard in Chambers. I intend to ask him to make his room available to us.'

'You're going to ask him to leave?' I wanted to get the situation perfectly clear.

'Exactly that.' Ballard made it perfectly clear, so I stood up.

'If Uncle Tom goes, I go,' I told him.

'That would seem to make the departure of Uncle Tom even more desirable,' Soapy Sam was saying with a faint smile as I left the room.

*

So that was how I decided, after so many years enduring the splendours and miseries of an Old Bailey Hack, to leave our Chambers in Equity Court and perhaps quit the Bar for ever. The decision was one which I couldn't wait to tell that lately reunited couple of lovebirds, She Who Must Be Obeyed and Boxey Horne. As I entered the mansion flat that evening I was singing ' "You take the High Road and I'll take the Low Road, and I'll be in Zimbabwe before you!" ' I entered our sitting room and I spotted Hilda pouring Boxey a generous whisky. 'I have news for you both,' I told them. 'My feet itch!'

'What do you mean by that, Rumpole?' My wife seemed puzzled.

'I can smell the hot wind of Africa,' I told them. 'I hear the cry of the parrot in the jungle and the chatter of monkeys. I wish to see the elephant and the gazelle troop shyly up to the waterhole at night. You have inspired me, Boxey, my old darling. I'm leaving the Bar.'

'Don't talk nonsense!' Hilda was somewhat rattled.

'I have handed in my resignation.'

'You've *what?*'

'I have informed our learned Head of Chambers, Soapy Sam Ballard, Queen's Counsel, that I no longer wish to be part of an organization which can't tolerate golf in the clerk's room.'

'Uncle Tom!' Hilda got my drift.

'Of course.'

'I've never understood why he had to play golf in the clerk's room.'

'Because no one sends him any briefs,' I enlightened her. 'Do you think he wants to be seen doing nothing? Anyway. I've handed in my resignation. One more case – I intend to defeat Soapy Sam over a spot of illicit arms dealing – and then travels Rumpole East away!'

'You're not serious?' Boxey also looked alarmed.

'Farewell to dusty old law! No more nine to five in the office. Ask for me in the Nairobi Club in five years' time and the fellows might have news of me. Up country.'

'He's joking,' Hilda told her childhood sweetheart. 'Definitely joking.' But then she sounded uncertain. 'Aren't you, Rumpole?'

'I wish I could come back with you,' Boxey told me. 'But . . .'

'Oh, you can't do that, Boxey. Of course not. Somebody's got to stay here and look after Hilda.' I was gratified to see that they looked at each other with a wild surmise. They wanted to talk further, but I refused to discuss the matter until my Swan Song, the Queen against Stanley Culp, was safely over and, I hoped, won.

Some days later I invited Phillida for a drink in Pommeroy's. When we were safely seated with glasses in our hands, she asked me if I were really thinking of leaving Chambers. I told her that my future depended on Ballard, and Hilda's long-lost cousin, who rejoiced in the name of Boxey Horne. She Who Must Be Obeyed, I explained, said she might have married Boxey.

'And I might not have married Claude.' Our Portia stared thoughtfully into her vodka and tonic. As Shelley would probably have said, in the circumstances, '*We look before and after;/ We pine for what is not.*' 'I might,' she added, 'have had a husband full of energy, and jokes, with a taste for adventure. Someone unconventional. A rebel who hadn't been to Bogstead and Winchester.'

'Portia. You're flattering me.' I smiled modestly.

'What do you mean?'

'But mightn't I have been a little old for you?'

'Why did you ask me for this drink?' Portia looked at me and asked sharply. It was time for me to put my master plan into practice. I began, I hope, as tactfully as possible with: 'There's a bit of an east wind blowing between you and Claude on the subject of young Tristan's education . . .'

'I don't see why the family has to be split up.' She was quite clear on the subject.

'Exactly. A boy needs his father.'

'And his mother, don't forget.'

'Worst thing that can happen,' I argued profoundly, 'for families is to be separated, torn apart by society's unnatural laws and customs.'

'You understand that?' She looked at me with more than usual sympathy.

'Handing a small boy over for other people to bring up has to be avoided at all costs.'

'You ought to tell Claude that.'

'Oh, I certainly shall,' I promised her as I raised my glass. 'Family togetherness. Here's to it, Portia, and I hope you support it, whenever you sit in judgement.'

Mizz Liz Probert had her own, somewhat uncomfortable, standards of honesty, which were usually calculated to cause trouble to others. It will be recalled that when Claude had incautiously invited her to a night *à deux* at the Opera, she immediately told Phillida of the invitation, thus causing prolonged domestic disharmony.* It was therefore predictable that she should tell Claude that she had seen Phillida on a bench in the Embankment Gardens, drinking champagne and holding hands with a famous film star. My learned friend, Mr Erskine-Brown, gave me an account of this conversation at a later date. It seems that Mizz Probert had her own explanation for this event, one hard to understand by any-one not intimately connected with the North Islington Women's Movement. 'You drove her to it, Claude,' Liz said. 'If a woman does that sort of thing, it's always the man's fault, isn't it?'

'And if a man does that sort of thing?'

'Well, it's always his fault. Don't you understand? Phillida's just rebel-ling against your enormous power and sexual domination.'

'Oh?' Claude tried to reason with Mizz Probert. 'Phillida is a Queen's Counsel. She wears a silk gown. She's about to sit as a Recorder. In judge-ment at the Old Bailey. I'm still a junior barrister. With a rough old gown made of some inferior material. How can I possibly dominate her?'

'Because you're a man, Claude,' Liz told him. 'You were born for domination!'

'Oh, really? Do you honestly think so?' At the time, Claude was not entirely displeased by this view. Later, in the privacy of his home, Phil-lida told me, he apologized to his wife for his terrible habit of domination. 'I suppose I can't help it; it's a bit of a curse really. Men just don't know their own strength.'

'Claude' – Phillida tried to keep a straight face – 'I have to decide on the shirts you want to buy. When we went out to dinner with the Arthurian Daybells you asked me to remind you whether you like smoked mackerel!'

'Do I?' her husband asked seriously.

'Not very much.'

'Ah. That's right.'

'You seem to suffer from terminal exhaustion directly your head hits the pillow. Can you please tell me exactly how you are exercising this

* See 'Rumpole and the Official Secret' (*The Second Rumpole Omnibus*).

terrible power over me? Could you give me one single instance of your ruthless domination?'

'I suppose it's just the male role. I'll try not to play it, Philly. I honestly will.'

'Oh, Claude!' Portia could no longer contain her laughter. 'Do you think I ought to stay here and look after you?'

'Well, you'll have to stay here now, won't you, anyway?' Claude told his wife.

'Because you tell me to?' She was still laughing.

'No. Because you're a Recorder.'

Portia had become a part-time judge and Portia was devoted to the idea of keeping children within the family circle. There was only one element of my equation left to supply, and to do so I entered our clerk's room with the intention of having a confidential chat with Henry. As good luck would have it, I found him patiently addressing Dianne, who sat with a book on her typewriter. ' "I knew that suddenly, when we were dancing," ' Henry told her, ' "an enchantment swept over me. An enchantment that I've never known before and shall never know again. My heart's bumping. I'm trembling like a fool." '

' "Thumping",' Dianne insisted.

'What's that?'

' "My heart's thumping." Otherwise very good.'

'The late Sir Noël Coward, Henry?' I guessed.

'Oh, yes, Mr Rumpole. The Bexley Thespians. We're putting on *Tonight at 8.30*, sir. We likes his stuff. I do happen to have the starring role.'

'With your usual co-star?' Fate was giving me unusual help with *R. v. Stanley Culp*.

'I shall be playing opposite Miss Osgood from the Old Bailey List Office. As per always.'

'Miss Osgood, who fixes the hearings and the Judges. A talented actress, of course?'

'Sarah Osgood has a certain magic on stage, Mr Rumpole.'

'And considerable powers in the List Office also, Henry. Remind me to send her a large bouquet on the first night. And for our Portia's début on the Old Bailey Bench, I thought it would be nice if Miss Osgood gave her something worthy of her talents.'

'No doubt you had something in mind, sir?' Our clerk wasn't born yesterday.

'*R. v. Culp.*' I told him what I had in mind. 'A drama of gun dealing in Notting Hill Gate. Likely to run and run. It might be Portia's way to stardom. Mention it to your fellow Thespian during a break in rehearsals, why don't you?' My hint dropped, I moved out of the room past our ever-putting oldest inhabitant. 'Still golfing, Uncle Tom?'

'Ballard wants to see me,' he said, almost proudly.

'Oh, yes. When?'

'Any time at my convenience before the end of the month. Do you think he's fixed me up with a junior brief?'

'Would you like that?'

'I'm not sure. I haven't kept my hand in at the law.'

'Never mind, Uncle Tom. Your putting's coming on splendidly!' And I left him to it.

And so it came about that fate spun its wheel and, with a little help from my good self and Miss Osgood at the List Office, the Queen against Culp was selected as the case to be tried by Mrs Recorder Erskine-Brown when she made her first appearance on the Old Bailey Bench. She sat there, severely attractive, a large pair of horn-rimmed glasses balanced on that delicate nose which has sent the fantasies whirling in the heads of many barristers, distinguished and otherwise. I thought how I had advised and trained her up, from white-wig to judge's wig, to lean to the defence, particularly when the defendant has a twelve-year-old son who is the apple of his eye. I also thought that there was no judge in England better suited to try the case against Stanley Culp.

As I rose to cross-examine the Special Branch Superintendent, Portia selected a freshly sharpened pencil and prepared to make a note. This was in great contrast to such as Judge Bullingham who merely yawns, examines his nails or explores his ear with a little finger during cross-examination by the defence, that is, if he's not actively heckling.

'Superintendent Rodney,' I began. 'Have you, as a Special Branch officer, ever heard of the Loyalist League of Welfare and Succour for Victims of Terrorist Attack?'

'Not till your client told us they sent him those packing cases.'

'Or of a Mr Banks, who apparently runs that philanthropic organization?'

'Not till your client told us his story.'

'A story you believed?'

'If I had we wouldn't be here, would we, Mr Rumpole?' Rodney smiled as though he'd won a point, but the Judge interrupted for the first time.

'Mr Rumpole. What does it matter what this officer believes? It's what the jury believes that matters, isn't it?'

'Your Ladyship is, of course, perfectly right. A Daniel come to judgement,' I whispered to Mizz Probert. 'Yea, a Daniel!' I then asked, 'Did my client, Mr Culp, give you a description of Banks, the man who had asked him to store the packing cases for him?'

'Superintendent,' her Ladyship said quite properly, 'you may refresh your memory from your notes, if you wish to.'

'Thank you, my Lady.' He turned a page or two in his notebook. 'Yes. Culp said, "Mr Banks called on me and asked me to store some . . . medical supplies. He was a man of average height, he had gold-rimmed glasses with . . ."'

'Slightly tinted lenses?' I suggested.

'Tinted lenses. Yes.'

'Well. You know perfectly well who that is, don't you?' I asked, looking at the jury.

'Excuse me, Mr Rumpole' – the Superintendent rather overacted complete bewilderment – 'I have absolutely no idea.'

'Really?' And I asked, 'Have the Special Branch made any effort whatsoever to find this elusive Banks? Have you sought him here, Superintendent? Have you sought him there?'

'My Lady' – Soapy Sam arose with awful solemnity – 'it is my duty to object to this line of questioning.'

'*Your duty*, Mr Bollard?' I thought his duty was to sit still and let me get on with it.

'My patriotic duty!' The fellow seemed about to salute and run up a small Union Jack. 'My Lady. This is a case in which the security of the realm is involved. The activities of the Special Branch necessarily take place in secret. The inquiries they have made cannot be questioned by Mr Rumpole.'

'What do you say, Mr Rumpole?' Portia was ever anxious to know both sides of the question.

'What do I say?' I came to the defence of the legal system against the Secret Police. 'I say quite simply that contrary to what Mr Ballard seems to believe, this trial is not taking place behind the Iron Curtain. We are in England, my Lady, breathing English air. The Special Branch is not the KGB. They are merely a widely travelled department of our dear Old Bill.' This got me a little refreshing laughter from the jury-box. 'I should be much obliged for an answer to my question.'

'Is the whereabouts of this man Banks vital to your defence?' Portia asked judicially.

'My Lady, they are.'

'And you wish me to make a ruling on this matter?'

'The first, I'm sure, of many wise judgements your Ladyship will make in many cases.'

'Then in my judgement . . .' I whispered to Liz to keep her fingers crossed, but happily justice triumphed and her Ladyship ruled, '. . . Mr Rumpole may ask his question.' A wise and upright Judge, a Daniel come to judgement, but Superintendent Rodney stonewalled our efforts by saying, 'We have not been able to trace Mr Banks or the Loyalist League of Welfare.'

'Much good did that do you!' Ballard muttered to me, and I muttered back, 'Wait for it. I'm not finished yet, Comrade Bollardski!' I said to the witness, 'Superintendent. You arrived at breakfast time on the 4th of May outside the shop in Notting Hill Gate to arrest my client. Who was in the car with you?'

'Detective Inspector Blake and Detective Sergeant Trump, my Lady.'

'And who had told you that a transaction in arms was likely to take place in Mr Culp's shop that morning?'

'My Lady . . .' the Superintendent appealed to the Judge, who ruled with a smile I found quite charming, 'I don't think the officer can be compelled to give the name of his informer, Mr Rumpole.' I accepted her decision gratefully and asked, 'Was your informer, let's call him Mr X, in the car with you and the other officers when you arrived at the shop?'

'My Lady.' Ballard rose again to maintain secrecy. 'The Court no doubt understands that any information about a police informer on terrorist activities would place the man's life in immediate danger.'

'Very well.' Portia saw the point. 'I don't think you can take the matter further, can you, Mr Rumpole?'

I could and did with my next question. 'Let me just ask this, with your Ladyship's permission. Did a man wearing gold-rimmed spectacles and tinted lenses get out of the police car in front of the shop that morning and walk away before the arrest took place?'

'I'm not prepared to answer that, my Lady,' the Superintendent stonewalled again.

'And was that man "Mr Banks"?' I pressed on.

'I have already told you, sir. We don't know Mr Banks.'

'But you do know whoever it was, an officer of your Special Branch, perhaps, who stored the packing cases in Mr Culp's shop, who told Mr Culp they were medical supplies, and arranged for this man MacRobert, who wanted to buy arms for his Ulster terrorists, to walk into your trap?'

'All I can tell you is that the cases of arms were in the shop and Mac-Robert called for them.' The Superintendent sighed, as though my defence were no more than a waste of his precious time.

'Had MacRobert met Mr Banks?'

'I can't say.'

'And the jury will never know because MacRobert has been silenced forever.'

'Detective Inspector Blake saw him in the act of pulling out a weapon. He fired in self-defence.'

'No doubt he did. But it leaves us, doesn't it, a little short of evidence?'

We weren't entirely bereft of evidence, of course. All through my cross-examination I had been aware of a small, solemn, spectacled boy sitting outside the Court with his social worker, longing to help his father. I had hoped to get enough out of the Superintendent to avoid having to put young Matthew through the rigours of the witness-box, but I hadn't succeeded. Now, Bernard whispered to me, 'The little lad's just longing to go in. Are you going to call him?' The business of being a barrister involves the hard task of making decisions, instantly and on your feet. You may make the right decision, you may often get it wrong. The one luxury not open to you is that of not making up your mind. I stood silent as long as I dared and then committed myself.

'Fortunately,' I told the Superintendent, 'I am in a position to call a witness who might be able to tell us a little more about the damned elusive Banks.'

'Oh, please, Mr Rumpole' – Sam Ballard's whispered disapproval echoed through the Court – 'don't swear, particularly in front of a lady Judge.'

Dressed in his best brown suit, a white shirt and a red bow tie, in the dock Stanley somehow looked more crumpled and less impressive than ever. He sat slumped like a sack of potatoes; the Court seemed too hot for him and he frequently dabbed his forehead with a folded handkerchief. However, when his son, a more alert figure, stepped into the witness-box and had the nature of the oath gently explained to him by Portia, Stanley pulled himself together. He sat up straight, his eyes shone with pride and he looked like a devoted parent whose son has just stood up to collect the best all-rounder prize at the school Speech Day. His pride only seemed to increase as I led young Matthew through his examination-in-chief.

'Matthew. Do you remember a man coming to ask your father to store some boxes?'

'I was in the shop.'

'You were in the shop when he arrived?'

'Yes. He said he was Mr Banks and I went and fetched Dad from the back. He was mending something.' The boy answered clearly, without hesitation.

The jury seemed to like him and I felt encouraged to ask for further details.

'Can you remember what Mr Banks looked like?'

'He had these gold-rimmed glasses. And they were coloured.'

'What was coloured?'

'The glass in them.'

'Did your father talk to Mr Banks?'

'Yes. I went upstairs. To finish my homework.' Portia was listening carefully and noting down the evidence. Matthew was doing well and his ordeal, I hoped, was almost over. I asked him, 'Did you see Mr Banks again?'

'Oh, yes.'

'When?'

'When the policemen arrived for Dad. Mr Banks got out of the police car.'

I looked at the jury and repeated slowly, 'Mr Banks got out of the police car. What did he do then?'

'He walked away.' I smiled at Matthew, who didn't smile back, but remained standing seriously at attention. 'Yes. Thank you, Matthew. Oh, just wait there a minute, will you?' I had to sit down then, and leave him to the mercy of Ballard. I had no particular fear, for Soapy Sam had never been a great cross-examiner. His first question, however, was not badly chosen. 'Matthew. Are you very fond of your father?'

'We look after each other.' For the first time Matthew looked, unsmiling, at the dock. His father beamed back at him.

'Oh, yes. I'm sure you do.' Ballard tried the approach cynical. 'And you want to help him, don't you? You want to look after him in this case?'

'I'd like him to come home.' I was pleased to see Portia give Matthew a small smile before busying herself with her notes.

'I'm sure you would. And have you and your father discussed this business of Mr Banks getting out of the police car?' Ballard asked an apparently innocent question.

'I told Dad what I saw.'

'And did he tell you it was going to be his story that the police had set up this deal, through Mr Banks?'

'He said something like that. Yes.' It wasn't exactly the best answer we could have expected.

'So does it come to this? You'd say anything to help your father's defence?'

'My Lady. That was a completely uncalled for—' I rose with not entirely simulated rage, anxious to give the boy a little respite.

'Yes, Mr Rumpole,' Portia agreed and then turned to the young witness. 'Matthew. Are you sure you saw a man with glasses get out of the police car?'

I subsided. My interruption had been a mistake. I had changed a poor and unsympathetic cross-examiner for a humane and understanding one who might put our case in far more damage. 'Yes, I am. Quite sure.'

'Apart from the fact that he had gold-rimmed glasses with tinted lenses, can you be sure it was the same man who came to your father's shop and said he was Mr Banks?' Portia probed gently and Ballard got on the bandwagon with a sharp 'You can't be *sure*, can you?'

'Please, Mr Ballard.' Unhappily, Phillida didn't let Soapy Sam show himself at his worst. 'Just think, Matthew,' she said. 'There's absolutely no hurry.'

There was a long silence then. Matthew was frowning and worried.

'I *think* it was the same man,' he said, and my heart sank.

'You think it was.' The Judge made a perfectly fair note and Ballard's voice rose triumphantly as he repeated. 'You *think* it was! But you can't be sure.'

'Well . . . Well, he looked the same. He *was* the same!' And then Matthew turned from a carefully controlled, grown-up witness to a child again. He called across to his father in the dock, 'He was, Dad? Wasn't he?'

And Stanley looked at him helplessly, unable to speak. The jury looked embarrassed, fiddled with their papers or stared at their feet. The blushing, confused child in the witness-box stood beyond the reach of all of us until the Judge mercifully released him. 'I don't think we should keep Matthew here a moment longer,' she said. 'Have either of you gentlemen any further questions?'

Ballard had done his worst and there was no way in which I could repair the damage. Phillida said, 'Thank you, Matthew. You can go now.' And the boy walked down from the witness-box and towards the door of the Court. His social worker rose to follow him. As he got to the dock he looked at his father and said quietly, 'Did I let you down, Dad?'

I could hear him, but Stanley couldn't. All the same his father raised his thumb in a hopeful, encouraging signal as Matthew left us to be taken back into care.

Henry told me that, whilst we were on our way back from Court, the world-famous film star called at our clerk's room in search of Phillida. When he was told that she had been sitting as a Judge down at the Old Bailey, he looked somewhat daunted.

'Isn't she too pretty to be a Judge?'

'I don't think the Lord Chancellor considered that, sir' – Henry was at his most dignified – 'when he made Mrs Erskine-Brown a Recorder.'

'A Judge, ugh!' Cy seemed to think this new position of Phillida's was something of a bar to romance. 'Anyway. Tell her I called by, will you? I'm getting the red-eye back to the Coast tonight. Say, that's a great gimmick!' This came as a direct result of seeing Uncle Tom putting in the corner of the room. 'What a great selling-point for your legal business.'

On his way downstairs, Cy met Soapy Sam Ballard and engaged him in some conversation which our Head of Chambers later reported to me. It seems that Cy had asked Ballard if he worked with Phillida and, on being told that Sam was Head of our Chambers, said, 'You run the shop! What a great gimmick you got, having an old guy playing golf in reception.' When Ballard explained he meant to put an end to it, Cy said, 'Are you crazy? Wait till I let them know on the Coast. There's a British lawyers' office, I'll tell them, where they keep an old guy to play golf in reception. Kind of traditional. I tell you. You'll get so much business from American lawyers! They'll all want to come in here and they won't *believe* it!'

'You think Uncle Tom'll bring us business?' Ballard was puzzled.

'You wait till I spread the word. You won't be able to handle it.'

In due course we made our final speeches and I sat back, my duty done, to hear her Ladyship sum up. 'Members of the jury,' she concluded, 'the defence case is that this arms sale was staged by the police to trap the man, MacRobert. Mr Rumpole has said that the arms were deposited in the shop by a Mr Banks, who was a police officer in plain clothes, and that Mr Culp was simply told they were medical supplies. He was a quite innocent man, used as bait to trap the terrorist MacRobert. Are you sure that Mr Culp knew what was in those packing cases? They must have been extremely heavy for medical supplies. Do you accept young Matthew's identification of Mr Banks as the man in the police car? He *thinks* it was Banks but, you remember, he couldn't be sure. Members of the jury, the decision on the facts is entirely for you. If there's a doubt, Mr Culp is entitled to the benefit of that doubt. Now, please, take all the time you need and, when you're quite ready, come back and tell me what you have decided. Thank you.'

So the usher swore to conduct the jury to their room and not to communicate with them until they had reached a verdict. As I said to my learned friend Mizz Liz Probert, it had been an utterly fair summing up by a completely unbiased Judge – always a terrible danger to the defence.

The jury were out for almost three hours and then returned with a unanimous verdict of guilty. Of course, an Old Bailey Hack should take such results as part of the fair wear and tear of legal life. 'Win a few, lose a few', should be the attitude. I have never managed to do this, but I still hoped, by an argument which I thought might be extremely sympathetic to our particular Judge, to keep Stanley out of prison.

Accordingly, when the time came for my speech in mitigation, I aimed straight for our Portia's maternal instincts. 'Whoever may be guilty in this case,' I ended, 'one person is entirely innocent. Young Matthew Culp has broken no laws, committed no offence. He is a hard-working, decent little boy and his only fault may be that he loves his father and wanted to help him. But if you sentence his father to prison, you send Matthew also. You sentence him to years in council care. You sentence him to years as an orphan, because his mother has long gone out of his life. You sentence him to being cut off from his only family, from the father he needs and who needs him. You sentence this small boy to a lonely life in a crowd of strangers. I ask your Ladyship to consider that and on behalf of Matthew Culp I ask you to say . . . no prison for this foolish father!'

Phillida looked somewhat moved. She said quietly, 'Yes. Thank you, Mr Rumpole. Thank you for all your help.'

'If your Ladyship pleases.' I sat and then Stanley Culp was told to stand for sentence. The fact that the Judge was an extremely pretty woman in no way softened the awesome nature of the occasion. 'Culp,' she began, 'I have listened most carefully to all your learned Counsel has said, and said most eloquently, on your behalf.' So far so good. 'Unhappily, all the crimes we commit, all the mistakes we make, affect our innocent children. I am very conscious of the effect any prison sentence would have on your son, to whom I accept that you are devoted.' So far so hopeful, but this wasn't the end. 'However, I have to protect society. And I have to remember that you were prepared to deal in murderous weapons which might have left orphans in Northern Ireland.' This was not encouraging, and Portia then concluded, 'The most lenient sentence I can impose on you is one of four years' imprisonment. Take him down.'

Stanley Culp was looking hopelessly round the Court as though searching for his son Matthew before the dock officer touched his arm and removed him from our sight.

Pommeroy's was the place to attempt to drown the memory of my failure, and Stanley's four years. I sat alone at my corner table and there my old pupil, her day of judging done, sought me out. 'I'm sorry about Culp,' Portia said.

'Never plead guilty,' I advised her.

'I was only . . .'

'Doing your job?'

'Well, yes.'

'It is your job, isn't it, Portia?' I told her. 'Deciding what's going to happen to people. Judging them. Condemning them. Sending them downstairs. Not a very nice job, perhaps. Not as agreeable as cleaning out the drains or holding down a responsible position as a pox doctor's clerk. Every day I thank heaven I don't have to do it.'

'Shouldn't I have become a Recorder? Is that what you're saying?'

'Oh, no. No. Of course you should. Someone's got to do it. I just thank God it's not me.'

'You're lucky.' She looked at me and I think she meant it.

'I enjoy the luxury of defending people, protecting them where I can, keeping them out of chokey by the skin of my teeth. I've said a good many hard words in my time but "take him down" is an expression I've never used.'

'Rumpole!' She was hurt. 'Do you imagine I enjoyed it?'

'No, Portia. No, of course not. I never imagined that. You had to do your job and you did it so bloody fairly that my fellow got convicted. He was caught in a trap. Like the rest of us.'

'Cheer up, Rumpole.' Then she smiled. 'I'll buy you a large Pommeroy's plonk.'

'I am greatly obliged to your Ladyship.' I drank up. 'And what about young Tristan? Is he to pay his debt to society?'

'I don't know what you mean. He's going to Bogstead.' She announced another verdict.

'Your Ladyship passed judgement in favour of my learned friend Mr Claude Erskine-Brown?' I couldn't believe it.

'Well. Not exactly. As a matter of fact Tristan passed judgement on himself.'

What had happened, it seemed, was that, saying goodnight to her son, Phillida had been amazed to hear him say that he was eagerly looking forward to Bogstead. 'But don't you want to stay with us?' his mother asked, and Tristan confessed that being in the bosom of his family all the time was a bit of a strain on his nerves as his father was forever listening to operas and his mother always had her nose inside some brief or other. It was difficult to talk to either of them.

'I told him I'd talk to him whenever he wanted, that I'd tell him what I'd been doing, being a Judge, and all that sort of thing.'

'And what did young Tristan say to that?' I asked her.

'He thought he'd find more to talk about with the chaps at Boggers,' Phillida said more than a little sadly.

I went back to Chambers to collect a brief for the next day, and there I met Sam Ballard, who was still unusually excited by his conversation with Cy Stratton, and had decided not to fire Uncle Tom, which made it unnecessary for me to set out for darkest Africa. I bought some flowers for Hilda at the Temple Underground station, and when I got home and presented them to her I noticed our so-called 'mansion' flat was strangely silent.

'Boxey's gone.' Hilda spoke in a businesslike tone, concealing whatever emotion she may have felt. 'And what are *they* for?'

'Oh, to stick in a vase somewhere.' I restrained myself, with difficulty, from dancing with joy.

'He must have gone when I was out buying chops for our supper and he didn't even say goodbye. Why would Boxey do a thing like that?'

'Certainly not running away from the prospect of looking after you, Hilda. Never mind.' We went into the sitting room and I poured her a large gin and tonic and myself a celebratory Pommeroy's. 'He was always such *fun* as a young man was Boxey,' Hilda said.

> *'We look before and after;*
> *We pine for what is not;*
> *Our sincerest laughter*
> *With some pain is fraught,'*

I told her.

'Quite honestly, Rumpole' – Hilda was becoming daring – 'did you think Boxey had become a bit of a bore in his old age?'

'*Our sweetest songs are those that tell of saddest thought.* I'm not going to Africa, Hilda.'

'I didn't think you were.'

'I shall never see the elephant and gazelle gathering at the water-hole. I shall never see zebra stampeding in the dawn. I shall get no nearer Africa than Boxey did.'

'What on earth do you mean, Rumpole?'

'All that talk about evening dress to impress the natives. I bet he got that straight out of H. Rider Haggard. And didn't it occur to you, Hilda? There are absolutely no tigers in Kenya!'

There was a long silence, and then Hilda said with a rueful smile, 'Boxey asked me for a thousand pounds to start a smallholding, with battery hens.'

'I don't believe he's been further East than Bognor. You didn't give him anything?'

'Out of the overdraft? Don't be foolish, Rumpole. So you're staying here.'

'Soapy Sam Ballard told Uncle Tom to carry on golfing; he thinks it'll bring us a great deal of business with American lawyers.' I poured myself another comforting glass. 'You know, I lost the case against Ballard.'

'I thought so. You're not so unbearable when you lose.' She thought the situation over and then said, 'So we'll have to get along without Boxey.'

'How on earth shall we manage?'

'As we always do, I suppose. Just you and I together.'

'Nothing changes, does it, Hilda?' The day had given me an appetite and I was looking forward to Boxey's chops. 'Nothing changes very much at all.'

Rumpole à la Carte

I suppose, when I have time to think about it, which is not often during the long day's trudge round the Bailey and more downmarket venues such as the Uxbridge Magistrates' Court, the law represents some attempt, however fumbling, to impose order on a chaotic universe. Chaos, in the form of human waywardness and uncontrollable passion, is ever bubbling away just beneath the surface and its sporadic outbreaks are what provide me with my daily crust, and even a glass or two of Pommeroy's plonk to go with it. I have often noticed, in the accounts of the many crimes with which I have been concerned, that some small sign of disorder – an unusual number of milk bottles on a doorstep, a car parked on a double yellow line by a normally law-abiding citizen, even, in the Penge Bungalow Murders, someone else's mackintosh taken from an office peg – has been the first indication of anarchy taking over. The clue that such dark forces were at work in La Maison Jean-Pierre, one of the few London eateries to have achieved three Michelin stars and to charge more for a bite of dinner for two than I get for a legal aid theft, was very small indeed.

Now my wife Hilda is a good, plain cook. In saying that, I'm not referring to She Who Must Be Obeyed's moral values or passing any judgement on her personal appearance. What I can tell you is that she cooks without flights of fancy. She is not, in any way, a woman who lacks imagination. Indeed some of the things she imagines Rumpole gets up to when out of her sight are colourful in the extreme, but she doesn't apply such gifts to a chop or a potato, being quite content to grill the one and boil the other. She can also boil a cabbage into submission and fry fish. The nearest her cooking comes to the poetic is, perhaps, in her baked jam roll, which I have always found to be an

479

emotion best recollected in tranquillity. From all this, you will gather that Hilda's honest cooking is sufficient but not exotic, and that happily the terrible curse of *nouvelle cuisine* has not infected Froxbury mansions in the Gloucester Road.

So it is not often that I am confronted with the sort of fare photographed in the Sunday supplements. I scarcely ever sit down to an octagonal plate on which a sliver of monkfish is arranged in a composition of pastel shades, which also features a brush stroke of pink sauce, a single peeled prawn and a sprig of dill. Such gluttony is, happily, beyond my means. It wasn't, however, beyond the means of Hilda's Cousin Everard, who was visiting us from Canada, where he carried on a thriving trade as a company lawyer. He told us that he felt we stood in dire need of what he called 'a taste of gracious living' and booked a table for three at La Maison Jean-Pierre.

So we found ourselves in an elegantly appointed room with subdued lighting and even more subdued conversation, where the waiters padded around like priests and the customers behaved as though they were in church. The climax of the ritual came when the dishes were set on the table under silvery domes, which were lifted to the whispered command of '*Un, deux, trois!*' to reveal the somewhat mingy portions on offer. Cousin Everard was a grey-haired man in a pale grey suiting who talked about his legal experiences in greyish tones. He entertained us with a long account of a takeover bid for the Winnipeg Soap Company which had cleared four million dollars for his clients, the Great Elk Bank of Canada. Hearing this, Hilda said accusingly, 'You've never cleared four million dollars for a client, have you, Rumpole? You should be a company lawyer like Everard.'

'Oh, I think I'll stick to crime,' I told them. 'At least it's a more honest type of robbery.'

'Nonsense. Robbery has never got us a dinner at La Maison Jean-Pierre. We'd never be here if Cousin Everard hadn't come all the way from Saskatchewan to visit us.'

'Yes, indeed. From the town of Saskatoon, Hilda.' Everard gave her a greyish smile.

'You see, Hilda. Saskatoon as in *spittoon*.'

'Crime doesn't pay, Horace,' the man from the land of the igloos told me. 'You should know that by now. Of course, we have several fine-dining restaurants in Saskatoon these days, but nothing to touch this.' He continued his inspection of the menu. 'Hilda, may I make so bold as to ask, what is your pleasure?'

During the ensuing discussion my attention strayed. Staring idly round the consecrated area I was startled to see, in the gloaming, a distinct sign of human passion in revolt against the forces of law and order. At a table for two I recognized Claude Erskine-Brown, opera buff, hopeless cross-examiner and long-time member of our Chambers in Equity Court. But was he dining *tête-à-tête* with his wife, the handsome and successful QC, Mrs Phillida Erskine-Brown, the Portia of our group, as law and order demanded? The answer to that was no. He was entertaining a young and decorative lady solicitor named Patricia (known to herself as Tricia) Benbow. Her long golden hair (which often provoked whistles from the cruder junior clerks round the Old Bailey) hung over her slim and suntanned shoulders and one generously ringed hand rested on Claude's as she gazed, in her usual appealing way, up into his eyes. She couldn't gaze into them for long as Claude, no doubt becoming uneasily aware of the unexpected presence of a couple of Rumpoles in the room, hid his face behind a hefty wine list.

At that moment an extremely superior brand of French head waiter manifested himself beside our table, announced his presence with a discreet cough and led off with '*Madame, messieurs*. Tonight Jean-Pierre recommends, for the main course, *la poésie de la poitrine du canard aux céleris et épinards crus.*'

'*Poésie . . .*' Hilda sounded delighted and kindly explained, 'That's poetry, Rumpole. Tastes a good deal better than that old Wordsworth of yours, I shouldn't be surprised.'

'Tell us about it, Georges.' Everard smiled at the waiter. 'Whet our appetites.'

'This is just a few wafer-thin slices of breast of duck, marinated in a drop or two of Armagnac, delicately grilled and served with a celery remoulade and some leaves of spinach lightly steamed . . .'

'And mash . . . ?' I interrupted the man to ask.

'*Excusez-moi?*' The fellow seemed unable to believe his ears.

'Mashed spuds come with it, do they?'

'Ssh, Rumpole!' Hilda was displeased with me, but turned all her charms on Georges. 'I will have the *poésie*. It sounds delicious.'

'A culinary experience, Hilda. Yes. *Poésie* for me too, please.' Everard fell into line.

'I would like a *poésie* of steak-and-kidney *pudding*, not pie, with mashed potatoes and a big scoop of boiled cabbage. *English* mustard, if you have it.' It seemed a reasonable enough request.

'Rumpole!' Hilda's whisper was menacing. 'Behave yourself!'

'This . . . "pudding"' – Georges was puzzled – 'is not on our menu.'

' "Your pleasure is our delight." It says that on your menu. Couldn't you ask Cookie if she could delight me? Along those lines.'

' "Cookie"? I do not know who M'sieur means by "Cookie". Our *maître de cuisine* is Jean-Pierre O'Higgins himself. He is in the kitchen now.'

'How very convenient. Have a word in his shell-like, why don't you?'

For a tense moment it seemed as though the looming, priestly figure of Georges was about to excommunicate me, drive me out of the Temple or at least curse me by bell, book and candle. However, after muttering, '*Si vous le voulez. Excusez-moi*', he went off in search of higher authority. Hilda apologized for my behaviour and told Cousin Everard that she supposed I thought I was being funny. I assured her that there was nothing particularly funny about a steak-and-kidney pudding.

Then I was aware of a huge presence at my elbow. A tall, fat, red-faced man in a chef's costume was standing with his hands on his hips and asking, 'Is there someone here wants to lodge a complaint?'

Jean-Pierre O'Higgins, I was later to discover, was the product of an Irish father and a French mother. He spoke in the tones of those Irishmen who come up in a menacing manner and stand far too close to you in pubs. He was well known, I had already heard it rumoured, for dominating both his kitchen and his customers; his phenomenal rudeness to his guests seemed to be regarded as one of the attractions of his establishment. The gourmets of London didn't feel that their dinners had been entirely satisfactory unless they were served up, by way of a savoury, with a couple of insults from Jean-Pierre O'Higgins.

'Well, yes,' I said. 'There is someone.'

'Oh, yes?' O'Higgins had clearly never heard of the old adage about the customer always being right. 'And are you the joker that requested mash?'

'Am I to understand you to be saying,' I inquired as politely as I knew how, 'that there are to be no mashed spuds for my delight?'

'Look here, my friend. I don't know who you are . . .' Jean-Pierre went on in an unfriendly fashion and Everard did his best to introduce me. 'Oh, this is Horace Rumpole, Jean-Pierre. The *criminal* lawyer.'

'*Criminal* lawyer, eh?' Jean-Pierre was unappeased. 'Well, don't commit your crimes in my restaurant. If you want "mashed spuds", I suggest you move down to the workingmen's caff at the end of the street.'

'That's a very helpful suggestion.' I was, as you see, trying to be as pleasant as possible.

'You might get a few bangers while you're about it. And a bottle of OK sauce. That suit your delicate palate, would it?'

'Very well indeed! I'm not a great one for wafer-thin slices of anything.'

'You don't look it. Now, let's get this straight. People who come into my restaurant damn well eat as I tell them to!'

'And I'm sure you win them all over with your irresistible charm.' I gave him the retort courteous. As the chef seemed about to explode, Hilda weighed in with a well-meaning, 'I'm sure my husband doesn't mean to be rude. It's just, well, we don't dine out very often. And this is such a delightful room, isn't it?'

'Your husband?' Jean-Pierre looked at She Who Must Be Obeyed with deep pity. 'You have all my sympathy, you unfortunate woman. Let me tell you, Mr Rumpole, this is La Maison Jean-Pierre. I have three stars in the Michelin. I have thrown out an Arabian king because he ordered filet mignon well cooked. I have sent film stars away in tears because they dared to mention Thousand Island dressing. I am Jean-Pierre O'Higgins, the greatest culinary genius now working in England!'

I must confess that during this speech from the patron I found my attention straying. The other diners, as is the way with the English at the trough, were clearly straining their ears to catch every detail of the row whilst ostentatiously concentrating on their plates. The pale, bespectacled girl making up the bills behind the desk in the corner seemed to have no such inhibitions. She was staring across the room and looking at me, I thought, as though I had thoroughly deserved the O'Higgins rebuke. And then I saw two waiters approach Erskine-Brown's table with domed dishes, which they laid on the table with due solemnity.

'And let me tell you,' Jean-Pierre's oration continued, 'I started my career with salads at La Grande Bouffe in Lyons under the great Ducasse. I was rôtisseur in Le Crillon, Boston. I have run this restaurant for twenty years and I have never, let me tell you, in my whole career, served up a mashed spud!'

The climax of his speech was dramatic but not nearly as startling as the events which took place at Erskine-Brown's table. To the count of '*Un, deux, trois!*' the waiters removed the silver covers and from under the one in front of Tricia Benbow sprang a small, alarmed brown mouse, perfectly visible by the light of a table candle, which had presumably been nibbling at the *poésie*. At this, the elegant lady solicitor uttered a piercing scream and leapt on to her chair. There she stood, with her skirt held down to as near her knees as possible, screaming in an ever-rising scale towards some ultimate crescendo. Meanwhile the stricken Claude looked just as a man who'd planned to have a quiet dinner with a lady and wanted to attract no one's attention would look under such circumstances. 'Please, Tricia,' I could hear his plaintive whisper, 'don't scream! People are noticing us.'

'I say, old darling,' I couldn't help saying to that three-star man O'Higgins, 'they had a mouse on that table. Is it the *spécialité de la maison?*'

A few days later, at breakfast in the mansion flat, glancing through the post (mainly bills and begging letters from Her Majesty, who seemed to be pushed for a couple of quid and would be greatly obliged if I'd let her have a little tax money on account), I saw a glossy brochure for a hotel in the Lake District. Although in the homeland of my favourite poet, Le Château Duddon, 'Lakeland's Paradise of Gracious Living', didn't sound like old Wordsworth's cup of tea, despite the 'king-sized four-poster in the Samuel Taylor Coleridge suite'.

'Cousin Everard wants to take me up there for a break.' Hilda, who was clearing away, removed a half-drunk cup of tea from my hand.

'A break from what?' I was mystified.

'From you, Rumpole. Don't you think I need it? After that disastrous evening at La Maison?'

'Was it a disaster? I quite enjoyed it. England's greatest chef laboured and gave birth to a ridiculous mouse. People'd pay good money to see a trick like that.'

'*You* were the disaster, Rumpole,' she said, as she consigned my last piece of toast to the tidy bin. 'You were unforgivable. Mashed spuds! Why ever did you use such a vulgar expression?'

'Hilda,' I protested, I thought, reasonably, 'I have heard some fairly fruity language round the Courts in the course of a long life of crime. But I've never heard it suggested that the words "mashed spuds" would bring a blush to the cheek of the tenderest virgin.'

'Don't try to be funny, Rumpole. You upset that brilliant chef, Mr O'Higgins. You deeply upset Cousin Everard!'

'Well' – I had to put the case for the defence – 'Everard kept on suggesting I didn't make enough to feed you properly. Typical commercial lawyer. Criminal law is about life, liberty and the pursuit of happiness. Commercial law is about money. That's what I think, anyway.'

Hilda looked at me, weighed up the evidence and summed up, not entirely in my favour. 'I don't think you made that terrible fuss because of what you thought about the commercial law,' she said. 'You did it because you have to be a "character", don't you? Wherever you go. Well, I don't know if I'm going to be able to put up with your "character" much longer.'

I don't know why but what she said made me feel, quite suddenly and in a most unusual way, uncertain of myself. What was Hilda talking about exactly? I asked for further and better particulars.

'You have to be one all the time, don't you?' She was clearly getting into her stride. 'With your cigar ash and steak and kidney and Pommeroy's Ordinary Red and your arguments. Always arguments! Why do you have to go on arguing, Rumpole?'

'Arguing? It's been my life, Hilda,' I tried to explain.

'Well, it's not mine! Not any more. Cousin Everard doesn't argue in public. He is quiet and polite.'

'If you like that sort of thing.' The subject of Cousin Everard was starting to pall on me.

'Yes, Rumpole. Yes, I do. That's why I agreed to go on this trip.'

'Trip?'

'Everard and I are going to tour all the restaurants in England with stars. We're going to Bath and York and Devizes. And you can stay here and eat all the mashed spuds you want.'

'What?' I hadn't up till then taken Le Château Duddon entirely seriously. 'You really mean it?'

'Oh, yes. I think so. The living is hardly gracious here, is it?'

On the way to my place of work I spent an uncomfortable quarter of an hour thinking over what She Who Must Be Obeyed had said about me having to be a 'character'. It seemed an unfair charge. I drink Château Thames Embankment because it's all I can afford. It keeps me regular and blots out certain painful memories, such as a bad day in Court in front of Judge Graves, an old darling who undoubtedly passes iced water every time he goes to the Gents. I enjoy the fragrance of a small cigar. I relish an argument. This is the way of life I have chosen. I don't have to do any of these things in order to be a character. Do I?

I was jerked out of this unaccustomed introspection on my arrival in the clerk's room at Chambers. Henry, our clerk, was striking bargains with solicitors over the telephone whilst Dianne sat in front of her typewriter, her head bowed over a lengthy and elaborate manicure. Uncle Tom, our oldest inhabitant, who hasn't had a brief in Court since anyone can remember, was working hard at improving his putting skills with an old mashie niblick and a clutch of golf balls, the hole being represented by the waste-paper basket laid on its side. Almost as soon as I got into this familiar environment I was comforted by the sight of a man who seemed to be in far deeper trouble than I was. Claude Erskine-Brown came up to me in a manner that I can only describe as furtive.

'Rumpole,' he said, 'as you may know, Philly is away in Cardiff doing a long fraud.'

'Your wife,' I congratulated the man, 'goes from strength to strength.'

'What I mean is, Rumpole' – Claude's voice sank below the level of Henry's telephone calls – 'you may have noticed me the other night. In La Maison Jean-Pierre.'

'Noticed you, Claude? Of course not! You were only in the company of a lady who stood on a chair and screamed like a banshee with tooth-ache. No one could have possibly noticed you.' I did my best to comfort the man.

'It was purely a business arrangement,' he reassured me.

'Pretty rum way of conducting business.'

'The lady was Miss Tricia Benbow. My instructing solicitor in the VAT case,' he told me, as though that explained everything.

'Claude, I have had some experience of the law and it's a good plan, when entertaining solicitors in order to tout for briefs, *not* to introduce mice into their *plats du jour*.'

The telephone by Dianne's typewriter rang. She blew on her nail lacquer and answered it, as Claude's voice rose in anguished protest. 'Good heavens. You don't think I did *that*, do you, Rumpole? The whole thing was a disaster! An absolute tragedy! Which may have appalling consequences . . .' 'Your wife on the phone, Mr Erskine-Brown,' Dianne interrupted him and Claude went to answer the call with all the eager cheerfulness of a French aristocrat who is told the tumbril is at the door. As he was telling his wife he hoped things were going splendidly in Cardiff, and that he rarely went out in the evenings, in fact usually settled down to a scrambled egg in front of the telly, there was a sound of rushing water without and our Head of Chambers joined us.

'Something extremely serious has happened.' Sam Ballard, QC, made the announcement as though war had broken out. He is a pallid sort of person who usually looks as though he has just bitten into a sour apple. His hair, I have to tell you, seems to be slicked down with some kind of pomade.

'Someone nicked the nail-brush in the Chambers loo?' I suggested helpfully.

'How did you guess?' He turned on me, amazed, as though I had the gift of second sight.

'It corresponds to your idea of something serious. Also I notice such things.'

'Odd that you should know immediately what I was talking about, Rumpole.' By now Ballard's amazement had turned to deep suspicion.

'Not guilty, my Lord,' I assured him. 'Didn't you have a meeting of your God-bothering society here last week?'

'The Lawyers As Christians committee. We met here. What of it?'

' "Cleanliness is next to godliness." Isn't that their motto? The devout are notable nail-brush nickers.' As I said this, I watched Erskine-Brown lay the telephone to rest and leave the room with the air of a man who has merely postponed the evil hour. Ballard was still on the subject of serious crime in the facilities. 'It's of vital importance in any place of work, Henry,' he batted on, 'that the highest standards of hygiene are maintained! Now I've been instructed by the City Health Authority in an important case, it would be extremely embarrassing to me personally if my Chambers were found wanting in the matter of a nail-brush.'

'Well, don't look at me, Mr Ballard.' Henry was not taking this lecture well.

'I am accusing nobody.' Ballard sounded unconvincing. 'But look to it, Henry. Please, look to it.'

Then our Head of Chambers left us. Feeling my usual reluctance to start work, I asked Uncle Tom, as something of an expert in these matters, if it would be fair to call me a 'character'.

'A what, Rumpole?'

'A "character", Uncle Tom.'

'Oh, they had one of those in old Sniffy Greengrass's Chambers in Lamb Court,' Uncle Tom remembered. 'Fellow called Dalrymple. Lived in an absolutely filthy flat over a chemist's shop in Chancery Lane and used to lead a cat round the Temple on a long piece of pink tape. "Old Dalrymple's a character," they used to say, and the other fellows in Chambers were rather proud of him.'

'I don't do anything like that, do I?' I asked for reassurance.

'I hope not,' Uncle Tom was kind enough to say. 'This Dalrymple finally went across the road to do an undefended divorce. In his pyjamas! I believe they had to lock him up. I wouldn't say you were a "character", Rumpole. Not yet, anyway.'

'Thank you, Uncle Tom. Perhaps you could mention that to She Who Must?'

And then the day took a distinct turn for the better. Henry put down his phone after yet another call and my heart leapt up when I heard that Mr Bernard, my favourite instructing solicitor (because he keeps quiet, does what he's told and hardly ever tells me about his bad back), was coming over and was anxious to instruct me in a new case which was 'not on the legal aid'. As I left the room to go about this business, I had one final question for Uncle Tom. 'That fellow Dalrymple. He didn't play golf in the clerk's room did he?'

'Good heavens, no.' Uncle Tom seemed amused at my ignorance of the world. 'He was a character, do you see? He'd hardly do anything normal.'

Mr Bernard, balding, pinstriped, with a greying moustache and a kindly eye, through all our triumphs and disasters remained imperturbable. No confession made by any client, however bizarre, seemed to surprise him, nor had any revelation of evil shocked him. He lived through our days of murder, mayhem and fraud as though he were listening to 'Gardeners' Question Time'. He was interested in growing roses and in his daughter's nursing career. He spent his holidays in remote spots like Bangkok and the Seychelles. He always went away, he told me, 'on a package' and returned with considerable relief. I was always pleased to see Mr Bernard, but that day he seemed to have brought me something far from my usual line of country.

'My client, Mr Rumpole, first consulted me because his marriage was on the rocks, not to put too fine a point on it.'

'It happens, Mr Bernard. Many marriages are seldom off them.'

'Particularly so if, as in this case, the wife's of foreign extraction. It's long been my experience, Mr Rumpole, that you can't beat foreign wives for being vengeful. In this case, extremely vengeful.'

'Hell hath no fury, Mr Bernard?' I suggested.

'Exactly, Mr Rumpole. You've put your finger on the nub of the case. As you would say yourself.'

'I haven't done a matrimonial for years. My divorce may be a little rusty,' I told him modestly.

'Oh, we're not asking you to do the divorce. We're sending that to Mr Tite-Smith in Crown Office Row.'

Oh, well, I thought, with only a slight pang of disappointment, good luck to little Tite-Smith.

'The matrimonial is not my client's only problem,' Mr Bernard told me.

'*When sorrows come*, Mr Bernard, *they come not single spies, But in battalions!* Your chap got something else on his plate, has he?'

'On his plate!' The phrase seemed to cause my solicitor some amusement. 'That's very apt, that is. And apter than you know, Mr Rumpole.'

'Don't keep me in suspense! Who is this mysterious client?'

'I wasn't to divulge the name, Mr Rumpole, in case you should refuse to act for him. He thought you might've taken against him, so he's coming to appeal to you in person. I asked Henry if he'd show him up as soon as he arrived.'

And, dead on cue, Dianne knocked on my door, threw it open and announced, 'Mr O'Higgins.' The large man, dressed now in a deafening checked tweed jacket and a green turtlenecked sweater, looking less like a chef than an Irish horse coper, advanced on me with a broad grin and his hand extended in a greeting, which was in strong contrast to our last encounter.

'I rely on you to save me, Mr Rumpole,' he boomed. 'You're the man to do it, sir. The great criminal defender!'

'Oh? I thought *I* was the criminal in your restaurant,' I reminded him.

'I have to tell you, Mr Rumpole, your courage took my breath away! Do you know what he did, Mr Bernard? Do you know what this little fellow here had the pluck to do?' He seemed determined to impress my solicitor with an account of my daring in the face of adversity. 'He only ordered mashed spuds in La Maison Jean-Pierre. A risk no one else has taken in all the time I've been *maître de cuisine*.'

'It didn't seem to be particularly heroic,' I told Bernard, but O'Higgins would have none of that. 'I tell you, Mr Bernard' – he moved very close to my solicitor and towered over him – 'a man who could do that to Jean-Pierre couldn't be intimidated by all the Judges of the Queen's Bench. What do you say then, Mr Horace Rumpole? Will you take me on?'

I didn't answer him immediately but sat at my desk, lit a small cigar and looked at him critically. 'I don't know yet.'

'Is it my personality that puts you off?' My prospective client folded himself into my armchair, with one leg draped over an arm. He grinned even more broadly, displaying a judiciously placed gold tooth. 'Do you find me objectionable?'

'Mr O'Higgins.' I decided to give judgement at length. 'I think your restaurant pretentious and your portions skimpy. Your customers eat in a dim, religious atmosphere which seems to be more like Evensong than a good night out. You appear to be a self-opinionated and self-satisfied bully. I have known many murderers who could teach you a lesson in courtesy. However, Mr Bernard tells me that you are prepared to pay my fee and, in accordance with the great traditions of the Bar, I am on hire to even the most unattractive customer.'

There was a silence and I wondered if the inflammable restaurateur were about to rise and hit me. But he turned to Bernard with even greater enthusiasm. 'Just listen to that! How's that for eloquence? We picked the right one here, Mr Bernard!'

'Well, now. I gather you're in some sort of trouble. Apart from your marriage, that is.' I unscrewed my pen and prepared to take a note.

'This has nothing to do with my marriage.' But then he frowned unhappily. 'Anyway, I don't think it has.'

'You haven't done away with this vengeful wife of yours?' Was I to be presented with a murder?

'I should have, long ago,' Jean-Pierre admitted. 'But no. Simone is still alive and suing. Isn't that right, Mr Bernard?'

'It is, Mr O'Higgins,' Bernard assured him gloomily. 'It is indeed. But this is something quite different. My client, Mr Rumpole, is being charged under the Food and Hygiene Regulations 1970 for offences relating to dirty and dangerous practices at La Maison. I have received a telephone call from the Environmental Health Officer.'

It was then, I'm afraid, that I started to laugh. I named the guilty party. 'The mouse!'

'Got it in one.' Jean-Pierre didn't seem inclined to join in the joke.

'The *wee, sleekit, cow'rin, tim'rous beastie,*' I quoted at him. 'How delightful! We'll elect for trial before a jury. If we can't get you off, Mr O'Higgins, at least we'll give them a little harmless entertainment.'

Of course it wasn't really funny. A mouse in the wrong place, like too many milk bottles on a doorstep, might be a sign of passions stretched beyond control.

I have always found it useful, before forming a view about a case, to inspect the scene of the crime. Accordingly I visited La Maison Jean-Pierre one evening to study the ritual serving of dinner.

Mr Bernard and I stood in a corner of the kitchen at La Maison Jean-Pierre with our client. We were interested in the two waiters who had attended table eight, the site of the Erskine-Brown assignation. The senior of the two was Gaston, the station waiter, who had four tables under his command. 'Gaston Leblanc,' Jean-Pierre told us, as he identified the small, fat, cheerful, middle-aged man who trotted between the tables. 'Been with me for ever. Works all the hours God gave to keep a sick wife and their kid at university. Does all sorts of other jobs in the daytime. I don't inquire too closely. Georges Pitou, the head waiter, takes the orders, of course, and leaves a copy of the note on the table.'

We saw Georges move, in a stately fashion, into the kitchen and hand the order for table eight to a young cook in a white hat, who stuck it up on the kitchen wall with a magnet. This was Ian, the sous chef. Jean-Pierre had 'discovered' him in a Scottish hotel and wanted to encourage his talent. That night the bustle in the kitchen was muted, and as I looked through the circular window into the dining room I saw that most of the white-clothed tables were standing empty, like small icebergs in a desolate polar region. When the prosecution had been announced, there had been a headline in the *Evening Standard* which read GUESS WHO'S COMING TO DINNER? MOUSE SERVED IN TOP LONDON RESTAURANT and since then attendances at La Maison had dropped off sharply.

The runner between Gaston's station and the kitchen was the commis waiter, Alphonse Pascal, a painfully thin, dark-eyed young man with a falling lock of hair who looked like the hero of some nineteenth-century French novel, interesting and doomed. 'As a matter of fact,' Jean-Pierre told us, 'Alphonse is full of ambition. He's starting at the bottom and wants to work his way up to running a hotel. Been with me for about a year.'

We watched as Ian put the two orders for table eight on the serving table. In due course Alphonse came into the kitchen and called out, 'Number Eight!' 'Ready, frog face,' Ian told him politely, and Alphonse came back with, '*Merci*, idiot.'

'Are they friends?' I asked my client.

'Not really. They're both much too fond of Mary.'

'Mary?'

'Mary Skelton. The English girl who makes up the bills in the restaurant.'

I looked again through the circular window and saw the unmemorable girl, her head bent over her calculator. She seemed an unlikely subject for such rivalry. I saw Alphonse pass her with a tray, carrying two domed dishes and, although he looked in her direction, she didn't glance up from her work. Alphonse then took the dishes to the serving table at Gaston's station. Gaston looked under one dome to check its contents and then the plates were put on the table. Gaston mouthed an inaudible '*Un, deux, trois!*', the domes were lifted before the diners and not a mouse stirred.

'On the night in question,' Bernard reminded me, 'Gaston says in his statement that he looked under the dome on the gentleman's plate.'

'And saw no side order of mouse,' I remembered.

'Exactly! So he gave the other to Alphonse, who took it to the lady.'

'And then . . . Hysterics!'

'And then the reputation of England's greatest *maître de cuisine* crumbled to dust!' Jean-Pierre spoke as though announcing a national disaster.

'Nonsense!' I did my best to cheer him up. 'You're forgetting the reputation of Horace Rumpole.'

'You think we've got a defence?' my client asked eagerly. 'I mean, now that you've looked at the kitchen?'

'Can't think of one for the moment,' I admitted, 'but I expect we'll cook up something in the end.'

Unencouraged, Jean-Pierre looked out into the dining room, muttered, 'I'd better go and keep those lonely people company', and left us. I watched him pass the desk, where Mary looked up and smiled and I thought, however brutal he was with his customers, at least Jean-Pierre's staff seemed to find him a tolerable employer. And then, to my surprise, I saw him approach the couple at table eight, grinning in a most ingratiating manner, and stand chatting and bowing as though they could have ordered doner kebab and chips and that would have been perfectly all right by him.

'You know,' I said to Mr Bernard, 'it's quite extraordinary, the power that can be wielded by one of the smaller rodents.'

'You mean it's wrecked his business?'

'No. More amazing than that. It's forced Jean-Pierre O'Higgins to be polite to his clientele.'

After my second visit to La Maison events began to unfold at breakneck speed. First our Head of Chambers, Soapy Sam Ballard, made it known to me that the brief he had accepted on behalf of the Health Authority, and of which he had boasted so flagrantly during the nail-brush incident, was in fact the prosecution of J.-P. O'Higgins for the serious crime of being in charge of a rodent-infested restaurant. Then She Who Must Be Obeyed, true to her word, packed her grip and went off on a gastronomic tour with the man from Saskatoon. I was left to enjoy a lonely high-calorie breakfast, with no fear of criticism over the matter of a fourth sausage, in the Taste-Ee-Bite café, Fleet Street. Seated there one morning, enjoying the company of *The Times* crossword, I happened to overhear Mizz Liz Probert, the dedicated young radical barrister in our Chambers, talking to her close friend, David Inchcape, whom she had persuaded us to take on in a somewhat devious manner – a barrister as young but, I think, at heart, a touch less radical than Mizz Liz herself.*

'You don't really *care*, do you, Dave?' she was saying.

'Of course, I care. I care about you, Liz. Deeply.' He reached out over their plates of muesli and cups of decaff to grasp her fingers.

'That's just physical.'

'Well. Not just physical. I don't suppose it's *just*. Mainly physical, perhaps.'

'No one cares about old people.'

'But you're not old people, Liz. Thank God!'

'You see. You don't care about them. My Dad was saying there's old people dying in tower blocks every day. Nobody knows about it for weeks, until they decompose!' And I saw Dave release her hand and say, 'Please, Liz. I *am* having my breakfast.'

'You see! You don't want to know. It's just something you don't want to hear about. It's the same with battery hens.'

'What's the same about battery hens?'

'No one wants to know. That's all.'

'But surely, Liz. Battery hens don't get lonely.'

* See 'Rumpole and the Quality of Life' (*The Third Rumpole Omnibus*).

'Perhaps they do. There's an awful lot of loneliness about.' She looked in my direction. 'Get off to Court then, if you have to. But do *think* about it, Dave.' Then she got up, crossed to my table, and asked what I was doing. I was having my breakfast, I assured her, and not doing my yoga meditation.

'Do you always have breakfast alone, Rumpole?' She spoke, in the tones of a deeply supportive social worker, as she sat down opposite me.

'It's not always possible. Much easier now, of course.'

'Now. Why *now*, exactly?' She looked seriously concerned.

'Well. Now my wife's left me,' I told her cheerfully.

'Hilda!' Mizz Probert was shocked, being a conventional girl at heart.

'As you would say, Mizz Liz, she is no longer sharing a one-on-one relationship with me. In any meaningful way.'

'Where does that leave you, Rumpole?'

'Alone. To enjoy my breakfast and contemplate the crossword puzzle.'

'Where's Hilda gone?'

'Oh, in search of gracious living with her Cousin Everard from Saskatoon. A fellow with about as many jokes in him as the Dow Jones Average.'

'You mean, she's gone off with another man?' Liz seemed unable to believe that infidelity was not confined to the young.

'That's about the size of it.'

'But, Rumpole. *Why?*'

'Because he's rich enough to afford very small portions of food.'

'So you're living by yourself? You must be terribly lonely.'

'*Society is all but rude,*' I assured her, '*To this delicious solitude.*'

There was a pause and then Liz took a deep breath and offered her assistance. 'You know, Rumpole. Dave and I have founded the Y.R.L. Young Radical Lawyers. We don't only mean to reform the legal system, although that's part of it, of course. We're going to take on social work as well. We could always get someone to call and take a look at your flat every morning.'

'To make sure it's still there?'

'Well, no, Rumpole. As a matter of fact, to make sure you are.'

Those who are alone have great opportunities for eavesdropping, and Liz and Dave weren't the only members of our Chambers I heard engaged in a heart-to-heart that day. Before I took the journey back to the She-less flat, I dropped into Pommeroy's and was enjoying the ham roll and bottle of Château Thames Embankment which would constitute my dinner, seated in one of the high-backed, pew-like stalls Jack Pommeroy has installed, presumably to give the joint a vaguely medieval appearance and attract the tourists. From behind my back I heard the voices of our Head of Chambers and Claude Erskine-Brown, who was saying, in his most ingratiating tones, 'Ballard. I want to have a word with you about the case you've got against La Maison Jean-Pierre.'

To this, Ballard, in thoughtful tones, replied unexpectedly, 'A strong chain! It's the only answer.' Which didn't seem to follow.

'It was just my terrible luck, of course,' Erskine-Brown complained, 'that it should happen at my table. I mean, I'm a pretty well-known member of the Bar. Naturally I don't want my name connected with, well, a rather ridiculous incident.'

'Fellows in Chambers aren't going to like it.' Ballard was not yet with him. 'They'll say it's a restriction on their liberty. Rumpole, no doubt, will have a great deal to say about Magna Carta. But the only answer is to get a new nail-brush and chain it up. Can I have your support in taking strong measures?'

'Of course, you can, Ballard. I'll be right behind you on this one.' The creeping Claude seemed only too anxious to please. 'And in this case you're doing, I don't suppose you'll have to call the couple who actually *got* the mouse?'

'The couple?' There was a pause while Ballard searched his memory. 'The mouse was served – appalling lack of hygiene in the workplace – to a table booked by a Mr Claude Erskine-Brown and guest. Of course he'll be a vital witness.' And then the penny dropped. He stared at Claude and said firmly, '*You'll* be a vital witness.'

'But if I'm a witness of any sort, my name'll get into the papers and Philly will know I was having dinner.'

'Why on earth *shouldn't* she know you were having dinner?' Ballard was reasoning with the man. 'Most people have dinner. Nothing to be ashamed of. Get a grip on yourself, Erskine-Brown.'

'Ballard. Sam.' Claude was trying the appeal to friendship. 'You're a married man. You should understand.'

'Of course I'm married. And Marguerite and I have dinner. On a regular basis.'

'But I wasn't having dinner with Philly.' Claude explained the matter carefully. 'I was having dinner with an instructing solicitor.'

'That was your guest?'

'Yes.'

'A solicitor?'

'Of course.'

Ballard seemed to have thought the matter over carefully, but he was still puzzled when he replied, remembering his instructions. 'He apparently leapt on to a chair, held down his skirt and screamed three times!'

'Ballard! The solicitor was Tricia Benbow. You don't imagine I'd spend a hundred and something quid on feeding the face of Mr Bernard, do you?'

There was another longish pause, during which I imagined Claude in considerable suspense, and then our Head of Chambers spoke again. 'Tricia Benbow?' he asked.

'Yes.'

'Is that the one with the long blonde hair and rings?'

'That's the one.'

'And your wife knew nothing of this?'

'And must never know!' For some reason not clear to me, Claude seemed to think he'd won his case, for he now sounded grateful. 'Thank you, Ballard. Thanks awfully, Sam. I can count on you to keep my name out of this. I'll do the same for you, old boy. Any day of the week.'

'That won't be necessary.' Ballard's tone was not encouraging, although Claude said, 'No? Well, thanks, anyway.'

'It *will* be necessary, however, for you to give evidence for the prosecution.' Soapy Sam Ballard pronounced sentence and Claude yelped, 'Have a heart, Sam!'

'Don't you "Sam" me.' Ballard was clearly in a mood to notice the decline of civilization as we know it. 'It's all part of the same thing, isn't it? Sharp practice over the nail-brush. Failure to assist the authorities in an important prosecution. You'd better prepare yourself for Court, Erskine-Brown. And to be cross-examined by Rumpole for the defence. Do your duty! And take the consequences.'

A moment later I saw Ballard leaving for home and his wife, Marguerite, who, you will remember, once held the position of matron at the Old Bailey. No doubt he would chatter to her of nail-brushes and barristers unwilling to tell the whole truth. I carried my bottle of plonk round to Claude's stall in order to console the fellow.

'So,' I said, 'you lost your case.'

'What a bastard!' I have never seen Claude so pale.

'You made a big mistake, old darling. It's no good appealing to the warm humanity of a fellow who believes in chaining up nail-brushes.'

So the intrusive mouse continued to play havoc with the passions of a number of people, and I prepared myself for its day in Court. I told Mr Bernard to instruct Ferdinand Isaac Gerald Newton, known in the trade as 'Fig' Newton, a lugubrious scarecrow of a man who is, without doubt, our most effective private investigator, to keep a watchful eye on the staff of La Maison. And then I decided to call in at the establishment on my way home one evening, not only to get a few more facts from my client but because I was becoming bored with Pommeroy's ham sandwiches.

Before I left Chambers an event occurred which caused me deep satisfaction. I made for the downstairs lavatory, and although the door was open, I found it occupied by Uncle Tom who was busily engaged at the basin washing his collection of golf balls and scrubbing each one to a gleaming whiteness with a nail-brush. He had been putting each one, when cleaned, into a biscuit tin and as I entered he dropped the nail-brush in also.

'Uncle Tom!' – I recognized the article at once – 'that's the Chambers nail-brush! Soapy Sam's having kittens about it.'

'Oh, dear. Is it, really? I must have taken it without remembering. I'll leave it on the basin.'

But I persuaded him to let me have it for safe keeping, saying I longed to see Ballard's little face light up with joy when it was restored to him.

When I arrived at La Maison the disputes seemed to have become a great deal more dramatic than even in Equity Court. The place was not yet open for dinner, but I was let in as the restaurant's legal adviser and I heard raised voices and sounds of a struggle from the kitchen. Pushing the door open, I found Jean-Pierre in the act of forcibly removing a knife from the hands of Ian, the sous chef, at whom an excited Alphonse Pascal, his lock of black hair falling into his eyes, was shouting abuse in French. My arrival created a diversion in which both men calmed down and Jean-Pierre passed judgement on them. 'Bloody lunatics!' he said. 'Haven't they done this place enough harm already? They have to start slaughtering each other. Behave yourselves. *Soyez sages!* And what can I do for *you*, Mr Rumpole?'

'Perhaps we could have a little chat,' I suggested as the tumult died down. 'I thought I'd call in. My wife's away, you see, and I haven't done much about dinner.'

'Then what would you like?'

'Oh, anything. Just a snack.'

'Some pâté, perhaps? And a bottle of champagne?' I thought he'd never ask.

When we were seated at a table in a corner of the empty restaurant, the patron told me more about the quarrel. 'They were fighting again over Mary Skelton.'

I looked across at the desk, where the unmemorable girl was getting out her calculator and preparing for her evening's work. 'She doesn't look the type, exactly,' I suggested.

'Perhaps,' Jean-Pierre speculated, 'she has a warm heart? My wife Simone looks the type, but she's got a heart like an ice cube.'

'Your wife. The vengeful woman?' I remembered what Mr Bernard had told me.

'Why should she be vengeful to me, Mr Rumpole? When I'm a particularly tolerant and easy-going type of individual?'

At which point a couple of middle-aged Americans, who had strayed in off the street, appeared at the door of the restaurant and asked Jean-Pierre if he were serving dinner. 'At 6.30? No! And we don't do teas, either.' He shouted across at them, in a momentary return to his old ways, 'Cretins!'

'Of course,' I told him, 'you're a very parfait, gentle cook.'

'A great artist needs admiration. He needs almost incessant praise.'

'And with Simone,' I suggested, 'the admiration flowed like cement?'

'You've got it. Had some experience of wives, have you?'

'You might say, a lifetime's experience. Do you mind?' I poured myself another glass of unwonted champagne.

'No, no, of course. And your wife doesn't understand you?'

'Oh, I'm afraid she does. That's the worrying thing about it. She blames me for being a "character".'

'They'd blame you for anything. Come to divorce, has it?'

'Not quite reached your stage, Mr O'Higgins.' I looked round the restaurant. 'So, I suppose you have to keep these tables full to pay Simone her alimony.'

'Not exactly. You see she'll own half La Maison.' That hadn't been entirely clear to me and I asked him to explain.

'When we started off, I was a young man. All I wanted to do was to get up early, go to Smithfield and Billingsgate, feel the lobsters and smell the fresh scallops, create new dishes and dream of sauces. Simone was the one with the business sense. Well, she's French, so she insisted on us getting married in France.'

'Was that wrong?'

'Oh, no. It was absolutely right, for Simone. Because they have a damned thing there called "community of property". I had to agree to give her half of everything if we ever broke up. You know about the law, of course.'

'Well, not everything about it.' Community of property, I must confess, came as news to me. 'I always found knowing the law a bit of a handicap for a barrister.'

'Simone knew all about it. She had her beady eye on the future.' He emptied his glass and then looked at me pleadingly. 'You're going to get us out of this little trouble, aren't you, Mr Rumpole? This affair of the mouse?'

'Oh, the mouse!' I did my best to reassure him. 'The mouse seems to be the least of your worries.'

Soon Jean-Pierre had to go back to his kitchen. On his way, he stopped at the cash desk and said something to the girl, Mary. She looked up at him with, I thought, unqualified adoration. He patted her arm and went back to his sauces, having reassured her, I suppose, about the quarrel that had been going on in her honour.

I did justice to the rest of the champagne and pâté de foie and started off for home. In the restaurant entrance hall I saw the lady who minded the cloaks take a suitcase from Gaston Leblanc, who had just arrived out of breath and wearing a mackintosh. Although large, the suitcase seemed very light and he asked her to look after it.

Several evenings later I was lying on my couch in the living room of the mansion flat, a small cigar between my fingers and a glass of Château Fleet Street on the floor beside me. I was in vacant or in pensive mood as I heard a ring at the front doorbell. I started up, afraid that the delights of *haute cuisine* had palled for Hilda, and then I remembered that She would undoubtedly have come armed with a latchkey. I approached the front door, puzzled at the sound of young and excited voices without, combined with loud music. I got the door open and found myself face to face with Liz Probert, Dave Inchcape and five or six other junior hacks, all wearing sweatshirts with a picture of a wig and YOUNG RADICAL LAWYERS written on them. Dianne was also there in trousers and a glittery top, escorted by my clerk Henry, wearing jeans and doing his best to appear young and swinging. The party was carrying various bottles and an article we know well down the Bailey (because it so often appears in lists of stolen property) as a ghetto blaster. It was from this contraption that the loud music emerged.

'It's a surprise party!' Mizz Liz Probert announced with considerable pride. 'We've come to cheer you up in your great loneliness.'

Nothing I could say would stem the well-meaning invasion. Within minutes the staid precincts of Froxbury mansions were transformed into the sort of disco which is patronized by under-thirties on a package to the Costa del Sol. Bizarre drinks, such as rum and blackcurrant juice or advocaat and lemonade, were being mixed in what remained of our tumblers, supplemented by toothmugs from the bathroom. Scarves dimmed the lights, the ghetto blaster blasted ceaselessly and dancers gyrated in a self-absorbed manner, apparently oblivious of each other. Only Henry and Dianne, practising a more old-fashioned ritual, clung together, almost motionless, and carried on a lively conversation with me as I stood on the outskirts of the revelry, drinking the best of the wine they had brought and trying to look tolerantly convivial.

'We heard as how Mrs Rumpole has done a bunk, sir.' Dianne looked sympathetic, to which Henry added sourly, 'Some people have all the luck!'

'Why? Where's your wife tonight, Henry?' I asked my clerk. The cross he has to bear is that his spouse has pursued an ambitious career in local government so that, whereas she is now the Mayor of Bexley-heath, he is officially her Mayoress.

'My wife's at a dinner of South London mayors in the Mansion House, Mr Rumpole. No consorts allowed, thank God!' Henry told me.

'Which is why we're both on the loose tonight. Makes you feel young again, doesn't it, Mr Rumpole?' Dianne asked me as she danced minimally.

'Well, not particularly young, as a matter of fact.' The music yawned between me and my guests as an unbridgeable generation gap. And then one of the more intense of the young lady radicals approached me, as a senior member of the Bar, to ask what the hell the Lord Chief Justice knew about being pregnant and on probation at the moment your boyfriend's arrested for dope. 'Very little, I should imagine,' I had to tell her, and then, as the telephone was bleating pathetically beneath the din, I excused myself and moved to answer it. As I went, a Y.R.L. sweatshirt whirled past me; Liz, dancing energetically, had pulled it off and was gyrating in what appeared to be an ancient string-vest and a pair of jeans.

'Rumpole!' The voice of She Who Must Be Obeyed called to me, no doubt from the banks of Duddon. 'What on earth's going on there?'

'Oh, Hilda. Is it you?'

'Of course it's me.'

'Having a good time, are you? And did Cousin Everard enjoy his sliver of whatever it was?'

'Rumpole. What's that incredible noise?'

'Noise? Is there a noise? Oh, yes. I think I do hear music. Well . . .' Here I improvised, as I thought brilliantly. 'It's a play, that's what it is, a play on television. It's all about young people, hopping about in a curious fashion.'

'Don't talk rubbish!' Hilda, as you may guess, sounded far from convinced. 'You know you never watch plays on television.'

'Not usually, I grant you,' I admitted. 'But what else have I got to do when my wife has left me?'

Much later, it seemed a lifetime later, when the party was over,

I settled down to read the latest addition to my brief in the O'Higgins case. It was a report from Fig Newton, who had been keeping observation on the workers at La Maison. One afternoon he followed Gaston Leblanc, who left his home in Ruislip with a large suitcase, with which he travelled to a smart address at Egerton Crescent in Knightsbridge. This house, which had a bunch of brightly coloured balloons tied to its front door, Fig kept under surveillance for some time. A number of small children arrived, escorted by nannies, and were let in by a manservant. Later, when all the children had been received, Fig, wrapped in his Burberry with his collar turned up against the rain, was able to move so he got a clear view into the sitting room.

What he saw interested me greatly. The children were seated on the floor watching breathlessly as Gaston Leblanc, station waiter and part-time conjuror, dressed in a black robe ornamented with stars, entertained them by slowly extricating a live and kicking rabbit from a top hat.

For the trial of Jean-Pierre O'Higgins we drew the short straw in the shape of an Old Bailey judge aptly named Gerald Graves. Judge Graves and I have never exactly hit it off. He is a pale, long-faced, unsmiling fellow who probably lives on a diet of organic bran and carrot juice. He heard Ballard open the proceedings against La Maison with a pained expression, and looked at me over his half-glasses as though I were a saucepan that hadn't been washed up properly. He was the last person in the world to laugh a case out of Court and I would have to manage that trick without him.

Soapy Sam Ballard began by describing the minor blemishes in the restaurant's kitchen. 'In this highly expensive, allegedly three-star establishment, the Environmental Health Officer discovered cracked tiles, open waste-bins and gravy stains on the ceiling.'

'The ceiling, Mr Ballard?' The Judge repeated in sepulchral tones.

'Alas, yes, my Lord. The ceiling.'

'Probably rather a tall cook,' I suggested, and was rewarded with a freezing look from the Bench.

'And there was a complete absence of nail-brushes in the kitchen handbasins.' Ballard touched on a subject dear to his heart. 'But wait, members of the jury, until you get to the—' 'Main course?' I suggested in another ill-received whisper and Ballard surged on '—the very heart of this most serious case. On the night of May the 18th, a common house mouse was served up at a customer's dinner table.'

'We are no doubt dealing here, Mr Ballard,' the Judge intoned solemnly, 'with a defunct mouse?'

'Again, alas, no, my lord. The mouse in question was alive.'

'And kicking,' I muttered. Staring vaguely round the Court, my eye lit on the Public Gallery where I saw Mary Skelton, the quiet restaurant clerk, watching the proceedings attentively.

'Members of the jury' – Ballard had reached his peroration – 'need one ask if a kitchen is in breach of the Food and Hygiene Regulations if it serves up a living mouse? As proprietor of the restaurant, Mr O'Higgins is, say the prosecution, absolutely responsible. Whomsoever in his employ he seeks to blame, members of the jury, he must take the consequences. I will now call my first witness.'

'Who's that pompous imbecile?' Jean-Pierre O'Higgins was adding his two pennyworth, but I told him he wasn't in his restaurant now and to leave the insults to me. I was watching a fearful and embarrassed Claude Erskine-Brown climb into the witness-box and take the oath as though it were the last rites. When asked to give his full names he appealed to the Judge.

'My Lord. May I write them down? There may be some publicity about this case.' He looked nervously at the assembled reporters.

'Aren't you a member of the Bar?' Judge Graves squinted at the witness over his half-glasses.

'Well, yes, my Lord,' Claude admitted reluctantly.

'That's nothing to be ashamed of – in most cases.' At which the Judge aimed a look of distaste in my direction and then turned back to the witness. 'I think you'd better tell the jury who you are, in the usual way.'

'Claude . . .' The unfortunate fellow tried a husky whisper, only to get a testy 'Oh, do speak up!' from his Lordship. Whereupon, turning up the volume a couple of notches, the witness answered, 'Claude Leonard Erskine-Brown.' I hadn't know about the Leonard.

'On May the 18th were you dining at La Maison Jean-Pierre?' Ballard began his examination.

'Well, yes. Yes. I did just drop in.'

'For dinner?'

'Yes,' Claude had to admit.

'In the company of a young lady named Patricia Benbow?'

'Well. That is . . . Er . . . er.'

'Mr Erskine-Brown' – Judge Graves had no sympathy with this sudden speech impediment – 'it seems a fairly simple question to answer, even for a member of the Bar.'

'I was in Miss Benbow's company, my Lord,' Claude answered in despair.

'And when the main course was served were the plates covered?'

'Yes. They were.'

'And when the covers were lifted what happened?'

Into the expectant silence, Erskine-Brown said in a still, small voice, 'A mouse ran out.'

'Oh, do speak up!' Graves was running out of patience with the witness, who almost shouted back, 'A mouse ran out, my Lord!'

At this point Ballard said, 'Thank you, Mr Erskine-Brown,' and sat down, no doubt confident that the case was in the bag – or perhaps the trap. Then I rose to cross-examine.

'Mr Claude Leonard Erskine-Brown,' I weighed in, 'is Miss Benbow a solicitor?'

'Well. Yes . . .' Claude looked at me sadly, as though wanting to say, *Et tu*, Rumpole?

'And is your wife a well-known and highly regarded Queen's Counsel?'

Graves's face lit up at the mention of our delightful Portia. 'Mrs Erskine-Brown has sat here as a Recorder, members of the jury.' He smiled sickeningly at the twelve honest citizens.

'I'm obliged to your Lordship.' I bowed slightly and turned back to the witness. 'And is Miss Benbow instructed in an important forthcoming case, that is the Balham Minicab Murder, in which she is intending to brief Mrs Erskine-Brown, QC?'

'Is – is she?' Never quick off the mark, Claude didn't yet realize that help was at hand.

'And were you taking her out to dinner so you might discuss the defence in that case, your wife being unfortunately detained in Cardiff?' I hoped that made my good intentions clear, even to a barrister.

'Was I?' Erskine-Brown was still not with me.

'Well, weren't you?' I was losing patience with the fellow.

'Oh, yes.' At last the penny dropped. 'Of course I was! I do remember now. Naturally. And I did it all to help Philly. To help my wife. Is that what you mean?' He ended up looking at me anxiously.

'Exactly.'

'Thank you, Mr Rumpole. Thank you very much.' Erskine-Brown's gratitude was pathetic. But the Judge couldn't wait to get on to the exciting bits. 'Mr Rumpole,' he boomed mournfully, 'when are we coming to the mouse?'

'Oh, yes. I'm grateful to your Lordship for reminding me. Well. What sort of animal was it?'

'Oh, a very small mouse indeed.' Claude was now desperately anxious to help me. 'Hardly noticeable.'

'A very small mouse and hardly noticeable,' Graves repeated as he wrote it down and then raised his eyebrows, as though, when it came to mice, smallness was no excuse.

'And the first you saw of it was when it emerged from under a silver dish-cover? You couldn't swear it got there in the kitchen?'

'No, I couldn't.' Erskine-Brown was still eager to cooperate.

'Or if it was inserted in the dining room by someone with access to the serving table?'

'Oh, no, Mr Rumpole. You're perfectly right. Of course it might have been!' The witness's co-operation was almost embarrassing, so the Judge chipped in with 'I take it you're not suggesting that this creature appeared from a dish of duck breasts by some sort of miracle, are you, Mr Rumpole?'

'Not a miracle, my Lord. Perhaps a trick.'

'Isn't Mr Ballard perfectly right?' Graves, as was his wont, had joined the prosecution team. 'For the purposes of this offence it doesn't matter *how* it got there. A properly run restaurant should not serve up a mouse for dinner! The thing speaks for itself.'

'A talking mouse, my Lord? What an interesting conception!' I got a loud laugh from my client and even the jury joined in with a few friendly titters. I also got, of course, a stern rebuke from the Bench. 'Mr Rumpole!' – his Lordship's seriousness was particularly deadly – 'this is not a place of entertainment! You would do well to remember that this is a most serious case from your client's point of view. And I'm sure the jury will wish to give it the most weighty consideration. We will continue with it after luncheon. Shall we say, five past two, members of the jury?'

Mr Bernard and I went down to the pub, and after a light snack of shepherd's pie, washed down with a pint or two of Guinness, we hurried back into the Palais de Justice and there I found what I had hoped for. Mary Skelton was sitting quietly outside the Court, waiting for the proceedings to resume. I lit a small cigar and took a seat with my instructing solicitor not far away from the girl. I raised my voice a little and said, 'You know what's always struck me about this case, Mr Bernard? There's no evidence of droppings or signs of mice in the kitchen. So someone put the mouse under the cover deliberately. Someone who wanted to ruin La Maison's business.'

'Mrs O'Higgins?' Bernard suggested.

'Certainly not! She'd want the place to be as prosperous as possible because she owned half of it. The guilty party is someone who wanted Simone to get nothing but half a failed eatery with a ruined reputation. So what did this someone do?'

'You tell me, Mr Rumpole.' Mr Bernard was an excellent straight man.

'Oh, broke a lot of little rules. Took away the nail-brushes and the lids of the tidy bins. But a sensation was needed, something that'd hit the headlines. Luckily this someone knew a waiter who had a talent for sleight of hand and a spare-time job producing livestock out of hats.'

'Gaston Leblanc?' Bernard was with me.

'Exactly! He got the animal under the lid and gave it to Alphonse to present to the unfortunate Miss Tricia Benbow. Consequence: ruin for the restaurant and a rotten investment for the vengeful Simone. No doubt someone paid Gaston well to do it.'

I was silent then. I didn't look at the waiting girl, but I was sure she was looking at me. And then Bernard asked, 'Just who are we talking about, Mr Rumpole?'

'Well, now. Who had the best possible reason for hating Simone, and wanting her to get away with as little as possible?'

'Who?'

'Who but our client?' I told him. 'The great *maître de cuisine*, Jean-Pierre O'Higgins himself.'

'No!' I had never heard Mary Skelton speaking before. Her voice was clear and determined, with a slight North Country accent. 'Excuse me.' I turned to look at her as she stood up and came over to us. 'No, it's not true. Jean-Pierre knew nothing about it. It was my idea entirely. Why did *she* deserve to get anything out of us?'

I stood up, looked at my watch and put on the wig that had been resting on the seat beside me. 'Well, back to Court. Mr Bernard, take a statement from the lady, why don't you? We'll call her as a witness.'

Whilst these events were going on down the Bailey, another kind of drama was being enacted in Froxbury mansions. She Who Must Be Obeyed had returned from her trip with Cousin Everard, put on the kettle and surveyed the general disorder left by my surprise party with deep disapproval. In the sitting room she fanned away the barroom smell, drew the curtains, opened the windows and clicked her tongue at the sight of half-empty glasses and lipstick-stained fag ends. Then she noticed something white nestling under the sofa, pulled it out and saw that it was a Young Radical Lawyers sweatshirt, redolent of Mizz Liz Probert's understated yet feminine perfume.

Later in the day, when I was still on my hind legs performing before Mr Justice Graves and the jury, Liz Probert called at the mansion flat to collect the missing garment. Hilda had met Liz at occasional Chambers parties but when she opened the door she was, I'm sure, stony-faced, and remained so as she led Mizz Probert into the sitting room and restored to her the sweatshirt which the Young Radical Lawyer admitted she had taken off and left behind the night before. I have done my best to reconstruct the following dialogue, from the accounts given to me by the principal performers. I can't vouch for its total accuracy, but this is the gist, the meat you understand. It began when Liz explained she had taken the sweatshirt off because she was dancing and it was quite hot.

'You were *dancing* with Rumpole?' Hilda was outraged. 'I knew he was up to something. As soon as my back was turned. I heard all that going on when I telephoned. Rocking and rolling all over the place. At his age!'

'Mrs Rumpole. Hilda . . .' Liz began to protest but only provoked a brisk 'Oh, please. Don't you Hilda me! Young Radical Lawyers, I suppose that means you're free and easy with other people's husbands!' At which point I regret to report that Liz Probert could scarcely contain her laughter and asked, 'You don't think I fancy Rumpole, do you?'

'I don't know why not.' Hilda has her moments of loyalty. 'Rumpole's a "character". Some people like that sort of thing.'

'Hilda. Look, please listen,' and Liz began to explain. 'Dave Inchcape and I and a whole lot of us came to give Rumpole a party. To cheer him up. Because he was lonely. He was missing you so terribly.'

'He was *what*?' She Who Must could scarcely believe her ears, Liz told me. 'Missing you,' the young radical repeated. 'I saw him at breakfast. He looked so sad. "She's left me," he said, "and gone off with her Cousin Everard."'

'Rumpole said that?' Hilda no longer sounded displeased.

'And he seemed absolutely broken-hearted. He saw nothing ahead, I'm sure, but a lonely old age stretching out in front of him. Anyone could tell how much he cared about you. Dave noticed it as well. Please can I have my shirt back now?'

'Of course.' Hilda was now treating the girl as though she were the prodigal grandchild or some such thing. 'But, Liz . . .'

'What, Hilda?'

'Wouldn't you like me to put it through the wash for you before you take it home?'

Back in the Ludgate Circus verdict factory, Mary Skelton gave evidence along the lines I have already indicated and the time came for me to make my final speech. As I reached the last stretch I felt I was making some progress. No one in the jury-box was asleep, or suffering from terminal bronchitis, and a few of them looked distinctly sympathetic. The same couldn't be said, however, of the scorpion on the Bench.

'Ladies and gentlemen of the jury.' I gave it to them straight. 'Miss Mary Skelton, the cashier, was in love. She was in love with her boss, that larger-than-life cook and "character", Jean-Pierre O'Higgins. People do many strange things for love. They commit suicide or leave home or pine away sometimes. It was for love that Miss Mary Skelton caused a mouse to be served up in La Maison Jean-Pierre, after she had paid the station waiter liberally for performing the trick. She it was who wanted to ruin the business, so that my client's vengeful wife should get absolutely nothing out of it.'

'Mr Rumpole!' His Lordship was unable to contain his fury.

'And my client knew nothing whatever of this dire plot. He was entirely innocent.' I didn't want to let Graves interrupt my flow, but he came in at increased volume, 'Mr Rumpole! If a restaurant serves unhygienic food, the proprietor is guilty. In law it doesn't matter in the least how it got there. Ignorance by your client is no excuse. I presume you have some rudimentary knowledge of the law, Mr Rumpole?'

I wasn't going to tangle with Graves on legal matters. Instead I confined my remarks to the more reasonable jury, ignoring the Judge. 'You're not concerned with the law, members of the jury,' I told them, 'you are concerned with justice!'

'That is a quite outrageous thing to say! On the admitted facts of this case, Mr O'Higgins is clearly guilty!' His Honour Judge Graves had decided but the honest twelve would have to return the verdict and I spoke to them. 'A British judge has no power to direct a British jury to find a defendant guilty! I know that much at least.'

'I shall tell the jury that he is guilty in law, I warn you.' Graves's warning was in vain. I carried on regardless.

'His Lordship may tell you that to his heart's content. As a great Lord Chief Justice of England, a Judge superior in rank to any in this Court, once said, "It is the duty of the Judge to tell you as a jury what to do, but you have the power to do exactly as you like." And what you do, members of the jury, is a matter entirely between God and your own consciences. Can you really find it in your consciences to condemn a man to ruin for a crime he didn't commit?' I looked straight at them. 'Can any of you? Can you?' I gripped the desk in front of me, apparently exhausted. 'You are the only judges of the facts in this case, members of the jury. My task is done. The future career of Jean-Pierre O'Higgins is in your hands, and in your hands alone.' And then I sat down, clearly deeply moved.

At last it was over. As we came out of the doors of the Court, Jean-Pierre O'Higgins embraced me in a bear hug and was, I greatly feared, about to kiss me on both cheeks. Ballard gave me a look of pale disapproval. Clearly he thought I had broken all the rules by asking the jury to ignore the Judge. Then a cheerful and rejuvenated Claude came bouncing up bleating, 'Rumpole, you were brilliant!'

'Oh yes,' I told him. 'I've still got a win or two in me yet.'

'Brilliant to get me off. All that nonsense about a brief for Philly.'

'Not nonsense, Leonard. I mean, Claude. I telephoned the fair Tricia and she's sending your wife the Balham Minicab Murder. Are you suggesting that Rumpole would deceive the Court?'

'Oh' – he was interested to know – 'am I getting a brief too?'

'She said nothing of that.'

'All the same, Rumpole' – he concealed his disappointment – 'thank you very much for getting me out of a scrape.'

'Say no more. My life is devoted to helping the criminal classes.'

As I left him and went upstairs to slip out of the fancy dress, I had one more task to perform. I walked past my locker and went on into the silks' dressing-room, where a very old QC was seated in the shadows snoozing over the *Daily Telegraph*. I had seen Ballard downstairs, discussing the hopelessness of an appeal with his solicitor, and it was the work of a minute to find his locker, feel in his jacket pocket and haul a large purse out of it. Making sure that the sleeping silk hadn't spotted me, I opened the purse, slipped in the nail-brush I had rescued from Uncle Tom's tin of golf balls, restored it to the pocket and made my escape undetected.

I was ambling back up Fleet Street when I heard the brisk step of Ballard behind me. He drew up alongside and returned to his favourite topic. 'There's nothing for it, Rumpole,' he said, 'I shall chain the next one up.'

'The next what?'

'The next nail-brush.'

'Isn't that a bit extreme?'

'If fellows, and ladies, in Chambers can't be trusted,' Ballard said severely, 'I am left with absolutely no alternative. I hate to have to do it, but Henry is being sent out for a chain tomorrow.'

We had reached the newspaper stand at the entrance to the Temple and I loitered there. 'Lend us 20p for the *Evening Standard*, Bollard. There might be another restaurant in trouble.'

'Why are you never provided with money?' Ballard thought it typical of my fecklessness. 'Oh, all right.' And then he put his hand in his pocket and pulled out the purse. Opening it, he was amazed to find his ten pees nestling under an ancient nail-brush. 'Our old nail-brush!' The reunion was quaintly moving. 'I'd recognize it anywhere. How on earth did it get in there?'

'Evidence gets in everywhere, old darling,' I told him. 'Just like mice.'

When I got home and unlocked the front door, I was greeted with the familiar cry of 'Is that you, Rumpole?'

'No,' I shouted back, 'it's not me. I'll be along later.'

'Come into the sitting room and stop talking rubbish.'

I did as I was told and found the room swept and polished and that She, who was looking unnaturally cheerful, had bought flowers.

'Cousin Everard around, is he?' I felt, apprehensively, that the floral tributes were probably for him.

'He had to go back to Saskatoon. One of his clients got charged with fraud, apparently.' And then Hilda asked, unexpectedly, 'You knew I'd be back, didn't you, Rumpole?'

'Well, I *had* hoped . . .' I assured her.

'It seems you almost gave up hoping. You couldn't get along without me, could you?'

'Well, I had a bit of a stab at it,' I said in all honesty.

'No need for you to be brave any more. I'm back now. That nice Miss Liz Probert was saying you missed me terribly.'

'Oh, of course. Yes. Yes, I missed you.' And I added as quietly as possible, 'Life without a boss . . .'

'What did you say?'

'You were a great loss.'

'And Liz says you were dreadfully lonely. I was glad to hear that, Rumpole. You don't usually say much about your feelings.'

'Words don't come easily to me, Hilda,' I told her with transparent dishonesty.

'Now you're so happy to see me back, Rumpole, why don't you take me out for a little celebration? I seem to have got used to dining *à la carte*.'

Of course I agreed. I knew somewhere where we could get it on the house. So we ended up at a table for two in La Maison and discussed

Hilda's absent relative as Alphonse made his way towards us with two covered dishes.

'The trouble with Cousin Everard,' Hilda confided in me, 'is he's not a "character".'

'Bit on the bland side?' I inquired politely.

'It seems that unless you're with a "character", life can get a little tedious at times,' Hilda admitted.

The silver domes were put in front of us, Alphonse called out, '*Un, deux, trois!*' and they were lifted to reveal what I had no difficulty in ordering that night: steak-and-kidney pud. Mashed spuds were brought to us on the side.

'Perhaps that's why I need you, Rumpole.' She Who Must Be Obeyed was in a philosophic mood that night. 'Because you're a "character". And you need me to tell you off for being one.'

Distinctly odd, I thought, are the reasons why people need each other. I looked towards the cashier's desk, where Jean-Pierre had his arm round the girl I had found so unmemorable. I raised a glass of the champagne he had brought us and drank to their very good health.

Rumpole on Trial

I have often wondered how my career as an Old Bailey Hack would terminate. Would I drop dead at the triumphant end of my most moving final speech? 'Ladies and gentlemen of the jury, my task is done. I have said my say. This trial has been but a few days out of your life, but for me it is the *whole* of my life. And that life I leave, with the utmost confidence, in your hands', and then keel over and out. 'Rumpole snuffs it in Court'; the news would run like wildfire round the Inns of Court and I would challenge any jury to dare to convict after that forensic trick had been played upon them. Or will I die in an apoplexy after a particularly heated disagreement with Mr Injustice Graves, or Sir Oliver Oliphant? One thing I'm sure of, I shall not drift into retirement and spend my days hanging around Froxbury mansions in a dressing-gown, nor shall I ever repair to the Golden Gate retirement home, Weston-super-Mare, and sit in the sun lounge retelling the extraordinary case of the Judge's Elbow, or the Miracle in the Ecclesiastical Court which saved a vicar from an unfrocking. No, my conclusion had better come swiftly, and Rumpole's career should end with a bang rather than a whimper. When thinking of the alternatives available, I never expected I would finish by being kicked out of the Bar, dismissed for unprofessional conduct and drummed out of the monstrous regiment of learned friends. And yet this conclusion became a distinct possibility on that dreadful day when, apparently, even I went too far and brought that weighty edifice, the legal establishment, crashing down upon my head.

The day dawned grey and wet after I had been kept awake most of the night by a raging toothache. I rang my dentist, Mr Lionel Leering, a practitioner whose company I manage to shun until the pain becomes unbearable, and he agreed to meet me at his Harley Street rooms at nine o'clock, so giving me time to get to the Old Bailey, where I was engaged in a particularly tricky case. So picture me at the start of what was undoubtedly the worst in a long career of difficult days, stretched out on the chair of pain and terror beside the bubbling spittoon. Mr Leering, the smooth, grey-haired master of the drill, who seemed perpetually tanned from a trip to his holiday home in Ibiza, was fiddling about inside my mouth while subliminal baroque music tinkled on the cassette player and the blonde nurse looked on with well-simulated concern.

'Busy day ahead of you, Mr Rumpole?' Mr Leering was keeping up the bright chatter. 'Open just a little wider for me, will you? What sort of terrible crime are you on today then?'

'Ans . . . lorter,' I did my best to tell him.

'My daughter?' Leering purred with satisfaction. 'How kind of you to remember. Well, Jessica's just done her A-levels and she's off to Florence doing the History of Art. You should hear her on the Quattrocento. Knows a great deal more than I ever did. And of course, being blonde, the Italians are mad about her.'

'I said . . . Ans . . . lorter. Down the Ole . . . Ailey,' I tried to explain before he started the drill.

'My old lady? Oh, you mean Yolande. I'm not sure she'd be too keen on being called that. She's better now. Gone in for acupuncture. What were you saying?'

'An . . . cord . . . Tong . . .'

'Your tongue? Not hurting you, am I?'

'An . . . supposed . . . Illed is ife.'

'Something she did to her back,' Leering explained patiently. 'Playing golf. Golf covers a multitude of sins. Particularly for the women of Hampstead Garden Suburb.'

'Ell on the ender . . .'

The drill had stopped now, and he pulled the cottonwool rolls away from my gums. My effort to tell him about my life and work had obviously gone for nothing because he asked politely, 'Send her what? Your love? Yolande'll be tickled to death. Of course, she's never met you. But she'll still be tickled to death. Rinse now, will you? Now what were we talking about?'

'Manslaughter,' I told him once again as I spat out pink and chemi-cated fluid.

'Oh, no. Not really? Yolande can be extremely irritating at times. What woman can't? But I'm not actually tempted to bash her across the head.'

'No' – I was showing remarkable patience with this slow-witted dentist – 'I said I'm doing a case at the Old Bailey. My client's a man called Tong. Accused of manslaughter. Killed his wife, Mrs Tong. She fell down and her head hit the fender.'

'Oh, really? How fascinating.' Now he knew what I was talking about, Mr Leering had lost all interest in my case. 'I've just done a tem-porary stopping. That should see you through the day. But ring me up if you're in any trouble.'

'I think it's going to take a great deal more than a temporary stop-ping to see me through today,' I said as I got out of the chair and struggled into the well-worn black jacket. 'I'm before Mr Justice "Ollie" Oliphant.'

As I was walking towards the Old Bailey I felt a familiar stab of pain, warning me that the stopping might be extremely temporary. As I was going through the revolving doors, Mizz Liz Probert came flying in behind me, sent the door spinning, collided into my back, then went dashing up the stairs, calling, 'Sorry, Rumpole!' and vanished.

'Sorry, Rumpole!' I grumbled to myself. Mizz Probert cannons into you, nearly sends your brief flying and all she does is call out, 'Sorry, Rumpole!' on the trot. Everyone, it seemed to me, said, 'Sorry, Rumpole!' and didn't mean a word of it. They were sorry for sending my clients to chokey, sorry for not showing me all the prosecution statements, sorry for standing on my foot in the Underground, and now, no doubt, sorry for stealing my bands. For I had reached the robing room and, while climbing into the fancy dress, searched for the little white hang-ing tabs that ornament a legal hack's neck and, lo and behold, these precious bands had been nicked. I looked down the robing room in des-peration and saw young Dave Inchcape, Mizz Liz Probert's lover and co-mortgagee, carefully tie a snow-white pair of crisp linen bands around his winged collar. I approached him in a hostile manner.

'Inchcape' – I lost no time in coming to the point – 'have you pinched my bands?'

'Sorry, Rumpole?' He pretended to know nothing of the matter.

'You have!' I regarded the case as proved. 'Honestly, Inchcape. Nowadays the barristers' robing room is little better than a den of thieves!'

'These are my bands, Rumpole. There are some bands over there on the table. Slightly soiled. They're probably yours.'

'Slightly soiled? Sorry, Rumpole! Sorry whoever they belonged to,' and I put them on. 'The bloody man's presumably got mine, anyway.'

When I got down, correctly if sordidly decorated about the throat, to Ollie Oliphant's Court 1 I found Claude Erskine-Brown all tricked out as an artificial silk and his junior, Mizz She Who Cannons Into You Probert.

'I want to ask you, Rumpole,' Claude said in his newly acquired QC's voice, 'about calling your client.'

'Mr Tong.'

'Yes. Are you calling him?'

'I call him Mr Tong because that's his name.'

'I mean,' he said with exaggerated patience, as though explaining the law to a white-wig, 'are you going to put him in the witness-box? You don't have to, you know. You see, I've been asked to do a murder in Lewes. One does have so many demands on one's time in silk. So if you're not going to call Mr Tong, I thought, well, perhaps we might finish today.'

While he was drooling on, I was looking closely at the man's neck. Then I came out with the accusation direct. 'Are those my bands you're wearing?' I took hold of the suspect tabs, lifted them and examined them closely. 'They look like my bands. They *are* my bands! What's that written on them?'

'C.E.B. stands for Claude Erskine-Brown.' This was apparently his defence.

'When did you write that?'

'Oh really, Rumpole! We don't even share the same robing room now I'm in silk. How could I have got at your bands? Just tell me, are you calling your client?'

I wasn't satisfied with his explanation, but the usher was hurrying us in as the Judge was straining at the leash. I pushed my way into Court, telling Erskine-Brown nothing of my plans.

I knew what I'd like to call my client. I'd like to call him a grade

A, hundred-per-cent pain in the neck. In any team chosen to bore for England he would have been first in to bat. He was a retired civil servant and his hair, face, business suit and spectacles were of a uniform grey. When he spoke, he did so in a dreary monotone and never used one word when twenty would suffice. The only unexpected thing about him was that he ever got involved in the colourful crime of manslaughter. I had considered a long time before deciding to call Mr Tong as a witness in his own defence. I knew he would bore the jury to distraction and no doubt drive that North Country comedian Mr Justice Oliphant into an apoplexy. However, Mrs Tong had been found dead from a head wound in the sitting room of their semi-detached house in Rickmansworth, and I felt her husband was called upon to provide some sort of an explanation.

You will have gathered that things hadn't gone well from the start of that day for Rumpole, and matters didn't improve when my client Tong stepped into the witness-box, raised the Testament on high and gave us what appeared to be a shortened version of the oath. 'I swear by,' he said, carefully omitting any reference to the Deity, 'that the evidence I shall give shall be the truth, the whole truth and nothing but the truth.'

'Mr Rumpole. Your client has left something out of the oath.' Mr Justice Oliphant may not have been a great lawyer but at least he knew the oath by heart.

'So I noticed, my Lord.'

'Well, see to it, Mr Rumpole. Use your common sense.'

'Mr Tong,' I asked the witness, 'who is it you swear by?'

'One I wouldn't drag down to the level of this place, my Lord.'

'What's he mean, Mr Rumpole? Drag down to the level of this Court? What's he mean by that?' The Judge's common sense was giving way to uncommon anger.

'I suppose he means that the Almighty might not wish to be seen in Court Number 1 at the Old Bailey,' I suggested.

'Not wish to be seen? I never heard of such a thing!'

'Mr Tong has some rather original ideas about theology, my Lord.' I did my best to deter further conversation on the subject. 'I'm sure he would go into the matter at considerable length if your Lordship were interested.'

'I'm not, Mr Rumpole, not interested in the least.' And here his Lordship turned on the witness with, 'Are you saying, Mr . . . What's your name again?'

'Tong, my Lord. Henry Sebastian Tong.'

'Are you saying my Court isn't good enough for God? Is that what you're saying?'

'I am saying that this Court, my Lord, is a place of sin and worldliness and we should not involve a Certain Being in these proceedings. May I remind you of the Book of Ezekiel: "And it shall be unto them a false divination, to them that have sworn oaths." '

'Don't let's worry about the Book of Ezekiel.' This work clearly wasn't Ollie Oliphant's bedtime reading. 'Mr Rumpole, can't you control your client?'

'Unfortunately not, my Lord.'

'When I was a young lad, the first thing we learned at the Bar was to control our clients.' The Judge was back on more familiar territory. 'It's a great pity you weren't brought up in a good old commonsensical Chambers in Leeds, Mr Rumpole.'

'I suppose I might have acquired some of your Lordship's charm and polish,' I said respectfully.

'Let's use our common sense about this, shall we? Mr Tong, do you understand what it is to tell the truth?'

'I have always told the truth. During my thirty years in the Ministry.'

'Ministry?' The Judge turned to me in some alarm. 'Is your client a man of the cloth, Mr Rumpole?'

'I think he's referring to the Ministry of Agriculture and Fisheries, where he was a clerk for many years.'

'Are you going to tell the truth?' The Judge addressed my client in a common-sense shout.

'Yes.' Mr Tong even managed to make a monosyllable sound boring.

'There you are, Mr Rumpole!' The Judge was triumphant. 'That's the way to do it. Now, let's get on with it, shall we?'

'I assure your Lordship, I can't wait. Ouch!' The tooth Mr Leering had said would see me through the day disagreed with a sharp stab of pain. I put a hand to my cheek and muttered to my instructing solicitor, the faithful Mr Bernard, 'It's the temporary stopping.'

'Stopping? Why are you stopping, Mr Rumpole?' The Judge was deeply suspicious.

Now I knew what hell was, examining a prize bore before Ollie Oliphant with a raging toothache. All the same, I soldiered on and asked Tong, 'Were you married to the late Sarah Tong?'

'We had met in the Min of Ag and Fish, where Sarah Pennington, as she then was, held a post in the typing pool. We were adjacent, as I well remember, on one occasion for the hot meal in the canteen.'

'I don't want to hurry you.'

'You hurry him, Mr Rumpole.'

'Let's come to your marriage,' I begged the witness.

'The 13th of March 1950, at the Church of St Joseph and All Angels, in what was then the village of Pinner.' Mr Tong supplied all the details. 'The weather, as I remember it, was particularly inclement. Dark skies and a late snow flurry.'

'Don't let's worry about the weather.' Ollie was using his common sense and longing to get on with it.

'I took it as a portent, my Lord, of storms to come.'

'Could you just describe your married life to the jury?' I tried a short cut.

'I can only, with the greatest respect and due deference, adopt the words of the psalmist. No doubt they are well known to his Lordship?'

'I shouldn't bet on it, Mr Tong,' I warned him, and, ignoring Ollie's apparent displeasure, added, 'Perhaps you could just remind us what the Good Book says?'

' "It is better to dwell on the corner of a housetop than with a brawling woman in a wide house",' Mr Tong recited. ' "It is better to dwell in the wilderness than with a contentious and angry woman." '

So my client's evidence wound on, accompanied by toothache and an angry Judge, and I felt that I had finally fallen out of love with the art of advocacy. I didn't want to have to worry about Mr Tong or the precise circumstances in which Mrs Tong had been released from this world. I wanted to sit down, to shut up and to close my eyes in peace. She Who Must Be Obeyed had something of the same idea. She wanted me to become a judge. Without taking me into her confidence, she met Marigold Featherstone, the Judge's wife, for coffee in Harrods for the purpose of furthering her plan. 'Rumpole gets so terribly tired at night,' Hilda said in the Silver Grill, and Marigold, with a heavy sigh, agreed. 'So does

Guthrie. At night he's as flat as a pancake. Is Rumpole flat as a pancake too?'

'Well, not exactly.' Hilda told me she wasn't sure of the exact meaning of this phrase. 'But he's so irritable these days. So edgy, and then he's had this trouble with his teeth. If only he could have a job *sitting down*.'

'You mean, like a clerk or something?'

'Something like a judge.'

'Really?' Marigold was astonished at the idea.

'Oh, I don't mean a Red Judge,' Hilda explained. 'Not a really posh Judge like Guthrie. But an ordinary sort of circus judge. And Guthrie does know such important people. You said he's always calling in at the Lord Chancellor's office.'

'Only when he's in trouble,' Marigold said grimly. 'But I suppose I might ask if he could put in a word about your Horace.'

'Oh, Marigold. Would you?'

'Why not? I'll wake the old fellow up and tell him.'

As it happened, my possible escape from the agonies of the Bar was not by such an honourable way out as that sought by Hilda in the Silver Grill. The route began to appear as Mr Tong staggered slowly towards the high point of his evidence. We had enjoyed numerous quotations from the Old Testament. We had been treated to a blow-by-blow account of a quarrel between him and his wife during a holiday in Clacton-on-Sea and many other such incidents. We had learned a great deal more about the Ministry of Agriculture and Fisheries than we ever needed to know. And then Ollie, driven beyond endurance, said, 'For God's sake—'

'My Lord?' Mr Tong looked deeply pained.

'All right, for all our sakes. When are we going to come to the facts of this manslaughter?'

So I asked the witness, 'Now, Mr Tong, on the night this *accident* took place.'

'Accident! That's a matter for the jury to decide!' Ollie exploded. 'Why do you call it an accident?'

'Why did your Lordship call it manslaughter? Isn't that a matter for the jury to decide?'

'Did I say that?' the Judge asked. 'Did I say that, Mr Erskine-Brown?'

'Yes, you did,' I told him before Claude could stagger to his feet. 'I wondered if your Lordship had joined the prosecution team, or was it a single-handed effort to prejudice the jury?'

There was a terrible silence and I suppose I should never have said it. Mr Bernard hid his head in shame, Erskine-Brown looked disapproving and Liz appeared deeply worried. The Judge controlled himself with difficulty and then spoke in quiet but dangerous tones. 'Mr Rumpole, that was a quite intolerable thing to say.'

'My Lord. That was a quite intolerable thing to do.' I was determined to fight on.

'I may have had a momentary slip of the tongue.' It seemed that the Judge was about to retreat, but I had no intention of allowing him to do so gracefully. 'Or,' I said, 'your Lordship's well-known common sense may have deserted you.'

There was another sharp intake of breath from the attendant legal hacks and then the Judge kindly let me know what was in his mind. 'Mr Rumpole. I think you should be warned. One of these days you may go too far and behaviour such as yours can have certain consequences. Now, can we get on?'

'Certainly. I didn't wish to interrupt the flow of your Lordship's rebuke.' So I started my uphill task with the witness again. 'Mr Tong, on the night in question, did you and Mrs Tong quarrel?'

'As per usual, my Lord.'

'What was the subject of the quarrel?'

'She accused me of being overly familiar with a near neighbour. This was a certain Mrs Grabowitz, my Lord, a lady of Polish extraction, whose deceased husband had, by a curious coincidence, been a colleague of mine – it's a small world, isn't it? – in the Min of Ag and Fish.'

'Mr Tong, ignore the neighbour's deceased husband, if you'd be so kind. What did your wife do?'

'She ran at me, my Lord, with her nails poised, as though to scratch me across the face, as it was often her habit so to do. However, as ill luck would have it, the runner in front of the gas-fire slipped beneath her feet on the highly polished flooring and she fell. As she did so, the back of her head made contact with the raised tiling in front of our hearth, my Lord, and she received the injuries which ultimately caused her to pass over.'

'Mr Rumpole, is that the explanation of this lady's death you wish to leave to the jury?' The Judge asked with some contempt.

'Certainly, my Lord. Does your Lordship wish to prejudge the issue and are we about to hear a little premature adjudication?'

'Mr Rumpole! I have warned you twice, I shall not warn you again. I'm looking at the clock.'

'So I'd noticed.'

'We'll break off now. Back at ten past two, members of the jury.' And then Ollie turned to my client and gave him the solemn warning which might help me into retirement. 'I understand you're on bail, Mr Tong, and you're in the middle of giving your evidence. It's vitally important that you speak to no one about your case during the lunch-time adjournment. And no one must speak to you, particularly your legal advisers. Is that thoroughly understood, Mr Rumpole?'

'Naturally, my Lord,' I assured him. 'I do know the rules.'

'I hope you do, Mr Rumpole. I sincerely hope you do.'

The events of that lunch hour achieved a historic importance. After a modest meal of bean-shoot sandwiches in the Nuthouse vegetarian restaurant down by the Bank (Claude was on a regime calculated to make him more sylph-like and sexually desirable), he returned to the Old Bailey and was walking up to the silks' robing room when he saw, through an archway, the defendant Tong seated and silent. Approaching nearer, he heard the following words (Claude was good enough to make a careful note of them at the time) shouted by Rumpole in a voice of extreme irritation.

'Listen to me,' my speech, which Claude knew to be legal advice to the client, began. 'Is this damn thing going to last for ever? Well, for God's sake, get on with it! You're driving me mad. Talk. That's all you do, you boring old fart. Just get on with it. I've got enough trouble with the Judge without you causing me all this agony. Get it out. That's all. Short and snappy. Put us out of our misery. Get it out and then shut up!'

As I say, Claude took a careful note of these words but said nothing to me about them when I emerged from behind the archway. When we got back to Court I asked my client a few more questions, which he answered with astounding brevity.

'Mr Tong. Did you ever intend to do your wife the slightest harm?'

'No.'

'Did you strike her?'

'No.'

'Or assault her in any way?'

'No.'

'Just wait there, will you?' – I sat down with considerable relief – 'in case Mr Erskine-Brown can think of anything to ask you.' Claude did have something to ask, and his first question came as something of a surprise to me. 'You've become very monosyllabic since lunch, haven't you, Mr Tong?'

'Perhaps it's something he ate,' I murmured to my confidant, Bernard.

'No' – Erskine-Brown wouldn't have this – 'it's nothing you ate, is it? as your learned Counsel suggests. It's something Mr Rumpole said to you.'

'*Said* to him?' Ollie Oliphant registered profound shock. 'When are you suggesting Mr Rumpole spoke to him?'

'Oh, during the luncheon adjournment, my Lord.' Claude dropped the bombshell casually.

'Mr Rumpole!' Ollie gasped with horror. 'Mr Erskine-Brown, did I not give a solemn warning that no one was to speak to Mr Tong and he was to speak to no one during the adjournment?'

'You did, my Lord,' Claude confirmed it. 'That was why I was so surprised when I heard Mr Rumpole doing it.'

'You heard Mr Rumpole speaking to the defendant Tong?'

'I'm afraid so, my Lord.'

Again Bernard winced in agony, and there were varying reactions of shock and disgust all round. I didn't improve the situation by muttering loudly, 'Oh, come off it, Claude.'

'And what did Mr Rumpole say?' The Judge wanted all the gory details.

'He told Mr Tong he did nothing but talk. And he was to get on with it and he was to get it out and make it snappy. Oh, yes, he said he was a boring old fart.'

'A boring old what, Mr Erskine-Brown?'

'Fart, my Lord.'

'And he's not the only one around here either,' I informed Mr Bernard. If the Judge heard this he ignored it. He went on in tones of the deepest disapproval to ask Claude, 'And, since that conversation, you say that the defendant Tong has been monosyllabic. In other words, he is obeying Mr Rumpole's quite improperly given instructions?'

'Precisely what I am suggesting, my Lord.' Claude was delighted to agree.

'Well, now, Mr Rumpole.' The Judge stared balefully at me. 'What've you got to say to Mr Erskine-Brown's accusation?'

Suddenly a great weariness came over me. For once in my long life I couldn't be bothered to argue and this legal storm in a lunch hour bored me as much as my client's evidence. I was tired of Tong, tired of judges, tired of learned friends, tired of toothache, tired of life. I rose wearily to my feet and said, 'Nothing, my Lord.'

'Nothing?' Mr Justice Oliphant couldn't believe it.

'Absolutely nothing.'

'So you don't deny that all Mr Erskine-Brown has told the Court is true?'

'I neither accept it nor deny it. It's a contemptible suggestion, made by an advocate incapable of conducting a proper cross-examination. Further than that I don't feel called upon to comment. So far as I know I am not on trial.'

'Not at the moment,' said the Judge. 'I cannot answer for the Bar Council.'

'Then I suggest we concentrate on the trial of Mr Tong and forget mine, my Lord.' That was my final word on the matter.

When we did concentrate on the trial it went extremely speedily. Mr Tong remained monosyllabic, our speeches were brief, the Judge, all passion spent by the drama of the lunch hour, summed up briefly and by half past five the jury were back with an acquittal. Shortly after that many of the characters important to this story had assembled in Pommeroy's Wine Bar.

Although he was buying her a drink, Liz Probert made no attempt to disguise her disapproval of the conduct of her learned leader, as she told me after these events had taken place. 'Why did you have to do that, Claude?' she asked in a severe manner. 'Why did you have to put that lunchtime conversation to Tong?'

'Rather brilliant, I thought,' he answered with some self-satisfaction and offered to split a half-bottle of his favourite Pouilly Fumé with her. 'It got the Judge on my side immediately.'

'And got the jury on Rumpole's side. His client was acquitted, I don't know if you remember.'

'Well, win a few, lose a few,' Claude said airily. 'That's par for the course, if you're a busy silk.'

'I mean, why did you do that to Rumpole?'

'Well, that was fair, wasn't it? He shouldn't have talked to his client when he was still in the box. It's just not on!'

'Are you sure he did?' Liz asked.

'I heard him with my own ears. You don't think I'd lie, do you?'

'Well, it has been known. Didn't you lie to your wife, about taking me to the opera?'* Liz had no compunction about opening old wounds.

'That was love. Everyone lies when they're in love.'

'Don't ever tell me you're in love with me again. I shan't believe a single word of it. Did you really mean to get Rumpole disbarred?'

'Rumpole disbarred?' Even Claude sounded shaken by the idea. 'It's not possible.'

'Of course it's possible. Didn't you hear Ollie Oliphant?'

'That was just North Country bluff. I mean, they couldn't do a thing like that, could they? Not to Rumpole.'

'If you ask me, that's what they've been longing to do to Rumpole for years,' Liz told him. 'Now you've given them just the excuse they need.'

'Who needs?'

'The establishment, Claude! They'll use you, you know, then they'll throw you out on the scrapheap. That's what they do to spies.'

'My God!' Erskine-Brown was looking at her with considerable admiration. 'You're beautiful when you're angry!'

At which point Mizz Probert left him, having seen me alone, staring gloomily into a large brandy. Claude was surrounded with thirsty barristers, eager for news of the great Rumpole–Oliphant battle.

Before I got into conversation with Liz, who sat herself down at my table with a look of maddening pity on her face, I have to confess that I had been watching our clerk Henry at a distant table. He had bought a

---

* See 'Rumpole and the Summer of Discontent' (*The Third Rumpole Omnibus*).

strange-looking white concoction for Dot Clapton, and was now sitting gazing at her in a way which made me feel that this was no longer a rehearsal for the Bexley Heath Thespians but a real-life drama which might lead to embarrassing and even disastrous results. I didn't manage to earwig all the dialogue, but I learned enough to enable me to fill in the gaps later.

'You can't imagine what it was like, Dot, when my wife was Mayor.' Henry was complaining, as he so often did, about his spouse's civic duties.

'Bet you were proud of her.' Dot seemed to be missing the point.

'Proud of her! What happened to my self-respect in those days when I was constantly referred to as the Lady Mayoress?'

'Poor old Henry!' Dot couldn't help laughing.

'Poor old Henry, yes. At council meetings I had to sit in the gallery known as the hen pen. I was sat there with the wives.'

'Things a bit better now, are they?' Dot was still hugely entertained.

'Now Eileen's reverted to Alderperson? Very minimally, Dot. She's on this slimming regime now. What shall I go back to? Lettuce salad and cottage cheese – you know, that white stuff. Tastes of soap. No drink, of course. Nothing alcoholic. You reckon you could go another Snowball?'

'I'm all right, thanks.' I saw Dot cover her glass with her hand.

'I know you are, Dot,' Henry agreed enthusiastically. 'You most certainly are all right. The trouble is, Eileen and I haven't exactly got a relationship. Not like *we've* got a relationship.'

'Well, she doesn't work with you, does she? Not on the fee notes,' Dot asked, reasonably enough.

'She doesn't work with me at all and, well, I don't feel close to her. Not as I feel close to you, Dot.'

'Well, don't get that close,' Dot warned him. 'I saw Mr Erskine-Brown give a glance in this direction.'

'Mr Erskine-Brown? He's always chasing after young girls. Makes himself ridiculous.' Henry's voice was full of contempt.

'I *had* noticed.'

'I'm not like that, Dot. I like to talk, you know, one on one. Have a relationship. May I ask you a very personal question?'

'No harm in asking.' She sounded less than fascinated.

'Do you like me, Dot? I mean, do you like me for myself?'

'Well, I don't like you for anyone else.' Dot laughed again. 'You're a very nice sort of person. Speak as you find.'

And then Henry asked anxiously, 'Am I a big part of your life?'

''Course you are!' She was still amused.

'Thank you, Dot! Thank you very much. That's all I need to know.' Henry stood up, grateful and excited. 'That deserves another Snowball!'

I saw him set out for the bar in a determined fashion, so now Dot was speaking to his back, trying to explain herself, 'I mean, you're my boss, aren't you? That's a big part of my life.'

Things had reached this somewhat tricky stage in the Dot–Henry relationship by the time Liz came and sat with me and demanded my full attention with a call to arms. 'Rumpole,' she said, 'you've got to fight it. Every inch of the way!'

'Fight what?'

'Your case. It's the establishment against Rumpole.'

'My dear Mizz Liz, there isn't any case.'

'It's a question of free speech.'

'Is it?'

'Your freedom to speak to your client during the lunch hour. You're an issue of civil rights now, Rumpole.'

'Oh, am I? I don't think I want to be that.'

And then she looked at my glass and said, as though it were a sad sign of decline, 'You're drinking brandy!'

'Dutch courage,' I explained.

'Oh, Rumpole, that's not like you. You've never been afraid of Judges.'

'Judges? Oh, no, as I always taught you, Mizz Liz, fearlessness is the first essential in an advocate. I can cope with Judges. It's the other chaps that give me the jim-jams.'

'Which other chaps, Rumpole?'

'Dentists!' I took a large swig of brandy and shivered.

Time cures many things and in quite a short time old smoothy-chops Leering had the nagging tooth out of my head and I felt slightly better-tempered. Time, however, merely encouraged the growth of the great dispute and brought me nearer to an event that I'd never imagined possible, the trial of Rumpole.

You must understand that we legal hacks are divided into Inns, known as Inns of Court. These Inns are ruled by the benchers, judges and senior barristers, who elect each other to the office rather in the manner of the Council which ruled Venice during the Middle Ages. The benchers of my Inn, known as the Outer Temple, do themselves extremely proud and, once elected, pay very little for lunch in the Outer Temple Hall, and enjoy a good many ceremonial dinners, Grand Nights, Guest Nights and other such occasions, when they climb into a white tie and tails, enter the dining hall with bishops and generals on their arms, and then retire to the Parliament Room for fruit, nuts, port, brandy, Muscat, Beaumes de Venise and Romeo y Julieta cigars. There they discuss the hardships of judicial life and the sad decline in public morality and, occasionally, swap such jokes as might deprave and corrupt those likely to hear them.

On this particular Guest Night Mr Justice Graves, as Treasurer of the Inn, was presiding over the festivities. Ollie Oliphant was also present, as was a tall, handsome, only slightly overweight QC called Montague Varian, who was later to act as my prosecutor. Sam Ballard, the alleged Head of our Chambers and recently elected bencher, was there, delighted and somewhat overawed by his new honour. It was Ballard who told me the drift of the after-dinner conversation in the Parliament Room, an account which I have filled up with invention founded on a hard-won knowledge of the characters concerned. Among the guests present were a Lady Mendip, a sensible grey-haired headmistress, and the Bishop of Bayswater. It was to this cleric that Graves explained one of the quainter customs of the Outer Temple dining process.

'My dear Bishop, you may have heard a porter ringing a handbell before dinner. That's a custom we've kept up since the Middle Ages. The purpose is to summon in such of our students as may be fishing in the Fleet River.'

'Oh, I like that. I like that *very* much.' The Bishop was full of enthusiasm for the Middle Ages. 'We regard it as rather a charming eccentricity.' Graves was smiling but his words immediately brought out the worst in Oliphant. 'I've had enough of eccentricity lately,' he said. 'And I don't regard it as a bit charming.'

'Ah, Oliver, I heard you'd been having a bit of trouble with Rumpole.' Graves turned the conversation to the scandal of the moment.

'You've got to admit, Rumpole's a genuine eccentric!' Montague Varian seemed to find me amusing.

'Genuine?' Oliphant cracked a nut mercilessly. 'Where I come from we know what genuine is. There's nothing more genuine than a good old Yorkshire pudding that's risen in the oven, all fluffy and crisp outside.'

At which a voice piped up from the end of the table singing a Northern folk song with incomprehensible words, 'On Ilkley Moor Ba Tat!' This was Arthur Nottley, the junior bencher, a thin, rather elegant fellow whose weary manner marked a deep and genuine cynicism. He often said he only stayed on at the Bar to keep his basset hound in the way to which it had become accustomed. Now he had not only insulted the Great Yorkshire bore, but had broken one of the rules of the Inn, so Graves rebuked him.

'Master Junior, we don't sing on Guest Nights in this Inn. Only on the Night of Grand Revelry.'

'I'm sorry, Master Treasurer.' Nottley did his best to sound apologetic.

'Please remember that. Yes, Oliver? You were saying?'

'It's all theatrical,' Oliphant grumbled. 'Those old clothes to make himself look poor and down-at-heel, put on to get a sympathy vote from the jury. That terrible old bit of waistcoat with cigar ash and gravy stains.'

'It's no more than a façade of a waistcoat,' Varian agreed. 'A sort of dickie!'

'The old Lord Chief would never hear argument from a man he suspected of wearing a backless waistcoat.' Oliphant quoted a precedent. 'Do you remember him telling Freddy Ringwood, "It gives me little pleasure to listen to an argument from a gentleman in light trousers"? You could say the same for Rumpole's waistcoat. When he waves his arms about you can see his shirt.'

'You're telling me, Oliver!' Graves added to the horror, 'Unfortunately I've seen more than that.'

'Of course, we do have Rumpole in Chambers.' Ballard, I'm sure, felt he had to apologize for me. 'Unfortunately. I inherited him.'

'Come with the furniture, did he?' Varian laughed.

'Oh, *I'd* never have let him in,' the loyal Ballard assured them. 'And I must tell you, I've tried to raise the matter of his waistcoat on many occasions, but I can't get him to listen.'

'Well, there you go, you see.' And Graves apologized to the cleric, 'But we're boring the Bishop.'

'Not at all. It's fascinating.' The Bishop of Bayswater was enjoying the fun. 'This Rumpole you've been talking about. I gather he's a bit of a character.'

'You could say he's definitely got form.' Varian made a legal joke.

'Previous convictions that means, Bishop,' Graves explained for the benefit of the cloth.

'We get them in our business,' the Bishop told them. 'Priests who try to be characters. They've usually come to it late in life. Preach eccentric sermons, mention Saddam Hussein in their prayers, pay undue attention to the poor of North Bayswater and never bother to drop in for a cup of tea with the perfectly decent old ladies in the South. Blame the government for all the sins of mankind in the faint hope of getting their mugs on television. "Oh, please God," that's my nightly prayer, "save me from characters."'

Varian passed him the madeira and when he had refilled his glass the Bishop continued: 'Give me a plain, undistinguished parish priest, a chap who can marry them, bury them and still do a decent Armistice Day service for the Veterans Association.'

'Or a chap who'll put his case, keep a civil tongue in his head and not complain when you pot his client,' Oliphant agreed.

'By the way,' Graves asked, 'what did Freddy Ringwood *do* in the end? Was it that business with his girl pupil? The one who tried to slit her wrists in the women's robing room at the Old Bailey?'

'No, I don't think that was it. Didn't he cash a rubber cheque in the circuit mess?' Arthur Nottley remembered.

'That was cleared. No' – Varian put them right – 'old Freddy's trouble was that he spoke to his client while he was in the middle of giving evidence.'

'It sounds familiar!' Ollie Oliphant said with relish, 'and in Rumpole's case there was also the matter of the abusive language he used to me on the Bench. Not that I mind for myself. I can use my common sense about that, I hope. But when you're sitting representing Her Majesty the Queen it amounts to *lèse majesté*.'

'High treason, Oliver?' suggested Graves languidly. 'There's a strong rumour going round the Sheridan Club that Rumpole called you a boring old fart.'

At which Arthur Nottley whispered to our leader, 'Probably the only true words spoken in the case!' and Ballard did his best to look disapproving at such impertinence.

'I know what he said.' Oliphant was overcome with terrible common sense. 'It was the clearest contempt of court. That's why I felt it was my public duty to report the matter to the Bar Council.'

'And they're also saying' – Varian was always marvellously well informed – 'that Rumpole's case has been put over to a Disciplinary Tribunal.'

'And may the Lord have mercy on his soul,' Graves intoned. 'Rumpole on trial! You must admit, it's rather an amusing idea.'

The news was bad and it had better be broken to She Who Must Be Obeyed as soon as possible. I had every reason to believe that when she heard it, the consequent eruption of just wrath against the tactless, bloody-mindedness of Rumpole would register on the Richter Scale as far away as Aldgate East and West Hampstead. So it was in the tentative and somewhat nervous way that a parent on Guy Fawkes night lights the blue touchpaper and stands well back that I said to Hilda one evening when we were seated in front of the gas-fire, 'Old thing, I've got something to tell you.'

'And I've got something to tell *you*, Rumpole.' She was drinking coffee and toying with the *Telegraph* crossword and seemed in an unexpectedly good mood. All the same, I had to confess, 'I think I've about finished with this game.'

'What game is that, Rumpole?'

'Standing up and bowing, saying, "If your Lordship pleases, In my very humble submission, With the very greatest respect, my Lord" to some old fool no one has any respect for at all.'

'That's the point, Rumpole! You shouldn't have to stand up any more, or bow to anyone.'

'Those days are over, Hilda. Definitely over!'

'I *quite* agree.' I was delighted to find her so easily persuaded. 'I shall let them go through their absurd rigmarole and then they can do their worst.'

'And you'll spend the rest of your days sitting,' Hilda said. I thought that was rather an odd way of putting it, but I was glad of her support and explained my present position in greater detail. 'So be it!' I told her. 'If that's all they have to say to me after a lifetime of trying to see that some sort of justice is done to a long line of errant human beings, good luck to them. If that's my only reward for trying to open their eyes and understand that there are a great many people in this world who weren't at Winchester with them, and have no desire to take port with the benchers of the Outer Temple, let them get on with it. *From this time forth I never will speak word!*'

'I'm sure that's best, Rumpole, except for your summings-up.'

'My what?' I no longer followed her drift.

'Your summings-up to the jury, Rumpole. You can do those sitting down, can't you?'

'Hilda,' I asked patiently, 'what *are* you talking about?'

'I know what *you're* talking about. I had a word with Marigold Featherstone, in Harrods.'

'Does *she* know already?' News of Rumpole's disgrace had, of course, spread like wildfire.

'Well, not everything. But she was going to see Guthrie did something about it.'

'Nothing he can do.' I had to shatter her hopes. 'Nothing anyone can do, now.'

'You mean, they told you?' She looked more delighted than ever.

'Told me what?'

'You're going to be a judge?'

'No, my dear old thing. I'm not going to be a judge. I'm not even going to be a barrister. I'm up before the Disciplinary Tribunal, Hilda. They're going to kick me out.'

She looked at me in silence and I steeled myself for the big bang, but to my amazement she asked, quite quietly, 'Rumpole, what is it? You've got yourself into some sort of trouble?'

'That's the understatement of the year.'

'Is it another woman?' Hilda's mind dwelt continually on sex.

'Not really. It's another man. A North Country comedian who gave me more of his down-to-earth common sense than I could put up with.'

'Sir Oliver Oliphant?' She knew her way round the Judiciary. 'You weren't rude to him, were you, Rumpole?'

'In all the circumstances, I think I behaved with remarkable courtesy,' I assured her.

'That means you were rude to him.' She was not born yesterday. 'I once poured him a cup of tea at the Outer Temple garden party.'

'What made you forget the arsenic?'

'He's probably not so bad when you get to know him.'

'When you get to know him,' I assured her, 'he's much, much worse.'

'What else have you done, Rumpole? You may as well tell me now.'

'They say I spoke to my client at lunchtime. I am alleged to have told him not to bore us all to death.'

'Was it a woman client?' She looked, for a moment, prepared to explode, but I reassured her. 'Decidedly not! It was a retired civil servant called Henry Sebastian Tong.'

'And when is this Tribunal?' She was starting to sound determined, as though war had broken out and she was prepared to fight to the finish.

'Shortly. I shall treat it with the contempt it deserves,' I told her, 'and when it's all over I shall rest:

> *'For the sword outwears its sheath,*
> *And the soul wears out the breast,*
> *And the heart must pause to breathe,*
> *And love itself have rest.'*

The sound of the words brought me some comfort, although I wasn't sure they were entirely appropriate. And then she brought back my worst fears by saying, 'I shall stand by you, Rumpole, at whatever cost. I shall stand by you, through thick and thin.'

Perhaps I should explain the obscure legal process that has to be gone through in the unfrocking, or should I say unwigging, of a barrister. The Bar Council may be said to be the guardian of our morality, there to see we don't indulge in serious crimes or conduct unbecoming to a legal hack, such as assaulting the officer in charge of the case, dealing in dangerous substances round the corridors of the Old Bailey or speaking to our clients in the lunch hour. Mr Justice Ollie Oliphant had made a complaint to that body and a committee had decided to send me for trial before a High Court Judge, three practising barristers and a lay assessor, one of the great and the good who could be relied upon to uphold the traditions of the Bar and not ask awkward questions or give any trouble to the presiding Judge. It was the prospect of She Who Must Be Obeyed pleading my cause as a character witness before this august Tribunal which made my blood run cold.

There was another offer of support which I thought was far more likely to do me harm than good. I was, a few weeks later, alone in Pommeroy's Wine Bar, contemplating the tail end of a bottle of Château Fleet Street and putting off the moment when I would have to return home to Hilda's sighs of sympathy and the often-repeated, unanswerable question, 'How *could* you have done such a thing, Rumpole? After all your years of experience', to which would no doubt be added the information that her Daddy would never have spoken to a client in the lunch hour, or at any other time come to that, when I heard a familiar voice calling my name and I looked up to see my old friend Fred Timson, head of the great South London family of villains from which a large part of my income is derived. Naturally I asked him to pull up a chair, pour out a glass and was he in some sort of trouble?

'Not me. I heard you was, Mr Rumpole. I want you to regard me as your legal adviser.'

When I explained that the indispensable Mr Bernard was already filling that post at my trial he said, 'Bernard has put me entirely in the picture, he having called on my cousin Kevin's second-hand car lot as he was interested in a black Rover, only fifty thousand on the clock and the property of a late undertaker. We chewed the fat to a considerable extent over your case, Mr Rumpole, and I have to inform you, my own view is that you'll walk it. We'll get you out, sir, without a stain on your character.'

'Oh, really, Fred' – I already felt some foreboding – 'and how will you manage that?'

'It so happened' – he started on a long story – 'that Cary and Chas

Timson, being interested spectators in the trial of Chas's brother-in-law Benny Panton on the Crockthorpe post-office job, was in the Old Bailey on that very day! And they kept your client Tongue – or whatever his name was—'

'Tong.'

'Yes, they kept Mr Tong in view throughout the lunch hour, both of them remaining in the precincts as, owing to a family celebration the night before, they didn't fancy their dinner. And they can say, with the utmost certainty, Mr Rumpole, that you did not speak one word to your client throughout the lunchtime adjournment! So the good news is, two cast-iron alibi witnesses. I have informed Mr Bernard accordingly, and you are bound to walk!'

I don't know what Fred expected but all I could do was to look at him in silent wonder and, at last, say, 'Very interesting.'

'We thought you'd be glad to know about it.' He seemed surprised at my not hugging him with delight.

'How did they recognize Mr Tong?'

'Oh, they asked who you was defending, being interested in your movements as the regular family brief. And the usher pointed this Tong out to the witnesses.'

'Really? And who was the Judge in the robbery trial they were attending?'

'They told me that! Old Penal Parsloe, I'm sure that was him.'

'Mr Justice Parsloe is now Lord Justice Parsloe, sitting in the Court of Appeal,' I had to break the bad news to him. 'He hasn't been down the Bailey for at least two years. I'm afraid your ingenious defence wouldn't work, Fred, even if I intended to deny the charges.'

'Well, what Judge was it, then, Mr Rumpole?'

'Never mind, Fred.' I had to discourage his talent for invention. 'It's the thought that counts.'

When I left Pommeroy's a good deal later, bound for Temple tube station, I had an even stranger encounter and a promise of further embarrassment at my trial. As I came down Middle Temple Lane on to the Embankment and turned right towards the station, I saw the figure of Claude Erskine-Brown approaching with his robe bag slung over his shoulder, no doubt whistling the big number from *Götterdämmerung*, perhaps kept late by some jury unable to make up its mind. Claude had been the cause of all my troubles and I had no desire to bandy words with the fellow, so I turned back and started to retrace my steps in an easterly direction. Who should I see then but Ollie Oliphant issuing from Middle Temple Lane, smoking a cigar and looking like a man who has been enjoying a good dinner. Quick as a shot I dived into such traffic as there was and crossed the road to the Embankment, where I stood, close to the wall, looking down into the inky water of the Thames, with my back well turned to the two points of danger behind me.

I hadn't been standing there very long, sniffing the night air and hoping I had got shot of my two opponents, when an unwelcome hand grasped my arm and I heard a panic-stricken voice say, 'Don't do it, Rumpole!'

'Do what?'

'Take the easy way out.'

'Bollard!' I said, for it was our Head of Chambers behaving in this extraordinary fashion. 'Let go of me, will you?'

At this, Ballard did relax his grip and stood looking at me with deep and intolerable compassion as he intoned, 'However serious the crime, all sinners may be forgiven. And remember, there are those that are standing by you, your devoted wife – and me! I have taken up the burden of your defence.'

'Well, put it down, Bollard! I have nothing whatever to say to those ridiculous charges.'

'I mean, I am acting for you, at your trial.' I then felt a genuine, if momentary, desire to hurl myself into the river, but he was preaching on. 'I think I can save you, Rumpole, if you truly repent.'

'What *is* this?' I couldn't believe my ears. 'A legal conference or a prayer meeting?'

'Good question, Rumpole! The two are never far apart. You may achieve salvation, if you will say, after me, you have erred and strayed like a lost sheep.'

'*Me*? Say that to Ollie Oliphant?' Had Bollard taken complete leave of his few remaining senses?

'Repentance, Rumpole. It's the only way.'

'Never!'

'I don't ask it for myself, Rumpole, even though I'm standing by you.'

'Well, stop standing by me, will you? I'm on my way to the Underground.' And I started to move away from the man at a fairly brisk pace.

'I ask it for that fine woman who has devoted her life to you. A somewhat unworthy cause, perhaps. But she is devoted. Rumpole, I ask it for Hilda!'

What I didn't know at that point was that Hilda was being more active in my defence than I was. She had called at our Chambers and, while I was fulfilling a previous engagement in Snaresbrook Crown Court, she had burst into Ballard's room unannounced, rousing him from some solitary religious observance or an afternoon sleep brought on by over-indulgence in bean-shoot sandwiches at the vegetarian snack bar, and told him that I was in a little difficulty. Ballard's view, when he had recovered consciousness, was that I was in fact in deep trouble and he had prayed long and earnestly about the matter.

'I hope you're going to do something a little more practical than pray!' Hilda, as you may have noticed, can be quite sharp on occasions. She went on to tell Soapy Sam that she had called at the Bar Council, indeed there was no door she wouldn't open in my cause, and had been told that what Rumpole needed was a QC to defend him, and if he did his own case in the way he carried on down the Bailey 'he'd be sunk'.

'That seems to be sound advice, Mrs Rumpole.'

'I said there was no difficulty in getting a QC of standing and that Rumpole's Head of Chambers would be delighted to act for him.'

'You mean' – there was, I'm sure, a note of fear in Ballard's voice – 'you want me to take on Rumpole as a *client*?'

'I want you to stand by him, Sam, as I am doing, and as any decent Head of Chambers would for a tenant in trouble.'

'But he's got to apologize to Mr Justice Oliphant, fully and sincerely. How on earth am I going to persuade Rumpole to do that?' Ballard no doubt felt like someone called upon to cleanse the Augean stables, knowing perfectly well that he'd never be a Hercules.

'Leave that to me. I'll do the persuading. You just think of how you'd put it nice and politely to the Judge.' Hilda was giving the instructions to Counsel, but Ballard was still daunted. 'Rumpole as a client,' he muttered. 'God give me strength!'

'Don't worry, Sam. If God won't, I certainly will.'

After this encounter Ballard dined in his new-found splendour as a bencher and after dinner he found himself sitting next to none other than the complaining Judge Ollie Oliphant, who was in no hurry to return to his bachelor flat in Temple Gardens. Seeking to avoid a great deal of hard and thankless work before the Disciplinary Tribunal, Soapy Sam started to soften up his Lordship, who seemed astonished to hear that he was defending Rumpole.

'I am acting in the great tradition of the Bar, Judge,' Soapy Sam excused himself by saying. 'Of course we are bound to represent the most hopeless client, in the most disagreeable case.'

'Hopeless. I'm glad you see that. Shows you've got a bit of common sense.'

'Might you take' – Ballard was at his most obsequious – 'in your great wisdom and humanity, which is a byword at the Old Bailey; you are known, I believe, as the Quality of Mercy down there – a merciful view if there were to be a contrite apology?'

'Rumpole'd rather be disbarred than apologize to me.' Oliphant was probably right.

'But if he would?'

'If he would, it'd cause him more genuine pain and grief than anything else in the world.' And then the Judge, thinking it over, was heard to make some sort of gurgling noise that might have passed for a chuckle. 'I'd enjoy seeing that, I really would. I'd love to see Horace Rumpole grovel. That might be punishment enough. It would be up to the Tribunal, of course.'

'Of course. But your attitude, Judge, would have such an influence, given the great respect you're held in at the Bar. Well, thank you. Thank you very much.'

It was after that bit of crawling over the dessert that I spotted Oliphant coming out of Middle Temple Lane and Ballard imagined he'd saved me from ending my legal career in the cold and inhospitable waters of the Thames.

It soon became clear to me that my supporters expected me to appear as a penitent before Mr Justice Oliphant. This was the requirement of She Who Must Be Obeyed, who pointed out the awful consequences of my refusal to bow the knee. 'How could I bear it,

Rumpole?' she said one evening when the nine o'clock news had failed to entertain us. 'I remember Daddy at the Bar and how everyone respected him. How could I bear to be the wife of a disbarred barrister? How could I meet any of the fellows in Chambers and hear them say, as I turned away, "Of course, you remember old Rumpole. Kicked out for unprofessional conduct."'

Of course I saw her point. I sighed heavily and asked her what she wanted me to do.

'Take Sam Ballard's advice. We've all told you, apologize to Sir Oliver Oliphant.'

'All right, Hilda, you win.' I hope I said it convincingly, but down towards the carpet, beside the arm of my chair, I had my fingers crossed.

Hilda and I were not the only couple whose views were not entirely at one in that uneasy period before my trial. During a quiet moment in the clerk's room, Henry came out with some startling news for Dot.

'Well, I told Eileen last night. It was an evening when she wasn't out at the Drainage Inquiry and I told my wife quite frankly what we decided.'

'What did we decide?' Dot asked nervously.

'Like, what you told me. I'm a big part of your life.'

'Did I say that?'

'You know you did. We can't hide it, can we, Dot? We're going to make a future together.'

'You told your wife that?' Dot was now seriously worried.

'She understood what I was on about. Eileen understands I got to have this one chance of happiness, while I'm still young enough to enjoy it.'

'Did you say "young enough", Henry?'

'So, we're beginning a new life together. That all right, Dot?'

Before she could answer him, the telephone rang and the clerk's room began to fill with solicitors and learned friends in search of briefs. Henry seemed to regard the matter as closed and Dot didn't dare to reopen it, at least until after my trial was over and an historic meeting took place.

During the daytime, when the nuts and fruit and madeira were put away and the tables were arranged in a more threatening and judicial manner, my trial began in the Outer Temple Parliament Room. It was all, I'm sure, intended to be pleasant and informal: I wasn't guarded in a dock but sat in a comfortable chair beside my legal advisers, Sam Ballard, QC, Liz Probert, his junior, and Mr Bernard, my instructing solicitor. However, all friendly feelings were banished by the look on the face of the presiding Judge; I had drawn the short straw in the shape of Mr Justice Graves – or Gravestone, as I preferred to call him – who looked as though he was sick to the stomach at the thought of a barrister accused of such appalling crimes, but if someone had to be he was relieved, on the whole, that it was only Horace Rumpole.

Claude gave evidence in a highly embarrassed way of what he'd heard and I instructed Ballard not to ask him any questions. This came as a relief to him as he couldn't think of any questions to ask. And then Ollie Oliphant came puffing in, bald as an egg without his wig, wearing a dark suit and the artificial flower of some charity in his buttonhole. He was excused from taking the oath by Graves, who acted on the well-known theory that Judges are incapable of fibbing, and he gave his account of all my sins and omissions to Montague Varian, QC, for the prosecution. As he did so, I examined the faces of my Judges. Graves might have been carved out of yellowish marble; the lay assessor was Lady Mendip, the headmistress, and she looked as though she were hearing an account of disgusting words found chalked up on a blackboard. Of the three practising barristers sent to try me only Arthur Nottley smiled faintly, but then I had seen him smile through the most horrendous murder cases.

When Varian had finished, Ballard rose, with the greatest respect, to cross-examine. 'It's extremely courteous of you to agree to attend here in person, Judge.'

'And absolutely charming of you to lodge a complaint against me,' I murmured politely.

'Now my client wants you to know that he was suffering from a severe toothache on the day in question.' Ballard was wrong; I didn't particularly want the Judge to know that. At any rate, Graves didn't think much of my temporary stopping as a defence. 'Mr Ballard,' he said, 'is toothache an excuse for speaking to a client during the luncheon-time adjournment? I should have thought Mr Rumpole would have been anxious to rest his mouth.'

'My Lord, I'm not dealing with the question of rudeness to the learned Judge.'

'The boring old fart evidence,' I thought I heard Nottley whisper to his neighbouring barrister.

And then Ballard pulled a trick on me which I hadn't expected. 'I understand my client wishes to apologize to the learned Judge in his own words,' he told the Tribunal. No doubt he expected that, overcome by the solemnity of the occasion, I would run up the white flag and beg for mercy. He sat down and I did indeed rise to my feet and address Mr Justice Oliphant along these lines. 'My Lord,' I started formally, 'if it please your Lordship, I do realize there are certain things which should not be said or done in Court, things that are utterly inexcusable and no doubt amount to contempt.'

As I said this, Graves leant forward and I saw, as I had never in Court seen before, a faint smile on those gaunt features. 'Mr Rumpole, the Tribunal is, I believe I can speak for us all, both surprised and gratified by this unusually apologetic attitude.' Here the quartet beside him nodded in agreement. 'I take it you're about to withdraw the inexcusable phrases.'

'Inexcusable, certainly,' I agreed. 'I was just about to put to Mr Justice Oliphant the inexcusable manner in which he sighs and rolls his eyes to heaven when he sums up the defence case.' And here I embarked on a mild imitation of Ollie Oliphant: ' "Of course you can believe that if you like, members of the jury, but use your common sense, why don't you?" And what about describing my client's conduct as manslaughter during the evidence, which was the very fact the jury had to decide? If he's prepared to say sorry for that, then I'll apologize for pointing out his undoubted prejudice.'

Oliphant, who had slowly been coming to the boil, exploded at this point. 'Am I expected to sit here and endure a repetition of the quite intolerable . . .'

'No, no, my Lord!' Ballard fluttered to his feet. 'Of course not. Please, Mr Rumpole. If it please your Lordship, may I take instructions?' And when Graves said, 'I think you'd better', my defender turned to me with 'You said you'd apologize.'

'I'm prepared to *swap* apologies,' I whispered back.

'I heard that, Mr Ballard.' Graves was triumphant. 'As I think your client knows perfectly well, my hearing is exceptionally keen. I wonder what Mr Rumpole's excuse is for his extraordinary behaviour today. He isn't suffering from toothache now, is he?'

'My Lord, I will take further instructions.' This time he whispered, 'Rumpole! Hadn't you better have toothache?'

'No, I had it out.'

'I'm afraid, my Lord' – Ballard turned to Graves, disappointed – 'the answer is no. He had it out during the trial.'

'So, on this occasion, Mr Ballard, you can't even plead toothache as a defence?'

'I'm afraid not, my Lord.'

'Had it out . . . during the trial.' Graves was making a careful note, then he screwed the top back on his pen with the greatest care and said, 'We shall continue with this unhappy case tomorrow morning.'

'My Lord' – I rose to my feet again – 'may I make an application?'

'What is it, Mr Rumpole?' Graves asked warily, as well he might.

'I'm getting tired of Mr Ballard's attempts to get me to apologize, unilaterally. Would you ask *him* not to speak to his client over the adjournment?'

Graves had made a note of the historic fact that I had had my tooth out during the trial, and Liz had noted it down also. As she wrote she started to speculate, as I had taught her to do in the distant days when she was my pupil. As soon as the Tribunal packed up business for the day she went back to Chambers and persuaded Claude Erskine-Brown to take her down to the Old Bailey and show her the *locus in quo*, the scene where the ghastly crime of chattering to a client had been committed.

Bewildered, but no doubt filled with guilt at his treacherous behaviour to a fellow hack, Claude led her to the archway through which he had seen the tedious Tong listening to Rumpole's harangue.

'And where did you see Rumpole?'

'Well, he came out through the arch after he'd finished talking to his client.'

'But *while* he was speaking to his client.'

'Well, actually,' Claude had to admit, 'I didn't see him then, at all. I mean, I suppose he was hidden from my view, Liz.'

'I suppose he was.' At which she strode purposefully through the arch and saw what, perhaps, she had expected to find, a row of telephones on the wall, in a position which would also have been invisible to the earwigging Claude. They were half covered, it's true, with plastic hoods, but a man who didn't wish to crouch under these contrivances might stand freely with the connection pulled out to its full extent and speak to whoever he had chosen to abuse.

'So Rumpole might have been standing *here* when you were listening?' Liz had taken up her position by one of the phones.

'I suppose so.'

'And you heard him say words like, "Just get on with it. I've got enough trouble without you causing me all this agony. Get it out!"?'

'I told the Tribunal that, don't you remember?' The true meaning of the words hadn't yet sunk into that vague repository of Wagnerian snatches and romantic longings, the Erskine-Brown mind. Liz, however, saw the truth in all its simplicity as she lifted a telephone, brushed it with her credit card in a way I could never manage, and was, in an instant, speaking to She Who Must Be Obeyed. Miss Probert had two simple requests: could Hilda come down to the Temple tomorrow and what, please, was the name of Horace's dentist?

When the Tribunal met next morning, my not so learned Counsel announced that my case was to be placed in more competent hands. 'My learned junior, Miss Probert,' Sam Ballard said, 'will call our next witness, but first she wishes to recall Mr Erskine-Brown.'

No one objected to this and Claude returned to the witness's chair to explain the position of the archway and the telephones, and the fact that he hadn't, indeed, seen me speaking to Tong. Montague Varian had no questions and my Judges were left wondering what significance, if any, to attach to this new evidence. I was sure that it would make no difference to the result, but then Liz Probert uttered the dread words, 'I will now call Mr Lionel Leering.'

I had been at a crossroads; one way led on through a countryside too well known to me. I could journey on for ever round the Courts, arguing cases, winning some, losing more and more perhaps in my few remaining years. The other road was the way of escape, and once Mr Leering gave his evidence that, I know, would be closed to me. 'Don't do it,' I whispered my instructions to Miss Probert. 'I'm not fighting this case.'

'Oh, Rumpole!' She turned and leant down to my level, her face shining with enthusiasm. 'I'm going to win! It's what you taught me to do. Don't spoil it for me now.'

I thought then of all the bloody-minded clients who had wrecked the cases in which I was about to chalk up a victory. It was her big moment and who was I to snatch it from her? I was tired, too tired to win, but also too tired to lose, so I gave her her head. 'Go on, then,' I told her, 'if you *have* to.'

With her nostrils dilated and the light of battle in her eyes, Mizz Liz Probert turned on her dental witness and proceeded to demolish the prosecution case.

'Do you carry on your practice in Harley Street, in London?'

'That is so. And may I say, I have a most important bridge to insert this morning. The patient is very much in the public eye.'

'Then I'll try and make this as painless as possible,' Liz assured him. 'Did you treat Mr Rumpole on the morning of May the 16th?'

'I did. He came early because he told me he was in the middle of a case at the Old Bailey. I think he was defending in a manslaughter. I gave him a temporary stopping, which I thought would keep him going.'

'Did it?'

'Apparently not. He rang me around lunchtime. He told me that his tooth was causing him pain and he was extremely angry. He raised his voice at me.'

'Can you remember what he said?'

'So far as I can recall he said something like, "I've got enough trouble with the Judge without you causing me all this agony. Get it out!" and, "Put us out of our misery!"'

'What do you think he meant?'

'He wanted his tooth extracted.'

'Did you do it for him?'

'Yes, I stayed on late especially. I saw him at 7.30 that evening. He was more cheerful then, but a little unsteady on his feet. I believe he'd been drinking brandy to give himself Dutch courage.'

'I think that may well have been so,' Liz agreed.

Now the members of the Tribunal were whispering together. Then the whispering stopped and Mr Justice Gravestone turned an ancient and fishlike eye on my prosecutor. 'If this evidence is correct,

Mr Varian, and we remember the admission made by Mr Claude Erskine-Brown and the position of the telephones, and the fact that he never saw Mr Rumpole, then this allegation about speaking to his client falls to the ground, does it not?'

'I must concede that, my Lord.'

'Then all that remains is the offensive remarks to Mr Justice Oliphant.'

'Yes, my Lord.'

'Yes, well, I'm much obliged.' The fishy beam was turned on to the defence. 'This case now turns solely on whether your client is prepared to make a proper, unilateral apology to my brother Oliphant.'

'Indeed, my Lord.'

'Then we'll consider that matter, after a short adjournment.'

So we all did a good deal of bowing to each other and as I came out of the Parliament Room, who should I see but She Who Must Be Obeyed, who, for a reason then unknown to me, made a most surprising U-turn. 'Rumpole,' she said, 'I've been thinking things over and I think Oliphant treated you abominably. My view of the matter is that you shouldn't apologize at all!'

'Is that your view, Hilda?'

'Of course it is. I'm sure nothing will make you stop work, unless you're disbarred, and think how wonderful that will be for our marriage.'

'What *do* you mean?' But I'd already guessed, with a sort of dread, what she was driving at.

'If you can't consort with all those criminals, I'll have you at home all day! There's so many little jobs for you to do. Repaper the kitchen, get the parquet in the hallway polished. You'd be able to help me with the shopping every day. And we'd have my friends round to tea; Dodo Mackintosh complains she sees nothing of you.' There was considerably more in this vein, but Hilda had already said enough to make up my mind. When my Judges were back, refreshed with coffee, biscuits and, in certain cases, a quick drag on a Silk Cut, Sam Ballard announced that I wished to make a statement, the die was cast and I tottered to my feet and spoke to the following effect. 'If your Lordship, and the members of the Tribunal, please. I have, I hope, some knowledge of the human race in general and the judicial race in particular. I do realize that some of those elevated to the Bench are more vulnerable, more easily offended than others. Over my years at the Old Bailey, before your Lordship and his brother Judges, I have had to grow a skin like a rhinoceros. Mr Justice Oliphant, I acknowledge, is a more retiring, shy and sensitive plant, and if anything I have said may have wounded him, I do most humbly, most sincerely apologize.' At this I bowed and whispered to Mizz Liz Probert, 'Will that do?'

What went on behind closed doors between my Judges I can't say. Were some of them, was even the sea-green incorruptible Graves, a little tired of Ollie's down-to-earth North Country common sense; had they been sufficiently bored by him over port and walnuts to wish to deflate, just a little, that great self-satisfied balloon? Or did they stop short of depriving the Old Bailey monument of its few moments of worthwhile drama? Would they really have wanted to take all the fun out of the criminal law? I don't know the answer to these questions but in one rather athletic bound Rumpole was free, still to be audible in the Ludgate Circus Palais de Justice.

The next events of importance occurred at an ambitious Chambers party held as a delayed celebration of the fact that Mrs Phillida Erskine-Brown, our Portia, was now elegantly perched on the High Court Bench and her husband Claude had received the lesser honour of being swathed in silk. This beano took place in Ballard's room and all the characters in Equity Court were there, together with their partners, as Mizz Liz would call them, and I had taken the opportunity of issuing a few further invitations on my own account.

One of the most dramatic events on this occasion was an encounter, by a table loaded with bottles and various delicacies, between Dot and a pleasant-looking woman in her forties who, between rapid inroads into a plate of tuna-fish sandwiches, said that she was Henry's wife Eileen, and wasn't Dot the new typist, because 'Henry's been telling me all about you'?

'I don't know why he does that. He has no call, really.' Dot was confused and embarrassed. 'Look, I'm sorry about what he told you.'

'Oh, don't be,' Eileen reassured her. 'It's a great relief to me. I was on this horrible slimming diet because I thought that's how Henry liked me, but now he says you want to make your life together. So, could you just whirl those cocktail sausages in my direction?'

'We're not going to make a life together and I don't know where he got the idea from at all. I mean, I like Henry. I think he's very sweet and serious, but in a boyfriend, I'd prefer something more muscular. Know what I mean?'

'You're not going to take him on?' Henry's wife sounded disappointed.

'I couldn't entertain the idea, with all due respect to your husband.'

'He'll have to stay where he is then.' Eileen lifted another small sausage on its toothpick. 'But I'm not going back on that horrible cottage cheese. Not for him, not for anyone.'

By now the party was starting to fill up and among the first to come was old Gravestone, to whom, I thought, I owed a very small debt of gratitude. I heard him tell Ballard how surprised he was that I'd invited him and he congratulated my so-called defender (and not my wife, who deserved all the credit) on having got me to apologize. Ballard lied outrageously and said, 'As Head of these Chambers, of course, I do have a little influence on Rumpole.'

Shortly after this, another of my invitees came puffing up the stairs and Ballard, apparently in a state of shock, stammered, 'Judge! You're here!' to Mr Justice Oliphant.

'Of course I'm here,' Ollie rebuked him. 'Use your common sense. Made Rumpole squirm, having to apologize, did it? Good, very good. That was all I needed.' Later Mr Justice Featherstone arrived with Marigold and among all these judicial stars Eileen, the ex-Mayor, had the briefest of heart to hearts with her husband. 'She doesn't want you, Henry,' she told him.

'Please!' Our clerk looked nervously round for earwiggers. 'How on earth can you say that?'

'Oh, she told me. No doubt about it. She goes for something more muscular, and I know exactly what she means.'

Oblivious of this domestic drama, the party surged on around them. Ballard told Mr Justice Featherstone that it had been a most worrying case and Guthrie said things might be even more worrying now that I'd won, and Claude asked me why I hadn't told him that I was talking to my dentist.

'Your suggestion was beneath contempt, Erskine-Brown. Besides which I rather fancied being disbarred at the time.'

'Rumpole!' The man was shocked. 'Why ever should you want that?'

'*For the sword outwears its sheath,*' I explained, '*And the soul wears out the breast, / And the heart must pause to breathe.* – But not yet, Claude. Not quite yet.*'

At last Henry managed to corner Dot, while Claude set off in a bee-line for the personable Eileen. The first thing Henry did was to apologize. 'I never wanted her to come, Dot, but she insisted. It must have been terribly embarrassing for you.'

'She's ever so nice, isn't she? You're a very lucky bloke, Henry.'

'Having you, you mean?' He still nursed a flicker of hope.

'No' – she blew out the flame – 'having a wife who's prepared to eat cottage cheese for you.'

Marigold said to Hilda, 'I hear Rumpole's not sitting as a judge. In fact I heard he was nearly made to sit at home permanently.' Marguerite Ballard, ex-matron down at the Old Bailey, told Mr Justice Oliphant that 'his naughty tummy was rather running away with him'. I told Liz that she had been utterly ruthless in pursuit of victory and she asked if I had forgiven her for saving my legal life.

'I think so. But who fed Hilda that line about having me at home all day?'

'What are you talking about, Rumpole?' She Who Must joined us.

'Oh, I was just saying to Liz, of course it'd be very nice if we could spend all day together, Hilda. I mean, *that* wasn't what led me to apologize.'

'That's the trouble with barristers.' She gave me one of her piercing looks. 'You can't believe a word they say.'

Before I could think of any convincing defence to Hilda's indictment, the last of my personally invited guests arrived. This was Fred Timson, wearing a dark suit with a striped tie and looking more than ever like a senior member of the old Serious Crimes Squad. I found him a drink, put it into his hand and told him how glad I was he could find time for us.

'What a do, eh?' He looked round appreciatively. 'Judges and sparkling wine! Here's to your very good health, Mr Rumpole.'

'No, Fred,' I told him, 'I'm going to drink to yours.' Whereupon I banged a glass against the table, called for silence and proposed a toast. 'Listen, everybody. I want to introduce you to Fred Timson, head of a noted family of South London villains, minor thieves and receivers of stolen property. No violence in his record. That right, Fred?'

'Quite right, Mr Rumpole.' Fred confirmed the absence of violence and then I made public what had long been my secret thoughts on the relationship between the Timsons and the law. 'This should appeal to you, my Lords, Ladies and gentlemen. Fred lives his life on strict monetarist principles. He doesn't believe in the closed shop; he thinks that shops should be open all night, preferably by jemmy. He believes firmly in the marketplace, because that's where you can dispose of articles that dropped off the back of a lorry. But without Fred and his like, we should all be out of work. There would be no Judges, none of Her Majesty's Counsel, learned in the law, no coppers and no humble Old Bailey Hacks. So charge your glasses, fill us up, Henry, and I would ask you to drink to Fred Timson and the criminals of England!'

I raised my glass but the faces around me registered varying degrees of disapproval and concern. Ballard bleated, 'Rumpole!', Hilda gave out a censorious, 'Really, Rumpole!', Featherstone, J, said, 'He's off again,' and Mr Justice Oliphant decided that if this wasn't unprofessional conduct he didn't know what was. Only Liz, flushed with her success in Court and a few quick glasses of the Mèthode Champenoise, raised a fist and called out, 'Up the workers!'

'Oh, really!' Graves turned wearily to our Head of Chambers. 'Will Rumpole never learn?'

'I'm afraid never,' Ballard told him.

I was back at work again and life would continue much as ever at 3 Equity Court.

Rumpole and the Model Prisoner

Quintus Blake, OBE and the staff cordially invite

Horace Rumpole Esq.

to a performance of *A Midsummer Night's Dream* by
William Shakespeare
15th September at 7 p.m. sharp.

Entry by invitation only. Proof of identity will be required.

RSVP
The Governor's Office
Worsfield Prison
Worsfield, Berks.

I had been to Worsfield gaol regularly over the years and never without breathing a sigh of relief, and gulping in all the fresh air available, after the last screw had turned the last lock and released me from custody. I never thought of going there to explore the magical charm of a wood near Athens.

'Hilda,' I said, taking a swig of rapidly cooling coffee and lining myself up for a quick dash to the Underground, 'can you prove your identity?'

'Is that meant to be funny, Rumpole?' Hilda was deep in the *Daily Telegraph* and unamused.

'I mean, if you can satisfy the authorities you're really She – I mean (here I corrected myself hastily) that you're my wife, I'll try for another ticket and we can go to the theatre together.'

'What's come over you, Rumpole? We haven't been to the theatre together for three years – or whenever Claude last dragged you to the opera.'

'Then it's about time,' I said, 'we went to the *Dream*.'

'Which dream?'

'The *Midsummer Night*'s one.'

'Where is it?' Hilda seemed prepared to put her toe in the water. 'The Royal Shakespeare?'

'Not exactly. It's in Her Majesty's Prison, Worsfield. Fifteenth September. 7 p.m. sharp.'

'You mean you want to take me to Shakespeare done by criminals?'

'Done, but not done in, I hope.'

'Anyway' – She Who Must Be Obeyed found a cast-iron alibi – 'that's my evening at the bridge school with Marigold Featherstone.'

Hilda, I thought, like most of the non-criminal classes, likes to think that those sentenced simply disappear off the face of the earth. Very few of us wonder about their wasted lives, or worry about the slums in which they are confined, or, indeed, remember them at all.

'You'll have to go on your own, Rumpole,' she said. 'I'm sure you'll have lots of friends there, and they'll all be delighted to see you.'

'Plenty of your mates in here, eh, Mr Rumpole? They'll all be glad to see you, I don't doubt.' I thought it remarkable that both She Who Must Be Obeyed and the screw who was slowly and carefully going over my body with some form of metal detector should have the same heavy-handed and not particularly diverting sense of humour.

'I have come for William Shakespeare,' I said with all the dignity I could muster. 'I don't believe he's an inmate here. Nor have I ever been called upon to defend him.'

Worsfield gaol was built in the 1850s for far fewer than the number of prisoners it now contains. What the Victorian forces of law and order required was a granite-faced castle of despair whose outer appearance was thought likely to deter the passers-by from any thoughts of evil-doing. Inside, five large cellular blocks formed the prison for men, with a smaller block set aside for the few women prisoners. In its early days all within was secrecy and silence, with prisoners, forbidden to speak to each other, plodding round the exercise yard and the treadmill – the cat-o'-nine-tails and the rope for ever lurking in the shadows. When it was built it was on the outskirts of a small industrial town, a place to be pointed out as a warning to shuddering children being brought back home late on winter evenings from school. Now the town has spread over the green fields of the countryside and the prison is almost part of the city centre. This, I thought, as my taxi passed it on the way from the station, looked in itself, with its concrete office blocks, grim shopping malls and multi-storey car parks, as if it were built like the headquarters of a secret police force or a group of houses of correction.

Inside the prison there were some attempts at cheerfulness. Walls were painted lime green and buttercup yellow. There was a dusty rubber plant, and posters for seaside holidays, in the office by the gate where I filled in a visitor's form and did my best to establish my identity. But the scented disinfectant was fighting a losing battle with the prevailing smell of stale air, unemptied chamber pots and greasy cooking.

The screw who escorted me down the blindingly lit passages, with his keys jangling at his hip, told me he'd been a schoolteacher but became a prison warder for the sake of more pay and free membership of the local golf club. He was a tall, ginger-haired man, running to fat, with that prison pallor which can best be described as halfway between sliced bread and underdone potato chips. On one of his pale cheeks I noticed a recent scar.

The ex-teacher led me across a yard, a dark concrete area lined with borders of black earth in which a few meagre plants didn't seem to be doing well. A small crowd of visitors from the outer world – youngish people whom I took to be social workers and probation officers with their partners, grey-haired governors of other prisons with their wives, enlightened magistrates and a well-known professor of criminology – was waiting. Their voices were muted, serious and respectful, as though, instead of having been invited to a comedy, they were expecting a cremation. They stood in front of the chapel, a gaunt Gothic building no doubt intended to put us all in mind of the terrible severity of the Last Judgement. There, convicted murderers had prayed while their few days of life ticked away towards the last breakfast. *'Puts the wretch that lies in woe/In remembrance of the shroud'* – I remembered the lines at the end of the play we were about to see. Then the locked doors of the chapel opened and we were shepherded in to the entertainment.

'"I have a device to make all well. Write me a prologue; and let the prologue seem to say, we will do no harm with our swords, and that

Pyramus is not kill'd indeed; and for the more better assurance, tell them that I Pyramus, am not Pyramus but Bottom the weaver. This will put them out of fear!"' The odd thing was – I had discovered by a glance at my programme before the chapel lights dimmed and the cold, marble-paved area in front of the altar was bathed in sunlight and became an enchanted forest – the prisoner playing Nick Bottom was called Bob Weaver. What he was in for I had no idea, but this weaver seemed to be less of a natural actor than a natural Bottom. There was no hint of an actor playing a part. The simple pomposity, the huge self-satisfaction and the like-ability of the man were entirely real. When the audience laughed, and they laughed a good deal, the prisoner didn't seem pleased, as an actor would be, but as hurt, puzzled and resentful as bully Bottom mocked. And, when he came to the play scene, he acted Pyramus with intense seriousness which, of course, made it funnier than ever.

We were a segregated audience, divided by the aisle. On one side, like friends of the groom, sat the inmates in grey prison clothes and striped shirts – and trainers (which I used to call sandshoes when I was a boy) were apparently allowed. On the other side, the friends of the bride were the great and the good, the professional carers and concerned operators of a curious and notoriously unsuccessful system. Of the two sides, it was the friends of the groom who coughed and fidgeted less, laughed more loudly and seemed more deeply involved in the magic that unfolded before them:

> 'But we are spirits of another sort.
> I with the morning's love have oft made sport,
> And like a forester the groves may tread
> Even till the eastern gate, all fiery red,
> Opening on Neptune with fair blessèd beams
> Turns into yellow gold his salt green streams.'

I hadn't realized how handsome Tony Timson would look without his glasses. His association, however peripheral, with an armed robbery (not the sort of thing the Timson family had any experience of, nor indeed talent for) had led him to be ruler of a fairy kingdom. Puck, small, energetic and Irish, I remembered from a far more serious case as a junior member of the clan Molloy. All too soon, for me anyway, he was alone on the stage, smiling a farewell:

> '*If we shadows have offended,*
> *Think but this, and all is mended:*
> *That you have but slumbered here,*
> *While these visions did appear . . .*'

Then the house lights went up and I remembered that all the lovers, fairies and Rude Mechanicals (with the exception of the actresses) were robbers, housebreakers, manslaughterers and murderers, there because of their crimes and somebody's – perhaps my – unsuccessful defence.

'I think you'll all agree that that was a pretty good effort.' The Governor was on the stage, a man with a ramrod back, cropped grey hair and pink cheeks, who spoke like some commanding officer congratulating his men after a particularly dangerous foray into enemy territory. 'We owe a great deal to those splendid performers and all those who helped with the costumes. I suggest we might give a hand to our director who is mainly responsible for getting these awkward fellows acting.'

A small, middle-aged man with steel-rimmed spectacles rose up from the front row of the inmates and lifted a hand to acknowledge the applause. This the Governor silenced with a brisk mutter of words of command. 'Now will all those of you who live in, please go out. And those of you who live out, please stay in. You'll be escorted to the boardroom for drinks and light refreshments.'

The screws who had been waiting, stationed round the walls like sentries, reclaimed their charges. I saw the director who had been applauded walking towards them with his knees slightly bent, moving with a curious hopping motion, as though he were a puppet on a string. I hadn't seen his face clearly but something in the way he moved seemed familiar, although I couldn't remember where I'd met him before, or what crime he might, or might not, have committed.

'Never went much for Shakespeare when I was at school,' Quintus Blake, the Governor, told me. He was holding a flabby sausage roll in one hand and, in the other, a glass of warmish white wine which, for sheer undrinkability, had Pommeroy's house blanc beaten by a short head. 'Thought the chap was a bit long-winded and couldn't make his meaning clear at times. But, by God, doesn't he come into his own in the prison service?'

'You mean, you use him as a form of punishment?'

'That's what I'd've thought when I was at school. That's what I'll tell Ken Fry if he complains we're giving the chaps too good a time. If they misbehave, I'll tell him we put them on Shakespeare for twenty-eight days.' Ken Fry is our new, abrasive, young Home Secretary who lives for the delighted cheers of the hangers and floggers at party conferences. Given time, he'll reintroduce the rack as a useful adjunct to police questioning.

'The truth of the matter' – Quintus bit bravely into the tepid flannel of his sausage roll – 'is that none of the fellows on Shakespeare duty have committed a single offence since rehearsals began.'

'Is that really true?'

'Well, with one exception.' He took a swig at the alleged Entre Deux Mers, decided that one was enough and put his glass down on the boardroom table. 'Ken Fry says prison is such a brilliant idea because no one commits crimes here. Well, of course, they do. They bully each other and get up to sexual shenanigans which put me in mind of the spot behind the fives court at Coldsands. I don't know what it is about prison that always reminds me of my schooldays. Anyway, as soon as they landed parts in the *Dream*, they were as good as gold, nearly all of them. And for that I've got to hand it to Gribble.'

'Gribble?'

'Matthew Gribble. Inmate in charge of Shakespeare. Just about due for release as he's got all the remission possible.'

'He produced the play?'

'And even got a performance out of that human bulldozer who played bully Bottom. One-time boxer who'd had his brains turned into mashed potatoes quite early in his career.'

'Gribble was the man who stood up at the end?'

'I thought I'd get this lot to give him a round of applause.' The Governor looked at the well-meaning elderly guests, the puzzled but hopeful social workers, who were taking their refreshments, as they took all the difficulties in their lives, with grim determination. It was then I remembered Matthew Gribble, an English teacher at a Berkshire polytechnic, who had killed his wife.

'I think,' I said, 'I defended him once.'

'I know you did!' The Governor smiled. 'And he wants you to do the trick again before the Board of Visitors. I said I'd try and arrange it because, so far as I'm concerned, he's an absolutely model prisoner.'

All this happened at a time when Claude Erskine-Brown (who had not yet become a QC – I call them Queer Customers) took to himself a young lady pupil named Wendy Crump. Mizz Crump was a person with high legal qualifications but no oil painting – as Uncle Tom, of blessed memory, would have been likely to say. She had, I believe, been hand-picked by Claude's wife, the Portia of our Chambers, who had not yet got her shapely bottom on to the Bench and been elevated to the title of Mrs Justice Phillida Erskine-Brown, a puisne judge of the High Court.

'Your Mizz Crump,' I told Claude, when we met at breakfast time in the Taste-Ee-Bite eatery a little to the west of our Chambers, 'seems a bit of an all-round asset.'

'All round, Rumpole. You've said it. Wendy Crump is very all round indeed.' He gave a mirthless laugh and spoke as a man who might have preferred a slimline pupil.

'Hope you don't mind,' I told him, 'but I asked her to look up the effect of self-induced drunkenness on crimes of violence. She came up with the answer in a couple of shakes, with reference to all the leading cases.'

'I'll agree she's a dab hand at the law.'

'Well, isn't that what you need a pupil for?' I knew it was a silly question as soon as I'd asked it. An ability to mug up cases on manslaughter was not at all what Claude required of a pupil. He wanted someone willing, husky-voiced and alluring. He wanted a heart-shaped face and swooping eyelashes which could drive the poor fellow insane when they were topped by a wig. He wanted to fall in love and make elaborate plans for satisfying his cravings, which would be doomed to disaster. What the poor old darling wanted was yet another opportunity to make a complete ass of himself, and these longings were unlikely to be fulfilled by Wendy Crump.

'What a barrister needs, Rumpole, in a busy life with heavy responsibilities and a great deal of nervous tension is, well, a little warmth, a little adoration.'

'I shouldn't be in the least surprised if Mizz Crump didn't adore you, Claude.'

'Don't even suggest it!' The clever Crump's pupil master gave a shudder.

'Anyway, don't you get plenty of warmth and affection from Philly?'

'Philly's been on circuit for weeks.' Claude took a quick swig of the coffee from the Old Bailey machine and didn't seem to enjoy it. 'And when she's here she spends all her time criticizing me.'

'How extraordinary.' I simulated amazement.

'Yes, isn't it? Philly's away and I have to spend my days stuck here with Wendy Crump. But not my nights, Rumpole. Never, ever, my nights.'

I lost his attention as Nick Davenant from King's Bench Walk passed us, followed by his pupil Jenny Attienzer. She was tall, blonde, willowy and carrying his coffee. Poor old Claude looked as sick as a dog.

That afternoon I was seated at my desk, smoking a small cigar and gazing into space – the way I often spend my time when not engaged in Court – when there was a brisk knock at the door and Wendy Crump entered and asked if I had a set of Cox's Criminal Reports. 'Not in here,' I told her. 'Try upstairs. Cox's Reports are Soapy Sam Ballard's constant reading.' And then, because she looked disappointed at not finding these alluring volumes at once, I did my best to cheer her up. 'Claude thinks you're a wonderful pupil.' I exaggerated, of course. 'I told him you were a dab hand at the law. He's very lucky.'

It's rare nowadays that you see anyone blush, but Wendy's usually pale cheeks were glowing. 'I'm the lucky one,' she said, and added, to my amazement, 'to be doing my pupillage with Erskine-Brown. Everyone I know is green with envy.' Everyone she knew, I thought, must be strangely ignorant of life at the Bailey, where prosecution by Claude has come to be regarded as the key to the gaolhouse door.

Wendy ended her testimonial with 'I honestly do regard it as an enormous privilege.' I supposed the inmates of Worsfield would consider basketball or macramé a privilege if it got them out of solitary confinement. Looking at the enthusiastic Mizz Crump I thought that Claude had been unfair about her appearance. It was just that she had acquired the look of an intelligent and cheerful middle-aged person whilst still in her twenties. She was, I suppose, what would be called considerably overweight, but there was nothing wrong with that. With her wiry hair scraped back, her spectacles and her willing expression, she looked like the photographs of the late Dorothy L. Sayers, a perfectly pleasant sight.

'I just hope I can be a help to him.'

'I'm sure you can.' Although not, I thought, the sort of help the ever-hopeful Claude was after.

'I could never rise to be a barrister like that.'

'Perhaps it's just as well,' I encouraged her.

'I mean I could never stand up and speak with such command – and in such a beautiful voice too. Of course he's handsome, which means he can absolutely dominate a courtroom. You need to be handsome to do that, don't you?'

'Well,' I said, 'thank you very much.'

'Oh, I didn't mean that. Of course *you* dominate all sorts of courtrooms. And it doesn't matter what you look like.' She gave a little gasp to emphasize her point. 'It doesn't matter in the least!'

'The extraordinary thing is that his name is Weaver. He was on the same floor as me, a couple of cell doors away.' Matthew Gribble spoke as if he were describing a neighbour in a country village. 'Bob Weaver. He used to laugh at me because I kept getting books from the library. He was sure I got all the ones with dirty bits in because I knew where to look for them. Of course, in those days, he couldn't tell the difference between soft porn and *Mansfield Park*. He was hardly literate.'

'You say he *was*.'

'Until I taught him to read, that is.'

'You taught him?'

'Oh, yes. I honestly don't know how I'd've got through the years here if I hadn't had that to do.' He gave a small, timid smile. 'As a matter of fact, I enjoyed the chance to teach again.'

'How did you manage it?'

'Oh, I read to him at first. I read all the stories I'd liked when I was a child. We started with *Winnie-the-Pooh* and got on to *Treasure Island* and *Kidnapped*. Then he began to want to read for himself.'

'So you decided to cast him?'

'If we ever did the *Dream*. He looked absolutely right. A huge mountain of a man with the outlook of a child. And kind, too. He *even* had the right name for it.'

'You mean, to play Nick, the weaver?'

'Exactly! I asked him to do it a long time ago. Two years at least. I asked him if he'd like to play Bottom.'

'And he agreed?'

'No.' The timid smile returned. 'He looked profoundly shocked. He thought I'd made some sort of obscene suggestion.'

We had been in the Worsfield interview room four and a bit years before, sitting on either side of the same table, with the bright blue paint and the solitary cactus, and the walls and door half glass so the screws could look in and see what we were up to. Then, we had been talking about his teaching, his production with the Cowshott drama group, the performances which he got out of secretaries and teachers and a particularly dramatic district nurse – and of his wife who apparently hated him and his amateur theatricals. When she flew at him and tore at his face with her fingernails during one of their nightly quarrels over the washing-up, he had stabbed her through the heart. I thought I had done the case with my usual brilliance and got the jury to find provocation and reduce the crime to manslaughter, for which the Judge, taking the view that a kitchen knife is not the proper reply to an attack with fingernails, had given him seven years. As the Governor told me, he was a model prisoner. With full remission he'd be out by the end of the month. That is, unless he was convicted on the charge I was now concerned with. If the Board of Visitors did him for dangerous assault on a prison warden, he'd forfeit a large chunk of his remission.

'The incident we have to talk about,' I said, 'happened in the carpenter's shop.'

'Yes,' he sighed, 'I suppose we have to talk about it.'

All subjects seemed to him, I guessed, flat, stale and unprofitable after the miracle of getting an illiterate East End prizefighter to enjoy acting Shakespeare. I remembered his account of the last quarrel with his wife. She had told him he was universally despised. She had mocked him for his pathetic sexual attainments while, at the same time, accusing him, quite without foundation, of abusing his child by a previous marriage. He had heard it all many, many times before. It was only when she told him that he had produced *Hamlet* as though it were a television situation comedy that their quarrel ended in violence.

'Yes, the carpenter's shop.' Matthew Gribble sighed. Then he cheered up slightly and said, 'We were building the set for the *Dream*.'

I had a note of the case given to me by the Governor. There were only four members of the cast working on the scenery, one civilian carpenter and a prison officer in overall charge. His name was Steve Barrington.

'Do you know' – my client's voice was full of wonder – 'Barrington gave up a job as a teacher to become a screw? Isn't that extraordinary?'

'Do you think he regrets it? He may not have got chisels thrown at him in class, with any luck.'

What was thrown was undoubtedly the tool which Matthew had been using. The screw was talking to one of the carpenters and didn't see the missile before it struck his cheek. The other cast members, except for one, said they were busy and didn't see who launched the attack.

'I put the chisel on the bench and I was just turning round to tack the false turf on to the mound we'd built. I didn't see who threw it. I only know that I didn't. I told you the truth in the other case. Why should I lie to you about this?'

Because you don't want to spend another unnecessary minute as a guest of Her Majesty, I thought of saying, but resisted the temptation. It was not for me to pass judgement, not at any stage of the proceedings. My problem was that there was a witness who said he'd seen Matthew Gribble throw the chisel. A witness who seemed to have no reason to tell lies about his friend and educator. It was Bob Weaver who had made the journey from illiteracy to Shakespeare, and been rewarded with the part of bully Bottom.

'Rumpole, a terrible thing has happened in Chambers!' Mizz Liz Probert sat on the edge of my client's chair, her face pale but determined, her hands locked as though in prayer, her voice low and doom-laden. It was as though she were announcing, to waiting relations on the quay-side, the fact that the *Titanic* had struck an iceberg.

'Not the nail-brush disappeared again?'

'Rumpole, can't you ever be serious?'

'Hardly ever when it comes to things that have happened in Chambers.'

'Well, this time, perhaps your attitude will be more helpful.'

'It depends on whether I want to be helpful. What is it? Don't tell me. Henry blew the coffee money on a dud horse?'

'Claude has committed the unforgivable sin.'

'You mean, adultery? Well, that's something of an achievement. His attempts usually end in all-round frustration.'

'That too, most probably. No. This is what he said in the clerk's room.'

'Go on. Shock me.'

'Kate Inglefield, who's an assistant solicitor in Damiens, heard him say it. And, of course, she was tremendously distressed.'

'Can you tell me what he said?' I wondered. 'Or are you too embarrassed? Would you prefer to write it down?'

'Don't be silly, Rumpole. He asked Henry if he'd seen his fat pupil about recently.'

There followed a heavy silence, during which I thought I was meant to say something. So I said, 'Go on.'

'What do you mean?'

'Go on till you get to the bit that caused Kate Inglefield – not, I would have thought, a girl who distresses easily – such pain.'

'Rumpole, I've said it. Do I have to say it again?'

'Perhaps if you do, I'll be able to follow your argument.'

'Erskine-Brown said to Henry, "Have you seen my fat pupil?" '

'Recently?'

'What?'

'He said recently.'

'Really, Rumpole. Recently is hardly the point.'

'So the point is my fat pupil?'

'Of course it is!'

I took out a small cigar and placed it between the lips. Sorting out the precise nature of the charge against Claude would require a whiff of nicotine. 'And he was referring – I merely ask for clarification – to his pupil Mizz Crump?'

'Of course he meant Wendy, yes.'

'And he called her fat?'

'It was' – Liz Probert described it as though murder had been committed – 'an act of supreme chauvinism. It's daring to assume that women should alter the shape of their bodies just for the sake of pleasing men. Disgusting!'

'But isn't it' – I was prepared, as usual, to put forward the argument for the defence – 'a bit like saying the sky's blue?'

'It's not at all like that. It's judging a woman by her appearance.'

'And isn't the other judging the sky by its appearance?'

'I suppose I should have known!' Mizz Probert stood up, all her sorrow turned to anger. 'There's no crime so contemptible that you won't say a few ill-chosen words in its favour. And, don't you dare light that thing until I'm out of the room.'

'I'm sure you're busy.'

'I certainly am. We're having a special meeting tonight of the Sisterhood of Radical Lawyers. We aim to blacklist anyone who sends Claude briefs or appears in Court with him. We're going to petition the Judges not to listen to his arguments and Ballard's got to give him notice to quit.'

'Mizz Liz,' I said, 'how would you describe me?'

'As a defender of hopeless causes.'

'No, I mean my personal appearance.'

'Well, you're fairly short.' The prosecutor gave me the once-over. 'Your nose is slightly purple, and your hair – what's left of it – is curly and you're . . .'

'Go on, say it.'

'Well, Rumpole. Let's face it. You're fat.'

'You said it.'

'Yes.'

'So should I get you blackballed in Court?'

'Of course not.'

'Why not?'

'Because you're a man.'

'I see.'

'I shouldn't think you do. I shouldn't think you do for a moment.'

Mizz Probert left me then. Full of thought, I applied the match to the end of the small cigar.

It was some weeks later that Fred Timson, undisputed head of the Timson clan, was charged with receiving a stolen video recorder. The charge was, in itself, something of an insult to a person of Fred's standing and sensitivity. It was rather as if I had been offered a brief in a case of a non-renewed television licence, or, indeed, of receiving a stolen video recorder. I only took the case because Fred is a valued client and, in many respects, an old family friend. I never tire of telling Hilda that a portion of our family beef, bread, marmalade and washing-up liquid depends on the long life of Fred Timson and his talent for getting caught on the windy side of the law. I can't say that this home truth finds much favour with She Who Must Be Obeyed, who treats me, on these occasions, as though I were only a moderately successful petty thief working in Streatham and its immediate environs.

The defence was elaborate, having to do with a repair job delivered to the wrong address, an alibi and the fact that the chief prosecution witness was a distant relative of a member of the Molloy family – all bitter rivals and enemies of the Timsons. While Fred and I were drinking coffee in the Snaresbrook canteen, having left the jury to sort out the complexities of this minor crime, I told him that I'd seen Tony Timson playing the King of the Fairies.

'No, Mr Rumpole, you're mistaken about that, I can assure you, sir. Our Tony is not that way inclined.'

'No, in *Midsummer Night's Dream*. An entirely heterosexual fairy. Married to the Fairy Queen.'

Fred Timson said nothing, but shook his head in anxious disbelief. I decided to change the subject. 'I don't know if you've heard of one of Tony's fellow prisoners. Bob Weaver, a huge fellow. Started off as a boxer?'

'Battering Bob Weaver!' Fred seemed to find the memory amusing. 'That's how he was known. Used to do bare-knuckle fights on an old airfield near Colchester. And my cousin Percy Timson's young Mavis married Battering Bob's brother, Billy Weaver, as was wrongly fingered for the brains behind the Dagenham dairy-depot job. To be quite candid with you, Mr Rumpole, Billy Weaver is not equipped to be the brains behind anything. Pity about Battering Bob, though.'

'You mean the way he went down for the Deptford minicab murder?'

'Not that exactly. That's over and done with. No. The way he's deteriorated in the nick.'

'Deteriorated?'

'According as Mavis tells Percy, he has. Can't hold a decent conversation when they visits. It's all about books and that.'

'I heard he's learnt to read.'

'Mavis says the family's worried desperate. Bob spent all her visit telling her a poem about a nightingale. Well, what's the point of that? I mean, there can't be all that many nightingales round Worsfield Prison. Course, it's the other bloke they put it down to.'

'Matthew Gribble?'

'Is that the name? Anyway, seems Bob thinks the world of this chap. Says he's changed his life and that he worships him, Mr Rumpole. But Mavis reckons he's been a bad influence on Bob. I mean that Gribble's got terrible form. Didn't he kill his wife? No one in our family ever did that.'

'Of course not. Although Tony Timson was rumoured to have attempted it.'

'Between the attempt and the deed, as you well know, Mr Rumpole, there is a great gulf fixed. Isn't that true?'

'Very true, Fred.'

'And Mavis says Bob's been worse for the last three months. Nervous and depressed like as though he was dreading something.' What, I wondered, had been bugging Battering Bob? It couldn't have been the fact that his friend was in trouble for attacking a warden; that had only happened a month before. 'I suppose,' I suggested, 'it was stage fright. They started rehearsing *Midsummer Night's Dream* around three months ago.'

'You mean like he was scared of being in a play?'

'He might have been.'

'I hardly think a bloke what went single-handed against six Molloys during the minicab war would be scared of a bit of a play.'

It was then that the tireless Bernard came to tell me that the jury were back with a verdict. Fred stood up, gave his jacket a tug and strolled off as though he'd just been called in to dinner at the local Rotary Club. And I was left wondering again why Battering Bob Weaver should decide to be the sole witness against a man he had worshipped.

I got back to Chambers in a reasonably cheerful mood, the jury having decided to give Uncle Fred the generous benefit of a rather small supply of doubt, and there waiting in my client's chair was another bundle of trouble. None other than Wendy Crump, Claude's pupil, clearly in considerable distress. 'I had to talk to you,' she said, 'because it's all so terribly unfair!'

Was unfair the right word, I wondered. Unkind, perhaps, but not unfair, unless she meant it as a general rebuke to the Almighty who handed out sylphlike beauty to the undiscerning few with absolutely no regard for academic attainment or moral worth. 'Of course,' I said, 'I think you look very attractive.'

'What?' She looked at me surprised and, I thought, a little shocked.

'In the days of Sir Peter Paul Rubens,' I assured her, 'a girl with your dimensions would have been on page three of the *Sun*, if not on the ceiling of the Banqueting Hall.'

'Please, Rumpole,' she said, 'there are more important things to talk about.'

'Well, exactly,' I assured her. 'People have suggested that *I'm* a little overweight. They have hinted that from time to time, but do I let it worry me? Do I decline the mashed spuds or the fried slice with my breakfast bacon? I do not. I let such remarks slide off me like water off a duck's back.'

'Rumpole!' she said, a little sharply, I thought. 'I don't think your physical appearance is anything to do with all this trouble.'

'Is it not? I just thought that we're birds of a feather.'

'I doubt it!' This Mizz Crump could be very positive at times. 'I came to see you about Erskine-Brown.'

'Of course, he shouldn't have said it.' I was prepared, as I have said, to accept the brief for the defence. 'It was just one of those unfortunate slips of the tongue.'

'You mean he shouldn't have told me about Kate Inglefield?'

'What's he told you about Mizz Inglefield? You mean that rather bright young solicitor from Damiens? She's quite skinny, as far as I can remember.'

'Rumpole, why do you keep harping on people's personal appearances?'

'Well, didn't Claude say . . . ?'

'Claude told me that Kate Inglefield had decided never to brief him again. And she's taken his VAT fraud away from him. And Christine Dewsbury, who's meant to be his junior in a long robbery, has said she'll never work with him again, and Mr Ballard . . .'

'The whited sepulchre who is Head of our Chambers?'

'Mr Ballard has been giving him some quite poisonous looks.'

'Those aren't poisonous looks. That's Soapy Sam's usual happy expression.'

'He's hinted that Erskine-Brown may have to look for other Chambers. He's such a wonderful advocate, Rumpole!'

'Well now, let's say he's an advocate of sorts.'

'And a fine man! A man with very high principles.' I listened in some surprise. Was this the Claude I had seen stumbling into trouble and lying his way out of it over the last twenty years? 'And he has absolutely no idea why he is being victimized.'

'Has he not?'

'None whatever.'

'But *you* know?'

'No, really. I have no idea.'

'Well' – I breathed a sigh of relief – 'that's all right then.'

'No, it's not all right.' She stood up, her cheeks flushed, her voice clear and determined. Mizz Crump might be no oil painting, but I thought I saw in her the makings of a fighter. 'We've got to find out why all this is happening. And we've got to save him. Will you help me get him out of trouble? *Whatever* it is.'

'Helping people in trouble,' I assured her, 'has been my job for almost half a century.'

'So you're with me, Rumpole?' She was, I was glad to see, a determined young woman who might go far in the law.

'Of course I am. We fat people should stick together.' Naturally, I regretted it the moment I had said it.

*

'The Governor says you're a model prisoner.'

'Yes.'

'Well, that's a kind of tribute.'

'Not exactly what I wanted to be when I was at university. I'd just done my first *Twelfth Night*. I suppose I wanted to be a great director. I saw myself at the National or the RSC. If I couldn't do that, I wanted to be an unforgettable teacher of English and open the eyes of generations to Shakespeare. I never thought I'd end up as a model prisoner.'

'Life is full of surprises.' That didn't seem too much of a comfort to Matthew Gribble as we sat together, back in the prison interview room. Spring sunshine was fighting its way through windows that needed cleaning. I had sat in the train, trees with leaves just turning green, sunlight on the grass. A good time to think of freedom, starting a new life and forgetting the past. 'If we can get you off this little bit of trouble, you should be out of here by the end of the month.'

'Out. To do what?' He was smiling gently, but I thought quite without amusement, as he stared into the future. 'I shouldn't think they'll ever ask me to direct a play for the Cowshott amateurs. "You'd better watch out for this one, darling," I can just hear them whispering at the read-through. "He stabbed his wife to death with a kitchen knife."'

'There may be other drama groups.'

'Not for me. Do you think they'd have me back at the poly? Not a hope.'

'Anyway' – I tried to cheer him up – 'you did a pretty good job with *A Midsummer Night's Dream*.'

'Shakespeare with violent criminals, deputy governors' wives and wardens' daughters. Not the RSC exactly, but I can put on a good show in Worsfield gaol. Wasn't Bob Weaver marvellous?'

'Extraordinary.'

'And you know what I discovered? He responds to the sound of poetry. He's got to know it by heart. Great chunks of it.' From Battering Bob to Babbling Bob, I thought, treating his bewildered visitors to great chunks of John Keats. It was funny, of course, but in its way a huge achievement. Matthew Gribble appeared to agree. 'I suppose I'm proud of that.' He thought about it and seemed satisfied. I turned back to the business in hand.

'Those other cast members in the carpenter's helping make the scenery – Tony Timson, the young Molloy? Do you think either of them saw who threw the chisel?'

'If they did, they're not saying. Grassing's a sin in prison.'

'But your protégé Babbling Bob is prepared to grass on you?'

'Seems like it.' He was, I thought, resigned and strangely unconcerned.

'Have you talked to him about it?'

'Yes. Once.'

'What did you say?'

'I told him to always be truthful. That's the secret of acting, to tell the truth about the character. I told him that.'

'Forget about acting for a moment. Did you ask him why he said you attacked the screw?'

There was a silence. Matthew Gribble seemed to be looking past me, at something far away. At last he said, 'Yes, I asked him that.'

'And what did he say?'

'He said' – my client gave a small, not particularly happy smile – 'he said we'd always be friends, wouldn't we?'

The master–pupil relationship – the instructing of a younger, less experienced person in the mysteries of some art, theatrical or legal – seemed a situation fraught with danger. While Matthew Gribble's devoted pupil was turning on his master with damaging allegations, Wendy Crump's pupil master was in increasing trouble, being treated by the Sisterhood of Radical Lawyers as a male pariah. As yet, neither Erskine-Brown, nor his alleged victim, had been informed of the charges against him, although Mizz Probert and her supporters were about to raise the matter before the Bar Council as a serious piece of professional misconduct by the unfortunate Claude, who sat, brooding and unemployed in his room, wondering what it was that his best friend wouldn't tell him which had led to him being shunned by female lawyers. I learnt about the proposed petitioning of the Bar Council when I visited the Soapy Head of our Chambers in order to scotch any plan to drive the unfortunate sinner from that paradise which is 3 Equity Court.

'There is no doubt whatever' – here Ballard put on his carefully modulated tone of sorrowful condemnation – 'that Erskine-Brown has erred grievously.'

'Which one of the Ten Commandments is it exactly, if I may be so bold as to ask, which forbids us to call our neighbour fat?'

'There is such a thing, Rumpole' – Ballard gave me the look with which a missionary might reprove a cannibal – 'as gender awareness.'

'Is there, really? And who told you about that then? I'll lay you a hundred to one it was Mizz Liz Probert.'

'Lady lawyers take it extremely seriously, Rumpole. Which is why we're in danger of losing all our work from Damiens.'

'The all-female solicitors? Not a man in the whole of the firm. Is that being gender aware?'

'However the firm is composed, Rumpole, they provide a great deal of valuable work for all of us.'

'Well, I'm aware of gender,' I told Soapy Sam, 'at least I think I am. You're a man from what I can remember.'

'That remark would be taken very much amiss, Rumpole. If made to a woman.'

'But it's not made to a woman, it's made to you, Ballard. Are you going to stand for this religious persecution of the unfortunate Claude?'

'What he said about Wendy Crump was extremely wounding.'

'Nonsense! She wasn't wounded in the least. None of these avenging angels has bothered to tell her what her pupil master said.'

'Did you tell her?'

'Well, no, I didn't, actually.'

'Did you tell Wendy Crump that Erskine-Brown had called her fat?' For about the first time in his life Soapy Sam had asked a good question in cross-examination. I was reduced, for a moment at least, to silence. 'Why didn't you repeat those highly offensive words to her?'

I knew the answer, but I wasn't going to give him the pleasure of hearing it from me.

'It was because you didn't want to hurt her feelings, did you, Rumpole? And you knew how much it would wound her.' Ballard was triumphant. 'You showed a rare flash of gender awareness and I congratulate you for it!'

*

Although a potential outcast from the gender-aware society, Claude hadn't been entirely deprived of his practice. New briefs were slow in arriving, but he still had some of his old cases to finish off. One of these was a complex and not particularly fascinating fraud on a bookmaker in which Claude and I were briefed for two of the alleged fraudsters. I needn't go into the details of the case except to say that the prosecution was in the hands of the dashing and handsome Nick Davenant who had a large and shapely nose, brown hair billowing from under his wig and knowing and melting eyes. It was Nick's slimline pupil, Jenny Attienzer, whom Claude had hopelessly coveted. This fragile beauty was not in Court on the day in question; whether she thought the place out of bounds because of the gender-unaware Claude, I'm unable to say. But Claude was being assisted by the able but comfortably furnished (slenderly challenged) Wendy Crump and I was on my own.

The case was being tried by her Honour Judge Emma MacNaught, QC, sitting as an Old Bailey Judge, who had treated Claude, from the start of the case, to a number of withering looks and, when addressing him in person became inevitable, to a tone of icy contempt. This Circus Judge turned out to have been the author of a slender handbook entitled 'Sexual Harassment in the Legal Profession'. (Wendy Crump told me, some time later, that she would challenge anyone to know whether they had been sexually harassed or not unless they'd read the book.)

Nick Davenant called the alleged victim of our clients' fraud – a panting and sweating bookmaker whose physical attributes I am too gender aware to refer to – and his last question was, 'Mr Aldworth, have you ever been in trouble with the police?'

'No. Certainly not. Not with the police.' On which note of honesty Nick sat down and Claude rose to cross-examine. Before he could open his mouth, however, Wendy was half standing, pulling at his gown and commanding, in a penetrating whisper, that he ask Aldworth if he'd ever been in trouble with anyone else.

'Are you intending to ask any question, Mr Erskine-Brown?' Judge MacNaught had closed her eyes to avoid the pain of looking at the learned chauvinist pig.

'Have you been in trouble with anyone else?' Claude plunged in, clay in the hands of the gown-tugger behind him.

'Only with my wife. On Derby night.' For this, Mr Aldworth was rewarded by a laugh from the jury, and Claude by a look of contempt from the Judge.

'Ask him if he's ever been reported to Tattersall's.' The insistent pupil behind Claude gave another helping tug. Claude clearly didn't think things could get any worse.

'Have you ever been reported to Tattersall's?' he asked, adding 'the racing authority' by way of an unnecessary explanation.

'Well, yes. As far as I can remember,' Mr Aldworth admitted in a fluster, and the jury stopped laughing.

'Ask him how many times!'

'How many times?' Wendy Crump was now Claude's pupil master.

'I don't know I can rightly remember.'

'Do your best,' Wendy suggested.

'Well, do your best,' Claude asked.

'Ten or a dozen times . . . Perhaps twenty.'

I sat back in gratitude. The chief prosecution witness had been holed below the waterline, without my speaking a word, and our co-defendants might well be home and dry.

At the end of the cross-examination, the learned Judge subjected Claude to the sort of scrutiny she might have given a greenish slice of haddock on a slab, long past its sell-by date. 'Mr Erskine-Brown!'

'Yes, my Lady.'

'You are indeed fortunate to have a pupil who is so skilled in the art of cross-examination.'

'Indeed, I am, my Lady.'

'Then you must be very grateful that she remains to help you. For the time being.' The last words were uttered in the voice of a prison governor outlining the arrangements, temporary of course, for life in the condemned cell. Hearing them, even my blood, I have to confess, ran a little chill.

When the lunch adjournment came Claude shot off about some private business and I strolled out of Court with the model pupil. I told her she'd done very well.

'Thank you, Rumpole.' Wendy took my praise as a matter of course. 'I thought the Judge was absolutely outrageous to poor old Claude. Going at him like that simply because he's a man. I can't stand that sort of sexist behaviour!' And then she was off in search of refreshment and

I was left wondering at the rapidity with which her revered pupil master had become 'poor old Claude'.

And then I saw, at the end of the wide corridor and at the head of the staircase, Nick Davenant, the glamorous prosecutor, in close and apparently friendly consultation with the leader of the militant sisterhood, Mizz Liz Probert of our Chambers. I made towards them but, as she noticed my approach, Mizz Liz melted away like snow in the sunshine and, being left alone with young Nick, I invited him to join me for a pint of Guinness and a plateful of steak-and-kidney pie in the pub across the road.

'I saw you were talking to Liz Probert?' I asked him when we were settled at the trough.

'Great girl, Liz. In your Chambers, isn't she?'

'I brought her up, you might say. She was my pupil in her time. Did she question your gender awareness?'

'Good heavens, no!' Nick Davenant laughed, giving me a ringside view of a set of impeccable teeth. 'I think she knows that I'm tremendously gender aware the whole time. No. She's just a marvellous girl. She does all sorts of little things for me.'

'Does she indeed?' The pie crust, as usual, tasted of cardboard, the beef was stringy and the kidneys as hard to find as beggars in the Ritz, but they couldn't ruin the mustard or the Guinness. 'I suppose I shouldn't ask what sort of things.'

'Well, I wasn't talking about that in particular.' The learned prosecutor gave the impression that he *could* talk about that if he wasn't such a decent and discreet young Davenant. 'But I mean little things like work.'

'Mizz Liz works for you?'

'Well, if I've got a difficult opinion to write, or a big case to note up, then Liz will volunteer.'

'But you've got Miss Slenderlegs, the blonde barrister, as your pupil.'

'Liz says she can't trust Jenny to get things right, so she takes jobs on for me.'

'And you pay her lavishly of course.'

'Not at all.' Still smiling in a blinding fashion, Nick Davenant shook his head. 'I don't pay her a thing. She does it for the sake of friendship.'

'Friendship with you, of course?'

'Friendship with me, yes. I think Liz is really a nice girl. And I don't see anything wrong with her bum.'

'Wrong with what?'

'Her bum.'

'That's what I thought you said.'

'Do you think there's anything wrong with it, Rumpole?' A dreamy look had come over young Davenant's face.

'I hadn't really thought about it very much. But I suppose not.'

'I don't know why she has to go through all that performance about it, really.'

'Performance?'

'At Monte's beauty parlour, she told me. In Ken High Street. Takes hours, she told me. While she has to sit there and read *Hello!* magazine.'

'You don't mean that she reads this – whatever publication you mentioned – while changing the shape of her body for the sake of pleasing men?'

'I suppose,' Davenant had to admit reluctantly, 'it's in a good cause.'

'Have the other half of this black Liffey water, why don't you?' I felt nothing but affection for Counsel for the prosecution, for suddenly, at long last, I saw a chink of daylight at the end of poor old Claude's long, black tunnel. 'And tell me all you know about Monte's beauty parlour.'

The day's work done, I was walking back from Ludgate Circus and the well-known Palais de Justice, when I saw, alone and palely loitering, the woman of the match, Wendy Crump. I hailed her gladly, caught her up and she turned to me a face on which gloom was written large. I couldn't even swear that her spectacles hadn't become misted with tears.

'You don't look particularly cheered up,' I told her, 'after your day of triumph.'

'No. As a matter of fact I feel tremendously depressed.'

'What about?'

'About Claude. I've been thinking about it so much and it's made me sad.'

'Someone told you?' I was sorry for her.

'Told me what?'

'Well' – I thought, of course, that the damage had been done by the sisterhood over the lunch adjournment – 'what Claude had said about you that caused all the trouble.'

'All what trouble?'

'Being blackballed, blacklisted, outlawed, outcast, dismissed from the human race. Why Liz Probert and the gender-aware radical lawyers have decided to hound him.'

'Because of what he said about me?'

'They haven't told you?'

'Not a word. But *you* know what it was?'

'Perhaps.' I was playing for time.

'Then tell me, for God's sake.'

'Quite honestly, I'd rather not.'

'What on earth's the matter?'

'I'd really rather not say it.'

'Why?'

'You'd probably find it offensive.'

'Rumpole, I'm going to be a barrister. I'll have to sit through rape, indecent assault, sex and sodomy. Just spit it out.'

'He was probably joking.'

'He doesn't joke much.'

'Well, then. He called you, and I don't suppose he meant it, fat.'

She looked at me and, in a magical moment, the gloom lifted. I thought there was even the possibility of a laugh. And then it came, a light giggle, just as we passed Pommeroy's.

'Of course I'm fat. Fatty Crump, that set me apart from all the other anorexic little darlings at school. That and the fact that I usually got an A-plus. It was my trademark. Well, I never thought Claude looked at me long enough to notice.'

When this had sunk in, I asked her why, if she hadn't heard from Liz Probert and her Amazonians, she was so shaken and wan with care.

'Because' – and here the note of sadness returned – 'I used to hero-worship Claude. I thought he was a marvellous barrister. And now I know he can't really do it, can he?'

She looked at me, hoping, perhaps, for some contradiction. I was afraid I couldn't oblige. 'All the same,' I said, 'you don't want him cast into outer darkness and totally deprived of briefs, do you?'

'Good heavens, no. I wouldn't wish that on anyone.'

'Then, in the fullness of time,' I told her, 'I may have a little strategy to suggest.'

'Hilda,' I said, having managed to ingest most of a bottle of Château Fleet Street Ordinaire over our cutlets, and with it taken courage, 'what would you do if I called you fat?' I awaited the blast of thunder, or at least a drop in the temperature to freezing, to be followed by a week's eerie silence.

To my surprise she answered with a brisk 'I'd call you fatter!'

'A sensible answer, Hilda.' I had been brave enough for one evening. 'You and Mizz Wendy Crump are obviously alike in tolerance and common sense. The only trouble is, she couldn't say that to Claude because he has a lean and hungry look. Like yon Cassius.'

'Like yon *who*?'

'No matter.'

'Rumpole, I have absolutely no idea what you're talking about.'

So I told her the whole story of Wendy and Claude and Mizz Probert, with her Sisterhood, ready to tear poor Erskine-Brown apart as the Bacchantes rent Orestes, and the frightened Ballard. She listened with an occasional click of the tongue and shake of her head, which led me to believe that she didn't entirely approve. 'Those girls,' she said, 'should be a little less belligerent and learn to use their charm.'

'Perhaps they haven't got as much charm as you have, Hilda,' I flannelled, and she looked at me with deep suspicion.

'But you say this Wendy Crump doesn't mind particularly?'

'She seems not to. Only one thing seems to upset her.'

'What's that?'

'She's disillusioned about Claude not because of the fat chat, but because she's found out he's not the brilliant advocate she once thought him.'

'Hero worship! That's always dangerous.'

'I suppose so.'

'I remember when Dodo and I were at school together, we had an art mistress called Helena Lampos and Dodo absolutely hero-worshipped her. She said Lampos revealed to her the true use of watercolours. Well, then we heard that this Lampos person was going to leave to get married. I can't think who'd agreed to marry her because she wasn't much of a catch, at least not in my opinion. Anyway, Dodo was heartbroken and couldn't bear the idea of being separated from her heroine so, on the morning she was leaving, Lampos could not find the blue silky coat that she was always so proud of.'

When she starts on her schooldays I feel an irresistible urge to apply the corkscrew to the second bottle of the Ordinaire. I was engaged in this task as Hilda's story wound to a conclusion. 'So, anyway, the coat in question was finally found in Dodo's locker. She thought if she hid it, she'd keep Miss Lampos. Of course, she didn't. The Lampos left and Dodo had to do a huge impot and miss the staff concert. And, by the way, Rumpole, there's absolutely no need for you to open another bottle of that stuff. It's high time you were in bed.'

At the Temple station next morning I bought a copy of *Hello!*, a mysterious publication devoted to the happy lives of people I had never heard of. When I arrived in Chambers my first port of call was to the room where Liz Probert carried on her now flourishing practice. She was, as the saying is, at her desk, and I noticed a new scarlet telephone had settled in beside her regulation black instrument.

'Business booming, I'm glad to see. You've had to install another telephone.'

'It's a hotline, Rumpole.'

'Hot?' I gave it a tentative touch.

'I mean it's private. For the use of women in Chambers only.'

'It doesn't respond to the touch of the male finger.'

'It's so we can report harassment, discrimination and verbally aggressive male barrister or clerk conduct direct to the S.R.L. office.'

'The S—?'

'Sisterhood of Radical Lawyers.'

'And what will they do? Send for the police? Call the fire brigade to douse masculine ardour?'

'They will record the episode fully. Then we shall meet the victim and decide on action.'

'I thought you decided on action before you met Wendy Crump.'

'Her case was particularly clear. Now she's coming to the meeting of the Sisterhood at 5.30.'

'Ah, yes. She told me about that. I think she's got quite a lot to say.'

'I'm sure she has. Now what do you want, Rumpole? I'm before the Divisional Court at 10.30.'

'Good for you! I just came in to ask you a favour.'

'Not self-induced drunkenness as a defence? Crump told me she had to look that up for you.'

'It's not the law. Although I do hear you work for other barristers for nothing, and so deprive their lady pupils of the beginnings of a practice.'

Mizz Probert looked, I thought, a little shaken, but she picked up a pencil, underlined something in her brief and prepared to ignore me.

'Is that what you came to complain about?' she asked without looking at me.

'No. I've come to tell you I bought *Hello!* magazine.'

'Why on earth did you do that?' She looked up and was surprised to see me holding out the publication in question.

'I heard you read it during long stretches of intense boredom. I thought I might do the same when Mr Injustice Graves sums up to the jury.'

'I don't have long moments of boredom.' Mizz Liz sounded businesslike.

'Don't you really? Not when you have to sit for hours in Monte's beauty parlour in Ken High Street?'

'I don't know what you're talking about . . .' The protest came faintly. Mizz Probert was visibly shaken.

'It must be awfully uncomfortable. I mean, I don't think I'd want to sit for hours in a solution of couscous and assorted stewed herbs with the whole thing wrapped up in tinfoil. I suppose *Hello!* magazine is a bit of a comfort in those circumstances. But is it worth it? I mean, all that trouble to change what a bountiful nature gave you – for the sake of pleasing men?'

I didn't enjoy asking this fatal question. I brought Mizz Liz up in the law and I still have respect and affection for her. On a good day she can be an excellent ally. But I was acting for the underdog, an undernourished hound by the name of Claude Erskine-Brown. And the question had its effect. As the old-fashioned crime writers used to say in their ghoulish way, the shadow of the noose seemed to fall across the witness-box.

'No one's mentioned that to the S.R.L.?'

'I thought I could pick up the hotline, but then it might be more appropriate if Wendy Crump raised it at your meeting this afternoon. That would give you an opportunity to reply. And I suppose Jenny Attienzer might want to raise the complaint about her pupil work.'

'What *are* you up to, Rumpole?'

'Just doing my best to protect the rights of lady barristers.'

'Anyone else's rights?'

'Well, I suppose, looking at the matter from an entirely detached point of view, the rights of one unfortunate male.'

'The case against Erskine-Brown has raised strong feelings in the Sisterhood. I'm not sure I can persuade them to drop it.'

'Of course you can persuade them, Liz. With your talent for advocacy, I bet you've got the Sisterhood eating out of your hand.'

'I'll do my best. I can't promise anything. By the way, it may not be necessary for Crump to attend. I suppose Kate Inglefield may have got hold of the wrong end of the stick.'

'Exactly. Claude said "that pupil". Not "fat pupil". Try it anyway, if you can't think of anything better.'

And so, with the case of the *Sisterhood* v. *Erskine-Brown* settled, I was back in the gloomy prison boardroom. When I'd first seen it, members of the caring, custodial and sentencing professions were feasting on sausage rolls and white wine after *A Midsummer Night's Dream*. Now it was dressed not for a party but for a trial, and had taken on the appearance of a peculiarly unfriendly Magistrates' Court.

Behind the table at the far end of the room sat the three members of the prisoners' Board of Visitors who were entitled to try Matthew Gribble. The Chairwoman centre stage was a certain Lady Bullwood, whose hair was piled up in a jet-black mushroom on top of her head and who went in for a good deal of costume jewellery, including a glittering chain round her neck from which her spectacles swung. Her look varied between the starkly judicial and the instantly confused, as when she suddenly lost control of a piece of paper, or forgot which part of her her glasses were tied to.

Beside her, wearing an expression of universal tolerance and the sort of gentle smile which can, in my experience, precede an unexpectedly stiff sentence, sat the Bishop of Worsfield, who had a high aquiline nose, neatly brushed grey hair and the thinnest strip of a dog-collar.

The third judge was an elderly schoolboy called Major Oxborrow, who looked as though he couldn't wait for the whole tedious business to be over, and for the offer of a large gin and tonic in the Governor's quarters. Beside them, in what I understood was a purely advisory capacity, sat my old friend the Governor, Quintus Blake, who looked as if he would rather be anywhere else and deeply regretted the need for these proceedings. He had, I remembered with gratitude, been so anxious to see Matthew Gribble properly defended that he had sent for Horace Rumpole, clearly the best man for the job. There was a clerk at a small table in front of the Visitors, whose job was, I imagined, to keep them informed as to such crumbs of law as were still available in prison. The prosecution was in the nervous hands of a young Mr Fraplington, a solicitor from some government department. He was a tall, gangling person who looked as though he had shot up in the last six months and his jacket and trousers were too short for him.

What I didn't like was the grim squadron of screws who lined the walls as though expecting an outbreak of violence, and the fact that my client was brought in handcuffed and sat between two of the largest, beefiest prison officers available. After Matthew had been charged with committing an assault, obstructing an officer in the course of his duty and offending against good order and discipline, he pleaded not guilty on my express instructions. Then I rose to my feet. 'Haven't you forgotten something?'

'Do you wish to address the Court, Mr Rumpole?' The clerk, a little ferret of a man, was clearly anxious to make his presence felt.

'I certainly do. Have you forgotten to read out the charges of mass murder, war crimes, rioting, burning down E-wing and inciting to mutiny?'

The ferret looked puzzled. The Chairwoman sorted hopelessly through her papers and Mr Fraplington for the prosecution said helpfully, 'This prisoner is charged with none of those offences.'

'Then if he is not,' I asked, with perhaps rather overplayed amazement, 'why is he brought in here shackled? Why is this room lined with prison officers clearly expecting a dreadful scene of violence? Why is he being treated as though he were some hated dictator guilty of waging aggressive war? My client, Mr Gribble, is a gentle academic and student of Shakespeare. And there is no reason for him to attend these proceedings in irons.'

'Your client, as I remember, was found guilty of the manslaughter of his wife.' The handsome Bishop was clearly the one to look out for.

'For that,' I said, 'he has almost paid his debt to society. Next week, subject to the dismissal of these unnecessary charges, that debt will be fully and finally settled and, as I'm sure the Governor will tell you, during his time in Worsfield he has been a model prisoner.'

Quintus did his stuff and whispered to the Chairwoman. She found her glasses, yanked them on to her nose and said that, in all the circumstances, my client's handcuffs might be removed.

After that the proceedings settled down like an ordinary trial in a Magistrates' Court, except for the fact that we were all in gaol already. Mr Fraplington nervously opened the simple facts. Then Steve Barrington, the screw who received the flying chisel, clumped his way to the witness stand and gave the evidence which might keep Matthew Gribble behind bars for a good deal longer. He hadn't seen the chisel thrown. The first he knew about it was when he was struck on the cheek. Gribble had been the only prisoner working with a chisel and he had seen him using it immediately before he turned away to answer a request from prisoner D41 Molloy. Later he took statements from the prisoners, and in particular from B19 Weaver. What Weaver told him led to the present charges against A13 Gribble. What Weaver told him, I rose to point out, had better come from Weaver himself.

'Mr Barrington' – I began my cross-examination – 'you were a teacher once?'

'Yes, I was.'

'And you gave it up to become a prison officer?'

'I did.'

'Is that because you found teaching too difficult?'

'I wonder if this is a relevant question?' Young Fraplington had obviously been told to make his presence felt and interrupt the defence whenever possible.

'Mr Fraplington, perchance you wonder at this question? *But wonder on, till truth make all things plain.*'

'Mr Rumpole, I'm not exactly sure what you mean.' The Chairwoman's glasses were pulled off and swung gently.

'Then you didn't see *A Midsummer Night's Dream*? You missed a treat, Madam. Produced brilliantly by my client and starring Prisoner Weaver as bully Bottom. You enjoyed it, didn't you, Mr Barrington?'

'I thought they did rather well, yes.'

'And I don't suppose, as a teacher who gave up the struggle, you could have taught a group of hard-boiled villains to play Shakespeare?'

'Mr Rumpole, I *must* agree with Mr Fraplington. How is this in the least relevant to the charge of assault?' The Bishop came in on the act.

'Because I think we may find, Bishop, that this isn't a case about assault, it's a case about teaching. Mr Barrington, you would agree that my client took Weaver and taught him to read, taught him about poetry and finally taught him to act?'

'To my knowledge, yes, he did.'

'And since this pupillage and this friendship began, Weaver, too, has been a model prisoner?'

'We haven't had any trouble from him lately. No.'

'Whereas before the pupillage, he was a general nuisance?'

'He was a handful. Yes. That's fair enough. He's a big man and . . .'

'Alarming when out of control?'

'I'd have to agree with you.'

'Good. I'm glad we see eye to eye, Mr Barrington. So before Matthew Gribble took him on, so to speak, there'd been several cases of assault, three of breaking up furniture, disobeying reasonable orders, throwing food. An endless list?'

'He was constantly in trouble. Yes.'

'And since he and Gribble became friends, nothing?'

'I believe that's right.'

'So you believe Matthew Gribble's influence on Weaver has been entirely for the good.'

'I said, so far as I know.'

'So far as you know. Well, we'll see if anyone knows better. Now, you questioned the other prisoners, Timson and Molloy, about this incident in the carpenter's shop?'

'Yes, I did.'

'And what did they tell you?'

'They said they hadn't seen anything.'

'And did you believe them?'

'Do I have to answer that question?'

'I have asked the question, and I'll trouble you to answer it.'

'No, I didn't altogether believe it.'

'Because prisoners don't grass.'

'What was that, Rumpole?' The Chairwoman asked for an explanation.

'Prisoners don't tell tales. They don't give evidence against each other. On the whole. Isn't that true, Mr Barrington?'

'I thought they might have seen something, but they were sheltering the culprit. Yes.'

'So Timson might have seen Molloy do it. Or Molloy might have seen Timson do it. Or either of them might have seen Weaver do it. But they weren't telling. Is that possible?'

'I suppose it's possible. Yes.'

'Or Weaver might have seen Timson or Molloy do it and blamed it on Gribble to protect them?'

'He wouldn't have done that.' There was an agitated whisper from my client and I stooped to give him an ear.

'What?'

'He wouldn't have blamed it on me. I know Bob wouldn't do that.'

'Matthew,' I whispered sternly, 'your time to give evidence will come later. Until it does, I'd be much obliged if you'd take a temporary vow of silence.' I went back to work. 'Yes, Officer. What was your answer to my question?'

'B19 Weaver had a particular admiration for A13 Gribble, sir. I don't think he'd have blamed him. Not just to protect the other two.'

'He wouldn't have blamed him just to protect the other two, eh?' The Bishop, who seemed to have cast himself as the avenging angel, dictated a note to himself with resonant authority.

Bottom the Weaver towered over the small witness table and the screws that stood behind him. He looked at the Visitors, his head slightly on one side, his nose broken and never properly set, and smiled nervously, as he had stood before the court of Duke Theseus, awkward, on his best behaviour, likely to be a bore, but somehow endearing. He didn't look at A13 Gribble, but my client looked constantly at him, not particularly in anger but with curiosity and as if prepared to be amused. That was the way, I thought, he might have watched Bob Weaver rehearsing the play.

Mr Fraplington had no trouble in getting the witness to tell his story. He was in the carpenter's shop in the morning in question. They were making the scenery. He was enjoying himself as he enjoyed everything about the play. Although he was dead nervous about doing it, it was the best time he'd ever had in his life. A13 Gribble was a fantastic producer, absolutely brilliant, and had changed his life for him. 'Made me see a new world', was the way he put it. Well, that morning when all the others were busy working and Mr Barrington was turned away, he'd seen A13 Gribble pick up the chisel and throw it. It struck the prison officer on the cheek, causing bleeding which he fully believed was later seen to by the hospital matron. He kept quiet for a week, because he was reluctant to get the best friend he ever had into trouble. But then he'd told the investigating officer exactly what he saw. He felt he had to do it. Doing the play was the best day in his life. Standing there, telling the tale against his friend, was the worst. Sometimes he thought he'd rather be dead than do it. That was the honest truth. To say that Battering Bob was a good witness is an understatement. He was as good a witness as he was a Bottom; he didn't seem to be acting at all.

'The first question, of course, is why?'

'Pardon me?'

'Why do you think your friend Matthew threw a chisel at the officer? Can you help me about that?' It would have been no use trying to batter the batterer – he had clearly won the hearts of the Visitors – so I came at him gently and full of smiles. 'He's always been a model prisoner. Not a hint of violence.'

'Perhaps' – Bob Weaver closed one eye, giving me his careful consideration – 'he kind of had it bottled up, his resentment against Mr Barrington.'

'We haven't heard he resented Mr Barrington?'

'Well, we all did to an extent. All of us actors.'

'Why was that?'

'He put Jimmy Molloy on a charge, so he lost two weeks' rehearsal with Puck.'

The Visitors smiled. I had gone and provided my client with a motive. Up to now this cross-examination seemed a likely candidate for the worst in my career so I tried another tack.

'All right. Another why.'

'Yes, sir.'

'If you feel you'd rather be dead than do it, why did you decide to grass against your friend?'

'I don't know why you have adopted the phrase "grass" from prison argot, Mr Rumpole.' The Bishop was clearly a circus judge manqué. 'This inmate has come here to give evidence.'

'Evidence which may or may not turn out to be the truth. Very well then. The Bishop has told us to forget the argot.'

'Forget the what?' Bob looked amicably confused and the Bishop smiled tolerantly. 'Slang,' he translated. 'I should have called it slang.'

'Why did you decide to give evidence against your friend?'

'Let me tell you this quite honestly.' The Batterer turned from me and faced the Visitors. 'Years ago, I might not have done it. In fact, I wouldn't. Grass on a fellow inmate. Never. Might have given him a bit of a hiding like. If I'd felt the need of it. But never told the tale. Rather have had me tongue cut out. But then . . . Well, then I got to know Matthew. I'd still like to call him that. With all respect. And he taught me . . . Well, he taught me everything. He taught me to read. Yes. He taught me to like poetry, which I'd thought worse than a punch in the kidneys. Then he taught me to act and to enjoy myself like I never did even in the old days of the minicab battles, which now seem a complete waste of time, quite honestly. But Matthew taught me more than that. "You have to be truthful, Bob", those were his words to me. Well, that's what I remembered. So, when it came to it, I remembered his words. That's all I've got to say.'

'You took his advice and told the truth.' The Bishop was clearly delighted, but I was looking at Bob. It had never happened before. It certainly didn't happen when he performed in the *Dream*, but now I knew that he was an actor playing a part.

And then something clicked in my mind. A picture of Dodo

Mackintosh at school, not wanting to let her heroine go, and I knew what the truth really was.

'You've told us Matthew Gribble is the friend who meant most to you.'

'Meant everything to me.'

'The only real friend you've ever had. Would you go as far as to say that?'

'I would agree with that, sir. Every word of it.'

'And one who has let you into a new world.'

'He's already told us that, Mr Rumpole.' I prayed for the Bishop to address himself to God and leave me alone.

'It's too true. Too very true.'

'I don't suppose life in Worsfield Category A Prison could ever be compared to a holiday in the Seychelles, but he has made your life here bearable?'

'More than that, Mr Rumpole. I wouldn't have missed it.'

'And in a week, if he is acquitted on this charge, Matthew Gribble will be free.'

It was as if I had got in a sudden, unexpectedly powerful blow in the ring. Bob closed his eyes and almost seemed to stop breathing. When he shook his head and answered, he had come back, it seemed to me, to the truth.

'I don't want to think about it.'

'Because you may never see him again?'

'Visits. There might be visits.'

'Are you afraid there might not be?' Matthew appeared to be about to say something, or utter some protest. I shot some *sotto voce* advice into his earhole to the effect that if he uttered another sound, I would walk off the case. Then I looked back at the Batterer. He seemed not to have recovered from the punch and was still breathless.

'It crossed my mind.'

'And did it cross your mind that he might move away, to another part of England, get a new job, work with a new drama group and put on new plays with no parts in them for you? Did you think he might forget the friend he'd made in prison?'

There was a long silence. Bob was getting his breath back, preparing to get up for the last round, but with defeat staring him in the face.

He said, 'Things like that do happen, don't they?'

'Oh yes, Bob Weaver. They happen very often. If a man wants to make a new life, he doesn't care to be reminded of the people he met inside. Did that thought occur to you?'

'I did worry about that, I suppose. I did worry.'

'And did you worry that all that rich, fascinating new world might vanish into thin air? And you'd be left with only a few old lags and failed boxers for company?'

There was silence then. Bob didn't answer. He was saved by the bell. Rung, of course, by the Bishop.

'Where's all this leading up to, Mr Rumpole?'

'Let me suggest where it led you, Bob.' I ignored the cleric and concentrated on the witness. 'It led you to think of the one way you could stop Matthew Gribble leaving you.'

'How was I going to do that?'

'Quite a simple idea but it seems to have worked. Up to now. The way to do it was to get him into trouble.'

'Trouble?'

'Serious trouble. So he'd lose his remission. I expect you thought of that some time ago and you waited for an opportunity. It came, didn't it, in the carpenter's shop?'

'Did it?'

'Matthew turned away to fix the grass covering on the mound. No one else was looking when you picked up his chisel. No one saw you throw it. Like all successful crimes it was helped by a good deal of luck.'

'Crime? Me? What are you talking about? I done no crime.' Bob looked at the Visitors. For once even the Bishop was silent.

'I suppose I'm talking about perverting the course of justice. Of assaulting a prison officer. I've got to hand it to you, Bob. You did it for the best of motives. You did it to keep a friend.'

Bob's head was lowered, but now he made an effort to raise it and looked at the Visitors. 'I didn't do it. I swear to God I didn't. Matthew did it and he's got to stay here. You can't let him go.' By then I think even they thought he was acting. But that wasn't the end of the story.

'Why did you do it?' The trial, if you could call it a trial, was over. Matthew and I were together for the last time in the interview room. We were there to say goodbye.

'I told you. What've I got outside? Schools that won't employ me. Actors and actresses who wouldn't want to work with me. What would they think? If I didn't like their performances, I might stab them. They'd be talking about me, whispering, laughing perhaps. And I'd come in the room and they'd be silent or look afraid. Here, they all want to be in my plays. They want to work with me, and I want to work with them. I thought of *Much Ado* next. Won't Bob make a marvellous Dogberry? Then, I don't know, do you think he could possibly do a Falstaff?'

'Become an old English gent? Who knows. You've got plenty of time. They knocked a year and a half off your remission.'

'Yes. A long time together. You were asking me why I threw the chisel?'

He knew I wasn't asking him that. At the end of Battering Bob's evidence I had to decide whether or not to call my client. Matthew had kept quiet when I'd told him to, and I knew he'd make a good impression. He walked to the witness table, took the oath and looked at me with patient expectation.

'Matthew Gribble. We've heard you were a model prisoner.'

'I've never been in trouble here, if that's what you mean.'

'And of all you've done for Bob Weaver.'

'I think it's been a rewarding experience for both of us.'

'And you are due to be released next week.'

'I believe I am.'

I drew in a deep breath and asked the question to which I felt sure I knew the answer. 'Matthew, did you ever throw that chisel at Prison Officer Barrington?'

The answer, when it came, was another punch in the stomach, this time for me. 'Yes, I did. I threw it.' Matthew looked at the Visitors and said it as though he was talking about a not very interesting part of the prison routine. 'I did it because I couldn't forgive him for putting Puck on a charge.' After that, the case was over and Matthew's exit from Worsfield inevitably postponed.

'You know I wasn't asking you why you threw the chisel because you didn't throw it. I'm asking you why you said you did.'

'I told you. I've decided to stay on.'

'You knew Battering Bob did it and he blamed you to keep you here because he thought he needed you.'

'Don't you think that's rather an extraordinary tribute to a friendship?'

There seemed no answer to that. I didn't know whether to curse Matthew Gribble or to praise him. I didn't know if he was the best or the worst client I ever had. I knew I had lost a case unnecessarily, and that is something I don't like to happen.

'You can't win them all, Mr Rumpole, can you?' Steve Barrington looked gratified at the result. He took me to the gate and, as he waited for the long unlocking process to finish, he said, 'I don't think I'll ever go back to teaching. They seem half barmy, some of them.'

At last the gates and the small door in the big one were open. I was out and I went out. Matthew was in and he stayed in. Damiens sent a brief in a long case to Claude and I told him he had a brilliant pupil.

'I suppose she'll be wanting a place in Chambers soon?' Claude didn't seem to welcome the idea.

'So far as I'm concerned she can have one now.'

'Young Jenny Attienzer is apparently not happy with Nick Davenant over in King's Bench Walk. Do you think I might take her on as a pupil?'

'I think,' I told him, 'that it would be a very bad idea indeed. I'm sure Philly wouldn't like it, and I'd have to start charging for defending you.'

'Rumpole' – Claude was thoughtful – 'do you know why everyone went off me in that peculiar way?'

'Not really.'

But Claude had his own solution. 'It never ceases to amaze me,' the poor old darling said, 'how jealous everyone is of success.'

Six months later I saw a production of *Much Ado About Nothing* in Worsfield gaol with Bob Weaver as Dogberry. I enjoyed it very much indeed.

Rumpole and the Old Familiar Faces

In the varied ups and downs, the thrills and spills in the life of an Old
Bailey Hack, one thing stands as stone. Your ex-customers will never
want to see you again. Even if you've steered them through the rocks
of the prosecution case and brought them out to the calm waters of a
not-guilty verdict, they won't plan further meetings, host reunion
dinners or even send you a card on your birthday. If they catch a glimpse
of you on the Underground, or across a crowded wine bar, they will
bury their faces in their newspapers or look studiously in the opposite
direction.

This is understandable. Days in Court probably represent a period of
time they'd rather forget and, as a rule, I'm not especially keen to renew
an old acquaintance when a face I once saw in the Old Bailey dock reap-
pears at a 'Scales of Justice' dinner or the Inns of Court garden party.
Reminiscences of the past are best avoided and what is required is a
quick look and a quiet turn away. There have been times, however,
when recognizing a face seen in trouble has greatly assisted me in the
solution of some legal problem, and carried me to triumph in a difficult
case. Such occasions have been rare, but like number thirteen buses,
two of them turned up in short order round a Christmas which I
remember as being one of the oddest, but certainly the most rewarding,
I ever spent.

'A traditional British pantomime. There's nothing to beat it!'

'You go to the pantomime, Rumpole?' Claude Erskine-Brown asked
with unexpected interest.

'I did when I was a boy. It made a lasting impression on me.'

'Pantomime?' The American Judge who was our fellow guest round
the Erskine-Brown dinner table was clearly a stranger to such delights.

'Is that some kind of mime show? Lot of feeling imaginary walls and no one saying anything?'

'Not at all. You take some good old story, like Robin Hood.'

'Robin Hood's the star?'

'Well, yes. He's played by some strapping girl who slaps her thighs and says lines like "Cheer up, Babes in the Wood, Robin's not far away."'

'You mean there's cross-dressing?' The American visitor was puzzled.

'Well, if you want to call it that. And Robin's mother is played by a red-nosed comic.'

'A female comic?'

'No. A male one.'

'It sounds sexually interesting. We have clubs for that sort of thing in Pittsburgh.'

'There's nothing sexual about it,' I assured him. 'The dame's a comic character who gets the audience singing.'

'Singing?'

'The words come down on a sort of giant song-sheet,' I explained. 'And she, who is really a he, gets the audience to sing along.'

Emboldened by Erskine-Brown's claret (smoother on the tongue but with less of a kick than Château Thames Embankment), I broke into a stanza of the song I was introduced to by Robin Hood's masculine mother.

> *I may be just a nipper,*
> *But I've always loved a kipper . . .*
> *And so does my loving wife.*
> *If you've got a girl just slip her*
> *A loving golden kipper*
> *And she'll be yours for life.*

'Is that all?' The transatlantic Judge still seemed puzzled.

'All I can remember.'

'I think you're wrong, Mr Rumpole.'

'What?'

'I think you're wrong and those lines do indeed have some sexual significance.' And the Judge fell silent, contemplating the unusual acts suggested.

'I see they're doing *Aladdin* at the Tufnell Park Empire. Do you think the twins might enjoy it, Rumpole?'

The speaker was Mrs Justice Erskine-Brown (Phillida Trant as she was in happier days when I called her the Portia of our Chambers), still possessed of a beauty that would break the hearts of the toughest prosecutors and make old lags swoon with lust even as she passed a stiff custodial sentence. The twins she spoke of were Tristan and Isolde, so named by her opera-loving husband Claude, who was now bending Hilda's ear on the subject of Covent Garden's latest *Ring* cycle.

'I think the twins would adore it. Just the thing to cure the Wagnerian death wish and bring them into a world of sanity.'

'Sanity?' The visiting Judge sounded doubtful. 'With old guys dressed up as mothers?'

'I promise you, they'll love every minute of it.' And then I made another promise that sounded rash even as I spoke the words. 'I know I would. I'll take them myself.'

'Thank you, Rumpole.' Phillida spoke in her gentlest judicial voice, but I knew my fate was sealed. 'We'll keep you to that.'

'It'll have to be after Christmas,' Hilda said. 'We've been invited up to Norfolk for the holiday.'

As she said the word 'Norfolk', a cold, sneeping wind seemed to cut through the central heating of the Erskine-Browns' Islington dining room and I felt a warning shiver.

I have no rooted objection to Christmas Day, but I must say it's an occasion when time tends to hang particularly heavily on the hands. From the early-morning alarm call of carols piping on Radio Four to the closing headlines and a restless, liverish sleep, the day can seem as long as a fraud on the Post Office tried before Mr Injustice Graves.

It takes less than no time for me to unwrap the tie which I will seldom wear, and for Hilda to receive the annual bottle of lavender water which she lays down rather than puts to immediate use. The highlights after that are the Queen's speech, when I lay bets with myself as to whether Hilda will stand to attention when the television plays the National Anthem, and the thawed-out Safeway's bird followed by port (an annual gift from my faithful solicitor, Bonny Bernard) and pudding. I suppose what I have against Christmas Day is that the Courts are all shut and no one is being tried for anything.

That Christmas, Hilda had decided on a complete change of routine. She announced it in a circuitous fashion by saying, one late November evening, 'I was at school with Poppy Longstaff.'

'What's that got to do with it?' I knew the answer to this question, of course. Hilda's old school has this in common with polar expeditions, natural disasters and the last war: those who have lived through it are bound together for life and can always call on each other for mutual assistance.

'Poppy's Eric is Rector of Coldsands. And for some reason or other he seems to want to meet you, Rumpole.'

'Meet me?'

'That's what she said.'

'So does that mean I have to spend Christmas in the Arctic Circle and miss our festivities?'

'It's not the Arctic Circle. It's Norfolk, Rumpole. And our festivities aren't all that festive. So, yes. You have to go.' It was a judgement from which there was no possible appeal.

My first impression of Coldsands was of a gaunt church tower, presumably of great age, pointing an accusing finger to heaven from a cluster of houses on the edge of a sullen, gunmetal sea. My second was one of intense cold. As soon as we got out of the taxi, we were slapped around the face by a wind which must have started in freezing Siberia and gained nothing in the way of warmth on its journey across the plains of Europe.

In the bleak mid-winter/Frosty winds made moan ... wrote that sad old darling, Christina Rossetti. Frosty winds had made considerable moan round the Rectory at Coldsands, owing to the doors that stopped about an inch short of the stone floors and the windows which never shut properly, causing the curtains to billow like the sails of a ship at sea.

We were greeted cheerfully by Poppy. Hilda's friend had one of those round, childishly pretty faces often seen on seriously fat women, and she seemed to keep going on incessant cups of hot, sweet tea and a number of cardigans. If she moved like an enormous tent, her husband Eric was a slender wraith of a man with a high aquiline nose, two flapping wings of grey hair on the sides of his face and a vague air of perpetual anxiety, broken now and then by high and unexpected laughter. He made cruciform gestures, as though remembering the rubric 'Spectacles, testicles, wallet and watch' and forgetting where these important articles were kept.

'Eric,' his wife explained, 'is having terrible trouble with the church tower.'

'Oh dear.' Hilda shot me a look of stern disapproval, which I knew meant that it would be more polite if I abandoned my overcoat while tea was being served. 'How worrying for you, Eric.'

The Rev. Eric went into a long, excited and high-pitched speech. The gist of this was that the tower, although of rare beauty, had not been much restored since the Saxons built it and the Normans added the finishing touches. Fifty thousand pounds was needed for essential repairs, and the thermometer, erected for the appeal outside the church, was stuck at a low hundred and twenty, the result of an emergency jumble sale.

'You particularly wanted Horace to come this Christmas?' Hilda asked the Man of God with the air of someone anxious to solve a baffling mystery. 'I wonder why that was.'

'Yes. I wonder!' Eric looked startled. 'I wonder why on earth I wanted to ask Horace. I don't believe he's got fifty thousand smackers in his back pocket!' At this, he shook with laughter.

'There,' I told him, 'your lack of faith is entirely justified.' I wasn't exactly enjoying Coldsands Rectory, but I was a little miffed that the Reverend couldn't remember why he'd asked me there in the first place.

'We had hoped that Donald Compton would help us out,' Poppy told us. 'I mean, he wouldn't notice fifty thousand. But he took exception to what Eric said at the Remembrance Day service.'

'Armistice Day in the village,' Eric's grey wings of hair trembled as he nodded in delighted affirmation, 'and I prayed for dead German soldiers. It seemed only fair.'

'Fair perhaps, darling. But hardly tactful,' his wife told him. 'Donald

Compton thought it was distinctly unpatriotic. He's bought the Old Manor House,' she explained to Hilda. From then on the conversation turned exclusively to this Compton and was carried on in the tones of awe and muted wonder in which people always talk about the very rich. Compton, it seemed, after a difficult start in England, had gone to Canada where, during a ten-year stay, he laid the foundations of his fortune. His much younger wife was quite charming, probably Canadian and not in the least stand-offish. He had built the village hall, the cricket pavilion and a tennis court for the school. Only Eric's unfortunate sympathy for the German dead had caused his bounty to stop short at the church tower.

'I've done hours of hard knee-work,' the Rector told us, 'begging the Lord to soften Mr Compton's heart towards our tower. No result so far, I fear.'

Apart from this one lapse, the charming Donald Compton seemed to be the perfect English squire and country gent. I would see him in church on Christmas morning, and we had also been invited for drinks before lunch at the Manor. The Reverend Eric and the smiling Poppy made it sound as though the Pope and the Archbishop of Canterbury would be out with the carol singers and we'd been invited to drop in for high tea at Windsor Castle. I also prayed for a yule log blazing at the Manor so that I could, in the true spirit of Christmas, thaw out gradually.

'Now, as a sign of Christmas fellowship, will you all stand and shake hands with those in front and behind you?' Eric, in full canonicals, standing on the steps in front of the altar, made the suggestion as though he had just thought of the idea. I stood reluctantly. I had found myself a place in church near to a huge, friendly, gently humming, occasionally belching radiator and I was clinging to it and stroking it as though it were a new-found mistress (not that I have much experience of new-, or even old-found mistresses). The man who turned to me from the front row seemed to be equally reluctant. He was, as Hilda had pointed out excitedly, the great Donald Compton in person: a man of middle height with silver hair, dressed in a tweed suit and with a tan which it must have been expensive to preserve at Christmas. He had soft brown eyes which looked, almost at once, away from me as, with a touch of his dry fingers, he was gone and I was left for the rest of the service with no more than a well-tailored back and the sound of an uncertain tenor voice joining in the hymns.

I turned to the row behind to shake hands with an elderly woman who had madness in her eyes and whispered conspiratorially to me, 'You cold, dear? Like to borrow my gloves? We're used to a bit of chill weather round these parts.' I declined politely and went back to hugging the radiator, and as I did so a sort of happiness stole over me. To start with, the church was beautiful, with a high timbered roof and walls of weathered stone, peppered with marble tributes to dead inhabitants of the manor. It was decorated with holly and mistletoe, a tree glowed and there were candles over a crib. I thought how many generations of Coldsands villagers, their eyes bright and faces flushed with the wind, had belted out the hymns. I also thought how depressed the great Donald Compton – who had put on little gold half-glasses to read the prophecy from Isaiah: ' "For unto us a child is born, unto us a son is given: and the government shall be upon his shoulder: and his name shall be called 'Wonderful' " ' – would feel if Jesus's instruction to sell all and give it to the poor should ever be taken literally.

And then I wondered why it was that, as he touched my fingers and turned away, I felt that I had lived through that precise moment before.

There was, in fact, a huge log fire crackling and throwing a dancing light on the marble floor of the circular entrance hall, with its great staircase leading up into private shadows. The cream of Coldsands was being entertained to champagne and canapés by the new Lord of the Manor. The decibels rose as the champagne went down and the little group began to sound like an army of tourists in the Sistine Chapel, noisy, excited and wonderstruck.

'They must be all his ancestors.' Hilda was looking at the pictures and, in particular, at a general in a scarlet coat on a horse prancing in front of some distant battle.

My mouth was full of cream cheese enveloped in smoked salmon. I swallowed it and said, 'Oh, I shouldn't think so. After all, he only bought the house recently.'

'But I expect he brought his family portraits here from somewhere else.'

'You mean, he had them under the bed in his old bachelor flat in Wimbledon and now he's hung them round an acre or two of walls?'

'Do try and be serious, Rumpole, you're not nearly as funny as you think you are. Just look at the family resemblance. I'm absolutely certain that all of these are old Comptons.'

And it was when she said that that I remembered everything perfectly clearly.

He was with his wife. She was wearing a black velvet dress and had long, golden hair that sparkled in the firelight. They were talking to a bald, pink-faced man and his short and dumpy wife, and they were all laughing. Compton's laughter stopped as he saw me coming towards him. He said, 'I don't think we've met.'

'Yes,' I replied. 'We shook hands briefly in church this morning. My name's Rumpole and I'm staying with the Longstaffs. But didn't we meet somewhere else?'

'Good old Eric! We have our differences, of course, but he's a saintly man. This is my wife Lorelei, and Colonel and Maudy Jacobs. I expect you'd like to see the library, wouldn't you, Rumpole? I'm sure you're interested in ancient history. Will you all excuse us?'

It was two words from Hilda that had done it: 'old' and 'Compton'. I knew then what I should have remembered when we touched hands in the pews, that Old Compton is a street in Soho, and that was perhaps why Riccardo (known as Dicko) Perducci had adopted the name. And I had received that very same handshake, a slight touch and a quick turn away when I said goodbye to him in the cells under the Old Bailey and left him to start seven years for blackmail. The trial had ended, I now remembered, just before a long-distant Christmas.

The Perducci territory had been, in those days, not rolling Norfolk acres but a number of Soho strip clubs and clip joints. Girls would stand in front of these last-named resorts and beckon the lonely, the desperate and the unwary in. Sometimes they would escape after paying twenty pounds for a watery cocktail. Unlucky, affluent and important customers might even get sex, carefully recorded by microphones and cameras to produce material which was used for systematic and highly profitable blackmail. The victim in Dicko's case was an obscure and not much loved Circus Judge; so it was regarded as particularly serious by the prosecuting authority.

When I mitigated for Dicko, I stressed the lack of direct evidence against him. He was a shadowy figure who kept himself well in the background and was known as a legend rather than a familiar face round Soho. 'That only shows what a big wheel he was,' Judge Bullingham, who was unfortunately trying the case, bellowed unsympathetically. In desperation I tried the approach of Christmas on him. 'Crimes forgiven, sins remitted, mercy triumphant, such was the message of the story that began in Bethlehem,' I told the Court, at which the Mad Bull snorted that, as far as he could remember, that story ended in a criminal trial and a stiff sentence on at least one thief.

'I suppose something like this was going to happen sooner or later.' We were standing in the library, in front of a comforting fire and among leather-bound books, which I strongly suspected had been bought by the yard. The new, like the old, Dicko was soft-eyed, quietly spoken, almost unnaturally calm; the perfect man behind the scenes of a blackmailing operation or a country estate.

'Not necessarily,' I told him. 'It's just that my wife has so many old school friends and Poppy Longstaff is one of them. Well now, you seem to have done pretty well for yourself. Solid citizens still misconducting themselves round Old Compton Street, are they?'

'I wouldn't know. I gave all that up and went into the property business.'

'Really? Where did you do that? Canada?'

'I never saw Canada.' He shook his head. 'Garwick Prison. Up-and-coming area in the Home Counties. The screws there were ready and willing to do the deals on the outside. I paid them embarrassingly small commissions.'

'How long were you there?'

'Four years. By the time I came out I'd got my first million.'

'Well, then I did you a good turn, losing your case. A bit of luck his Honour Judge Bullingham didn't believe in the remission of sins.'

'You think I got what I deserved?'

I stretched my hands to the fire. I could hear the cocktail chatter from the marble hall of the eighteenth-century manor. ' "Treat every man according to his deserts and who shall escape whipping?" ' I quoted *Hamlet* at him.

'Then I can trust you, Rumpole? The Lord Chancellor's going to put me on the local Bench.'

'The Lord Chancellor lives in a world of his own.'

'You don't think I'd do well as a magistrate?'

'I suppose you'd speak from personal experience of crime. And have some respect for the quality of mercy.'

'I've got no time for that, Rumpole.' His voice became quieter but harder, the brown eyes lost their softness: that, I thought, was how he must have looked when one of his clip-joint girls was caught with the punters' cash stuffed in her tights. 'It's about time we cracked down on crime. Well now, can I trust you not to go out there and spread the word about the last time we met?'

'That depends.'

'On what?'

'How well you have understood the Christmas message.'

'Which is?'

'Perhaps, generosity.'

'I see. So you want your bung?'

'Oh, not me, Dicko. I've been paid, inadequately, by legal aid. But there's an impoverished church tower in urgent need of resuscitation.'

'That Eric Longstaff, our Rector – he's not a patriot!'

'And are you?'

'I do a good deal of work locally for the British Legion.'

'And I'm sure, next Poppy Day, they'll appreciate what you've done for the church tower.'

He looked at me for a long minute in silence, and I thought that if this scene had been taking place in a back room in Soho there might, quite soon, have been the flash of a knife. Instead, his hand went to an inside pocket, but it produced nothing more lethal than a chequebook.

'While you're in a giving mood,' I said, 'the Rectory's in desperate need of central heating.'

'This is bloody blackmail!' Dicko Perducci, now known as Donald Compton, said.

'Well,' I told him, 'you should know.'

★

Christmas was over. The year turned, stirred itself and opened its eyes on a bleak January. Crimes were committed, arrests were made and the courtrooms were filled, once again, with the sound of argument. I went down to the Old Bailey on a trifling matter of fixing the date of a trial before Mrs Justice Erskine-Brown. As I was leaving, the usher came and told me that the Judge wanted to see me in her private room on a matter of urgency.

Such summonses always fill me with apprehension and a vague feeling of guilt. What had I done? Got the date of the trial hopelessly muddled? Addressed the Court with my trousers carelessly unzipped? I was relieved when the learned Phillida greeted me warmly and even offered me a glass of sherry, poured from her own personal decanter. 'It was so kind of you to offer, Rumpole,' she said unexpectedly.

'Offer what?' I was puzzled.

'You told us how much you adored the traditional British pantomime.'

'So I did.' For a happy moment I imagined her Ladyship as Principal Boy, her shapely legs encased in black tights, her neat little wig slightly askew, slapping her thigh and calling out, in bell-like tones, 'Cheer up, Rumpole, Portia's not far away.'

'The twins are looking forward to it enormously.'

'Looking forward to what?'

'*Aladdin* at the Tufnell Park Empire. I've got the tickets for the 19th of Jan. You do remember promising to take them, don't you?'

'Well, of course.' What else might I have said after the fifth glass of the Erskine-Brown St Émilion? 'I'd love to be of the party. And will old Claude be buying us a dinner afterwards?'

'I really don't think you should go round calling people "old", Rumpole.' Phillida now looked miffed, and I downed the sherry before she took it into her head to deprive me of it. 'Claude's got us tickets for Pavarotti. *L'Elisir d'Amore*. You might buy the children a burger after the show. Oh, and it's not far from us on the tube. It really was sweet of you to invite them.'

At which she smiled at me and refilled my glass in a way which made it clear she was not prepared to hear further argument.

It all turned out better than I could have hoped. Tristan and Isolde, unlike their Wagnerian namesakes, were cheerful, reasonably polite and seemed only too anxious to dissociate themselves, as far as possible, from the old fart who was escorting them. At every available opportunity they would touch me for cash and then scamper off to buy ice cream, chocolates, sandwiches or Sprite. I was left in reasonable peace to enjoy the performance.

And enjoy it I did. Aladdin was a personable young woman with an upturned nose, a voice which could have been used to wake up patients coming round from their anaesthetics, and memorable thighs. Uncle Abanazer was played, Isolde told me, by an actor known as a social worker with domestic problems in a long-running television series. Wishy and Washy did sing to electric guitars (deafeningly amplified) but Widow Twankey, played by a certain Jim Diamond, was all a Dame should be, a nimble little cockney, fitted up with a sizeable false bosom, a flaming red wig, sweeping eyelashes and scarlet lips. Never have I heard the immortal line, 'Where's that naughty boy Aladdin got to?' better delivered. I joined in loudly (Tristan and Isolde sat silent and embarrassed) when the Widow and Aladdin conducted us in the singing of 'Please Don't Pinch My Tomatoes'. It was, in fact and in fairness, all a traditional pantomime should be, and yet I had a vague feeling that something was wrong, an element was missing. But, as the cast came down a white staircase in glittering costumes to enthusiastic applause, it seemed the sort of pantomime I'd grown up with, and which Tristan and Isolde should be content to inherit.

After so much excitement I felt in need of a stiff brandy and soda, but the eatery the children had selected for their evening's entertainment had apparently gone teetotal and alcohol was not on the menu. Once they were confronted by their mammoth burgers and fries I made my excuses, said I'd be back in a moment, and slipped into the nearby pub which was, I noticed, opposite the stage door of the Empire.

As the life-giving draught was being poured I found myself standing next to Washy and Uncle Abanazer, now out of costume, who were discussing Jim the Dame. 'Very unfriendly tonight,' Washy said. 'Locked himself in his dressing-room before the show and won't join us for a drink.'

'Perhaps he's had a bust-up with Molly?'

'Unlikely. Molly and Jim never had a cross word.'

'Lucky she's never found out he's been polishing Aladdin's wonderful lamp,' Abanazer said, and they both laughed.

And as I asked the girl behind the bar to refill my glass, in which the tide had sunk to a dangerous low, I heard them laugh again about the Widow Twankey's voluminous bosom. 'Strapped-on polystyrene,' Abanazer was saying. 'Almost bruises me when I dance with her. Funny thing, tonight it was quite soft.'

'Perhaps she borrowed one from a blow-up woman?' Washy was laughing as I gulped my brandy and legged it back to the hamburgers. In the dark passage outside the stage door I saw a small, nimble figure in hurried retreat: Jim Diamond, who for some reason hadn't wanted to join the boys at the bar.

After I had restored the children to the Erskine-Browns' au pair, I sat in the tube on my way back to Gloucester Road and read the programme. Jim Diamond, it seemed, had started his life in industry before taking up show business. He had a busy career in clubs and turned down appearances on television. ' "I only enjoy the living show," Jim says. "I want to have the audience where I can see them." ' His photograph, without the exaggerated female make-up, showed a pale, thin-nosed, in some way disagreeable little man with a lip curled either in scorn or triumph. I wondered how such an unfriendly-looking character could become an ebullient and warm-hearted widow. Stripped of his make-up, there was something about this comic's unsmiling face which brought back memories of another meeting in totally different circumstances. It was the second time within a few weeks that I had found an old familiar face cast in a new and unexpected part.

The idea, the memory I couldn't quite grasp, preyed on my mind until I was tucked up in bed. Then, as Hilda's latest historical romance dropped from her weary fingers, when she turned her back on me and switched out the light, I saw the face again quite clearly but in a different setting. Not Diamond, not Sparkler, but Sparksman, a logical progression. Widow Twankey had been played by Harry Sparksman, a man who trained as a professional entertainer, if my memory was correct, not in clubs, but in Her Majesty's prisons. It was, it seemed, an interesting career change, but I thought no more of it at the time and, once satisfied with my identification, I fell asleep.

*

'The boy couldn't have done it, Mr Rumpole. Not a complicated bloody great job to that extent. His only way of getting at a safe was to dig it out of the wall and remove it bodily. He did that in a Barkingside boutique and what he found in it hardly covered the petrol. Young Dennis couldn't have got into the Croydon supermarket peter. No one in our family could.'

Uncle Fred, the experienced and cautious head of the Timson clan, had no regard for the safe-breaking talent of Dennis, his nephew and, on the whole, an unskilled recruit in the Timson enterprise. The Croydon supermarket job had been highly complicated and expertly carried out and had yielded, to its perpetrators, thousands of pounds. Peanuts Molloy was arrested as one of the lookouts, after falling and twisting an ankle when chased by a nightwatchman during the getaway. He said he didn't know any of the skilled operators who had engaged him, except Dennis Timson who, he alleged, was in general charge of the operation. Dennis alone silenced the burglar alarm and deftly penetrated the lock on the safe with an oxyacetylene blowtorch.

It had to be remembered, though, that the clan Molloy had been sworn enemies of the Timson family from time immemorial. Peanuts's story sounded implausible when I met Dennis Timson in the Brixton Prison interview room. A puzzled twenty-five-year-old with a shaven head and a poor attempt at a moustache, he seemed more upset by his Uncle Fred's low opinion of him than the danger of a conviction and subsequent prolonged absence from the family.

Dennis's case was to come up for committal at the South London Magistrates' Court before 'Skimpy' Simpson, whose lack of success at the Bar had driven him to a job as a stipendiary beak. His nickname had been earned by the fact that he had not, within living memory, been known to splash out on a round of drinks in Pommeroy's Wine Bar.

In the usual course of events, there is no future in fighting proceedings which are only there to commit the customer to trial. I had resolved to attend solely to pour a little well-deserved contempt on the evidence of Peanuts Molloy. As I started to prepare the case, I made a note of the date of the Croydon supermarket break-in. As soon as I had done so, I consulted my diary. I turned the virgin pages as yet unstained by notes of trials, ideas for cross-examinations, splodges of tea or spilled glasses of Pommeroy's Very Ordinary. It was as I had thought. While some virtuoso was at work on the Croydon safe, I was enjoying *Aladdin* in the company of Tristan and Isolde.

'Detective Inspector Grimble. Would you agree that whoever blew the safe in the Croydon supermarket did an extraordinarily skilful job?'

'Mr Rumpole, are we meant to congratulate your client on his professional skill?'

God moves in a mysterious way, and it wasn't Skimpy Simpson's fault that he was born with thin lips and a voice which sounded like the rusty hinge of a rusty gate swinging in the wind. I decided to ignore him and concentrate on a friendly chat with DI Grimble, a large, comfortable, ginger-haired officer. We had lived together, over the years, with the clan Timson and their misdoings. He was known to them as a decent and fair-minded cop, as disapproving of the younger, Panda-racing, evidence-massaging intake to the Force as they were of the lack of discretion and criminal skills which marked the younger Timsons.

'I mean the thieves were well informed. They knew that there would be a week's money in the safe.'

'They knew that, yes.'

'And was there a complex burglar-alarm system? You couldn't put it out of action simply by cutting wires, could you?'

'Cutting the wires would have set it off.'

'So putting the burglar alarm out of action would have required special skills?'

'It would have done.'

'Putting it out of action also stopped a clock in the office. So we know that occurred at 8.45?'

'We know that. Yes.'

'And at 9.20 young Molloy was caught as he fell, running to a getaway car.'

'That is so.'

'So this heavy safe was burnt open in a little over half an hour?'

'I fail to see the relevance of that, Mr Rumpole.' Skimpy was getting restless.

'I'm sure the Officer does. That shows a very high degree of technical skill, doesn't it, Detective Inspector?'

'I'd agree with that.'

'Exercised by a highly experienced peterman?'

'Who is this Mr Peterman?' Skimpy was puzzled. 'We haven't heard of him before.'

'Not Mr Peterman.' I marvelled at the ignorance of the basic facts of life displayed by the magistrate. 'A man expert at blowing safes, known to the trade as "peters",' I told him and turned back to DI Grimble. 'So we're agreed that this was a highly expert piece of work?'

'It must have been done by someone who knew his job pretty well. Yes.'

'Dennis Timson's record shows convictions for shoplifting, bag-snatching and stealing a radio from an unlocked car. In all of these simple enterprises, he managed to get caught.'

'Your client's criminal record!' Skimpy looked happy for the first time. 'You're allowing that to go into evidence, are you, Mr Rumpole?'

'Certainly, sir.' I explained the obvious point. 'Because there's absolutely no indication he was capable of blowing a safe in record time, or silencing a complicated burglar alarm, is there, Detective Inspector?'

'No. There's nothing to show anything like that in his record . . .'

'Mr Rumpole,' Skimpy was looking at the clock; was he in danger of missing his usual train back home to Haywards Heath? 'Where's all this heading?'

'Back a good many years,' I told him, 'to the Sweet-Home Building Society job at Carshalton. When Harry Sparksman blew a safe so quietly that even the dogs slept through it.'

'You were in that case, weren't you, Mr Rumpole?' Inspector Grimble was pleased to remember. 'Sparksman got five years.'

'Not one of your great successes.' Skimpy was also delighted. 'Perhaps you wasted the Court's time with unnecessary questions. Have you anything else to ask this officer?'

'Not till the Old Bailey, sir. I may have thought of a few more by then.'

With great satisfaction, Skimpy committed Dennis Timson, a minor villain who would have had difficulty changing a fuse, let alone blowing a safe, for trial at the Central Criminal Court.

'Funny you mentioned Harry Sparksman. Do you know, the same thought occurred to me. An expert like him could've done that job in the time.'

'Great minds think alike,' I assured DI Grimble. We were washing away the memory of an hour or two before Skimpy with two pints of nourishing stout in the pub opposite the beak's Court. 'You know Harry took up a new career?' I needn't have asked the question. DI Grimble had a groupie's encyclopedic knowledge of the criminal stars.

'Oh yes. Now a comic called Jim Diamond. Got up a concert party in the nick. Apparently gave him a taste for show business.'

'I did hear,' I took Grimble into my confidence, 'that he made a comeback for the Croydon job.' It had been a throwaway line from Uncle Fred Timson – 'I heard talk they got Harry back out of retirement' – but it was a thought worth examining.

'I heard the same. So we did a bit of checking. But Sparksman, known as Diamond, has got a cast-iron alibi.'

'Are you sure?'

'The time when the Croydon job was done, he was performing in a pantomime. On stage nearly all the evening, it seems, playing the Dame.'

'*Aladdin*,' I said, 'at the Tufnell Park Empire. It might just be worth your while to go into that alibi a little more thoroughly. I'd suggest you have a private word with Mrs Molly Diamond. It's just possible she may have noticed his attraction to Aladdin's lamp.'

'Now then, Mr Rumpole,' Grimble was wiping the froth from his lips with a neatly folded handkerchief, 'you mustn't tell me how to do my job.'

'I'm only trying to serve,' I managed to look pained, 'the interests of justice!'

'You mean, the interests of your client?'

'Sometimes they're the same thing,' I told him, but I had to admit it wasn't often.

As it happened, the truth emerged without Detective Inspector Grimble having to do much of a job. Harry had, in fact, fallen victim to a tip-tilted nose and memorable thighs; he'd left home and moved into Aladdin's Kensal Rise flat. Molly, taking a terrible revenge, blew his alibi wide open. She had watched many rehearsals and knew every word, every gag, every nudge, wink and shrill complaint of the Dame's part. She had played it to perfection to give her husband an alibi while he went back to his old job in Croydon. It all went perfectly, even though Uncle Abanazer, dancing with her, had felt an unexpected softness.

I had known, instinctively, that something was very wrong. It had, however, taken some time for me to realize what I had really seen that night at the Tufnell Park Empire. It was nothing less than an outrage to a Great British Tradition. The Widow Twankey was a woman.

DI Grimble made his arrest and the case against Dennis Timson was dropped by the Crown Prosecution Service. As spring came to the Temple Gardens, Hilda opened a letter in the other case which turned on the recognition of old, familiar faces and read it out to me.

'The repointing's going well on the tower and we hope to have it finished by Easter,' Poppy Longstaff had written. 'And I have to tell you, Hilda, the oil-fired heating has changed our lives. Eric says it's like living in the tropics. Cooking supper last night, I had to peel off at least one of my cardigans.' She Who Must Be Obeyed put down the letter from her old school friend and said, thoughtfully, '*Noblesse oblige.*'

'What was that, Hilda?'

'I could tell at once that Donald Compton was a true gentleman. The sort that does good by stealth. Of course, poor old Eric thought he'd never get the tower mended, but I somehow felt that Donald wouldn't fail him. It was *noblesse.*'

'Perhaps it was,' I conceded, 'but in this case the *noblesse* was Rumpole's.'

'Rumpole! What on earth do you mean? You hardly paid to have the church tower repointed, did you?'

'In one sense, yes.'

'I can't believe that. After all the years it took you to have the bathroom decorated. What on earth do you mean about *your noblesse*?'

'It'd take too long to explain, old darling. Besides, I've got a conference in Chambers. Tricky case of receiving stolen surgical appliances. I suppose,' I added doubtfully, 'it may lead, at some time in the distant future, to an act of charity.'

Easter came, the work on the tower was successfully completed, and I was walking back to Chambers after a gruelling day down the Bailey when I saw, wafting through the Temple cloisters, the unlikely apparition of the Rev. Eric Longstaff. He chirruped a greeting and said he'd come up to consult some legal brains on the proper investment of what remained of the Church Restoration Fund. 'I'm so profoundly grateful,' he told me, 'that I decided to invite you down to the Rectory last Christmas.'

'*You* decided?'

'Of course I did.'

'I thought your wife Poppy extended the invitation to She . . .'

'Oh yes. But I thought of the idea. It was the result of a good deal of hard knee-work and guidance from above. I knew you were the right man for the job.'

'What job?'

'The Compton job.'

What was this? The Rector was speaking like an old con. The Coldsands caper? 'What *can* you mean?'

'I just mean that I knew you'd defended Donald Compton. In a previous existence.'

'How on earth did you know that?'

Eric drew himself up to his full, willowy height. 'I'm not a prison visitor for nothing,' he said proudly, 'so I thought you were just the chap to put the fear of God into him. You were the very person to put the squeeze on the Lord of the Manor.'

'Put the squeeze on him?' Words were beginning to fail me.

'That was the idea. It came to me as a result of knee-work.'

'So you brought us down to that freezing Rectory just so I could blackmail the local benefactor?'

'Didn't it turn out well!'

'May the Lord forgive you.'

'He's very forgiving.'

'Next time,' I spoke to the Man of God severely, 'the Church can do its blackmailing for itself.'

'Oh, we're quite used to that.' The Rector smiled at me in what I thought was a lofty manner. 'Particularly around Christmas.'

Rumpole and the Primrose Path

The regular meeting of the barristers who inhabit my old Chambers in Equity Court took place, one afternoon, in an atmosphere of particular solemnity. Among those present was a character entirely new to them, a certain Luci Gribble, whom our leader, in a momentary ambition to reach the status of an 'entrepreneur', had taken on as Director of Marketing and Administration.

Mizz Liz Probert, observing the scene, later described Luci (why she had taken to this preposterous spelling of the name of Wordsworth's great love was clear to nobody) as in her thirties, with a 'short bob', referring to hair which was not necessarily as blonde as it seemed, a thin nose, slightly hooded eyes and a determined chin. She wore a black trouser suit and bracelets clinked at her wrists. The meeting was apparently interrupted from time to time, as she gave swift instructions to the mobile phone she kept in her jacket pocket. She also wore high-heeled black boots which Liz Probert priced at not far short of three hundred pounds.

'I'm vitally concerned with the profile of Equity Court.' Luci had a slight Northern accent and a way, Liz noticed, of raising her voice at the end of her sentence, so every statement sounded like a question. 'I take it that it's in the parameters of my job description to include the field of public relations and the all-important question of the company's – that is to say' (here Liz swears that Luci corrected herself reluctantly) 'the *Chambers'* image. Correct, Chair?'

This was an undoubted question, but it seemed to be addressed to an article of furniture, one of that old dining-room set, now much mended and occasionally wobbly, which had been bequeathed to Equity Court in the will of C. H. Wystan, my wife Hilda's father and once Head of our Chambers. However, Soapy Sam Ballard, as our present

Head and so Chairman of the meeting, appeared to follow the new arrival's drift.

'Of course that's your job, Luci.' Soapy Sam was on Christian-name terms with the woman who called him Chair. 'To improve our image. That's why we hired you. After all, we don't want to be described as a group of old fuddy-duddies, do we?' Chair, who might be thought by some to fit the description perfectly, smiled round at the meeting.

'It's not so much the fuddy-duddy label that concerns me at the moment, although I shall be including that in a future presentation. It's the heartless thing that worries me.'

'Heartless?' Ballard was puzzled.

'The public image of barristers,' Luci told the meeting, 'equals money-grabbing fat cats, insincere defenders of clients who are obviously guilty, chauvinists and outdated wig-wearing shysters.'

'Did you say "shysters"?' Claude Erskine-Brown, usually mild mannered, ever timid in Court, easily doused by a robust opponent or an impatient Judge, rose in his seat (once again this is the evidence of Liz Probert) and uttered a furious protest. 'I insist you withdraw that word "shyster".'

'No need for that, Erskine-Brown.' Ballard was being gently judicial. 'Luci is merely talking us through the public perception.'

'You put it, Chair, succinctly and to the point.' Once again, Luci was grateful to the furniture.

'Oh, well. If it's only the public perception.' Erskine-Brown sank back in his seat, apparently mollified.

'What we have to demonstrate is that barristers have outsize hearts. There is no section of the community, and we can prove this by statistics, which cares more deeply, gives more liberally to charity, signs more letters to *The Times* and shows its concern for the public good by pointing out more frequent defects in the railway system, than the old-fashioned, tried-and-trusted British barrister.'

'You can prove anything by statistics.' Erskine-Brown was still out, in a small way, to cause trouble.

'Exactly so.' Luci seemed unexpectedly delighted. 'So we have chosen our statistics with great care, and we shall use them to the best possible advantage. But I'm not talking statistics here. I'm talking of the situation, sad as I'm sure we all agree it may be, which gives us the opportunity to show that we *do* care.' Luci paused and seemed, for a moment, moved with deep emotion. 'So much so that we should all join in a very public display of heartfelt thanks.'

'Heartfelt thanks for what?' Erskine-Brown was mystified. 'Surely not our legal aid fees?'

At this point, Luci produced copies of a statement she invited Erskine-Brown to circulate. When Liz Probert got it, she found that it read:

We wish to give heartfelt thanks for the life of one of our number. An ordinary, work-aday barrister. An old warhorse. One who didn't profess to legal brilliance, but one who cared deeply and whom we loved as a fellow member of number 3 Equity Court.

'By this act we shall show that barristers have hearts,' Luci summed up the situation.

'By what act is that, exactly?' Erskine-Brown was still far from clear.

'The Memorial Service. In the Temple Church for the late Horace Rumpole, barrister-at-law. Chair, I'm sure we can rely on you for a few remarks, giving thanks for a life of quiet and devoted service.'

It later emerged that at this stage of the Chambers meeting Liz Probert, undoubtedly the most sensible member of the gathering, suggested that a discussion of a Memorial Service was a little premature in view of the fact that there had as yet been no announcement of Rumpole's death. Erskine-Brown told her that he had spoken to She Who Must Be Obeyed, who was, he said, 'putting a brave face on it', but admitted that I had been removed from the hospital to which I had been rushed after a dramatic failure in the ticker department, brought about by an unusually brutal encounter with Judge Bullingham, to the Primrose Path Home in Sussex, and would not be back in Chambers for a very long time indeed. In that case, Liz suggested, all talk of a Memorial Service might be postponed indefinitely.

'Put our programme on hold?' Luci was clearly disappointed. 'It'd be a pity not to continue with the planning stage. Naturally, Mrs Rumpole's hoping for the best, but let's face it, at his age Rumpole's actuarial chances of survival are approximate to a negative-risk situation—'

'And one knows, doesn't one,' Erskine-Brown asked, 'what places like the Primrose Path are like? They call themselves "Homes", but the reality is they are—'

'What do you think they are?' Liz Probert was cynical enough to ask. 'Houses of ill fame? Gambling dens? Five-star hotels?'

'They are places,' Erskine-Brown was looking at her, she said, more in sorrow than in anger, 'where people are sent to end their days in peace. They call themselves "convalescent homes" to reassure the relatives. But the truth of it is that not many people come out of them alive.'

'We'll need to put together a programme.' Ballard was seriously worried. 'And we can hardly ask Mrs Rumpole for her help. As yet.'

'I have an aunt in Godalming.' Erskine-Brown seemed unnaturally proud of the fact. 'I can call in on Rumpole when I go down to see her next.'

'And I'm sure your visit, Erskine-Brown,' Ballard said, 'will be a welcome treat for Rumpole.'

As usual, our Head of Chambers had got it completely wrong.

So now Claude and I were together in my room in the Primrose Path Home, somewhere on the sleepy side of Sussex. It was a place of unremitting cleanliness, and so tidy that I was homesick for the unwashed ashtray, resting place for the butt ends of small cigars, the pile of unreturned briefs, the dusty, yellowing accounts of ancient crimes (for which those found guilty must have now completed their sentences), outdated copies of Archbold on Criminal Law and Procedure, and the Old English Law Reports, bound in crumbling leather and gathering dust, as did the collapsing umbrella left by some long-forgotten client. On the mantelpiece I kept a few souvenirs of my notable cases: the bullet found embedded in the radiogram in the Penge Bungalow affair, the china mug inscribed to a 'Perfect Dad' from which Leonard Peterson had drunk his last, arsenic-flavoured cup of tea, and the sheet music of 'In a Monastery Garden', which Mrs Florence Davenport had been playing as she awaited the news of her husband's death after his brakes had been partially severed by her lover.

By contrast, the Primrose Path Home was uncomfortably tidy. The atmosphere was heavy with the smell of furniture polish, chemical air fresheners and disinfectant. There was a constant hum of hoovering and the staff seemed to handle everything, including the patients, with rubber gloves.

'What's your favourite music, Rumpole?'

'Music, Erskine-Brown?'

'Schubert Trio? Mozart Concerto? We know you're absurdly prejudiced against Wagner. What about "When I was a little page" from Verdi's *Falstaff*?'

'I never was a little page! Don't babble, Erskine-Brown.'

'Or Elgar? Typically English, Elgar.'

'When I sing to myself, which is only very occasionally—' Poor old Claude seemed, for no particular reason, to be in some distress, and I was doing my best to help him out.

'Yes. Yes!' His nose twitched with excitement. 'Tell me, Rumpole. When you sing to yourself, what do you sing?'

'Sometimes "Pop Goes the Weasel". Occasionally "Knock'd 'em in the Old Kent Road". More often than not a ballad of the war years, "We're going to hang out the washing on the Siegfried Line". You remember that, don't you?'

'No, Rumpole, I'm afraid I don't.' Erskine-Brown's nose twitched again, though this time it was a sign of displeasure. He tried another tack. 'Tell me, Rumpole. Talking of the war years, did you ever serve your country overseas?'

'Oh yes,' I told Claude, in answer to his ridiculous question. 'I flew Spitfires in the war. I shot down the Red Baron and was the first British pilot to enter Berlin.'

Claude looked at me sadly and said, 'I only ask because Ballard wants material for his speech.'

'His speech about me?' I was puzzled.

'About your life. To give thanks for your existence.'

It sounded extremely improbable. 'Ballard's going to do that?'

'We shall celebrate you, Rumpole.'

'You mean—' I was hoping against all the probabilities that they were contemplating some sort of party '—a Chambers piss-up in Pommeroy's Wine Bar? Drinks on the Soapy Sam Memorial Fund?'

'Not exactly that, Rumpole.' Claude glanced, nervously I thought, at his watch. 'I'd better be getting back. I've got a rating appeal tomorrow.'

'I envy you, Erskine-Brown. You seem to lead a life of perpetual excitement.'

'Oh, there's just one more thing.' The man was already on his feet. 'Do you have a favourite prayer?'

'Why do you ask?'

'To help us, Rumpole, to celebrate your life.'

'Then I pray to God to be left alone. So I can get out of here as quickly as possible. It's all far too clean for my liking.'

'I'm sure you're quite comfortable here, Rumpole.' Erskine-Brown gave me a smile of faint encouragement. 'And I know they'll look after you extremely well. For as long as you have left.'

At which he stood up and stole silently out of the room with the guilty look of a man leaving a funeral early.

When Erskine-Brown had gone, I watched morning television. A group of people had been assembled, having, it seemed, only one thing in common. They had each had sexual intercourse with someone who turned out to be a close relative. This incident in their lives, which many people might wish to keep discreetly under wraps, led them to speak out at length, as cheerfully as though they were discussing gardening or cookery, to the huge audience of the unemployed, the pensioned-off and the helpless in hospitals. As their eager, confiding faces filled the screen I began to doze off – the best way, I had found, of enjoying life at the Primrose Path Home.

Whoever had christened this place of eternal rest the Primrose Path betrayed insufficient knowledge of English literature. According to Ophelia in *Hamlet*, it's the path of dalliance – and any dalliance in the home was confined strictly to the television. The porter in *Macbeth*, however, said that the primrose way led ' "to the everlasting bonfire" '. This may have been a more accurate description. The inhabitants of the rooms down the corridor were given to disappearing quietly during the night and leaving the Primrose Path, I felt sure, for the nearest crematorium.

I woke up, it seemed hours later, to my untouched lunch, a tray mainly loaded with a plethora of paper napkins, much unwelcome salad and a glass of orange juice. I was searching for a mouthful of edible cheese under the stationery when I caught a sound, unusual, even unknown in the Primrose Path. A woman was sobbing. People died there, but you heard no cries of agony, no angry slamming of doors, or wailing of relatives. The sobs I heard were restrained, but they were undeniably heartfelt. I abandoned my lunch, switched off the television and moved, as quietly as I could manage it, into the corridor.

At the end of the passage, with its linoleum shining like polished shoes, a woman was sobbing as she watered a bowl of hyacinths. She was, perhaps, in her late forties, her chestnut hair fading a little, but with high cheekbones, usually amused eyes and a generous mouth. She was Nurse Albright, my favourite member of staff, known to me as Dotty Dorothy, owing to her habit of occasionally promising to dust off my aura by polishing the surrounding air. She also brought me an assortment of roots, herbs and leaves, which, if added to my tea, she promised, would soon make me fit to run a mile, spend a day defending in a murder trial and learn to tango at evening classes. She was, above all, cheerful and unfailingly kind, and we would sing together songs we both loved, songs I had kept from the prying ears of Erskine-Brown, such as 'Night and Day', 'That Old Black Magic' and 'Bewitched, Bothered and Bewildered', which I had danced to in a far-distant time, before Hilda's and my fox-trotting days were over.

Dotty Dorothy's singing, her use of herbs and strange roots and, on many occasions, her kindness got her into frequent trouble with her boss, Sister Sheila Bradwell, who ruled the Primrose Path with the kind of enlightened and liberal principles which guided Captain Bligh when he was in charge of the *Bounty*. Sister Sheila recognized no superior being, except for one called Nanki-Poo, an evil-tempered, spoiled and domineering Pekinese whom I had seen the Sister kiss, fondle, feed with chocolate biscuits and generally spoil in a way she would never treat a patient. Like many of the inhabitants of the Primrose Path, Nanki-Poo suffered a degree of incontinence which littered the garden and added some significance to his name. He would also, when out walking, sit down if a leaf attached itself to his trailing hair, and yelp until a nurse came and relieved him of the encumbrance.

It was the sudden appearance of the powerful Sister Sheila, with or without her pet, that Nurse Dotty Albright feared as we stood chatting in the corridor.

'Get back into your room, Mr Rumpole,' Dotty swallowed a sob and wiped an eye on the back of her hand, 'before Sister spots you.'

'Never mind about Sister Sheila.' I had grown impervious to the icy disapproval of the Head Girl. 'Tell me what's the matter.'

'A terrible night, Mr Rumpole. It's been the most ghastly night ever at the Primrose Path.'

'Tell me what happened.'

'Poor Mr Fairweather . . . He passed away during the night. They took him away. It was my night off and they took him away without even telling me.'

I had caught a glimpse of Fairweather – Freddy, Dotty often called him – a short, beady-eyed, bald-headed, broad-shouldered man in a dressing-gown being pushed in a wheelchair to his room down the corridor. He was recovering, Dotty told me, from a massive heart attack, but she brought him roots and herbal remedies and he made jokes and flirtatious suggestions. Freddy and I, she assured me, were her two favourite patients.

'Can you imagine that?' Dotty said as she took out a crumpled handkerchief and blew her nose gently. 'Sister let them take him without even a chance of saying goodbye. Freddy would have hated that. He was full of rude suggestions, of course he was. He was a bit of a jack the lad, we know that, even in his condition of health. But underneath all that, he had the most perfect manners. Even if he'd gone, even if it was too late, he'd have liked me to be there to hold his hand and say goodbye before he passed away. But *she* wouldn't have that. *She* has to know best, always.'

As Dotty went on talking, it appeared that the sad death of Freddy Fairweather wasn't the only disaster of that long, eventful night. A certain Michael Masklyn, high up on the list of unpopular patients, had, in Dotty's words, 'done a runner' and strayed from the Primrose Path under the cover of darkness. Masklyn was an unknown quantity; he seemed to have few friends and no visitors except an older woman who had visited him once and, as their voices were raised in a quarrel, was heard to vow never to come near him again. He'd been transferred from a hospital which had, as might be expected, run out of beds, and found a place in the Primrose Path under some sort of government scheme. He had, Dotty assured me, a vile temper, was thankful for nothing and had once thrown a glass containing his urine sample at the head of a trainee nurse who would do no harm to anybody.

'I never thought he was well enough to get out of here.' Dotty had stopped crying now and her voice was full of anger. 'Sister's security's just hopeless. His clothes were in his room, just as yours are, and Gavin was fast asleep at his desk downstairs. So Mr Masklyn just walked off and left us. I hate to say this to you, Mr Rumpole, but there's just no organization in this place. No organization at all. It's all rules and no practice. Not the place for either of us really, is it?'

Strangely enough, after that sad and eventful evening, the Primrose Path became, in some elusive and quiet way, more interesting. I tried to discuss the break-out of Michael Masklyn with Sister Sheila, but was met with pursed lips and the shortest of possible answers.

'He was an impossible patient,' Sheila Bradwell told me. 'In one way we were glad to get rid of him. But of course we had our duty of care. You can't keep an eye on everyone twenty-four hours a day.'

'Do the police know he's gone missing?' I felt a stirring of the old need to cross-examine the witness.

'We reported it, naturally, Mr Rumpole, if you're so interested. There was no sign of him at his last known address.'

'Did he have a family?'

'Someone he said was his sister came once. No one's been able to track her down either.'

'My friend Dotty says his door was locked in the morning when she came on duty.'

'Your friend Nurse Albright says a lot of things we don't have to take too much notice of. Of course the door wasn't locked at night. We locked it in the morning, until the police came to see if there were any clues to where he'd gone. You don't want the evidence disturbed. You know all about that, don't you, Mr Rumpole?'

'I suppose I do. All the same, it must have been a terrible night for you. I was sorry to hear about Mr Fairweather.'

Sister Sheila Bradwell stood looking at me, a straight-backed, straight-haired woman, born to command. I thought I saw in her eyes not sorrow for the passing of another patient, but a faint amusement at the fact that I had bothered to raise the subject.

'These things happen, Mr Rumpole, at a place like this. They're very sad, but they happen all the time. We've got used to it, of course. And we deal with it as kindly as possible, whatever your friend Nurse Albright may say about the matter.'

'She said she was very fond of Mr Fairweather. He was kind to her, and she enjoyed looking after him.'

'And did your friend tell you that dear old Mr Fairweather had also said he'd left her money in his will?' Sister Bradwell was smiling as she said that, and it came as something of a shock. After being clearly disapproved of for asking impertinent questions, it suddenly seemed as though I was being drawn into an argument from which, for the moment, I retreated.

'She never said anything like that. Only that she was upset because he died so suddenly.'

'Well, it's nothing for you to worry about, Mr Rumpole, is it? You can concentrate on getting a good rest. Shall I switch your telly on for you?'

'Please don't.'

'Very well then, Mr Rumpole. And if you take my advice, you'll steer very clear of your friend's herbal remedies. Some of them may have unfortunate results.'

In the days that followed, Dotty seemed unusually busy, but late one afternoon, as I woke from a light doze, I found her sitting by my bed with a surprise present. It was half a bottle of claret she had managed to get opened in an off-licence and smuggled in under her mac. We shared a toothglassful of a wine in the same humble class as Château Thames Embankment, but nonetheless welcome to a palate starved of alcohol. So the old friendly Dotty was back, but quieter and sadder, and I didn't dare suggest even a muted rendition of 'Bewitched, Bothered and Bewildered'.

'They don't want me to go to the funeral,' she said.

'Who doesn't want you to? The family?'

'No, Sister Sheila. And Freddy's special doctor. Freddy wouldn't see anyone else.'

The common run of patients, myself included, were attended to by one of the local GPs. However, the Primrose Path was visited almost daily by a tall, elegantly dressed man in a well-cut suit who moved down the corridor in a deafening smell of aftershave, always escorted by Sister Sheila and referred to by the staff, in tones of considerable awe, as Doctor Lucas.

'I've never got on with that Lucas. Well, they won't even tell me where the funeral's going to be.'

'They won't?'

'They said it was Freddy's special wish. He hated funerals . . .'

'Well, none of us like them. Particularly our own.'

'So he didn't want anyone to be there. That was his last wish, they told me. And, of course, he wanted to be cremated.'

' "The primrose way" ', I thought, ' "to the everlasting bonfire".'

'You know what happened? Doctor Lucas and Sister Sheila were with him when he died. They rang the undertaker, they said, and they had him taken away at once. During the night. As though . . . Freddy was something to be ashamed of.'

'You miss him, don't you?'

'Poor old darling. Sometimes he said he was in love.' She put a hand into the pocket of her uniform and pulled out a photograph, a bald-headed, suntanned, bright-eyed elderly man with a nose which looked as though it had, at some distant time in his life, been broken in hostility or sport. He was sitting up in bed, smiling, with his arm round Nurse Dotty. It had been taken, Dotty told me, by trainee Nurse Jones, and they had all been laughing a good deal at the time.

'Sister Sheila said something.' I hesitated before I asked the question. 'Was he going to leave you money in his will?'

'Oh, he told everyone that.' She was smiling now. 'Not that I ever really expected anything, of course. But it just showed how well we got on. He said he didn't have much of a family left to provide for.'

We talked a little more, and she told me that Freddy had a business somewhere in the North of England and he 'wasn't short of a bob or two', and then she asked for my legal advice, adding, 'Do you mind if I pay you with this glass of wine?'

'That makes it as profitable as a conference on legal aid,' I told her.

'I'm going to find out about Freddy's funeral. When I've found out, I'm going to it. I don't care what Sister Sheila has to say about it. I'm entitled to do that, aren't I?'

'I'm sure,' I gave her my best legal opinion, 'you're entitled to go to any funeral you choose. I'd even invite you to mine.'

'Don't be silly.' She smiled and, for an unexpected moment of delight, held my hand. 'That's not going to happen. And we're not going to stay here much longer, are we? Either of us. The Primrose Path's really just not our sort of place.'

'Not our sort of place.' Dotty's words, together with her account of the ease with which the awkward customer Masklyn had escaped from the Primrose Path, fired my enthusiasm. I waited for a night when Dotty was not only off duty but had gone to stay with her sister in Haywards Heath. I made sure that she couldn't be blamed by the Obergruppen-führer for my having gone missing from the list of inmates. And I wanted to avoid any lengthy argument with the Primrose Path (whose bill had been paid to the end of this month) or my wife Hilda, which might prolong my term of imprisonment.

The clothes I was wearing when my ticker overreacted so dramatically to the strain put upon it by an appearance before the raging Judge Bullingham had come with me to hospital and from there to the Primrose Path. They were hanging in a cupboard in my room, so I was able to change the pyjamas for my regulation uniform of black jacket and waistcoat, a pair of striped trousers supported by braces, a white shirt with detachable collar, and dark socks with, by this time, dusty and unpolished black shoes. I had kept charge of my wallet, which had four ten-pound notes and a travel pass in it, so I was soon prepared for the dash to freedom. I paused only to scribble a note for Dotty, which contained simply my four-line version of an old song:

> The way you feel my pulse
> The way you test my pee
> The memory of much else
> They can't take that away from me.

I wasn't particularly proud of rhyming 'pulse' with 'else', but time was pressing and I had a journey to make. I signed the message 'Love Rumpole', put the dressing-gown back on over my clothes and moved out stealthily towards the staircase.

The gods who look after the elderly trying to escape the clutches of the medical profession were on my side. That night a poll was being taken on television to decide the Sexiest Footballer of the Year, an event which had aroused far more interest than any recent election. So the television sets were humming in the rooms, and the nurses had withdrawn to their staffroom to watch. The desk in the hallway was, more often than not, manned by Gavin, a quiet and serious young man to whom a shaven head and an overlarge brown jumper gave a curiously monkish appearance. He was studying somewhere, but turned up for nights at the Primrose Path, where he read until dawn. His attendance was irregular, and, as on the night that Michael Masklyn walked free, he was away from his desk. I slid back bolts, undid chains and passed out into the night.

Somewhere in the backstreets of the town I discarded the dressing-gown, tossing it over a hedge into somebody's front garden as a surprise present. I found a spotted bow tie in a jacket pocket and fixed it under my collar. Accoutred as though for the Old Bailey, I presented myself at the railway station, where the last train to Victoria was, happily, half an hour late.

My first call in London was to Equity Court. Our Chambers were silent and empty, the clerk's room was fuller than ever of screens and other mechanical devices and I searched in vain for briefs directed to me. I went into my room, which seemed on first glance to be depressingly tidy. However, the eagle eyes of the tidier-up had missed a half-full packet of small cigars at the back of a drawer. I lit one, puffed out a perfect smoke ring, and then I noticed a glossy little folder, which looked like the advertisement for a country hotel or a tour of the Lake District, except that the cover bore the words 'Equity Court Chambers' with the truncated address 'bestofthebar.com'. There was an unappealing photograph captioned 'Samuel Ballard, QC, Chair and Head of Chambers' standing in the doorway as though to tempt in passing trade.

Inside, on the first page, was a list of our Chambers' members. My eye was immediately drawn to one entry, 'Horace Rumpole, BA Oxon', against which someone had written with a felt-tip pen, 'Deceased?' I immediately lifted the telephone and called my home in Froxbury mansions.

'Rumpole, is that you?' Hilda sounded as though I had woken her from a deep sleep.

'Yes. It's me, Rumpole. And not Rumpole deceased either. It's Rumpole alive and kicking.'

'Isn't it way past bedtime in the Primrose Path?'

'I don't care what bedtime is in the Primrose Path. I'm not in the Primrose Path any more. I've put the Primrose Path far behind me. I'm in Chambers.'

'You're in Chambers? Whatever are you doing in Chambers? Go back to the nursing home at once!' Hilda's orders were clear and to be disobeyed at my peril. I took the risk.

'Certainly not. I'm coming home to Gloucester Road. And I don't need nursing any more.'

It would be untrue to say that there was – at first, anyway – a hero's welcome for the returning Rumpole. There were no flowers, cheers or celebratory bottles opened. There was the expected denunciation of the defendant Rumpole as selfish, ungrateful, irresponsible, opinionated, wilful and, not to put too fine a point upon it, a pain in the neck to all who had to deal with him. But behind these stiff sentences, I got the strange and unusual feeling that Hilda was fairly pleased to see me alive and kicking and to discover that I had, so far as could be seen, passed out of the Valley of the Shadow of Death and had come back home, no doubt to give trouble, probably to fail to co-operate with her best-laid schemes, but at least not gone for ever.

I have to admit that our married life has not been altogether plain sailing. There have been many occasions when the icy winds of Hilda's disapproval have blown round Froxbury mansions. There have been moments when the journey home from the Temple felt like a trip up to the front line during a war which seemed to have no discernible ending. But, in all fairness, I have to say that her behaviour in the matter of the Rumpole Memorial Service was beyond reproach. She told me of the impending visit of the two QCs, and when Ballard let her know, over the telephone, that they planned a 'fitting tribute to Rumpole's life', she guessed what they were after and even suffered, she admitted with apparent surprise, a curious feeling of loss. She had telephoned the Primrose Path and spoken to Sister Sheila, who was able to tell her, much to her relief, that 'Mr Rumpole was being as awkward as ever!' Now that I appeared to be back in the land of the living, she was prepared to fall in with my master plan and enable me to eavesdrop, as the two leading pompositities of our Chambers unfolded their plans to mark the end of Rumpole's life on earth.

Accordingly, I was shut away in the kitchen when Ballard and Erskine-Brown arrived. Hilda left the sitting-room door ajar, and I moved into the hall to enjoy the conversation recorded here.

'We're sure you would like to join us in offering up thanks for the gift of Rumpole's life, Mrs Rumpole,' Soapy Sam started in hushed and respectful tones.

'A gift?' She Who Must Be Obeyed sounded doubtful. 'Not a free gift, certainly. It had to be paid for with a certain amount of irritation.'

'That,' Ballard had to concede, 'is strictly true. But one has to admit that Horace achieved a noticeable position in the Courts. Notwithstanding the fact that he remained a member of the Junior Bar.'

'Albeit a rather elderly member of the Junior Bar,' Claude had to remind Hilda.

'It's true that he never took a silk gown *or* joined us in the front row. The Lord Chancellor never made him a QC,' Ballard admitted.

'His face didn't fit,' Claude put it somewhat brutally, I thought, 'with the establishment.'

'All the same, many of the cases he did brought him—' Ballard hesitated and Claude supplied the word:

'Notoriety.'

'So we want to arrange a Memorial Service. In the Temple Church.'

It was at this point that She Who Must Be Obeyed offered a short, incredulous laugh. 'You mean a Memorial Service for *Rumpole*?'

'That, Mrs Rumpole, Hilda if I may,' Ballard seemed relieved that the conversation had, at last, achieved a certain clarity, 'is exactly what we mean.'

'We're sure that you, of course, Hilda, and Rumpole's family and friends would wish to join us in this act of celebration.'

'Friends?' Hilda sounded doubtful and added, I thought unkindly, 'Rumpole has friends?'

'Some friends, surely. From all sections of society.'

'You mean you're going to invite that terrible tribe of South London criminals?' I thought this ungrateful of Hilda. The Timsons' addiction to ordinary decent crime had kept us in groceries, including huge quantities of furniture polish, washing-up liquid and scouring pads, and had frequently paid the bill at the butcher's and several times redecorated the bathroom over the long years of our married life.

'I hardly think,' Claude hastened to reassure her, 'that the Timsons would fit in with the congregation at the Temple Church.'

'I'm sure there will be many people,' Ballard was smiling at She Who Must, 'who aren't members of the criminal fraternity and who'll want to give Rumpole a really good send-off.'

It was at this point that I entered the room, carrying a bottle of Château Thames Embankment and glasses. 'Thank you for that kind thought, Ballard,' I greeted him. 'And now you're both here, perhaps we will all drink to Rumpole revived.'

Hamlet, happening to bump into his father's ghost on the battlements, couldn't have looked more surprised than my learned friends.

The return to life was slow and, in many ways, painful. At first there was a mere trickle of briefs. Bonny Bernard, my favourite solicitor, had given up hope of my return and sent a common theft charge against two members of the Timson clan to Hoskins in our Chambers. I'm only too well aware of the fact that Hoskins has innumerable daughters to support, but I had to make sure that the Timsons knew I was no longer dead, and had to finance a wife with a passion for cleaning materials, as well as the life-giving properties of Pommeroy's Very Ordinary Claret.

I was sitting in my room in Chambers, wondering if I would ever work again, when our clerk Henry put through a phone call and I heard, to my delight, the cheerful voice of Sister Dotty, although on this memorable occasion the cheerfulness seemed forced and with an undertone of deep anxiety. After the usual inquiries about whether or not I was still alive, and the news that she was doing freelance and temporary nursing and had taken a small flat in Kilburn, she said, with a small and unconvincing laugh, 'I had a visit from the police.'

'You had a burglary?'

'No. They wanted me to help them with their inquiries.'

I felt a chill wind blowing. People who help the police with their inquiries often end up in serious trouble.

'Inquiries about what?'

'Poor old Freddy Fairweather's death. They suggest I call in at the station and bring my solicitor. And I haven't really got a solicitor.'

'Then I'll get you one. Where are you? I'll ring you back.'

This was clearly a job for my old friend Bonny Bernard. I called him to remind him that I was, in spite of all the evidence to the contrary, up for work, and put him in touch with Dotty. A few days later, they called in at my Chambers to report the result of an extraordinary conversation which had taken place with Detective Inspector Maundy and Detective Sergeant Thorndike in a nick not too far from the Primrose Path Home.

'They were a decent enough couple of officers,' Bernard told me. 'But they soon made their suspicions clear to me and the client.'

'Suspicions of what?'

'Murder.'

I looked at Dotty, all her smiles gone to be replaced with a bewildered, incredulous terror. I did my best to make light of the moment. 'You haven't done in Sister Sheila?'

'They're investigating the death of one of the patients,' Bernard said. 'A Mr Frederick Fairweather.'

'Freddy! As though I'd do anything to hurt him. We were friends. You know that. Just as we were, Mr Rumpole.'

'And what's she supposed to have done to Fairweather?'

'Digitalis.' Bernard looked at his notes.

'Foxgloves?' I remembered Dotty's collection of herbal remedies.

'It's used to stabilize the action of the heart.' Words began to pour out of Dotty. 'They asked me about the access I had to digitalis, they seemed to think that I had a huge collection of pills and potions . . .'

'Well, you had, hadn't you?'

'Herbal remedies, you know that. And, of course, I had digitalis, but I'd enter every dose I had to give a patient – and I never treated Freddy with it at all.'

'So what do they suggest?' I asked Bernard.

'That they have evidence my client used a whole lot of digitalis without entering it or keeping a note,' he told me. 'And that she was seen coming out of Fairweather's room an hour before he died. She also boasted she was going to benefit from the deceased's will.'

'It's all completely ridiculous!' Dotty could contain herself no longer. 'I went to bed early and never left my room until I went on duty next day. I didn't care a scrap about Freddy's will. I only wanted him to get better, that was all I wanted. Nothing would have made me harm him, nothing in the world!'

She was crying, I remembered, as she watered a bowl of hyacinths after Freddy Fairweather died. She was crying again now, but angrily, dabbing at her eyes with the clutched ball of a handkerchief.

'That Doctor. Lucas, was it? He must have entered the cause of death?' I asked Bernard.

'The cause of death was a heart attack. The deceased had heart problems. But Lucas told the Inspector that what he saw might also have been brought about by an overdose of digitalis.'

I made a note and then asked Dotty, 'You told me you were going to Freddy's cremation. Did you go?'

'It was very strange. I rang the undertakers that used to come to the Primrose Path, but they knew nothing about Freddy. Then I rang the crematorium and I got a date. It was terrible, Mr Rumpole, just terrible. There was no one there. Absolutely no one at all. Sheila had said Freddy didn't want anyone to see him go, but I couldn't believe it. I was alone, in that horrible place . . . I think they were waiting for someone to come. I don't know who they thought I was. One of the family, even a wife, perhaps. I told them I was his nurse and they said they might as well begin. There was some sort of music. I suppose they had it left over from someone else's funeral, but there was no one to say anything. Not a word. Not a prayer. And there was just me to watch the coffin slide away behind the curtains. Apart from me – he went quite alone.' She dabbed her eyes again and then looked up at me. A look full of unanswered questions.

'Did you tell the police that?'

'No. I just answered their questions.'

'And is there anything else you want to tell me?'

'Only that I'm angry. So angry.'

'Because you know who's been talking to the police?'

'Of course. Sister Sheila!'

'You think it's Sheila?'

'Who else could it be?'

I wasn't in Court, of course, and what I was about to do was calculated only to avoid the trial of Dotty on the unsubstantial charge against her. Greater love, I thought, has no man than this, that he give up a defence brief at the Old Bailey for a friend.

'I wonder if you could help me. There are a few little things I'd like to ask about Freddy.' The art of cross-examining, I have always believed, is not the art of examining crossly, and I started in my politest, gentlest and most respectful tone of voice. Lull the witness into a false sense of security was my way, and ask questions she has to agree to before you spring the surprises. 'Mr Fairweather had a company selling private pensions up in Leeds, hadn't he?'

'That was his business, was it? Then you know more than I do.' Sheila was expressionless, and now Nanki-Poo snorted.

'Oh, I doubt that. And his business was called Primrose Personal Pensions, wasn't it? And this is the Primrose Path Home.'

'A pure coincidence.' Sister Sheila was, for the first time, on the defensive.

'Really? There are a lot of coincidences, aren't there, about that eventful night? But let's stick to his business for a moment. Didn't he buy this home as an investment about ten years ago? That was when you'd started to run it, and you got to know him rather well. Isn't that the truth of the matter?'

'I really don't see why I should sit here answering questions about the home's private business. That is absolutely no concern of yours, Mr Rumpole.'

'I'm afraid it *is* my business, Mrs Fairweather.'

There was a silence then. A heavy stillness, during which the dog made no sound and Sister Sheila moved not at all. She sat looking at her undrunk cup of coffee, and the plate on which four chocolate biscuits lay in a neat pattern. Then she managed to whisper, 'What did you call me?'

'By your name. You married Freddy last year, didn't you, at a Leeds Register Office? He was the divorced husband of Barbara Elizabeth Threadwell, by whom he had one son, Gavin. A quiet boy who got into university to read theology and is occasionally on duty at the desk in the hallway. I suppose you got Freddy to marry you as part of the deal.'

'Deal?' The witness was now making the mistake of asking *me* questions. 'What sort of a deal are you suggesting?'

So I told her. 'Primrose Personal Pensions is in serious trouble, isn't it? The pensions just aren't there any more. The poor devils who subscribed to Primrose have no comfortable income to look forward to. God knows what'll happen to them. They'll be sleeping in doorways and dying on the National Health because the truth of the matter is that Freddy trousered their money. Then he had nowhere to hide, except a quiet nursing home run by his wife, where he could be treated by his company doctor, who would issue endless chits assuring the world and the Fraud Squad that Freddy was far too ill to come to Court.'

Had I been advising Sister Sheila at that moment, she would have refused to answer further questions on the grounds that they might incriminate her. Without the advantages of my advice, she tried to discover the strength of the evidence against her.

'Mr Rumpole, are you telling me you knew Mr Fairweather well?'

'Since I left here I've got to know him very well indeed.'

'You must be seriously ill, Mr Rumpole.' A faint smile appeared on Sister Sheila's face, a smile of derision. 'Since you left here Mr Fairweather has, as you well know, been dead.'

'Are you sure?'

'Sure?' She spoke as though there was no possible doubt about the matter. 'Of course I'm sure.'

'It would have been what he wanted.' I seemed to surprise her.

'You think he wanted to die?' The smile was overtaken by a brief, mirthless laugh. 'People who come here don't *want* to die, Mr Rumpole.'

'Not everyone has the Fraud Squad and the Pensions Watchdog breathing down their necks. Not everyone has filched thousands of pensioners' money. The time was coming when Dr Lucas's chits and Freddy's shelter in the Primrose Path might not have been enough. There was only one place left for him to hide in. Death.'

'Are you suggesting my patient committed suicide?'

'Of course not. Freddy wouldn't give up as easily as that. His way out, and I think you know this as well as I do, was a death which was as much a fake as his pensions.'

'That's a most outrageous suggestion!' Sister Sheila, as so many witnesses do when they strike a sticky patch, fell back on righteous indignation. 'My lawyers will make sure you pay for it. And never repeat it.'

'Oh, I think your lawyers will have more important business on their hands. I'm sure Freddy's death was discussed, but not planned exactly. No one could have planned the great opportunity of that night. It was more by luck, wasn't it, than good management?'

'Mr Rumpole,' Sister Sheila gave a magnificent display of patience with a questioner in an advanced stage of senile decay, 'Mr Fairweather died of heart failure. Confirmed by Doctor Lucas. His body was cremated, an event which was witnessed by your friend, Nurse Albright, who says he promised her something in his will.'

'Let me first deal with that.' I fed her tightly controlled fury by smiling tolerantly as I counted off the points on my fingers. 'Doctor Lucas had spent years as the official medical adviser to a fraudulent pension company. Like you, I'm sure he expected to share in the spoils. You did your best to keep the date and place of Freddy's funeral a secret, but Dotty made her own inquiries. It's true she saw a coffin slide into the everlasting bonfire, but whose coffin was it, exactly?'

'Freddy's, of course.' By now the witness was standing, furious, all pretence that we were just discussing another unfortunate patient gone. 'Who else could it have been?'

'A man called Masklyn?' I suggested. 'A transfer from a crowded hospital. A man no one knew much about. No apparent friends. No traceable relatives. He left the hospital that night. Was it, perhaps, the night *he* happened to die? I'm not saying you and Lucas killed him. I don't think you did, I just think his death was a stroke of luck. It meant that one of you could tell the undertaker that the dead man's name was Frederick Fairweather.

'And now, do you want to know why I've gone to the trouble of finding all this out? Because you got in a panic when you thought Dotty was asking too many questions and finding out too much about that dubious event in the crematorium. So what did you do? You decided Dotty would lose her credibility if she was a murder suspect and not a reliable witness. So you spun the police some ridiculous story about too much digitalis, as though she would have killed Freddy because he'd promised to remember her in his will! I'm sure he liked her. But there wasn't any will, any more than there was any fatal heart attack. When you next see Freddy, give him my regards and ask him if he's enjoying his death.'

I got up to go then, and the room, which had seemed so still, was suddenly full of movement. Nanki-Poo jumped out of his basket and started to bark, a high-pitched, irritable yelp like a particularly difficult patient complaining hysterically. At the same time, the door opened and Doctor Sydney Lucas stood in my way. He was looking at me in what I took to be a distinctly unfriendly fashion.

'He's mad!' I heard Sister Sheila tell him. 'He's come back to us and he's seriously insane. He's been talking nonsense to me about poor Freddy.'

Doctor Lucas filled the doorway, considerably younger, taller and a great deal stronger than I am.

'Excuse me' was all I could think of to say. 'Detective Inspector Maundy of the local Force is waiting for me outside. He'll be very worried if I don't emerge. I did warn him that I might have some difficulty leaving . . .'

Whatever they had done to help a crooked businessman disappear from the face of the earth, however outrageous and reckless that plan had been, and however dishonest the doctor's conduct, the mention of the local constabulary made him step away from the door. I walked past him and out into air no longer freshened by chemicals. A cloud had covered the sun, there was a stirring of wind and I felt heavy drops of rain. Wheelchairs were being hurriedly pushed into shelter. I walked away from the Primrose Path for the last time and towards the forces of law and order. I was prepared to make a statement.

*

The University of North Sussex is not an old foundation. The main hall is a modern glass and concrete building, in front of which stands a large piece of abstract statuary built, so far as I could see, of flattened and twisted girders and bits and pieces of motionless machinery. But inside the steeply raked amphitheatre the Chancellor, professors and lecturers were decked out in pink and scarlet gowns with slung-back medieval hoods.

I sat with Dotty among the parents, behind the rows of students. A cleric in a purple gown, the head of the theology department, was calling out names, and the Chairman of the local waste-disposal company, earlier granted an Honorary Doctorate of Literature, handed out the scrolls. Gavin, in his clean white shirt and rarely worn suit, looked younger than ever, hardly more than a schoolboy. As he waited his turn in the queue, his eyes were searching the audience. When he saw Dotty he gave her a small, grateful wave and a smile. Then his name was called and he stepped forward.

'Look now,' I gave Dotty an urgent instruction. 'Look at the entrances.'

She turned and I turned with her. High above us, at the top of the raked seats, there were three doorways. He was standing in the middle one. He must have just moved to where he could see his son, far below him, get his degree. He stood there, a small, broad-shouldered, square figure with a broken nose. It was a moment of pride he had not been able to resist and, as a great chancer, why shouldn't he have taken this risk to see Gavin get what he had never had – a university degree? Gavin shook hands with the waste-disposal magnate and went off with his scroll. Freddy Fairweather turned away, meaning to disappear again into the world of the dead. But he was stopped by Fig Newton and DS Thorndike, who had been waiting for him at my suggestion.

So the case of the Primrose Path never got me a brief. Neither Sister Sheila nor Doctor Sydney Lucas, when arraigned for their various offences, thought of employing Rumpole to defend them. Freddy Fairweather ended up in an open prison, from which he may expect an early release owing to the unexpected onset of Alzheimer's disease. Gavin has taken Holy Orders and returned to Leeds. I still meet Dotty, from time to time, for tea in the Waldorf Hotel, where we sing, quietly but with pleasure, the old standards together.

The day after Freddy Fairweather was arrested, Henry brought a brief into my room. 'Good news at last, Mr Rumpole,' he said. '*R. v. Dennis Timson*. Receiving stolen DVDs. It should be interesting. You won't get cases like that from our so-called Marketing Director.' But I have to say, it was to the Marketing Director I owed my greatest debt of gratitude when I came back to the land of the living and solved the mystery of the Primrose Path Home.

PENGUIN MODERN CLASSICS

THE TITMUSS NOVELS BY JOHN MORTIMER

PARADISE POSTPONED

'Ironic and elegant ... a panoramic human comedy of life in our times' *Evening Standard*

When Simeon Simcox leaves his entire fortune to the ruthless, social-climbing Tory MP Leslie Titmuss, the Rector's two sons react in very different ways. Henry decides to fight the will and prove their father was insane. Younger brother Fred takes a different approach, digging in Simeon's past, only to uncover an entirely unexpected explanation for the legacy.

A delicious portrait of English country life by a master satirist.

TITMUSS REGAINED

'Richly entertaining ... mercilessly funny in its observations on the way we live now' *Sunday Times*

The Right Honourable Leslie Titmuss has clawed his way up the Tory ranks and is now Secretary of State at the Ministry of Housing, Ecological Affairs and Planning. But seismic changes are afoot in the countryside where a new town threatens to engulf his back garden. Will Leslie bow to market forces? Or will he fight against the multi-storey car parks and shopping precincts that could sweep away Rapstone Valley?

The sequel to *Paradise Postponed*, *Titmuss Regained* is an affectionate elegy to a disappearing world.

THE SOUND OF TRUMPETS

'Delicious ... Mortimer in vintage form' *Observer*

When a Tory MP is found dead in a swimming-pool wearing a leopardskin bikini, the embittered Titmuss sees the ideal opportunity to re-enter the political arena. All he needs is a puppet, and Terry Flitton – inoffensive New Labourite – is perfect. Terry heads blindly for the by-election but is he too busy listening for the sound of victory trumpets to notice that the Tory dinosaur is not quite extinct?

The culmination of a masterly trilogy, *The Sound of Trumpets* is a devilishly witty satire on political ambition, spin and sleaze.

PENGUIN MODERN CLASSICS

CLINGING TO THE WRECKAGE
JOHN MORTIMER

Clinging to the Wreckage is the first part of John Mortimer's acclaimed autobiography. Here he recounts his solitary childhood in the English countryside, with affectionate portraits of his remote parents – an increasingly unconventional barrister father, whose blindness must never be mentioned, battling earwigs in the mutinous garden, and a vague and endlessly patient mother. As a boy dreaming of a tap-dancing career on the stage and forming a one-boy communist cell at boarding school, his father pushes him to pursue the law, where Mortimer embarks on the career that was to inspire his hilarious and immortal literary creations.

Told with great humour and touching honesty, this is a magnificent achievement by one of Britain's best-loved writers.

'A true masterpiece of the genre' *The Times*

'Enchantingly witty … should be held as the model for all autobiographies of our times' Auberon Waugh

PENGUIN MODERN CLASSICS

A VOYAGE ROUND MY FATHER
JOHN MORTIMER

In John Mortimer's most famous and highly autobiographical play, a young man looks back on an unconventional childhood and youth overshadowed by his irascible and eccentric father. Sent away to boarding school to be 'prepared for life', he finds teachers deranged by shell shock after the First World War and boys who try to coat their ordinary home lives with romance. As the Second World War begins, the mild-mannered protagonist tries to become a writer, but is compelled to become a barrister like his father – a towering character depicted with affection and exasperation.

Hugely popular since it was first performed, *A Voyage Round My Father* is a sublimely comic drama of warmth, nostalgia and wisdom.

'Generous and humane … Mortimer's fond tribute to his father could hardly be a finer tribute to himself' *Guardian*

'A skilful, witty and touching evocation of his extraordinary parent … a perfect synthesis of reality and art' *Daily Telegraph*

Contemporary ... Provocative ... Outrageous ...
Prophetic ... Groundbreaking ... Funny ... Disturbing ...
Different ... Moving ... Revolutionary ... Inspiring ...
Subversive ... Life-changing ...

What makes a modern classic?

At Penguin Classics our mission has always been to make the best
books ever written available to everyone. And that also means
constantly redefining and refreshing exactly what makes a 'classic'.
That's where Modern Classics come in. Since 1961 they have been an
organic, ever-growing and ever-evolving list of books from the last
hundred (or so) years that we believe will continue to be read over and
over again.

They could be books that have inspired political dissent, such as
Animal Farm. Some, like *Lolita* or *A Clockwork Orange*, may have
caused shock and outrage. Many have led to great films, from *In Cold
Blood* to *One Flew Over the Cuckoo's Nest*. They have broken down
barriers – whether social, sexual, or, in the case of *Ulysses*, the
boundaries of language itself. And they might – like *Goldfinger* or
Scoop – just be pure classic escapism. Whatever the reason, Penguin
Modern Classics continue to inspire, entertain and enlighten millions
of readers everywhere.

'No publisher has had more influence on reading habits than Penguin'
Independent

'Penguins provided a crash course in world literature'
Guardian

The best books ever written

PENGUIN 🐧 CLASSICS

SINCE 1946

Find out more at www.penguinclassics.com